MORE PRAISE FOR
THE FIRE DREAM

"Old-fashioned heroism in a saga of Vietnam . . . The reader [feels] he or she has been in the trenches. . . . It is the grand effort of a veteran dedicated to telling the story. It's the war as viewed from near, or at, the frontline. . . . In Leib's fictional remembrance, fighting men have nightmares but glory perches on every shoulder."

Newsday

"Fast-paced . . . Rich in tactical, strategic and technological detail. Yet Leib creates characters whom we care about and who reflect a variety of perspectives about the war, camaraderie, spirit, survival and coming home."

The Wichita Eagle-Beacon

"Good plot, lots of interesting high-tech warfare trivia but chief emphasis is on spinning the yarn . . . Recommended."

Indochina Chronology

"Moving and exciting. The battle scenes are hair-raising, and honor—a concept that has been sadly unfashionable for a long time—returns sounding wonderful."

The Kirkus Reviews

Also by Franklin Allen Leib
Published by Ivy Books:

FIRE ARROW

THE
FIRE
DREAM

Franklin Allen Leib

IVY BOOKS • NEW YORK

The Fire Dream is a work of fiction. Any resemblance between characters in this novel and persons living or dead, other than historical figures, is coincidental and unintentional.

The United States Army and Air Force units named are for the most part real, but they did not participate in any of the actions described, and most if not all were not in Southeast Asia during the time described. The actions described, with the exception of the relief of Hue in 1968, are wholly fictional. United States and Royal Australian Navy ships named and described were operating off Vietnam during the period, and in the roles portrayed.

Ivy Books
Published by Ballantine Books
Copyright © 1989 by Franklin Allen Leib

All rights reserved under International and Pan-American Copyright Conventions. Published in the United States by Ballantine Books, a division of Random House, Inc., New York, and simultaneously in Canada by Random House of Canada Limited, Toronto.

No part of this book may be reproduced or utilized in any form or by any means, electronic or mechanical, including photocopying, recording or by any information storage and retrieval systems, without permission in writing from the Publisher. Inquiries should be addressed to Presidio Press, 31 Pamaron Way, Novato, CA 94949.

Library of Congress Catalog Card Number: 88-28958

ISBN - 0-8041-0607-X

This edition published by arrangement with Presidio Press

Manufactured in the United States of America

First Ballantine Books Edition: September 1990

IN MEMORIAM

Rufus Hood
Hovey R. Curry
Socorro Pereira
Bobbie Joe Mounts
Philip E. Ruminski, Jr.

Five names taken at random from The Wall.

ACKNOWLEDGMENTS

The author wishes to thank the many people who gave this work critical readings and helped me to refine and polish the long manuscript. Deserving of special thanks are Jim and Marian Adams, John Ehrlichman, Carole Hall, Adele Horwitz, Lee Matthias, and Carl and Patricia Morton. Special acknowledgment to Maj. Stewart Brown, Armor, United States Army, for his invaluable assistance as to Armor weapons and tactics, and to Col. Robert Kane, USA (Ret.), for his thoughtful help in working through the battles.

PROLOGUE

26 February 1968   Quang Tri Province, Vietnam

The lieutenant lay face down on the muddy bank, where he had fallen. Pain gripped him, a tight steel ring around his temples. He gagged on the taste of gasoline, but his throat was dry, and he could not spit. He forced his mind to see outward; his eyes remained tightly shut.

The jungle seemed blurred beyond the low fire, and there were no jungle sounds. The advancing, encircling flames were yellow and crackling, arising like pointed tongues from the jungle floor itself, from the mud and the water, but as they rose and joined together they became almost colorless, like a thick lace curtain rippled by a strong breeze. He became vaguely aware of the heat.

His right hand, numb and beyond his control, stretched out toward the small stream. The flames reached the hand as they gradually encircled his body. The cuff of his uniform began to smoke as the nylon material melted and ran. He could not move his arm despite the growing pain.

The flames engulfed him completely, and he saw nothing but the fire immediately before his eyes. He breathed the flames and tasted them, harsh and fiercely hot. He could hear a singing, a rhythm, a chant. He listened intently, hearing the song but not the words. Increasingly he felt the sadness of great loss, but couldn't remember why.

He became nauseated by the tastes and smells of his own burning body, sweet, greasy, corrupt. The fire inside burned his leg bones to agonizing red heat, and the bones cooked the muscles of his legs from within. His lungs flared brightly like old dry leaves, and emptied without a sound. There was a dull pop as his skull exploded.

The last flames died and the darkness and silence were total. He felt the sudden rush of cooling rain. He trembled violently at the chill.

The lieutenant awoke in the field shelter soaked with sweat. Moser knelt beside him, motionless. Only when he moved did Moser speak. "You OK, sir?"

The lieutenant shook his head clear. The fever made his legs and arms burn and ache, yet he was cold. He tried to speak but his voice choked in his parched throat.

The big man held a cup of green Vietnamese tea. He reached around with his other hand and lifted the lieutenant's head. The lieutenant drank the lukewarm liquid.

"OK, thank you, Moser."

"The same dream?"

"Yes. It's familiar now, almost like a friend."

The big man touched his face gently with his thick, calloused fingers. "You're still awful hot, sir."

"It's the malaria; nothing serious."

"You could get outa this. You should, that sick."

The lieutenant forced himself to a sitting position. He felt dizzy, but his strength was returning. "It's just malaria. Everybody has malaria."

Moser handed the officer a towel. He rubbed his torso, then his arms and legs, vigorously against the chill.

"You could git out, home. You bin wounded. You way overtime on this fuckin' assignment."

The lieutenant looked up. "You want me to do that?"

The big man shifted, stood. "I think you done enough."

The lieutenant felt very tired. "I am OK. And you know it." He hoped the words carried conviction.

"Yes, sir."

He wished he could say more. He shook off the fever, and pulled on a semidry T-shirt. "Wake me at 0530, then."

"It's 0600 now, sir. The grunts are gettin' ready to move out. You goin' to the briefin', or you want to send the sergeant?"

The lieutenant felt suddenly weary, angry at his sickness and at his fear. "I'll go." He rose slowly, fighting to conceal the unsteadiness in his legs. Maybe I should go home, he thought, rubbing his eyes. But what difference could it possibly make? Big Moser is right, Nam is everything, and everything is Nam. At least here you could sometimes feel the pain coming. The lieutenant pulled on his shirt, picked up his rifle, and walked through the rainy darkness to the officers' call.

USA

4 April 1966   Survival, Escape, Reconnaissance, and Evasion (SERE) Training School, Camp Pettigrew, North Carolina

Ensign William McGowen Stuart, USNR, shivered in the cold, steady rain. He was wet through, and had been since he and the rest of his five-man SERE team had been dropped off the truck that had brought them out from the camp at 1000 hours in the morning. It was now nearing dark. The only shelters the men had been provided were five tattered parachutes. They had no equipment and no food or water.

The senior officer in the group was an air force captain, Carter Peters. Two others were naval aviator lieutenants, one an F-4 Phantom pilot, Harrigan, and the other his radar intercept officer, or RIO, Martini. Neither man had offered his first name. The fifth man in the group was Billy Hunter, a bone-hard athletic-looking marine private first class, just finished his basic training at San Diego and headed for Pathfinder School at Camp Pendleton in California.

Stuart had never felt so chilled and miserable as he tried to concentrate on the training problem. Remain undetected by the "enemy" patrols, and maneuver down the ridges and across the coastal plains back to the main camp. Note useful terrain details. Keep track of "enemy" positions and movements. Above all, the men in this and three other teams dropped off at other locations were to evade capture for three days. Capture meant the prison camp.

At first, Stuart thought he was going to like SERE training. The first day the trainees were given fatigue uniforms and boots and organized into the teams. The rest of the day was all classroom; a cheerful marine gunnery sergeant explained the purpose of the training and the rules of engagement with "enemy" instructors.

The training was designed for aviators and other personnel likely to find themselves behind enemy lines, but not likely to have ground combat experience or training. The concept was developed in response to the military's conviction that POWs in Korea had failed to resist so-called "brainwashing" because they had not known what to expect, and had not been thoroughly enough drilled in the discipline required to remain a cohesive unit and help each other under the stress and hardship of prison camp. The course would also give the trainees some rudiments of survival and evasion tactics.

Another sergeant had instructed the men on map and terrain reading and evasive tactics. A skinny lance corporal showed slides of all the edible, and the dangerously inedible, plants to be found in the area, and told them in gruesome detail what parts of small mammals could be eaten raw should the men be lucky enough to snare one. The cheerful gunnery sergeant returned and told them that while the edible plants described by the lance corporal were *theoretically* abundant, the area around Camp Pettigrew had been used for survival training of one kind or another since War Two, and that they should expect to get hungry. And then he lectured on how to maintain discipline and alertness while deprived of food and sleep.

The final phase would be the prison camp. Any teams not captured by the Red Forces by the morning of Field Day Four were to show themselves, and use smoke grenades to reveal their positions if necessary. In response to a question from Captain Peters, the gunny beamed, and said no—no team had ever evaded capture up to the morning of Field Day Four. There would be four teams of five men each coming in from different locations. The Red Forces outnumbered the SEREs roughly two to one, knew the country very well, and of course knew exactly where the trainees had to go.

Carter Peters was a raw-boned, red-faced, easygoing officer from Lubbock, Texas. He was determined to make the best of the training, then get on to his new assignment with a squadron of F-105s based in Nakhon Phanom, Thailand. As darkness thickened, he reviewed the map and the tactical situation with the team, and talked about how they would move as soon as it was fully dark and where they would go. They would move only at night, and very slowly. The entire distance to be covered in the three days and nights was little more than eight kilometers.

That's about five miles, thought Stuart. I will have to get used to klicks.

Captain Peters finished briefing and asked for suggestions. Hunter spoke first. "Captain, as long as the rain continues, there won't be a moon, and the rain itself will muffle the sound of our passage. Maybe we should try to cover ground while the weather is bad."

"The rain might keep the patrols in," added Martini. "Why, after all, would they get wet and cold if they didn't have to?"

Peters decided to cover at least half the distance the first night, and set as an objective a small canyon four kilometers away that might be expected to offer some cover for them to wait out the following day.

Each man carefully packed his parachute in its pack, making sure that none of the white or orange nylon could be seen. They checked each other for shiny objects, such as watches or belt buckles. Metal rank devices were removed from collars and sunk deep into pockets. Hunter compressed some winter green grass into a lump and stuck it in his cheek like a tobacco chaw. Stuart followed suit, but the rest of the team settled for handfuls of water from numerous puddles. The team moved out at 1930.

Hunter took the point, with Peters just behind him at slack. Harrigan and Martini were next, and Stuart took the tail-end position, called drag. They moved very slowly, working always downhill, as Hunter used the small compass from an air force survival pack to keep track of the turns away from the direct line to their objective that the terrain forced them to take. At first they stumbled a lot, and seemed to make a terrible racket in the rain-quiet night, but soon they got more accustomed to the techniques of bush-walking, stepping around sticks and things that could trip them, and maintaining the proper two-meter interval between each man and the next.

Just before 2300 Hunter found the creek that would lead them to the canyon farther downstream. The team halted briefly for a conference. Although there had been no sign of the Red Forces patrols, the men whispered. Harrigan leaned close to Peters, "Smoke OK, Cap?"

"I think not, old buddy," replied Peters. "We might be able to protect the light, but the smell could just call them enemigos right in on our AO."

Stuart was impressed by how seriously Peters was taking the

training, and also with the spirit of the team. I must be the only
one soft enough to be cold and sore, he thought. He decided he
liked Peters and Hunter. He smiled to himself at Peter's pickup
of the marine instructor's slang—AO meant area of operation;
to a mud marine, it meant wherever he was.

Hunter suggested that, since everybody had wet feet anyway,
they walk in the creek as long as it was shallow, to erase their
trail.

Martini sneered. "Shit, Hunter, if those bastards are trailing
us, and they come onta this stream, they know we gotta go
downstream, whether in it or alongside it."

Harrigan nodded. "I gotta figure they won't even patrol tonight. They want us cold and wet and miserable. They won't
even come for us until tomorrow, or maybe the third day."

"So how does that change what we do?" asked Peters, softly.

"Let's hump it right through, get as close to camp as possible," said Harrigan. "Maybe even right the way in. Make it
home-free-all while the Red Forces are staying dry." Harrigan's
nose was running and his voice was thick.

"I have a problem with that." Stuart was surprised to hear
his own voice.

"I got at least two problems with that," said Hunter.

Carter Peters held his hands in front of the men and gestured
for quiet. "Go ahead, William."

"Well, the drill is we stay out here and learn a little surviving.
Harrigan may be right about the enemy patrols staying in, but
if nothing else we've go to improve our movement technique
before the patrols do come."

"Aw, fuck that, *Ensign*," whispered Martini harshly. "The
answer to this kind of training is to get through it, period. I vote
we drive on, even get captured if necessary, just get it over
with."

Stuart was stung by Martini's rebuke, and especially by the
implied reminder that of all the men he had by far the least
experience and the least knowledge of the way the military *really*
operated. He felt the color rising in his cheeks and was glad of
the darkness, and glad as well that Peters turned to Hunter.

"Like I said, I got a coupla problems with the lieutenant's
suggestion we rabbit on in," said Hunter, measuring his words
slowly. "First is, I bet every time they run this drill, some team
tries that, so they will be ready, then we get two extra days at
the prison camp. No fuckin' way they just gonna let us get dry
and rest up even if we do make it in early. Second thing, Ensign
Stuart is right. We're here so we might's well learn it. I don't
know about you airdale officers, but I heard for enlisted marines

that if you fuck up this course *in any way* you get to repeat it.''
Hunter was looking hard at the two navy lieutenants.

Peters seemed amused. "Well, as your commander, gentlemen, I have decided we will hold to our original plan of operation and our original objective. Ensign Stuart will take the
point.''

Hunter handed Stuart the small, luminous-faced compass.
Stuart could make out his smile in the darkness. "Be real careful
of your footing in the stream, sir.''

"Thanks, Hunter," Stuart smiled back. He picked up his
parachute pack and led the unit down into the stream, feeling
for each foothold before putting weight on it. Slowly and almost
silently the team moved through the darkness. The rain abruptly
ceased, and Stuart began to feel better.

At 0115, Stuart was startled by shouting off to his right, followed by the popping sound of a light machine gun. He froze.
Peters touched his shoulder and beckoned him to climb up the
stream bank and crawl up into the thick undergrowth. The men
sat in silence and listened to more shouting, and a sound that
sounded like a hard slap.

"What the fuck are they shouting?" whispered Harrigan.

"Sounds like Chinese," offered Martini.

"Probably just part of the realism," said Carter Peters. "Does
send a chill up your spine, though, doesn't it?''

Sure does, thought Stuart. His heart was still pounding. "I
wonder how close they are?''

"Not very," whispered Hunter. "Half a mile, maybe.
Sound'll carry on a damp night.''

Harrigan crawled in closer. "I guess a patrol musta caught
one of the other teams.''

"Or at least that's what they want us to think," said Peters.
"In any event, let's lie up here for a while, real quiet. I make
us only about half a klick from that holler we're headed for.''

Stuart sat with his arms around his shins and began to feel
cold again. I wonder if anybody else is really afraid of all this,
he thought.

The team reached the little canyon at 0230, just as the moon
was rising behind thin clouds. Peters decided they should walk
all around the canyon before entering it, searching for any sign
of enemy presence. The search took almost an hour before Peters was satisfied. In the center of the canyon on the north bank
of the stream Harrigan found a small, dry cave. He gave a low
whistle and the team converged.

"Just the place to hole up, hey, Cap?''

"Looks cozy," agreed Peters.

"Enemy is bound to know about this place, sir," said Hunter.

I was just thinking the same thing, thought Stuart. "We might be better off near the other end. Walls aren't so steep, and we would be better able to move out if we spot a patrol."

Martini grinned derisively, and shook his head.

"This place is dry," said Harrigan, simply, as light rain began falling.

"It's a trap," said Hunter. "Enemy catch us here, we got no place to run to."

Martini snorted. "Hunter, you're not seriously considering *running* from the so-called enemy once they find us."

"Damn right, sir," said Hunter, crisply.

"Escape and evade," said Stuart. It just popped out.

Martini turned to Peters, who smiled, then slowly nodded. "Let's go take a look up the other end."

Once the campsite had been selected, the men worked quickly to gather brush to hide it. They would have to wrap themselves in the parachutes to keep warm, and no matter how much brush they gathered, Peters, walking the perimeter, could see the orange and white panels.

"It's no good, gentlemen. Anybody not even trained gonna see those chutes."

"We oughta bury 'em, Captain," said Hunter.

"I'm afraid you're right, Hunter."

"If we had shovels, we could dig in a bit, then cover ourselves with leaves," said Martini.

"If my aunt had balls she'd be my uncle," said Harrigan. "Besides, there's precious few leaves around."

"We're going to have to sleep like marines. Huddled up. Conserve warmth," Hunter said quietly. Carter Peters nodded.

"I feel too keyed up to sleep," said Stuart, rising. "I'll take the first lookout watch."

"Lemme have the parachutes," said Hunter. "I'll take 'em down by the stream and bury 'em."

"And I," said Martini with a lopsided grin, "will gather edible roots and berries."

Ensign Stuart found a sheltered position near the rim of the hollow, and sat to take his watch. The night was so quiet it was spooky, and once he sat down, he began to feel very cold. He felt physically tired, but his mind raced. He remembered the day of his commissioning as an ensign in the Naval Reserve, the same day he had graduated from Georgia Tech. Stuart was tall and slim, blond and blue-eyed; despite himself, he had thought himself a handsome figure in his dress-blue uniform, with gray gloves and gold- and ivory-hilted dress sword. His mother and father had complimented him, as had his fiancée, Karen Dyer, who had come up from Rollins College in Florida to his graduation and commissioning in Atlanta.

Stuart felt no particular desire to pursue a career in the armed forces, yet he was aware of the traditions of his people to serve in time of war. He had selected the Navy as the tiniest break with tradition. The first Stuarts in America had come as soldiers; an ancestor, James John, had been an ensign in the British Army that defeated the French at Fort George in the Carolinas in the French and Indian War of 1763, and later had followed his old colonel, George Washington, to Long Island, Valley Forge, Trenton, and Yorktown. A later Stuart, General J.E.B., had been the most famous cavalry commander of the Confederacy, while his first cousin Amos was killed leading his Sixth Connecticut Regiment at the Battle of Shiloh in 1863. Stuarts had rallied in the Spanish War of 1898, and in the First World War, and William's father had led a battalion of infantry across France with Patton's Third Army in 1944.

William had gotten his commission through NROTC. He had enjoyed the small but dignified ceremony, and he had a romantic view of his upcoming naval service in smart uniforms on a big ship. Now he was shivering and miserable in a wet North Carolina wood. He fought back the urge to curse, or to weep. He had been a serving officer for forty-two days.

The worst of this, he thought, watching the winter-quiet night, is that I practically volunteered for this program. Stuart had reported to the Fleet Anti-Air Warfare Center at Dam Neck, Virginia, in early March, and spent three weeks learning about the guns in the fleet. He was to receive training afterward in amphibious warfare at Little Creek, part of the huge Norfolk Naval Station, then join the USS *Valley Forge*, an old straight-deck World War II vintage carrier that had been converted to an amphibious assault ship and served in the Pacific Fleet.

After completing gunnery training at Dam Neck, Stuart reported to the sprawling naval base at Norfolk for housing during the five weeks of school at Little Creek. When he turned in his orders at transient officers' assignment, he was told that the next class did not begin for ten days. He asked the third-class yeoman on duty what he was expected to do in the meantime. The petty officer shrugged. "I can git you leave papers cut."

Stuart considered. "I don't really want to use up leave. I'm not even sure I have ten days coming."

The sailor shrugged again. "Up to you. I guess you can just

lounge around the luxurious BOQ, though the Navy don't like to see its new-minted en-signs do that. Maybe I can find you another school for a week.''

"Do that, please," said Stuart. He was beginning to worry the Navy was going to bore him to death before he ever saw blue water.

The yeoman seemed oppressed by the thought of the extra effort. "Anything you particularly like?"

Stuart's mind was blank. "I don't know. What's available?"

The other man shifted in his seat. "Why don't you go get checked in at the 'Q and come back around 1600. I'll see what I can find."

Stuart went to the junior officers' bachelor officers' quarters—the BOQ, or BOG, as it was affectionately called—and stowed his gear in the two-man room to which he was assigned. When he returned to the transit officers' office at 1600, he found the same yeoman grinning as he approached the counter. "What are my options, Robbins?" inquired Stuart, reading the plastic name tag.

"Well, *sir*, the onliest thing I could find that begins tomorrow and ends in time for you to start Amphib Officers' School is SERE training. You catch the bus to North Carolina at 0600 tomorrow, *sir*."

Stuart found the yeoman's taunting emphasis on the "sir" irritating, but kept his voice even. "And what is SERE training, Robbins?"

Robbins produced a pamphlet, and tossed it on the counter. "SERE, *sir*, is survival, escape, reconnaissance, and evasion. Good course for an en-sign going over toward Nam."

"What's it like?" Stuart did not want to reach for the pamphlet.

Robbins leaned forward, grinning happily, and patted the rating patch on his left shoulder with his right hand. "Well, I a *yeoman*, *sir*, so I don't rightly *know*, but I *hear* they leaves you in the woods for a few days, then takes you to a mock-up Vietnamese prison camp and beats the shit out of you, so's you'll know how to take it if'n you get caught over there."

Stuart waited for the "sir" that should have ended the sentence until he was sure it wasn't coming. "I'll be on a *ship* over there, Robbins."

Robbins leaned back and spread his arms in the universal military gesture that meant "hey, don't look at me, pal." "*Amphibs*, sir! You gonna be trained as a boat officer, just ten days away! You could need this shit! Sir!"

Stuart picked up the pamphlet, and the one-page temporary

duty order that instructed him to board a bus to Camp Pettigrew in North Carolina for one week's training, SERE. Well, screw it, he thought, at least I can run off some of my winter fat. "Thank you, Robbins," Stuart forced a smile. Robbins threw a half salute as Stuart departed.

He thinks I'm a dumb cherry to volunteer for anything, Stuart had thought at the time. Now, as the night grew colder and the drizzle increased, Stuart was sure the surly yeoman had been dead right.

Martini struggled up to Stuart's position, making a lot of noise and cursing as he tripped over an exposed root. "I got the watch, Ensign. Bed down."

The daylight hours passed slowly but uneventfully. Several times the watching members of the SERE team heard motor vehicles, and once gunfire, but all were distant, and to the west. It seemed that their long march of the previous night had gotten them ahead of the enemy's patrols.

Stuart walked point most of the following night. He was gaining confidence in his bush-walking, and the others seemed content to let him lead, except Hunter, who relieved him to let him rest when the bush got thick. During one rest period, Stuart departed from the unit to take a piss, and Hunter sought him out.

"Hey, Ensign Stuart, sir, what do you think of these guys?"

"They are OK, Hunter."

"Yeah, sir, maybe the captain, but these two nasal radiators, I don't know."

Stuart looked at Hunter's skeptical, agitated expression. In some strange way, the pressure of this exercise is affecting all of us, he thought. "Hunter, the whole point of this exercise is to instill in each of us the importance of the chain of command. We have a captain in the Air Force, and two navy lieutenants. You are a private first class, and I am an ensign. An ensign is said to be lower than whale shit, and you are fresh out of boot camp. We have to trust these guys."

Hunter stepped back. Stuart sensed his anger. "Sir, you got anything against fighting this war?"

"No, why?"

"Because I intend to fight it. I intend to come outa this course *with honors*. I intend to *evade* capture, and *escape* once captured."

"Well, that's what we all will try to do."

"Bullshit, sir. Those two navy crybabies will lie down, and the captain may want to be tough, but he ain't. Look, I'll play the role, kiss their asses, but when it comes time to run, or hide, or *escape and evade*, I would like to team up with you. Unofficial, of course.''

Stuart was startled and confused by Hunter's outburst. He was flattered that Hunter saw potential in him that he didn't see in himself. Still, he felt that he had to straighten the kid out. ''Now *listen*, Hunter,'' Stuart whispered urgently, seeing Captain Peters waving to them to form up to resume the march, ''number one, we have to stick together as a unit. That's number one in the training. Number two, I'm a total boot! I just got commissioned!''

''Don't mean nothin'. You got heart. You and me, unofficial, OK?''

Nothing in NROTC prepared me for this situation, thought Stuart. Nothing prepared me for an enlisted man trashing officers. Yet somehow I know Hunter is a little bit right.

Stuart shrugged, ''OK. We get caught, we team. But when those patrols find us, and you and I both know they will, we try to get all the guys to resist, to run. We try, Hunter, OK?''

Hunter frowned. ''OK, sir, but if their hands go up at the first blank, we go together, and fast. Deal?''

Stuart sighed. It is a real situation, yet it is training, yet it is real! I wish I could stop the problem, ask the instructors. I can't. ''Deal.''

Hunter smiled. ''OK, now I know. We'll try to get the captain through, at least.''

''All, Hunter.''

Hunter nodded. ''OK, sir, all, your rules. The rules of the game. Let's get this gang bang on the road.''

They camped the third morning under a huge copper beech tree, among the spreading roots. The cover was minimal, but the team had decided that the first priority in any campsite was ease of escape. All day the men were kept awake by the sounds of trucks and jeeps, some with loudspeakers, calling to them in English, and in the Oriental-sounding gibberish, calling them in, saying that they would be well treated. Harrigan's cold had been driven deep into his chest, and he was running a high fever. Martini sat despondent, saying nothing. Captain Peters agonized over his conflicting responsibilities. ''Look men, Harrigan is near pneumonia. Maybe we should pop smoke, get him in.''

Hunter spoke up. ''Lieutenant Harrigan, you want to go on?''

Harrigan coughed, a deep, racking, wet rumble, and spit out a stream of yellow mucus. ''Yeh.''

''You sure?'' asked Peters.

"Yeh. You guys are right, we got to finish this thing. I have a smoke grenade; I can't make it, I'll drop back, pop when you guys are off."

Carter Peters shook his head. "I don't think we should split up."

Harrigan coughed and grimaced, then looked up with red-rimmed eyes. "We would if this was real, Cap."

"No." Stuart was surprised at the firmness in his voice. "We'll carry you. If this was real, we couldn't leave you."

Peters looked at the boot ensign and nodded slowly. As night fell, he gave the orders to move. "This night, we'll circle the camp and try to make it in from the east. It won't likely work, but we'll try."

The night was clear and cold. A nearly full moon would rise at about 0300, so the night's march and the establishment of a place of concealment had to be completed before then. Captain Peters picked out a small swale in the middle of a flat plain barely above sea level less than one klick from the camp perimeter as the night's objective. He also decided to cross over the ridge rather than stick to the creek bottom, thus shortening the route and getting away from the creek, which seemed to draw the enemy like a road the closer they came to the camp. Once they reached the night position, they would decide whether to rush for the lighted perimeter, or hide and pop smoke in the morning.

Stuart had the point with Peters at slack, then the two naval aviators, finally Hunter at drag. Stuart felt a slight tug at his ankle, heard a sound like zip! ding! and whisper-yelled "Grenade!" as he fell backward away from his feet. There was a soft pop just in front of him, followed by a cloud of white smoke and, fifty feet up the trail, a deafening explosion.

Stuart low-crawled back, and grabbed the captain's shoulder, "We gotta move out! This place will crawl with Red Forces."

Peters looked up at Stuart blankly, then nodded. Harrigan and Martini got to their feet slowly as Peters yelled at Hunter to pick up point and move rapidly up over the ridge. No point trying to be quiet now, thought William, as the men ran away from the booby trap. If that mine had been where the smoke grenade was, we'd be gone. Just gone.

Hunter floated over the ridge at a trot. The others were having trouble keeping pace, and Peters hissed at Hunter to slow down. Stuart saw disgust in Hunter's eyes as he turned, but he slowed, and the intervals were more or less reestablished.

Once across the ridge, the team came upon a well-defined path. Peters moved up to slack, and decided to risk it at least until they put some distance between themselves and the land-mine site. Hunter led off, and they jogged down the clear trail. Half a klick along, the trail seemed to end abruptly, or to be blocked by a dense object unidentifiable in the darkness. Hunter slowed, and stepped off the trail fifty meters short of the block-age. A second explosion, from behind them on the trail, sent them sprawling in an untidy heap, lungs empty. From the block-age on the trail a powerful floodlight split the night.

Stuart saw his teammates as in a still photograph, faces fixed in shock, eyes reflecting light like terrified animals. Hunter was up quickly as automatic weapons opened up from the right side of the trail. In the gaps between the deafening bursts of fire, the night was further assaulted by piercing yells.

Stuart found himself up and running, half dragging Martini by the shoulder. Martini tore his hand away and dove into a bush. Hunter was ahead of him, moving out. Harrigan lay where he had fallen, doubled over, apparently in pain. Carter Peters was running after Hunter. Stuart saw the first enemy soldiers emerge into the light, still firing their weapons. Stuart heard one yell, in accented English, "Hands up, Yankee dogs! Hands up! Hands up."

Stuart ran. He looked back one more time, and saw Martini crawl out from under his bush, with his hands up.

Stuart ran in the direction he had seen Hunter and the captain take. The Reds had swiveled their powerful light at him, illu-minating the woods brightly all around him except directly in front of him, where his own body left a strip of inky shadow. He juked right and left, running through gaps he could see, gaps that often disappeared from vision just when he reached them as the searchlight shifted. He was aware of moving shadows, less dense, of the enemy soldiers pursuing.

Rushing through the darkness, Stuart misjudged a gap, and struck his right shoulder on a tree. Off balance, he tripped and fell forward down a steep slope. He slid face first all the way to the bottom, feeling sand and leaf mold driven into his eyes and mouth. At the bottom, he found a small stream, and immedi-ately splashed water into his burning eyes.

He was now again in total darkness, and his eyes adjusted. Looking up, he could see the bright light and dense shadows dancing back and forth, but the light did not reach down into the streambed. He put his hands into the water to feel which way it was flowing, to see which way was downstream, then moved off in that direction. He had splashed for about twenty meters through the tiny stream when he heard a "Sssst!" He dropped to a crouch and froze, listening.

"Sssst! Redsign!"

Redsign was the team's recognition signal. They had not yet used it. "Red Rover!" whispered Stuart. In spite of the situation, and his own very real terror, he felt a little silly using these passwords.

Hunter emerged from the darkness. "Jesus fucking Christ, Mr. Stuart! You OK?"

"Yeah, Hunter. You?"

"Yeah, fine." Hunter grasped Stuart's chin and tilted his face upward to catch the first dim moonlight. "Your face is cut to shit."

Stuart put his hands on his face, felt the slick blood on his palms. He knelt, and once again rinsed with handfuls of cool water. "Wow, that stings! But I'm OK. Where's the captain?"

"He fell, said his ankle gave out. He told me to leave him, find you. Boy, you were running through those trees like a striped ass ape!"

Stuart chuckled. His breathing was slowing toward normal. Hunter helped him up and took the point, and they moved out at a fast walk down the stream. They could neither see nor hear evidence of pursuit by the Red Forces.

"What about those other assholes, sir?"

Stuart took a deep breath. Try to be an officer, he thought. Try to be a leader. "Let's call 'em teammates, Hunter, or officers, OK?"

Stuart could see Hunter's shoulders shrug. "Uh, yessir. Sorry, sir." Hunter's voice was without expression.

Gently, thought Stuart, gently. "Lieutenant Harrigan looked hurt. Lieutenant Martini was captured." How did one lead a man tougher, and better suited to the task? Maybe that's part of what I'm here to learn.

Hunter suddenly stopped, turned. "So we got away. What do we do now, sir? You are the honcho now."

Thank you, Hunter, thought Stuart. "We don't have the map. I do have the compass. We'll continue east, but as soon as we find a deep hole, I think we ought to hide. Remember, tomorrow is Field Day Four, and if we can evade capture until dawn, we've beaten this phase."

Hunter nodded in the darkness. "Yeah. We probably oughta slow down until we find a good spot. This place is crawling with made-up dinks."

Off to the left, they heard a whooosh! then a dull pop, pop. The sky to the north lit up with stark white magnesium illumination flares. From the same direction, they heard automatic weapons fire, and distant shouting. Stuart looked at the compass, and took the point.

Hunter and Stuart made very slow progress through the thickening forest. The creek they had been following turned sharply south after they made a kilometer's march away from the scene of the ambush, so they struck eastward across country. The night continued to hiss, pop, and brighten with parachute flares as the Red Forces closed in, and shouts and distant gunfire forced them to move cautiously, staying under cover. It was just after 0300; they had lain in a deep puddle under an uprooted tree for ten minutes, first watching a patrol of the Reds lead a SERE team, tied and blindfolded, down a narrow path toward the road where trucks waited, then watched another patrol sweep very carefully along the same track. Stuart felt his heart racing and wondered why the enemy couldn't hear the beat. He concentrated on his heart, and it slowed, and his blood cooled.

They had been about to move out when Hunter grasped Stuart's hand in an iron grip. A single soldier with a Browning automatic rifle on a sling slipped noiselessly along the trail in front of their AO. Hunter's grip relaxed slowly, "Trail watcher, with a BAR, waiting for stragglers," he whispered. "These bastards don't miss a trick."

Stuart nodded in the darkness. "I think we'd better find some kind of hole to hide in. The patrols are everywhere."

"Which way, sir?"

Stuart pointed. "See that big beech, on the ridge line? Let's cross the trail and work our way up. I don't figure there will be another patrol along immediately on the same trail."

Hunter rose up to a squat. "That's pretty open country to cross."

"I reckon we have to chance it. With luck we'll get through between patrols."

"Reckon we can find cover up there?"

"I really don't know, Hunter, but it seems to me these patrols are concentrating on paths and streambeds, rather than the ridges."

"That's how they told us to move."

"Right, and I'm sure it's the right way to move, but given what we've seen, the wrong way to hide."

Hunter nodded. The movement was barely visible. Both men had darkened their faces with mud. "Let's go, then, sir. I point?"

"You got it. Quickly across the road, then quietly, straight up to the tree."

The climb to the beech tree was slow and hard, and the men

felt much more exposed to the light from the popping flares, as well as the moonlight shining around racing, low clouds. They crawled the last two hundred yards across an open slope, listening to distant gunfire and the maniacal mock-Asian screaming.

At the base of the big beech they found a triangular enclosure, formed by a granite boulder on one side, the tree itself on another, and a fallen branch some four feet thick closing off the third. Stuart sat down exhausted with his back to the branch while Hunter conducted a brief and largely fruitless search of the surrounding area for edible plants. He wadded up the leaves of a few perennial grasses and shared them with Stuart.

"How long you reckon till dawn, sir?"

Stuart tilted his watch to the moonlight. "It's 0345. Moonrise was about 0300, if I remember right. Dawn about 0630, I'd guess." Stuart suddenly felt very weary. His stomach growled audibly.

Hunter chuckled, "Didn't think much of my cooking, eh, sir?"

Stuart yawned. "Hunter, I'd take a walking tour again with you anytime, but a chef you're not."

Hunter got up from his crouch. "Get a little sleep, sir. I'll take the first watch."

"Thanks, Hunter. Wake me if you start to nod, or in one hour, max."

"Yes, sir."

Stuart stretched out along the base of the log, hugging himself against the chill. His legs ached from the exertion. The cuts on his face burned, and he felt his left eye swelling shut from either a cut or something caught below the eyelid. The sharp hunger pains had largely ceased after the second day, but they had been replaced by a dull and steady ache. He was also beginning to feel the lassitude and lack of focus the instructors had said would come with lack of food. Yet through it all, he felt in surprisingly good spirits.

"Sir?" whispered Hunter.

"Yes?"

"We are going to get through this, sir."

Stuart closed his eyes. "No problem, Marine."

He was instantly asleep.

Stuart came quickly awake with Hunter's hand on his shoulder. The sky had cleared, and the moon painted the wet landscape a ghostly silver. Stuart checked his watch, 0515. Hunter had let him sleep one-and-a-half hours.

"Any sign of the little Asiatic nightstalkers, Hunter?" Stuart whispered.

Hunter grinned. "No, sir. I think I saw another patrol go by on that path we crossed to get up here, but it's been real quiet for about an hour. No flares, no shouting, no gunfire, nothing."

Stuart stood up and stretched. I would give my soul and first-born son for a hot bath, something to soothe this eye, and a steak and a beer. "Maybe the bastards have packed it in for the night. Anyway, get some sleep. We'd better be ready to march in as soon as the sun is fully up."

"Roger, sir," Hunter sounded jubilant. "We gonna be the first guys ever to make it all the way." Hunter arranged himself in the exact spot against the branch Stuart had just left. "You got this spot nice and warm for me, sir. Good night."

"Good night, Hunter. Hey, and thanks for the extra rest."

"Don't mean nothin'. Good night." Hunter rolled his body toward the log and slept.

Stuart took a quick turn around the perimeter. The night seemed peaceful and undisturbed. The assholes must have stopped looking. Sadistic bastards. William was surprised to feel the heat of his hatred of these men who chased and pursued, and left him and his team and the others without food or shelter. In a flash, he felt that if he had a weapon, he could kill.

Steady, lad, he thought, this is training, just training. Just a camping trip in bad weather. At least when we turn ourselves in we can clean up and get dry. And they will have to feed us *something.*

The thought of food made his stomach turn, and rumble loudly. Stuart felt a liquid feeling in his bowels, a sudden urgency. I'll be damned, he thought, three days and nights with nothing to eat but Hunter's leaf sandwiches, and I have to take a shit.

Stuart got up quietly from the shadow of the boulder where he had been sitting. I should wake Hunter and tell him I am leaving the perimeter, he thought, but fuck it, let him sleep. He walked up the hill from the big tree and found another fallen branch, just the right height to sit across. He unbuttoned his trousers, and sat. Nothing happened. His guts rumbled, but nothing came.

Stuart caught a slight movement out of the corner of his left eye. He looked at the spot, saw nothing, but suddenly he was very alert. He started to rise, reaching for his trousers down around his ankles, as a Red Forces soldier fired an entire magazine of blanks from his BAR from fifteen feet away. Stuart felt the pressure in his bowels break suddenly, overcoming the constriction of his sphincter in a long, painful squirt.

The BAR gunner now stood behind him with the big gun leveled at Stuart's head. Stuart watched fascinated as three more soldiers rose from the grass in front of him. They had been perfectly concealed. He might easily have stepped on them. No one had spoken. To his right, Stuart saw Hunter peering over the fallen log of their hideout. Stuart looked away. Maybe they didn't know he was there. Suddenly it was important that Hunter evade until morning.

The three soldiers approached in a skirmish line. William knew that only seconds could have passed since the BAR man had fired, but time seemed slowed, as if caught in a viscous liquid. He sat stupidly on the log with his hands covering his ears.

The nearest soldier turned on a powerful flashlight, pointing it into Stuart's eyes. "GET UP! HANDS ON HEAD! *CHU MEN HA DO, DO!*"

Stuart stood, and moved his hands to the back of his neck. He felt completely unmanned, his trousers still down around his ankles.

"FILTHY SHIT-SPATTERED AMERICAN DOG!" shouted the soldier, who had red officer's tabs on the collar of his greatcoat. He swept the area with the light. "WHERE IS OTHER DOG? YOU COME HERE, YOU TELL ME!"

Stuart started forward, tripped in his trousers, and barely avoided falling. The soldiers laughed loudly, but the officer maintained his scowl. Stuart decided to reach for his trousers. Once again, the officer screamed, "CHU MEN HA DO! HANDS ON HEAD!"

The officer took two quick strides, shoved his face in front of Stuart's, and thrust the flashlight sharply under Stuart's chin. "ANSWER, SHIT-SPATTERED DOG! WHERE OTHER *CHO DE*? OTHER DOG!"

The officer's spittle stung Stuart's injured eye, and his breath reeked of garlic. Stuart felt his composure returning, and he found it easy to stare back at the shorter officer and say nothing.

"ANSWER! ANSWER!" The officer shoved violently on Stuart's chest, sending him sprawling on his bare ass. He clutched at his trousers and pulled them up, as the officer once again bellowed, "CHU MEN HA DO!" and kicked him swiftly in the ribs. The soldiers stepped closer, and noisily cocked their weapons.

Stuart felt the sharp pain in his ribs, then recognized the expertise with which it had been applied. Nothing broken and no real injury.

The officer continued shouting in his weird singsong accent. "You no good solja. You no even good trainee! We know two dogs run togetha! You should move, but you hide, keep red solja out late!" The next kick carried even less force. "Maybe you other dog come in now, before I kick this dog to death! Then all can go get warm, dry!" This time, the officer struck at his head with the butt of the flashlight, but the blow landed on his shoulder.

Stay down, Hunter, run away! Hunter will run, thought Stuart. He knows he can't do anything for me, and it is his duty to continue to evade. Stuart smiled inwardly. Keep the humps out all night, Hunter, good buddy.

Stuart was jerked to his knees from behind. While he was being blindfolded, he was allowed to button his trousers, then his hands were tied tightly behind him, once at the wrists and again at the elbows. He was pulled roughly to his feet, and the soldier behind him prodded with a rifle. "*TCHO DA!* MARCH!"

Hang in there, Hunter, thought Stuart, as he marched to the persistent prod of the soldier's weapon.

7 April 1966   Camp Pettigrew, North Carolina

Stuart reckoned he had walked blindfolded for about half a kilometer, under the constant prod of the soldier behind him. He fought his panic by trying to work out the direction he was being marched, and the distance. He also tried to figure out how many men were escorting him. They never talked, but from the footfalls he could sometimes hear in the damp earth, he guessed two. That meant two, at least, still looking for Hunter.

Stuart felt a road under his feet, and heard a motor idling. He was picked up and dumped without ceremony or comment into the bed of a truck. The truck sped off, banging his head against the side. He heard a soldier laugh as his head rang.

After perhaps five minutes, the truck stopped, and he was dumped out. Strong arms picked him up and frog-marched him up metal steps. He was sat in a chair, and his arms and legs were tied to it. His blindfold was removed, but the room was in total darkness.

Bright lights flared on. Stuart saw he was in a standard military trailer, fitted out as a medical clinic. A doctor, dressed in white, stood at a door at the far end, his hand on a light switch.

"You're late, Marine."

"Ensign, sir. United States Navy." Stuart felt his reply was correct, if a little formal.

27

The doctor pulled up a stool and faced Stuart. He looked to be a man in his fifties. He had a kindly smile, and he clucked sympathetically as he looked intently at Stuart's burning left eye.

"This is a break in your training, Ensign, the only one allowed. Your captors brought you to me because of the apparent injury to your eye. Let me see."

The doctor probed, and Stuart flinched. The doctor pressed compress after compress onto Stuart's left eye. The gritty feeling dissolved, and the pain diminished.

"How bad is it?" asked Stuart.

The doctor shrugged while continuing to probe and wash. "Bad enough for the sadistic bastards to bring you here. You have a cut in the lid, and a lot of dirt, but the eye itself seems not to be affected." The doctor paused. "You would be better off in a hospital."

"You mean I should withdraw from the training?"

"Ensign, you can withdraw from this course at any time."

Stuart felt heat in his cheeks and neck. "That's not what I meant, *sir*! I mean, is my eye in danger? Do I have to withdraw?"

The white-coated doctor leaned back. "Your eye is not in danger now, but infection could spread. And if you ask to see me again, you'll have to withdraw. Right now, I'd say you could go on, but I wouldn't advise it."

"Why not?"

The doctor sighed. "Ensign, I can pack the eye with boric acid, which will aid healing, and antibiotics to retard the infection. I can give you a massive shot of antibiotics, and I will. But when you go into that camp, you'll be roughed up. You will be denied medication, unless you withdraw. And even now, you are destined for an especially rough time."

Stuart's heart raced as he thought it out. Withdraw. Fail. Continue, lose an eye. Doubt made his bowels loosen again. He felt ill. Withdraw. Coward. Blind.

"Why a special rough time, then, Doctor?" he asked, calming himself.

The doctor finished up with a swab, cleaning the lower lid. "You are, I believe, the last one captured. They always, *here*, reserve something special for the last ones they have to chase the hardest and the longest."

"The others are all in?"

"They have all been in, and bedded down, I believe, since, at the latest, midnight."

Hunter is still out there, thought Stuart. "Pack the eye, Doc.

I'm staying." His mind screamed at him, idiot! Don't risk an eye!

"OK, Ensign, but against my advice." The doctor worked quickly, packing a patch over Stuart's eye, and taping it fast. The doctor washed Stuart's face with a strong, astringent-smelling soap, dried it, then painted the cuts with something that stung. Mom used to do that when I would hurt myself, mused Stuart. He felt the sharp prick of an injection in his forearm. "Antibiotics. Make you a little sick, because it's a strong dose, but those bastards would take away any pills I gave you."

Stuart felt genuinely grateful. "Thanks, Doc."

The doctor looked thoughtful. "I really don't advise you to stay, son."

Stuart smiled. "I got a buddy out there, Doc. Coming in later than me. We have to escape."

The doctor shook his head. "I'm going to put your blindfold back on, son. I assure you, I'll do it more gently than the guards. Then I have to leave. Remember two things." The doctor wrapped the dirty bandage around Stuart's head. He could smell the earthy smell. "You can always get medical attention if you agree to withdraw. And, as soon as those sadists get dirt under that bandage, get rid of it, and get clean water on the eye as often as you can."

"Thank you, Doctor. What should I worry about, with the eye?"

The doctor sighed. "I would like you out of this, Ensign, but if you insist on staying in, this: fever, badly blurred vision. Especially fever. Don't be a hero at your own expense."

Stuart felt cold and weak in his guts. "OK, I'll watch."

"Last chance to get out easy, son."

Stuart stiffened behind his blindfold. "I'll stay with it, sir."

The doctor patted Stuart on the shoulder. "Good luck. I'm leaving now; your gracious hosts will be back shortly."

"Thanks, Doc." Stuart sat perfectly still, listening intently to the sounds of the doctor leaving.

The Red officer stepped silently out of the shadows, to the back of Stuart's chair. The doctor, at the other end of the room, pointed to Stuart, and then gave a thumbs-up sign to the guard officer. The doctor left. The guard officer moved to the back of Stuart's chair, picked it up, and threw it and Stuart tied to it against the wall of the trailer. Stuart struck the wall with his shoulder, and he cried out in pain and anger. The guard officer stepped to him, cut his bonds to the chair, and pulled him to his feet.

"Welcome, Shit-Spattered Puppy Dog." Stuart recognized the

voice of the guard officer, even though it was whispered, and spoken without the phony Asian accent. "You should have taken the Doc's offer, asshole. You are mine, now."

Stuart was pulled roughly from the trailer, and down the metal steps. His mind raced. The doctor tried to fuck me. I will trust only Hunter.

And my fellow prisoners, and the chain of command, his training reminded him.

At the door of the medical trailer, the Red officer, with a muttered command, turned Stuart over to another soldier who prodded him forward. The day was warming, and his filthy uniform was gradually drying. Be good to get clean, he thought, but not bloody likely.

The surface underfoot changed from grass to gravel. Stuart could hear men shuffling, and a few low words: "well done, way to be, semper fi."

The soldier behind him put a hand on Stuart's shoulder. "*Dung lai!* Stop!" Stuart stopped. "*Ngoi xuong! Ngoi xuong!* Squat now!" The soldier's hand pushed downward, and, awkwardly, Stuart squatted. The blindfold was ripped off, and Stuart flinched and squinted against the sudden light. His right eye quickly focused; his left remained in blissful darkness.

Standing at attention before Stuart were the eighteen men of his and the other three SERE teams. Major Roberts, USAF, the senior American officer, stood in front, with the rest of the men arrayed in two ranks behind him. Stuart could see Carter Peters leaning on a crude crutch. Must have hurt his ankle badly, thought Stuart. Asshole doctor couldn't talk him out of the program, either.

Stuart heard a man walk around him, then saw his legs in short, highly polished boots and pressed gray trousers. A riding crop touched him gently under the chin, and he looked up into the man's face. Despite the man's savage scowl, and the strange uniform with red collar tabs and a red star on the soft cap, Stuart recognized him as the cheerful marine sergeant from the classroom. Stuart wanted to laugh, but suppressed it. This really is chicken shit, he thought. The sergeant withdrew the crop and stood up, at Stuart's right side. In a slightly singsong voice, the sergeant began to speak.

"For those of you American prisoners who were brought here only last night, or," Stuart felt the crop tap him lightly on his right shoulder, "this *morning*, allow me to introduce myself. I am Colonel Minh of the Red Forces. I am the camp commandant. The men you see behind me are my officers and men, all but one patrol who will soon bring in the last of you, who has foolishly refused to come in under safe conduct at dawn today. Your comrade will regret his disobedience, as will all you who disobey." The tapping on Stuart's shoulder became harder, more insistent, as the commandant punctuated each phrase. "This man here is a fine example. He evaded our search to the last minute, almost to the safe-conduct time. You should praise him. I honor him. I admire bravery and resourcefulness. HOWEVER!" The last blow of the riding crop grazed Stuart's ear, and stung sharply. "However, in camp, there must be no disobedience of *any* kind! THIS MAN!" Whap! Again the crop caught Stuart's ear. "This *brave* man, has already caused my officers and men much difficulty. Now, this man will be treated fairly, treated well! As will you all! My officers and men know that I insist on it! But my men work hard, and long hours, and they grow forgetful of their natural courtesy in the face of DISOBEDIENCE!" Stuart flinched to his left but the crop struck his ear hard. He bit back a cry as he rocked away from the blow.

Major Roberts stepped forward. "Colonel Minh, I must protest this brutal beating of an American officer—"

"SILENCE!" The crop struck again, from the side, and Stuart toppled over onto the gravel. Instinctively, he twisted his head to land on the back, protecting his eye.

As Stuart struggled to get back to his squatting position, there was a flurry of shouting and movement of the guards behind him, then a rush toward the left, where the camp gate stood. Stuart looked after them, and saw Hunter, standing just outside the high wood and wire gate. Slowly, almost casually, he took the smoke grenade from his belt, pulled the pin, and tossed it to the foot of the gate, where it gushed orange smoke. Stuart struggled to his feet and began cheering wildly. The other prisoners picked up the cheering, drowning the enraged screaming of the commandant. The guards opened the gate and surrounded Hunter. One struck him to the ground with a long staff of bamboo. Another bound his arms, and he was dragged into the center of the camp, face to face with the commandant. The cheering subsided as other guards brandishing their staffs moved toward the American ranks. Major Roberts grabbed Stuart's shoulder and pulled him into the re-forming American ranks. Strong fingers from behind him untied the ropes on his wrists and ankles. Someone gave him a light pat of welcome on his ass.

Two guards moved into the prisoners' rank, pushing men aside, and pulled Stuart back out toward the commandant. One of the guards screamed "Ngoi xuong!" Stuart was forced down to a squat. The commandant turned his back on Hunter, and walked him to within a foot of Major Roberts, tapping his palm lightly with his crop.

"Major, you have under your command a very *disobedient* group of men. I fear your time here will be difficult. But that is up to you. Now, your men will be given a delousing bath, and then a nice, cold shower, and clean uniforms. Then you will eat, then your men will clean their quarters for inspection. Who is your second in command?"

"Captain Peters, sir."

"Very well. Place him in charge. You will be quartered separately, in the main building."

"I prefer to stay with my men, Colonel."

The commandant smiled thinly. "But *I* want you where I can observe you, Major."

The major shrugged. "Captain Peters, take charge."

"Yes, sir," said Carter Peters, moving forward, leaning on his crutch. "Two of you men help Hunter up."

The commandant continued to stare at Major Roberts. He held up his left hand, and the two men who had started toward Hunter stopped. Without turning, the commandant pointed toward Hunter with the crop. "That man will not be joining you just yet, Captain. He is late for his training, and must get caught up. That man goes in the box."

"But, Colonel—" protested Major Roberts.

"As does that one." The commandant pointed to Stuart. Two guards pulled him to his feet, and he was marched away following Hunter and his two guards.

The box turned out to be a cramped plywood chamber, probably once a packing crate of some sort. It was designed so that it was too short for a man to stand, and too narrow for him to sit or kneel. Stuart, blindfolded once again, was shoved roughly into one chamber; he heard Hunter bounce into the other side, and both doors were shut.

Stuart waited a minute in the silence. He sensed rather than heard the guards still close outside, waiting for him to speak.

"Sir, can you hear me?" whispered Hunter.

Immediately the guards began pounding on the outside of the box with their bamboo staffs, screaming, "*Im lang di! Im lang di!* Silence!"

"They'll leave off soon, Hunter," Stuart whispered.

Stuart pressed his toes against the front wall of the box and tried to force his ass down the back wall far enough to allow him to straighten out his neck. He was not entirely successful, but he was able to transfer most of the pressure from his neck to his back and thighs, and at least rotate his neck. He thought that Hunter, two inches taller, must be really suffering.

The pounding and shouting ceased, and Stuart waited for what he thought was about five minutes before whispering cautiously, "Hunter?"

"Yes, sir." No shouting, no pounding.

"You OK?"

"Yes, sir. I found a way to kinda lean. They won't leave us here long, d'ya think?"

"I doubt it. They can't risk anything that could really hurt our backs. Say, congratulations on making it all the way in. When I saw that smoke pop right in those play-dinks' faces, I almost died."

"Weren't nothing, really. After they took you off, two of the soldiers just waited. Finally they came in and searched the hideout, but I was lying on top of the log. They looked under everything, but they never looked up. I thought about jumping the hump with the BAR."

Stuart smiled in the darkness, imagining Hunter charging the camp gate with the BAR. "Well done, anyway."

"How bad is that eye?"

"I doubt it's bad at all. On the way in I was taken to a doctor, who tried to talk me into withdrawing. He acted as though he wasn't part of the training, but I think he was."

"So, how we gonna get outa this fucked-up summer camp?"

He is already thinking of escape, thought Stuart. "Well, to get credit for the escape, we have to make it work, assuming the guards had real bullets."

"Which means we have to get, say, twenty meters beyond the wire before they see us."

"Yeah. Under a truck, with a work detail, something."

Suddenly the pounding on the outside of the box began again. "Im lang di! You bad prisna, get nutha half hour for talk! Im lang di, or *nevah* get out!" The pounding ceased.

Stuart counted slowly to two hundred twenty before Hunter spoke. "Fuck 'em. We ain't been here no half hour, and no way they can keep us in here much longer."

The door to Stuart's box was jerked open. Hands grabbed him, yanked him out, and sent him sprawling on the gravel. Once again he managed to roll to protect the eye.

"You dirty, shit-smelling dog! You go now shower, then solitary! You stink up box!"

Stuart was pulled to his feet. "What about the other man?" He felt he had to talk to these animals, to make them see him as human.

The guard forced a high-pitched laugh. "He make fool of Red Forces with smoke grenade! He stay in box forever! Ha! Ha!" The guard poked Stuart sharply in the ribs with his bamboo staff. Stuart moved off, with the guard guiding by tapping first one side, then the other with the staff. Like you drive a camel, thought Stuart. "Hey Red, what's the word in your language for 'escape'?"

The guard barked his high-pitched laugh. "For you, Shit-Spattered Dog, no such word."

"Hell, man, I know I won't escape, but what's the word?"

The guard was silent for a minute. "*Di-di. Di-di* mean run away. But for you, forget it." For punctuation, the guard put a little more emphasis into the staff.

They reached the bathhouse, and Stuart's blindfold was removed, as were his bonds. He was directed to strip, then step into a pool of evil-smelling, milky liquid and squat. The frigid liquid reached up to his neck. Tilting his head to the right, he carefully dipped some of the stuff onto his hair. He was then directed to stand under a shower head. The guard pulled a chain, and a heavy rush of cold water rinsed him. The guard tossed him a bar of yellow soap and a small washcloth. Stuart washed and rinsed quickly but thoroughly, avoiding wetting the eye patch, then washed and rinsed again. He was shivering uncontrollably. The guard directed him to drop the soap in one bucket and the washcloth in another, threw him a thin gray towel. Stuart rubbed himself vigorously, especially his hair, and felt a little warmer. The guard gestured with his staff for Stuart to go into the next room, where he was able to select a rough cotton shirt, canvas trousers with a drawstring, and a loose, quilted jacket. The shirt and trousers were dull gray, and the jacket was an incongruously cheerful bright blue. Stuart put them on. "Boots?" he said to the guard.

"Boots go to Red Forces. Take shoes, there."

Stuart picked through a box of canvas slippers with what appeared to be cardboard soles until he found two that fit. Won't get far in these, he thought.

"Now what, Red, old buddy?" Stuart tried a bright smile on the guard, who, underneath the uniform and the accent, looked like your average Chinese kid from San Francisco.

The guard smiled briefly in return. "You go solitary. Later see Di-wee.* Di-wee very angry, out all night."

"Di-wee is the officer?"

"Di-wee is captain. You learn fast, Shit-Spattered Dog."

*Dai-uy.

* * *

The guard marched Stuart across the yard, this time without the blindfold. He saw his fellow prisoners hoeing the barren ground into long, parallel rows, under the watchful eye of the Di-wee. The Di-wee smiled at Stuart, pointed a finger and cocked his finger and thumb like a pistol, and mock-fired. Stuart made a point of smiling back.

Stuart was prodded into a narrow room, smelling of fresh cement, with one tiny window some fifteen feet above the ground. He heard the door locked behind him. There was a bucket, for the obvious necessities, a drain in the middle of the floor, and a thin mattress with an even thinner blanket on it. Stuart sat on the mattress, then lay down to try to sleep. He was too keyed up, and too hungry. A small iron door in the main door opened, and a bowl of something, and a mug of something, were shoved through onto the cement floor. The iron door clanged shut.

Stuart scrambled forward like an animal. The mug was green tea, the bowl, a thick rice gruel. Stuart shoved the gruel down his throat as quickly as he could without choking. It was bland, flavorless. It was delicious. His shrunken stomach would take only half the bowl. He drank the tea slowly, then managed to eat some more gruel. No telling how often they feed you, he thought. He lay back on the thin mattress, the blanket pulled under his chin, and slept.

Out in the chilly, damp air, the camp routine gradually became established. The acting senior American officer, Capt. Carter Peters, demanded to speak to Major Roberts, and was refused. The men were fed, as promised, but the food was a heavily salted rice gruel, which many couldn't eat, and others ate, only to throw it up again. Captain Peters demanded to know the disposition of Ensign Stuart and Private First Class Hunter, and the guards laughed, and kicked at his injured ankle. The men hoed on.

Stuart awoke with a start. He had been dreaming of his capture, of grinning yellow men probing his injured eye with their staffs, and of the doctor in his white coat, beckoning him to a clean bed with a warm blanket. Stuart sat up, gathering the thin blanket around him. I have no idea of the time that has passed, he thought. He heard a door slam to his right, then silence. He drifted off to sleep.

He awakened again in darkness. A persistent, light tapping on the wall to his right gradually brought him back to consciousness.

Stuart brought his ear close to the wall. There was a definite pattern to the tapping. Three taps, pause for the space of one tap, two taps, a longer pause. During the next long pause, Stuart repeated the pattern, tapping with his ring.

The tapping changed, slowly, like deliberate counting. The taps stopped after Stuart counted nineteen. The instructors had told them that the crudest code among prisoners was to spell by counting through the alphabet. The nineteenth letter in the alphabet was S. The three-tap was a question mark. S with a question mark—are you there, Stuart. Stuart answered with one tap. Yes. Stuart then tapped slowly eight taps, followed by the rapid three, and got back one. H for Hunter. The guy never gives up, thought Stuart. So he is next door.

Stuart began to search with his hands along the wall and at the juncture between the wall and the floor for cracks or holes. Only the floor of the cell was cement; the government hadn't wasted much on the structure. The walls felt like a light composition board. Stuart pushed against it and it moved slightly. But no cracks. Almost no light came in from the small window. Stuart tried whispering, then talking, but Hunter did not answer. They used the tap code to exchange "OKs," and "fed?" and then tired of the laborious process. Stuart felt good about a full night's sleep ahead, and returned to the mattress and wrapped the blanket tightly around him against the increasing chill. Cold is better than cold and wet, he thought, and then he slept.

Stuart shook himself awake, as the small iron door clanged shut. Stuart smelled the rice porridge and felt an immediate and ravenous hunger. He slid out of bed and picked up the bowl, and began eating rapidly with his fingers. Buried in the sticky gruel he found a piece of fatty bacon. He finished the bowl easily, and sipped and savored the cup of tea.

After letting his breakfast settle, Stuart performed ten minutes of calisthenics. He was straining through the fiftieth sit-up when the cell door opened. I tire quickly, he realized.

Two guards stood at the door, each with his bamboo staff. Without speaking, the smaller guard motioned Stuart to come forward. Stuart stood. "Where to, little buddy?"

The guard scowled. "Wash. Then go see Di-wee."

Stuart was led down a short passageway to a head and given a sliver of soap and a towel. There was a mirror on the wall, so he decided to remove the eye patch and see how his eye looked. The cut seemed all right, but the eyelids, both top and bottom, were red and swollen and very tender to the touch. He forced the eye open with his fingers and squinted his right eye shut. His vision through the left eye was blurry, but rapidly it cleared. He found he could keep the eye slightly open without his fingers.

Conjunctivitis, he thought. I had that one summer at swimming camp. A few days of antibiotics once I get out of this zoo. Drive on, he thought, as the tears seeped onto his reddish cheek.

The patch looked dirty, so he threw it away. He washed the eye carefully, then washed the rest of his body as best he could and dried it. The smaller guard pointed to a clean gray prison uniform on a hook. Stuart dressed, and put his quilted jacket back on over the uniform. Again without speaking, the guard motioned for Stuart to follow.

Stuart was marched back along the passage, past the cells. When he passed in front of Hunter's cell, he called loudly, "Morning, Hunter." He got no response from the cell, but a sharp jab in the ribs for his trouble.

At the end of the passageway was a guard station. Another guard came forward and swiftly bound Stuart's arms. The feeling of being bound again sent a chill through Stuart. It is meant to do that, he thought. The corridor continued to the right, and Stuart was prodded rapidly forward, with the new guard leading. At the last door, the lead guard knocked. An Asian-sounding shout came from within. The guard opened the door and shoved Stuart in. The door slammed behind Stuart. Stuart came to attention, he guessed by instinct. Maybe I should slouch, he thought. Who the hell knows?

The Di-wee was seated with his feet up on the metal table before him, grinning and smoking a cigarette. He was a small man with small feet in highly polished boots, neat, even slightly effeminate in appearance. The smoke from his cigarette smelled delicious.

"Hello, Shit-Spattered Dog," he said softly.

"My name is Ensign Stuart."

"Your name is of no importance to me, dog."

Stuart stood silent. I have to understand this, he thought.

"I demand to see Major Roberts."

The Di-wee blew smoke at Stuart. "You are in no position to demand anything, Shit-Spattered Dog. But I am *rude*! A cigarette, *Ensign*?" The Di-wee offered a pack of Marlboros.

A bit difficult, thought Stuart, with my arms bound. Sure would like one. "No, thank you."

"It would be 'no, thank you, *Di-wee*,' wouldn't it?" The man's manner was playful. What is his game?

"Aye, Captain," said Stuart. See where it leads.

The Di-wee swung his legs down and under the table. He lit a fresh cigarette, and pressed it between Stuart's lips. "We have to talk, Ensign Stuart. Training is not proceeding satisfactorily. I fear I may have to fail this entire class." The Di-wee's face was composed, his expression caring.

"Sir," said Stuart, around the cigarette. Sound noncommittal, he thought.

"You, and the marine next door to you, had to be made examples," the Di-wee spread his hands, "because you lasted rather longer outside the wire than the others did. But the example has failed. Do you understand?"

"I'm afraid I don't, Captain."

The Di-wee sighed. "Your friends, Ensign, remain out there, hoeing stupid rows in the soil. They do not resist, they do not try to escape, and, Ensign, they do not care about you and the jarhead, locked away in my little fort. Doesn't that depress you?"

"I demand to see Major Roberts. I demand to be returned to the company of my fellow prisoners."

The captain slammed his fist down hard on the tabletop. "Spare me this school-yard shit! We have something to get done here, Troop! We have a *message* to impart!"

What is he doing to me? thought Stuart. Which role is he playing? "I wish to be returned to my unit, sir."

The captain stood, and threw up his hands. "And so you shall, Shit-Spattered Dog! So you shall! But in *my* time, and for *my* purposes!" He leaned across the table, close to Stuart's face. "You, Shit-Spattered Dog, and that absurd gung-ho marine will indeed be returned to the company of your gallant unit. And then, dog, or Ensign, whichever you prefer, you will demonstrate your mettle. You will escape."

Stuart relaxed. So that's the game, he thought. "Are you saying you'll let us escape?"

The Di-wee sat, and once again propped his feet on the table. "No. Of course not. You will try, and I will catch you, and I will punish you. But your act will, I *hope*, put some life into your comrades."

Stuart puzzled. "When you release us back to the camp, we will become subject to the chain of command. We will escape only if we're told to try by competent authority."

The captain laughed. It sounded like a bark. "No, dog, you will go because *I will it*!" his fist slammed the table. "If you don't, I will force you, and that asshole marine, to *withdraw* from this program! Your military career will be over before it has even begun, *Ensign*!"

Stuart felt strangely detached, cool. "I thought the purpose of this training, *Captain*, was to prepare men for captivity, not to wash them out.''

The Di-wee's eyes took on a cunning cast. ''Asshole, the purpose is, first, to find out who can *take* it, who we can count on. And the rest, we watch.''

This has to be bullshit, thought Stuart. ''When Hunter and I go back to our unit, we'll follow the chain of command, Di-wee.''

The captain laughed. ''No, you won't, Shit-Spattered Dog. Because I won't let you, and your yellow comrades won't let you. You will ache to escape. I will catch you, and you will withdraw, *voluntarily*. You will be the sacrifice needed to teach this class. Dismiss. *DO MANHG!*''

The door flew open, and Stuart was marched roughly back to his cell. He immediately began the tap code for Hunter, but there was no reply.

8 April 1966   **Camp Pettigrew, North Carolina**

Stuart did some calisthenics in his cell, then rested. As the shadows through the high window lengthened, the iron door opened, and another bowl of rice and a cup of tea were thrust through, followed by an open can of C-rations, which proved to contain peaches in syrup. The iron door clanged shut.

Stuart ate slowly, savoring the bland food. He ate the peaches between sips of tea, trying to make them last, but in a few minutes all the food was gone.

I have to make some sense of the Di-wee's story, he thought, lying on the mattress, digesting. How can he make us escape? Why? Were the men outside in the camp truly failing the course? The instructors had said that men would be separated, that hostilities would develop, but that the purpose of the training was to let men see the effects and to understand that they must remain a cohesive unit, stick together, maintain the chain of command. So the Di-wee wants to make Hunter and me believe that we'll be punished because of the failures of the others, failures we have no reason to believe have happened, other than the word of the Di-wee. That has to be it. If he can get us to distrust the others, to try an escape without the consent of the senior officers, he'll have broken the discipline. Stuart smiled to himself. Cunning bastard.

On the gravel courtyard in front of the prison barracks, Capt. Carter Peters stood at attention, bracing himself with his crude crutch. He shivered in the cold. Before him stood one of the junior guard officers, in his neat green uniform and long green overcoat with red collar tabs. Behind Peters, in the barracks, the men rested and bitched. Carter Peters felt very tired. The steady diet of thin, salty gruel gave little energy, and the close conditions of the barracks, plus frequent nighttime turnouts and inspections, meant the men had not slept much. And what little energy the men could glean from the gruel was sapped each day by the cold, damp hours hoeing and planting the commandant's "vegetable garden." The men were surly. Some were scared. Two had become so ill from not being able to keep the food down that they had been forced to ask for medical attention, with the full agreement of Peters, and had therefore been "withdrawn" from the camp, and from the program.

Behind the guard officer stood two guards with bamboo staffs, dressed warmly in quilted trousers and jackets. Captain Peters began his twice-a-day litany: "I demand to see Major Roberts."

"De-NIED, Cho de," the guard officer sneered. "The major does not wish to see you."

Peters sighed. "I demand to see the commandant."

"Denied." The officer smiled. "The commandant is indisposed."

Indisposed, thought Peters. This training has lost touch with reality. "Lieutenant, my men are sick, and they're cold, and they're weak. We need proper food. We need blankets. According to the rules regarding the treatment of prisoners of war, we are entitled—''

The officer held up his hand. "Captain Pe-ter, your men have food. They have blankets. Do you think the fighters of the Red Forces live in luxury? A bowl of rice is enough for a *soldier* of the Red Forces; is it not enough for sissy fliers of great America? Fliers who have nothing to do but sleep, and hoe a bit in the colonel's garden?''

Peters shifted his weight, and adjusted the crutch. An angry flush rose in his cheeks. He looked down at the pudgy officer, some four inches shorter than his own five-eleven. "You *fighters* look pretty well fed.''

The officer jabbed his gloved finger into the chest of the air force captain. "Maybe, Captain, we can do with less. Anyway, as more of your men *withdraw*, there may be more of the people's rations to go around. Have you finished with your stupid *demands*, Captain?''

Peters shifted his weight again. The pain in his ankle rose in waves. "You have two of my men, Ensign Stuart and Private First Class Hunter, held incommunicado. As acting senior American officer, I have the right to see them.''

The guard officer stood stone-faced. The two guards behind him giggled. "You will have them back soon enough. The Di-wee tires of them.'' The officer took one step back and saluted, concluding the interview. Bleakly, Captain Peters returned the salute, and hobbled back to the barracks. This is *training*, he thought. It will *end*. Imagine, *imagine* the real thing!

And why do the guards giggle when I ask about Stuart and Hunter?

Stuart was sound asleep. In a dream, he saw Karen in the grip of the grinning Di-wee, behind a glass wall. She didn't know, of course, who he was, or that he held her lover in captivity. Karen smiled at the Di-wee, and let him touch her hand. Stuart pounded on the glass wall, which gave back no sound. The dream ended with the repeated crash of a gong.

Stuart awakened quickly. The gong continued, along with Asian-sounding shouting over the camp's public address speakers. Bright light flooded in through the high window, as the whole camp came awake. Stuart looked at his wrist, futilely. He could not get used to living without a watch, even though the guards had confiscated all watches on the first day of prison camp. The instructors had said something during orientation about autonomous time management. A joke then. Stuart realized with a chill that he was not even sure how many days had passed.

The din outside his cell increased. Stuart could hear guards running to and fro, shouting.

Shit! he thought, someone must have gone through the wire!

Three guards burst through the door of his cell. They quickly bound his arms and hustled him into the passageway and down it to a small room with a table and several metal folding chairs. He was roughly pushed into a chair and tied to it. The guards left, closing the door behind them. Someone must have gotten out! Nothing else could explain this commotion, he thought. The door opened again, and three other guards entered, dragging Hunter. They bound him to a chair across the table from Stuart, and once again left, closing the door.

"Hunter! Jesus, am I glad to see you! What's happening?"

Hunter grinned. "No idea, sir, how are you?"

Hunter looks fit enough, thought Stuart. "I'm OK. The Di-wee talk to you today?"

"Shit, sir, half the afternoon. Told me I was a traitor, taking it easy in my cell, not even trying to escape. Says you an' me goin' back to the camp tonight, best try something, or he's gonna fix something so we have to withdraw."

"He told me more or less the same thing. You got any idea what he's thinking about?"

"I think we're being set up somehow."

"How?"

"No idea, really, but I think he's still pissed about you and me evading capture so long. I think he means to fuck us up, if he can. Sir, you and me are a team now, an escape team, whether we like it or not."

Stuart smiled. "Still think we can get out?"

"Fuckin' A. I ain't been thinkin' about nothin' else in that shithole cell."

He is a better man than I am, thought Stuart.

The door opened quickly and two guards came in, followed by the Di-wee and a bewildered-looking Major Roberts.

The Di-wee held a short swagger stick in his right hand. "*Major Roberts*, you have demanded to see your solitary-confined comrades. Here they are. You have two minutes."

Major Roberts looks disoriented, or drugged, thought Stuart. That is not possible. This is training.

The major said nothing, just started, swallowing slowly. Finally Stuart spoke. "Are you all right, Major?"

The major seemed to pull himself together. "Yes, fine, Stuart. You? Hunter, you OK?"

"Fine, sir," said Stuart. Hunter merely nodded.

"You're going out of here tonight, to the barracks," Major Roberts's thought seemed to escape him.

"And you, sir?" asked Hunter.

"The-the, ah Di-wee, keeps me here. Here. You have to tell Captain Peters to resist! To, ah, struggle!" The major's head fell. He mumbled "shtruggle," then slumped.

"Enough, Major," said the smiling Di-wee, taking his arm and leading him from the room. Once again the door closed.

"What do you make of that, Hunter?"

"Bastard looked drunk."

Stuart pondered. The major had appeared flushed, and, yes, he thought, even fat. How does this fit the Di-wee's plan?

The Di-wee opened the door quietly, and walked to the head of the table. He looked at the two bound men for a minute. "So, Shit-Spattered Dog, and ridiculous Pathfinder, it is time for you to return to your comrades. I am sure they will welcome you. And I am sure you will find my *advice* appropriate." With an elaborate bow, he motioned toward the door, as guards entered and untied Stuart and Hunter from the chairs. They were marched out of the room and down the passage through an open door. Outside in the brilliantly lit courtyard, they were prodded toward the single rank of prisoners arrayed behind Captain Peters. On a little stage in the center of the yard stood the commandant, and next to him, Major Roberts. Stuart saw the prisoners, and stopped dead, despite the prodding. My God, he thought.

Healthy young men who have been deprived of food for three days developed a hollow-eyed look, and discomfort in their innards, but a couple of days of moderate intake of food and some rest brings their appearance back to nearly normal. Men starved for five days look far different. Captain Peters and the prisoners behind him looked truly emaciated. Stuart looked at Hunter, who was patting his hard belly. He sees it too, thought Stuart. This is the setup. We'll be seen as having accepted privilege.

"Here are your *comrades*, Captain Peters," shouted the commandant in his high, reedy voice. "You may now *care* for them! And here is your senior officer, well, as you all can see! Now you are dismissed!"

Stuart felt his bonds suddenly released. He steeled himself, and walked steadily toward the thin and ragged rank of prisoners. Hunter walked at his side, his face set in anger.

Hunter and Stuart sat on narrow cots facing Captain Peters. For nearly an hour they had gone over everything of significance that had happened since they had been taken from the box on the morning of the first day. The men were all tired, but Captain Peters continued. In other parts of the barracks, a few men slept, but most watched and listened. Some looked as if they were afraid of us, thought Stuart. Some looked openly hostile, and some had a listless, uncaring stare.

"OK," Carter Peters paused. "Now, once more before we sack out. Tell me about your meetings with the Di-wee. Hunter?"

"The guards brought me to his office, hands tied. He called me hero marine, or Pathfinder, and said I had angered him by making him stay up all night looking for me. He said he was going to find a way to wash me out. He said he wanted me to lead an escape attempt so he could have a little fun chasing 'the gardeners'—he calls you all 'the gardeners.' "

Peters shifted his posture. How degrading, he thought. "Continue, Hunter."

"Yes, sir. Well, he said he would like to chase you sorry-ass—sorry, sir, but those were his words—"

"Just continue, Hunter."

"Well, then maybe make something out of a dismal training class."

"And what did you say?"

"Nothing, sir, just kept repeating the classroom crap about demanding to see the senior American officer, demanding to be returned to my unit."

"Did he mention Ensign Stuart?"

"Yes, sir. He said he'd already agreed to the phony escape."

"Anything else?"

Hunter thought for a moment, his hard eyes moving from face to face. That asshole Martini wants to say something, he thought. "Nothing else, sir."

Stuart then repeated his account of his interview with the Di-wee. Carter Peters probed a bit, then fell silent.

"May I say something, Captain?" asked Stuart.

"Go ahead."

"It occurs to me, sir, that this is right out of the training manual. Major Roberts is separated, and appears to be collaborating. Hunter and I are separated, apparently for punishment, but then you find, we *all* find, that we have indeed been better treated. We're told that your inaction may cause all of us to fail this course. You're told—we don't know what you've been told, but the effect of this *training*, sir, is to engender distrust, and to break down discipline. And," Stuart paused, and looked straight into the angry face of Lieutenant Martini, "it seems to be working."

Martini exploded. "That's easy for you to say, with two days warm and dry to feed up and rest up. Well, I don't buy it, Stuart. I think you gave something up."

"Just what do you think we gave up?"

Martini sneered, "From what the guards say, maybe your pretty pink asses!"

Stuart bolted upright, striking his shoulders on the upper bunk. He was shocked speechless. He felt Hunter's restraining hand on his arm. Carter Peters was speaking.

"Martini, that was uncalled for!"

Uncalled for? thought Stuart. Martini continued, "Sorry, Carter, but let me finish. You want to know what we heard, *Ensign*? OK, maybe you're right, maybe this *training* is just more than any of us could have expected. But whenever anyone asked for you two, the guards would giggle, and say something like, 'they with Di-wee now, hee, hee! the Di-wee *special* friend now, not like you, peasant heroes!' And face it! That Di-wee looks like a fruit!"

Stuart sat, controlling his anger. Hunter spoke, ice in his voice. "Surely you didn't *believe* these slurs against your comrades, Lieutenant?"

Martini shook his head and looked at his muddy slippers. All his anger had suddenly disappeared; he looked tired and without hope. "I'm sorry, guys. I don't know what I believe." He looked up, his face twisted in anguish. "The fuckers are getting to us, aren't they?"

"Just like they said they would," said Peters. "They're following their own script to the letter."

Stuart nodded. "They're far more creative than we thought."

"And more brutal," offered Hunter. "But when you think of it, nobody has really been hurt. Your bellies ache more than ours, but they took the guys out who were really sick."

"It's still training, Carter," said Stuart.

"What do you suggest, William?"

"That we try an escape."

"No-oo, Carter!" cried Martini. "We haven't got a chance with the Di-wee's goons! Most of us can barely walk!"

"Just Hunter and me, Captain, while we're still strong." Stuart's voice was very soft, and very insistent.

"Oh, that's *great*, Stuart!" shouted Martini, his voice high-pitched and quavering. "Just you two, to play footsie with your friend, the almighty fucking Di-wee down at the safe house, while the rest of us are left to the mercy of his goons!"

Stuart felt his anger rising. Peters spoke sharply. "Shut up, Martini! Shut UP!" Martini slumped, his head in his hands.

"How about it, Carter?" Stuart thrust his angry, flushed face into Peters's, "Do we have command authorization to attempt to escape?"

"Do you want to try, Hunter?" asked Peters.

"Yes, sir!" said Hunter, without hesitation.

"Then do it." Peters felt old and tired. "Do it well."

"Thank you, sir," chorused Hunter and Stuart.

Peters looks up bleakly. "Do you have some sort of a plan?"

"Lots of 'em," said Hunter, grinning.

Reveille was held at 0530 in the stuffy barracks where the seventeen prisoners slept. The men were marched to the wash-house, then back to the barracks, where breakfast was served— gruel from a big pot, and tea. Each man was responsible for his own bowl, made of plastic, and his tin cup. The portions were slightly smaller than Stuart and Hunter had been served in solitary, and the tea was cold.

"Hm," said Carter Peters, as he squatted between Stuart and Hunter, "how does this compare to the chow up topside at the big house?"

" 'Bout the same," said Hunter.

"Maybe a little less of it," said Stuart. He thought to himself with a twinge of guilt that the only detail he had left out about his solitary confinement was the can of peaches. Wouldn't have done the others any good to know.

"Tastes the same?" probed Peters.

"Sure. Why?" asked Hunter.

"Because up to today, the stuff they gave us was watery, and very salty. Some of the men couldn't hold it down. What do you make of that?"

"Sorry to hear that, sir," said Hunter, without expression.

What's he getting at? thought Stuart. "Maybe a new gruel chef checked in." The joke fell flat.

"Or maybe the captain thinks we sold the plans to the Polaris missile to the dinks to get our food from the commandant's personal mess?" Hunter's voice had taken on its edge.

"Easy, Hunter," said Stuart, quickly.

"No, that's OK," said Peters, rocking back on his heels and smiling. "One of the things I came over to you for was to apologize for last night. Especially for Martini, ah, who has had a difficult time of it, especially since Lieutenant Harrigan had to withdraw, close to pneumonia."

"We were in the bush with Lieutenant Martini, Captain. We know about Lieutenant Martini," said Hunter.

Peters looked hard at Hunter. "Remember why you are here, Hunter."

"Yes, sir." Expressionless.

"So," said the captain, cleaning his bowl and setting it aside, "how are you going to try it?"

Stuart was about to say he hadn't any idea when Hunter cut in. "Better you don't know, sir." Hunter smiled.

Carter Peters's brows arched.

"Security, sir." Hunter fairly beamed.

Peters smiled and stood up. "Quite, Hunter. Well, good luck with it."

As the captain shuffled off, Stuart whispered, "You sure do know how to tread the fine line of insubordination, Hunter."

"Thank you, sir! United States Marine Corps, sir!" Hunter tried to look solemn, but didn't quite bring it off. Despite himself, Stuart grinned.

A gong sounded, and the prisoners were formed up for a short harangue from a junior guard officer. The wooden hoes were distributed, and the prisoners set off in the pinkish dawn to work in the commandant's garden.

Hunter's escape plans, formulated in the isolation of his cell, did not stand up to the light of day. The wire was a little farther from the barracks than he had remembered, the gate higher, the guards more numerous. There were no guard towers, except right by the gate, and, although the fence looked as if it could be easily climbed, the only way to get up and over even at night would be to have the guards' attention diverted, and Hunter didn't trust the other prisoners to get a diversion done right, or even agree to try.

That asshole Martini, thought Hunter. He would probably turn them in for an extra bowl of rice if he knew the plan. Imagine him accusing Stuart and me of dropping trow for the Di-wee! Jesus!

Hunter looked across at Stuart, hoeing but looking around. The guy's a boot ensign. Still, I think he's a goer. His eye looks like shit; must hurt. He could see tears seeping in a steady stream from the nearly closed left eye. We'd better do this quickly, if at all, he thought.

After evening chow was passed out, and the prisoners once again paraded, the guards distributed mimeographed forms of a germ-warfare confession. The prisoners took the forms, and stuffed them in the pockets of their quilted jackets. Hunter read his: "The undersigned officer of the Imperialist Forces of the

United States of America willingly confesses to having dropped
from aircraft dusts and gases containing agents designed to
sicken and kill the civilian population of the Democratic Republic of. . . ." Hunter balled it up and threw it away. As the
prisoners were once again marched to the washhouse, an army
second lieutenant named Loonfeather approached him.

"Hey, Gung-ho, saw you throw away the Di-wee's confession
form. Not smart."

Hunter hissed, "Surely the lieutenant does not advocate signing that shit."

Loonfeather grinned, "Ease off, Bro. Not everyone here is
Martini. But that confession is *genuinely useful*."

"How so?" I can talk to this guy, thought Hunter.

Loonfeather leaned in close. "Not much toilet paper on the
evening watch, Bro."

Hunter grinned. "OK, Bro, I learn. You Indian, or what?"

"Yep. Dakota. White people say Sioux."

"Don't you want to get out?"

"Fuckin' A, Troop. Only I got a sprained ankle, slow you
down too much. You steal a truck, you tap my shoulder."

Hunter liked the Indian, and took a chance. "If we need a
diversion, will you lead it?"

Loonfeather grinned. "Fuckin' A." He disappeared into the
latrine.

One trooper, maybe, in this sorry-ass circle-jerk, thought
Hunter.

The night was interrupted once, for a bed-toss. Guards
shouted, pushed the men around, and threw bunks on the floor.
Hunter watched the prisoners. Most seemed almost to sleep
through it, even while standing. Loonfeather tipped him a wink,
then slowly closed his eyes. When the guards left and the overhead lights were put out, the barracks seemed instantly asleep.
Hunter lay awake, fighting his fatigue. We need a workable plan,
he thought. In the end fatigue prevailed, and he slept dream-
lessly.

At breakfast the following morning, the rumor was passed:
third-to-last day. Hunter felt his opportunity slipping away. If we
don't go, the Di-wee wins. And these assholes win. He thought
again of Martini, and of the look of shock and pain on Ensign
Stuart's face when Martini all but called him a queer. Ten minutes in a room alone with Martini, thought Hunter. Wouldn't
need but five. Then the Di-wee.

Hunter was suddenly aware of his thoughts. It was the first

time in his life that he wanted to hurt someone, really hurt. It was a physical need, and it was strong.

It has to be today, he decided.

Hunter squatted down beside Stuart, and whispered, "Sir, I'm not sure how, but we di-di today."

"OK, Hunter," Stuart replied without looking at him. The short, fat guard the prisoners called Watermelon was looking at them. "Look, you have to know, this eye is getting bad again."

Hunter's heart rammed inside his chest. "You don't want to go, sir?"

Watermelon turned away. Stuart looked at Hunter sharply. The eye does look a mess, thought Hunter. "Fuck me, Marine. I'm *going*!" He grinned. "But you'll have to lead."

Hunter patted Stuart on the shoulder, felt the fever. "You sure?"

"No-o doubt."

Hunter was hoeing his row in the barren earth, thinking, thinking. The Di-wee and two guards marched across the gravel to the farmers. The two guards grabbed Stuart, threw away his crude hoe, forced him to his knees, and tied his arms. Captain Peters stepped forward to protest. The Di-wee held up his hand and shouted, "Bunk inspection for Shit-Spattered Dog! Continue gardening, heroic peasants! Ha!" Stuart was marched toward the barracks. Hunter left his row, and, carrying his hoe, quietly slipped around to the back of the barracks, an idea forming in his mind.

The Di-wee left his guards at the door of the barracks and, taking one of the guard's bamboo staffs, stepped inside behind Stuart. With the staff, he prodded Stuart to sit on his bunk.

"The eye gets worse, Shit-Spattered Dog."

Stuart held the Di-wee's eyes with his one good one. "It will carry, Di-wee."

"You have not escaped. Your opportunity has come, and you have done nothing of what I told you."

Stuart forced a smile. "The ides of March have come, Di-wee, but they have not gone."

The Di-wee smiled, propped the staff against the wall, and squatted in front of Stuart. "Cute, but not enough. I don't think you have either the strength, or the *balls*, to try to make it out. Therefore, I have decided you will teach the commandant's gardeners a lesson in a different way. You will voluntarily withdraw, because of the condition of your eye."

Stuart smiled, "You'd like that."

"And I shall have it."

Stuart considered. The pain was bad, but endurable. He knew he was feverish, but he was having no problem seeing out of the eye, to the extent he could open it. "No way, man."

The Di-wee gripped his chin. "Look at me, asshole. You can't even see out of the left side of your face, can you?"

"Well enough, Di-wee."

The Di-wee's open-handed blow to the left side of his head took Stuart completely by surprise. He felt a sharp yelp of pain and rage escape from his throat, and warm fluid flood down his cheek. The world turned white-hot, then cooled to red behind his closed eyes. Pain pushed his breakfast suddenly upward, but he held it, swallowing the acid. He opened his eyes when he heard a sharp grunt. He saw the Di-wee's face inches from his, his eyes protruding, his head pressed upward by the forearm of a powerful man gripping him in a choke hold. He looked up and saw the face of Hunter above that of the Di-wee. Hunter's face was contorted with anger.

"K-kill him," choked Stuart.

Hunter released the choke hold and threw the Di-wee on his back. He picked up the Di-wee's bamboo staff and held it vertically, like a harpoon over the Di-wee's head. He stepped astride his prone body, ready to use the staff or to do a knee drop on the man's chest if he moved. The Di-wee's face went from purple to red as oxygen flowed back up the vessels in his neck. His eyes were still closed. I really choked the hump out, thought Hunter.

Stuart shook his head slowly and opened his eyes.

"Shake it off, sir," said Hunter, gently.

"Yeah. Jesus, that hurt." Stuart looked at the mess of blood and pus on his shirt. "Can you reach me a towel or something?"

"Ensign. Look, leave it. It's a mess. It looks disgusting, but it's just a little cut. And it will divert attention. I'll get you fixed up as soon as we get out."

"We, we are going out?"

"Just as soon as I get into this asshole's uniform."

Stuart shook his head, trying to clear it. "I'm a little groggy, man."

"Don't mean nothing. Look, I'm the Di-wee, and I'm taking you out to the medical trailer. You have agreed to withdraw."

Stuart forced his left eye open. The vision was blurry, but cleared as tears flooded, dripping more of the mess onto his shirt. He smiled at Hunter. "Yeah. Di-di time."

The Di-wee moaned, a rattling sound in his throat. Hunter raised the staff. "Well, *Di-wee*, is it *prisoner*, or do I dash your brains out here and now?"

"Pris-" the Di-wee winced at the pain in his throat. "Prisoner." The word came out in a whistle.

Hunter took a step back, and relaxed his grip on the staff. "Good choice. Now, don't get up, just wriggle out of that uniform."

The Di-wee got to his knees, and unbuttoned his long woolen coat. "I'll have your ass for this, Hunter. Not just the escape, but for assaulting an officer."

Hunter raised the staff again. "You're a *dink* officer, asshole. And you just assaulted Ensign Stuart. Hurry up, right down to your jockeys."

The Di-wee removed his polished boots, his trousers, and his loose woolen tunic.

"Now untie Ensign Stuart." Stuart stood and turned around. Now that the pain is receding, I think my eye feels better with less pressure. I can keep it open, he thought. He felt the cord come off his arms, which tingled.

Hunter handed the staff to Stuart, who pointed it at the Di-wee while Hunter tied him up good and tight, wrists and ankles together with one cord. He tore a towel in half lengthwise for a gag.

"There's no need to gag me, Hunter. Under the rules, once taken prisoner, I'll have to remain here quietly until I'm found."

"In a pig's eye," said Hunter, and gagged him tightly. He shoved the Di-wee under Stuart's bunk, all the way to the wall. "Your rules just don't give me much comfort."

Hunter undressed quickly and pulled on the Di-wee's uniform. It was too small, and it bound in all the wrong places. He rammed his feet into the shiny half boots. "Whew! Ain't walking far in these!" He shrugged into the long overcoat, and put his own cloth slippers into the pocket. The boots pinched horribly. He picked up Stuart's blanket from the bunk, and draped it over the ensign's shoulders, leaving the messy shirt exposed.

"You feel OK, sir?"

Stuart nodded and smiled, "Yeah. My head's clear. I can run when we get outside."

"That's plan B. Just follow my lead. I'm the Di-wee, and I'm taking you out. Clear?"

"Roger."

Hunter pulled the Di-wee's soft, peaked cap low on his brow, and picked up the staff. "Try to walk like your hands are still tied. Keep your face down until I prod you, then look right at the guards. Ready?"

"Ready?"

"Let's do it."

They stepped out of the barracks and toward the gate, Stuart leading, his head down. The two guards who had accompanied the Di-wee earlier stood about twenty feet away, watching the gardeners. The nearest looked up, and started toward them. Hunter jabbed Stuart in the back, and he looked up quickly. The guard's chin dropped, and he looked away quickly. "Di-wee?" chirped the guard.

"Gate. Open," barked Hunter, and the kid ran to the gate. The other guard continued to stare dumbly at Stuart. Look away, dammit, thought Hunter. We're going to have to pass very close to the second guard.

Hunter walked directly behind Stuart, to keep the guard from seeing past the ensign. At ten feet, he tapped Stuart between the shoulder blades and said sharply, "Dung lai!"

Stuart stopped. Hunter speaks good dinkese, thought Stuart. I'll have to try to hold this guard's attention. The gate was opened, and several guards gathered there, enjoying the show. Two guards manned the tower above the gate.

Shit, thought Hunter. Have to change the game plan. He put his hand on Stuart's shoulder, and turned him away from the gate to face the gardeners. Several men looked away quickly. Carter Peters was closest. He put his hand to his mouth, but held his eyes on Stuart's. He opened his mouth to make the required protest, then with a thrill he recognized Hunter.

"You listen, you stupid peasant heroes!" boomed Hunter. "This man withdraw. But this no ordinary prisna! This Shit-Spattered Dog! He defy commandant! He defy Di-wee! He no brave! He quit, get treatment. No brave man should look at him! Maybe all prisna like quit, huh?"

Jesus, Hunter, don't overdo it, thought Stuart, though he does sound remarkably like the Di-wee.

"I can't take any more a' this shit! Arrgh!" screamed Lieutenant Loonfeather as he threw down his hoe and hobbled toward the open gate. The guard near Stuart swung his staff at Loonfeather's legs, tripping him, but he was up quickly and kept going. The Di-wee's other escort, without his staff, tried to tackle Loonfeather, but was sent sprawling by a neat stiff arm to the jaw. The remaining guards by the gate gang-tackled the lieutenant, who continued to struggle and howl like a madman.

"That prisna go in the box," shouted Hunter. "Put prisna in box! Di-wee see prisna first get back." Hunter paused. Beautiful. "Now all get to work. You, Shit-Spattered Dog, Tcho da."

Hunter marched Stuart directly through the gate, keeping Stuart's body between himself and the lone guard standing by the gate, ready to close it behind them. The guard was holding his jaw in obvious pain, and saw nothing. The guards in the tower saw Stuart's bloody face, and the top of the Di-wee's cap, then turned to watch the continuing struggle of four men trying to get Loonfeather into the box. The gate was closed and secured.

Jesus, Mary, and Joseph, thought Carter Peters, hoeing slowly. He looked straight at the ground to hide his grin. He was trying so hard not to laugh that tears came to his eyes.

Outside the gate, Hunter marched Stuart quickly toward the medical trailer. "Now what?" whispered Stuart.

"Keep going. Right up the steps, into the trailer."

Stuart mounted the steps and pushed the door open. Hunter followed him through and closed the door behind him. The doctor stood up from his chair, setting a book aside. "Well, I see you're finally going to take my advice and withdraw—what the fuck?" Hunter had the doctor by the throat.

"OK, dink doctor, very quiet. Now, quickly, clean up that eye."

The doctor's eyes showed fear. Good, thought Hunter. "I can't treat him unless he withdraws."

Hunter tightened his grip. The doctor grasped at Hunter's wrists, and struggled feebly. "OK, OK. You win." Once released, the doctor smiled. "Jesus, you guys got balls. No one has ever tried this. How'd you get out?"

"Never mind that," said Hunter, "just fix the eye, and quickly."

"Yeah, OK. Sit over here, son."

The doctor quickly cleaned the eye, probing carefully. "Probably was a good thing you got cut. Lotta pus came out." The doctor squeezed gently, and Stuart winced as more mess flowed down his cheek. "Sorry, son, but let's get all we can."

The doctor worked deftly, cleaning, then taping an ointment-soaked patch over the eye. Stuart felt better than he had in days. The doctor prepared an injection.

"What's in that needle," said Hunter, quickly.

The doctor stopped. "Antibiotics. Bicillin. Why?"

"No shit?"

"Of course not. I *am* a doctor."

"Gonna make him drowsy, or sick?"

"A little queasy, maybe, if he hasn't eaten. But shit, man, he needs it."

Stuart felt detached, savoring the cool ointment on the hot eye. "Go ahead, Doc. I can stand the queasiness." The needle jabbed his arm.

Stuart's arm tingled. "Can you give me a clean shirt, Doc?"

The doctor smiled, and pulled a blue navy working shirt from a locker. "Why not? In for a penny, in for a pound." He handed the shirt to Stuart, who shrugged out of the blood- and pus-stained prison shirt and dropped it on the floor of the trailer.

Hunter picked up a roll of adhesive tape. "Gotta tie you, Doc, sorry."

"OK. Gotta play along, I guess. Not too tightly, though. Can't lose circulation in my fingers."

Hunter taped the doctor to his chair. "What size shoes you wear, Doc?"

"Eleven. You gonna take my shoes?"

"Got to," said Hunter, and did.

"You gonna run through the woods in white shoes?"

"They will get dirty soon enough." Hunter smeared petroleum jelly on the shoes. That should pick up dirt, he thought. "There another door outa this trailer?"

The doctor's eyes twinkled. "Yep. Behind the filing cabinets, other end. You fuckers are crazy."

"Thanks, Doc." Hunter gagged him with gauze, leaving plenty of room to breathe. "Let's di-di, Ensign."

The guard at the gate tower became suspicious some fifteen minutes after the Di-wee and his prisoner had passed through the gate, because the Di-wee hadn't returned. He shouted down to another guard, who went to find Lieutenant Tranh, the duty guard officer. Lieutenant Tranh walked down to the medical tent, and found Doctor Fredericks bound and gagged. Lieutenant Tranh thought that the doctor was altogether too amused about the escape. The officer hurried back to the camp, and sounded the gong. The off-duty guards hurriedly assembled, and the prisoners cheered.

The guards swarmed through the barracks, and quickly found the Di-wee. They untied the cord binding his wrists and ankles, and removed the gag. The Di-wee was pale and disoriented. A guard was sent running for a new uniform for the Di-wee. As soon as he was dressed, he was helped across the compound to the main block, where the offices and the solitary confinement cells were located. The doctor was waiting.

The doctor looked at the angry purple bruises on the Di-wee's neck, and whistled. Two guards held the Di-wee steady on the stool while the doctor looked into his eyes and tested his reflexes. "You OK, Mac?"

The Di-wee blinked his eyes as the doctor's light was withdrawn. "Could use some water," he rasped.

"Coming up, sir," said Lieutenant Tranh, and brought a glass.

"Thanks, Tommy. Look, you better call Base, and make sure that safe house is manned. We haven't had a successful escape in the last sixteen programs."

"Consider it done, Captain," said the lieutenant, and left the doctor and the Di-wee alone.

"What do you think, Doc?"

The doctor shrugged, and rubbed some petroleum jelly on the bruises. "No damage from the choking. Dehydration from the gag. Drink some water, get some rest."

"Lieutenant Tranh—ah, Tommy, says they found you taped to your chair."

"Right! The fuckers marched right in, one of them in your uniform! He stood me up by the throat; I mean, Mac, look at these bruises!" The doctor pulled his collar open. The Di-wee saw a dark purple welt on either side of the doctor's throat.

"How do your bruises compare with mine?"

"Well, shit, Mac, no way, but that was one scary dude."

"What did he say to you?"

"Well, I told him I couldn't do anything, lessen he withdrew, I mean, like procedure. But he made, and I mean *forced* me to treat the other one's eye!"

The Di-wee leaned forward. "That's good. I was going to bring him to you anyway. Doc, I didn't hurt that kid, did I? Shit, I just gave him a sharp slap, and his whole face practically exploded."

The doctor shook his head. "No, Mac, the eye is clean. Must have been swollen really tight. You probably opened the original cut."

"Would that have been really painful?"

"Yep, damn straight."

The Di-wee shook his head. "I gotta tell you, Doc, I'm glad this is my last class. I hate this shit."

"But the training is important, you say."

"Yeah, I guess. But if that crazy marine hadn't grabbed me, I think I would have hugged that Navy kid."

"I know. So what happens now? Send out the chasers, bring 'em back alive?"

The Di-wee smiled. The movement hurt his neck. "No, Doc, we don't have the chasers except in the Field Phase. They're marines getting trained in night infiltration up at Quantico, down for a little Practical."

"So, what, then?"

The Di-wee stood up, and drank another glass of water from the sink. "Well, Doc, we will just let them stumble through the jungle for a couple of hours, find the safe house, and get their milk and cookies. Then we will go pick them up.''

''Bet you're going to dance on them really good.''

The Di-wee smiled again, and it hurt again. ''Oh, yeah, we will. Seems almost sad, Doc. The more you try in this program, the more you get fucked up. But in a real prison camp, that's what they do. Go for the natural leaders; break them, and the rest, the sheep, just lay down.''

''I get the funny feeling you're not entirely sad, or even pissed off, about this escape, Mac.''

The Di-wee smiled. I have got to stop doing that, he thought, rubbing his throat. ''Oh, I am not *pleased*. I wanted an *attempt*, not an outright breakout. But at least the thing was done by a United States Marine.''

''Semper fi, right?''

The Di-wee put on his regulation Di-wee scowl. ''Fuck you, *navy* dockta! Gotta get me Shit-Spattered Dog, and *specially*, Pathfinda! Ha! Ha!'' The Di-wee walked from the office. The ha! ha! really hurt.

Hunter and Stuart made easy time through the scrubby pine woods, and reached the safe house in a little over two hours, by the Di-wee's watch, now strapped to Hunter's wrist. Training doctrine required any escapees to proceed immediately to the safe house, which was as easy as going downhill. If they made it, they had been told, their escape would be rated a success, and they would be given food and water, and then returned to training without prejudice.

The safe house was a metal hut, located in a clearing beside a dirt road. A jeep with marine corps markings was parked in front. Stuart and Hunter watched from the trees, and saw no movement.

''What do you think, sir?'' whispered Hunter.

''Well, it's supposed to be manned. Let's move up quietly, then rush the door.''

''Go.''

Hunter, carrying the bamboo staff, reached the door. They had detected no movement in the hut as they approached in staggered rushes. Hunter waited, silently, for five minutes, then offered a thumbs-up sign to Stuart. Stuart nodded, and returned the thumbs-up. Hunter kicked the flimsy wooden door off its hinges, and lunged into the room. He was greeted by a scream. Pressed against the far wall of the hut was a uniformed navy nurse, her hand tight over her mouth, ending her scream. Hunter lowered the staff.

"Howdy, ma'am," said Hunter, with his best home-boy grin.

The nurse dropped her hand. "They told me you guys were crazy."

Hunter threw the staff in the corner. "Mad marines, ma'am. Crazed to kill the enemy, but always courteous to womenfolk."

Stuart stepped through the doorway, and propped the broken door back in place. "Sorry about the fright, ma'am."

The nurse smiled. She was young, and quite pretty, thought Stuart. "You guys want some chow?"

"Damn right, ah, yessum," said Hunter.

The nurse opened a Styrofoam cooler, and produced two wrapped sandwiches and a half gallon of milk. She put the sandwiches on paper plates on a plain wooden table, poured milk into paper cups, and gestured the men to stools. "Been a while since anybody made it all the way down here."

" 'At a fact," said Hunter, his mouth full of chicken sandwich.

"Now, you marines eat *very slowly*! Chew! After what you've been eating, that sandwich is mighty rich."

"I'm a marine. This here officer is only Navy. Sorry, sir!" Hunter smiled at Stuart, who was grinning while chewing slowly. She has a beautiful smile, thought Hunter. "What's yer name, lovely lady?"

The nurse blushed, and smiled despite herself. "Clarissa Meadows. *Lieutenant* Clarissa Meadows." She turned to Stuart for help. "Why don't you say anything, sir?"

Stuart grinned as he swallowed his mouthful of sandwich and took a long drink of milk. I have never enjoyed a meal as much as this, not in the finest restaurants of Atlanta or New York, he thought. "The mission of the amphibious Navy, ma'am, is to bring the marines to battle, not tell them how to fight it."

"And the mission of navy nurses is to get you to eat slowly. Really, if you wolf that down after not eating much for days, you will lose it."

Hunter put down his sandwich and drank a little milk. "Feel free to interrupt me, Lieutenant, at any time." The big, boyish grin.

Stuart could see the nurse was halfway between nervous and charmed. "Don't let him bother you, Lieutenant. He just hasn't had anybody to smile at in a week."

They finished the sandwiches, slowly, and drank most of the milk. They were smoking the nurse's cigarettes when the sounds of a jeep and a heavy truck arriving broke up the banter. "We run, Ensign?" said Hunter, stubbing out the cigarette.

"No, Hunter. We made it. The game is ours."

There was a pounding on the door. Hunter leaned over to the pretty nurse, "Will you marry me, if'n I live?" The nurse blushed and smiled, and moved away. The door fell down, and two guards with BARs walked in, followed by the Di-wee, his face white with rage.

"Bind them, tight!" rasped the Di-wee.

Two more guards entered, and tied the men's arms in the now-familiar manner. Stuart kept his face impassive, but Hunter grinned happily at the Di-wee.

The Di-wee turned to the nurse, "You, out!" The nurse blanched, picked up her field jacket and the cooler, and fled. The Di-wee paced in the small room like a caged lion. They heard the nurse's jeep start, and drive off. After a minute of pacing, the Di-wee spoke. "Shit-Spattered Dog will be returned to the camp to complete his training. Pathfinda—but it's over for you, so you can be Private First Class Hunter once again—will go with me to the lockup at Camp Pettigrew, to await trial for assault with intent to kill—"

Hunter exploded, "You can't do that! What I did was perfectly justified by rules—"

The Di-wee stepped forward and slapped Hunter, hard. "No more training for you, Hunter! If you are lucky, they will *only* bust you out of the Marine Corps!" He turned to the guards, "Take him to the jeep, and watch him closely."

The two unarmed guards hustled Hunter out of the hut, followed by the men with the BARs. Stuart spoke for the first time. "I want to go with him, Captain."

"You took no part in the assault."

"I want to speak for him, about the assault, and about his staying in the program."

The Di-wee looked at Stuart steadily. "To go with him, you will have to withdraw. Is that what you want."

"No, sir. But if I've learned anything in this program, it's to protect a comrade."

The Di-wee spat. "Well, he is out of the program. Maybe your testimony will keep him in the Corps, as a permanent E-1. But anyway, I am not going to let you withdraw. There is one more lesson you will teach the peasant gardeners."

A guard came in and blindfolded Stuart. Even under the high blindfold, the left eye felt good. "I don't believe you're going to do this to Hunter, Captain."

The Di-wee built a sneer into his voice, "And why not? The bastard practically killed me."

"Because I think you're a better man than that."

The Di-wee smiled at Stuart's blindfold. I hope I can convince that murderous bastard Hunter of that, he thought. He turned to the guard. "Put Shit-Spattered Dog in the truck. Get him back to camp, put him in BOX!"

"Ha, *Hun hao*, Di-wee!" replied the guard. Stuart was led out of the hut and boosted into the truck. A guard sat on either side of him as the truck moved off on the gravel road.

The Di-wee was smoking a cigarette when Hunter was brought back into the hut. Jesus, if looks could kill, I'd be gone, thought the Di-wee. I have to do this very carefully. "Marine, during the course of this training, I've told you many things that were not true. Now I'm going to tell you the truth. My name is Joseph MacIntyre, Captain, USMC." The Di-wee took his green military ID card and held it in front of Hunter's face.

Hunter's eyes smoldered. "Don't mean nothin'. So you got a name."

The Di-wee sighed. "Private Hunter, I told you that you're out of the program. You are, but not withdrawn. Graduated. Graduated, I might say, with distinction.

Hunter remained silent, looking fury at a spot two inches above the Di-wee's nose.

"And, of course, no court-martial. You overstepped the rules, Marine, but within reason. You did make your escape, and with an injured man."

Hunter frowned deeply, and thought a moment, "This is another trick, right?"

"No trick."

"So how come I'm still tied up?"

The Di-wee smiled. "Because you looked, a moment ago, like you wanted to kill me—"

"Might could," interrupted Hunter.

"—And I want to make sure you believe me before I cut you loose."

"Just one other question."

"Before or after I cut you loose?"

"Before. If I'm graduated, why did you tell me I was out, and headed for a court-martial?"

The Di-wee began to pace again. "That wasn't for you, it was for Ensign Stuart. I was less sure of him than you. I wanted to see how he would react."

"And how did he react?"

"Well, very well. He volunteered to remain with you, to make sure your side got told, even if he had to withdraw to do it."

Hunter smiled, and began to relax. "He's a good man. What happens to him now?"

"Nothing bad. They'll take him back to camp, rough him up in front of the rest, then put him in the box. But this time, he'll go in the side you were in, which is big enough so he'll be comfortable. I need him to try one more time to drive home the lesson of staying together to your comrades."

"What do you think of those guys, Captain?"

"Well, you, and Stuart, and especially Captain Peters, have responded beautifully."

The guard moved behind Hunter, and prepared to loosen the ropes. He looked at the captain, who nodded. Hunter said, "I mean the rest of the guys, Captain."

"About average, for this program."

Hunter stretched his shoulders and rubbed his wrists. "Those assholes—excuse me, sir, those *guys* are *average*?"

Captain MacIntyre held his face expressionless. "Yes, Hunter."

"That's not good, sir."

"Now, perhaps, you begin to understand your own ordeal."

Hunter looked at the captain. "Maybe I do. But I would still like to kick your ass, sir."

MacIntyre's face darkened. "OK. Outside."

Hunter rocked on the balls of his feet in the gravel in front of the hut, in an easy boxing stance. He had a good four inches in height and plenty of weight on MacIntyre, a fact brought home by the tightness of the Di-wee's uniform, which Hunter was still wearing. He circled the captain wearily, then stopped. "Aren't you even going to put up your hands?"

"When I need to. Yours to open."

Hunter smiled, and moved in, throwing a hard left jab, ready with the right cross. The jab struck air. The captain had ducked it. Hunter circled, jabbing carefully with the left. MacIntyre never actually backed up, but he always pulled his head away from the blows. The best Hunter could account for was a grazing of the captain's hair. Hunter timed the jab, saw which way MacIntyre leaned, and followed with a vicious right hand. MacIntyre blocked the blow with his left forearm, and deflected the arm to Hunter's left. Hunter lost his balance for a fraction of a second. MacIntyre pivoted compactly on his left foot, then, his back to the reeling Hunter, drove his right heel into Hunter's solar plexus. Hunter landed flat on his ass, doubled over and gasping for breath.

Captain MacIntyre waited, arms crossed, while Hunter regained his breath. "Sorry, Marine, but that love tap was for the choke hold."

Hunter smiled, and got slowly to his feet, rubbing his chest. He nodded.

"Do you feel any better, Marine?" asked the captain.

Hunter took a ragged deep breath, then another. "You know I do, because now I can see you as a fighting marine, and not as some sadistic bastard. Sir."

MacIntyre smiled crookedly. "I guess that's a compliment. Come on, I'll drop you off at Pettigrew before I return to form at the camp."

"I still got questions, sir."

"We'll talk in the jeep. Let's go."

---

10 April 1966   Camp Pettigrew, North Carolina

The truck carrying Stuart bumped into the camp, and stopped. Stuart was dumped onto the gravel and frog-marched to the center of the grinder. He was made to squat, and his blindfold was removed. The guards scurried about, forcing the prisoners to line up at attention. Captain Peters grinned at Stuart, and gave him a thumbs-up. Stuart thought the rest of the men looked merely apprehensive. Loonfeather was missing from the formation.

The junior guard officer strode to the front of the assembled guards, and addressed the prisoners. "Here, peasant heroes of the commandant's garden, you see your brave comrade, the Shit-

Spattered Dog! The *escape artist*! He wants to tell you about his adventures!'' The guard officer prodded Stuart with his boot, and Stuart lost his balance and rolled over onto his side. He was pulled back to his squat by guards standing on either side of him.

The guard officer continued, ''The *Di-wee* will decide punishment for dog when he return. But now, let us hear of his adventures. What did you find when you reached the safe house, dog?''

''We were met there by a nurse.''

''A *nurse*! A *pretty* nurse?''

Stuart grinned. This means nothing. This asshole looks entirely different since we escaped. Smaller, and comic. ''Yes, a pretty nurse.''

The guard barked an order, and Stuart was dragged to his feet. The guard officer stood close to Stuart, and looked up into his face. ''So, Shit-Spattered Dog, a pretty, *round-eyed* nurse met you. And what did she do?''

Behind the officer, Stuart could see the prisoners. Most seemed expressionless. Captain Peters grinned. Stuart spoke loudly, trying to hearten the prisoners, trying for a response, ''She gave us food.''

''Food! What kind of food, Shit-Spattered Dog?''

''A chicken sandwich and milk.''

The guard officer stepped back, grinning, and turned to look at the prisoners. ''A *chicken* sandwich! And *milk*! Was it a *big* chicken sandwich?''

''Yes.''

''And the milk was fresh, I trust?''

''Yes,'' said Stuart, to the officer's back.

The guard addressed the prisoners, ''So, the *heroic* Shit-Spattered Dog, and the *heroic* Pathfinda hurt our Di-wee, make *illegal* escape, and eat chicken sandwiches and drink fresh milk with pretty round-eyed nurse, *while comrades starve*!''

This is funny, thought Stuart. Why don't these guys even smile?

The officer turned back to face Stuart. ''For your selfish act, all must suffer! There will be *no chow* tonight, for any prisna!''

Carter Peters spoke, his voice level, his smile evident. ''We're proud of you and Hunter, Stuart.''

''Proud!'' scoffed the officer, ''Proud, and hungry! These men break rules! Otha dog, Pathfinda, go with Di-wee, withdraw! He *afraid* come back, face hungry comrades.''

''That's not true!'' shouted Stuart.

''*Im lang di!* Silence!'' shouted the officer. ''*You* liar! All can see Pathfinda no come back! No here, face comrades! You, Shit-

Spattered Dog, get good food, fresh milk, eat like pig, not share with comrades.''

"I would have shared if I could!'' shouted Stuart.

"Ah, so? Well maybe still can.'' The officer gave an order to the two guards, who tightened their grips on Stuart's arms. The officer delivered a vicious uppercut punch to Stuart's abdomen. Stuart's knees buckled, but the guards jerked him upright. Waves of nausea passed through his body, but he fought them back. The second punch was harder than the first, and Stuart felt a warm, acid rush as the contents of his stomach rose and flowed out of his mouth in a foamy stream. The guards dropped him on his knees, facing the spreading mess, and stepped back. Stuart got up, fighting the pain, and looked at the prisoners. Some looked back in horror, some in sympathy. One man gagged and turned away. Stuart spat, and shook his head to clear it.

The guard spoke softly. "So share, after all. Put Shit-Spattered Dog in the box, wait for Di-wee.'' The officer gestured grandly toward the mess on the ground. "All prisna welcome,'' he said as he turned his back and strode back to the camp offices.

Captain MacIntyre drove the jeep slowly up through gravel track. "So ask your questions, Hunter.''

I don't want to give this bastard any satisfaction, thought Hunter, but I want to know. "Ah, well, sir, like the language you guards speak. I mean, that's kinda chicken shit, isn't it?''

MacIntyre smiled. "Sure it is, but the shrinks say it helps us to break down your morale, forces you to respond to us in a strange way, and prevents you from communicating with us. Later, it aids in making you *feel* like a prisoner, by making you learn several phrases.''

Interesting, thought Hunter. I did learn several phrases. "Is it a real language?''

"No. Some Vietnamese, some Chinese, but mostly it's gibberish. There are only about twenty phrases, almost all commands.''

"Does 'Di-wee' mean anything?''

"Yep. *Dai-uy* is Vietnamese for captain.''

"Oh.''

They rode in silence for a minute. "What's really on your mind, Hunter?''

Hunter felt angry and confused, his tired mind flashing between the man who was the Di-wee, and this ordinary marine officer sitting beside him.

"Well, sir, I'm not *complaining*, but how come Ensign Stuart and I seemed to get an extra ration of shit? Was it really because we kept you out looking for us all night?''

MacIntyre looked quizzically at Hunter, and slowly smiled. This kid is still furious, he thought. ''The fact that you evaded successfully is not the reason you two were singled out—and I admit you were singled out—but it's related to it. Every group of men has natural leaders, natural achievers. There's no reason to believe that the natural leader will be the one with the highest rank, especially in a mixed group like these classes. We try to separate the natural leaders and discredit them, to see whether the group discovers a new leader in its midst, or simply falls apart.''

''So for that you had to continually fuck us up. Sir.''

MacIntyre spoke quietly, ''We also have to find out how those leaders will function, Hunter. From what we know, that's exactly what the enemy will do.''

Hunter thought about that, and his anger ebbed. ''So Ensign Stuart and I are natural leaders.''

''Don't forget Captain Peters. In many ways he'd had it far rougher than you two.''

I guess that's fair enough, thought Hunter, remembering the starved look of the prisoners when he and Stuart had rejoined them after the two days in solitary. ''Is that why you took away Major Roberts, to see if Captain Peters could take command?''

Once again MacIntyre smiled. ''You're learning.''

''So, whatever became of Major Roberts?''

''For that, Hunter, you will have to wait for the debriefing.''

They rode in silence the last half mile to the main barracks, where the captain stopped the jeep. ''OK, Hunter, go in and get cleaned up, get some rest. See you again real soon.''

''One last question. How long will Ensign Stuart be in the box?''

''I'm sure he is already out. The final act is beginning, but his part, like yours, has been played. You'll see him soon.''

Hunter got out of the jeep. ''Sir, or Di-wee, either way, I'm proud of that escape.''

Captain MacIntyre put the jeep in gear. ''So am I, Marine.''

After Stuart had been dumped in the box and the junior guard officer walked away, the other prisoners were herded back into their barracks, and told to prepare for inspection by the Di-wee as soon as he returned. Once they were inside, Stuart was removed from the box and marched up to the camp office, sent to the hot shower in the officers' end of the building, and given clean green fatigues to put on. He was then led back to his old cell in solitary. He was quickly asleep.

In the barracks, the men set about straightening up their bunks, and getting themselves as clean as possible at the cold taps at the end of the room.

"I don't know if I can really take two more days of this shit. I'm getting really sick," said Lieutenant Martini to no one in particular.

"Buck up, Lieutenant," said Captain Peters. "It's the same for all of us."

"I bet that crazy Loonfeather is eatin' good up there in solitary."

"Lieutenant, stop bitching! Feeling sorry for yourself won't help."

"Yes, sir," said Martini, barely above a whisper.

The Di-wee waited until 1800, fully one hour after the men would have expected the evening meal, to call the prisoners out on parade. Darkness was falling rapidly and a cold, damp wind was starting up under a leaden, turbulent sky.

Next to 4 A.M., the shrinks tell us, 6 P.M. is the time of day when the spirit is lowest. Time to test them one more time.

Carter Peters took his place in front, and came to awkward attention with the aid of his crutch. "Fourteen men present and correct, Di-wee."

The Di-wee returned the salute and studied the men. All tired. Some sick, but none seriously. Pain on many faces, pain of hunger. Carter Peters looked determined, but few of the other faces showed any spirit at all.

The Di-wee unbuttoned his warm overcoat and then his tunic. He wanted the prisoners to see the purple bruises on his throat. It is now, when morale is lowest, that these men must harden up. If Hunter, Stuart, and Loonfeather had been in the parade, they would have shown spirit to the others, which is why the Di-wee had removed them—Hunter back at the base camp, Stuart and Loonfeather in solitary.

The Di-wee looked at each man in turn, then at Carter Peters. He spoke softly, with only a trace of the fake accent. "Well, Captain?"

"Sir, I protest the mistreatment of Ensign Stuart. I demand he be returned to the barracks."

The Di-wee waved his hand, a dismissive gesture. "We will deal with him presently. What else?"

"Sir, I demand we be fed. These men—"

The Di-wee rubbed the bruises on his throat gently, forcing

Carter Peters to look at them. "Captain Peters, the prisoner we call Pathfinder, and another, Shit-Spattered Dog, conducted an illegal escape from this camp this morning. I can only conclude that you, as senior American officer, gave them your blessing, and that they had the support of *all* your men. For this, *all* must be punished. The loss of one meal hardly seems severe, nor will it be the only punishment."

Carter Peters said nothing. His throat was tight. The Di-wee continued, speaking just loudly enough so that all the prisoners could hear. "There is a rumor going around that this program ends in two days. That is not true. This program can be extended, on my sole authority, for an additional two days, if I am not satisfied with the progress of the training." The Di-wee heard a deep sigh from behind Peters, but could not tell its origin in the deep shadows. "I have today decided training should be extended."

"Thank you for giving us an opportunity to improve, Di-wee," said Captain Peters, evenly, "but the men still need food."

The Di-wee allowed himself a slight smile. Good shot, Peters, he thought. "Which brings me to my next topic. Each day, you men are given an opportunity to sign a simple confession. It is unimportant, really, but it would please the commandant. What pleases the commandant pleases me. So, your men will be given another opportunity to sign."

"None of my men will sign that paper, Di-wee," said Peters, strongly.

"No? Perhaps a hungry man might. Remember, any man who signs will be given double rations."

"My men aren't that hungry, sir."

"Good! Then why all this bellyaching about needing to be fed?" Once again, a deep sigh could be heard from the ranks. Shut *up*, you bastard thought Captain Peters, you will make it worse. "So, if food is not enough to tempt your brave men, I offer additional inducements. One: you have had a comrade in the box since 1500. You have all seen the box; it is very small and cramped. I intend leaving Shit-Spattered Dog in there until taps, two more hours. Every signature I get reduces his time by fifteen minutes. Fifteen minutes. Surely it is a little thing to help a comrade, Captain?"

"None of my men will sign that paper. And I'm sure Stuart wouldn't ask us to."

"Perhaps, perhaps. But any man who signs helps himself, helps his comrade, and helps me. So, each man will go to the table over there by Lieutenant Tranh. He will be given a numbered form. He will sit at the table and mark the form, and put it in the box. No man need know what another writes on the form. Maybe not sign, maybe sign, up to you. Maybe smart fella write 'fuck you, Di-wee.' Ha! Ha! But remember, all the forms are numbered.''

"We won't sign.''

"Maybe, maybe not! But just for taking time to reconsider, maybe a little tea and rice.''

"Even if no one signs?''

"Of course. A promise. More food, of course, for signers, but a little tea and rice for everyone.''

"All right, I'll go first, but *no one signs*!'' Captain Peters tossed this last phrase over his shoulder to his men. This is a trap, but I don't see how it works, he thought.

"Good, Captain, it is your honor to begin, but before you do, you should see this.'' The Di-wee reached inside his coat and produced a document. It was the familiar germ-warfare confession. At the bottom of the page was a signature: Peter Roberts, MAJ, USAF. Peters was stunned. "Do you recognize *Major Roberts's* signature, Captain?''

"No, I don't. I'm sure it's a forgery.''

"Oh, I assure you, I assure *all* of you, that it is quite genuine. Now, if your own superior officer thinks this piece of paper is of no importance,'' the Di-wee folded the document and put it back inside his coat, "then why should you men deprive yourselves and punish your comrade in the box? But let us begin. Captain?''

Angrily, Carter Peters sat at the table, wrote something in block capitals, crumpled the paper, and threw it in the box. The Di-wee smiled benevolently as each man in turn sat down and wrote. Lieutenant Tranh wrote each man's name on his clipboard next to a number, and handed the forms to the men as each approached the table. He was not standing close enough to the table to see what any man wrote. Some looked at him furtively; a couple smirked. After the last prisoner had placed his form in the box, Lieutenant Tranh closed it and handed it to the Di-wee. "Very well. You men may return to your barracks. Your snack will be along presently, and,'' he tapped the box, "for some a decent meal.''

The Di-wee walked back to his office and opened the box. The first paper he drew out was Peters's, the only crumpled one. He smoothed it and smiled. Peters had indeed written "fuck you, Di-wee,'' and had boldly circled the number one in the corner. Most men had just scribbled. There were two bullshits. The Di-wee opened the last paper, still smiling. A look of disgust spread across his face. At the bottom of the very last form was a clear and legible signature. The Di-wee tore the signed confession into tiny pieces and dropped it into the waste basket with the others.

Carter Peters lay in his bunk, racking his brain about the germ-warfare confession ploy. Surely no one had signed, because no one had been taken away, but there had to be a trick in it, some-where. I wish I weren't so tired, he thought. I wish I could think.

"Fuckin' Di-wee lied. Ain't gonna be no food," said Martini to his shoes.

Most of the men dozed, or slept fitfully in their bunks. Some lay in the fetal position, fists pressed against empty stomachs.

The camp gong sounded, and light penetrated the dim hut as all the outside lighting came on. The door of the barracks was thrown open, and a guard stood silhouetted in the doorway. "Captain Peters? Everybody out on parade."

Men got up stiffly, sighing and bitching, and filed out, taking up their usual places. As Peters's eyes became accustomed to the bright lights, he saw the commandant and the Di-wee stand-ing in their usual places, and next to them, Stuart and Loon-feather. As his men formed up, Stuart and Loonfeather walked down to Peters, saluted, and took places at the end of the rank behind him. Peters noticed with mild curiosity that the two pris-oners were wearing pressed green utilities. Then he realized that the commandant wore the uniform of a marine gunnery ser-geant, and the Di-wee that of a marine captain. Now what's happening? His brain fought through fatigue.

The Di-wee took a step forward, and faced Peters. "Captain Peters, I'm Captain Joseph MacIntyre, the officer in charge of this school. The Camp Phase of SERE training is over. You and your men have successfully completed the training."

Peters looked at the Di-wee. He fought for a clear head. "But the extension—"

"No extension, Captain. It's over."

"Thank Christ," whispered Peters.

"You men will be bused back to the base camp, where all this began. You will be given hot showers, clean uniforms, and a simple meal, then a good night's sleep. Medical corpsmen will be there to take care of any minor medical problems, and there will be a barber standing by to help with the cleanup. Tomorrow we will have a short debriefing, then each man will receive his certificate and transportation arrangements."

Peters stared at the captain. Somehow he had nothing to say.

"Congratulations, Captain," said Captain MacIntyre.

"Ah, thank you, sir."

Captain MacIntyre stepped up and extended his hand. Captain Peters shook it. "Captain, the bus is waiting just outside the gate. Do you, do any of your men, need help?" This guy looks all in, thought Captain MacIntyre.

Peters drew himself up, and felt his mind clearing as anger cut through the fog of fatigue. We have had about all the help from you bastards a man could want, he thought. "We'll be fine, sir," he said to the Di-wee.

Awkwardly, because he was still using the crutch, Peters did an about-face and looked at the men. All looked weary, but most looked happy, and some looked proud. Martini looked strangely distraught. Odd, thought Peters, I would have thought he'd be gladder than anyone to hear the camp was over. "SERE Team Seven-oh-two, ten-HUT!" Peters was glad to see some military bearing return to the ragged men. "Right, HACE! Forward, HARCH!"

Captain MacIntyre watched as the men shambled toward the waiting bus. Jesus, I'm glad I'm leaving this place!

Most of the men were asleep by 2100, and they were not called for reveille until 0800 the following day. Many men found themselves up very early, a leftover from camp life, and these took leisurely hours at breakfast of fruit, cereal, and soft-boiled eggs. They were warned by sympathetic mess cooks that several more days would pass before they would be ready for the traditional military, hearty bacon-and-egg breakfast, but there was plenty of rich, hot coffee, and that made it all right by Ensign Stuart. And there was tobacco. Stuart screwed a Player's Navy Cut cigarette into his grandfather's short black holder, and deeply inhaled the strong Virginia tobacco as the debriefing was about to begin.

Nineteen men were there, all graduates. Even the men who had been forced to withdraw for medical reasons were there. Stuart was especially glad to see Hunter, who had told him about his conversation with the Di-wee—it was still hard to think of him as simply Captain MacIntyre—after the escape.

At 1000, Captain MacIntyre took his place at the podium in the small classroom where the men of SERE Team 702 had originally been briefed. He looked so different, so *ordinary*, thought Stuart, in the crisp, fitted marine working green uniform, khaki gabardine shirt with khaki tie and tight-fitting olive-drab blouse and trousers.

"Men, this debrief is the last chapter of this SERE training cycle," Captain MacIntyre began, "but it is perhaps the most important. All of you men will receive certificates of completion for this course, and they will all look the same. That's not because you all performed equally well under the stress of the curriculum," MacIntyre paused, but seemed to look at no one, "but because the worth of this course, for each of you, is not how you performed here, but how well you are now prepared to stand up to a real enemy, in a real prison environment, should that ever occur." Once again, MacIntyre paused, letting the words sink in. The only eyes really meeting his belonged to Peters and Hunter.

"By now I believe each of you can understand the reality of what may have seemed unbelievable just seven short days ago. You now know that with deprivation of sleep, harassment, and lack of adequate food, you rapidly became disoriented. You began to doubt your comrades, and you lost faith in your senior officers. You began to hate your guards, and even hate your comrades. Yet some of you tried to curry favor with the very guards you hated, and some of you even thought to betray your own comrades. And through all of this, each and every one of you *knew*, fucking *knew*, that you were in a training environment in North Carolina, U. S. of A!"

Stuart sat bolt upright at the Di-wee's—Captain MacIntyre's—shouted last sentence. Many of the men shifted nervously as the captain let his words sink in deep. The relaxed atmosphere of the debrief disappeared.

Captain MacIntyre began again, in a very soft voice. "This training is rough. It is meant to be. But just *imagine* what the real thing would be like!"

MacIntyre stopped completely, and appeared to be studying his notes. Stuart lit another cigarette, and looked furtively at Hunter, who seemed angry. Carter Peters's eyes were half closed, his breathing shallow.

"So," began the captain once again, "each of you must evaluate his own performance here. We won't. But remember, if this training is ever *needed* by any of you," once again, he let it sink in, "remember how vulnerable each of you were here. Remember, most of all, how you must stay together." MacIntyre paused. The SERE trainees coughed and exchanged glances, some proud, some sheepish. MacIntyre stood away from the lectern, and finished. "Now, in closing, I would like to congratulate all of you, especially your commander, Captain Peters. You got through, and you emerged as credits to your respective branches. Questions?

Carter Peters raised his hand, "Captain, I want to ask the same question I asked two or three times a day in camp. Where is Major Roberts?"

Captain MacIntyre smiled. "Let me ask you, Captain Peters, did you accept his germ-warfare confession as genuine?"

"No."

"Did you believe he was collaborating with the enemy?"

"I didn't want to. No, I don't think I did."

"Well, let's ask him. Sergeant, would you go and ask Major Roberts to step in?"

The smiling gunnery sergeant left, and returned in less than a minute. Major Roberts followed him into the room and stood beside Captain MacIntyre. It is the same man, all right, thought Peters. Same silver hair, same correct military bearing. But instead of brass oak leaves of a major on the collar points of his utilities there were the chevrons and rockers of a sergeant major.

Captain MacIntyre clapped him on the shoulder. "Well *Major* Roberts, did you collaborate with us?"

The sergeant major grinned. "Sure did. Signed that dumb confession, too. Must make thirty times in the last two years."

Captain Peters spoke quietly, "So 'Major Roberts,' the senior American officer, never existed."

"That's right, Captain. We wouldn't want to pack up a real trainee for the whole Camp Phase, yet the enemy is almost certain to separate the senior officer, and any others who show any exceptional initiative."

"I suppose I should have thought of that myself," said Captain Peters.

"It's not surprising that you didn't. You never knew when he might be returned. And besides, given the level of disorientation brought on by stress, the illusion of the camp is pretty convincing."

Several men laughed and nodded in agreement, and the men seemed to relax again. The sergeant major waved and left, and Captain MacIntyre stepped from behind the podium and said, "Let's break here for coffee, gentlemen, then we will wrap this up."

The men began departing after lunch. Hunter and most of the others were put on a bus to Raleigh to catch commercial flights to their next assignments. Stuart was scheduled to be picked up by a navy bus at 1400, along with Harrigan and Martini and another navy pilot–RIO team, and taken back to Norfolk.

Martini and Harrigan were drinking coffee and playing gin when Captain MacIntyre walked into the mess hall. "Lieutenant Martini, a word please? My office."

Martini followed the captain into a small cubicle at the end of the passageway. MacIntyre picked up a telex off the bare desk, and handed it to Martini.

FM: BUPERS AVIATION ASSIGNMENT SECTION, WASHINGTON, DC

TO: MARTINI, LOUIS R. LTJG, USN 700423

VIA: OIC SERE, CAMP PETTIGREW, NC

REPORT IMMED BUPERS AA SEC WDC TEMPORARY DUTY PEN PERMANENT CHANGE OF STATION (PCS) ORDERS. SIGNED ROGERS RADM USN

Martini stared at the paper, reading it over and over. "You read this, Captain?"

"Yes."

"I don't get it. I was all set to go out to join the F-4 squadron on the *Enterprise*, at Pearl. With Lieutenant Harrigan. We been training together for nine months."

"The needs of the Navy change, Martini." Captain MacIntyre's voice revealed no interest in Martini's problem.

Martini crumpled up the telex, and stuffed it into his pocket. "Probably just some foul-up. Shit, I was looking forward to getting out to Pearl."

MacIntyre walked to the door of the office. "Could be. No better place to fix a screwup in orders than BuPers."

"Yeah, I guess so. Well, OK, thanks, Captain, for a lovely time."

"A pleasure," said Captain MacIntyre, his voice even.

10 April 1966   United States Naval Station, Long Beach, California

Bobby Coles filed into the gray navy school bus in the chilly, dark fog of predawn. His name was checked against a list by a yawning marine corporal, who repeated his instructions to each man to fill the seats in the bus from the back to the front, leaving no gaps. Bobby threw his toilet kit onto the overhead rack and slid into a seat next to a scared-looking white man with a shaky grin, who hadn't even waited for the boot-camp barbers to shave his head.

"Hi, uh, m-my name is J-John Blake," said the kid. Bobby gave him a low-intensity street stare, then a very slow nod, and leaned back as well as he could in the straight bench seat and closed his eyes. The corporal dropped into the driver's seat, pulled the door closed, and drove slowly toward the main gate, the light of the headlamps reflected and smothered by the fog.

Bobby squirmed to settle his six feet two inches into the cramped space. So it is, Bobby, he thought. Robert Richmond Coles, honors graduate of the University of Southern California, standout football player for the PAC-8 champion Trojans, drafted by the New York Giants on the day of his best game against UCLA, the first man in his family to graduate from anything, the first with a future as bright as even a white man, to be a lawyer, a leader. And then drafted by the U.S. Army, right out of the middle of that future.

Bobby pounded one fist gently against the other, keeping his eyes closed as the bus bounced over surface streets, seeking in the fog for the San Diego Freeway. Bobby thought over the last eight weeks of his life, from the time he had received his draft notice to his enlistment in the Marine Corps to this dismal muster for the bus at five o'clock in the morning on the wet pavement of the naval base at Long Beach. "Hurry up, girls!" shouted the first marine Bobby had ever met outside the recruiting office. "Wouldn't do to give you pukes less than a full day, your first day as boot marines!" The corporal had grinned at the self-conscious, nervous, and just-plain-scared gaggle of recruits, standing at attention against the bus, having buttoned up every button on their bodies at the corporal's bawled command.

Bobby cracked his eyes open as the bus swung slowly onto the ramp for the freeway south. The kid next to him was staring out the window, his Adam's apple working up and down. Shit, Bobby thought, the pussy is crying. Bobby settled back, and thought about when he was small, and about growing up with Simon, twelve years his senior, and their sister Rebecca, four years older than Bobby.

Bobby rubbed his shoulders and the back of his neck, then massaged his face. He was already getting stiff in the small seat. He was lean but heavily muscled, a conditioned athlete. He had straight, almost aquiline features and large, expressive eyes. He had been called handsome. Like Simon, he was very dark, and he liked that; it made him feel that his blood had not been polluted by white trash during slave times. Becky was curiously light, by contrast, with translucent, almost ivory skin. She was the prettiest woman Bobby had ever known.

Simon wasn't pretty. Simon had raised Bobby and Rebecca after their mother had died and their father drifted away nine years before. To support himself and the younger children, Simon had supplemented his earnings as a laborer by working illegal clubs as a boxer. He was an inch shorter than Bobby, but a good thirty pounds heavier, most of it muscle. He had learned to fight in the street, and to box in the Marine Corps. His power had made him formidable in the ring, but he was never quick enough to avoid taking punches, and his strong brows and prominent cheekbones caused the cuts to be deep, and to scar. His face had a fierce, dangerous look, which Simon had used to good advantage, both inside and outside the ring. Bobby thought it was mostly bluff, but he was always glad his big brother loved him.

Simon had been taken away from Bobby and Becky when Bobby had just turned eighteen. Simon was hit from behind on La Cienega Boulevard by a beach-blond Malibu type in a Corvette, whose friend and he decided that Simon was at fault and should be prepared to pay for damages. Simon walked to a phone booth to call the police, saying he had no intention of telling anyone he was at fault for getting hit from behind while standing at a stop light. One of the boys blocked his way, and the other one stepped up and punched Simon in the back of the head. Simon laid them out end to end, then called the police. The driver of the Corvette had a long history of traffic violations, and a record of other trouble as well. He also had a prominent judge for a father. Simon was charged with assault. Simon had friends on the police force, who had turned a blind eye on the illegal clubs where Simon had boxed, but they could do nothing, were *told* to do nothing. All they could do, and did do by silencing the street people who knew, was to conceal Simon's professional if illegal boxing. Had that come out, the charge could have been increased to assault with a deadly weapon.

Simon was convicted and sentenced to two to five years in prison. First offenders in cases of simple street altercations didn't normally go to prison, but the white judge of whom no one would speak had fixed Simon good. So Simon went to prison, and the judge's son managed to kill himself a year later by running the Corvette off Latigo Canyon Road.

Prison ended Simon's active role as surrogate father for his sister and brother. Fortunately, Rebecca was already working, and could support her continuing studies, and Bobby had just entered SC on a full athletic scholarship. Simon was out of prison in the minimum two years, a model prisoner. After he got out, life seemed to go easier for him. He seemed to have ways of making money, of which he never spoke and Bobby never asked. A year after leaving prison, he had managed to buy a small house in Watts, the old neighborhood. The house they had grown up in had been seized and sold for taxes while Simon was in prison. Last year Simon had acquired an interest in a saloon. When Bobby visited his older brother in his new surroundings, he was able to see that Simon had a lot of power and respect in the neighborhood. Bobby was a little uneasy at first about the source of that power and respect, but he figured any breaks Simon was getting were well deserved.

Simon had never expressed any resentment at having two years carved out of his life by the white power structure for no reason other than that the bastards *could*. Bobby was bitter, and thought he always would be. Simon would say that certain things were facts, and it didn't serve a man to complain about facts. Well, it might be that a rich white man could put a poor black man in prison at will, but Bobby would never accept the fact as *necessarily* true. Bobby had heard the campus intellectuals, both black and white, talk of using the advantages of their education to effect change through the system, and he heard the fringe radicals, mostly black, plot violent attacks on that very system, pledging to burn it down and root out all the oppressors. Bobby had kept his head with the counselors of reason, but the radicals tugged at his soul, even though he found their vision of the world after the revolution far bleaker than the present conditions, and their methods for bringing about their vision terrifying. But when the intellectuals said they couldn't understand the appeal to young blacks of the Muslims or the Black Panthers, Bobby felt like telling them to ask his brother, Simon, about working through the system. But Simon, of course, would have agreed with the moderate, gradualist view.

Bobby had written his political science thesis on "The Socialization of Black People in America, 1865–1915," and he had originally included a long argument on the effects of the eradication of black traditions, both slave and the older African. Bobby felt he should be able to identify some deliberate effort on the part of the white power structure, determined to keep blacks out of the mainstream of American growth, to muddle and erase black roots. It was a demonstrable fact that blacks in general were worse off, more dispossessed and more socially isolated on the eve of the First World War than they had been at the end of the Civil War. But Bobby just couldn't find a link between the white man and the loss of the black culture. The traditions seemed simply to have slipped away rather than to have been taken. Whites seemed not to have interfered in the growth of black churches; if anything, the churches' role in preserving and developing spiritual hymns from African music should have helped any effort to preserve and pass along tradition. In the end, Bobby had pulled the entire argument from the thesis. He still felt he was right, but the thesis had to be closely reasoned on the facts. One unsupported idea would taint the whole thesis, and Bobby felt he had already said, and substantiated, several important and worthwhile things.

The nasal voice of the corporal driving the bus buzzed in the PA system. "Getting closer to marine country, girls. There's the turnoff for El Toro, just ahead. We will make Dago in under two hours." Bobby dozed.

* * *

Simon Coles drove north through the darkness along the Harbor Freeway, leaving Long Beach and his baby brother behind. He had wanted to stay and wait for the bus to leave, but Bobby urged him to go. He remembered well his own first minutes in the Marine Corps in 1951; the shouting, the confusion, and the humiliation. Bobby would want those minutes to himself, so Simon had hugged him, and driven away.

He left the freeway at Manchester Avenue in south central Los Angeles, and drove east into Watts, parked his new Buick, and went inside, lighting the lamps in the kitchen. Dawn was still an hour away. Simon got out eggs and ham for his breakfast, and boiled water and chicory for coffee.

He looked at the street in front of his house, the house bought for his family with blood and pain, and with something darker since his prison days. All his people had worked with their hands, and the muscles of their bodies. He had done so, and toiled as well with his fists and his face. But his two, pretty Rebecca and fine, handsome Robert Richmond, were getting out of the shit, up and away. That was why Simon had done what he had, and continued to do what he did, because he loved the kids in a way that neither of his work-weary parents ever had time to love him, or them. Rebecca, and Robert, and their kids and grandkids would never have to dig up the street, or fight, or clean other people's houses, because of Simon's love. Now the kid had to risk his ass in the mud to fight in Vietnam, a place Simon hadn't even known existed until Robert's notice had come, and Simon had called his old topkick down at Camp Pendleton. Robert had faced the danger with his pride, and his anger, and he would risk Simon's dream as well. Robert had railed against the system and the structure when his notice came, but then he faced facts and signed up with the marines. Robert said he hated the idea of fighting a war to defend the power structure of the imperialists who oppressed the black man at home and all the brown and yellow men abroad, yet he had taken the oath, and become a marine, to be the best.

Simon poured the savory, bitter chicory coffee and watched the ham sizzle. Maybe Bobby had his own dream, and maybe he had to have the physical proof that all brave men require of their ability to stand up to pain and fight on. Maybe Bobby was showing the yearnings of youth for passage into manhood through struggle. Simon had had manhood and pain thrust upon him so early he had never had a youth. Bobby's success in college, his desire to become a lawyer, his very *being* had come out of having a time while young to think and dream. Youth, then, too, was part of Simon's gift of love.

Simon ate his breakfast slowly, watching the hazy morning press through the low-lying fog. He washed the breakfast dishes and puttered around the house, neating things up. He wished someone would come by; he didn't want to think about Robert in the marines, Robert in Vietnam.

Simon took his coffee into the living room and picked up his easy reading, easy because it was so familiar, the words comforting or disquieting, but always the same, the same words with which Simon's mother had taught him to read:

In the beginning, God created the heaven and the earth.
And the earth was without form, and void and darkness was upon the face of the deep.
And the spirit of God moved upon the face of the waters.
And God said, Let there be light: and there was light.

God hadn't created the light that was Bobby simply to destroy it. Yet Simon knew his own life would not pass much scrutiny in final judgment. Simon thought of the suffering of Job, and he a righteous man.

Man that is born of woman is of few days, and full of trouble.
He cometh forth like a flower, and is cut down, he fleeth also as a shadow, and continueth not.

His sons come to honour and he knoweth it not, and they were brought low, but he perceiveth it not of them.
But his flesh upon him shall have pain, and his soul within him shall mourn.

A semitrailer rumbled past the slow-moving navy bus, its horn moaning. Bobby pulled himself upright in the hard seat, his back and shoulders stiffer from his brief sleep. He nudged the white boy next to him, who continued to stare out the window. The sky had lightened from black to wet gray. "Where are we, man?"

The goofy kid looked at Bobby, all smiles. "C-camp P-pendleton. We get AIT here, after Basic. Look, there's miles of it."

Bobby looked over the kid's shoulder at the green country, nodded, and screwed himself into a new position, knees up in front of him. He didn't know what AIT was, but figured he would, soon enough. He thought back to the day two weeks after he had received his draft notice, the day before he had enlisted in the Marine Corps.

Bobby had driven his brother's Buick home after spending the day talking to the clerk of his draft board, to his coaches at SC, and finally to the front office of the New York Giants. Each had been sympathetic, and each had told him that in the spring of 1966 the draft was hungry, the deferments were gone, and the phony National Guard billets had been used up.

Bobby arrived home frustrated and angry. He found Simon studying his old, crumpled Bible. As usual, Simon had read into the dusk without remembering to turn on a lamp. Bobby turned one on and sat on the sofa across from his brother's chair. He watched while his brother made his way slowly through the text, his lips moving silently. Simon would stop when he reached the end of the chapter. It was Simon's way. Bobby waited. Simon's lips stopped. He laid the old book aside, and looked at his brother.

"You do any good?" Simon asked.

"No, I don't guess. I have to write to the draft board, but I doubt anything will come of it."

"The Giants?"

"No. Nor the school. You?"

Simon sighed. How to say this? Tell the horror, or conceal it? "I talked to Tolliver, my old sergeant in the corps. He's a master gunnery sergeant now at Camp Pendleton."

"What the hell good's he gonna do?"

Simon rose. "He told me why you got drafted. The government wants this war in Vietnam to grow."

"To what? Nobody even knows where Vietnam is, except a few demonstrators, and they aren't too sure. What do we have there, five or ten thousand advisers?"

"One hundred and seventy thousand men, a third in combat units," said Simon. "Tolliver told me that the military just went in for a commitment of enough troops to defeat the guerrillas whether the South Vietnamese fight or not. The government has gone along. The services have been told to get ready to train, then deploy, the forces required."

Bobby had thought of army service as mostly two boring years wasted out of his life. He hadn't thought about actual fighting. "How many people?"

Simon looked sadly at baby brother, saw his child's face from long ago. "They want a presence in eighteen months of a half million, net."

"Net? Net of what?"

Simon looked at Bobby for a long time. Why had he always known the punishment would come? Why had he not known how soon? "Net of the casualties."

Bobby's mind froze on the word "casualties," stunned, as if

by a hard tackle. He forced himself to resume thought. His head tingled. Casualties. He rubbed his eyes till they hurt.

Simon put his hands on his brother's shoulders. "Bobby—"

Bobby said, "And what of the *facts*, of the *system*, big brother?"

"Bobby—"

"Simon, the coaches at the school checked. Of the guys drafted for the pros off the team, all but one of the black guys were also drafted by the Army."

"Bobby, we got to think—"

"None of the white guys."

"Bubba! OK, you're right! Dammit, I know shit and pain and misery come from the white man! Better than you! Far better! But you got to learn, as I had to learn, that a black man has got to be his *own*, not a reflection of fear of the white man, or hatred of the white man!"

Simon turned abruptly and walked across the room to the front window. Bobby missed the warmth of the big hands on his shoulders. "So you do hate."

"Of course."

"Then what about your facts."

"Hatred is one of my facts."

"Why did you always deny your hatred?"

"I wanted you out of it. You and Rebecca."

"And now?"

Simon walked to his brother, squatted in front of the couch, and placed his hands on Bobby's cheeks. "Bubba, I have done many wrong things, but I always loved you and your sister."

"Big brother?"

"I want you to pray with me now."

They prayed. Simon aloud, "The Lord is my shepherd—" Bobby silently. "Now go to bed," said Simon, gently. "Tomorrow we are going to reason this out, like men."

Like black men, thought Bobby. Like scared black men.

Simon got right to the point as they sat down to breakfast. "Sergeant Tolliver says there ain't no way you'll get out of it."

"Figures," Bobby shrugged. "When the bastards want you, they get you, right? You got prison for being black; I get the Army."

Simon looked at his brother awhile, as he chewed and swallowed his ham. "That shit ain't doing us no good, Bubba."

Bobby shrugged again. "OK, I won't argue with you. But what *is* going to do any good? I'll write the draft board, but they aren't going to care, so I go in the Army."

"Tolliver thinks you should go in the marines."

"Oh, that's a *great* idea! Aren't they the 'first to fight?' I'd be even more likely to get blown away in the marines than in the fucking Army!"

"Tolliver says you'd get better training. Better training is what helps you—" the words tasted like a copper penny, "—survive."

Bobby sat quietly, chewing on the hard-cooked ham, and on his brother's words. Simon rattled the pans on the stove, then returned with the chipped enamel coffeepot. Bobby looked at his older brother, and saw sadness in his tired, scarred face.

"So you think I should join the marines?"

Simon sat back down at the table. "Only you can decide that. But I can tell you, Bubba, that Tolliver said a lot of things. Things he never said about Korea. He said that the communists were everywhere, in every village, in every piece of jungle. He said there were no front lines, and no way to tell the friendly people from the enemy." Bobby shifted in his chair. Simon stopped, his great head bowed over his folded hands.

"He said one more thing, something I never thought to hear Tolliver say."

Simon looked up intently at his kid brother. "He said that no matter how many boys we sent over there to die, we would never win."

Bobby felt his body tighten in the expectation of physical pain, just as it did when he had stretched out going for a football and he knew a hit was coming.

"What is Tolliver going to do? Will he go back?"

Simon shook his head slowly. "Not if he can help it."

The bus geared down and left the freeway, and passed immediately through the main gate of the marine base. Bobby sat up straight. He felt he understood his brother much more, now that the differences between them had largely dropped away. Bobby could see that Simon had always felt that he should have a different destiny, that he should escape the seemingly inevitable fate of the black man to get fucked by the system. That explained why Simon had concealed his hatred of white people. Simon had expected Bobby and Rebecca would live with whites as equals, wouldn't need to hate to survive. Now that Bobby had been fucked over, he and Simon were more alike than different. So Bobby felt closer to his brother than before. An odd result of the new closeness was that the brothers had hardly talked in the last few weeks. Their communication had been driven inside by the system that crushed them, like the communication of prisoners who had been ordered not to speak.

The bus bumped into the middle of the main grinder at the Marine Corps Recruit Depot, joining perhaps a dozen identical gray buses already parked in a long row. Fog blew in from the cold sea, spreading and softening the sunlight of early morning. By the time the bus stopped, Bobby felt he was already conditioned to accept and even thrive on the well-known brutality of marine corps basic training. The recruits were herded off the gray school bus by a swarm of bellowing drill instructors in Smoky Bear hats. Bobby dropped his flight bag and fell to doing pushups in the mud along with the rest of his class. The other men looked frightened; Bobby had accepted. How easily one accepts the oppressor, Bobby thought, as a DI bellowed at him to keep his back straight. Bobby smiled. Fuck you, man, I can do this. I'm going to be a fighting man.

After the DIs had had enough fun watching out-of-shape recruits collapse in the mud in the only civilian clothes they had been allowed to bring with them, they formed the recruits into a swaying line and allowed them to practice saluting the outgoing class as they were marched to the same gray buses that had just brought the MCRD its next meal. The survivors looked neater than any men Bobby had ever seen, and they sang a cadence to welcome "new meat" as they marched in perfect unison. Bobby wondered where the buses would take them. Direct to Vietnam, he supposed. A DI about five-foot-five yelled up at Bobby to wipe the grin off his face. Bobby folded into his badass street stare, but inside he was laughing.

The DIs turned the recruits and herded them across the parade ground and into the barracks, the way Bobby thought sheepdogs probably worked sheep, though he had never seen it. Everyone here is an animal, but the dogs are stronger than the sheep. Lesson One already learned, Oppressors.

17 April 1966   USS *Valley Forge*, Long Beach, California

Douglas MacArthur Moser left the mess deck early and returned to the 2d Division berthing space. The mess deck had been nearly empty; most of the sailors had taken the three-day liberty and gone home, or to the homes of friends, for Easter. Moser couldn't have made it home to Georgia and back, and he hadn't wanted to spend Easter with someone else's family, even though the chief had encouraged men from towns in southern California to take a shipmate home with them.

The holiday dinner the mess cooks had served up had been good, and as always, plentiful. Moser lay back on his bunk contented, his belly feeling good and warm, full of ham and yams and apple pie. He had been in the Navy almost six months, yet the quality and the plenty of the food continued to amaze him. He had been a big man at six-foot-five when he enlisted, but rawboned at 210. He now weighed almost 250, and none of it was fat. He felt good, and strong, and quite contented to be lying in his bunk on Easter Sunday with nothing whatever to do. He even felt a little grateful to the red-faced Georgia circuit judge who had gotten him to join the Navy in the first place.

Moser let his mind wander back to the mountains of northeastern Georgia. That ole judge sure had hollered. He had yelled "I oughter lock you up ten years at least, what you done to these boys, not to mention the winda of the tradin' post, and the windshield of the county cruiser.'' Moser smiled to himself. He could remember every word. ''But I'm agonna give you a chance to straighten yoursel' out. I know you was provoked some. I'm agonna suspend sentence for thirty days, and then I'll jest forget it, if'n you enlist in one o' the Armed Forces of the U-nited States, and agree to allot twenny dollars a month outa your pay to pay for the winda and the po-lice car windshield. Well?''

So Moser had hitchhiked to Gainesville, the nearest town to have a recruiting station, and joined the Navy. He chose the Navy because his cousin had been in the Army and said it sucked. Nobody from around Breaker's Holler had been in the Navy.

At the time, Moser had thought it damned unfair he should have to be in that courtroom to be yelled at by that old judge at all. The fight had started because Clem Watkins had said Moser's mother was a whore. Clem hadn't seen Moser in the back of the store, doing inventory, and so Moser thought to let it pass. He knew his mother had a lot of men friends since his daddy had wandered off two years past, but he didn't think she deserved the things he knew people said about her. He knew what they said, though folks were careful not to say them when he could hear. Moser had no reputation as a fighter, but his great strength was well known. Folks had seen him throw hundred-weight sacks of cement into a wagon like they were feather pillows. Folks had seen him swing an ax.

Anyway, Moser figured Clem just hadn't seen him, so he decided to let it pass. But Bobby Joe Emry had nudged Clem and giggled, and pointed to Moser in the back of the store. Clem turned and faced Moser with a slow grin. ''Sorry if'n you heard that, boy.''

Moser sighed. No ignoring it now. ''Jest don't say that no more. Ain't right to say that.''

''Said I was sorry, kid.''

''Sheet. You heard it said, Bubba Moser,'' taunted Bobby Joe. ''You gonna let ole Clem jest walk away jest cause he says he's sorry?''

Moser stepped out from behind the counter and faced the men seated at the rough-plank bar. Clem standing, thumbs hooked in his belt, trying to hold back a grin. Bobby Joe seated on a barrel with his legs crossed. Ben Winny leaning back against the bar. Big Bill Otis next to him, whittling on a tobacco plug. All big, hard men, thought Moser, though none as big as me. Older, maybe better fighters. I don't care. I just think this is stupid. I don't want to hurt nobody over a word. But a man couldn't let his own mother be called a whore.

"I reckon you truly sorry you said that, Clem Watkins, I can let it pass. You sayin' you truly sorry you said that about Momma?" Moser moved close to Clem, balanced on the balls of his feet, his hands loose. We'll just drift into this fight, and for what? he thought.

Clem's smile became tight. He don't want this either, thought Moser. But he ain't going to back down for a seventeen-year-old kid.

"Well, now Bubba, I'm truly sorry you *heard* what I—"

Bobby Joe guffawed loudly, interrupting Clem's words. Moser's left hand swung up from his side in an arc and his fist struck Clem's chin with enough force to lift him off his feet. Clem's head struck the bar and he fell in a heap on the sawdusty floor, his neck at an odd angle. Ben Winny jumped on Moser's back, but Moser threw him off, and pivoted to his left and kicked the barrel out from under Bobby Joe, who hit the wall face first. Moser whirled and crouched as Ben came at him again, and landed two quick lefts and a roundhouse right, which smashed Ben's nose in a bright splash of blood. In exchange Moser received a stinging blow to the ear and an ineffective punch to the ribs. As Ben went down, Moser could see Big Bill still seated, whittling the tobacco plug.

Bobby Joe jumped on Moser's back, getting his elbow under Moser's chin in a choke hold. Moser reached around and grasped a handful of Bobby Joe's hair, then ran backward into the edge of the bar. There was a grunt and the choke hold abruptly released. Moser turned, and planted two hard punches into Bobby Joe's gut. It was you who wanted this fight, thought Moser, so you can have a little extra. Bobby Joe landed a good right to Moser's left eye, and tried to back away. Moser trapped him against the bar and pounded his face and body. Big Bill stabbed his knife into the bar and stood up. "Could be that's enough, Bubba."

Moser shook the blood from his eye and looked at Big Bill quickly. He wasn't coming. "Not just yet," he replied. He grabbed the nearly limp Bobby Joe by the collar of his shirt and his belt, raised him over his head, and hurled him through the window in front of the store. Bobby Joe bounced off the hood of the deputy sheriff's Ford and slid through the windshield into the front seat, just as Deputy Barnes, summoned by passersby, stepped through the front door of the trading post.

Moser was charged with assault. Probably wouldn't have been, they told him, but both Clem and Bobby Joe had landed up in the hospital, Clem with a cracked neck, though fortunately not broken, and Bobby Joe with two broken ribs and deep cuts on his face. The county prosecutor got Big Bill Otis to say that he heard Clem apologize, but he cut him off when Big Bill started to say the apology hadn't sounded right. The prosecutor hadn't let Moser tell his story at all, but Moser kind of thought the judge could see how things had been, despite the prosecutor's fast talking. Since Moser didn't have a lawyer, the judge asked a few questions himself. Moser felt that the judge understood.

Moser still felt bad about the hurt he had caused, but he wasn't sorry about leaving Breaker's Holler. He liked the Navy, and he looked forward to going to sea on a real ship, and seeing the world. He had never learned to read well, and some of the classroom stuff was hard, but he liked the military training, and he especially liked being well fed every day, and warm and dry every night.

He did miss his Momma, Jean-Ann. She was still a pretty woman despite the hard, poor life she had led, and Moser had always felt she loved him. His father was a less distinct figure to him, drifting in and out of their lives until gone, apparently for good, just three years ago this coming spring. He had lost an arm fighting in Korea, and had trouble holding work, so he drifted. Moser was the only child, born when Jean-Ann was just sixteen, and they kind of grew up friends. He wrote letters home when he could and she answered in spurts.

Seaman Apprentice Douglas MacArthur Moser felt pretty good to be where he was. He swung his legs over the edge of the bunk. Think I might just ease down to the mess deck and see if I can get me another slab of that apple pie, he thought. Navy going to be all right.

Moser and his friend, Juan Mendoza, had finished fleet training on February 4, 1966, and received orders to report to the USS *Valley Forge* at her home port of Long Beach, California. The *Valley* was an aging World War II–vintage aircraft carrier that most of her crew of 1,200 thought overdue for the scrap yards. Her life in service had been extended through her conversion to an LPH, a helicopter assault ship, designed to carry a battalion landing team of 800 marines, all their gear, and a squadron of marine medium helicopters close inshore, then launch the laden helicopters at the enemy in the new marine doctrine of vertical assault. There were newer LPHs, but not enough for the demands of Vietnam, so the aging *Valley Forge* and her sister ship, USS *Princeton*, were continued in service until enough new ships were ready.

Moser and Mendoza were assigned to the 2d (Deck) Division, and began learning the ways of shipboard navy life. Since the *Valley* had just emerged from a three-month in-port period, she stayed tied to the dock while her own crew as well as many civilian yardworkers sweated to put her back together and get her ready for sea. For Moser and Mendoza, most of this work consisted of cleaning out filthy lockers, and chipping and painting. Standing or sitting for hours pounding the ancient and pitted layers of paint off the *Valley*'s deck and bulkhead plates was dirty and tiring work, but Mendoza soon discovered in working with the chipping details that here the information one really needed to survive and prosper in this man's Navy was to be found.

Mendoza learned from his fellow "deck apes" that serving in the amphibious forces, Pacific Fleet, had a character different from serving in subs, destroyers, or in the big attack carriers. Subs and destroyers were considered the "real Navy," and got all the glory, so the gung-ho Naval Academy type of officers went to them, along with most of the ambitious petty officers in the technical ratings. Hotshot aviators had to fly jets, so they naturally went to the big carriers. As they got more senior, they hoped to command the big carriers as the final step to rear admiral.

The importance of this, the experienced sailors informed Mendoza and Moser, was that while all officers and most petty officers (other than bosun's mates) were assholes, you had to learn there were different types of assholes, some more dangerous to a sailor's peace than others. The recognition rules were these:

The Captain, always an aviator, must have fucked up somewhere else, or he'd have gotten command of a big attack carrier. He'd be pissed off about that, and therefore mean.

Any Naval Academy man found on an amphib had to have fucked up. Very mean.

The other aviators on the ship must have fucked up in order to be stuck flying helos. Real aviators flew fixed-wing jets. Watch out.

The rest of the officers were mostly short-time reserves, college kids doing their hitch to avoid the Army. They could be good or bad.

Any officer who looked too old for his rank was probably a

Mustang, an officer who had started out as an enlisted man. Since these officers really knew what went on, they could be especially dangerous, and always the harshest disciplinarians.

The 2d Division officer, Ensign Siegel, the son of a Chicago plumber, was of the short-time reserve type, a loudmouth who liked to bust balls. He was a small, strutting man who gloried in lording over men of no meaner background than his own. Salute him a lot, the experienced seamen told the new boots, and forget him. The chief ran the division.

The chief was Senior Chief Boatswain's Mate Brown, a quiet man from Alabama who was considered by the deck sailors the best chief in the *Valley Forge*. Moser liked him because his gentle demeanor and soft Southern accent were familiar and easy to understand. Moser understood practically nothing of Mr. Siegel's rapid-fire speech, and kept away from him as much as possible. This was difficult, because Siegel prided himself on giving frequent counseling to the new boots who came into 2d Division in a steady trickle as the *Valley* got closer to her next deployment. The more experienced deck apes said that this was because Mr. Siegel was such an asshole that only the boots would talk to him, because they didn't know any better. Mendoza liked the officer because he was easy to lie to, and disliked the chief because he wasn't.

While Mendoza was acquiring wisdom in the subtle arts of fucking the system and avoiding work, Moser began to learn about the ship itself. When he had first seen it up close, Moser thought it about the biggest man-made thing in the world. Tied to the dock day after day, the *Valley* didn't seem at all shiplike. She didn't seem to move, and with all the bustle of activity had more in common with a big factory. Moser wandered around the ship when he wasn't on duty, asking shy questions in his slow, halting way. In a few weeks he was familiar with most of the ship's miles of passageways, including such truly exotic spaces as main engineering control, the flight deck, the bridge, and the combat information center. During the same period, Mendoza had seen little of the vast ship beyond the 2d Division spaces, the mess decks, and the way aft to the afterbrow where the men mustered to go ashore for liberty.

Moser's favorite discoveries were the *Valley*'s five-inch guns, two double enclosed mounts to starboard, and two open single mounts to port. He especially liked the open mounts, mount 52 forward, and mount 58 aft, because he could see the whole gun in one glance. Moser found out that the leading petty officer of the gunnery division, which owned these beautiful guns, was from near Caesar's Head, in the western mountains of South Carolina, not more than twenty miles from Moser's birthplace in Clayton, Georgia. Gunner's Mate First Class Jason Everson didn't think Moser talked funny at all, although even Everson thought the big man spoke slowly. Moser showed such an interest in the guns that Everson made a note of his name. G Division had been drawn down during the yard period, and he would soon be looking for raw seamen like Moser to bring the division up to strength.

Even though the *Valley* was old, Moser learned that she had several advantages over the newer LPHs, and over other amphibs in general. First, she was big, at 899 feet long and displacing 35,000 tons. The newer ships were only 600 feet long and 18,000 tons. Chief Brown told the sailors that that meant the *Valley* could carry more, and do her job better. That sounded good to Moser, but Mendoza kidded him for being gung-ho. Just as important, the chief told them, the *Valley* was faster and more reliable, because she had eight boilers and four engines, developing 150,000 horsepower to the four propellers. The old *Valley* could do more than thirty knots, and carry enough fuel to do it all the way across the Pacific. The newer LPHs had only two pissant boilers, one engine, and one propeller. They could do eighteen knots at best, and couldn't cross the Pacific without a stop. That means we can get from here to the war six to eight days faster (boos), said the chief. We also get home six to eight days faster when the cruise is done. Even Mendoza cheered for that. The chief told them the *Valley* handled better in rough seas. The newer ships rolled their guts out, not good for tender boot stomachs. The men cheered again, and Moser felt more a part of the crew. Mendoza said it was all chicken shit.

On the third of April the *Valley* got underway for the first time since Moser and Mendoza had joined the ship. It was a short, one-day trip to test the engines and to give the largely new crew a chance to get a first taste of their at-sea duty stations. Moser and Mendoza had been assigned to the special sea detail, the group of officers and men, serving in various capacities from the bridge to the main deck to main engine control, whose responsibility it was to take the ship into and out of port, and to sea.

Moser and Mendoza were assigned to a line-handling party just forward of the forward brow. (The what? asked Mendoza: The gangway to you, Boot, replied a fresh-faced kid who had been on the *Valley* six whole months.) The detail that had to steady the heavy brow in the wind as it was lifted clear of the ship by the huge crane on the dock was also 2d Division, but under the personal command of the first lieutenant, the officer in overall charge of the three deck divisions. Lieutenant Commander Donald was a mustang and a Southerner, and considered by Chief Brown the most able sea officer on the ship. Chief Brown stood a few feet from Donald, directing the groups of sailors holding the steadying lines as the brow was swung up and across to the dock. Since Donald was watching the brow away, and directing the rest of the line-handling crews by means of the phones clipped over his head, there was little for Ensign Siegel to do but strut around Moser's line-handling party making loud, jocular remarks. Moser didn't know, but he kind of thought the first lieutenant and the chief were unimpressed. Moser thought if he were an ensign, he'd be a lot quieter.

The chief caught the eye of the first lieutenant, who nodded. The chief advanced to the rail, and shouted across to the line handlers on shore, and Moser and his party were told to slack off all the tension. One by one the lines were taken off the bollards on the dock, and dropped into the water, to be hauled aboard by teams of sailors encouraged by brawling petty officers, and, of course, Mr. Siegel. As the last line was hauled aboard, the 1-mc public address system barked "Shift colors, the ship is underway," and the *Valley* slid slowly into Long Beach Harbor. Mendoza punched Moser's shoulder lightly, "Hey, big fella, we're real sailors now!"

"Yep," Moser smiled out at the gray waters of the harbor as the ship picked up speed and the breakwater sped past. He wanted to say something, but couldn't find the words. There was a lump in his throat.

Stuart dozed in his seat in the back of the plane. Following SERE training, he had completed the amphibious warfare course; once again, as in gunnery training, he had enjoyed the practical phases—driving World War II–vintage landing craft onto beaches, and learning to extract the awkward craft back out through the surf without broaching—but the classroom material had been boring.

Stuart had never really thought about the war in Vietnam. As a shipboard officer, he didn't expect to see much of Vietnam, or of the fighting, except perhaps through the eyes of the marine grunts and helicopter pilots who would operate from the *Valley Forge*. He certainly never expected to be in danger.

SERE had changed his thinking. For the first time, the war in Nam felt real and immediate, even fascinating. Crazy, he thought, coming fully awake as the pilot announced the start of their descent into Los Angeles. This is no time to be getting romantic. Three years on the ship, and out. Probably go to law school. Maybe business. Raise a family.

Karen threw her arms around his neck as he entered the terminal. They kissed and smiled at each other. Karen looked radiant. She had completed her studies at Rollins and received her degree, but had foregone the graduation ceremony to spend Stuart's last few days in the U.S. with him, before he departed to join the *Valley Forge* at Subic Bay, in the Philippines.

They walked arm in arm to the baggage claim area. Karen put her hands on Stuart's shoulders, and looked at him at arm's length.

"You look very handsome in uniform, William, dearest."

William grinned, and felt a little foolish. "Thanks, my love. I will say I'm beginning to feel at home in this outfit. While I was in ROTC, it always felt like a costume."

Karen pulled close, and rested her head on his shoulder. Stuart lightly stroked her fine golden hair. He felt a tightness in his throat and an aching fullness in his groin. God help me, he thought, I love this woman more than life.

Stuart's seabag and his B-4 finally emerged, and he gathered them up. They walked out to the parking lot and Karen retrieved her brother's new Buick. Karen's brother, ten years older than she and a vice president of Bank of America, lived in a house on the strand in Manhattan Beach.

It was only a short ride from the airport, and they talked little during the trip. William was content just to watch his lovely fiancée as she attacked the traffic expertly, long, slim, golden-tanned thighs wrapped in a short beige skirt. The love he felt caused his breathing to become shallow; it almost hurt.

Karen parked the Buick in the short driveway beside the beach house. William carried his bags inside, and Karen threw her arms around his neck again, this time kissing him deeply, prob-ing fiercely inside his mouth with her tongue, pressing her body urgently against his. William felt his erection straighten painfully inside his tight-fitting uniform trousers, and pressed it against Karen. She broke the kiss, and he urgently pulled her back. She reached a hand down and pressed it against his swollen groin. A low moan escaped from William's throat and once again their mouths separated. "Come on," she said, huskily, and pulled him into the bedroom.

"Where's Robert?" asked William, as Karen unbuttoned his uniform jacket.

"In San Francisco for the week," she said, as William's hands moved lightly over her breasts, unbuttoning her silk blouse.

"I'm sorry to miss him," lied William, shrugging free of his shirt, and pulling Karen close by the waist of her skirt, fighting the side zipper with shaking fingers.

"I'll bet," giggled Karen, as they fell onto the king-sized bed and removed the last of each other's clothing.

They rolled together, clutching, kissing. Karen's hands were everywhere, touching, caressing, brushing ever so lightly over William's chest, his belly, his penis and below, lightly squeezing his painfully anxious scrotum. Karen had been a virgin when she and William had first become lovers, and William had had a few women before, but her passion and her boldness always made him feel the less experienced. It was almost frightening. He felt clumsy as he first stroked her breasts with his thick fingers, then took first one nipple, then the other into his mouth. He probed each nipple with the point of his tongue, felt them become firm and prominent. Karen alternately moaned, and cried out sharply, as William gently forced her thighs open, and touched the silky mound between. Karen continued her urgent kissing, her tongue probing deeply between gasps for breath as his fingers sought and touched within. She bucked and seemed to struggle as he stroked her. She withdrew her right hand from around his neck and placed it on his chest, digging her nails in slightly, pushing him away. She looked at him, her expression twisted as if with pain, her eyes bright, "Baby, I want to feel you inside me, please, William!"

William stroked her face, caressing, "I won't be able to hold it very long, dearest. It's been too long; I'm just too excited."

Karen dug her nails a bit more, and bit her lower lip. "That's all right, I want you *now*!"

William rolled on top of Karen, guided himself inside her. Her cries became more frantic, and she bucked so hard that William had to hold her beneath her hips to avoid being thrown off. Her nails in his chest became genuinely painful as he pushed his chest down onto her breasts and kissed her deeply, wildly. He tried to take his mind away, to prolong the moment, but he could feel the warmth rising through his body, and the ache in his genitals become unbearable. His body took control, and despite his wish to hold off, he felt the pace of his thrusting increase. He pushed his weight up with his elbows, closed his eyes tightly, and came explosively at the end of his deepest thrust. Karen screamed, long and high-pitched, tapering off into a low moan, her wild humping seeming to draw William's softening penis in deeper. William tensed the muscles of his back and legs, trying to keep up with Karen's ecstasy. Gradually she subsided. They lay together, clinging. Karen smiled, and kissed him lightly on the nose. William knew she hadn't reached a climax.

"I'm sorry I was so quick, babe. You just get me too excited."

Karen hugged his neck, and kissed him harder. "It was fine, lover. I'm flattered I do that to you."

William rolled onto his back. "You surely do."

Karen got up, slowly. "I'll get you a cigarette. Then I have a surprise for you."

I wish you would just lie here, thought William. He took the cigarette and inhaled deeply. I'll never be able to love this woman as much as I want to, as much as she deserves.

Karen went into the kitchen, and returned with a chilled bottle of champagne and two glasses. "I thought you would probably be tired after your flight, so I marinated a couple of steaks, and made a big salad. OK?"

Stuart smiled, "Wonderful. Perfect. I love you so much, Karen."

"I love you, too, sailor." She poured the champagne and handed a glass to William. They touched glasses. "To love, and welcome to California, Ensign."

"To love, and to you, my angel."

Karen put her glass down, and took William's. Once again, they embraced, and savored each others' mouths with eager tongues. Karen looked out the window. It was fully dark. "Damn! I wanted to watch the sun sink into the Pacific, with the champagne."

"Tomorrow, my love," said Stuart, lying back, drinking in the tastes of Karen and the champagne. "Tomorrow."

Stuart woke before dawn. The combination of the time-zone change and the habits of military training awakened him early, and he could not go back to sleep. Karen lay next to him, on her side, with her back to him, her hair a fine-spun golden halo on the pillow. William ached with love to look at her, and gently kissed her shoulder. She didn't stir.

William got up carefully, and dug out of his seabag a pair of running shorts and a gray sweatshirt with "USN" front and back, which he had bought at the PX at Norfolk. The sun was rising brassy-hot through the smog over the Los Angeles basin, and the day was already warming as he walked across the deck and dropped onto the beach.

He *needed* to be physical, to burn energy. He ran, alternately for pace, then short sprints. His muscles warmed, but did not tire.

He and Karen had enjoyed the steaks marinated in wine vinegar and herbs, and then grilled. The salad was mostly spinach, crisp and bitter, and richly garnished with mushrooms, shallots, cherry tomatoes, wine vinegar, oil, and garlic. They finished two bottles of Louis Martini cabernet sauvignon, which, following the hastily consumed champagne, made them decidedly mellow. The time change had Stuart yawning uncontrollably by ten o'clock, and Karen led him gently back to the big bed, and they once again made love. William felt much more relaxed, and the loving was slow, and he felt more in control of his urgent passion and more responsible to Karen's. They fell asleep in each other's embrace.

William turned about a mile and a half down the beach, and started back toward the house. He continued to run effortlessly, strongly, enjoying the sweat, and the swishing sound of his bare feet scuffing the caked sand just above the high-water line.

He felt more strongly than ever that he and Karen would be together forever when he got back from the western Pacific. He would be there in just a few days! He thought about Vietnam, and his mind pictured rich, exotic, rotting jungles vividly colored birds and flowers, and the lurking enemy, fading before tightly knit units of American soldiers. Of course he would never see the jungle, but the picture in his mind was very strong. I'll just do my three years, he thought. Then Karen, and life.

He reached the house, hot and finally a little tired. He considered a plunge into the ocean, but thought better of it. He knew the water would be very cold, and didn't want to risk a cramp.

He reentered the house, and heard Karen in the shower, singing softly. He poured himself a glass of orange juice from the pitcher in the fridge, then picked up his GI douche kit from the bureau in the bedroom, and found the other shower. He shaved quickly, then took a long, hot shower, ending with the water cooler, then cold. The cold brought back SERE. He dried himself, put on soft jeans and a cotton sweater. He found Karen in the kitchen, drinking coffee and eating an English muffin. She poured him a cup.

"Do you want some breakfast, Ensign?"

She looked lovely in a crisp blue silk suit and a creamy silk blouse and high-heeled blue shoes. "You look great, babe. Why the smart outfit?"

"Did I forget to tell you? Of course I did. Robert has arranged a series of job interviews with his bank, downtown."

William sipped the coffee, and began to collect eggs, sausages, and English muffins to prepare his breakfast. "I'll cook something up, love. I know you're not a breakfast person. What kind of job interviews?"

Karen wrinkled her nose as the sausages hit the hot griddle. William turned on the exhaust fan. "Well, one is with the head of the marketing department, which sounds kind of interesting, and one with the head of banking credit training. Wouldn't it be great if I could get a job right away, and have an apartment all ready by the time your ship gets back to Long Beach?''

"Yeah, very good indeed." William broke two eggs into the pan to fry in the hot grease. Karen backed away.

"I can never get used to those big, greasy breakfasts."

"Remember, I's a country boy, love."

"I guess. Anyway, if you want to use Robert's car, you'll have to drive me downtown.''

William kissed Karen lightly, respecting the precise makeup. "You go ahead, love. I'll just laze around here, maybe walk into the village. When do you think you'll be back?''

Karen picked up the car keys. "I'm not really sure. In time for sundowners, anyway."

William smiled and threw a mock salute. "I'll be sure the wine is appropriately chilled, ma'am."

William sat down to eat his breakfast. All food had seemed more enjoyable since SERE, but especially breakfast. He glanced without interest at the front page of the *L.A. Times*. It occurred to him that he and Karen had not had anything of a conversation since his arrival. We can talk with the sundowners, he thought. They had always been able to talk about anything, and Stuart wanted to share with her his new feelings about himself, and to hear about her new feelings as a graduate. Prior to this morning, it had never occurred to him that she had thought about getting a job. Somehow the idea of Karen as a professional woman made her seem even more interesting.

Karen returned at four-thirty to find William dozing in a lawn chair on the deck overlooking the beach. She kicked off her shoes, fell on top of him with a giggle, and hugged his neck. He stroked her silky hair and kissed her nose, then her eyes, and then her mouth. "How was your day, Ensign?" she asked, biting his ear. He winced; her teeth were very sharp.

"Very relaxing, my love. How was yours?"

Karen got up. "It was interesting. I'll tell you after I change. How are we off for champagne?''

"Well off. I found a nearby merchant, and replenished the stock. I'll have it organized when you return, ma'am."

Karen sat in William's lap, one arm around his neck, her champagne glass in her other hand. The sun was hanging inches above the horizon, setting out a golden path hemmed with red, from the edge of the world to the beach house. William stretched and pulled the champagne bottle from the ice bucket on the deck beside him, and refilled both glasses.

"That's where you're going, isn't it," said Karen, pointing lazily at the western ocean and the brilliant sunset.

"Yes. To the land and sea beyond the sunset."

"Is the same sun shining there now?"

"Maybe just barely. Must be about dawn."

Karen kissed him. There was a tear in her eye, and it fell on his cheek. "William, you must think of me, each day, when you first see the sun."

"And you must think of me each night at sundown."

"We must try to communicate with our minds. Do you think we can?"

"We must try to feel each other's love. I'll need that, to endure the separation."

"And I. My love will reach out strongest at sundown. You will feel it."

William stroked her fine gold hair, red and orange in the dying glow. "I know I will, my love."

"My love."

The sun slipped beneath the horizon with a final blaze of fiery red. A cool wind sprang up from the sea.

Karen put walnuts and raisins on boneless chicken breasts, preparing them for the oven. William had offered to take her to a restaurant, but she wanted the time with him alone. William worked on the salad, and watched the steaming rice. They stopped often to touch each other, and kiss.

"Tell me about the interviews, love."

Karen smiled, and slid the seasoned chicken breasts into the oven. "The first one was with the bank credit training director. It was fairly awful. I can't imagine anything more boring than analyzing financial statements and making credit checks over the phone, then ending up in some dreary branch approving car loans. I honestly don't see how Robert stands it, although at least he's in International, now."

"How bout the marketing job?"

Karen pushed him away from the salad, and put her arms around his neck, nestling her head under his chin. Stuart kissed her hair, inhaling the subtle, flowery fragrance. "Do you think I could be any good at business, William?"

"I don't see why not. What would they want you to do?"

Karen pulled away to set the table. "We talked mostly about a job selling the BankAmericard to merchants. You know, signing up more shops and restaurants who'll accept the card. He really made it sound interesting, and competitive, with Diners

Club, and Carte Blanche, and American Express all so entrenched in the marketplace.''

William laughed. '' 'Entrenched in the marketplace?' You sound like you're already selling.''

"I think he liked me.''

"I'm sure he did. You are *very* likable.'' William tickled her ribs, then gently touched her breasts. Karen pulled away, and gave him a look of mock outrage and a light slap.

"I really think I might like it.''

"Great, how's the pay?''

"Probably around $6,800 a year.''

"That's not too bad. More than I'll be making.''

"Would that bother you?''

William laughed as he inserted the corkscrew carefully into a bottle of cabernet. "Hell, no, love. Any wage below an ensign's pay is probably illegal. Besides, you're smarter than I am, and *much* better looking.''

Karen spooned the rice onto plates, and laid the bubbling chicken breasts on the rice beds, covering them with the fragrant sauce. William put the salad bowl on the table and poured wine into their glasses.

"You really think I should go to work, I mean, even start a career? We've never talked about it.''

Stuart tasted the wine. "If it's what you want, darling, sure. Besides, if you change your mind, you can give it up when I get back.''

Karen smiled. "You sound very possessive.''

"Well, we are getting married, aren't we?''

"Next spring, my love, if you still want to after seeing the exotic Orient.''

William picked up her delicate hand and kissed it. "I will only want you more.''

Karen leaned across the table and they kissed, deeply. She pushed him away, gently. "Eat your dinner, Ensign.''

William sat, and tasted the chicken. He raised his glass to his wife-to-be. "This is delicious, love.''

Karen smiled, and touched his hand. "William, you haven't told me about your training. What was it like?''

William told Karen about the training in gunnery, and then, more slowly, about the amphibious course. He felt vague, abstract. He wanted to talk about SERE, but he couldn't think of a way to make the experience comprehensible to so gentle a person as Karen, so he stalled, rambling on about the other training.

"You don't seem terribly interested in talking about this, William," said Karen, softly.

William sat silent, smoking. I don't know what SERE means to me, yet I want to share it. I guess I should. "More coffee, love?"

"Yes. Let's have it in front of the fire."

They cuddled in the deep leather sofa, in front of a small fire the evening didn't really need. The mesquite popped in the fireplace, and shot tiny flames of green and blue. William felt the gut-wrenching pain of his love. "Let me love you, darling."

"Please," breathed Karen, into his neck.

Karen sat upright in bed, her face twisted and teary, clutching the sheets tightly around her body. "I can't believe it. William, I can't *stand* it! Such brutality!"

"Well, darling, it was just realistic training."

"It makes me sick. Why did they do it to you?"

William felt puzzled. He had tried to make SERE sound positive, even fun. Clearly he had failed. "It was just hard training. I didn't mind it."

"But you told me you were just going to a ship. Off Vietnam. Not in it. Why *you*?" Karen's voice was pleading.

"Baby, I wasn't really due for this training; it just came up, in a gap between the other schools. Don't take it so seriously; I was never in any danger."

Karen hugged the sheets tighter, seemed to shrink from him. "But that's *it*, isn't it, William? You *are* going into danger."

William tried to put his arms around her shoulders, tried to pull her back to him. She shook him off, then settled back into the bed, her back to him and still clutching the sheet around her like a protective shield. William spoke very softly. "There's always a little danger, my love. More training is always better than less. I'm going to be on a great big ship, miles offshore."

"I can't bear the thought of you in danger." Karen was suddenly crying heavily. "You never told me you would be in danger. I won't be able to sleep any night while you're gone."

William pulled himself to a sitting position and embraced her, fighting the stiffness in her body. "Baby, you know I would never do anything to spoil our happiness. Don't think about it."

Karen turned and hugged his chest, wetting his skin with her tears, and kissing the tears. "You should never have told me."

Maybe not, thought Stuart, stroking her hair. But why not? Isn't this me? Isn't this part of loving, part of the deal?

William did not mention SERE again, or Vietnam, but the subject hung between them, creating little frowns and long looks at the end of laughter. Early the next afternoon, Karen got a call from the personnel office at Bank of America, asking that she return for more interviews the next week. Karen was gleeful and they got into the last of the champagne a little early. He had but two days left of his leave.

William's orders required him to report to Travis Air Force Base, north of San Francisco, at 0500 on 1 June. Karen's father had given her an air ticket and a reservation at the Mark Hopkins Hotel so she could fly up with her fiancé the day before his departure and spend the evening with him. He had also reserved a rental car so she could drive William to Travis.

On the way to the airport and on the flight, Karen talked excitedly about her upcoming interviews, and the possible career that could follow. William encouraged her, fighting to suppress his sense of foreboding at the coming separation, a feeling he had never before experienced. Karen's reaction to his description of SERE had brought home to him that this separation would be very real, not like semesters apart while at school, punctuated by stolen weekends. They would be truly apart, and William felt already that Karen was shunning the part of him that was drawn to the rotting jungles of Nam.

They had dinner at Alexis, near the hotel—delicious food with a Middle Eastern flavor, and more champagne. They returned to the Mark early and went to bed. They would have to start for Travis by 0400. William had felt increasingly preoccupied during dinner, and he realized as he paid the bill that he couldn't remember what he had eaten. As they made love in the big hotel bed, William felt the pain increasing in his gut. The agony of being pulled apart so slowly racked him. He sat, doubled over on the edge of the bed, smoking cigarette after cigarette while Karen slept quietly. Part of him wished he were already on the plane, already gone. He was still awake when the hotel operator phoned at 0330.

Karen drove north and east into the pinkish gray dawn. They reached the big air base just before five in the morning, and William presented his orders, nervous at arriving so close to the deadline. The airman at the desk gave him his boarding plaque in exchange for several copies of the orders, and told Stuart the flight would depart at 0900.

"Jesus, man, it's that late already?"

The airman smiled, "Ain't late, sir. That's the time she goes."

Stuart looked at his orders in disgust. "Then why did I have to report at 0500?"

Once again, the airman smiled. "You in the military, sir, and you still have to ask?"

Stuart walked back to the curb, where Karen sat in the car. She, too, had assumed his departure would be immediate. When he told her of the snafu, she laughed, and brightened. "Get in, sailor, we passed a motel just outside the gate."

They made love a last time in the dingy motel. Karen's passion and intensity no longer frightened him; he tried to absorb it, to store it up. He felt his own lovemaking had matured over the last few precious days, and was at last sure of Karen's orgasm, shuddering, scratching, crying, pleading. He knew they loved each other, but he was afraid of the gulf that had already come between them, and he felt chilled to the bone.

2 July 1966   Camp Pendleton, California

Private First Class Bobby Coles turned in his orders to the clerk of the training battalion at Camp Pendleton, and was assigned a bunk in the Alpha Company barracks. He had completed boot camp a week previously, and had taken six days' boot leave to visit Simon in Los Angeles. Simon had driven him down to Camp Pendleton this morning.

Coles had hated boot camp, not for the physical hardships, which he had handled easily, but for the phony, macho camaraderie that the drill instructors had insisted the men play at. As a result of his thesis research, Coles thought he knew something of methods of manipulation and repression, and he had been amused, and sometimes appalled, at how easily the DIs had gotten the recruits to handle their own discipline. Virtually all the dirty side of the military training had been performed by the boot noncoms—men in the Marine Corps only weeks—rather than by the DIs themselves. A clear objective of basic training had been to reduce individuality and promote a team spirit, but at a very low level. The men had been taught to respond to commands and even to lectures on such subjects as dangers of venereal disease (beware of Suzy Rottencrotch!) with grunts of hu-yet! and growls of hoo-RAUGH! rather than with words.

Coles found the Alpha barracks and reported to the company clerk. Coles got listed on the company roll, then stowed his gear in the empty barracks. The other members of the company arrived in small groups toward evening, taking noisy showers and dressing in class A uniforms for chow. They were a company for administrative purposes only; the men were spread out through a variety of schools from advanced infantry training (AIT), where Bobby was headed, through artillery, communications, supply, vehicle maintenance—just about everything.

The bunk below Bobby's was occupied by a tough-looking white PFC named Billy Hunter. Bobby thought he had seen the face before, and said so. Hunter grinned. "I saw you at Dago, day you got there. I was going out as you came in."

Coles shook hands. "Yeah, I remember. You looked me right in the eye, like you knew me."

Hunter tapped the plastic name tag on Coles's sharply creased gabardine shirt. "I knew you, all right. Bobby Coles, defensive corner for USC. I played tight end at Arkansas. Our coach had a thing about USC pass defense, made us watch films of what a real defensive secondary looked like."

Bobby grinned. "I sure wish I was back playing ball."

"They got a team here, plays other bases," said Billy Hunter. "They're practicing already. They play all fall, and into January. You be going out, I expect."

"Well, I might. It has to beat this military shit."

Hunter shrugged. "They take it pretty seriously. Word is, if you are really good, they keep you here, as an instructor of some kind. You got drafted by the NFL, right?"

"Right. Maybe I could still play, after I get out. What about you, you gonna play?"

Hunter shrugged. "I just finished AIT, and I'll be starting Pathfinder School. I kind of like the training. I kind of like the Marine Corps."

Coles knotted his tie carefully, and they headed out to the mess hall. "So, Hunter, what do you figure happens to us here?"

"After Pathfinder School, I expect to be assigned to a line unit for more training, then off to Nam."

"Nam is bad shit, I heard," said Coles, not wanting to say too much, since he was a cherry in the outfit.

They entered the brightly lighted mess hall and joined the long line of marines at the cafeteria entrance. "Well, Bobby, around here, that's all anybody wants. Can't be a mad marine killing machine anywhere's else but Nam."

Bobby winced at the boot camp jargon. I hope Hunter does not turn out to be one of those instant lifers, as the boots who were just too gung-ho were termed. "Yeah, Billy, maybe. But I'm not sure I'm all that keen to go.'

Hunter grinned and handed Bobby a tray. "Neither am I, Brother. But that's what we're trained to do."

Coles fell easily into the routine of Advanced Infantry Training. He found the instruction more focused and the problems more interesting than in boot camp, but he was frustrated by the slow pace at which field problems were developed, as every lesson had to be taught at the pace of the slowest-witted marine.

Hunter spent many nights outside the barracks on exercises, training for long-range patrols behind enemy lines. When he did see Coles, he spoke animatedly about the seven- to twelve-man reconnaissance units, and the tactics they were being taught. Coles found Hunter's enthusiasm amusing and infectious at the same time, and he soon fell in, at least in public, with the idea that the marines at Pendleton were being readied to do their job as an elite fighting force, and that meant for most of them duty in Vietnam. He wondered at times what the feeling would be like in a training unit in the Army, with the new men composed mostly of draftees.

Hunter finished Pathfinder School in early September, and was assigned to Charlie Company, 2d Battalion, 17th Marines. When Coles finished AIT a few days later, he was assigned to the same unit. That evening, as they walked from the mess hall to their new barracks, a buck sergeant they didn't know stopped them by the company office.

"Hi, guys. You're Cole, and Hunter, right?"

"Coles, with an 's,' " said Coles.

"I'm Billy Hunter, Sergeant," said Hunter.

"Yeah, well I'm LaSalle. Now as you guys are in a real unit, *outward bound*, I was wondering we might talk about a little football."

"Go ahead, Sergeant," said Coles, seating himself on the step in front of the barracks. Hunter sat down beside him, and the sergeant squatted in front of them. Hunter thought the approach felt like a little conspiracy being discussed.

"Call me Frenchie," the sergeant continued. "You guys probably have heard we have a team here, a team the commanding general takes great pride in."

"We heard he bets a lot on them," said Coles.

"Yeah, well, you hear a lot of things. Anyway, in terms of talent, this team could take out most first-rate colleges, though I gotta admit we don't have anything like the same kind of coaching."

Coles studied the sergeant. He was about thirty, six feet or a bit less, and looked in shape. "You on this team, Frenchie?"

"Nah. Not good enough. But I am the defensive backfield coach." The sergeant grinned pleasantly.

"Where'd you play college ball?" asked Hunter.

"Purdue, until I flunked out. Anyway, the sergeant major who is the head coach asked me to come see you fellows. The Training Command personnel sergeant tips him when anybody who played for a major school comes into the camp. So, are you interested?"

Coles shrugged. For some reason he couldn't quite identify, he felt he should conceal his enthusiasm. "Yeah, I guess. You, Billy?"

"Sure, to take a look. What do we have to do?"

"Let me speak to your company sergeant. He'll authorize it, and you show up at the field behind the big gym for practice tomorrow at 1600. You'll have to try out, of course, but either one of you will have had to have forgotten an awful lot in the last nine months not to make it."

Coles and Hunter each shook hands with the sergeant. "We look forward to trying out, then," said Coles.

"Yeah," said Hunter. "Be fun to play."

Billy Hunter lay in his bunk in the dark barracks, thinking about football. He had played three good seasons at the University of Arkansas, but had never gotten his degree. Billy wasn't stupid, and he knew it. He was just plain bored. College to him had been nothing more than football, and football had given him an easy life. He had had a vague notion that if he played well enough, a pro contract might set him free—from Sparkman, Arkansas, from dirt farming, and from his father's shadow. But he knew in his heart that he was drifting, making nothing of himself, and he felt ashamed. He had clung to the thought that his

flashy catch against Texas for the winning score might get him
a pro football contract. The bidding wars between the NFL and
the AFL which had forced the draft for both leagues to occur as
early as it possibly could, right after the last games for most
major colleges, meant there were a lot more pro bids, but the
draft results had been posted in the field house on the Sunday
following the Texas game, and he had not been selected. After
football season was over, the tutors who the coaches had re-
cruited to hold up Billy's precarious grade-point average had
disappeared. He felt he just couldn't sit around and wait to be
flunked out, like so many finished athletes, so he just left and
went home to Sparkman. He filed all his courses as incomplete,
so he could return and re-enroll to finish without having to be
re-admitted, but somehow he doubted he ever would.

His jammed knee from the Texas game had come back all
right without surgery, but its continuing stiffness gave him an
excuse for light workouts rather than heavy farming. And he was
enjoying the notoriety that came from his successes in Fayetteville. The good old boys bought him beers, and such girls and
women who were around paid him all kinds of attention. The
skinny, reserved farm boy nobody had noticed very much had
come back filled out, handsome, and with a reputation of his
own. It was different, and Little Billy liked it. He knew the
attention wouldn't last, and he'd be back in his parents' shadow
again. He fretted as autumn turned to winter.

Little Billy was not little by any reasonable standard. At six-
two and two hundred twenty, he was well over average size just
about everywhere except on the football field. As the first born
of Big Bill Hunter, who had owned the biggest and most pros-
perous farm in not-very-prosperous Sparkman, he automatically
became "Little Billy." Big Bill had had a seat on the board of
the Farmers' Co-op; in the fifties he had twice been mayor of
Sparkman. He had died of cancer in 1963 but his presence was
still felt, and as long as Little Billy stayed around Sparkman, he
would always be Little Billy. Hell, he didn't mind. Shit, he hated
it.

Little Billy took it easy now, driving around the farm pretending to take an interest in what the men were doing; going over
the accounts with the hired foreman and his mother, who understood the numbers better than either of the men; drinking
with his good buddies in one of the local honky-tonks, some of
which were legal, depending on which side of the county line
they stood; or getting lucky with wholesome farm girls, as well
as a few slightly less wholesome but generally more interesting
young wives, and in some of the darndest places.

Little Billy got more restless each day. He wasn't fooling anybody. He felt an increasing pressure all around him to get on with it—something, anything. His mother never said anything outright; she just looked at him with a hint of sadness in her eyes, which hurt more than words could have. Billy lay upstairs in his room for long, silent hours, hearing the whispers in the old house, trying to figure out ways to make himself want to be in Sparkman, want to look after the little empire his father had built, and look after his mother. Neither, he knew, had any real need of his care, even if he had known how to give it. Then three weeks after he had come home, his notice of induction into the United States Army arrived. The postman, old Mr. Whithers knew what it was by the shape of the envelope. He had brought it right into the parlor, where Billy was reading the local newspaper.

"Looks like you bin called to the colors, Little Billy," the old man had grinned. Billy was stunned when he read the notice, and horrified. The Army! It had never occurred to him that his student deferment would lapse as soon as he left college. He hadn't even thought about it. In this part of Arkansas there had always been enough poor kids who joined up after high school to fill the draft quota. Yet here it is, Billy had thought, as he stared dumbly at the paper in his hands.

On December 28, 1965, Billy went to Little Rock for his pre-induction physical. He knew many football players, healthy enough to stay in the game even at the pro level, who could not pass an army physical. One little cartilage operation, one brown scar curving around the left knee he had jammed, and he could have walked out of the physical with a 4-F on his draft classification card, and no obligation to serve. But he passed the casual physical, and was given a date, January 11, 1966, to report for induction.

Billy walked out of the dingy old hospital, crossed the square by the war memorial, and headed toward the lot where he had parked the battered pickup. A big man with a crinkly red face and a gray crew cut, wearing an olive-drab uniform with three red-backed chevrons and two rockers beneath crossed rifles on his sleeves, stood in Billy's way on the sidewalk, grinning a friendly grin. He pointed to the induction orders Billy held in his left hand, and called out in a hearty, jovial voice, "I know what you got there, boy!"

Billy smiled sheepishly, and handed the papers to the man when he reached for them. The man read them quickly and handed them back. "Looks like you got one more choice to make, William Hunter."

Billy laughed. "I think this paper says I'm plumb outa choices, sir."

The man clapped Billy on the shoulder, and steered him toward a storefront with signs in the windows proclaiming "Join the Navy and See the World," and "Be the Best! Marines!" "Come on into my parlor, William. Let's have us a little talk about the United States Marine Corps."

Three days later, when the good old boys had let him sober up, Little Billy joined the United States Marine Corps. If he was going to go, he'd go with the best, dammit. Maybe Big Billy would have been proud. Maybe Rose Ellen would be. Somehow he especially wanted his mother to be proud.

The Army was taking people so fast that they had basic training programs starting virtually every week somewhere in the country. The marines, still a tiny outfit by comparison, started boot camps every other month, and only at two places—Parris Island, South Carolina, and San Diego, California. Billy Hunter was to report to San Diego on January 13, 1966. Soon enough.

Little Billy decided he should spend the short time he had left with his family on the farm, and give up most of his forays to the saloons of Arkadelphia and Little Rock. He spent time talking to his mother, cool and distant as always; running the farm with the quiet efficiency and detachment that had allowed folks to believe Big Billy had really been the brains and imagination in the family. Big Billy had been a good salesman, and a good organizer of other peoples' ideas, but if he hadn't married Rose Ellen Loving he'd never have gotten much beyond the struggling small farmer he had become as the Depression was ending. Little Billy himself hadn't known the true secret of Big Billy's success until after his father had died—suddenly after only a year of being really sick.

After the funeral Billy had taken his mother aside and said he'd be coming home from Fayetteville to pick up running the farm. His middle brother, just about to start at the university in the fall, had volunteered as well. They had all sat in the parlor, and Little Billy could feel Rose Ellen observing them coolly, knowing that neither he nor Henry wanted to come back. Little Billy was sure, however, that she also knew that if she asked, either or both would have done so without complaint.

She said that she had confidence in the foreman and the hands, and with the help of her youngest son, Joseph, then fifteen, she was sure she could carry on as she had during their father's illness. How she protected the old man's pride even after death.

It would be all right, boys, but thank you anyway. Rose Ellen had sat in the shadowy parlor, dry-eyed and composed.

Little Billy and his two brothers had grown up close to one another. They were just far enough apart in age to avoid the competitive fights brothers have. The younger boys looked to Billy for leadership, comfort and protection. Their father traveled a lot and their genteel, busy mother seemed to notice their growing up accomplishments more for the dirt and disruption they caused than for their true and obvious value. The boys became self-reliant allies, a society of their own that had no other permanent members and few transient ones.

Their games seemed always to take them down to the creek bottom where the creek now ran cool and clear through the gray-green Laurel grass. The small pool that had sustained Big Bill and his parents through the Dust Bowl years had been widened and dammed, and was ideal for swimming and fishing.

The boys played their games intensely, running, climbing, and they grew up swift and strong. When they went to school, they all moved naturally into sports. Little Billy played football right from grade school, and was quarterback and team captain by consensus in his senior year in high school. Henry, by then old enough to want to show his differences from his older brother, played baseball. The youngest, who worshipped both his older brothers, played both football and baseball. Little Billy thought young Joseph had the finest athletic potential of them all, and Little Billy looked forward to seeing his younger brother play in college.

Little Billy remembered that it had been football that caused the only long-running disagreement he ever had with his father. When the other two boys had been too little to play games with him, his father got out his Dick Williams baseball glove and threw a baseball, and hit him fly balls in the field south of the house. When Little Billy began to play football in the cub league at the age of thirteen, Big Billy told him to be careful. When he began to play Little League baseball, his father came to the games. Billy mostly sat on the bench. He never really had a talent for baseball, and the more he sat on the bench, the more discouraged he became. Yet his father always came, and made jovial banter as they drove home from every game in which Little Billy had not played. He felt he had let his father down. Yet, when Little Billy played cub football, and began to excel, his father stayed away. When, in the fall of his sophomore year in high school, he announced with embarrassed pride that he had made the varsity football team, his father was furious. Big

Billy rarely let his anger show, and had schooled the boys never to give in to temper. Yet at the point of Little Billy's halting, proud announcement, Big Billy exploded.

The boy had been terrified. Why wasn't his father proud? Little Billy knew he would be as good a football player as he had been a bad baseball player, and he wanted his father to see him play and not warm a bench. Yet his father raged. High school football was absolutely forbidden. The sport was brutal and dangerous, and a fine boy soon to be a man with responsibilities had no business getting himself hurt and maybe crippled playing a silly game. Billy was too light, too skinny, and could get broken in half (he had his full height at fifteen, but he weighed only 160 pounds). The son had never seen his father like that. Little Billy started crying, blubbering how he wanted to play, how he would be good. No, his father raged. Absolutely not. Rose Ellen tried to calm her husband, and when he told her to leave it to him, Rose Ellen's blue eyes blackened like a thunderhead, and she ordered Little Billy and his brothers from the room. He fled upstairs to the comfort of his brothers, who were as terrified and bewildered as he was.

There was never any supper that night, though Rose Ellen brought the boys soup and sandwiches upstairs. She told them that their father had a severe headache, and had gone to bed. The boys felt the world shifting beneath them. Their father had never lost his temper like that, and he had never gone to bed, or let them go to bed, without saying good night, when he was home.

In the morning, Big Billy sat very calmly at breakfast and apologized to his family, and especially to Little Billy, for losing his temper. Rose Ellen and he, he said, had decided that Little Billy could play, if he promised to be very careful, but that he should remember how the game and its violence worried his father. So Little Billy played, and got better, and became team captain, and was awarded a scholarship to play at the university, and his father never, ever came to a game. When Little Billy came home Saturday evenings in the fall, tired and perhaps bruised from a game, his father would look at him with great sadness, as if he hadn't expected him to come home whole, or come home at all. His father never repeated his command that his son give up the game, but Little Billy knew his father hated it. And Little Billy never found out why.

As daylight faded into evening the day of Big Billy's funeral, Little Billy had asked his mother why his father had such a boundless hatred of the game of football. Rose Ellen's eyes filled quickly, and she told him there had been a side of Big Billy she never understood, a side of him fiercely protective of her and the boys, and at the same time deeply fearful that something would happen to them, something painful, violent. Every night Big Billy spent away from home, through all the years, he had called, or tried to call, his wife. And always there was fear in his voice, the fear that would not be quieted by any of Rose Ellen's assurances. She supposed that was the reason he hated football.

By that time his mother was crying freely, something she had not previously done in Little Billy's sight. He did not ask again. Rose Ellen reached out for her boys. Billy tried to say comforting things, but no words came. They stood together in the darkened parlor and wept for the man they had loved but never completely known.

So Billy Hunter wasn't at all sure his father would have been proud he had gone into the Marine Corps, though he supposed the old man would have played the role with the local Rotarian patriots. The violence of military service, perhaps even actual combat if President Johnson kept sending people to Vietnam, would surely have pained his father. Little Billy felt a twinge of sudden fear in his gut. At least whatever pain and fear of pain lay ahead for him, his father would not feel it. That realization made him feel very alone, and, for the first time, afraid.

On January 11, his orders to report to San Diego had arrived, along with travel vouchers and instructions as to what he should bring with him. Practically nothing. Billy made the rounds, saying good-bye. It all felt very final. He walked for hours down by the creek that had sustained the brothers' boyhood games. The creek seemed small and rather ordinary. He tried to drink in the people, the places, to fix them in his mind for the dark and lonely times ahead. He tried to talk to his mother, but with little success. His brother, Henry, came down for the weekend, then drove Billy back to Little Rock where his journey would begin. Little Billy felt sad and scared, like a kid, really, leaving home at an early age. His brother made all the conversation at first, then fell silent. Little Billy stared at the passing farmland he had seen hundreds of times but never really looked at.

At the airport, Henry had insisted on carrying his brother's tiny airline bag. After exchanging the first of the travel coupons plus a copy of his orders for a boarding pass, Billy followed his brother into the tacky airport bar for a beer. The plane was to be one hour late, and Henry said he would wait until it arrived. The beer tasted sour. Little Billy looked at his brother, and wanted suddenly to be alone. He told Henry that the delay could be longer, and he'd miss his classes. The look of forced good cheer Henry had been wearing all morning disappeared, and Little Billy saw in the young and familiar face the look of great and distant sadness with which his father used to greet Little Billy on autumn Saturday evenings after high school football. Oh God, thought Little Billy, oh sweet Jesus. He embraced his brother, and momentarily put his head on the smaller man's shoulder. He then straightened up and held his brother by the shoulders, trying to meet the sad, penetrating gaze with one of equal steadiness.

"You're going to do all right, big brother," Henry had said. "You're going to be fine."

"I know, young Henry, but I'm going to have to live away from family for a while, and I think I had best begin now." When they had said their final good-byes and Henry walked out of the terminal, Little Billy felt he had said good-bye to himself as well. He sat back down in the deserted bar and had another beer, more sour than the first, then another, which began to taste better.

And now I'm a marine, soon to go to war, and I'm playing football, he thought, lying in his rack. I hope my father rests and doesn't fret.

Billy closed his eyes and slept.

There were fifty-two marines on the squad, organized into offensive, defensive, and specialty units. The guys seemed to be having fun, but the practice was hard. Bobby felt good to be in pads again, and although he was a little rusty on his coverages, it was readily apparent that he would be very welcome in the defensive secondary. The only receiver who beat him deep in the first scrimmage was Billy Hunter.

They continued to participate in the routine of training with their company, although the topkick, First Sergeant Phillips, a bullet-headed black man about forty years old who reportedly ate nails, showed disgust when they went off each afternoon after training to "play games."

Two weeks after their tryout, Phillips called Hunter and Coles to the company office just as they were leaving for practice. He pointed at two sets of temporary orders on his desk.

"Well, looks like you two pussies are really getting ahead. You've been ordered to report to Squad Leaders' School, next class. Tomorrow." Hunter felt that had Phillips not been standing in his own spotless office, he would have spat.

"What's Squad Leaders' School, Top?" asked Hunter. It was the first he had heard of it.

"The Corps is short of noncoms. Not enough old bastards like me stay in. So they take a few cherries, especially college boys like you, and send them to some twelve-week school, then they just make them *sergeants*! Let 'em wear three stripes just like *real* sergeants!" Once again, the Top seemed ready to spit.

"We didn't ask for this, Top." Hunter felt he had to defend himself, although he liked the idea of being a sergeant.

"We," said Phillips, stroking the rockers under his own three stripes, "call 'em ready-mixes."

"Well, gee, Top, what do you expect us to do?" Coles felt a little hot. "We didn't ask for this."

"And I didn't ask for the school for you, and neither did the lieutenant, nor the captain. So who does that leave, pussies?"

Coles and Hunter stood silent.

"Maybe ask your pals down at the old playground behind the gym."

The Squad Leaders' School did indeed contain many of the more promising men on the football team, and Sergeant Major Jackson, who was in charge of the general's team, was one of the instructors. Billy Hunter didn't like the idea of getting a deal, especially one so obvious, because of playing football, but he was mollified somewhat to find the school was hard, and the training taken very seriously. Most of the guys had at least two years of college, and a lot had never been near football practice in this or any other life. Billy figured he'd get back in grace with the Top when the unit got ready to ship out.

On September 18th, the Camp Pendleton team hosted El Toro Marine Air Station, and beat them 24–7. The game had been hard fought, but sloppy. Hunter caught three balls, one for a touchdown, and Coles was a standout at free safety, knocking down El Toro passes all afternoon. Two weeks later, the team traveled north to Alameda Naval Air Station. The Alameda team had been decidedly better than El Toro, but once again Pendleton won, and was rewarded with a night of liberty in San Francisco before returning to camp and the Squad Leaders' School. Hunter liked playing, but somehow there was far less passion than he had felt at Arkansas. Maybe it was the lack of big crowds, but Billy kind of thought he was really past football, and ready to be a marine.

Bobby Coles took the practices seriously, gradually rebuilding skills and timing. He worked with LaSalle and with the other defensive backs, trying to teach them as much of the USC flexing zone as he could. He thought the team played reasonably well, although most treated it more like a job than a game. He supposed it would be like that in the NFL.

Bobby studied hard at the school as well. He could guess the school was part of the scheme to keep the better players at Pendleton after their units were sent overseas, but he wasn't about to rely on football alone to ensure that he finished at the top of his class. He also didn't want to give the Topkick any additional excuses to ridicule him, not that the Top cared for or needed any excuse. Bobby was beginning to resent the Top's constant gibing about boys who play games while men became fighting marines. Fuck him, thought Bobby. Lots of mess cooks are marines. Lots of clerks.

Rumor Control reported that the battalion would be going to Okinawa sometime around the end of December, the last stop before Vietnam.

Coles and Hunter and all of their class graduated from Squad Leaders' School on the 18th of December. Their graduation ceremony was deferred, even after they had received and sewn on their E-5 buck sergeant's stripes, because the following day the football team was taken in two olive-drab buses down the road to Miramar Naval Air Station for the biggest game of the schedule. Rumor had it the commanding officer at Miramar collected ringers just like their own good general.

The game was rough. The men said the stakes were high, but Billy found himself listless and uninspired. He caught a pass for thirty-five yards in the first quarter, then dropped two in the second, and got a chewing out from the sergeant major. Bobby intercepted a pass thrown by the Miramar quarterback from his own end zone, and walked in for the first half's only score.

Early in the third quarter, Billy caught a pass over the middle, and was brutally speared in the back by the Miramar safety. He landed on his right shoulder, which blazed with pain. He was helped off the field, and watched as Pendleton scored again. The pain subsided, and he knew that if he wanted to, he could go back in. He sat on the bench with ice on his shoulder and said nothing.

The game ended with Pendleton's ringers beating Miramar's 14–7. Billy took no joy in the victory, though he hoo-raughed with the other men as they rode back to Pendleton in the dark, drinking beer from a cooler provided by the grateful commandant. When the bus reached the camp, the men went to the enlisted men's club for their celebration—the last, for many, as they would now join the sergeants' mess. Sergeant Billy Hunter pulled Sergeant Bobby Coles to a corner, away from the noise and the splashing beer.

"You got an idea what happens now, pardner?"

Bobby slugged back his beer. He was a little drunk. "I reckon we can stay with this *winning* team, redneck."

"Stay here and play football. Pass on the war," said Hunter.

Bobby's eyes focused carefully. "Ain't necessarily my war, redneck."

Billy resented the redneck gibe. He had never seen Bobby drink like this. "You sure about this, Bobby? Them letting us stay on, as 'instructors' in the general's private ringer team?"

Bobby giggled. "I been kind of figuring on it, Bro. What's eating at you?"

Hunter leaned his face in close to Coles. "Just why did you join the Marine Corps, *Sergeant*?"

Coles frowned, and let out a slow breath. "OK, red—, sorry, OK, Billy, we feel differently about this, you know that. Let's just have some fun, OK?"

"Why did you join?" said Hunter, sitting down across from Bobby.

Coles put down his mug and pulled himself together. "OK, OK. I was drafted into the Army, same time practically as into the NFL. I still want that pro career. I joined the Corps because I thought I would get better training, to help me *survive*." Bobby paused, and looked hard at his friend. "I want to survive, man. So why did you join?"

Billy returned Bobby's stare. He shrugged, "I guess it's fairest to say I was bored."

"So what are you getting at me for? What's the gung-ho all about?"

Billy leaned back. "The training hasn't changed your mind? The Corps doesn't mean anything?"

Bobby slumped in the chair. The party seemed to recede. "I know what you mean, man. But I just want to get by. I'll soldier if I have to, but if the general wants me to play football, hell, I gotta say no? Lighten *up*, Bro!"

Billy leaned back and drank some beer, forcing himself to relax. "Bobby, I guess what I'm saying is I really don't know what to do if they ask me to leave the company—stay here and play ball."

"Shit, man, why are you personally responsible for what the government does with your ass? Did you vote for this war? Are you personally needed to kill a bunch of little yellow people in a country no American citizen could have found on a map five years ago? What's this guilt you're haulin' around, Bro?''

"I don't know, man," said Billy, his eyes downcast, staring into the beer stein. "Being in the Marine Corps, doing *well*, was going to mean something to me."

Coles refilled both mugs from the pitcher between them. "Roll with it, brother mine. *Non morituri te salutamus.*"

"What the hell does that mean?"

Bobby raised his mug and clinked it against Hunter's. "Old Roman soldier's saying. Roughly, it means let the other guy do it."

"Ten-HUT!" bawled First Sergeant Phillips as Hunter and Coles filed into the company office. The two ready-mix sergeants snapped to attention, eyes rigidly forward. First Sergeant Phillips stood beside the big gray steel desk. The company commander, Captain Leitner, sat behind the desk, his hands resting on two olive-drab folders on the otherwise empty surface of the desktop.

"At ease, men," said Captain Leitner.

The topkick came around in front of the desk and faced Hunter and Coles. He looked into Coles's eyes from below. Coles thought First Sergeant Phillips's eyes looked yellowish, like a wild animal's, and dangerous. The topkick passed on to stare into Hunter's eyes, and Coles felt a relieving of the tension that seemed to crackle from those jungle eyes. The topkick sat with one haunch on the edge of the desk, and began in a low voice, all the more menacing because of the sense that the rage beneath was barely in control. Intimidation and manipulation, thought Bobby.

"OK, pussies. Excuse *me*! *Sergeant* pussies! Well, the captain has asked me to have a short career guidance session with you *sergeants*. As you both know, this battalion is very shortly to be going off to do its duty in the Republic of Vietnam. We had, of course, hoped you two would be joining us, but something has come up.''

Bobby's heart, already pounding, gave an extra leap. We made the team, he thought.

The topkick got up off the desk and began pacing slowly in the tiny office. The captain sat, impassive, his hands clasped on top of the folders that must contain orders for the transfer of Coles and Hunter. Coles stared at the folders, and willed the captain's hands to rise

"Battalion has received, just this morning," continued the topkick, his voice even but gradually losing its edge, "a *request* from the camp commandant to transfer you two fine young men to the camp staff, as instructors.''

Hot *damn*! thought Bobby. He wanted to shout.

"Sergeant Hunter, you are requested to become a team instructor in Pathfinder School! Did you know you had done so *well* in that school?''

"Yes, Top. I was at the top of my class.''

"You probably learned enough to practice your pathfinder's skill *in the field*, wouldn't you say, *Sergeant*?''

"Yes, Sergeant,'' said Hunter. Coles could hear the strain in his voice.

"And you, *Sergeant* Coles, you are to teach marines in AIT! A course you only recently completed! Were you at the top of *your* class, too?''

"They don't issue individual grades in AIT, as the First Sergeant well knows.'' Bobby planted an edge in his voice and earned a baleful stare from the topkick in return. For a long minute the room was silent.

The topkick resumed his pacing. "Naturally, the colonel would find it very hard to refuse the general's *request*, even though it would deprive one of his line companies of two trained *sergeants*,'' the topkick spat the word at Coles's boots, "just at the point of overseas deployment. But the colonel has asked the captain, and the captain has asked me, to determine whether you men might want the colonel to ask the commandant on your behalf to *cancel* his request, and allow you to deploy with this company as you have been *prepared* and *trained* to do.''

Not fucking likely, thought Coles. Phillips stopped directly in front of Hunter. "Well, Sergeant Pathfinder, do you want to be a football hero, or a *marine*?''

The bastard knows Billy has doubts, that's why he's starting on him, though Bobby.

The captain spoke for the first time since putting the men "at ease.'' "That's enough, Top. The man has an important choice to make; let him think about it.''

Good cop, bad cop, thought Bobby.

Sergeant Phillips turned to Coles. "I'll bet I know your answer already, *Sergeant* Coles.'' The voice was loaded with contempt.

"Yes, Sergeant. I have no desire to contest the general's request. I'm quite happy to be an instructor on the staff.''

"And to play football with the general's team.''

"And to play football, too, if that's what the Marine Corps wants of me.''

The topkick flared, "You have no right to call yourself a *marine*! You're a fucking *football player*, nothing more!"

Coles let his own anger up a notch. "That's not fair, First Sergeant!"

"And why isn't it? Marines *fight*! Marines *kill*! Marines don't play fucking games!"

"Let the man talk, Top," put in the captain, mildly.

"There are marines who are cooks, marines who pound typewriters, marines who keep track of our fucking *pay*, Top! And when a class at AIT graduates, they have a parade, and there are marines in the band playing fucking *sousaphones*! And they don't have to listen to this shit!"

First Sergeant Phillips stared at Coles, his expression shifting between amazement and outrage. The captain picked up one of the olive-drab folders. "What do you think of that, First Sergeant Phillips?"

The topkick took the folder from the captain and slapped it into Coles's chest, hard enough to rock him back slightly on his heels. Coles took the folder and tucked it neatly under his left arm, and came to attention. "I got no need in my outfit for a *marine* who'd rather play football than kill dinks, Captain," growled the Topkick.

"Then that's all, Sergeant Coles," said the captain, with a hint of sadness. "Good luck instructing."

Coles saluted. "Thank you, sir." He executed a smart about-face, concentrating very hard to get it perfect. "Don't let them bullshit you, Billy."

"I said, that's all, Sergeant," said the captain.

"OUT!" roared the Topkick.

"You must think me a total asshole."

Bobby Coles looked up from his beer. He was sitting, alone, at the end of the bar in the sergeant's mess, having tired of the hoo-RAUGH bullshit of the party of the ready-mix sergeants following the football victory over El Toro. He was surprised to see the face of Billy Hunter.

"Hey, sit down, man."

"I mean, shit, about me letting the Top and the captain talk me into, well, staying with the unit, moving out."

Bobby clapped Hunter on his shoulder, and motioned to the barkeep to bring him a beer. "Shit, man, *never*! I would have thought you'd think me the asshole for stayin', playing ball while you guys head out for Nam."

Billy sat, and toasted with his beer. "Wasn't a man in the outfit wouldn't a done what you did, having the pro prospects you have. Way you told the Top, you're a legend in the company."

"The guys don't think I'm some kinda, ah, quitter?" Bobby fought back the word "coward," which had been whispering in his mind.

Billy looked surprised. "Hell, no, Bobby. They understand. They know. For us, I guess the Corps is part of the way we try to grow up. You are *there*, man, you *know* what you want to do. Most of us don't, and that's why we're here."

Coles thought about that, wondering. I don't really know *any-thing*, he mused. Why do they think different? "When you shipping out, Bro?"

Hunter took a long draw of his beer. "Three days. Parade tomorrow. You come by and see us, tomorrow night in the barracks, OK?"

"The guys would like that? Billy, I still feel a little bit small, you know, about staying here—"

"They would. They know what you're doing, breaking away. Takes balls, maybe more than we got, just following on, you know?"

I wonder, thought Coles, after Hunter had left. I really wonder if the topkick wasn't right.

Bobby watched the battalion pass in review the following afternoon, under brilliantly sunny skies. The men looked smart in their dress-blue uniforms, probably the last time they would wear them for quite a while. He looked at the faces of the marching marines, and noted that the men looked proud and happy. The junior officers mostly tried to look fierce, executing sword salutes as each marching unit's first sergeant bawled "Eyes, RIGHT!" as the unit passed the reviewing stand. Why do they look so happy? wondered Bobby. They're going into a war even the lifers in the sergeant's mess whispered was awful. And why do I suddenly feel I want to go with them? Put it right out of your mind, brother mine, thought Bobby. Hoo-raugh is still bullshit, and not every black man in the United States has to go overseas to fight for his country.

Bobby tried very hard to think up a reason not to go over to his old barracks after the parade, to share in the beer and revelry he knew would go on the last night before the men started the full-time packing of gear. The vehicles and heavy equipment had already been packed up weeks before, and had left by ship from San Pedro.

Bobby couldn't get over the feeling that the men about to go and fight would resent his decision to "accept" an instructor's

billet and stay at Pendleton. Still, he thought, if I don't show up
after Hunter has asked, it will look as though I'm really ashamed
of what I did and afraid to face them. And, dammit, I'm not
ashamed. Bobby set his jaw and pulled on his green uniform
blouse over his freshly pressed khaki gabardine shirt and match-
ing tie. He looked at himself in the mirror and straightened his
cap. The ready-mix sergeant's stripes felt warm against his upper
arms, and seemed to mock him. Fuck it, he thought; let's get
this done.

It all worked out like Hunter had said. The men of his platoon
gathered around him, clapping him on his back and hooting as
wildly exaggerated accounts of his confrontation with the Topkick were told and embellished and retold. Bobby had been instantly relieved upon entering the barracks to find that the Top
himself had declined the men's halfhearted invitation to join the
lash-up party.

Most of the men had removed blouses and ties, and Bobby
quickly did the same. Some of the marines sang raucous songs
of war, including boot-camp favorites such as ''Born to Zap
Gooks'' and ''Storm the Town and Kill the People,'' as well as
a new one, said to be the anthem of a newly formed navy-marine
outfit in Da Nang called the 7th ANGLICO:

> You're goin' home in a body bag, do-da, do-da!
> You're goin' home in a body bag, it's the only way!
> Shot between the eyes!
> Shot between the thighs,
> You're goin' home in a body bag, zip! da-do-da-day!

After drinking more beer than he really wanted to, Bobby
made a little speech about how he was going to miss his good
friends, and how much he wished them well. It sounded thin as
he said it, but Bobby knew he meant it, and so, it seemed, did
his comrades. Hunter stood up, and said they would save some
little bitty dinks for him, if ever he wanted to come back to the
outfit, and the men responded with the inevitable shouts of ''hoo-
RAUGH!'' and cheers. Bobby left the party at its height, and
walked as steadily as he could back to his room in the empty
instructor's barracks. He carefully removed and hung up his uniform and sat on the edge of his bed. His head fell into his open
hands and he choked back a sob. He had never felt more miserable in his life.

taller and slier at Pendleton. Still, he thought, if I don't show up
after Hunter has asked, it will look as though I don't really approve
of what I did and what to face them. And, damnit, I'm not
ashamed. Bobby set his jaw and pulled on his front uniform
blouse over his freshly pressed khaki pants and shirt and cinch-
ing his tie. He looked at himself in the mirror and straightened his
cap. The ready-with sergeant's stripes felt warm against his upper
arm, and seemed to bind tight. Hell, it, he thought, let's get
this over.

It all worked out like Hunter had said. The men of his platoon
gathered around him, clapping him on the back, and another as
wildly exaggerated accounts of his confrontation with the British were told and embellished and retold. Bobby had been instantly relieved upon entering the barracks to find that the Top
himself had declined the men's half-hearted invitation to join the
fish-fry party.

Most of the men had removed blouses and ties, and Bobby
quickly did the same. Some of the platoon sang raucous songs
of war, including boot-camp favorites such as "Born to Raise
Cocoa," and "Storm the Hogs and Kill the People" as well as
a new one, said to be the anthem of a newly formed navy-marine
outfit in Da Nang called the 7th ARCLIGHT.

> You're going home in a body bag, do-dah!
> You're going home in a body bag, it's safe only, way!
> Shot between the eyes,
> Shot between the thighs,
> You're going home in a body bag, all-night de-do-da-day!

After drinking more beer than he really wanted to, Bobby
made a little speech about how he was going to miss his good
friends, and how much he valued them well. It sounded lake as
he said it, but Bobby knew he meant it, and so, it seemed, did
his comrades. Hunter stood up, and said they would save some
little beer Stones for him, if ever he wanted to come back to the
outfit, and they then responded with the inevitable shouts of "Hoo
RAGH!" and others. Bobby left the party as his height and
wished to steady, as he could back to his room in the Supply
nonchalantly casual. He carefully removed and hung up his uniform and sat on the edge of his bed. His head felt numb his open
hands and he choked back a sob. He had never felt more alive,
or more in his life.

NAM

5 June 1966   **USS** *Valley Forge*

Moser woke promptly at 0500 when the brig chaser on duty sounded the buzzer. This was his third wake-up in the tiny cell, the day he would be getting out.

Moser ran his hand over his shaven skull and breathed the sharp pain in his ribs. That third class radioman sure had a hell of a kick. His hand found the lump on the back of his head from the shore patrol dude's nightstick, and massaged it gently. He then rolled out of the bunk and began to collect his shaving gear for the morning trip to the head. Reveille for the ship as a whole was not until 0600, but Moser and the other sailor in the brig, a black airman named Johnson, had to be through washing up before the other sailors needed the head.

The brig chaser coming on watch shouted from the top of the trunk, and Moser and the airman started climbing the three decks of ladders to the second deck, where the heads they used were located. The brig chaser on duty followed, his billy club banging on the ladders as he climbed. The new chaser led off, and the little parade marched quietly to the head. Moser looked at the other prisoner, who grinned. Brig prisoners were not allowed to talk to each other, but the way the black dude grinned all the time, whatever he had done must have been worth the brig time.

The men washed and shaved quickly, and were returned to

123

their cells. As deep inside the ship as the brig was, it was always steamy hot, and it stank of sweat and hot paint. Moser was very determined to avoid ever having to come back down here, once he got out. They would now wait for two hours until after the crew had breakfast, then they would be marched to the mess deck to have their own chow. Moser hated these trips more than the brig time itself, with the brig chaser in front bellowing "Make way for prisoners from the brig!" which made sure everybody noticed them, in their dungarees stenciled with a big P, and their shaven heads. Any time an officer was encountered along the route, the prisoners had to snatch off their white hats, and slam themselves face first against the bulkheads, screaming "By your leave, sir!" The drill was the work of First Lieutenant Vogel, the marine combat cargo officer who was permanently assigned to the *Valley*, and it was meant to humiliate. The brig chasers themselves were handpicked by Lieutenant Vogel, and were prize ball-busters.

Moser leaned back on his bunk. One more trip to the mess hall, then he would be let out and sent back to his duties in the ship's armory. He ran over in his mind the events that had earned him Captain's Mast and three days in this stinking cage.

Mendoza and I went on liberty over to Olangapo, he remembered, just a week ago. Juan had wanted to find a card game, and soon did in the dark interior of a bar far enough from the main gate of the Subic Bay Naval Base to likely escape the attention of either the shore patrol or curious junior officers. Moser didn't particularly like playing cards; for one thing, it was against regulations and could get you in trouble, and anyway, the rules of the different games confused him. Mendoza always insisted, saying that Moser was his good luck, and Moser usually went along. Mendoza seemed to win all the time, and Moser did OK when he didn't do something stupid, like not betting a straight that Juan once dealt to him pat, having failed to see the order in the five cards. Mendoza had been real mad about that one, calling Moser a dumb motherfucker right in front of the other players.

The game that Mendoza found had four sailors already playing, and a shifty Filipino civilian the others called Yardbird. Mendoza and Moser sat in, and after a few bad hands, Mendoza and Moser began to win. It seemed every time Mendoza dealt the cards, Moser got at least one high pair, and sometimes two pairs.

The last hand was dealt by common consent at 2100, so the men could hit the bars and streetside food stalls. Some of the sailors were grumbling that they would have to go straight back to their ships, because nearly all their money was gone. Mendoza was cheerful. Most of the money on the table was in front of him. Moser was about even. He had been ahead earlier, but when Mendoza had dealt him a pair of aces and a pair of sixes, he had bet heavily, but had been beaten by Mendoza himself with three ladies.

It seemed natural that Mendoza had the deal again for the last hand. The game was five card draw, one of the easier ones to follow. Mendoza dealt the cards with a fluid grace that Moser had often admired. Juan's long, tapering fingers seemed to caress every card from the deck to the neat piles in front of each player. The men bet their cards cautiously. The bets were small, and only the little Filipino threw in his hand in disgust rather than call the bet. Mendoza neated up Yardbird's discards with his left hand, and the remaining players called for various numbers of new cards. As each man threw in his discards, Moser pushed them into a pile with his left hand before dealing out the replacements. Finally, Mendoza dealt himself two new cards, and the betting resumed.

Moser looked over his cards. There was a lot of tension in the room. Only Mendoza continued to chatter as the bets went around. Moser noticed a particular intensity in the gaze of Yardbird, seated immediately to Mendoza's left. During the exchange of new cards for old, the Filipino's hard black eyes never left Mendoza's swift, graceful fingers.

Moser and one more sailor dropped out in the first round of betting after the draw. The second round bumped the bet to five dollars, the limit for any one round, and two more sailors dropped their cards on the table. Only Mendoza and a third class radioman from the USS *Dubuque* were left, and, once again the raises went up the limit. Mendoza's call was the last, and the radioman laid down a full house, kings over sixes, and leaned across the table to scoop up the money. Mendoza held up his empty left hand in a gesture that said hold on, and with a flourish laid down four tens and a five.

"Damn!" exploded the radioman, and Juan started stacking the bills and coins. "*Nobody* draws two cards and comes up with four of a kind."

"Better to be lucky than smart," said Mendoza, careful not to gloat. Moser felt a dangerous electric feeling in the room.

"He cheated." The voice, very quiet, almost a hiss, was Yardbird's. He had hardly spoken all evening. The room became tautly silent for half a heartbeat.

"Hey, what the fuck, Flip! I don't have to cheat!" blustered Mendoza, getting quickly to his feet and stuffing the money into his pockets. Moser thought he saw fear jump into the Mexican's quick eyes.

The big radioman stood and placed his hand on Mendoza's shoulder, sitting him back down. "I think we want to hear about this, Mex." There was clearly menace in his voice.

"Hey, man! Lay off! This guy is just sore he lost money! Hey, Moser! Tell this guy lay off, we got to go!" Mendoza squirmed but was unable to get out of the chair.

"How come you say my friend cheats, Yardbird?" Moser let the question out flat and gentle. He didn't want this to be a fight. He'd heard these Flips carried knives, and could use them.

Yardbird spoke slowly, carefully. "I watch. I see, all night, but not sure. Last hand, I watch real close when I throw in cards. The Mex, he palmed one of those tens, right from my discards. I watch real close." The soft, hissing voice held the attention of every man in the room.

Moser looked at Mendoza's face, sweaty and drawn. "What you got to say, Juan?"

Mendoza's eyes darted from face to face. "Moser! How are you, how are *any* of you sailors gonna take the word a some fuckin' Huk against an American sailor!"

"Maybe give the money back, we let you live," breathed the big radioman.

"No fuckin' way!" Mendoza finally managed to squirm free of the radioman, and got up and backed to the wall. "Look, I'm gonna throw in five bucks, here!" He pulled the bill out of his front pocket and dropped it on the table. "Buy you guys a coupla rounds. Come *on*, Moser!"

Moser got up quickly, kicking his chair back, letting the men see his size in the dim, smoky light. "Anybody else see him cheat?" The sentence came out like a growl. The sailors looked quickly at Moser, then looked away. Only Yardbird held his gaze. Moser felt a tightness in his stomach as he thought about the Filipino's hidden knife. Moser let the silence go a full minute, then stepped back from the table and spoke again, holding his voice flat. "Then I guess he didn't cheat."

Mendoza stepped around the table and toward the door. Moser followed, watching Yardbird's hands carefully, but they remained flat on the table surface. As Mendoza and Moser reached the door, the big radioman shook his fist and shouted, "Don't neither you assholes come back here!"

Moser stepped out into the street to see Mendoza walking rapidly up the sidewalk in the direction of the center of Olongapo and toward the main gate. Moser caught up in a few long strides, and grabbed his friend by the bicep.

"What's the hurry, Juan?"

Mendoza shook his arm free, and took a rapid glance over his shoulder. Moser looked back, too, but there was no pursuit. Mendoza kept walking rapidly. "Hey, man, those guys are *pissed off*! They might decide to come after us!"

"They gotta reason to, Juan?" asked Moser, once again grabbing the arm, this time with enough force to bring Mendoza to a halt.

Mendoza looked into Moser's face. His eyes still darted back down the dark street. "Hey, man, I won close to fifty bucks! Sure they're pissed! You don't believe that crazy Huk asshole, do you?"

"Did you cheat, Juan, or didn't you? I want you to tell me."

Mendoza managed one of his winning smiles. Moser thought it made him look like a little kid. "Hey, man, *no*! *I didn't cheat!* But let's get outa here anyway!"

"Ain't got nothing to hide, let's get us a beer at Ramona's first," said Moser, watching Juan's darting eyes.

"Not me, man, I'm going back to the ship and put this money in a safe place." He reached into his front pocket and pulled out a wad of dirty bills, shoving them into Moser's hand. "Have a San Mig on me, big guy. I'll check you later." Mendoza hurried away, and Moser walked at an easy pace to Ramona's, on the main drag. He looked at the bills in his hand, all ones, of course, but Moser had never known Juan to be so generous with his money. Still, it would buy several San Miguels if you didn't let the girls talk you into buying them "brandies," which every sailor knew were really cold tea.

I got nothing to hide, and I'm going to have a beer, thought Moser as he entered the saloon.

Moser lay back in his cell, going over it slowly. He hadn't wanted to believe Juan was a cheat; he still didn't. Yet the pattern in the card game, especially how Moser always got good cards when Juan dealt, and how Juan almost always seemed to clean him out late in the game, had been the same in previous games. Moser was surprised he had never noticed it before, but he didn't know cards, or odds. Nobody had ever said Mendoza cheated before, although Moser had heard sailors in 2d Division, and later in G Division, say Mendoza stole things. I wish I had some other friends, thought Moser. Someone to talk to. Juan is really the only sailor who takes any time with me; the others just think I'm dumb. I wonder if I am dumb, he mused, as his mind returned to the night of the last card game.

* * *

Moser had had two beers at the bar at Ramona's, and even bought a "brandy" for one of the bar girls he kind of liked, named Lola. He decided he didn't want to eat the monkey meat on a sliver of bamboo the street vendors sold, but would rather grab a hamburger at the EM club back at the base. He picked up what was left of his bar cash and shoved it in the front pocket of his white uniform trousers, jammed his white hat on the back of his head, and ambled out of the saloon. He turned up the street toward the main gate. The big third class and three of the sailors from the game met him at the first corner.

"Hey, Moser, wait up. We want to talk to you." The radioman's tone was neutral.

" 'Kay," said Moser, stopping about six feet away from the little group.

"Where's yer greaser friend?" said the radioman.

"Juan went back to the ship."

The radioman shifted on his feet, seemed uneasy. "Moser, look, we went over it with Yardbird, ah, what he saw. We think the Mex was cheating."

Moser was relieved to see the Filipino with his hidden knife was not with them, but decided to play on the point. "He ain't here to say it to me."

"He works on the base, man. Any trouble with a sailor, he could get fired."

"So what do y'all want from me?" asked Moser, holding his voice even.

"Well, we want our money back."

"I ain't got it. You sayin' I cheated too?" Moser let a little edge come into his voice.

"Well, like maybe you were partners, you and the Mex," said one of the other sailors who hadn't spoken before. Moser shot him an angry look, and the man took an uneasy half step backward.

"I ain't no cheat, an' I ain't got nothin' a' yours. An' I'm done talkin', goin' back to my ship." Moser took a step to go around the radioman, who moved quickly to block his path. Moser stopped short and looked the radioman full in the eyes. "Y'all *do not* want to fuck with me," said Moser, very softly.

The radioman clearly isn't liking this, but his mind is made up, thought Moser. The radioman spoke, trying to be firm but not provocative. "Hey, Moser, OK, you're big, but there's four of us. Just give us whatever money you got, and we will forget it."

Moser took a step forward, and once again the third class blocked his path. Moser put his right hand in the middle of the man's chest and shoved as hard as he could. The man staggered back several paces, almost fell. Moser took another step toward the main gate.

Moser massaged the lump on the back of his head. The rest of it had happened pretty quickly. One of the sailors jumped on his back, getting an elbow under his chin in a choke hold. Another man tackled him around the knees, and Moser went down in the muddy road. As Moser clawed at the man with the choke hold, the radioman kicked him savagely in the ribs. It hurt like blazes, and he gasped for air. The radioman kicked him again. Moser broke the choke hold by pulling the man behind him completely over his head and throwing him halfway across the street. He shook the smaller sailor free of his legs and went after the third class. The man was a fair boxer, but Moser soon had him pinned against the wall of a bar and was pounding his body and face with his huge fists. He heard the whistles of the approaching shore patrol, but his anger at being held down and kicked kept him throwing punches even after the third class had stopped trying to fight back. Somebody cracked him over his head from behind, and he woke up in the holding pen of the shore patrol just inside the main gate. He was covered with mud and blood, and his ribs and head felt like they were on fire. As he sat up in the cell, his head seemed ready to explode, and he let out a low moan. The shore patrol officer got up from behind his desk and came over, leaning his elbows on the bars.

"Well, Mighty Joe Young awakens."

Moser looked around. The only other occupant of the cell was a drunken marine, sound asleep. "Where's the other guys, sir?"

"What other guys, sailor?"

"There was four of 'em, sir. Three seamen an' a third class radioman. They jumped me in the street, knocked me down an' kicked me!"

The lieutenant jg picked up a clipboard off the desk and studied it. "So they jumped *you*, eh? I don't suppose you have noticed that none of that blood on your uniform is yours?"

"Yes, sir, I just defended myself!"

The officer pointed to the clipboard. "That's not what it says here, sailor. According to the report of the arresting petty officer, you were beating up on a third class, who is, by the way, at the hospital with a probable broken jaw. He made a statement as best he could that you assaulted him for no reason. There's no mention of any other sailors."

"That's bullshit! Er, sorry, sir, but they musta run off when the SPs got close!"

The officer sighed. He hated this duty. Absolutely *everyone* lied. "Well, sailor, you will get to tell your side of it, but this report says clearly that you were beating the hell out of a man who was not fighting back."

Moser hung his head. "He kicked me, sir, while his friends held me down."

The door to the shore patrol station was flung open, and Lieutenant Hooper, Moser's division officer, marched into the room in his dress whites. He had been called from an excellent dinner at the Kalayan officers' club to pick up Moser, and he was visibly angry. He read the report the SP officer handed him, and signed for a copy. He then signed the release order, and a second class in pressed dungarees and a white duty belt unlocked the cell door. "Come along, Moser," said Lieutenant Hooper.

"You want someone to go with you, Lieutenant?" asked the SP officer. "This guy is some bruiser."

"What? No, I'll be fine, thanks."

As they walked out to the gray pickup truck that belonged to the *Valley*, Lieutenant Hooper looked over Moser's ruined uniform in disgust. "Boy, you really fucked up this time, Moser."

"B-but sir! It wasn't like that! I can explain—"

"Don't even talk to me, Moser. Just get in the truck."

5 June 1966   USS *Valley Forge*

Stuart rubbed his eyes awake as reveille was passed over the ship's 1-mc public address system. 0600. He didn't really have to be anywhere until 0930, when he was finally going to be told by the ship's executive officer, Commander Simon, what his assignment would be, so he lay back and dozed.

This is my fourth day on this ship, he thought, and so far no one seems to care. It is almost just as well; I'm going to need a month just to get used to this heat. As the boot, the most junior ensign on the ship, Stuart had been assigned the top bunk in a two-man stateroom, too low down in the ship to have a porthole. Stuart guessed the mean nighttime temperature in his bunk to be about ninety-five degrees. A noisy old fan pushed the muggy air around, but the air was just too hot and too laden with moisture for the fan to have any cooling effect.

Stuart swung his legs over the side of the bunk and sat up. He was naked except for his skivvy shorts, and his watch, which said 0625. The sheet clung wetly to his back. He reached around and peeled it off and dropped to the linoleum-covered steel deck.

The occupant of the lower bunk, one Ensign Corris, was on emergency leave in the States, so Stuart had yet to meet him. I hope he is an OK guy, thought William. We will be living pretty close in here. Stuart shaved quickly at the stateroom's small sink, then wrapped a towel around himself and went to the head for the first shower of the day.

He felt a little afraid of the big, old ship, constantly humming with machinery sounds as she sailed across the calm South China Sea at twenty knots, making little more motion than she had moored at the huge U.S. naval station at Subic Bay, from which she had sailed the day before. She had miles of passageways, and in every one officers and enlisted men were rushing in all directions, apparently on urgent business. Stuart alone had nothing to do but eat and sleep until it was time to see the executive officer. He followed the passages and ladders to the wardroom for breakfast.

The wardroom consisted of two rooms, a reading room with padded chairs and sofas, and a dining room with many round tables. Stuart marveled at the houselike appointments of the wardroom, with its wooden and overstuffed furniture, table-cloths, and oil paintings. He had expected something much more spartan—metal furniture bolted to the deck, et cetera. He wondered what would happen in a storm.

The wardroom was air-conditioned to a tepid seventy-five degrees, which felt like an icebox when Stuart first went in. He would have liked to spend time reading the various technical publications that lay around on wooden tables, but junior officers were not encouraged to loiter in the wardroom, so he had not.

Breakfast was served buffet style, although the senior officers could be served at a table if they wished. At lunch and dinner, all the officers were served by Filipino stewards. Stuart served himself fresh grapefruit juice, bacon, scrambled eggs, toast, and coffee, and picked up the orange antimalaria pill from a bowl on a table near the entrance to the dining area.

The seating in the wardroom was in theory unrestricted, but in fact a strict pecking order was observed. The round table nearest to the entrance was the executive officer's parliament, and only other commanders who were department heads sat there, usually in the same chairs every day. The tables nearest to the XO's table were filled up by other commanders and lieutenant commanders, and a few senior lieutenants, especially those trying to be seen. The lieutenants (junior grade) and the ensigns and warrant officers filled up the tables in the outer rings. Some of the lieutenants and lieutenant commanders preferred to sit with the junior officers. Not surprisingly, these men were generally well liked.

Stuart sat down next to Ensign Buck Thomas, the Fire Control Officer, who was in earnest conversation with a full lieutenant

Stuart hadn't met. Others who filled the table as breakfast proceeded were the ship's boatswain, WO Leo Maralit, a Filipino who had been a chief boatswain's mate with eighteen years' service before becoming a warrant officer; Lieutenant Commander Donald, the ship's first lieutenant, in charge of all of the deck divisions; Lieutenant Johnson, the ship's senior dentist; Ensign Hayes, who did something in communications, and Lieutenant jg Ward, an aviator, the Assistant Air Operations Officer. Stuart was introduced by Ensign Thomas to those he had not met, and all made polite inquiry as to how he was settling in. The lieutenant sitting next to Buck Thomas was introduced as Phillip Hooper, the Gunnery Division Officer.

"You're the new boot ensign. Ken Howard's numerical relief."

"Yes, Phillip."

"Everybody calls me Hoop. You've been the subject of much conversation, young William." Hooper smiled a wolfish grin. He was a big man, maybe six-three, 230 pounds, with a shock of blond hair and a ruddy complexion.

Stuart was puzzled. He was beginning to feel he had been completely forgotten. "Why?"

Hooper laughed, a deep rumble. "Hell, man, every division officer on this or any ship wants a boot. Me included. I put in for you as soon as I heard you had orders in."

"Why is that?" Stuart felt the question sounded lame.

"Because we all want to get off this stinkin' amphib, young'un! Come on, I want to show you the excellent G Division office, just in case, unlikely, the XO gives you a choice." Hooper wiped his mouth, and waited, expectantly. Buck Thomas just grinned.

"You could do worse, William," said Lieutenant Commander Donald. "G Division is a for-sure challenge." The other officers laughed. Stuart felt the laughs were friendly.

"Do I really have a choice?" asked William.

"Probably not," grinned the First Lieutenant, "but let me know if they want to make you a snipe. Hooper's mob is a lesser fate."

Stuart knew that a snipe was an engineer, officer or man who served in the engineering spaces of the big carrier. He thought that his engineering degree made such an assignment likely, but his one visit to main control, where it was *really* hot, had discouraged him about the prospect. "I'd rather be on deck, sir."

Donald got up. "Then ask for it. Commander Skelly, the Weapons officer—my boss, as well as the boss of the Gunnery and Fire Control divisions—is shorter of officers than any other department head. You ever do any sailing?''

"Uh, yes, sir, Lightnings, and Dyer dinghys." Stuart felt a bit embarrassed to speak of such small boats.

"Excellent. Hoop, you have my permission, unofficial, of course, to recruit this man." The first lieutenant left the table.

Hooper's long strides took them rapidly aft and out of officers' country. They both had to stoop as they passed through watertight doors about every twenty-five feet. As they came abreast the mess decks, a sailor in pressed dungarees wearing a white guard belt with a billy club approached, calling "Make way for the prisoners from the brig!" and more softly, "Good morning, sir." Behind the brig chaser came two men in dungarees and white hats. They made a quick right-face and pressed themselves against the bulkhead.

"By your leave, *sir*!" they chorused.

"Carry on," said Hooper, mildly, and continued on, stopping at the next ladder, and pointing downward. When they reached the next deck down, Hooper opened a door that was half steel plate, half wire mesh, stenciled "G Division Office—Armory. Authorized Personnel Only," and gestured Stuart to a seat in front of a gray metal desk. Hooper sat behind the desk, lit a cigarette, and passed the pack to Stuart, who did likewise, screwing the lit cigarette into his black holder.

"What was that commotion we just passed, Hoop?"

Hooper exhaled the smoke above his head. "Brig prisoners, returning to their cells after breakfast. Ah, did you notice the big man?"

"Yes. A giant. What did he do?"

"Fighting. While on liberty. Sent a guy to the hospital. He is, ah, one of mine. Ours." Hooper grinned his wolf grin.

"Jesus, a guy that big and a disciplinary problem? Maybe engineering is safer."

Hooper drew on the cigarette. "Moser is not a bad guy. Unfortunately, he lets himself get led astray by another of G Division's charmers, a slick little weasel named Mendoza he went through boot camp with. My own intelligence is that Mendoza was almost caught cheating in a card game, and the guys in the game caught up with Moser later on, and jumped him. It was essentially self-defense."

"So why did Moser get the brig?"

"Well, I couldn't prove anything, and of course Mendoza wouldn't come forward to help his 'friend.' Besides, the sailor Moser whomped was off the *Dubuque*, same squadron as us, and her captain made a stink."

"So Moser got a court-martial?"

"Nah. The asshole from the *Dubuque* wanted one, for assault, because his radioman is still in the hospital and had to miss movement when the squadron sailed. But our captain is senior, and he just had Moser up before him at Captain's Mast, and gave him three days in the brig. Wanted to bust him back to seaman apprentice too, but I talked him out of that." Hooper ground out his cigarette in a tin ashtray. Stuart had already finished his, not liking the taste.

Stuart pulled out his own cigarettes and offered the pack to Hooper. Hooper took one and smiled. "English, hey? Very nice." Hooper lit both cigarettes with a battered lighter.

"So why do you want me in this division, Hoop?"

"Well, you gotta start somewhere, and these guys ain't bad— mostly just kids trying to be men too early in their lives. The only one I'd get rid of if I could is that slime Mendoza."

"Why don't you?"

"Well, we're short-handed, and he does do some work, if one of the petty officers is looking right at him. The truth is the chief—Chief Gunner's Mate Everson, just promoted, by the way, a really good man except when we're in Long Beach, where he beats up his wife—agreed to take Mendoza from 2d Division in order to get Moser, who'll be taking the test for third class this month and may actually pass it. Second Division probably got the best of us, but sooner or later Mendoza will get caught, and we'll get rid of him. I'd wager a week's drinking money that fine lad will finish his naval service in the big brig in San Diego."

Stuart grinned, "Once again, Lieutenant, why do you want me?"

Hooper looked up, sheepish. "Well, yes, I do digress. I won't shit you, Stuart, you seem like a good lad. I'm regular Navy, but what I really like is UDT—underwater demolition teams."

"I know. Frogmen. Divers."

"Right. Well, I'm fully qualified, and I want to get one of the SEAL teams in Vietnam, as a command. But since I'm regular Navy, I have to do some ship-driving, qualify as underway Officer of the Deck, all that crap. Well, I've done all that, but the old man won't approve my transfer request until I recruit and train a relief. You." Once again, Hooper grinned broadly. Stuart decided he would like working for the big lieutenant.

Stuart had considered asking for training for the SEALs, Sea-Air-Land Commandos, but had not wanted to extend his time in service for the extra year that was a condition. He looked across the desk. Hooper looked back with an encouraging grin. "How long would you be here to train me?"

"Hey, that depends on you, and how soon the old man thinks you can handle it. Three months? Maybe four? Most ensigns are deemed lucky indeed to have their very own division in less than a year." Hooper looked a little sideways, but his candor and humor were getting to Stuart. "Besides, the big guns are fun to play with."

Stuart grinned. "Any chance to meet the men, especially the chief, before I see the XO?"

Hooper got up quickly. "Morning muster, in here, 0745." There was a clatter as several men came down the ladder and into the outer part of the office. "Right now, it seems," grinned the big lieutenant.

Stuart stood stiffly at attention at the open door to the XO's stateroom, and knocked. Commander Simon motioned Stuart inward, and toward a chair. Stuart entered, remaining at attention. When in doubt, said boot lore, stand at attention and say nothing. The XO's stateroom had a porthole, open to the warm and humid morning breeze.

"Sit down, Mr. Stuart." The XO's voice was soft, and faintly Southern. He peered at Stuart above half glasses.

"Sir," said Stuart, and sat. The commander continued to study Stuart's personnel jacket, which was spread out on his desk.

"Welcome." The XO swiveled in his chair, and extended a hand, which Stuart shook, half standing. "You are indeed welcome. We are, as you may have heard, short of junior officers."

"Yes, sir."

The XO smiled. "You are very military, young Stuart. You have even had SERE training. Are you, as the young officers say, gung-ho?"

Stuart shifted in his seat. "I want to be a good officer, sir."

The commander looked positively fatherly. Stuart remained on guard.

"Well, Ensign, we are short of junior officers in virtually every department, except supply. You wouldn't be looking for supply, I would hope?"

"No, sir. I'm a line officer."

"I recognize your insignia, son," the exec continued dryly, returning his gaze to the personnel jacket before him. "You have an engineering degree. What concentration?"

"Mostly civil, Commander," Stuart lied. His degree had been about evenly concentrated between civil and mechanical, but Stuart had already decided he wanted to stand his watches on the bridge, and not in main control.

"If, *if*, I were to give you a choice, Mister, do you have any idea what you would like to accomplish on board this vessel?" The soft voice had a hint of testing in it.

Stuart stiffened to attention while still seated. "I would like to qualify as Officer of the Deck, Commander."

The XO laughed without mirth. "Are you tough, Mister?"

Stuart found the question disconcerting. What was the answer he expected? "I'm fair, sir, I believe."

"Tough enough for the thugs of G Division?"

Thugs? thought Stuart. "Ah, yes, sir, I think so. I'm told that the chief is first rate. I'd rely on him."

"Not entirely, I hope, Ensign. The division officer is responsible; the chief is only his best adviser."

"Yes, sir."

The XO sat back and beamed. "Sure you wouldn't like a safe billet in engineering, son?"

"No, sir. Thank you, sir."

The XO took off his half glasses, and rubbed the red marks on his nose. Stuart saw that his eyes were pale gray and watery. "So Hooper sold you. That's OK by me, Mr. Stuart, I need a good officer to replace Hooper. But to run G Division, you're going to have to be as tough as they come." The commander jabbed at Stuart's file on the desk.

"Will I be on the bridge watch bill, Commander?"

The XO turned back to his desk. Stuart sensed the interview was over. "If Lieutenant Commander Donald will have you, and if the captain will, you will. In the meantime, learn the guns, and learn the men. Report to Lieutenant Hooper, Mister Stuart."

"Aye, aye, sir," said Stuart, backing to the doorway and retreating from the stateroom. The XO did not look up from his desk, or otherwise acknowledge Stuart's departure.

Moser packed his shaving kit in his tiny locker in the G Division berthing space and changed into his own not very pressed dungarees and blue baseball cap. He threw the brig clothes in the laundry hamper; they would find their way back to the brig after they were washed. He walked swiftly to the G Division office, anxious to be back in his solitary duty in the armory, not really wanting to face any of the guys yet, and especially puzzled about what to say to Mendoza. Juan had flat lied to Lieutenant Hooper about the card game, thus failing to back Moser's claim that a bunch of guys had reason to jump him. Sure, Juan could have gotten into some trouble about gambling, but nothing like three days in the brig.

The division office was empty when he arrived, so Moser unlocked the armory with his own key. Nothing had been disturbed after he had last cleaned up. Only the chief and Lieutenant Hooper had keys besides his.

Laid out on the big metal workbench, fully disassembled, was an old machine gun, a Browning air-cooled .50-caliber that the chief said probably killed Japs in World War Two. Moser had been restoring the old weapon, replacing worn parts and changing the tension on the cam that controlled the loading and ejection mechanism, but the weapon still had a tendency to jam. I'll try to get the chief to let me take her back to the fantail and fire her off this afternoon, he thought, if I ain't still in the doghouse.

Moser assembled the weapon slowly, carefully. His last adjustment was to a tensioning pin in the receiver, below the cam. Newer Marks of this weapon did not even have this arrangement, so the manual Moser had open on the workbench gave him little assistance. But the action felt smoother when he pulled it through several times. Lastly he screwed in the long, solid barrel, and rubbed the machine gun with fine oil till it shone. Ole Betsy, he thought. Accurate and deadly to more than a mile.

Moser heard a clatter on the ladder, and Mendoza appeared at the armory door. "Hey, man, I heard you were out! Was it bad?"

"Hello, Juan," said Moser, not looking up from his work.

Mendoza frowned. "Hey, man, you're not pissed at me, are you?"

Moser looked at Mendoza. "Lieutenant Hooper said I coulda stayed out of the brig, if'n you'd've come forward about that card game."

Mendoza laughed. "You believe that asshole? Come on, man, officers always try to fuck you, you know that. Hey, I checked with a guy in the legal office, see, just to see how I could help you, man. He tole me, I say you and me was gambling before you got jumped, they just add a new charge, then maybe you get a court-martial, serious shit!"

Moser looked hard at Mendoza's eyes. They seemed steady above his friendly smile. I wish there was someone I could talk to besides Juan. Still, it could be true.

"Ain't you got no work, Juan?" said Moser, quietly, working the action of the machine gun in his big hands, feeling and listening for friction.

Mendoza stepped through the armory door, something he knew regulations forbade him to do. He slapped Moser on the shoulder. Moser continued with his work. "Hey, Moser! Fuckin' chief got me chippin' paint in that big bomb magazine again.

How am I ever gonna be a gunner's mate when I don't hardly ever see the guns? Anyway, I hadda come down and see my main man!''

"Outa the armory, Juan. You know you ain't allowed."

Mendoza looked shocked and hurt. Moser felt a twinge of guilt. "Yeh. Right, *amigo!* All the times I help you out, you one hour outa the fuckin' brig, and you gone fuckin' *military!*"

Moser sighed. How could anyone know anything? The chief wouldn't really talk to him, and the rest of the men avoided him. He'd heard men say Mendoza stole, and that if any complained, Moser would drop on them hard, but he had no way of knowing why these things were said, because he had no one to ask. "Take it easy, Juan. I'm edgy, from the brig, I guess."

Mendoza smiled his infectious smile. "That's better, good buddy. Now, I gotta tell you the news! We gettin' a brand-new cherry boot division officer!"

Moser looked up. Now that was interesting. "Mr. Hooper's leavin' the division?"

"Yeah, that's what I heard. I can hardly wait."

Moser was puzzled. "Mister Hooper seems a pretty good man. The guys like him all right."

"Yeah, maybe, but I don't. He lets the chief bust my balls all the time. At least that wimp Siegel used to stop Chief Brown from giving me absolutely *every* shit detail, even if it was only to show the chief he had some say in things."

Moser smiled. "Might could be the chief go easier, you do a little more work, Juan."

"Ah, fuck you, man. Easy enough for you sittin' all day in this fuckin' armory. Christ, with that big ventilation blower in the overhead, it's practically air-conditioned. It gets fuckin' hot up in those gun mounts, and even hotter in the magazines."

"So how is a new officer gonna change any of that?"

"Shit, I don't know. But this Hooper, he's regular navy for one, and a lieutenant for two. He knows too much, or thinks he does. A nice cherry reserve ensign will be a lot easier to deal with, you'll see."

Moser locked away the big fifty in the small-arms locker, and opened a well-worn paperbound manual on the bench in front of him. The manual was entitled *Taking the Written Test for Gunner's Mate, Guns, Third Class (GMG-3).* Mendoza looked at the publication with distaste as Moser found his place. "How come you bother with that shit, Moser? You'll never pass that test."

"Gonna pass it. Gonna make rate."

"Who the fuck cares?"

"Don't you wanna make rate, Juan?"

"Nah!" Mendoza looked at his watch, won last night in a card game. Just about fifteen minutes left until he was supposed to secure his magazine and head for noon chow. Fuck it, he thought, might's well get head of the line. "You ready for chow, man?"

"I better wait for the Chief. He left a note for me."

"Bye!" said Mendoza, and started up the ladder to the mess decks. He surely had no desire to see the Chief just then. He found the thought of Moser even taking the test for third class immensely amusing. Dumb motherfucker could barely read.

Moser had the manual open to a section on the different types of projectiles and fuses used in the five-inch, .38 caliber guns the *Valley* carried. His blunt fingers moved slowly beneath the words, but when they came to diagrams, they fairly flew. Moser's lips moved silently past words and numbers, but he only smiled as the diagrams flashed into memory.

18 July 1966   USS *Valley Forge*

Ensign Stuart, standing Junior Officer of the Watch on the bridge, stood at the starboard surface-search radar repeater trying to make sense of the many small contacts on the screen. The weather was rainy and the winds gusted to near gale force as the *Valley* pushed aside the heavy swells of the Taiwan Straits en route to Okinawa. The embarked marine battalion landing team, 1st of the 26th Marines, had moved inland in force the week of 10–16 June, to the western border of I Corps, and shifted, or "chopped," its command in country. The *Valley* was racing north to pick up a fresh BLT and replacement helicopters for its squadron of marine medium helos.

"What do you make of it, William?" asked the Officer of the Deck, Lieutenant Hooper.

"Probably fishing boats, Hoop." Stuart dialed up the gain on the radar, and many more points of light emerged. He dialed it back down. "Lots of sea return. Combat is tracking as six contacts, Lima through Quebec. They're all pretty much in our track, moving slowly northward."

The carrier put her bow into a particularly large swell, and shuddered as a green wave six feet high swept aft along the empty flight deck, streaming onto the catwalks and over the side. "Where is contact, ah, Delta, the freighter with no IFF?"

"Inland of us, Hoop, to port," answered Ensign Thomas, the Junior Officer of the Deck. "He's clear."

"Thanks, Buck," said Hooper, staring intently through the rain-spattered window of the bridge. "Who has the watch in combat?"

Thomas looked at the Plexiglas status board angled between the top of the windows and the overhead. "Lieutenant jg Simonds, Hoop. And Chief Hanes."

Hooper continued to fight the return of the red lights inside the bridge from the raindrops on the forward windows. "You check them out on the way up, Buck? They standing a proper watch?"

Buck Thomas frowned. "Looked all right to me, Hoop. 'Course, Gordy Mason had the watch then; Simonds relieved him just as I came up."

"Shit," said Hooper, without inflection. "Since Warrant Officer Bright left the ship, those turkeys in combat haven't been able to find their asses with both hands. William, range to the nearest 'fishing boat.' "

William moved the cursor he had been keeping on the nearest contact, designated Mike by combat, a quarter inch closer to the center of the screen as the sweep passed. He read the meter next to the cursor control with a cupped red flashlight. "Ninety-six hundred yards, Hoop."

"Give me a course to miss the lot of them by twenty-five hundred yards, leaving all to starboard."

"Aye, aye, sir," said Stuart. He had already set up the solution on the maneuvering board, a circular plotting paper that enabled him to plot all objects on the screen in course and speed relative to the *Valley*. He quickly updated the solution to account for the *Valley*'s continuing progress, then checked the entire setup. "Recommend coming left to three-four-five, time to turn zero-one-five-five."

Hooper looked at the maneuvering board. "Seems reasonable. Buck, you have the conn, make it so. William, figure what our course will be to return to track after we pass clear."

"Already have, sir. Just back to three-five-eight. No correction at this range."

"You gonna wake the old man, Hoop?" asked Thomas.

Hooper sighed. "I guess so. I hate to wake him for something this trivial, but the Night Orders are quite clear. Remember Captain Drover, Buck?"

"Yeah. Always slept in his in-port cabin. Wake him for World War Three, at least."

Hooper grinned, remembering the elegant gentleman-captain who had preceded the rasp-edged Captain Ryan. "The old man usually likes to talk when I wake him. Go ahead and execute if I don't come right back. And try for a visual sighting." Hooper disappeared along the short catwalk into the enclosed bridge. The captain's sea cabin was just aft.

Buck Thomas checked his watch, and pressed down a switch on the 5-mc squawk box. "Signal bridge, conn. Keep looking for lights to starboard ahead."

"Sigs, aye," rasped the squawk box.

"William, do me a favor, go out and get wet, take a good look."

"Sure, Buck." Stuart was still new enough at the game to like night watches, especially if something happened. He shrugged into his rain parka and stepped out onto the starboard wing of the bridge with his binoculars slung around his neck. He first swept the entire horizon forward of the ship, then concentrated on the 12 o'clock to 3 o'clock quadrant. Nothing. He reentered the bridge just as Ensign Thomas gave the command to commence the turn.

"Helmsman, left five degrees rudder, steady on course three-four-five."

"Helmsman aye," came back from the red-lit interior of the closed, or armored, bridge. Ten seconds later, "Sir, steady on course three-four-five."

"Very well," said Thomas. "See anything, William?"

"Not yet, Buck. I don't guess we'll see them until we're practically by them, if at all." Chinese fishing boats rarely carried any lights unless they were fishing at night, and the seas were too rough for that. Stuart checked the radar. Soon the *Valley*'s turn would begin to affect the relative movement of the contacts.

"What time will we turn back?"

Stuart rechecked the maneuvering board. "Safe, say oh-two-oh-five. Might's well be sure."

"You're quick with that maneuvering board, Boot."

"Yeah, well, my daddy's money for four years at Georgia Tech was not entirely wasted."

Thomas laughed. "How you liking G Division?"

Stuart smiled, "Good. Hooper is a first-rate teacher; of course, the sooner he gets me qualified, the sooner he leaves. The Chief is OK; I think he's afraid I'm such a shavetail that the men will try to get round me once Hoop leaves."

"Which leaves the men."

Stuart sighed, "Yeah, what a bunch. The second class, Collins, is OK when he's sober. The only third class is Wasakonis, and the division should have four. The rest of the men are, well, a challenge."

Buck Thomas smiled, "Or a trial."

Stuart grinned, peering down into the radar repeater. The contacts were sliding down the right side of the screen, responding to the effect of the carrier's course change. "I envy you your technicians, Buck."

"Well, at least the FTs are motivated, and they have to be a bit bright. How's your brig rat?"

"Moser? I don't know. Hard to reach, very shy, really. I'm sure he would be fine if we could just keep him away from Mendoza."

"You've said that to Moser?"

"Once. He just clams up, says Mendoza is his only friend, et cetera. The sad part is the other men in the division do avoid him, because they think he's Mendoza's enforcer."

Hooper came back on the bridge. "We by 'em yet, Buck?"

Stuart, at the radar repeater, answered for Thomas, "Just about. One minute to turn."

Hooper looked at the radar repeater, and briefly at Stuart's maneuvering board solution. "Fine. Say, Buck, give the kid the conn; I'll go over your correspondence course with you."

Buck Thomas pointed his index finger at Stuart, with a grin. Stuart turned to the open armored porthole, and pronounced, "This is Ensign Stuart. I have the conn."

"Ensign Stuart has the conn," chorused the helmsman and the Quartermaster of the Watch.

Stuart felt a rush of pride and importance every time he was granted the conn. In theory, he controlled every man and every action aboard the giant warship as soon as the Quartermaster of the Watch recorded the magic words. In fact, he knew, he wasn't really responsible for *doing* anything; the helmsman steered, the engineers far below managed the plant, Hoop was there to take over at the slightest need, and the Captain slept not twenty feet away.

"Sir!" the talker for combat manning sound-powered phones called, "Combat wants to scrub contacts Lima and Mike, moving astern."

"Permission granted," intoned Stuart, grinning into the radar repeater. Hooper and Thomas retreated to the far starboard corner of the bridge, and were going over some school pub in low tones.

"Sir! Combat wishes to scrub contacts Delta, November, Oscar—"

"Permission is granted to scrub them all, Combat."

"Combat, aye, sir."

The night flew by. Stuart drank the strong coffee that was continually passed up by the men back in the armored conning tower. Stuart checked his radars, talked to main control about shifting a new boiler on line and another off, and enjoyed himself. He felt his first six weeks at sea had been a success.

The XO had said learn the guns, and learn the men. Well, he felt his daily tours of the ship's six five-inch guns with the chief and the second class, plus a lot of time with the technical manuals, had made him pretty cognizant of the guns. His training at Dam Neck hadn't hurt, either. Learning the men was another matter; G Division sailors were at once ignorant and streetwise, and the shortage of petty officers made the job harder.

Hooper had told him, his first day as junior division officer, that Moser was to be his "special project." Stuart's first clumsy efforts at counseling had been rebuffed with shy politeness, so he sought another approach. One of his other charges from Hooper had been to square away the division's equipment maintenance ledgers, which had been neglected due to the lack of qualified petty officers, and to ready the records for conversion to the navy's new planned maintenance system. This was a real challenge for a World War II ship like the *Valley*, for although the guns themselves continued in service in many older ships throughout the fleet, G Division had under its control such things as bomb elevators and ammunition hoists that had been manufactured under wartime contracts by companies long since out of business. Hooper had decided it was more important for the chief to work full-time on getting the guns truly operational, and to delegate the records to the junior division officer. Stuart didn't like being cooped up in the division office, but he recognized the rightness of the decision.

The only advantage of being tied to the office and the maintenance records was that it kept him in close proximity to Moser, who worked in the adjacent armory. In an almost ritual way, like two people meeting from different cultures, the two men began feeling each other out. Moser had a small and unauthorized coffee maker in the armory, made of scrounged diesel engine parts and heated by an old soldering iron Moser had modified. Moser made excellent coffee, which he began offering to the JDO each morning. Hooper had turned over the small arms in the armory to Stuart, which meant each weapon had to be compared by serial number to the official records, and signed for. Stuart found that Moser's records corresponded to no known system, but were accurate, and he showed the big man how to make the job easier. The inventory also joined them in their first joint conspiracy; the armory contained a few extra components not on the rolls, acquired from marines in trade, or previously logged out as useless and expended, but which Moser had repaired. There was even a fully assembled, and operational, Russian-made light machine gun, an unauthorized souvenir belonging to one of the sergeants of the 1/26. These were petty secrets, but secrets bind, and Stuart felt he could see the beginnings of trust in the big man.

The bulkhead door on the port side of the bridge slammed behind Stuart, and he looked around. "Permission to come onto the open bridge, sir," said Ensign Siegel.

Stuart glanced at his watch, 0340. Siegel, coming up to relieve Buck Thomas as JOOD, was late, as usual. "Permission granted."

"Well, well!" sneered Siegel. "The boot has the conn!"

"None of that crap on my bridge, Siegel," said Hooper from the darkened starboard corner.

"Yes, sir! Just trying to instill a little naval tradition in the boot, sir."

"Fine, but not on my bridge."

Siegel sought out Buck Thomas. "Ready to relieve you, sir. What have we got?"

"Stuart will brief you, Marty," said Thomas, packing his correspondence course pubs into his plastic briefcase.

Siegel unzipped his green jacket and turned to face Stuart. "What have we got, Boot?"

Stuart ran the situation down. He reviewed the radar contacts they were tracking, none now closer than six miles. He went over the state of the plant; which boilers on line to which engines, and other details; the ship's course and speed, and the course changes that would occur during the next watch; the Night Orders; and the navigation plot. Without acknowledging the briefing, Siegel turned back to Lieutenant Hooper. "Request permission to relieve the Junior Officer of the Deck, sir!" Siegel raised his hand in salute.

Hooper returned the salute. "Permission granted."

Siegel then saluted Ensign Thomas. "I relieve you, sir."

Thomas returned the salute, then saluted Hooper, informing him formally that he had been properly relieved, and left the bridge.

The formality of all that might seem antiquated, even comic, to someone unfamiliar with the Navy and its history, mused Stuart. But I find it appropriate, and strangely reassuring. Now he saluted Lieutenant Hooper, "Sir, I have no relief, permission to secure?" Junior Officer of the Watch was a training position only, and at present there were only two others on the watch bill, and neither was assigned to the oncoming watch.

"Permission granted, William, and thanks. See you bright and early in the office. Take the conn, Marty."

"This is Ensign Siegel! I have the conn! G'night, Boot."

Stuart made his way through the darkened ship to his steamy stateroom. He undressed quickly and climbed into bed. Below him, Ensign Corris snored on, deep in the sleep of a supply corps officer, never disturbed by watch-standing duties.

Stuart was instantly asleep, and, as so often when he slept as dawn approached, he felt the warming presence of Karen.

23 September 1966   *Valley Forge*, off the Cua Viet River, Vietnam

Good my love,

Time passes in a very strange way on this ship. It is, the docs say, the angst of indefinite waiting. Every day is much like the one before, and there is no expectation that the next day will be any different. My days revolve around standing my watches, which vary with the schedule, but as the ship is now in Condition III, we have to man one gun mount and one fire-control director all the time, and that cuts the bridge steaming watch teams from six to three. Buck Thomas and I alternate standing JOOD watches and director watches each week, so at least that makes a change, though I must say there is nothing on earth as boring as a director watch, especially at night. We try to train by locking on to passing aircraft, but at night there are very few, so mostly we just sit, cold and damp in the mist at night, broiling in the sun during the day. It is truly awful.

During the day, we conduct air operations, resupplying the marines of the battalion landing team, which is operating only a few miles inshore in a place they call the Leatherneck Square. Judging by the casualties we're receiving by the medevac helos, the fighting must be rough, but once again, nobody on this ship really knows. At night, at least every other night, we steam farther offshore to rendezvous with a supply ship—sometimes an oiler for fuel, sometimes an ammo ship, sometimes a reefer for fresh food. Theoretically, we could remain here forever.

With the watch-standing four hours on and eight hours off, we never really get a proper night's sleep, and of course the regular work of the ship must continue to get done. Days really aren't days any more, there are just watches and work and snatches of sleep. I have to work hard not to hate my roommate, a supply corps officer in charge of the wardroom mess who works what amounts to a nine-to-five day, and sleeps at least nine hours every night.

We have been on the line here for nearly nine weeks since the five days spent in Okinawa, and away from Subic nearly thirteen weeks, so we will have to go back to Subic soon for maintenance and repairs. One of our four propeller shafts has been locked for two weeks with bearing trouble, but fortunately (or unfortunately) there are still the other three. Rumor has it that one of the reasons we have been here so long is that the *Okinawa*, one of the new LPHs, has propeller shaft problems of her own, but since she has only one shaft, she sits in port while we carry on the war. I think that secretly the men are proud of the toughness of this old ship, which is not to say most are not ready to kill for a little liberty.

I'm pleased your new job is developing so well. It doesn't surprise me at all that you're a super salesman. You sure could sell me anything, and I would do anything to be there with you to let you do it.

I don't know whether you have been trying to think of me at sunset, but I really believe I can feel you in a special way around dawn. Maybe it's just the lack of sleep, but it feels nice.

I have to close this, my beloved Karen, and post it in time for the afternoon mail bird to Da Nang. Then I can take a shower, have dinner, and go back on watch from eight to twelve tonight. We will refuel tonight, probably around 2 A.M., so I really will get virtually no sleep before going back on watch at eight o'clock in the morning.

Please try to write when you can; your letters are not only my link to you but to a real world.

I love you,
William

18 October 1966

Moser stood on the fantail with Ensign Stuart, holding the eighty-four-pound restored "fifty" in his huge right hand the way another man might hold a broomstick. He waited while Wasakonis removed the gun that was normally manned from its mounting, then carefully put the old gun in its place. To the untrained eye, the two looked the same, but to Moser the newer Mark looked almost crude, and certainly dirty.

Stuart had gotten permission to test fire the machine guns to conduct training for the gunner's mates and boatswain's mates who stood the machine gun watches when the ship was in Vietnamese coastal waters. A dozen men stood in a knot, eagerly awaiting their turns, but Stuart knew the training would not be done on the old gun, that only Moser ever fired it.

Moser fed in a belt of linked ammunition and locked the cover down. "Ready any time, sir."

Stuart turned to the fantail watch, a sailor who wore a sound-powered phone headset connected to the bridge. "Dobbs, ask the OOD for permission to test fire machine guns."

The kid spoke into his mouthpiece. In a moment he had a reply, "OOD says permission granted, sir."

Moser pulled back the bolt and chambered the first round. He nodded to one of three white-clad mess cooks who loitered on the fantail to see the show. They had brought up two bins of garbage for dumping, and were supplying the day's targets. The first two cardboard boxes went over the side. Moser let the boxes drift back about fifty yards, tossing in the turbulence of the ship's wake, then fired a burst of five rounds. Bullets tore both boxes in half. The men cheered and the cooks threw more garbage over the side.

"Throw lotta shit, man," said Moser, firing burst after burst. Every can, every box seemed to be hit as the big bullets turned the wake to froth. The last round on the belt fired, and its metal link clinked on the deck. Stuart felt deafened in the silence. Sailors gathered around and picked up the steel links and the brass shell casings and dropped them over the side, each trying to be noticed by Gunner's Mate Third Class Moser, each eager for his chance to fire the big gun.

Let 'em wait, thought Moser, carefully locking in a new belt. "Mr. Stuart? Y'all wanta try Ole Betsy?"

Stuart was surprised. Moser had never let anyone else even touch the antique, always making some excuse about the action not being quite right. Stuart was genuinely flattered. "Thank you, Moser, I certainly would."

Stuart gripped the left handle tightly and pulled back the bolt, chambering the first round. He had not been prepared for the strength required to pull the bolt back—Moser had made it look so easy—and he almost didn't get it. "Give Mr. Stuart lotta boxes, y'all," said Moser to the mess cooks.

Stuart crouched behind the gun, gripping both handles with both thumbs on the twin trigger. The gun began firing almost before he wanted it to, and he could see the tracers and shell splashes well beyond the garbage. The gun bucked like a live animal, and Stuart had to set his feet and hold on for dear life. The second burst destroyed some garbage, but that was likely because there was now a continuous carpet behind the ship.

"Give her a coupla real long bursts, sir," said Moser.

Stuart concentrated, flexed his numb hands. He took careful aim at a big tin can bobbing in the wake and squeezed the trigger slowly. Once again the big gun bucked, but Stuart adjusted, and was pleased to see the can fly high in the air, turning over as it fell. He trained until he saw a box, and cut it in half. He got another box, and another, and was feeling pretty good about his shooting when the belt ran out. The men cheered politely, but Stuart knew they wished he would back off and let them at it.

"Pretty good shootin', sir," said Moser with a grin. "Notice somethin'?"

"What, Moser?" said Stuart, returning the grin.

"She don't jam no more! I done fixed her good."

"Hey, congratulations, Moser! You surely have."

"Thank you, sir." Moser looked happy and bashful.

"Hey, Moser, when do we get to fire?" asked Mendoza, wanting to be first.

"Jest holt on. Make a line behind Farly. Wasakonis, put that other gun back up, this'n here's too hot."

Moser put on a hot-caseman's protective mitt, and removed Ole Betsy from the mount and laid her carefully on the deck. That Mr. Stuart is all right. I bet he'd be a good friend.

20 October 1966

Stuart was working alone in the G Division office, trying to make some sense of the maintenance log for mount 58, the single five-inch gun on the portside aft catwalk. The gun had more problems than the others, largely because of its location in the steady stream of the corrosive stack gases from the ship's steam plant that swirled across the flight deck and down over the gun whenever the ship was making any speed. Repairs had been made over the years, parts ordered, others traded, others custom-machined, and the log was hopelessly out of date. Without wanting to admit it to himself, Stuart had fallen into the practice of "gun-decking" the logs—just writing up the periodic entries corresponding to regular maintenance that had never been logged and indeed may never have been performed. Just get the damn thing current, he thought, and then we can shift it to PMS.

Lieutenant Hooper burst into the office, his face split by a grin that Stuart had come to recognize as the high-jinx grin. "Grab your hat, Ensign, we have a mission of utmost delicacy to perform."

Stuart laughed, and put the maintenance logs aside. "What are you taking about, Hoop?"

"We're flying down to Saigon to pick up some highly secret documents. Moser!"

Moser emerged from the armory, wiping his huge hands on a rag. "Yessir?"

"Two forty-fives, Moser—holsters, belts, two full clips each. The junior division officer and I are going in harm's way."

"Yessir." Moser looked bewildered as he ducked back into the armory.

And not just him, thought Stuart. "Come on, Hoop, what is this?"

"Secrets, secrets," said Hooper, pacing about the small office and rubbing his hands. "We're to take a bag of secret stuff to Saigon, and exchange it for another. The fall of empires, should we fail."

"We don't have any secrets, Hoop."

"No, laddie, but Lieutenant jg Epstein, the top secret control officer, does, and he actually *does not* want to go to Saigon! Methinks he fears danger! So I volunteered us."

Moser reappeared with the pistols in holsters. Feeling a bit silly, Stuart buckled the canvas belt around his waist and adjusted the holster. Hooper did the same. "Is there any danger, Hoop?" Stuart drew the pistol and checked the full magazine.

"Nah! We fly into Da Nang, catch a flight to Long Binh or Ton Son Nhut, helo to the embassy, drop the bag, wander down to Tu Do Street for a leisurely lunch and all the French wine we can get down our throats, then go back to the embassy, pick up the new bag, and reverse the whole process."

Stuart slowly smiled. "A boondoggle. A skate."

Hooper arched his brows in mock surprise. "Your mental quickness continues to amaze me, Ensign. Now, shall we go?"

Still Stuart hesitated. Seems a little irresponsible, but a chance to see Saigon. "How long we be gone, Hoop?"

"Back by 2000, latest."

"I have the afternoon watch."

"So do *I*, you idiot! I've swapped us for the four-to-eight tomorrow morning. Now, *come on*, before Epstein or the XO changes his mind."

It had been a morning of firsts for Stuart. His first ride in a helo from the *Valley*'s deck, his first sighting from the air of Da Nang and the vast complex of military bases around its harbor, his first landing in country. The marine helo dropped them at the naval base at camp Tien Shaw, and they lugged the heavy, sealed bags to a bus stop, where a blue bus driven by an air force sergeant picked them up, and dropped them in front of the transport squadron Da Nang terminal, a nondescript metal building next to the long runway. Flights of F-105 Thunderchief fighter-bombers—called Thuds—were taking off into the squally sky with heavy bomb loads. Hooper presented their priority transport orders, and they were soon aboard a dirty and dented C-130 transport.

As the big aircraft climbed out over the South China Sea, Stuart felt a damp draft on his neck, and looked up to find a neat row of bullet holes above the small window. When the crew chief came by, Stuart pointed to the holes. "Khe Sanh. Way west," shouted the crew chief over the deafening racket of the big cargo plane. "This run," the sergeant shouted, pointing down, "piece a cake." Fair enough, thought Stuart, but he was glad nonetheless when the aircraft proceeded south over the water.

The C-130 landed at the army's sprawling base at Long Binh, and Stuart and Hooper exchanged yet another copy of their transport orders for a ride on an army UH-1E Huey helo, which took off with five other passengers. Stuart watched the passing countryside with wonder. Vivid flame and bougainvillea trees lined quiet lanes, and Vietnamese people and animals crowded the roads that passed by European-looking farmhouses, then sub-

urbs, and finally entered into the city itself. Stuart grinned at
his fellow passengers, but they all looked bored. Stuart thought
Vietnam looked exotic, sensuous, and seductively beautiful.

The Huey landed on the roof of the embassy, and Hooper led
the way down several flights of stairs. They were stopped at the
door of the second floor code room, and a marine in dress uniform checked the seal numbers on the bags against their orders,
and signed for the bags. "You got one bag goin' back."

"We'll pick it up later, Corporal," said Hooper, with as much
gravity as he could muster. "Other business first."

The marine smiled amiably, "Try the Cafe Metropole, on the
square at the end of the road next to the Continental Palace
Hotel, Lieutenant."

Hooper favored the marine with his most avuncular grin,
"Would that we had the time, Corporal." Stuart bit his lip and
turned away quickly, barely stifling his laughter, and they left
the embassy by the side entrance.

They found the Cafe Metropole without difficulty, and Hooper
pronounced it acceptable. Since it was not yet 1100, the restaurant was nearly empty, and the two officers were seated at a
sidewalk table under a yellow and white umbrella by an obse-
quious waiter who spoke French. Soon they were presented with
an iced bottle of champagne, Veuve Clicquot Ponsardin. Hooper
took the first delicate sip, then a larger one, his eyes closed.
When he opened his eyes, he seemed supremely happy, as though
he had just won a great prize after a long and difficult struggle.

Hooper raised his glass, "To *la guerre*, laddie, our lovely but
remorseless mistress."

Stuart laughed, and clinked his glass on Hooper's. The champagne tasted like nectar of the old gods. He decided to remember the name.

"Well, Mr. Stuart, it seems there is no finer way to enjoy a
few hours of discreet but serious drinking than in doing so with
the knowledge, nay, the *certainty*, that our masters would not
approve."

Stuart swallowed a bit more of the icy, tingling liquid. "Freely
translated, we are goofing off."

"Precisely, William, precisely. But we deserve it, you, especially." Once again, Hooper raised his glass in salute.

"Why so, Hoop?"

"You have worked hard. No, you have, and it's been noticed.
Commander Donald says you stand a very good watch, and he
will probably qualify you as OOD before we get home. That is
fast, especially considering we have some ensigns and even some
jgs who haven't qualified, even though they've been standing

watches longer than you have." Hooper emptied his glass and the waiter rushed in to refill both.

"And," continued Hooper, after another sip with his eyes closed, "you are doing a good job with the division. The records are in better shape than they've ever been, and the chief grudgingly concedes you don't baby the men. He was pissed off when he heard Moser let you fire his pet machine gun, though. He says Moser snuffles and growls like an old bear whenever he even gets near the armory."

Stuart smiled at the picture. The first bottle was emptied, and the waiter raced to the bar for another. The restaurant was gradually filling, mostly with Europeans and Americans.

Hooper tasted the first glass from the new bottle and nodded to the waiter, who filled Hooper's glass and a fresh one for Stuart. William liked the light buzz he was feeling, but decided he'd better slow down. He knew from prior experience he couldn't hope to keep pace with Hooper.

"I really appreciate your telling me all that, Hoop. It feels good. You have been a good teacher."

"Hell, man, the *best*! Remember, I have added incentive!"

"Hey, that's right! I almost forgot, the SEAL detachment. How is that coming?"

Hooper grinned and leaned forward, grasping Stuart's free hand. "The best news for last. When I went into the XO to get his sign-off on this little skate, the old bastard told me he had finally signed and forwarded my request for transfer. He's ready to give you G Division!"

Stuart felt more and more mellow. The waiter brought menus, which Hooper ignored, so Stuart did likewise. The conversation rose and fell, and Stuart began to worry about falling asleep.

In the middle of the square in front of the restaurant a procession of saffron-robed Buddhist monks had stopped. While two policemen tried to dissuade them, the monks formed a ring around one of their number, who sat in the lotus position on the pavement. One of the policemen left, and soon the high-low sound of an approaching siren could be heard in the distance. The waiter poured more champagne in Stuart's glass, and one of the monks poured fluid from a can over the head of the sitting monk. The light breeze brought the sharp smell of gasoline across the square, overpowering the delicate bouquet of the champagne. Hooper turned around in his seat, and said, quietly, "Oh, my God." The gasoline caught fire at one edge of the pool surrounding the seated monk, and quickly spread to his body with a soft whumpf. The chattering lunchtime crowd in the restaurant was suddenly hushed.

Stuart stood and started forward into the street. He was stopped and pushed back to the sidewalk by one of the monks. He felt drawn to the horror, and repelled, and the effect left him fixed to the spot where he stood.

The flames rose in a tall cone above the seated monk, yellow and red at the top, mixing into black smoke. Surrounding the monk himself, the flames were almost colorless, distorting the image of the seated man like a thick lace curtain rippled by a strong breeze. Stuart became vaguely aware of the heat.

One of the monk's arms rose from his lap and seemed to gesture. Stuart watched with increasing horror as the arm broke off at the shoulder and fell to the pavement. Still the monk sat, and still he burned. The head, blackened and seemingly stripped of flesh, lolled forward, and with a soft, barely audible pop, the skull exploded. Stuart tried to shut his eyes against the sight, but he could not. The smell and taste of gasoline and burning flesh reached his nose and mouth. Finally the body toppled over on its side, and the flames subsided. Stuart shut his eyes tightly, and tried to hold his breath. He felt himself dizzy, swaying, his knees rubbery. Strong hands grasped him and swung him around. He opened his eyes and saw the frightened face of the waiter, who was speaking to him loudly in a language he could not understand. The waiter pushed him into the dim interior of the restaurant. Stuart found himself in a small, brightly lit bathroom. He fell to his knees in front of the French-style toilet and closed his eyes again as all the contents of his stomach rushed out of his mouth. He braced his hands on the floor and heaved until he was empty.

Stuart got to his feet and staggered to the sink. He washed his pale, sweaty face and rinsed away the tears. He cupped his hands under the tap and diverted the water into his mouth. Gradually the sour taste of the vomit faded, but the stink of the gasoline and burning flesh seemed lodged in his nose. He inhaled water into his nose and blew it out. The smell remained.

By the time Stuart found his way back to the table on the sidewalk, the body and the monks were gone. A fire truck had arrived and its crew was hosing down the scorched spot on the pavement. Several policemen watched. Otherwise the scene was completely ordinary. The crowd had thinned, but the restaurant was still nearly full. As Stuart took his seat, Hooper pushed a glass of pinkish, bubbly liquid toward him. "Drink that, William."

Stuart took a sip. "What is it?"

"Seltzer water with bitters. It will settle your stomach, and take the bad taste away."

Stuart took another sip, then drank the whole glass. He did feel better. "Je-jesus, Hoop, what a horrible thing to do!"

"Yeah." Hooper's voice was hoarse, and very soft. "I've heard they did that, but I never expected to see it. I guess the Buddhists started that when Diem was still in power; now they just keep protesting." Hooper leaned forward. "Kid, you got to harden yourself. This is Nam. Even out on that ship, it's Nam."

"I don't know if I could ever get hard enough to watch something like that."

Hooper leaned back and twisted around, pulling the champagne bottle from the bucket, and filled both glasses. "I don't know if I can drink that, Hoop. I'm still a little queasy."

Hooper tried to smile, but ended up looking grave. He is shaken up, too, realized Stuart. William picked up the glass and took a cautious sip, then another, finding the cool drink pleasing, if tasteless. He smiled at Hooper, knowing the smile wasn't working.

"The champagne will go very nicely with the lunch I have ordered, William."

Stuart put his glass down. "How can you think of food after seeing that?" William looked toward the empty square, then looked quickly back.

Hooper's face was impassive. He is really holding himself in, thought Stuart. I guess that is what it is all about. "We came here for lunch," said Hooper, his voice low but insistent. "We are going to have lunch. You will find your appetite in good order, Ensign."

The luncheon was served by the same waiter, who made solicitous noises at Stuart before Hooper shooed him away. The first course was chilled vichyssoise. Stuart tasted it, aware of Hooper's eyes on him. The soup was delicious, and suddenly Stuart felt very hungry. The main course was a large river fish steamed in the Chinese style. William ate ravenously, and drank his share of the champagne. They each had two cups of coffee with sweet dessert cakes, and, at Hooper's insistence, a large cognac. By the end of the meal, their conversation was once again relaxed, and the spectacle that had occurred not forty feet away was not mentioned.

Hooper and Stuart strolled back to the embassy and picked up the sealed code bag. They then retraced their morning's journey back to the *Valley*, arriving at 1745. Stuart took a shower and washed his hair. When he closed his eyes he saw the monk, beckoning through the flames. He opened his eyes quickly, and his eyes burned with soap.

Stuart dressed in a clean uniform, and lay down on his bunk.

Very carefully, he closed his eyes, concentrating on his memory of Karen's last kiss, at Travis the day he flew out. Karen's face did not appear in his mind's eye, but neither did the burning monk.

Stuart woke with a start to the ringing phone. It was 1930 and time to relieve Lieutenant jg Edwards on the bridge.

4 November 1966

Hooper strode into the division office looking for Stuart. Stuart was going over maintenance records with the chief and the new second class, Danello. "Ah, there you are, William. All set to go ashore?"

Stuart laughed. "Liberty call, Mr. Hooper?"

"In a sense. A word with you, in private?" Hooper beckoned with his finger.

Stuart followed Hooper into the inner office, and closed the door. They sat on opposite sides of the metal desk. Hooper opened a pack of Dunhill cigarettes, took one, and tossed the pack to Stuart. Stuart picked up the red and gold box reverently, and carefully withdrew one of the long, gold-ringed cigarettes. Hooper lit both with his battered Zippo. "Where the hell did you find Dunhills, Hoop?"

"There's an army helo driver in the wardroom, dropped in for lunch. Sold me the pack for a buck. Gets 'em at the officers' club in Quang Ngai. A present."

A buck was steep. American cigarettes on the *Valley* were a buck twenty a *carton*, but, of course, English cigarettes were simply unobtainable. Stuart drew the first drag deep into his lungs, and let it out slowly. "Hey, thanks, Hoop. A real nice thought."

"Good," said Hooper, brightly. "Now, about your shore leave."

Stuart frowned. "Another Saigon run?"

"Er, no. We're landing the landing force this afternoon, both the airborne and seaborne forces. *Dubuque* has asked us for a boat officer, and, I, ah, volunteered. Volunteered *you*, that is."

Stuart sat up straight. "I had that boat officer course in Norfolk."

"Fortunately, the Commander knows that."

Stuart shrugged. "So what's the big deal? I'll do it. I'm sure the marines aren't going to try a landing any place they don't already control."

"Nah! It's just more wet and cold, that's all."

"By the way, Hoop, why me?"

"Well! Is this the way we respond to duty's clarion call, young Stuart?"

William just waited. He knew Hooper would spar forever, given any response.

"So, OK, OK. *I* went the last time, before you reported aboard, and now I'm too *short*, and far too *senior*, to go." Hooper stroked his lieutenant's twin silver bars for emphasis. "I suggested to Commander Skelly that he send that asshole Siegel, but the way the little whiner squirmed would have made you sick. Anyway, the Commander knows the XO would never let Siegel off the ship on something like this. He'd just fuck it up somehow, and embarrass the captain." Stuart took another long, heady drag on the strong Virginia cigarette, and waited.

Hooper looked at Stuart, his expression finally serious. "Look, it's good to take a little risk now and again. It looks good on your record, and it will get into your record, because I'm writing your fitness report tonight, my last official act before I depart this rust bucket forever. Besides, as you say, the marines will have secured the landing zone."

Stuart smiled, slowly, as he stubbed out the Dunhill. Going to have to hoard these, he thought, sliding the box into his shirt pocket. "Hey, Hoop, I don't mind."

"Well, then don't give me that hard-ass look. It's good for you." I didn't even know I *had* a hard-ass look, thought Stuart. "I suggest you take along one of the guys to watch your back"

Stuart's smile fell in on him. "Really? Well, who would you take?"

Hooper jerked his thumb in the direction of the armory, "I would suggest someone familiar with small arms."

Of course. "Moser, Douglas M.?"

"Moser, Douglas M., his ownself." It was a joke among officers that since enlisted men in the Navy were addressed only by their last names, any man known by his full name had to have been written up on charges often enough for the officers to remember.

"Do you think he's the right man? With his record?"

"Yes. He's steady, if none too bright, and he can shoot. And without Mendoza to lead him to it, he will find no trouble. Besides, he likes you, and he'll be handy if the marines panic, which does happen on landing craft."

Moser stood next to Mr. Stuart at the starboard boat pocket, carrying an M-1 rifle in his left hand. He had a canvas bandolier of ammo slung over his shoulder. Mr. Stuart had a .45 pistol and two clips, about as useful in a fight as tits on a boar, in Moser's opinion. They waited as the LCM-8 landing craft approached, two big tracked vehicles already in her well-deck. The marines scheduled for this trip waited on the hangar deck in full battle gear.

Moser was excited to be going on the trip upriver, and pleased that Mr. Stuart had chosen him as his gunner. An M-1 wasn't much in the way of firepower, but the only other choice was a .45-caliber Thompson submachine gun, which had no more range than Mr. Stuart's pistol. I'd like to find a way to get Ole Betsy into this hunt, he thought.

The coxswain of the LCM-8 brought the square-ended landing craft alongside the boat pocket with a thump and a roar of backing diesel engines. The bowman caught the line suspended from the boat boom, and the mike boat settled in under the cargo net that hung down the side of the carrier. The marines formed up and started to load, quiet and businesslike.

Moser could see what looked like a tripod machine gun mount all the way aft, behind the coxswain's little armored conning tower. He borrowed the bullhorn from Chief Brown. "Ahoy, you, cox'n! That mount behind you take a fifty cal?"

The coxswain shouted above the idling diesels, "I think so, but we ain't got no fifty cal."

"That thing, gotta swivel on a top? Take a look!"

The coxswain stepped back and put his hand on top of the central pipe. "Yeah. Swivel, four bolt holes."

Moser gave the cox a thumbs-up sign, and handed the bullhorn back to Chief Brown. He turned to find Mr. Stuart, who was watching the marines loading, and talking to the First Lieutenant. " 'Scuse me, Commander. Mr. Stuart?"

"Yes, Moser?"

"Sir, lemme go get that fifty I bin workin' on. This ole rifle no damn use." Moser held the M-1 away from him in his huge hand in a gesture of contempt.

Stuart looked thoughtful. "You sure that mount aft will take it?"

"Yeah. Yessir, I'll bring some tools. I'll git her up, no sweat."

"Well, I think it's a good idea. Better hurry, though. The marines are halfway loaded."

Moser grinned, "Back in two shakes of a lamb's tail." He turned, racing for the armory.

Lieutenant Commander Donald smiled. "That Moser is going to be a pretty good sailor, William."

"I always liked the kid," said Chief Brown, in his soft

Southern drawl. "I'm glad he got his third class crow. That promotion has made him more careful on liberty."

"Yeah. He didn't break up a single radioman last time in Subic," laughed the first lieutenant.

"He ain't really trouble, Commander," said Chief Brown. "He's just so big and strong. Trouble gets brought to him."

Moser reappeared at the boat pocket at the head of an impromptu work party of Mendoza and Blackie Wilson. Moser carried the big machine gun in an oil-stained seabag in one hand and his toolbox in the other. Stuart doubted he could easily carry either load in both arms. Mendoza and Wilson each carried two cannisters of ammunition. Moser arranged the whole load on the small cargo net under the light crane at the boat pocket, and carefully tied the ammo cans to the toolbox and the seabag so they couldn't slip through the mesh. He picked up two corners of the net and put them on the cargo hook that dangled from the crane. A boatswain's mate attached the other two corners and closed the safety stop. The crane operator took up tension. Moser stuck his big boots into the mesh of the cargo net and grasped the net firmly just under the hook. "Goin' over, Mr. Stuart!" The load rose off the deck, and was swung out and lowered into the well of the mike boat. Marines in the well helped Moser unload, and the net was winched back up. Stuart watched as Moser organized three marines to help him get all the gear to the stern of the mike boat, where Moser stowed it inside the conning tower, and set to examining the gun mount.

"I guess I better get ready myself. She's almost loaded. See you later, Commander."

"I'd climb down, if I were you," said Lieutenant Commander Donald, mildly.

Stuart grinned. I'm going to hear about Moser's stunt with the crane later on. "Aye, aye, sir."

"Godspeed, William."

Stuart had read the summary of the operations plan for the landing. Heliborne units, approximately one reinforced company, would land on the main road, called Highway One, where it led into Dong Ha from the south. Another company would land on the beach just to seaward of the helicopter troops, and bring in their heavy equipment. Stuart's boat was to lead a column of five others up the Cua Viet River itself, with a tank platoon and most of a rifle platoon embarked. There were two M113 Scout vehicles in the well of the LCM-8 from *Dubuque*. The Mike-8 behind held two more, and the last three boats in the column carried one M48A3 tank each, plus troops and their gear. The operation was called Jackknife 4, and its objective was to open the road from the coast west to the marine outpost at Khe Sanh, near the Laotian border, and keep it open. Very few details about the marines' operations once ashore were in the summary; the Navy's job was just to land the marines and their gear swiftly and efficiently, and then to resupply them as needed by boat and helicopter.

The boats motored in a slow circle a thousand yards from the mouth of the Cua Viet. The air was spread with wisps of fog, mixed with occasional rain showers. They would remain where they were until all the elements were in place and ready to go. When the Commodore and his staff aboard the *Valley* had it all the way they wanted, they would broadcast a signal, which, when decoded with the day book in Stuart's jacket pocket, would say simply, "Land the airborne and seaborne landing force." When he got the signal, Stuart would start his column up the river, past the crumbling French-built lighthouse, and land his marines and their equipment at a broad beach with a good pool ten and a half kilometers upriver. The beach was marked on the chart at a point where the Cua Viet turned south and a tributary from the west, which flowed through the town of Dong Ha itself, joined the main stream. The area was described in the op plan as "secured." Piece of cake. Stuart lit a cigarette, not a Dunhill—they were in a drawer in his stateroom—but a far less tasty Tareyton, and screwed it into his black holder. "How's it going, Moser?"

Moser looked up from his work on the gun mount, "Be OK. Gonna vibrate a little. I got no idea what kinda gun s'posed to fit this mothafucka, but I pushed two big rubber washers in either side a' the mounting bolt. Should be plenty tight." Moser trained the gun around astern, careful not to point it at the boat circling behind them. He elevated and depressed the barrel, squatting behind the low mount to point it upward about thirty degrees. "Ain't gonna be any good agin airplanes, but I guess that ain't the need, sir," Moser grinned. The tank platoon leader, a stocky red-haired Second Lieutenant named Chandler, pulled himself up out of the well to the stern deck, and stood beside Stuart. He squinted at the dim, nearly featureless shore. "What do you think, Admiral? Where we going?"

Stuart pointed to the white ruin of a lighthouse, barely discernible against the sandy beach, and handed the marine officer his binoculars. The lieutenant took a look and handed the glasses back. "Doesn't look like much."

"Probably isn't much," said Stuart. "But the channel is deep right up to your beach, so it shouldn't be difficult."

"I sure hope not. this is my first trip in country. How about you?"

"Once before." Stuart decided not to go into detail.

"Oh, good. See you got your own firepower." Chandler nodded toward the fifty. Moser sat cross-legged at the base of the tripod and looked to be asleep. Stuart knew he wasn't.

"We aim to deliver you safely, Lieutenant."

Chandler grinned. "Well, good. this landing craft is so fuckin' deep we can't fire the machine guns on the scouts over the sides. I guess we might get some sniper fire from the riverbanks."

"I'm sure your brother marines are patrolling the banks."

"Yeah, sure. Still, there's been a lot of infiltration around here; it's part of the reason we are going in"

Stuart felt a little uneasy and very exposed. Surely this guy is just nervous. Surely the marines would have the banks covered. "We'll get you there, Chandler. How are your men holding up?"

Chandler shrugged, and accepted a cigarette and a light. "They're green, though mostly not as green as I am, and a little scared. Quite a few are seasick. These boats are pretty steady, but the diesel smoke gets to them."

And the cold, thought Stuart, and the damp, and the fear. "Things will smooth out once we enter the river, and the smoke will blow away from us to the north."

"Sir!" interrupted the coxswain. "Signal from the flagship, kilo mike charlie x-ray."

Stuart pulled the day code from his pocket and decoded the signal, knowing what he would find. "OK, that's it, we're going upriver. Cox'n, head her in, just to the left of the lighthouse."

"Aye, aye, sir."

Stuart blew the whistle on the lanyard around his neck, and hand-signaled the boats to close up and follow. He watched as each acknowledged, and lined up straight and close in his boat's wake. Moser opened the ammo can he had clamped to the side of the jury-rigged mount, and inserted the first linked round into the machine gun and slammed the lock.

The lighthouse was coming up rapidly as the column increased speed. Stuart looked at his watch, 1527. It will be dark on the way back, he realized. Won't that be the shits.

Stuart's Mike-8 glided into the still, green water of the river. The surface was smooth as glass, with only an eddy or two here and there to betray current. The only sound was the muffled pounding of the diesels, and the hollow echoes coming back from the banks on both sides of the river. Stuart looked back to see the column of five boats in close formation of line astern, moving together at the signalled speed of seven knots. Let's get in, get unloaded, and get clear, he thought.

His thought was shattered by the high-pitched bark of an automatic weapon, followed immediately by the sounds of bullets banging and whizzing off the conning tower. Instinctively, Stuart dropped to his knees on the steel deck, and pressed himself against the bulkhead. Below in the well, marines were scrambling over each other, some trying to climb up on top of the scout cars. Stuart shouted at them as another burst raked the sides of the landing craft, "Stay *down*, goddammit! Lieutenant, keep those men down!" Chandler looked back at him. His eyes were wide, and his mouth open, but he nodded and began motioning and pulling men down off the vehicles.

Stuart half-turned as Moser spoke. " 'Ques'p'mission ta op'n fire, sir!" Before Stuart could answer, his wind was taken by the deafening blast of the big fifty. A short burst, another, then a longer burst, then sudden silence, the only remaining sound the tinkle of brass cases and steel links bouncing across the steel deck and down into the well. Gradually Stuart became aware once again of the diesels and their echoes. "I got 'em, Mr. Stuart," said Moser, calmly. "You kin see."

Stuart rose slowly, and not to full height. He stepped quickly from the shelter of the conning tower to behind Moser's broad back. His knees felt a little shaky, and he put his hand on Moser's shoulder to steady himself. Moser pointed to a spot on the bank, just receding astern of the boat. At first, Stuart could see nothing, but he got his binoculars up to his eyes and saw two bodies, dressed in black, lying face down on the levee, and above them in a shallow foxhole a Russian light machine gun just like the one they were holding in the armory. "Well done, Moser. Cool hand."

Moser stood and stretched, but didn't turn around. "Thank you, sir."

Stuart scuttled back to the conning tower, trying to stand straight. He aimed his binoculars forward, and thought he could see the tall tree on the right bank that marked the last turn before they reached the landing beach. He looked down and saw Chandler scrambling up the ladder from the well, his M-2 carbine slung on his shoulder. "Chandler, please stay down and keep your men down!" His voice sounded harsh and high pitched.

Chandler held up his hands, and smiled crookedly. He was still pale. "OK, Admiral! But do I detect a trace of excitement in your voice?"

Scared shitless would better describe it, thought Stuart, noting that the marine's voice was soft and well controlled.

"Come on, Admiral, don't make me look bad. Let's have a smoke."

"OK, fine." Stuart took the cigarette from Chandler and put it between his lips quickly, not wanting to see if his hands were shaking. Chandler lit both cigarettes with cupped hands that seemed quite steady.

Chandler sat on the edge of the well, his legs swinging. "Just small arms, eh?"

"One light machine gun, Russian-made, feeds from a drum. I don't remember the mark."

"RPK," said Chandler, exhaling strongly. "Nice, quick job of suppression, your guy."

"Hey, we take good care. But we really don't want to have your men stick their heads up."

"OK, sorry. Inexperience on my part. I just never knew the Navy drew fire for the marines." His tone was friendly, and Stuart felt the tension going. He took the cigarette from his lips and held it away from him. He noted with satisfaction that his hand was steady, then he flicked the butt into the river.

"You guys will get plenty of chances to get shot after we leave you."

"Yeah," said Chandler, without expression. "Sure hope nobody takes it to mind to drop a mortar round into this old boat."

Stuart's heart was suddenly pounding again. He lit another cigarette, offering the pack to Chandler, who shook his head. "Now that, Chandler, is a decidedly unwelcome thought." Chandler shrugged and dropped down into the well.

The column of boats reached the landing beach at 1700. The beach was wide enough to take two mike boats at a time, and since most of their load was vehicles, the off-load was completed in less than thirty minutes. The last mike boat extracted from the beach at exactly 1730. Lieutenant Chandler shouted across to Stuart just as he was about to signal the landing craft to form up behind him. Stuart hoped there wouldn't be a delay. There was maybe thirty minutes of daylight left under the thick gray clouds, and he wanted to use it to get as far downriver as possible. Without their loads, the big mike boats could do better than ten knots. Chandler came down to the water's edge, and shouted, "I'm sending a scout with a rifle squad, and one a' my tanks back along the levee to cover your withdrawal. It's a pretty good track."

Stuart grinned and saluted, "Thanks, you're a good man. Good luck."

Chandler returned the salute. "You're under my protection now, Navy."

Stuart leaned into the conning tower, "Cox'n, let's go. Flank speed, or whatever."

"Aye, aye, sir." The coxswain opened the throttles wide, and the mike boat turned back north, downriver. Stuart hand-signed the other boats to follow, and they formed up smartly, big diesels blatting loudly. As they passed the big tree on the north bank, they saw the tank and the scout, rolling along the levee, guns trained out across the river. Stuart couldn't hear them over the boats' engines, so they seemed like silent monsters, seeing him safely back to the sea.

Running at top speed and with the slight current, they cleared the ruined lighthouse at 1814, as the last light faded. The monsters watched the last boat out of the river mouth.

The boats had a much greater motion now, being light and bucking into the swells from the southeast monsoon, but Stuart enjoyed the pitch and the spray. He radioed the flag, and asked for a bearing to return to the *Valley*. He was told to take the boat back to *Dubuque* and disembark to await orders. Fine with me, thought Stuart. Any luck, might get a full night's sleep. "Bearing to Iowa Bravo, please, Jackknife."

"This is Jackknife, Bluejacket Leader. Iowa Bravo will flash first letter of your last name from her yardarm blinker until you acknowledge, over."

"This is Bluejacket Leader, roger, over." Stuart decided he liked being Bluejacket Leader better than the name Hooper had suggested in jest, Task Force Stuart. He swept the horizon looking for the Morse code signal for S, which was simply three dots. The many ships were visible only as darker smudges on the dark horizon. Then he saw it, flash-flash-flash. Quickly he took a bearing on the light by the steering compass. "Steer one-two-zero, Cox'n. Back to *Dubuque*."

"Aye, aye, sir. Running lights, sir?"

"Yeah, we're out of range of the beach."

"Aye, aye, sir."

"Jackknife, we have Iowa Bravo, over."

"Jackknife, roger, out."

Stuart lit a cigarette and sat down on the steel deck to enjoy the last few minutes of his first command at sea.

21 November 1966   USS *Valley Forge*

Stuart and Moser and Moser's machine gun were picked up off the *Dubuque*'s small flight deck by helicopter and landed back on board the *Valley* just after 0900. Stuart was standing director watches that week, and when he passed by the weapons department office, he found his rotation was unchanged.

Seeing the watch schedule unaffected, and knowing that he ought to be on watch right now, for the forenoon watch, Stuart wondered who had stood his watches while he was gone. He wondered whether anyone had. It was widely accepted among the junior officers on the *Valley* that the only person on the ship who cared whether the ship remained at Condition of Readiness III was the captain. And many if not most believed that the captain himself did not really believe the ship was any more secure for being in Condition III, but was just covering his ass. Stuart smiled to himself. I'll bet no one stood my watches while I was gone. I wonder what would happen if I simply failed to show up for my next watch, the second dog.

Stuart shaved and took another shower, then got into a clean uniform in his stateroom. He then strolled to the wardroom and had a mug of coffee and a donut to supplement the full breakfast he had eaten on *Dubuque*. The wardroom was deserted, and he quickly became bored. He realized he had hoped to meet someone to tell the story of his adventures on the mike boat, as Blue-jacket Leader. Screw it, he thought, I might as well go to the office.

In the armory, Moser had stripped the .50-caliber machine gun he called Ole Betsy down to its tiniest component parts, and had placed all but the largest in a shallow steel tray flooded with nitro-powder solvent. He heard a clang as Stuart entered the division office. Without being asked, he poured a mug of coffee from his specially built coffee percolator, and took it in to the junior division officer.

"Mornin', sir," said Moser, setting down the JDO's coffee mug on the desk.

"Morning again, Moser," said Stuart, lighting a cigarette. "Sit down a minute."

Moser sat. "Yes, sir?"

"Moser, I've been thinking. That piece of gunnery you performed on the boat yesterday, well, not only was it good shooting, but you probably saved my life."

Moser felt himself blushing like some girl, and looked hard at the gray top of the desk. "I jest did, ah, what was needed, sir."

Stuart blew a plume of smoke at the ceiling. "Moser, listen to me. You stood behind that gun, and you spotted the enemy, and you fired and suppressed them, while I was crouched down behind the conning tower. Now, I wouldn't want you to tell that story around, but you and I know that is what happened, don't we?"

Moser blushed again, and felt acutely uncomfortable. "Hell, sir, I was jest alookin' out! You were takin' care a' the whole boat! I heared ya yelling at them fuckin' jarheads!"

Stuart smiled. "Thank you, Moser, you're a good man, and a good friend. If ever I need a man to watch my back again, I hope you will volunteer."

Moser stood up, and rubbed his hands in a wringing motion in front of him. "Damn straight, sir! Rebel yell, hell yeah! Thank you, sir!" Mr. Stuart stood, and smiled, and held out his hand. Moser stood and shook it, then watched as the junior division officer left the division office, a note in his hand. I wonder why he's thankin' me, thought Moser. He was the one who showed them marines who the boss was. And he called me his friend.

The note in Stuart's hand was from Lieutenant Hooper. It read, simply, "Find me the instant you return, asshole." Stuart smiled and crumpled the note. He now knew who was standing his director watches. He returned to his stateroom and sat down to write a letter to Karen. Doubtless the best place to find Hooper would be in the wardroom, during lunch.

Moser was just securing the armory to go to noon chow when Mendoza appeared. "Hey, big guy, I heard you shot a gook!"

Moser didn't like the tone of Mendoza's voice. Joyous and sneering, mixed. "I might have. Don' mean nothin' heah, Juan."

"But you're a hero! Maybe we can figure a way to make some money outa this."

Moser hung the keys back on his belt loop. "Leave it alone, Juan."

Mendoza smiled his little-boy grin. "Hey, man! I'm just happy for you! Anyway, let's go eat, I got somethin' else to discuss with you."

Stuart indeed found Hooper at lunch. As he walked into the wardroom, Hooper, already seated at a table in JO country, the outer ring, fixed him with a steady gaze and pointed emphatically at the empty chair beside his own. Stuart walked slowly across the deck, stopping to speak to several officers on the way, most of whom congratulated him on his "firefight" with the enemy. Stuart thought that two bursts of incoming and three of outgoing could hardly be deemed a firefight, but why spoil a good story? When he reached Hooper's table, he could see the boss was wavering between chewing him out and laughing at his insolence. Stuart put on his best smile, and slapped Hooper on his shoulder as he dropped into the chair. Hooper guffawed once, then set his face in a stern expression.

"Greetings, intrepid corsair," hissed Hooper through clenched teeth.

There was no one else yet at the table. Here goes a piece of my ass, thought Stuart. "Morning, Hoop."

"Good night's sleep on the comfy new *Dubuque*, William?"

"Hey, great, Hoop. That whole ship is air-conditioned! Bet you slept well too, off the bridge watch bill at last."

"You asshole! The fucking commander made me stand your watches in the fucking director."

Stuart arched his brows in mock horror, "They made *you* stand a director watch?"

"*Two* fucking director watches, Ensign. And where were you this morning, pray? I had an excellent view of your triumphal return on the flight deck far below me at exactly zero-niner-zero-eight."

Stuart laughed. He just couldn't help it; Hooper's anger at his own loss of dignity was just too comic. Fortunately, at that moment the first lieutenant and Doc Stevens sat down at the table, so the dressing-down couldn't continue. Stuart spent the rest of lunch telling an economic version of the boat trip up the Cua Viet, stressing Moser's cool presence, and his devastating marksmanship. Hooper was unusually silent, but Stuart knew him too well to worry about any lingering anger. Hooper finished quickly, and excused himself. As he stood, he placed a hand heavily on Stuart's shoulder. "Your next *director watch*, is, I believe, the *second dog*, William?"

Stuart wiped his mouth with his napkin to conceal his grin. "Yes, sir. Second dog, sir."

"Perhaps you would do me the kindness of dropping by my stateroom immediately after you are relieved? We will need to review your fitness report." Delivered with the maximum wolfish grin.

Oops, thought Stuart. But Hooper is too good a man to fuck me up over something like this. "Sure, Hoop. Yes, sir."

Hooper strode out of the wardroom. Lieutenant Commander Donald laughed his high-pitched laugh until tears came. Stuart blushed crimson, hurriedly finished his coffee, and fled from the wardroom.

The day had turned sunny and hot by the time Stuart relieved Ensign LaRue, the new boot, at 1745. The director crew of two of Buck Thomas's fire-control technicians and Stuart all took photographs of the swift but fiery display of the tropical sunset. There was a legend that if you looked at the western horizon just as the last trace of the huge orange ball slipped below, you would see a green flash, but Stuart never had, nor had he met anyone who had.

After sunset, the men took their proper positions and ran drills. There were plenty of aircraft in the area, and the old gear worked pretty well at acquiring the slow ones, as long as they didn't fly straight in toward the ship, like they would do in an actual attack. No one really expected the twenty-year-old Mark 37 system to be able to do much about an attack by modern aircraft, but Stuart sometimes daydreamed about how they might take on an attack by PT boats of the type the North Vietnamese had used to attack the destroyers *C. Turner Joy* and *Maddox* in the Gulf of Tonkin in 1964.

The two-hour second dog watch went quickly, and Stuart was relieved by Ensign Davis, the new JDO of 2d Division. Stuart tried to be helpful to Davis whenever he could, pitying the man the awful fate of being subordinate to Lieutenant jg Siegel.

Well, thought Stuart cheerfully, now to drop in on Hoop and get the rest of my reaming. I am sure he wouldn't really downgrade my fitness report for failing to get right up and relieve him on my return to the ship. I think I am sure. A bit of bad luck him being up there in the director as we landed. He reached the stateroom door and knocked.

"Enter." Stuart entered. "Sit." Stuart sat. Hooper was pretending to study some papers on his desk, but Stuart could see the topmost sheet was the ship's Plan of the Day, which absolutely no one studied. He is just doing this for effect, thought Stuart, and he gritted his teeth to stifle a smile that was fighting for control of his face. Hooper finally looked up, working on a schoolteacherish expression of frosty pleasantness. Stuart could feel himself losing control. "Is the door locked, Ensign?" Hooper said sweetly.

Stuart got up quickly and locked it. A laugh came up in a strangled snort as he sat back down.

"Smirkest thou, Ensign?" said the amiable Hooper, his wintry smile broadening.

"Shit, Hoop, I'm sorry I didn't come right up. Really! But it all seemed so funny, I—I, oh, shit!" All control left him, and Stuart laughed, laughed like he had not his entire time on the *Valley*. Hooper began to shake in his chair, and then his own control broke down. The two officers looked at each other across the tiny stateroom, and roared.

After about two minutes, they were down to snorts and giggles, though each bout of giggles in one set the other off again. Hooper got up and got a hand towel from the sink, and dabbed at tears streaming down his face, then threw it at Stuart, who did the same. Finally, Hooper opened his locker and produced a bottle of champagne stuffed down into a Styrofoam cooler of ice. Stuart recognized the orange label, Veuve Clicquot. He was a little surprised.

"Don't look at me with that idiotic Puritan smirk, William. You're a man, now, and old enough to face some difficult truths."

"Am I that naive? I really thought navy ships were dry."

"Not aircraft carriers, my boy. My roommate, Lieutenant Garner, is the flight deck officer; this is from his private stock."

Stuart winced as the cork came out, loudly.

"There's a saying here, William," said Hooper, filling two coffee cups. " 'What are they going to do, send you to Vietnam?' Really, as long as it doesn't get out of hand, it is tolerated. Anyway, it's my last evening on this slave ship, and I'm

celebrating. If you like, I'll make it a direct order, Ensign.''
Hooper raised his cup, and Stuart clinked it. Hooper stood. ''To
the new G Division officer, may the gods cover his back.''

''To the new officer in charge, SEAL Detachment, Danang,
Hoop, and good luck!''

Hooper drank deeply, then refilled both cups. ''You will have
far more need of luck than I, me lad. Just remember what your
sixth-grade teacher told you as she picked up her ruler, 'there is
no such thing as a bad boy.' ''

''I'll be OK, Hoop. Just don't get blown up in one of your
operations deep inside Haiphong Harbor.''

Hooper took another sip. ''Not to worry. But now, on to the
centerpiece of this evening's devilry, the review of your fitness
report.'' Here it comes, thought Stuart. ''Now, the captain hasn't
signed off yet, 'cause I just finished it last night, but since I'm
leaving *tomorrow*, if you're to have the appeal to which you're
entitled, but which will do you precious little good, it must be
here and it must be now!''

Stuart waited for Hooper to continue. When he did not, Stuart
asked, quietly, ''How did you rate my performance?''

Hooper grinned, and sipped his champagne before answering,
''Outstanding, in all respects. And I assure you, the old man will
sign it. Drink *up*, Ensign, you've survived the first six months!''

Stuart took a small sip. The champagne tasted as good as it
had in Saigon. ''Thanks, Hoop. You've been a good teacher. I
have to say, though I'm glad to be getting the division, I'll miss
you.''

''Bullshit. I've ridden your ass pretty hard, but you've learned,
and matured. And by the way, the old man *loved* your Stephen
Decatur act up the Cua Viet. I dressed it up a bit, but I think
he's going to ask for your silver bar early.''

Stuart's heart leaped. The only thing any ensign really coveted
was to get rid of the brown bar, and to become a lieutenant,
junior grade. He took a more generous sip of champagne, and
Hooper immediately refilled his cup. ''Well, Hoop, you must
have some criticism.''

''Only one,'' said Hooper, without an instant's hesitation.
''You're a bit of a tight-ass. Loosen up, enjoy being in the Navy,
enjoy, if you can, the war! The marines say, 'you might could
die here, so don't miss any chance to live here,' and it's true.''

Stuart studied Hooper in silence, letting the criticism sink in.
Stuart took another sip from the chipped wardroom cup. ''OK,
Hoop, fair enough. Maybe I was trying too hard, too afraid of
failure.''

''If you had done any less, you wouldn't be half as good as I think you are. But now you're in it, you know what's really important and what is not. You're a good officer, but stay as tight as you are, and you could become a prick.''

Stuart smiled, but his mood was sinking. ''Is that what the men think of me, Hoop?''

''Now, don't you go getting insecure on me, William. What the men think is their business, and I, for one, have never asked them, nor would I. Just take my advice, and loosen up.''

Stuart pulled himself up straight in the chair, and emptied his cup. Hooper refilled both one last time, then hid the empty bottle in a lower drawer. ''What other advice do you have, Hoop?''

''Write Moser up for a medal.''

''Really? What he did deserves a medal?''

''Sure. And even if it didn't, the captain will doubtless put you in for one, so it would be ungracious in the eyes of the men if your recommendation were not in first. Besides, it makes the captain look good to have decoration recommendations to forward.''

Stuart savored the idea. Of course Moser deserved a medal! ''What medal should I shoot for, Hoop?''

Hooper drained his cup and stared at it with fond regret. ''That depends on how you write it up. Now, for the Congressional Medal of Honor, which clearly is not appropriate, the citation has to say 'conspicuous gallantry at the risk of his life above and beyond the call of duty.' One of them, I think it's the Silver Star but it might be the Bronze, says something like 'selflessly exposed himself to enemy fire,' which seems nearer the truth. Warrant Officer Benson in the personnel office has a book that covers all that shit. Try for a Silver Star, because the RAMFs will knock it down one step, anyway.''

''What's a RAMF, Hoop?''

''In marineese, a rear area motherfucker. You know, the desk jockeys in Saigon and Honolulu and Washington who control our lives without muddying their uniforms with the unsightly mess of battle. For some reason, our army brethren call them REMFs, for rear echelon motherfuckers, but it works out the same.''

Stuart laughed. It was like learning the secret words, being admitted to the tribe. ''Shit, maybe he ought to get a Silver Star. He probably saved my life.''

Hooper looked at him with an expression of mock concern. ''Indeed, you were the probable target. I've heard it said that the VC places a value on American officers far above their actual worth.''

Stuart's smile froze. And there we have Hooper's final judgment of the mike boat run. And the real reason for his anger at lunch. Stuart felt his head shrinking rapidly, and it actually felt good, like an unwelcome pressure being released. "I am going to miss you, Hoop."

"Doubtless. And I will miss you. I doubt many of my Sealies will have a palate for champagne. Anyway, now that you've been shown the route, stay close to Lieutenant jg Epstein, and come for a visit."

"Right, Hoop. Sure I will."

"And now, if you will leave me, I have to finish packing. I'm getting off on the first ship's helo run at 0830. I'll say good-bye to the men in the division office at 0730."

"Shit! I'll be up in the director on the four to eight! But I'll see you when I get off. Anyway, good night, and thanks for helping me see things in, ah, perspective."

"Good night, me good lad."

28 November 1966

Stuart shook himself awake when the phone rang in his stateroom. The luminous dial on his watch said 0210. Ensign Corris murmured a protest from his lower bunk as Stuart turned on the light on the opposite side of the stateroom, near the sink. "Hey, man, you up 'n' down all night."

"It's called watch-standing, Corris. It's called Navy," said Stuart, scrambling into his trousers.

"Yeah, OK, better you 'n me, slugger. Try to get us some better movies." Corris rolled over and covered his head with the sheet.

Sure, thought Stuart. Sleep on through, asshole. Stuart shrugged into his green watch jacket, and turned out the light.

The call had been from the bridge. The OOD had set the special underway replenishment detail, which meant Stuart had the JOOD watch under Lieutenant Commander Donald. Stuart liked the assignment, but he had just stood the evening watch, the eight to twelve, and had been in his bunk less than two hours.

Way to be, thought Stuart, yawning as he made his way through the red-lit passageways to the wardroom, where coffee would be available, and maybe snacks. He filled his mug, and wrapped two doughnuts in a napkin and stuffed them in his jacket pocket. Two minutes later, he entered the Open Bridge.

The Steaming Watch was already chasing the oiler, the ancient *Ashtabula*. Stuart quickly got himself up to date, and relieved

Lieutenant jg Siegel, who went below to bully his line- and hose-handling parties at stations Three and Five.

Stuart took the conn, and worked out the approach solutions on the maneuvering board. He took a bearing circle out onto the starboard bridge wing and dropped it over the gyrocompass repeater, leaving the companionway door open behind him.

"The Captain is on the bridge!" called Lieutenant Broom, the Officer of the Deck, saluting as Captain Ryan stepped through the companionway and hoisted himself into his chair on the port side of the bridge.

Lieutenant Commander Bill Donald stepped onto the bridge and saluted the Captain. "Good evening, Skipper."

The captain returned the salute. "We all set up, Bill?"

The first lieutenant turned to face into the armored conning tower aft of the Open Bridge. "Situation reports, men?"

"Main Control, manned and ready, sir," said the lee helmsman, who transmitted engine-order commands to Main Control by means of the engine-order telegraph's brass handles, and who also could talk to them via sound-powered phones.

"After Steering, manned and ready, sir," said the helmsman.

"Combat, manned and ready, sir," said the talker for the Combat Information Center.

"Deck, manned and ready, Commander," said the talker who would be hooked up to another talker who would follow Warrant Officer Maralit around on the hangar deck, where hoses, cargo whips, and all other connections would be made.

"Navigation, manned and ready. Underway Replenishment Detail, manned and ready, sir," Said Quartermaster First Class Preston, the leading rate of N (Navigation) Division. That meant, among other things, that a picked and especially qualified helmsman from N Division was steering the ship during the critical maneuvers of Underway Replenishment. The man was a third class quartermaster named Fellows.

"I am ready to relieve Lieutenant Broom, sir," said Donald, saluting the captain.

"Permission granted, Bill; let's get this done."

"Aye, aye, sir."

"Captain, I have been properly relieved by Lieutenant Commander Donald."

"Thanks, Broom. Good night."

Bill Donald stepped onto the starboard bridge wing. "How does she look, William?"

Stuart raised himself from the bearing circle. "Usual *Ashtabula*, Commander, weaving a bit. Required course is one-seven-five; she's averaging about one-seven-seven."

"We on course to intercept?"

"Yes, sir. I have us in her wake, two thousand yards astern, at time 0234. Do you wish to take the conn?"

Donald leaned over the repeater and took a bearing. "Want to do the approach, William? Flat-calm moonlit night."

Stuart laughed. It was overcast and raining lightly, and the swells were running about six feet, spaced no more than forty feet apart. "As the commander wishes, sir."

"Take her in. Real careful."

Stuart was astonished. "Do you mean that, sir?"

"I do. I've told the captain you're ready. Don't embarrass me, William."

"Yes, sir. I mean, no, sir, I won't."

"I'll be right here. Don't hesitate to ask my help if you need it, but I want you to do it."

"Aye, aye, sir."

Stuart ran through the problems of an underway replenishment approach in his mind. The basic issue was one of relative movement. The oiler, a 24,000-ton vessel when fully loaded, would follow the course and speed laid down by the officer in tactical command, the commodore of the squadron, embarked aboard the *Valley*. The ships refueling would have to do all the maneuvering needed to approach the oiler, and to maintain position while hoses were passed across and fuel was pumped, and while any other cargo was transferred by the cranelike burton whips. The distance between the ships had to be maintained at 120 feet or less for fuel transfer, and as little as 80 feet for heavy cargo. The closer the ships got, the more they tended to be sucked toward each other. This was called bank effect; it had first been observed by ships and barges in canals. The *Valley* was almost 900 feet in length, the *Ashtabula* more than 550, so 80 feet was awfully close. And Stuart had observed, during the *Valley's* last two approaches to *Ashtabula*, that her steering was slightly erratic. *Ashtabula* was at least as old as the *Valley*.

As the carrier took preliminary station in the oiler's wake, Stuart took a bearing through the bearing circle on the starboard gyro repeater. By lining up the oiler's stern light with the aircraft-warning light on her mast, he could fix her true course far more accurately than by radar. Radar was more accurate for ranges. Stuart read the bearing, and therefore the course, as 177. He returned to the shelter of the Open Bridge, noting that the rain was increasing.

"Kick it, Bill," grunted the captain.

"Aye, aye, sir. How much speed you got on, William?"

"Uh, twenty knots, sir." Shit, thought William, don't make

me go in any faster. He thought about redoing his solution for a new speed, and his mind went suddenly blank as to how to make the calculation, and even as to how the maneuvering board actually worked. He felt himself close to panic.

"Twenty knots, Captain," said Commander Donald, knowing it was the standard speed for a daylight approach, a far easier maneuver than the night shot in progress.

"Kick it," repeated the captain.

"Twenty-four knots, OK, William?" Donald's voice was almost a whisper.

Stuart stepped back from the maneuvering board. He had torn off the top sheet and recalculated his entire solution. He had felt an unfamiliar, almost crazy rush as the solution came up under his fingertips. "Aye, aye, sir. Lee helm! All engines ahead flank! Indicate turns one-eight-zero!"

"Lee helm aye. All engines are ahead flank, turns one-eight-zero indicated and answered, sir!"

Donald put his hand on Stuart's shoulder as Stuart once again stood on the starboard wing, leaning over the gyro repeater. Stuart jumped at the touch. Adrenaline, he thought. Donald's voice was soft, but urgent, "Remember the bumps we'll feel when the bow crosses first the oiler's stern wake, then her quarter wake. The bow will tend to the left as you accelerate and drag back right as you slow into position."

"Aye, aye, sir." Stuart felt he knew it all by the book, but the rushing of the *Valley* toward the oiler was happening faster than he had remembered, and his confidence was shaky. Still, Donald would take over if he thought this was getting out of hand. Once in close, however, any mistake would turn into disaster so quickly that neither Donald's intervention nor the Captain's would really make any difference. It's my game to win or lose.

Racing along in the oiler's wake with twelve knots of speed advantage, Stuart took a final bearing. The 177 true was holding up. He had the carrier pointed straight at the oiler's stern as they closed. At a thousand yards, he would have to angle the ship to the left to achieve the offset that would allow the carrier to come to rest, relative to the oiler; both ships would then be steering 177 degrees and moving at exactly twelve knots, side by side, so that hoses could be passed over and fueling commenced. Once the hookup was achieved, it would be *Valley Forge*'s responsibility to maintain precise position on the oiler until all fueling and all other transfers were done. That could easily take three hours.

"Range to oiler," said Stuart into the conning tower.

"One-thousand-oh-fifty yards," answered Bill Donald, from the repeater on the open bridge.

"Roger," said Stuart. Here we go. "Left three degrees rudder, steer one-seven-zero." Might as well make a positive maneuver, he thought.

"My rudder is left three degrees. Steady on new course one-seven-oh, sir," Fellows intoned from the red-lit darkness of the conning tower.

"All engines ahead two-thirds, indicate zero-seven-zero rpms."

"All engines are ahead two-thirds, sir, zero-seven-zero rpms indicated and answered," called the lee helmsman.

"Very well. Fellows, right two degrees rudder, steer course one-seven-seven."

"Coming right to one-seven-seven, sir. Steady on course one-seven-seven, sir."

The oiler was growing larger by the minute. Stuart was trying to feel the space, and the speed, trying to feel how Lieutenant Commander Donald did it. "Lee helm, indicate turns niner-niner-niner, maneuvering combination." Maneuvering combination meant that the engineers were alerted to the possibility of radical changes in the orders for power, a difficult thing to manage in a twenty-year-old steam plant.

"Main control answers for maneuvering combination, sir."

I can do this, thought Stuart. "Indicate turns zero-eight-zero." Twelve knots was 090 turns, but Stuart sensed the approach was a little hot, and anyway, he knew it was better to come on station a little behind, then power into position, than it was to attempt to drop back from too far ahead.

The bow of the carrier was now some fifty feet ahead of the stern of the oiler, and moving forward smoothly. The swells were not creating a problem, and the interval looked about right. "Lee helm, zero-niner-five rpms."

"Zero-niner-five rpms, sir. Answered, sir."

Lieutenant Commander Donald came out onto the bridge wing and pushed himself into the raised chair behind Stuart. "It's all feel from here, William."

"Yessir," said William, glad of the encouragement and irritated at the distraction. The distance between the ships was widening. "Right one degree rudder, course one-seven-eight. Indicate zero-eight-eight rpms."

"Steady on course one-seven-eight, sir."

"Zero-eight-eight turns, indicated and answered, sir."

The ship slowed, relative to the oiler, and Stuart felt he had it. "Left, one degree rudder, steer one-seven-seven and nothing to the right of one-seven-seven. Indicate zero-niner-zero rpms."

"One-seven-seven and nothing to the right, sir."

"Zero-niner-zero rpms, sir."

There was a faint popping from the hanger deck, far below. The deck talker piped, "Bos'n reports shot lines over, sir."

"Very well," said Stuart. He felt suddenly relaxed, even though he knew he would have to keep maneuvering by one degree course changes and one- and two-revolution-per-minute speed changes for hours—unless Lieutenant Commander Donald relieved him. He smiled to himself, I feel good. "Captain, Officer of the Deck! The ship is on station!"

"Very well," grunted the captain, muffled in his pea jacket and slumped in his chair.

"Excellent," whispered Donald, from behind him. "Now hold us close."

The two giant ships had been gliding through the night, tied together with thick rubber hoses transferring fuel and by the burton whips lifting dry cargo, for more than two hours, and the time, 0445, was well into what should have been the next watch. Even with the concentration of constant, tiny course and speed changes needed to maintain the position on the oiler fore and aft, as well as the interval between the ships, Stuart felt himself getting very tired. The oiler had reported trouble with one of her fuel-transfer pumps about an hour ago, and the *Valley* was receiving fuel oil at two stations instead of the usual three, with the fourth starboard station receiving jet fuel and then aviation gasoline. Stuart's mind and body cried out for sleep.

Stuart felt Bill Donald's big hand on his shoulder and realized he had been drifting off. His heart racing, he checked his position. "What do you think, William?" asked Donald.

"About what, er, Bill?"

Donald laughed. "Steering this close does heighten your concentration, doesn't it? I'm sure if the voice had been the helm or lee helm, you would have heard it, but any other voice, you just tune it out."

"I guess so, sir." Jesus, thought Stuart, I hope that is what happened.

"Very well. Anyway, Deck is asking us to get in to eighty feet. They have two replacement helicopter engines to transfer."

Oh, shit, thought Stuart. Helicopter engines were just about the heaviest objects they ever received by burton whip transfer, and that meant the ships had to get close so that the angle between the whips that would lift and control the load across could be reduced. The greater the distance between the ships, the greater the angle; the greater the angle, the greater the strain on the cargo-handling gear. Stuart looked at the first lieutenant, still seated on the stool welded to the bulkhead behind him. Donald was sighting along the lighted distance line that ran between the signal bridges of the two tied ships. "You're at about 110 feet, William. We'll have to get closer."

Just like that, thought William, his throat drying. I would rather do the whole approach over than have to maneuver in to the oiler's side while maintaining station fore and aft so precisely that neither the transfer of the heavy engines nor the fuel transfers would be disturbed.

Donald looked up and smiled as William accepted another cup of coffee from the Quartermaster of the Watch. "Are you tired, William? Do you want me to take the conn?"

Of course I do, dammit, thought William, but he said, "I'm fine, Bill. I will continue, as you wish." Take it, Bill, he thought, take it, can't you feel I am not ready to do this?

Donald regarded Stuart with what looked like a thoughtful, detached air. He is going to take it, thought Stuart. "Carry on, William, close to eighty feet. I will call the ranges for you," said Donald.

Stuart took a sip of coffee. "Lee helm, indicate zero-niner-five rpms."

"Zero-niner-five rpms, indicated and answered, sir!"

Slowly Stuart inched the carrier closer, adding speed and taking it off as the fore-and-aft position changed. The hard part was the amount of anticipation required; the 37,500-ton *Valley* did not respond instantly to either helm or engines, and if he waited until the ship was either moving ahead or aft relative to the oiler, he would never get the relative movement back under control.

"One hundred feet," said Bill Donald.

Stuart ordered a little more starboard helm. He was sweating, and he had an odd tingling sensation behind his eyes. The oiler seemed to surge toward him.

He turned to call for left rudder.

"One hundred feet," said Donald.

Shit! William looked at the interval. I have got to anticipate, but if I'm going to fuck this up, it will be through excess caution. "Meet her," he called in to Fellows.

"Meet her, aye," said Fellows, as he turned the rudder left just enough to steady the ship on her current heading. "Course is one-seven-eight, sir."

"Very well. Lee helm, zero-niner-one rpms."

"Zero-niner-one, and answered, sir."

"Very well." Stuart looked over the bulkhead at the water rushing between the ships, glowing green with natural phosphorescence and from the floodlights on both ships. I am sure we are closer.

"Eighty-five feet," said the First Lieutenant.

"Thank you, Commander," said Stuart, relieved. Now just get her back in the groove. "Helmsman, come left to course one-seven-seven. Zero-niner-zero rpms."

"Very well."

"Officer of the Deck! The bos'n requests permission to begin heavy transfer!" called the telephone talker hooked up to the bosun's talker on the hangar deck.

"Bring 'em over, and smartly," said Donald, smiling at William. "My team is ready to go off watch."

Jesus, I'll say, thought Stuart, as he continued to watch the racing channel of water between the two ships, making minute adjustments of course and speed. As the watch had grown older, he had been able to hold in position with fewer and fewer changes of helm and engines.

He heard the scream of heavy winches as the first of the big aircraft engines was lifted off the deck of the oiler and swung over the water. "Distance to oiler, Commander?" he asked.

Donald looked at the water interval, then back at the lighted distance line. "Seventy-five to eighty feet. Looks good."

Stuart swallowed, and looked at the interval between the ships. It looks right, he thought. Down below, the first engine was unhooked on the *Valley*'s deck, and the hooks swung back to the oiler for the other. Hurry up, thought Stuart. "Range, Commander?"

Donald looked over the side at the interval, then at the distance line. He trusts his eyes more than the dancing lights, thought Stuart, and so do I. "As before, William. Recommend you hold her just as she is."

A nice way of saying calm down, thought Stuart. He looked over the side as the second engine, in its gray waterproof cannister, was swung across. Halfway, it was almost skimming the water, as the crane operators fought to keep the angles down. The load seemed to stop just then, and Stuart thought they might drop it, but slowly it started uphill toward the hangar deck, and disappeared from view.

"Commander! Bos'n says he's all done; requests permission to break away," said the deck talker.

"Stand by," said the First Lieutenant. He turned and shouted down to the starboard signal bridge, astern and below the open bridge. "Sigs, this is Lieutenant Commander Donald. Tell *Ashtabula* we're breaking away."

The signal was passed across by light and by semaphore flags. Stuart had a moment to think about the breakaway maneuver. He knew that you couldn't just turn left and pull away, like a car would be driven away from a curb, because the ship actually turned about a point just forward of the bridge, with the bow going in the direction of the rudder, and the stern swinging the opposite way.

"*Ashtabula* acknowledges breakaway, Commander," came the voice of the Petty Officer of the Watch on the signal bridge, rasping out of the squawk box inside the bridge. The captain, who hadn't moved all night, leaned forward and pressed the switch for signal bridge. "Conn, aye," he growled. "Cut her away, Bill."

So, continued Stuart in his mind, as the breakaway checklist continued, I'll put the helm over real slowly, while powering up. As my speed comes up, I may even have to turn back toward the oiler, to meet any tendency for the stern to be sucked in.

"Sir, bos'n reports all lines clear, all hoses clear."

"Very well. Let's go, William."

"Aye, aye, sir. All engines ahead standard, indicate turns one-one-five."

"All engines are ahead standard, one-one-five rpms, and answered."

Stuart waited until the movement forward relative to the oiler was quite apparent, and then he had the helm put left two degrees. He stood on the aft end of the bridge wing and watched the interval between the ships as far astern as he could see. At first the interval seemed to remain constant, even as the bow swung out, but then he could see the distance astern was gradually widening. "Left five degrees rudder."

"My rudder is left five degrees, sir."

The two ships were separating rapidly now, and Stuart felt his fatigue return in a rush. It was a good feeling. "Navigation, what is our course to return to night steaming station?"

"Three-five-zero, sir."

Stuart took one last look at the receding oiler, then at the gyro repeater. The ship's heading was sweeping past 090, and decreasing. "Helmsman, increase rudder to left ten degrees, steady on new course three-five-zero."

The helmsman answered. Stuart walked back onto the open bridge. Bill Donald slapped him on the back. "Damn fine job,

William. I'll take it from here. You have my permission to secure.''

"Thank you, sir, but my relief—''

"—Is the bos'n. He won't be cleaned up on deck for another hour. When's your next watch?''

Stuart groaned inwardly. He had been too busy to think about it. "The eight to twelve, Commander,'' he looked at his watch, 0530. "in exactly two hours.''

Donald grinned. "I'll sleep soundly through the morning with the knowledge, Mister Stuart, that you are watching. Now strike below.'' He turned to the porthole of the conning tower. "This is Lieutenant Commander Donald; I have the conn.''

"Officer of the Deck has the conn, sir.''

Donald turned to Stuart, "You are *relieved*, William.''

"Aye, aye, sir,'' said Stuart, saluting "Good night, and good night, Captain,'' he repeated, throwing a salute at the shapeless mound in the chair. He neither expected an acknowledgment nor received one. He started for the port-side companionway door.

"Mr. Stuart!'' growled the mound.

"Yes, Captain?''

"Good job. G'night.''

"Thank you, sir. Good night, Captain.''

7 December 1966   *Valley Forge*, off the Cua Viet

Good my lady love,

The rumors that have been flashing around the ship for several days have finally been confirmed. Our sister ship, the *Princeton*, is making a fast passage across the Pacific to relieve us, now four months late in coming home. It is estimated *Princeton* will reach Subic Bay in about fourteen days. We will turn over the marine squadron and their gear in Subic, then go to Yokosuka in Japan, and then home. I can hope to hold you in my arms by about the 25th of January.

To answer your last question first, yes, yes! the plans you have set forth for our wedding sound fine, even idyllic. March sounds fine, the sooner the better. The *Valley* is scheduled for a major overhaul, so I won't be going anywhere. I will want to bring several of my fellow officers as ushers, Buck Thomas, Gordy Mason, Phillip Hooper, if he can make it. I don't know if I will be able to match eight bridesmaids, though!

The rest sounds fine. Please call my mother, in Virginia, about the baptismal certificate.

Your letters sound excited. You cannot know how much I draw from your letters, or how much I wish for our reunion.

My love, yours,
William

* * *

Stuart sealed the envelope and answered the phone. It was the weapons officer, Commander Skelly, asking for a report that the chief had promised to furnish two weeks previously. Stuart liked the chief, but his failure to do even minimal paperwork was frustrating in the extreme. While Stuart was having his ear chewed by the commander, Lieutenant jg Epstein entered the division office, and sat.

Stuart smiled at Epstein, and pointed toward the armory, where Moser's special coffee was to be had, while still listening to the department head expound on the importance of proper record keeping.

Stuart had been put off at first by Epstein's aloofness, but had come to like his wry wit, and his playing on navy conventions. Epstein was ascetically handsome and very thin; his body seemed made for the high-collar service dress-white uniform. It was said that he had asked for crypto school at Pearl Harbor just for the parties.

Epstein returned from the armory with coffee in a plastic cup, and sat down just as the commander stopped his chewing out, so Stuart was able to hang up. Epstein took a packet of Pall Malls and lit one, and handed the pack to Stuart. "Thanks, David. I guess we're finally going home."

"So it seems. I hear we may not even stop at Pearl."

"How is Pearl for liberty, David? I flew straight out."

Epstein exhaled a long plume of smoke toward the ceiling, and smiled as though reliving a special experience. "Wonderful. Almost refined, in an old-fashioned navy way, as befits an outpost of empire. And a junior officer with reasonable table manners is sought after."

"I'm sorry we're going to miss it."

"Actually, officers from ships in transit get nowhere, and end up chasing tourist bimbos. But to be *stationed* there, ah!"

"Maybe you will go back."

"I'd kill for the chance. However, I could tell from a snatch of your last conversation that you have work to do, and work you will want to do quickly, so you can take advantage of my next proposition."

"Right. Some damned ammo status report the chief 'forgot' to submit. What's your proposition?"

"How would you like to fly courier for me, to Danang? At least get in a dinner at the officers' club. I have a crypto machine that's broken. I have to turn it in."

Maybe a chance to see Hooper, thought William. "I guess

so. I'll have to get off my department head's shit list, but I can do that if I can extract the report from Everson.''

"It has to go tomorrow, latest.''

"I'll try. Tell me, David, why don't you take these chances yourself to get off the ship?''

"Didn't Hooper tell you? He was always my most devoted courier.''

Stuart remembered some remark from Hooper about Epstein's fear of danger, but he wasn't about to say that. "No, he never did.''

"Well, in the first place, no Captain in his right mind would let his top secret control officer get off the ship in a combat zone. If anything came up, the skipper himself has the only other key to the vault, and I can't see him crawling through pubs when all hell would probably be breaking loose at the same time. I'm also one of only two crypto officers on board; the other is the ops officer, and he can barely type.'' Epstein paused to light another cigarette.

"And in the second place?'' asked Stuart.

"Well, my dear boy, think of the danger to the war effort should I be caught! If they catch you with my crypto rotor, they have a piece of hardware. Damaging, not catastrophic. And even though they pull out all your nails and crush various soft parts of your body with pliers, you will never be able to tell them how the device *works*!''

"We deck apes are expendable, hey?''

"Deplorably, that is so,'' said Epstein with a look of mock regret.

"Let me see what I can swing with the Commander. Hey, do me a favor, get a message off to Hooper at the SEAL detachment; see if he'll be on the base.''

"No problem. You will let me know, then?''

"Right. Now I just have to find the chief and stand over him while he writes the ammo report.''

The *Valley*'s helo lifted off the flight deck into the hazy heat at 1500, the mail run. Stuart was strapped into the canvas bench on the port side of the aircraft opposite the door-gunner, the sealed bag containing the broken code machine beneath the seat. The tail section of the aircraft was stacked with orange and blue sacks of mail. Stuart was looking forward to seeing Hooper after dropping the bag; Hooper's message had said he would meet Stuart at the Stone Elephant Officers' Club at Camp Tien Shaw, on the navy's end of Danang, at 1730.

Stuart dozed as the helicopter wop-wopped down the coast. The air felt cooler and dryer at 1,000 feet of altitude. Suddenly the aircraft rolled over to starboard, and began to descend. Stuart came quickly awake; he knew they were nowhere near Danang. The crew chief came aft to him, and handed Stuart his headset. "Yes, sir," said Stuart into the mike.

"Stuart, we're going over to fly backup to one of the marine helos, picking up an emergency medevac," said Lieutenant Ramirez through the static crackle. "You armed?"

"A forty-five, Jess. What about my bag?"

"I dunno. Wanna dump it?"

Better not, thought Stuart. If it was that simple, Epstein would have tossed it over the side in deeper water than this. "No, I'll keep it."

"OK, hang on. We'll just orbit until the squadron's bird makes the pickup."

Stuart handed the headset back to the crew chief. Nothing is ever easy, he thought, as the helo descended over thickening jungle.

The marines had marked the landing zone with smoke, and Stuart could see the tightly bunched men facing outward around the perimeter as the ship's helo banked again to starboard, and formed up behind the marine bird that would make the actual pickup. The marine bird side-slipped toward the LZ, and Stuart could see four marines holding onto a man on a stretcher. Just as the marine helo flared for landing, a thick stream of green tracers erupted from the hill that overlooked the LZ from the north. Stuart felt the sour taste of fear as the marine helo bucked and staggered over the LZ, then rose rapidly, the stream of tracers following it up. Stuart lost his view as the *Valley*'s helo heeled radically to port in a tight turn, then climbed away from the LZ and the menacing gun. Stuart picked up an extra headset, and plugged it into the board next to the crew chief, so he could listen to the intercom and radio chatter.

"Barker Six, you are going to have to suppress that fifty-one, or we can't get in and out." Stuart thought he recognized the voice of Major Brabham, the squadron operations officer, presumably the pilot of the marine helo.

"Roger, Angel Four. We have a flight of A-Ds inbound. Can you loiter to the west while we barbecue the bastard?"

"Roger, Angel Four standing by. Seabird, this is Angel Four."

"This is Seabird." The voice of Lieutenant Ramirez was loud in the headset.

"Jess, can you come up and take a look at my underside? We stopped a bunch of those rounds."

"Sure, coming up. You got any control problems?"

"Not yet. Take a look at the port side and underneath."

Stuart turned to watch the air strike come in as Ramirez maneuvered to inspect the marine bird. Two air force A1-Es, propellor-driven fighter-bombers that had first been produced by Douglas in World War II, flew over in formation, got their spot from Barker Six, then began their bomb run. For some reason—many said it was respect for the old war planes' stamina—pilots always called them A-Ds, or Able-Dogs, both the nomenclature and the phonetic alphabet relics of the Korean War, the old aircraft's heyday.

Stuart saw the bright smears of yellow and red flames as the napalm burst from the bomb cannisters and spread over fifty yards of the hillside. It looked to him that the column of flame and smoke had surely covered the spot from which the VC gunners had fired their .51-caliber machine gun.

"We have a problem, Major," said Ramirez. Stuart turned back facing forward as the A-Ds made their wide turn to return to Danang for more bombs.

"What do you see, Jess?" crackled Major Brabham through the static of nearby weather.

"Belly looks OK. You have about three or four holes in the engine cowling, but I can't see anything leaking out. But your port-side wheel is shot away."

"Shit. I can't risk landing or taking off on that uneven LZ with just the strut."

"I know. Fly cover for us; we'll take it."

"You ever pick anybody outa the jungle, Jess?"

"Nah, but flying is flying, hey, Major?"

"OK. Call Barker Six, I expect he's anxious."

"Roger," answered Martinez.

The headset clicked as Ramirez shifted frequencies up in the cockpit. " 'Gels Four, Angels Four, come in, over."

"Barker Six, this is Seabird. Angels Four has aircraft damage; we'll make the pickup."

"OK, Seabird. Appreciate it. This kid needs hospital."

"Roger, Seabird is comin' down."

Ramirez descended to a few feet above the treetops, and accelerated into a port turn. The trees rushed by beyond the gunner standing in the open door, and seemed to reach for the helicopter. He's making sure he's less exposed to gunners up the ridge, thought Stuart, watching. He's also giving the door-gunner a clear field of fire. The helo swerved violently left, then right, as a tree forty feet higher than their altitude flashed past. I hope he's not just showing off, thought Stuart, bleakly. I don't like this at all.

The helicopter tilted up sharply, losing all her forward motion as Ramirez pulled in the collective. The helo shuddered violently, then landed with a slight bounce. The door-gunner stepped aside and the stretcher was thrust aboard. The black marine in the stretcher was ashen around his full lips, and was shivering slightly. His chest was heavily bandaged. The medical corpsman handed Stuart the IV sack of plasma, already dripping into the wounded man's arm, gesturing at Stuart to hold the sack up over the stretcher. Stuart nodded; conversation was impossible over the roar of the helicopter's engine. The corpsman jumped out the door, and ran for the edge of the LZ, holding onto his helmet. Stuart heard the crew chief say "go!" over the intercom, and the bird lurched, tipped steeply forward, and took off. Stuart heard a loud clang, then two more, from up forward, and saw that once again tracers were rising up from the hillside like high-speed hornets. Stuart had to look out around the door-gunner, whose fat body was shaking from the recoil of the .30-caliber machine gun he was firing in short bursts. The helo appeared to be at the center of a cone of tracers. Stuart heard more pings and tearing sounds, as pieces of the aluminum skin of the aircraft were torn away by the pursuing machine gun bullets. The helo rose rapidly and turned away. The door-gunner stopped firing, and threaded in another belt of ammunition.

Stuart's breath escaped in a rush, taking his fear and tension with it. He felt a light pressure on his right hand, and saw that the wounded marine had grasped it, and was trying to talk. Stuart made sure the IV in his left hand was still flowing, then bent his ear close to the kid's mouth. He felt the wounded man's breath on his ear, but could make out no sound. Feeling helpless, and ever more scared, Stuart tried to smile, and squeezed the man's hand. "Hospital," he mouthed, "Danang. Maybe ten minutes." The young man nodded and smiled back through his pain.

The helicopter leveled off at about 1,500 feet, and flew straight for Danang. The marine helo had gone on ahead, very low on fuel. Stuart continued to hold the IV in his left hand, and the marine's hand in his right. If I ever survive this, he swore to himself, no more milk runs for David Epstein.

Stuart looked out the door, past the gunner still standing by the light machine gun. He noticed a dark and spreading stain on the left leg of the gunner's flight suit, and then saw that drips of something were flying from the forward edge of the door. He reached across, and stuck his hand in the steady stream of drips. He brought the warm fluid close to his face, and smelled the strong scent of warm oil. He caught the crew chief's eye, and held his hand forward. The chief smelled it, and said, "Shit!" into his lip mike.

"What is it, Bowen?" asked Ramirez.

"We leaking lube oil, sir. A lot of it."

"Yeah, I know. Pressure is dropping all the time."

"We gonna make it?"

"I dunno. You know these engines, Chief. When we run out of oil, she'll just seize up."

"How does the cylinder head temperature look?"

"Up, but not bad. We have to keep going; there's no place closer at this point. Oh, shit." There was a marked and sudden increase in the pitch of the engine sounds, and the helo began to vibrate and wobble in flight. "Call it in, Butterworth, while I look for a flat spot."

"OK, Jess," replied Lt. (jg) Fred Butterworth, the copilot. "Danang tower, this is Seabird. Mayday, mayday. My position is—"

Stuart crawled to the door and looked out. Rice paddies, mostly flooded for the winter transplanting, some fallow and dry. No sign of anything like a military installation, or even a town. Stuart listened to Butterworth calling in his position and progress, and requesting an emergency medevac chopper for the wounded man and a pickup for the rest of them. Danang said they would vector helos out to search, and to keep reporting position.

There was another loud bang forward, which shook the aircraft like a wet dog. Smoke began to flow in around the leading edge of the door. "OK, Butterworth, there. The field next to that little canyon," said Ramirez, his voice calm and unhurried.

"Looks a little narrow, Cap."

"It's all we have. I've got her."

Jesus, Mary, and Joseph, Stuart prayed, numbly. He knelt and got his arm around the wounded marine, who seemed to be asleep, and braced himself as best he could. He saw a line of trees rush past, then tall, dry grass. The aircraft struck the ground with enough force to propel him forward into the bulkhead, stunning him. The helo bounced, and the tail section slewed around out of control, and Stuart was thrown back toward the door. He realized he had lost the IV bag. The helo pitched, nose down, and slid into the narrow canyon, and Stuart was once again thrown forward, this time sliding into the crew chief. The aircraft came to rest, its nose just short of a creek, leaning on its left side against a tree. Stuart pushed himself aft to look for the IV.

"Everybody all right back there?" called out Ramirez. Before anyone could respond, the starboard side of the helo was raked with several long bursts of automatic weapons fire. The door-gunner spun around, his arms flying away from his sides. Stuart had the vague impression of a giant red stain on the man's chest as the gunner fell on top of him. Stuart felt the wind knocked out of his chest, and an excruciating pain as his left knee was twisted beneath the gunner's bulk. The fat man's body continued to absorb bullets, and by the way it did so without any response, Stuart knew he was dead.

Stuart heaved the gunner's body aside and pushed himself, sitting, toward the door. The .30-caliber Browning machine gun had been shot out of its mount, and lay in the doorway, its belt still locked in. Stuart pulled it toward him, up over his left shin, which was twisted at an odd angle from below the knee. Stuart looked out the door, and saw three soldiers in loose black clothing coming toward the helo in short rushes, covering each other with short bursts of fire from their AK-47s as they ran. There was no return of fire from the helo. Stuart braced the forward end of the barrel against the outside of his boot. The nearest VC was no more than ten yards away as he stopped and crouched. He had not taken cover. Stuart waited until the other two men were up and moving, then opened fire, training the barrel back and forth by moving his leg and body, and holding the jumping gun down with both hands. He fired, back and forth, until the gun jammed. He worked the bolt to clear the jam, then pulled himself forward, still seated, to look out. The three VC were all down. Two lay face down about ten yards away, with large blood stains on their backs from exit wounds. The third was less than ten feet from the helo, on his back with his legs twisted under him, with an arm nearly torn off at the shoulder, and his face a featureless red mask. Sweet Jesus, thought Stuart.

He hung his leg over the side and straightened it out. Only then did he notice that the machine gun barrel had burned right through his khaki trousers, and into the flesh of his shin. Smoldering cotton threads stuck to the blackened and blistering skin. The sweetish smell made Stuart feel slightly sick.

"Hey, hey, anybody back there?" Butterworth's voice was a wail of pain.

"Butterworth. Yeah, me, Stuart. Don't yell."

"I need help, man," said Butterworth, his voice an urgent whisper.

"Shut up." Stuart listened to the jungle. The only sounds were the dripping of moisture from the trees, the gurgle of the creek, and the pinging of the ruined aircraft engine as it cooled.

But there had to be more than three of them. "OK, Butterworth, what is your situation?"

"Broken leg. Ramirez is dead. Christ, Stuart, one minute he was flyin' the plane, then we stopped down here, and he looked out the window, and then his head just came off. I got his blood and brains all over me."

"Give me a minute, Butterworth, let me see who's OK back here." Stuart crawled back into the helo. One look at the door-gunner was enough. The crew chief was hanging from his harness. Stuart pushed his helmet back; there was nothing remaining of the left side of his face, and his tongue hung out obscenely. Stuart fought the acid back down his throat. He reached the side of the wounded marine, and touched him gently on his face, then his neck. There was no rhythm of life. For some reason, Stuart felt particularly sad about the young marine.

"Stuart, you gotta get me outta here. The helo could still burn."

Stuart didn't like the idea of being more exposed. Irrational, he thought. They know we're here, and the helo's fuel cells could be ignited by an electrical short, or a bullet. Better move it. "I'm coming, Butterworth."

Stuart swung himself down to the jungle floor. He tested his weight on his left leg. It felt OK, although he couldn't straighten the knee completely. The burns were beginning to hurt more than the knee. Bracing himself with his hand, he made his way forward past the strut, whose wheel, six inches off the ground, was spinning slowly. Planting his right foot in the recessed toe-hold, he pulled himself upward and grasped the handle of the cockpit door. His neck crawled at the thought of what might be going on in the jungle behind his back. There had to be more than three of them. Nobody sends out a three-man patrol. Because of the helo's position, tilted toward her port side, the door was difficult, but Stuart got it open and slid back. He reached in and unsnapped the harness buckle that held Lt. Jesus Ramirez's nearly headless corpse. Stuart could see the bits of bone and brains spattered around already covered with fat black flies, and once again he fought to control his stomach. The cockpit seemed literally awash with blood. Stuart got his arms around Ramirez and pulled him onto his shoulder. The body seemed surprisingly light. He lifted and pulled the pilot out of the aircraft, and laid him gently on the sandy creek edge. He swiped ineffectually at the flies, most of which did not even bother to rise from their feast. Stuart spat something bitter onto the beach, took a hurried look behind him, and went back up after Butterworth.

Stuart found a small hollow next to the creek for a shelter. There was a fallen tree in front, which gave some concealment from anyone approaching the helicopter. Stuart carried Butterworth to the hollow, and left him. His leg was indeed badly broken, the thigh bone jutting up beneath the thin fabric of the gray flight suit. His face was very pale and sweaty and his hands were cold. Shock, thought Stuart, absently, as he returned to the helo. Soon he had collected the machine gun, the last two belts of ammunition, the splintered first aid box, and the code bag. As he placed the last of these next to Butterworth, he heard the roar overhead of searching aircraft. He looked up, but saw nothing through the dense jungle canopy.

"A-Ds," said Butterworth.

"You radioed our position just before the crash, right?"

"Right. Can you see them?" Butterworth's eyes were closed.

Stuart stood a little, and looked up. He heard the A-Ds return, and this time he thought he saw a flash of metal. He heard the rotors of approaching helicopters. I can't see *shit*! thought Stuart, fighting panic. What if they can't find us?

"Can you see them, Stuart? My leg hurts."

"No, man, I can't. And they won't see us! We've got to do something.

"Smoke grenades. In the bird, under the right seat. Orange plastic can with flotation collar."

Stuart hobbled back to the helo as fast as he could. My leg hurts too, he thought. He heard more helicopters overhead. Stay with me, you guys! He found the cannister and wrenched it out from beneath the seat, and carried it like a baby back to the hollow. He unscrewed the cap and dumped out the flares of various types. He found two fat tubes of waxed cardboard, marked ORANGE SMOKE. "Butterworth, how do you light these things?"

"You just twist off the cap, and rub the abrasive surface against the top of the flare, like lighting a kitchen match. But you have to get out in the open, first."

"Hey, why, man? The smoke will rise through the trees." Stuart tore at the top of the first flare. You think I am going crawling out there among the entire VC army, you are *crazy*, thought Stuart.

Butterworth opened his eyes. They seemed to plead. "Stuart, pull yourself together, and listen. That smoke grenade is especially made to put out a thick smoke, which will lie flat on the sea surface, and point to the downed man. You have to get into the open."

Stuart stopped tearing at the top. Another helo wop-wopped overhead. It seemed farther away. Stuart felt close to tears.

"I'd go if I could, man. I know you've already done a lot," said Butterworth, quietly.

Stuart felt his body drain of tension, and his head clear. Fuck it, just fuck it, he thought. "I know you would, man." He stuffed the two smokes in his shirt, drew his .45, and stepped from the hollow. His left leg felt on fire from the knee down, and that increased his anger. Savagely he forced the leg straight, and stood. Fuck you, leg, just walk, he thought, as new waves of pain swept upward. Crouching low, with the .45 hanging loosely in his right hand, he began to walk, then jog, up the side of the canyon, following the path of crushed vegetation the helo had made on the way down. He kept moving his eyes right and left. Come on, VC. Just let me see you before you do it.

Stuart grabbed an exposed root, pulled himself over the last steep part, and rolled on his side at the edge of the dry paddy. He set the .45 on the ground, and carefully twisted off the cap of the first flare. He could hear helicopters all around, but none close. He struck the flare head smoothly, as the directions printed on the tube said, and as the flare caught, he tossed it as far as he could into the paddy. A thick coil of orange smoke rose up in the calm air, drifting away from him on an unfelt breeze. And it sure did hug the ground.

Stuart felt dizzy from the pain in his leg and the exertion. His blurred vision and lightheadedness told him he had suffered a concussion. He sat up and shook his head sharply to clear it. He picked up his .45 and waited.

Stuart's head snapped up and his eyes opened. The helo was a few feet from the ground, still coming toward him. The rotor wash dissipated the orange smoke and sent bits of straw and dirt stinging into Stuart's face. Stuart tried to shout, but the roar of the engine and the force of the rotor wash blew the words away unformed. Two men jumped from the chopper as it landed, followed by two more. The first man reached Stuart, and laid his M-14 rifle down next to him. Gently he pried the .45 from Stuart's hand, unloaded the chamber, and put it back in Stuart's holster. The act made Stuart feel slightly foolish. The man hauled Stuart to his feet, picking up his rifle as he did so. They started toward the helo. Stuart stopped the marine, shouting in his ear over the rotor and engine noise. "There's a wounded man, and four dead down there, by the downed bird." The man gave him a thumbs-up, and once again started them toward the helicopter. Another landed behind, and marines poured out to secure a perimeter. Stuart was helped into the marine CH-34, and made to lie on a stretcher. Almost immediately two marines appeared carrying Butterworth, who was put in a stretcher on the ground, then lifted in beside Stuart. His eyes were once again closed. The marine who had helped Stuart, a black sergeant with Morrow stenciled above his pocket, jumped into the helicopter as it tilted forward for takeoff. He placed a bag next to Stuart, who recognized it as the sealed code bag he was carrying to Danang. All that seemed so long ago. He wondered what time it was; the inside of the helicopter seemed dark as midnight. He hoped he wouldn't miss Hooper at the officers' club.

The medical corpsman gave Butterworth a shot of morphine. Butterworth smiled his thanks. "The other guy in pain?"

Sergeant Morrow looked at Stuart closely. "No, Doc, he's fast asleep."

9 December 1966   Navy Surgical Hospital, Danang

Stuart woke up in a hospital bed. He felt badly hung over, but knew at once no liquor had caused it. He couldn't see well; the room was fuzzy. He knew he had been awake before, but couldn't remember what happened then. His burned shin throbbed, but he knew he had felt that before. He wondered how bad his leg could be; it hadn't felt that bad when he walked in, but the medics seemed pretty concerned. Infection. It moved so quickly in the humid, living heat of Vietnam. Stuart's own backup medical training had taught him enough about how fast infection moved through burned or punctured flesh into the blood. He knew, but had had no opportunity to dress the wound after the helo went down.

Stuart's mind slipped. He didn't have any sense of the passage of time. The throbbing of his leg provided a pulse, a measure of time, but it could have been once a second or once a year. He felt he should get a grip, swim out of this foggy lethargy, but the effort seemed enormous, and reality illusive. He was in the hospital at Danang. What difference could it possibly make whether he really got his shit together today or next week? He slept.

The throbbing paced him along, through sleeping, waking, and the vague and dreamless state that intervened. It really didn't hurt very much, but then, infection didn't. He wondered whether he would lose the leg. Surely they would have cut off the leg in the hospital if his life were threatened. Suddenly he was fully awake. Suppose they had cut it off! He knew that he would still have the throbbing even if the leg had been amputated. He sat up, fighting the dizzy sickness, and touched his left leg through the damp sheet. He peered down his body and saw the tent made in the sheet by two feet. He still had both his legs.

The throbbing subsided, receded to the edge of consciousness. Stuart lay back, feeling the dizziness back off, and wiped the sweat from his face with the gray sleeve of his hospital garment.

Stuart felt his body probe itself, and he became gradually aware of a new sensation: a crawly itching in his left elbow, like the passage of a heavy insect. Risking the dizziness again, he raised and tilted his head and saw a tube in the large vein of his left elbow. Red. Blood. He was receiving a transfusion. He looked upward for the bottle of blood flowing in. He saw none. He refocused carefully on the itching elbow, squinting to clear his blurred vision. The tube ran down, over the side of the bed. The blood ran out, not in.

Stuart leaned as far left as he could, but could not see where the blood went. He did see a corpsman asleep in a chair, very far away, next to the bed, with a copy of *Stars and Stripes* spread open on his lap. Stuart realized the bottle must have fallen while the corpsman slept, that his transfusion had thus been reversed. He shouted to awaken the corpsman; no sound emerged. He raised himself up on his sore left shoulder and bellowed; a sound like the crushing of dry twigs came out.

The corpsman stirred, awakened, and smiled unconcernedly at Stuart. "How you doin', sir?"

Stuart croaked, gagged, fell off the fragile rest of his left shoulder. He swallowed, calmed himself a little. Tried again. "The bottle. Transf-trans-fus-ion?"

The corpsman stood up; suddenly his face was inches away. "There ain't no transfusion, sir. You don't need no blood. You're OK. The surgeon said it was OK to take a pint of yours. That's what I'm doing. It's almost done." The corpsman checked the probe in Stuart's arm. "It don't hurt, sir, does it? I tried to place the needle real careful, 'cause I thought you were asleep."

Stuart sank deeply into the pillows, and shut his eyes to block out the nausea.

"Sir?"

"Why," Stuart croaked. "Why?" a little stronger.

"Well, sir, you're all right. You'll be leaving here, maybe tomorrow. The docs said we could take blood from the nonserious casualties, sir, and you got type A, which they need real bad, on account of the new casualties."

"Why?" Stuart croaked again, once again weak.

"Well, gee, sir, we got a bunch of new casualties today, sir, one hundred sixty-three before four o'clock, when I came on. This is the first day the helos could fly in from the western mountains, since Sunday, sir."

Stuart fought to steady his mind. This couldn't be real. Not the bloodletting, not even the hospital. He forced back the urge to vomit, staring carefully at the light fixture on the ceiling. The room lost its spin, swayed, stopped. Stuart concentrated on making his voice steady, even. "What day is today?"

"Why, Tuesday, sir." The corpsman's face held a dumb, puzzled look.

"When did I come in here?" said Stuart, carefully but with newfound confidence in his voice as messenger.

The corpsman moved closer, his puzzled face showing more concern. "Sunday night, sir, the day before yesterday. They finished patching you up yesterday morning."

Oh, God, thought Stuart. I thought it must have been weeks.

"Are you feelin' bad, sir? Should I call the doc?"

Stuart held himself in, eyes closed. A moment only. "No, I'm OK. Where do these casualties come from?"

"From up north, sir. Near the Laotian border. Near the DMZ. A place called Khe Sanh. The fog kept the choppers out for three days. Awful casualties, sir."

Oh my God, thought Stuart, clamping his eyes shut against the face of the corpsman. That's where Chandler and his men were going after Moser and I took them up the Cua Viet. He felt a tug at his left elbow, a swabbing of cool alcohol.

"Donation's done, sir. I'll go now." Stuart could not open his eyes.

"You rest, sir. I'll take this blood down to the lab, and I'll bring the donation papers for you to sign tomorrow. You'll feel better then." The corpsman receded through the great depth of the room as Stuart watched through slitted eyes. The door closed with a soft clang, felt more than heard. This is a bad dream, thought Stuart. The throbbing of his leg rocked him to sleep.

The following afternoon, Stuart was given a green uniform and boots, then discharged and told to find his way back to his unit. His bed was needed for the increasing flow of more seriously wounded and dying from Khe Sanh.

Stuart took the transit bus from the hospital in Danang over to the naval installation at Camp Tien Shaw. He felt dizzy and bleary-eyed in the violent Vietnamese sun, and his body seemed unbalanced by the stiff bandages on his leg. He knew he should report to somebody, but he couldn't quite figure out whom. He knew the ship's helicopter from the *Valley* would land at the Tien Shaw pad around four o'clock, to discharge and pick up mail for the squadron. He could think of no reason why the *Valley* would have left station, especially with a major battle apparently in progress near the DMZ. Then again, he thought, since the *Valley* with her squadron of CH-34s and her two fully equipped operating rooms was a primary casualty evacuation and treatment ship, the marine aviators would probably be flying day and night to get the dead and wounded out from Khe Sanh, and the ship's helo would likely be flying medevac as well.

Stuart stopped short in front of the main administration building of the camp, his daydream shattered by the realization that the ship's helicopter he was relying on to get him back to the *Valley* lay broken and blood-soaked in the bottom of a ravine somewhere north of Danang. Vivid pictures of the scene, and especially of the bodies of Ramirez and the crew chief, and the three boys in black pajamas, flashed through his mind. He remembered the young marine he had tried to care for, who had died as well. With what seemed to be an audible bang inside his skull, Stuart's mind cleared. He looked blankly at the admin building. He swayed slightly as his heart slowed, and wiped the streaming sweat form his face. I was so close to death, he thought. The urgent need to report back to the *Valley* receded rapidly from his mind.

Stuart decided to check into the Transient Officers' Quarters until he could find out for sure where the *Valley* was and how he was meant to get back aboard.

Checking into the TOQ was easy. Stuart had his hospital discharge and treatment sheet and his ID, but no one asked to see them. He selected a bunk in an empty four-man room, and took a sponge bath. He locked up his gear, which consisted of a Red Cross shaving kit in a plastic pouch he had been given at the hospital, some underwear and socks he had been allowed to buy, and the receipt for David Epstein's code machine. He put on the second set of jungle greens he had been issued at the hospital, and put the new boots back on over fresh green socks. He checked his .45, noted it was dirty, decided it wasn't very dirty, and put it in the holster on his right hip. He abruptly remembered he would have to reach the *Valley* or some facility with a medical team tomorrow, to get his dressing changed. "Rebuilt," the fat burn specialist with the Texas drawl had said, pointing out to Stuart the detailed instructions on the discharge and treatment sheet.

Thinking about the leg brought the throbbing back into the foreground. Stuart pushed it away, back down through his brain into the dark. It didn't really hurt very much, and the fat specialist had been very proud of his work. Not even significant scarring, he had drawled. Stuart hated Texas accents.

He completed dressing. He wished he could have taken a real shower, but that was out for at least a week, and then only between dressing changes. His body was already sticking to the clean uniform. The heat was impossible to get used to. Only one thing to ease it, he thought, the Stone Elephant for drinks. I can call Hooper from there, tell him what happened. He will know what I should do.

Happy hour started at five; it was only four, but Stuart figured he deserved a head start. Somebody there would have some knowledge of the whereabouts of the *Valley*. Stuart walked out into the glare, wishing for the dark glasses he had lost in the helo crash, and walked the fifty meters to the Stone Elephant Officers' Club. The pain in his leg boomed up into his head.

Stuart slid onto a stool in the cool, nearly deserted bar. He decided to start with a beer, to see what his doped-up, overslept body could take. He assumed he was doped up; he still had not read his discharge and treatment sheet. The Vietnamese barman brought a large icy mug of beer. No so bad, thought Stuart, as half of it slid down his throat and spread out inside of him.

His mind drifted back to the crash and the firefight that had left four Americans and three VC dead. Part of his brief battlefield medicine course had been a couple of lectures on the psychological effects of combat. The doctors had listed the various ways otherwise healthy men react to the trauma of killing, watching their comrades die, and fear of pain and death and cowardice.

During the long minutes or seconds after the helo had crashed and the little VC field team charged firing into the clearing, Stuart was sure he killed three human beings. The one who had gotten closest to the aircraft, whose body Stuart looked at after he stopped firing, was no more than three meters from the aircraft when the bullets from the .30-caliber machine gun ripped into him. The slugs from the thirty were not very large, but arriving in large numbers they had the effect of a chain saw, smashing the boy's face and chest, and leaving one of his arms attached to his shoulder by only a piece of what might have been tendon behind the splintered and exposed bone. Stuart recalled vividly the appearance and position of all three bodies, and he recalled his first feeling while looking at them—curiosity.

Stuart ordered another beer. When the barman brought it, Stuart looked thoughtfully at his inevitably blank expression. I wonder what he would think if he knew I just wasted three of his brothers? Or were they his enemies? Probably wouldn't give a shit, Stuart decided. You didn't have to know everything in Vietnam to know the Vietnamese didn't exactly overflow with love for their fellow man, whatever his race.

He sipped the beer and tried to recall what the doctors had said about normal and abnormal reflections upon self as killer. The more intelligent the newly blooded killer, the doctors had said, the more thoughtful, the more introspective, the harder time they would have in understanding what their emotions were telling them. The thoughtful ones could never think of themselves as killers, it seemed. Most felt they could kill, but abhorred it as necessary in war and nothing to be proud of. They would disdain and even fear the macho types who swaggered about gleefully, bragging about wasting gooks and taking ears and reveling in the horror of war. If they had to kill, these thoughtful ones, they would have to steel themselves, before and especially after, against the revulsion they would feel about this lowly, animal act.

The bar was filling rapidly as five o'clock approached, and the barmen were getting busy. Stuart looked around for familiar faces, and found none. Someone from the *Valley* or the squadron would be along, he felt sure, or at least someone from the *Okinawa*'s squadron who could tell him what was going on up north. Stuart took a good pull of the cold beer. The medicine taste in his mouth and the sourness in his stomach were disappearing. He suddenly felt good, and wanted to talk to someone. He drank some more of the very cold beer, and realized he was grinning broadly. Something like a chill passed through his mind. He realized that his grin had coincided with a flashback of the fire-fight, of the gooks going down under his, *his* machine gun. The grin faded. Stuart knew it would return. He also knew he would talk about it when he saw his friends again. Those bastards had made their decision when they came into the clearing, firing into the downed helicopter full of people, *my* people. They would have killed us all (they did kill four out of six of us, for Christ's sake), so why should I not feel a little satisfied about putting them down and saving my ass? Of course it was a normal re-action. Stuart decided he wasn't even going to *think* about it. You didn't have to love people who tried to kill you. The beer, he realized, was beginning to make him feel a little drunk. He also realized he was grinning again.

A heavy hand clamped his shoulder, upsetting his balance. He struggled to retain his perch on the stool. "Hey, Stuart, how's the gentlemen's seagoing Navy? In which off-limits saloon did you get that fine set of black eyes? You are two days fucking late." Stuart pushed his head up against the weight of the hand and found himself looking into the grin of Lieutenant Hooper.

"Hello, Hoop. I was going to call you."

"Lucky I found you, then. I came over to pick up new weap-ons and equipment, and decided to vary the venue of at least my early-evening drinking. What happened to you Sunday night, and why aren't you fighting the hated Cong from the breezy bridge of the *Valley*?"

Lieutenant Hooper attracted the barman with a great com-manding sweep of his arm, and two more cold beers were pro-duced. Stuart told his story briefly, and, it seemed to him, modestly. Hooper shook his head thoughtfully. "You're one lucky son of a bitch. You're not supposed to walk away from that sort of ambush."

"Well, the river helped. They could only come from one side."

"Still, they must have thought you all were dead in the chop-per or they wouldn't have come straight in. They probably fig-ured to rob the chopper and the bodies before the whole thing burned."

"Yeah, Hoop. I guess so." Stuart felt a little queasy listening to Hooper tell him how he ought to be lying gut-shot and burned up in a helicopter skeleton by a steamy riverbank instead of sitting in the Elephant getting drunk. He ordered another round from the passing barman.

Hooper's evaluation took a bit of the edge off his earlier feeling of triumph. He felt a little mental shrug. Better, he supposed, to be lucky than smart.

Hooper suddenly gave a great shout of laughter and belted Stuart on the shoulder, slopping about a third of Stuart's beer onto the bar.

"Hey. What's the funny part?" Stuart asked, lifting his sleeve out of the spilled beer.

Hooper guffawed again. "I was just thinking you must have shocked the shit out of those dinks when you let fly with the thirty from the middle of a pile of bodies."

Stuart tried to adopt a thoughtful expression, but wound up with half a grin. "They did look a mite surprised."

Hooper laughed again. "Let's drink up, laddie, then go pick up the new weapons for my unit."

"I have to get back to the *Valley*."

"Not tonight. The war owes you a little rest."

"Well, maybe, but I've got to get somewhere I can get this dressing changed every day."

"Not to worry. Old Hoop will see you get your dressing changed."

Stuart joined Hooper in the black SEAL team jeep. Stuart felt relaxed from the combination of the slight beer buzz and the easy conversation. Now that he had told someone, someone well equipped to understand, he could begin to feel that the crash and the firefight, and his comparatively minor injuries, were part of the past. The experience would sink in, become part of him. Fuck it, he thought. The war didn't encourage too much introspection.

The jeep bounced into the yard behind the nondescript warehouse whose number corresponded to the number on the pickup notice in Hooper's hand. Stuart swung stiffly out of the jeep, allowed the dizziness to pass with both feet on the ground, then followed Hooper inside. The big lieutenant had already organized two civilian clerks, one American and one Vietnamese, who were scurrying around locating his order. Fourteen Stoner System carbines and related spares in three boxes, and two large crates of 5.56mm ammunition. These last two were obviously heavy, but in fifteen minutes Hooper and the two clerks had everything sweated into the jeep.

"You familiar with this system, Lieutenant?" the American clerk asked, as Hooper signed the delivery and custody receipts.

"Nope," said Hooper. "Never even seen one of the fuckers."

"Come on around the back," smiled the civilian. "We'll show you. Tran, get two guns and some ammo."

The two officers followed the skinny civilian around to the

back of the long row of warehouses, where there was a trash-choked ravine with steep grown-over sides. The little dead-eyed Vietnamese came through the back door of the warehouse carrying the two black rifles in front of him like cord wood, with an ammunition cannister balanced on top. The civilian took the ammunition off the top of the pile, then handed a carbine to each officer. The weapon was all black, steel and plastic, with no wooden stock at all. Stuart observed Hooper turning the rifle over every which way, examining it with an experienced eye.

"Goddam thing is so light, it feels like a toy," said Hooper. Right, thought Stuart.

The civilian grinned a toothy, country-boy grin. "Oh, it ain't no toy," he said. "It's a real gook splitter."

Stuart winced, and glanced beneath his eyebrows at Tran, who squatted in the dust a few paces away. The Vietnamese clerk's expression did not register the insult. Probably can't hate us any more than he does, no matter what we call them, thought Stuart.

The civilian handed each officer a curved thirty-round clip. Stuart's clip went in easily and locked solidly. "The firing selector is on the right side. Four positions from top to bottom: safe, single fire, stitch fire, full automatic. Try 'em on single fire. Just pick out any old can or box down there. Might even scare out a rat." Both officers raised the carbines to their shoulders and fired a few tentative rounds. It sure doesn't kick like the M-14, thought Stuart, though the muzzle jumped a bit. He fired again, splitting a Schlitz can. He was pleased. He had missed the same can on the previous shot.

"OK," the civilian said, holding up his hand, "now let her rip on full auto." Dutifully the two officers thumbed the selector switches down to the fourth position, sighted, then began firing short, then longer, bursts into the garbage at the bottom of the ravine. The weapons worked smoothly. Cans and other debris bounced around in a satisfying way. The damp evening air held the tangy smells of cordite and warm gun oil.

Stuart and Hooper stopped firing when their clips were exhausted. Hooper drew the bolt back twice to make sure the weapon was indeed empty, then set it down carefully. "Nice." He smiled, and gave a low whistle. "It really tears, even with that light ammunition. And that light ammunition will be easy to haul."

The civilian pulled another two clips from the can, picking up Hooper's carbine. "Whoo! You ain't see the best part!" His grin had become positively lupine, threatened to split his skinny, stupid face. Hooper took the cue. "OK," he almost growled, "what the fuck is stitch fire gonna do for us?" He had examined the selector, which made no mention of stitches, giving only choices of S, 1, 3, and FA. Hooper shot Stuart a wry look that Stuart read to mean I am sure we could have figured this out, but might as well let the goofy turd have his day. Stuart smiled.

The civilian positively beamed, reloaded Hooper's carbine, and swung it around on the gully. "Now this is really somethin'. The M-sixteen don't even *have* this! You ready?" The civilian conspicuously clicked the selector from S through 1 to 3. "Now, then. This little jewel allows the Stoner to put out three rounds every time you pull the trigger. You see how the muzzle kicks up and to the right, same's any automatic? Well, you remember that and the good old stitch switch, and you don't hardly have to aim the damn thing!"

Neither Hooper nor Stuart spoke. The skinny man seemed almost breathless with excitement. "Well, anyways, you don't have to aim it like *we* was taught, takin' it up to your shoulder and all. You just point it a little low and to the left, and let her rip!" The civilian chambered a round, pointed into the gully, and pulled the trigger. The Stoner snapped three times in rapid succession and a five-gallon can jumped and fell over.

"You see!" crowed the civilian.

"You hit what you aimed at?" drawled Hooper.

"Shore did. You call me a target."

"How about that yellow and green box that says somebody's peaches?"

Without hesitation, and without lifting the carbine from his hip, the clerk trained and fired. The peach carton tore in half. The clerk cackled, absolutely delighted. "Come on, you boys have a try. I ain't no trick shot." He handed the carbine back to Hooper. "Just like takin' a stitch."

Stuart and Hooper stepped up to the gully and took a few tentative "stitches." At first the stance felt stiff and awkward, but within a very few minutes and not too far into the next clips the civilian handed out, both officers were able to hit virtually anything they intended. Although the technique was meant to be used at close range against a target the size of a man, Stuart quickly found he could vary his grip on the carbine and therefore the tightness of the three-shot groups. Bottles and cans leaped and died.

Both officers stopped firing at the end of the third thirty-round clip. Hooper examined the weapon with new interest. "Potent," he said. Potent indeed, thought Stuart.

"You see," interjected the civilian, "you spot a gook, and you let him have a stitch. Now, if he's closer than you think, or if he's running at you, your first two slugs prob'ly get him while the third goes high and wide. But if he's really a little farther away, or if he ain't comin' an' you think he is, then the first one prob'ly goes in the dirt in front of him, while the next two tear him up. You see?''

Hooper looked almost reverently at the Stoner as he handed it to the civilian, who passed it on to the waiting Tran along with the other carbine and the ammunition box. Stuart and Hooper started back for the loaded jeep. Darkness was closing in rapidly now, and Stuart felt sure Hooper would want to get the Stoners unloaded and locked away before beginning the serious evening's drinking in the bars along Da Lat Street in the ville. The skinny civilian scurried along at their heels, hating to give up the conversation. Hooper stopped at the side of the jeep and turned to shake the civilian's hand.

''Hey, Lieutenant,'' the clerk beamed, ''another thing the techs mentioned, you see? You get some green kid, maybe, gets a little buck fever, maybe the first time under fire? So, maybe, he just pulls the old trigger and closes his eyes? The stitch, well, he just lets off three rounds into the trees—on full auto, he sprays thirty rounds every which-a-way, leaving him an empty piece, huh?'' A good thought, considered Stuart. Hooper let out the jeep's clutch.

''Potent, hey?'' said Hooper, wheeling the jeep around.

''Deadly potent, Hoop,'' Stuart responded.

Hooper shook Stuart awake. He raised himself from the sweat-soaked cot in Hooper's quarters, and sat sideways. Jesus. His head and leg throbbed in unison. If they have to cut one off, thought Stuart, it should be the head.

Stuart realized he had virtually no recollection of the previous evening beyond the first drink in the Broken Hand Bar in Da Lat Street. How long had he slept?

''Good morning, asshole,'' rasped Hooper.

Stuart probed his sore head with his fingers, expecting bruises. ''Merry Christmas to you, Hoop!''

''Come on, pardner,'' Hooper's voice reflected his own pain. ''It's eight o'clock. We gotta get your ass over to the hospital to get that dressing changed, then I'll drive you to Transient and they will cut you orders back to the *Valley*. Jesus, my head.''

''Any coffee?'' Stuart's voice was a croak.

''Sure. Full breakfast if you want it. But hustle up, it's down in the mess tent, on the left. I'll get your gear together,'' replied Hooper.

Stuart swayed as he got up, bolted out the door, and threw up as discreetly as possible in the ditch outside the hootch. No one seemed to be around. Searching more with his nose than any other senses, he found the mess tent and had a considerable breakfast. He felt immediately better, and realized that he really didn't know when he had last eaten solid food. He savored a third cup of rich coffee, and then returned to Hooper's quarters. Hooper had packed his hospital carryall and was sorrowfully sipping a warm beer.

"Ah, old buddy, I love you, but don't come back too often." Hooper cracked a painful grin as he swung Stuart's bag onto the jeep. Stuart wondered briefly why the bag clanked, then forgot about it as he swung his bad leg aboard.

Stuart emerged from the hospital he had left less than twenty-four hours before, with a new dressing and a feeling of well-being due to the painkillers he had cadged off the duty medical corpsman. He found Hooper slumped in a pool of sweat in the jeep's driver seat. "What kept you?" said Hooper.

"Had to pick up your breakfast," said Stuart, handing Hooper one of the beers the X-ray tech had sold him off the dry-ice cover of the film storage.

"Sweet Jesus," said Hooper as he finished the beer. Stuart opened another as Hooper started the jeep. "Maybe you can come back."

Stuart discovered at the transient desk that he might have to wait several days to get a flight up to Khe Hah, where the marine squadrons were operating a forward base from the carriers, or to one of the dirty, nameless towns along the Cua Viet River into which landing craft were bringing the heavy equipment for what had become a major operation around Khe Sanh. Everything Stuart heard about Khe Sanh sounded bad—a short airstrip surrounded by hills on which the marines were dug in, where they were pounded day and night by NVA artillery set up on other hills. Sometimes the marine outposts were overrun, and then the enemy brought up his guns and worked over the airstrip itself. Added to this was virtually constant fog and drizzle, which made both air resupply and air strikes ineffective and often impossible. Stuart felt a genuine foreboding about getting started in a transport system that was pointed at Khe Sanh. Once you got started on such a routing, there was no certainty you could just hop off at a convenient waypoint and pick up a returned boat or aircraft. Things tended to get swept along. Things and people. Stuart accepted the flight orders, noted the very low priority assigned to his movement, and rejoined Hooper in the jeep.

"You all set, pardner?" Hooper handed Stuart the last, no-longer-cold beer. Stuart explained.

"Bad shit," said Hooper. "Scuttlebutt is we may be heading north ourselves. Where you supposed to go now?"

"I'm supposed to go over to the air base, get quarters, then hang around with my low priority for an empty seat going anywhere north. Look, Hoop, I think I'll go back to the TOQ and try for at least a day or two to catch a ride on one of the squadron's helicopters if they come down for mail. If that doesn't work, I can begin my low-priority journey to nowhere in a couple of days." Stuart hoped his friend would approve.

"Seems a'right. I'll drop you there, but then I gotta turn up at operations to see what nasty little things those desk-bound assholes have dreamed up for me and my Sealies to do."

Well, at least Hooper didn't seem to *disapprove*, thought Stuart. He suddenly wondered why he cared. He was certainly obeying the spirit of his orders, and if he did catch a ship's helo, he would be back to his command sooner than if he obeyed his orders to the letter. Nevertheless, in the eleven months since he had received his commission, this was the first time he had varied even slightly from his orders, and Stuart wasn't sure how he felt about that.

Hooper stopped in front of the TOQ, and Stuart swung stiffly down from the jeep. " 'Bye, Hoop. Thanks for the stimulating evening."

"Not at all, my friend. With your demonstrated combat and drinking skills, you could almost be a SEAL."

Stuart turned to go. "Hey, shooter, don't forget your gear," called Hooper. Stuart went to the back of the jeep to get his bag. He couldn't remember why Hooper had thought it so important he have his gear last night. He picked up the bag and it rattled like a bag of steel bones.

"What'd you put in here, Hoop?"

"Well, a bottle of Scotch, among other things. I know how dry it gets at sea." Hooper twisted around in the seat and grinned. "I also disassembled and packed up one of those neat little sewing machines and a couple of clips."

"Hoop! What the hell am I going to do with that?" Again, Stuart's emotions were mixed.

"Well, old son, I'd say that was fairly obvious. If you insist on eschewing the important but admittedly safer contribution to the war effort of the seaborne serving officer to become rather more directly involved in the killing of the enemy, you'd best be suitably equipped." Hooper got down and took the bag from

Stuart and carried it inside, thereby seeming to make Stuart's decision for him.

"You can't just give it to me, Hoop."

"Not to worry. I requisitioned two more of the little darlings than I need for my team. I made a note of the number, and we'll lose this one on our very next nighttime walkabout." Hooper's grin was gone. "Besides, you're too good a friend to trust to the vagaries of a forty-five when we know there's something much better available."

They said their farewells and Hooper left Stuart to study his mixed emotions. Would I see combat again? How much should one bend the rules in order to survive?

Stuart caught a marine helicopter from the *Valley Forge* at four o'clock that same afternoon. An hour later he was back "home." He signed in the .45 he was accountable for, and asked Moser to lock up the Stoner in the back of the armory. He then went to his stateroom, washed as best he could, and slept for fourteen hours.

===

3 January 1967   *Valley Forge*, **en route Yokosuka–Long Beach**

Valley Forge pushed her bow into the white-capped gray swells of the northern Pacific, straining against the seas like a harness. Stuart looked into the conning tower as Quartermaster First Class

Preston turned the chart to show it to him. "Time forty still look good to turn, Preston?"

"Yes, sir. Eastward and home."

Stuart looked out into the cold rain. Off to port was the island of Ie Shima, which guarded the southern approaches to Tokyo Bay. At 1140, he would turn from his southerly course to 085, just north of east, the first leg in the great circle course to Long Beach, California, USA.

Stuart stood the JOOD watch on the special sea and anchor detail with Lieutenant Commander Donald. Donald had made Stuart his JOOD for all special evolutions, having added entering and leaving port to underway replenishment. Stuart had conned the ship into and out of Yokosuka Naval Base, and Donald never said a word. Yokosuka was difficult and dangerous, because of all the traffic going to and coming from Tokyo and Yokohama steaming in the narrow channel. Yokosuka lies seaward of both Yokohama and Tokyo, so to get into Yokosuka, a ship has to make a left turn across all the outbound traffic—ships of every nation and type, all going at different speeds in the confined channel.

"Coming up on time forty, Mr. Stuart."

Stuart walked over to the captain, who was slumped in his seat and staring at the rain-spattered windscreen. "Captain, the navigator recommends coming left to course oh-eight-five at this time."

"Make it so."

"Aye, aye, sir. Shall we continue at fifteen knots?"

The captain turned and looked at Stuart. He actually moved, thought Stuart. "What do you think?" The captain wore a sardonic expression.

Stuart mentally shrugged. "I expect you will want best speed, sir."

The captain pushed his long body up out of the chair. "Right, William, and best speed is flank speed. Bring her up slowly to thirty knots, and if she's handling the seas, thirty-two. If she isn't riding well, call me in my in-port cabin. Bill, set the steaming watch." The captain touched his brow in acknowledgment of the two salutes, and left the bridge.

"The captain has left the bridge," intoned the Quartermaster of the Watch.

"All engines ahead full, one-three-five rpms," said Stuart.

"All engines are ahead full, one-three-five rpms, sir," answered the lee helmsman.

"Left ten degrees rudder."

"My rudder is left ten degrees," answered the helmsman.

"Very well," said Stuart, watching the big ship turn into the easterly breeze, with Ie Shima on the port beam. "All engines ahead flank, one-five-five rpms."

The lee helm answered, and Stuart gave Fellows, the helmsman for special sea detail, his course. Gradually Stuart built the speed up to 195 rpms, 24 knots. The ship twisted a little in the long swells, but felt very good. He took her up to 26 knots, then 28, realizing he had never before felt the ship at speed, much less driven her. He ordered 30 knots.

Bill Donald leaned into the conning tower. "Bos'n's Mate of the Watch!"

"Yes, sir!"

"Secure the special sea and anchor detail."

"Aye, aye, sir!"

Stuart listened for the keening of the boatswain's pipe, amplified by the 1-mc public address system. The Boatswain's Mate of the Watch piped "attention,"—a short low note, followed by a long high note, then the low note, and the high note held even longer, then allowed to trail off to nothing. Stuart loved the sound. The boatswain made his announcement, "Now, secure the special sea and anchor detail, set the regular steaming watch, on deck, section three."

Stuart felt a thrill at the feel of the big ship moving under his feet, powering into the open Pacific at thirty knots. Each long swell threw a top of gray-white foam high over the bow and down the flight deck as the ship dropped into the trough, and the ship shook and shuddered as she pushed aside each succeeding crest with raw power. "Lee helm! Two-five-zero rpms!"

"Two-five-zero, and answered, sir!" Stuart heard excited chatter and spontaneous applause from the conning tower. The men knew that the ship was now coursing home at major speed, thirty-two knots.

Lieutenant Freitag came on the open bridge to relieve Lieutenant Commander Donald. They went over the nav plot and the few remaining contacts on the radar screen. Stuart had been on watch for nearly five hours, first preparing for the exit from Yokosuka and then doing it, but he was in tune with the rush of the carrier through the long swells of the Pacific, and he wanted to stay with it.

Donald leaned in to the Quartermaster of the Watch, Quartermaster Third Class Voytek. "I have been relieved, Voytek."

"Aye, aye, sir."

"This is Lieutenant Freitag, I have the deck and the conn."

Stuart's spirit contracted. He wanted to drive, drive the mighty

ship on. A particularly large wave top bounced off the bow and
sent spray all the way to the windows of the bridge.

"William," said Lieutenant Commander Donald.

"Yes, sir?"

"When you're relieved, come to the wardroom. I'd like a word
with you, over coffee and late lunch."

"Aye, aye, sir. Bill."

Ensign Fiedler, the new JO in Fire-Control Division, hauled
himself onto the bridge from the port companionway, unaccustomed to the motions of the *Valley* driving through fifteen-foot
swells at thirty-two knots. He slid across the wet linoleum-tiled
deck of the open bridge, and saluted Stuart, "Ready to relieve
you, sir."

Stuart gave Fiedler the briefing. William sensed that Fiedler
shared the electricity of the entire watch at the feeling of the
ship's being alive and racing through the real Pacific. Steaming
at five to ten knots in the relatively calm waters of the South
China Sea seemed a far lesser experience by comparison. Stuart
did not want to leave the bridge.

"Sir request permission to relieve Ensign Stuart as Junior Officer of the Deck."

"Permission granted," said Lieutenant Freitag.

"Sir, I have been properly relieved by Ensign Fiedler," said
Stuart, with regret.

"Roger, Stuart, and thanks," said Lieutenant Freitag.

Stuart joined Donald at one of the outer ring tables. The wardroom was nearly empty. "You handle the deck well, William."

"Thank you, Bill. You've given me a lot of opportunities."

Donald pushed aside his plate, and motioned to a steward for
coffee. William continued to eat his ham steak, which had been
dried out under a heat lamp while he was still driving the boat.
"Can you handle the *Valley*, William?" Donald's voice was even
softer than usual.

Stuart put his knife and fork together on the plate. "Yes, sir.
Yes, Bill, I believe I can."

"So do I." Donald sipped his coffee.

Stuart's heart raced. "Uh, thank you, Bill."

"And I believe you want it."

"Yes, sir! I surely do."

Donald reached down under his chair, and brought up a manila envelope. "The old man just signed this, William. Congratulations."

Stuart opened the envelope, slid the letter out, and read it. It
was his qualification as Officer of the Deck, underway, with

added paragraphs qualifying him for underway replenishment and entering and leaving port.

"The whole nine yards, William," said Lieutenant Commander Donald.

Stuart was dumbfounded. OOD, *and* unrep and sea detail? "Why, uh, all at once, Bill?"

"Because I'll be leaving the ship, as soon as we reach Long Beach."

Stuart took a deep breath, then exhaled slowly. "Why, Bill?" It felt like asking Daddy why he had to go away on your birthday.

Donald pushed himself back, and scratched a cigarette from the pack he never seemed to remove from his shirt pocket. "The *Valley* will be in the yard five months at least, more likely six or seven, the way we've pushed her this trip. Many officers will be pulled off. Some, like me, because a long yard period is not seen as conducive for advancement for ship drivers, have asked for reassignment."

Stuart felt puzzlement join his feeling of triumph. "What does this mean for me, Bill?"

"Nothing bad. You are a reserve. You will spend time in Long Beach, with your new wife. Your work while in the yard will be excruciatingly dull, but when the *Valley* rejoins the fleet in five or six or however many months, you will be the premium ship driver, and maybe the only one, so you will have to train the others. If you decide to continue your navy career, you will have a good jacket; if not, you will have spent much time with something approaching shore duty, and you will have had some fun."

Stuart sipped his tepid coffee. "Could I be transferred off the ship, Bill?"

"Unlikely. This old war lady will likely be pared of almost all regular navy officers, and worse, with respect, of her best petty officers as the yard period progresses. Guys like you, well-regarded USNR types, will form the backbone of the crew that gets this poor old fighter through the yard period and back out to sea."

"What about not-so-well-regarded USNR types?"

Donald smiled. "They remain, William, they remain. But enough of this lugubrious talk of life ashore for many months."

I'll take it, thought William. Ashore, get the marriage going, look after my Karen, I'll take it. Still, making OOD has been a goal, and playing the grizzled mariner to a bunch of new boots after the yard period couldn't be all bad, either. "When do I go on the OOD Watch bill, Commander?"

Donald grinned. "Luck is with you, William. You can begin

tonight, with the Midwatch. As of now, Bill Donald has disappeared from the watch bill.''

Stuart almost slumped. The fucking Mid. He had just gotten used to the idea of standing one watch in seven as JOOD; now it was one in five as OOD. But not a bad trade, he thought. "Aye, aye, sir.''

"So get some rest. And, William, congratulations." Bill Donald extended his hand as he stood. Stuart jumped to his feet. "Yes, sir! Thank you, Bill.''

Lieutenant Commander Donald looked into William's eyes long enough to make his eyelids twitch. "William, I'm not your counselor, but I think you might be happiest if you didn't rule out a career with us.''

Us, thought William. Navy. Men like Bill. But that is silly; Karen and I have plans. Service is service, but then, there is life. "Thanks, Bill, I will keep that thought.''

Stuart climbed down the ladders from the Open Bridge after the Morning Watch. He felt tired; the watch had seemed long. As the *Valley* had closed the coast of California, shipping traffic became heavier. They had a particularly vexing time with an elusive, faint radar contact that zigzagged in front of the ship at low and inconsistent speed, betraying no set pattern. In the early pink light of dawn, it turned out to be a large sailing yacht, beating toward Los Angeles. She was a lovely sight, with white topsides and teak decks, and the crew waved cheerfully as the carrier hurtled past.

The long-range air search radar had picked up the San Gabriel Mountains during the Midwatch, some two hundred miles out. Stuart knew the visual sighting of land would come in the forenoon; then the ship would slow to time her arrival in Long Beach for just before noon. The port captain had dictated the time for the *Valley*'s entry two days previously, and the ship had radioed the Naval Officers' Wives Association the arrival time and dock assignment. Stuart hoped that the wives' group would have reached Karen, and that she would be there to meet the ship. He felt the ache for Karen that had been suppressed for nearly eight months become more painful, more urgent with each passing hour. She is so close, he thought, so close. The last mail he had received in Yokosuka had contained pages of description of the wedding arrangements, and the date she had set, March 2nd. The enthusiasm of her letters infected him; he looked forward to the marriage as the formal and public affirmation of their love. March 2nd, barely one and a half months away.

Stuart stopped at the flight deck and stepped out, enjoying the crisp, damp breeze. He wanted a cigarette, but the smoking lamp was always out on the flight deck, even now, with the gasoline lines purged and filled with inert gas. His mind floated back over his first eleven months as a commissioned officer in the Navy. He thought with affection of Hoop, and Bill Donald, who had done the most to shape his shipboard development. He was, on balance, pleased; he felt he had developed rapidly from the confused and almost frightened novice who had walked aboard the *Valley* in June, and who now could drive the ship in all important evolutions, and could run a division. He thought as well of his three very different trips into the deeply mysterious heart of Vietnam: the festival-like foray into cosmopolitan Saigon, shattered by the monk's self-immolation; the terrifying but exhilarating run up the Cua Viet River with Moser saving his hide; and the disastrous helicopter ride to Danang, sudden killing and sudden death. He felt a lingering confusion about what each of the incidents really meant to him, or ought to mean.

Stuart ducked back in through the flight deck companionway, and ran down the last two long ladders to the hangar deck. He was hungry for breakfast and a little sleep before the sea detail, which would be set around 1100. As he strode forward toward officers' country, he heard the boatswain's pipe trilling attention, and calling the relief of the watch.

"Now, sweepers, sweepers, start your brooms, sweep down all ladders and passageways, take all trash and garbage to the fantail for dumping. Lifeboat crew of the watch to watch, and mus-ter, on deck, section one. Now, sweepers." Stuart strode on toward the wardroom, feeling proud and feeling good.

Stuart dropped from his bunk and caught the phone on its second ring. He glanced at his watch, 1030. "Stuart."

"Hey, William, Paul Freitag. The captain wants to set the special sea and anchor detail in fifteen minutes."

"OK, Paul. Thanks."

"Don't forget the uniform of the day is service dress blue."

"Who could forget? But, thanks."

"See you presently."

Stuart pulled the blue uniform with its single gold sleeve stripe out of his locker. He hadn't worn it since arriving on the *Valley*, and it had gotten a fine coating of mildew, but a vigorous brushing the previous evening had cured that. He dressed rapidly, tying his tie three times before he had it right. He hadn't tied a tie for eight months. Ten minutes later he stepped onto the bridge.

The *Valley* had slowed to fifteen knots, and the horizon ahead was filled with the vast coastline of greater Los Angeles. The sky was brilliant blue, though smudged with smog over the city itself. The *Valley* was surrounded by sailboats and other small craft, and the Captain cursed softly each time one got too close to the bow.

Stuart got up to date on the navigation plot, laid out right past the breakwater to the long dock on the southern end of the naval station. Stuart noted the wind was logged as east-northeast at ten knots, virtually perfect for a straight-in landing. Stuart stepped out onto the bridge wing, and confirmed the chilly wind in his face. Turn your head until both ears are evenly chilled, Lieutenant Commander Donald had told him; you are then facing the wind. More reliable than any instrument. Stuart watched as the sailors in dungarees and the officers in khaki were replaced by officers and men in dress blues. When Preston reported the sea detail manned and ready, Stuart relieved Lieutenant Freitag. "Captain, I have the deck and the conn. Request permission to slow to ten knots."

"Permission granted, William," the old man actually smiled, "permission granted to take her right the way in. We both hope you won't hear further from me until we're firmly tied up."

"Aye, aye, sir! Lee helm, all engines ahead two-thirds, zero-seven-five rpms."

The order was answered. Next Stuart called for maneuvering combination, ready to enter the confined waters inside the breakwater and into the harbor itself.

Many senior officers had crowded onto the starboard bridge wing, chattering and getting in the way, but there was no getting rid of them. Stuart saw Bill Donald and Commander Skelly come up together. Donald smiled and gave Stuart the thumbs-up sign.

As the ship slid past the light at the end of the outer breakwater, Stuart slowed to four knots, and ordered one prolonged blast of the ship's whistle, which meant changing occupation, from underway to in port. The long blast rumbled and echoed back to them. As the bow of the *Valley* passed the inner end of the breakwater, Stuart could see the dock, and the crowd of several thousand people, many waving American flags. I hope Karen is there. If only she could know that it's me driving! A railroad crane was already in position to lift the brows across as soon as the ship was in position.

"Everything going smoothly, William?" asked the Captain, softly. He sounds a little nervous, thought Stuart.

"Aye, aye, Captain." I am a little nervous, too, with everybody on and off the ship watching, but this really should be about the easiest docking I have done yet. "All engines stop."

"All engines are stopped," answered the lee helm.

"Right, five degrees rudder." Stuart wanted to get the bow pointed in toward the dock early, so he could gradually pull the stern into line with tiny increments of left rudder, and contrary orders of the engines.

"My rudder is right five degrees, sir."

"Very well." The bow was swinging nicely, and now was pointed directly at the crane. Stuart estimated the distance to the dock from the bow at three hundred yards. "Rudder amidships."

"My rudder is amidships."

"Left five degrees rudder. Port engine back one-third."

"My rudder is left five," answered the lee helmsman.

Stuart was now conning from the starboard bridge wing, and he was grateful that the chattering senior officers made way for him. The distance to the dock was down to fifty yards, but the ship had almost stopped. The wind was now a factor, shoving the bow off to the right, toward the dock. Stuart felt he had the solution just right, a little power into the wind, and the *Valley* would come to rest against the camels. I bet that crane won't have to move ten feet, he thought. "Port engine stop, starboard engine ahead one-third. Rudder amidships." The big ship glided ever closer, with the starboard engine holding the bow on the wind. When the crane was abreast the forward aircraft elevator, Stuart called all engines stop, and he heard the pop-pop of shot lines being fired, and saw the red padded bolts bounce on the dock to be seized by waiting line handlers. As the first line struck the dock, the Boatswain's Mate of the Watch piped attention, then announced, "Shift colors; the ship is moored," which brought a cheer from the spectators, held back beyond the crane by beribboned sawhorses.

The ship still inched forward as messenger lines were dragged across by the shot lines, and then the heavy hawsers pulled over after the messengers. As soon as the looped ends of the hawsers were dropped over the bollards on the concrete dock, the sailors on the forecastle, the hangar deck, and the fantail began to winch them in, and the *Valley* came to a complete halt. "Sir!" called the talker for the boatswain, "The bos'n says the ship is in position. He requests permission to have the forward brow swung over."

"Permission granted," said Stuart, and sure enough, the crane, its warning bell ringing a welcome, rolled forward about ten feet and dropped the brow. "Captain, request permission to tell Main Control we're finished with engines."

"Permission granted," boomed the captain, pushing himself away from the rail; then, more softly, "Damn fine landing, son."

"Thank you, sir," said William, saluting the captain's receding back. Most of the senior officers followed the captain off the bridge, and Stuart was able to get hold of a pair of binoculars to search the crowd for Karen. "Bos'n's Mate of the Watch?"

"Sir!"

"Secure the special sea and anchor detail, set the in-port watch on the quarterdeck."

"Aye, aye, sir!"

The crane had set the forward and after brows in place, and had rolled away on its rails, its bells ringing cheerfully. The crowd surged forward. Stuart watched the people cross the brow, two abreast. Five minutes into the stampede, he spotted Karen, in a blue and white silk dress, her golden hair shining. He waved, but she was not looking up, and didn't see him.

He passed the binoculars in to Preston, and made his way quickly down the ladders and onto the hangar deck. The quarterdeck was a small area at the end of the brow, with a highly polished linoleum deck and cordoned off with spotless white rope strung between polished five-inch shells. Standing in the center of the quarterdeck, receiving a great deal of attention from the Officer of the Deck, Gordy Mason, and his JOOD, David Epstein, was Karen. She caught William's eye and rushed into his arms.

"Hello, my good love."

"Oh, my god, William, you're really back."

"Tsk, tsk, Ensign, snogging on the holy quarterdeck?" said Mason, in a tone of offended piety.

"Tea and cookies in the wardroom, Mr. Stuart," added Epstein. Stuart flushed, but he saw both men were smiling. He led Karen toward the wardroom.

"William, when can I take you home?" whispered Karen, holding tightly to his arm.

"In a little while. I just want to show you off for a few minutes, then my department head will let us go. I'm as anxious as you are, my love."

"You couldn't be," said Karen, with a smile somewhere between sweetness and lust.

William brushed his face against her fine soft hair ever so briefly. His throat was tight. "Just a few minutes."

Their lovemaking was urgent, almost violent at first, but it soon subsided to the slower, gentler pace they both preferred. They had been in bed in the furnished apartment with the drapes drawn since early afternoon, and now it was fully dark. William felt incongruously hungry, then he remembered that he had not had lunch.

Karen returned from the kitchen with a bottle of champagne and two frosted glasses. William noted that she had abandoned her previous practice of putting on a wrap when walking about, and now moved easily, naked as a wild animal, sensuous beyond any measuring.

Karen filled the glasses, and put the bottle on the bedside table. They clinked glasses and toasted. William became more aware of his hunger. Karen put her glass down, and slid toward the bottom of the bed, stroking his belly and then his thighs with her long, strong fingers. She bowed her head, and kissed his navel. Stuart dozed, spent. He was alert with a jolt as he realized she had taken his limp penis into her mouth. He was shocked and delighted, frightened and ecstatic, as he sprang to full and fat erection. Will I hurt her, he thought? He raised his head from the neck, and saw Karen rolling her tongue around his shaft, across the swollen tip. Her eyes were closed; a moan escaped her lips. He threw back his head onto the pillow, and came violently, grasping Karen's golden head and calling her name.

Karen knelt between his legs, her head on his stomach, cradled in his caressing hands. After minutes of silence, she crawled up his chest and kissed him. "Umm," she said.

"That was a surprise. A nice surprise," said William, his voice weak and his breath short.

Karen rose up, and looked at him quizzically, "Surprise?"

William stroked her hair. "You never did that before."

Again, the questioning look. "I guess I always wanted to, love. Didn't you like it?"

"I loved it, my love, I love everything about you."

She gave him a mocking look, and settled her head back on his chest. A tiny doubt gnawed at his brain. He was sure he had never asked her to do that. Could she have perhaps? . . . He drove the thought away. It was disloyal to his love, and unwelcome in his own mind. It is just so good to be home.

17 January 1967   Camp Pendleton, California

Bobby Coles pushed himself to master all of the skills of a marine, even as he taught new boots the advanced infantry training course. He told himself he *was not* doing it to compensate for living out his life as a marine playing football. He just wanted to be the best prepared in case *they* changed his assignment.

He himself had been sent to a steady stream of special schools. He had been to a school in battlefield medicine, really just advanced first aid with special attention to stabilizing wounds and dressing to prevent infection, and the care of patients suffering from shock. He took a course in spotting artillery and air strikes. He had asked for parachute training, but the Topkick said he had to wait until the end of the football season, since the course took three full weeks out at Twentynine Palms, and worse, might cause an injury. So Coles learned, and taught, and practiced, and played football.

The team continued to win, and Bobby felt that the men were playing better as a team, especially the defense. In the last two games, neither March Air Force Base nor San Diego Naval Station had scored a touchdown. And then the word came down that the camp commandant had been given his third star, and ordered to take up a job in the office of the commandant of the Marine Corps in Washington. The new camp commandant was a young-looking major general who had been deputy commander of the 3d Marine Amphibious Force in Danang.

The day after General Dowd took over, the team had a home game against NAS Miramar, and, naturally, the general came to watch. The joke in the locker room was how do we make ourselves inconspicuous and win a football game at the same time. The men were far too nervous to laugh. No one knew how the new commandant would react to discovering he owned a team of ringers, kept on at Pendleton long after their training programs had been completed. The pessimists assumed that since the general was a Vietnam vet, he probably thought everyone should be one. Sergeant Major Jackson told them just to quit bitching and win the fucking game. The players shrugged and filed onto the sunlit field. Bobby saw the new commandant for the first time, saluting as the ''Star-Spangled Banner'' was played. Morituri te salutamus, thought Bobby, holding his hand salute against his football helmet.

Pendleton won the toss and received the kickoff. After two ineffective running plays, the quarterback, a new kid who had flunked out of Oregon State but who really had an arm, threw a bullet to a fleet black kid called Motor who had taken Billy Hunter's old starting position at tight end. The ball bounced off Motor's shoulder pad and into the arms of a Miramar linebacker. Touchdown. Shit, thought Coles, the offense is so tight it squeaks.

Pendleton received the kickoff again, and once again they failed to move the ball. Coles went in on fourth down and punted, a good, long spiral. Miramar started on offense from their own thirty-seven, and at last Pendleton got to play defense.

It seemed to Coles that the defense was as loose as the offense had been tight. The major strength of the defense was a corps of very fast, strong, and aggressive linebackers. The best of the bunch was a black marine named Lee from Midland, Texas, whom Bobby had come to like. Lee was in the Miramar backfield before the handoff from the quarterback to the tailback was quite completed, and his tackle drove the tailback hard into the ground. The second play was a reverse, which fooled no one on the Pendleton defense, and which was stopped for another loss. Third and eighteen, estimated Bobby, watching the linebackers in front of him shifting in and out between the down linemen as the Miramar quarterback called his signals. If they had had a commentator from a network, thought Bobby, he would have said that Pendleton was ''showing blitz.'' Bobby smiled as the count continued. That quarterback is about to be well and truly welcomed to Camp Pendleton.

The ball was snapped and the quarterback fled from the on-rushing linemen and linebackers. Bobby worked in his zone, keeping an eye on the rest of the coverage. The wide receiver on this side would be Bobby's responsibility, and, as the man feinted out and then turned in, the ball was thrown, hard and accurately. Bobby had to stretch full length, diving over the receiver, to knock the ball down. The receiver grumbled something about interference, and Bobby growled that the pussy should play the whistle. The apathetic crowd of off-duty marines and their wives and girlfriends began to make a little noise.

Fourth down, and the kicking and kick-receiving units came out. Bobby stayed on the field to catch the punt. Punting and catching punts were things he had never done in college, but he liked them. Besides, he knew a lot of young prospects clung to their pro teams through the first few difficult years of adjustment by playing well on special teams.

The kick was short, and very high, so Bobby had to make a fair catch. The offense would have the ball on their own forty-five. Bobby met the quarterback as he trotted out, and stopped him, putting his hands on his shoulder pads. "Just play loose, Lawrence. If the commandant doesn't like ringers, he sure isn't likely to like ringers who don't win!"

Lawrence grinned. "You fuckers just keep backin' 'em up; we'll get it in." They exchanged a hand slap and Bobby left the field. Now he watched the offense begin to play. Lawrence opened up immediately with quick, short passes, mostly timing patterns, and the offense began to move, four consecutive first downs, then a four-yard run for the six. Bobby sat on the bench, getting cold.

Lee sat beside him, watching intently. "Offense looks good, Bro."

"Yeah," said Bobby. "They loose, now."

"They had a meeting while you was catchin' that punt. They decided that if the new commandant decides to dump the team, it wasn't gonna be 'cause the team wasn't good."

Bobby smiled, and his spirits picked up. "Defense oughta go out in a blaze of glory, then, too, hey Bro?"

Lee butted his helmet against Bobby's. His smile was frightening; he was missing about eight teeth in the middle of his mouth. "Right, mothafucka. Offense, that big guard from Grambling, say they gonna cover the spread by halftime."

Coles had heard that Pendleton was favored by the betters by a spread of ten points. "So what do we say, Lee?"

"Total offense for them, running and passing, less than a hundred yards, the whole fuckin' game."

Ambitious, thought Coles. During the last game with Miramar, their quarterback had completed passes for close to two hundred yards and two touchdowns, and they had a good running tailback. "Why not, Bro? Let's get 'em."

Pendleton's place kicker had kicked the ball out of the end zone, and Miramar would start from the twenty. Lee and Coles and the rest of the defense trotted onto the field.

Lee punched Bobby's arm, hard. "Bro, you know what this strategy mean?"

Bobby laughed. "Yeah, it means you front horses are going to be swarming and blitzing all day."

"Right, and it mean any fuckin' ball that motherless white boy manage to squeeze past us gotta be caught, or knocked down, by you brave fuckas back *here*." Lee pointed at the ground at Bobby's feet for emphasis.

"You just stay in his face; the corners and the safeties will do the rest," said Bobby, now very much into the spirit of the game.

"Right," said Lee, as Miramar broke the huddle with a loud clap and came to the line of scrimmage.

Pendleton controlled the game through ferocious intensity. The score was 21–7 at halftime, so the offense made good its boast. Miramar managed total offense of 118 yards, so the defense came up a little short, but no one held it against them. The final score was 38–10. The players laughed and slapped and frolicked in the showers like a high-school team that had just won a state championship.

The commandant received congratulations from the admiral who commanded NAS Miramar, a little coolly, the admiral later remarked. The commandant asked the base personnel officer, Lieutenant Colonel Rogers, seated behind him in the stands, where in his command had all these fine football players come from. Colonel Rogers answered that they were nearly all from the training command. The general observed to himself that if Colonel Rogers had tried any harder to keep expression out of his face, he might just as well have blushed. When he returned to his office, he placed a call to Colonel Emrite, head of the training command, and congratulated him on the fine play of so many of his instructors. Colonel Emrite thanked the general. The commandant then invited the colonel to dinner, asking him to bring with him the service records of all of the players on the team who were attached to his command.

Colonel Emrite sat in the commandant's tiny den, trying to appear relaxed, as the commandant leafed through the last of

the service records. The general had a snifter of brandy and a
cigar in an ashtray next to him. He occasionally puffed at the
cigar, but had barely sipped the fine cognac. Emrite had long
since finished his brandy and wanted another. The commandant
set the last of the records aside, took a tiny sip of brandy, and
looked at the colonel over his reading glasses. "Mike, I see here
we have young marines, bright, most with some college, *three
college graduates*." The general paused, but Emrite did not feel
it was the time to speak. The commandant continued, "*Well
trained*, even *over trained*, mostly noncoms, even sergeants, all
with combat MOSs, and they're all in your command, and they're
a superb, even *professional quality*, football team." Once again
the general paused and Emrite waited. "Doesn't that strike you
as odd, given, Mike, that there is a nasty little war on?" The
general's voice was soft, but the colonel heard an edge of sar-
casm, and he felt his face redden. "Why weren't these men
deployed when their units were, Mike? Instructors shouldn't be
that hard to attract from among more seasoned NCOs."

Emrite took in his breath slowly. Surely the general had figured out that this scheme hadn't originated with training command. "General, these men were kept here at Pendleton to play
football."

The general stared at Emrite without expression. "You signed
the orders that these men be transferred from departing units
into your command."

So that's it. "Yes, sir, I did."

The general took off the half glasses and massaged his nose.
Emrite felt sweat trickling underneath his gabardine shirt, although the room was cold. The general leaned back in his chair,
his cigar in one hand, the other tapping ominously on the stack
of service records on the table beside him. "Colonel Emrite, I
want you to know that if your answers to those two questions
had been anything, *anything*, other than the ones you just gave,
I would have had you out of my command, and even out of the
Marine Corps. Do we understand each other?"

Emrite's throat was so dry he croaked. "Yes, General."

The commandant rose. "Give me your glass, Mike. I'm going
to need your advice as to how to unwind this mess without causing embarrassment to, ah, anyone."

The colonel leaped up, relief bringing a sudden smile to his
face, and held out his brandy glass to be filled. The general
poured slowly, and Emrite willed his hand not to shake.

The general sat, and resumed. "My predecessor took a great
interest in the team, I'm told."

"Yes, sir, he did. I believe, sir, he felt a winning team enhanced the prestige of the camp."

The general laughed, a loud, single bark. It was so unexpected, it made Emrite jump. "Shit, Mike, I've just admired your courage and forthrightness. Don't get political with me and ruin the favorable impression I have of you."

The colonel leaned back, and smiled weakly. He again felt the sweat trickling. "Yes, General."

"OK. Now, I don't suppose there will be any way to get these men back to the units they were assigned to before they, ah, made the team."

"I doubt it, sir. They will have been replaced."

"What we have to figure out, Mike, is how to get these men back into the mainstream of the Marine Corps without giving any suggestion that we're punishing them."

"We could make them available as replacements to field units.'

"Yes, some, maybe, but we don't want them thinking they just got dumped."

The colonel thought for a moment, being careful not to drink his brandy too quickly. "If at least some of them could be induced to volunteer for small, elite units," he let the thought hang between them.

The general smoked and sipped. "Perhaps. Find out what's out there, Mike. I just don't want anyone to think these boys are being dumped because they played ball well enough to serve a somewhat unorthodox need of a commander. Sorry, Mike, you never heard that implied criticism of my predecessor." The commandant smiled. "One other thing. I want to talk to some of these men, to see how they feel about themselves, and the Marine Corps. We really must try to handle this whole situation with great delicacy, Mike."

"Yes, sir, I completely agree." Fuck this up, he thought, and a lieutenant general in the office of the commandant of the Marine Corps gets pissed, and General Dowd and I will be guarding the embassy in Lagos for the rest of our days. "Which ones would you like to see, General?"

"I'll just take three or four at random," said the commandant, pulling several files from the stack. "These."

Emrite took the files from the general's hand. The one on top belonged to Coles, Robert R., Sergeant, USMC. Emrite thanked the general for the fine dinner and left, vowing to himself to do this thing as well as any man could, for his sake, for the men, and especially for the commandant, who probably stood to lose more than any of them if the thing went badly, and whom, Emrite had decided, he immensely liked.

* * *

Colonel Emrite finished explaining the nature of his dinner conversation with General Dowd to the topkick, Sergeant Major Jackson. Jackson looked puzzled, and took his time mulling over the revelations. "So you figure, Colonel, that all these boys goin' to line units?"

"Looks that way, Sergeant Major, nothing for it."

Jackson shrugged. "You know, Colonel, I think some of 'em be glad. These men too proud, too *good*, to be house marines."

"The important thing, Sergeant Major, and I'm echoing the general, is that none of them feel they're being punished. Bad feeling could mean difficulty, for, ah, well, everyone." Emrite smiled weakly.

Jackson grinned. "I hear you, Colonel, sir." He laughed without sound.

"Yeah, well, Sergeant Major, I guess you been covering for officers for most of your life—"

"Twenny-eight years, sir."

"Right. Anyway, the general wants to feel the thing is being done right, so he wants to speak to a sample of the men. The players."

"Who he got in mind, Colonel?"

"He picked four, at random. Take a look," Emrite handed Jackson the four service records.

Jackson opened each record slowly, and set each aside. Coles's was the last record. "Seems all right, Colonel. But this last man, Coles, he's a bit of a hard case. He was drafted to the NFL."

Emrite shifted uneasily. "Do you think he'll act up, Sergeant Major?"

Jackson shrugged again. "Not if I talk to him. I think he feels bad about not goin' up with the one-slash-twenty-six. Besides, he is a smart boy."

Emrite rose. "OK, Sergeant Major, talk to him. Talk to all of them, but don't coach them. This general, General Dowd, when he looks into your eyes, he sees the back of your marine-polished skull."

Jackson chuckled, "I hear you, sir."

General Dowd invited Sergeant Coles to be seated in his small office. Bobby sat at rigid attention while the general relit his pipe. Bobby tried to make himself as calm as possible, but he felt the stress in his body rising with the blue smoke from the general's pipe. The top had warned him that the general was a cold piece—marine corps jargon for a man who could not be read and who could not be fooled. Bobby waited.

The general put his matches aside and tamped down the burning tobacco with an empty rifle shell casing. "Sergeant Coles, I expect you know why you're here."

Coles shifted slightly in the hard chair, trying to gain some space. "Sergeant Major Jackson said you wanted to talk to—some of the men on the team, General. About new assignments." Leave it blank, thought Coles.

The general blew a cloud of sweet-smelling smoke at the roof of the office. "I want to get good assignments for you men, Sergeant. I want you to understand that."

"Yes, sir."

"Well, then, Sergeant, what would you like to do?"

Coles was surprised. He had been expecting to be hustled off to some repple depple—replacement depot—in Vietnam, without further ceremony. "Aren't we to be shipped off to Nam, General? Aren't we viewed, ah, beg the general's pardon, sir—"

"Speak frankly, Marine," said the general, around the pipe.

"—As a bunch of fuck-ups, ah, sir?"

The general seemed to breathe more energy through his pipe, increasing the smog. "Any reason why you should, Sergeant?"

"No, sir! Not to *my* mind, sir!" Sit and wait, he thought.

"Nor to my mind, either, Sergeant. Neither you, nor any of the other *marines*," the general stretched the word, filled it with meaning, "who were assigned to play on that team, have anything to explain."

OK, thought Bobby, warily. "So what should we do, General?"

"You tell me, Sergeant Coles. I have some flexibility in getting you orders."

Bobby relaxed his face into an even, noncommittal smile. "Any black outfits needing ready-mix sergeants, General?"

The general looked into Sergeant Coles's eyes, and saw the edge of defiance and defiance's sister, fear. "There haven't been any segregated outfits since War Two, Sergeant."

This is getting away from me, thought Coles. "I think Nam, General. I think some kind of special unit."

"Why a special unit, Sergeant?"

Bobby flushed with anger, or fear, or something in between. "Because, General, I know now, like I didn't know before, that I'm a *marine*, and I want to prove it, sir." There, dammit, he made me say it.

The general lit the pipe yet again. Each time the smoke was more noxious. "I believe I told you that you have nothing special to prove, Sergeant."

Bobby looked at his hands, clasped tightly against his belt

buckle. I really don't know what I want, he thought, but I don't ever want to feel again that I can't be part of it. The war. He remembered vividly the day his battalion left for Nam, and how they looked and felt, and how apart he had felt. It doesn't matter that no one, other than that asshole Sergeant Phillips, ever criticized my staying here. Marines are proud, he thought, his mind beginning to race. Yes, dammit, I know I'm right. It is fucking crazy, but I'm proud, too. Marine proud. "That's what I would like, General." Bobby listened to his own voice, heard it soft, and proud, and devoid of even the small measure of defiance he had brought into the general's office.

The commandant put the dead pipe down in a big glass ashtray. He looked at Bobby, and for the first time in the course of the interview, smiled in a friendly way. "Good, Sergeant, good. Give me a couple of days. I'll get you into a good outfit. With—" the general paused, and reached slowly across his desk with his hand extended, "my strongest recommendation."

Bobby shook the hand, and jumped up to attention, grinning. "Thank you, sir!"

"Thank you, Sergeant Coles. Good men like you make my job a pleasure."

2 February 1967   Quang Tri Province

Sergeant Billy Hunter took his tepid jungle shower slowly, shivering slightly despite the heat of early afternoon. He suspected the malaria was gaining a bit; it did that, waxed and waned, always there, yet never dominant, at least not yet. Clever parasite, he thought.

The 1st of the 26th Marines was mostly in its "safe" bivouac, called Camp Seven, fifteen kilometers west of Quang Tri City, in the northern end of I Corps. Hunter was leading the pathfinder squad since Sergeant Nigroni had gotten himself killed two weeks previously by tripping a wire. The antivehicle mine Nigroni had tripped had blown away Hammond, the M-60 machine gunner, and the new second lieutenant, Rains, in addition to the sergeant himself. Hunter felt sad about that, to the extent that he could feel anything about anything or anyone, after six weeks of nonstop, long-range recon patrols.

The mission of Hunter's battalion and two others was to work short distances westward along Highway 9, leading from Dong Ha to Khe Sanh in the west and across the border into Laos. The operations were meant to interdict the southward movement of supplies from North Vietnam to the Viet Cong forces who infested the otherwise nearly depopulated jungle. The marines held the coast against considerable opposition, and they held

Khe Sanh, and had held it against attacks that had been occurring for six months. Marine casualties had been steady, and at times heavy. The men speculated that at some point the Joint Chiefs would get the authority, as well as the men and materiel required, to force a passage all the way up Highway 9, and then to hold the road. But for now, there were barely enough resources to cling to the ends of the highway, and to try to cut off the supplies that flowed across the DMZ each night.

While most of the marines operated noisily and in daylight around Quang Tri and the outposts of the Leatherneck Square—the largest of which were Con Thien, Gio Linh, Dong Ha, and Cam Lo—Hunter's long-range recon patrols, or LRRPs, and those of two other units were mostly employed in quiet night operations. The men worked in the inky darkness of the tropical nights, watching road crossings or mining them, seeking out enemy troop concentrations, and more recently, penetrating enemy perimeters all the way to the Ben Hai River, which marked the middle of the DMZ and border between North and South Vietnam. Hunter had heard that the LRRPs might soon be extended beyond the river into the north, tracking movements of enemy men and materiel.

Hunter welcomed the week of respite his unit had been promised by the captain, but he felt as well the draw of the jungle, and of the nighttime battle for the darkness. He stepped from the shower and rubbed himself vigorously with his stowaway dry towel. The shivering stayed with him, but lighter, the fever soft, like the buzz of two strong drinks too quickly taken. Hunter dressed in clean marine greens, transferring only his cigarettes and his sergeant's chevrons from the old and dirty uniform. The brightly polished brass chevrons were pinned on the inside of the breast pocket, and the flap buttoned down over them. Brass chevrons had drawn many a bullet. Hunter stepped out of the latrine and encountered Trace, his leading noncom and machine-gunner. Corporal Trace was a quiet black man, tall and strong, from Nashville, Tennessee. He was a little older than Hunter, and had been in the Marine Corps for two years. Hunter valued the corporal's experience in the field, and the quiet way he helped Hunter learn the ropes of the night war. ''Let's take a walk, Sergeant, ease down.''

Hunter smiled. ''Ease down is good, Trace. Where to?''

''The ville, just outside the wire. Relaxing place, secure.''

''OK. I might could use some relax.''

Trace led Hunter down a steep slope to a collection of three small huts, apparently built on a marine rubbish dump. The huts were constructed of traditional bamboo frames walled with wo-

ven elephant grass, armored with tin cans beaten flat. The roofs
were of pilfered corrugated galvanized steel, and the foundations
were crudely sandbagged. Stretched from roof poles and poles
jutting from the dirt around the hootches were lengths of stolen
marine corps wire, from which hung drying marine corps laundry. Scrawny chickens pecked at imaginary food around the
hootches. Hunter felt uneasy, and thumbed the selector of his
M-14 from safe to fire. "Why are we here, Trace?"

"Relaxation, Sarge. Be cool. Thumb that safety back on."
Trace had his own weapon slung over his shoulder, muzzle
downward. "Ah Loan!" he called into the silent encampment.

Hunter marveled at the lack of voice in Vietnamese farm animals; the whole country hid from the terror of days and especially nights. Hunter looked right and left, and stooped to look
under the hootches. "Ah Loan!" called Trace a second time.

Hunter caught movement in the corner of his left eye and
trained the rifle rapidly. He carefully released the thumb pressure on the safety as he saw that his target was a young Vietnamese woman, a girl, really, standing in the dark doorway of
the largest of the three hootches. Ignoring the rifle leveled at her
heart, she beckoned, wordlessly, for the two marines to enter.
She disappeared inside the hootch. Trace followed her in, and,
after a moment's hesitation, so did Hunter.

The interior of the hootch was dark, and fragrant with incense. Trace was well-known to the occupants. As his eyes became accustomed to the smoky gloom, Hunter made out an old
man, an old woman, and the woman child. Trace engaged them
in urgent, low-toned conversation. The old man cackled and
nodded, and held out his hand. Trace placed a wad of bills in
the hand, which closed like a trap and disappeared inside the
old man's dirty black T-shirt.

"Sit here, Sergeant," said Trace, motioning to a dilapidated
mattress, covered in cheap yellow synthetic fabric. Trace sat on
a mattress opposite, pulling his legs into the lotus position under
him. The girl served the two marines tea as the older people
departed through a curtain wall into the adjoining hootch. The
girl then opened a wooden box inlaid with what appeared to be
mother of pearl, and extracted two long, thin, and expertly rolled
joints. She handed one to Hunter and the other to Trace, and
bowed and left the hootch.

Hunter held the unlit joint in his hand, and then sniffed it. It
was faintly perfumed. "Hey, Trace, man, I don't do drugs. I
mean, never." He continued to hold the joint, and to stare at it.

"It's harmless, man," answered Trace. "We're stood down,

and you're so tight you don't even sleep. Believe me, I'm your friend.''

The girl returned with a coal from the family's cooking fire held between two bamboo tongs. She took the joint from Trace and lit it carefully, inhaling just enough to get it going properly. She then took Hunter's, and lit it. It seemed that her eyes held his as she puffed the flame alive, then gently, wordlessly, placed the stick between his lips. Hunter could not refuse the gift, carried to him as it was in those dark and caressing eyes. He took a soft drag, then a bit more. The smoke was hot in his throat, and dry. He drank some tea, and watched Trace, who surged the smoke deep into his lungs.

Trace sat with his eyes closed, holding the smoke in, then slowly letting it escape through the corners of his mouth. The girl said something to Trace, and he nodded, still letting the smoke slide in thin spirals from the edges of his smile. Once again, the girl disappeared.

Hunter took another drag, and held it in a bit longer. He still felt nothing, but he noticed the incense scent was stronger, and that the details of the furniture in the room were clearer, and seemed to be more in harmony than he first had realized. ''Trace, hey, Trace?''

Trace cracked an eye open. It seemed the maximum effort of which he was capable. ''Relax, Billy, relax, relax.''

Hunter was relaxed, far more so than at any time since he had stepped off the landing craft near Dong Ha, however long ago that was. He took another little smoke. ''Trace, whad-whad is 'is shit?''

Trace smiled. ''You floatin' yet, Bro?''

''Floating. Floating.''

Trace laughed, very slowly. The laugh rolled and echoed in the hootch. The sound of the laugh had the richness of a bass fiddle. ''It's called five-sixths, Bro. Laotian grass, pinch of shaved opium. Harmless, harmless.''

Opium, thought Hunter, man, that is serious. Grass is bad enough, but opium! The joint had burned down to his fingers, and without thinking, he took another long drag before dropping the smoldering end in a cracked plate the girl had left in front of him. He could picture the girl very clearly in his mind, and he wished she would return.

The girl pushed through the curtain holding a teapot and a tray with three tiny china cups, and a fat candle in a holder made from a C-ration can. She placed the tray on the floor, and set the candle midway between Trace and Hunter. Her movements were curiously slow and exact. The skirts of her deep blue *ao dai* swung out like shimmering wings as she whirled with tantalizing slowness, knelt, and served Trace, then Hunter, from the teapot, passing each his cup with both hands, head bowed low. Hunter took the cup, watching her crown of shiny black hair as he did so. He could see each individual, brilliantly shining lock of her hair. How remarkable, he thought.

The drink was hot rice wine, very sweet and viscous. It soothed Hunter's throat from the harshness of the smoke. Once again the girl left the room.

"Hey, Trace, man."

"Hey, Trace, man." Didn't I just say that? thought Hunter. Did I ever say it? Trace was unmoving, across the small room, save for a slight swaying in his lotus position. Was he really swaying? Hunter was confused, yet he felt warm and safe, safe. The girl entered the room, this time carrying two bamboo tubes and two silver knitting needles, and a small rice bowl containing what looked to be black tar.

Hunter watched as the girl gathered the black tar from the bowl on one needle, and held it above the flame of the candle in front of him. Using the other needle to shape it, she slowly incredibly slowly, wound the tar into a ball, and added to it from the bowl, making the ball larger until it was a half inch in diameter. She then set aside the first needle, leaning it against the cracked plate to cool. She started another ball on the second needle, shaping it with her moistened finger and grimacing when the black paste stuck to her finger and burned. Hunter felt pain with her, and raised his hand to help her, but she didn't see him. Finally, she set the second needle, with its black glob of tar on the end, next to the first against the rim of the plate.

The girl floated over to Trace, handed him his wine cup, and waited while he drained it. She then took up one of the knitting needles and squeezed the ball of paste off the end, placing it in a silver cup attached to the side of one of the bamboo tubes. She tilted the cup next to the candle flame and sucked on the top of the bamboo tube. Hunter watched as the ball in the cup became cherry red, and smelled the sweet gray smoke that swirled in the silent room. The girl choked at the smoke in her throat and grimaced again. She handed the bamboo pipe to Trace, who put it to his lips and inhaled, slowly. The pill in the pipe's cup glowed.

The girl floated back to Hunter's side of the hootch, bowed, and offered him wine. He reached out and touched her hair, and she drew away. He wanted to apologize, but he couldn't, because she was holding the cup of wine to his lips. Sweet, sorrow, safe. She lit the second pipe and gave it to him. Watching Trace in the distance, he took a long, slow toke. Sweet smoke, very hot, burned in his throat and lungs, and in his eyes. He closed his eyes against the tears, and floated free, up and out of the hootch. The girl watched him, her face upturned, her eyes wide. Hunter held out his hand to her, but she shook her head. He floated over the fat, muddy Ben Hai River, and realized he was over North Vietnam. He tried to twist his body and turn back south, but he could not control his movement. Below him, he could see columns of men in black and blue uniforms sneaking down trails toward the south. They could easily have shot him, but they never looked up. Hunter floated out over the sea.

Billy felt he must have slept, for he now floated on in the night. Below him in the gray of false dawn were silent fields, and barns and houses, and Billy knew that he was home. He could see the old creek, and his two little brothers at the mouth of the cave where they had fought Indians. Billy shouted, but the two little children were watching the creek, and they did not look up. Billy struggled to break free of whatever was keeping him up, keeping him moving, but he could not. The scene from his boyhood drifted away behind him.

The pace of his movement quickened, and he could no longer see clearly what was below him. He was racing along, rocking from side to side. Ahead he could see a pinpoint of yellow light, which grew rapidly larger as he hurtled toward it. He recognized the light as the flames of the end of time. He felt the searing heat on his face and then he burst through into nothingness.

Hunter woke up in his own bed. His eyes were grainy and his mouth was sour. There was no one else in the hootch. He looked at his watch, six-thirty. Breakfast, he thought abstractly. He raised himself carefully from the cot, feeling nauseated. I wonder how I got back here, he thought. He felt suddenly sick with anxiety. I might have done anything. I've lost most of an afternoon and all of a night. I might have been caught, I don't even know.

Hunter picked up his douche kit and went to the head. There were a few marines still shaving and washing up, but most had gone on to chow. The men he knew said hello to him; nothing seemed out of place. He put his kit on the shelf and stuck his head under the cold water tap to get the cobwebs out. There was a searing pain on his cheek, and he pulled his head back quickly from the water stream. He looked at the cracked strip of mirror, and reached up and touched a red, blistered spot on his face.

"Nasty burn," said Trace, beside him. In a whisper, Trace added, "Let's go to chow, Sergeant. We got to talk a bit."

"Damn straight, Trace. What the hell did you get me into?"

"Not here, man. Everything is cool. Let's get over to the mess tent before all the bacon is gone."

Hunter brushed his teeth and shaved quickly. Fortunately the mysterious burn was above his beard, but the pressure of the razor on his cheek made him weep with pain. "I better get a dressing for this burn."

"Got it right here, Babe. All ready to go, burn ointment and all. Just pat it dry; the blister has burst." Hunter patted his face with the cleanest corner of his towel and Trace expertly taped the gauze pad in place. "Now let's go find us a quiet corner and get some eats. You must be hungry, after all that sleep."

Hunter followed Trace across the dusty grinder to the mess tent. He was aching to question Trace, but he understood the wisdom of waiting until they could get into a reasonably private spot. Trace's apparent lack of concern was by itself reassuring. Billy's stomach was still churning, but when he got in front of the cooks serving scrambled eggs and bacon, he found he was indeed hungry, and he took a generous portion. He followed Trace to a table at the far end that was just being vacated by a group of marines from Headquarters Company. Hunter and Trace exchanged greetings with the departing group and then had the table to themselves.

Trace took a swallow of coffee and said softly, "You gave me a bit of a scare last night, Sergeant Billy."

"I don't remember a thing. What the fuck happened?" Billy started eating. His appetite was enormous.

Trace touched a finger to his own cheek quickly. "Among other things, you keeled over into the candle. Little Nga had to pull you out."

"Jesus," said Billy, eating.

"And you were raving something about the flames of the end of time."

Hunter drank some coffee. His senses seemed especially keen. He wondered if the drug had completely worn off. "How did I get back to camp?"

"You walked, with me by your side."

"Jesus! Do you think anybody saw us?"

"Lots of people saw us. It was eight o'clock at night. We didn't run around naked, or bay at the moon; we just walked in. You were very quiet, and a little scared, I think. You kept asking me to hold you down if you started to float away."

"Christ, I don't remember any of this."

"You must have taken too much, too fast. And I shoulda warned you, 'cause I know you ain't been sleeping."

"How did it affect you?"

Trace shrugged. "Just very mellow, very relaxed, man. I had another pipe while you slept; then we walked back, took a shower, and I put you to bed. I dumped your uniform, by the way, because it reeked of smoke."

"Jesus, well, thanks for taking care of me, but we are not going to do that again. We coulda got caught and spent the rest of our natural lives in some brig."

Trace looked at Billy hard, the corners of his mouth pinching with anger. "Now, *look*, asshole, I was right there, I took care of you. You needed to relax, and if nothing else, you got around ten hours of sleep. You are my friend and my squad leader, and you need to relax."

Hunter looked at Trace. "I guess you're right, I have been awfully tight since the sergeant and that lieutenant got blown away. But I'm not sure I could handle another experience quite like that."

"Next time you will know to go slow."

Not for me, thought Billy. "That little girl sure was pretty."

Trace grinned. "She says she's seventeen. She liked you too; she cried when you burned her face. I promised to bring you back."

I will go back, then, but not for the dope, at least not for the serious dope, but to see Nga. Pretty name, I wonder what it means?

"It means moon," said Trace, grinning.

"What?" asked Billy.

"Nga means moon, Sergeant. Now, Sergeant, we have a war to run." Trace got up and took his empty tray in one hand and Hunter's in the other. Billy swallowed the last of his coffee, and followed.

Billy leaned back and closed his eyes, feeling the laced-up joint of five-sixths take effect, turning his mind loose to follow trails that passed from I Corps to anywhere. Nga lay with her head in his lap, warm and half asleep. Trace had gone off with one of the older girls, after giving the grinning Ah Loan more money. At first, Billy had wanted to sleep with Nga, but after Ah Loan had told him she was a virgin and therefore worth five hundred American dollars, he had decided he liked the idea of her virginity. Ah Loan continued to leer and make gestures of obvious meaning at Billy, but Billy just smiled. Fuck Ah Loan, he thought, drifting through the jungle night.

Since his first frightening experience, Billy had stayed well away from the pure opium. One, or at the most two of the tight, thin joints of five-sixths gave him all the space and relaxation he needed, and he felt he could almost direct his fantasy flights. He also thought he could come back down quickly if need be, though he didn't risk smoking unless he was sure his patrol squad was stood down for at least the next day. His refusal of the opium pipe irritated Ah Loan, who complained that the price of two joints hardly paid for his hospitality, and certainly not for the attendance of his prettiest "daughter." Fuck Ah Loan. Billy stroked Nga's lightly perfumed hair.

The problem is that the old bastard knows I really come here for the girl, and not for the dope, thought Billy, and sooner or later he is going to put the squeeze on me, somehow. Nga crawled up his arm and kissed him lightly, her lips closed, a child's kiss. "Mo' wine, Bi-lee?" she whispered, hugging him around his neck.

"No, my love, just stay with me."

"Yes, Bi-lee." She settled down again, her cheek against his groin. He felt himself stirring as Nga innocently, perhaps unknowingly, placed her tiny hand on his penis, which uncurled itself painfully inside his trousers. He dared not reach down to free it lest he break the spell. He forced his mind away from his body, and the painful fullness subsided. He drifted, the image of the innocent lady moon in his lap alternating with that of the leering, yellow-eyed, gap-toothed Ah Loan. Billy wished he could get the girl away from the old panderer before he did manage to get his filthy five hundred American dollars from some corrupt Vietnamese general. He knew no marine would come up with it; marines didn't care about virginity, unless, like Billy, they respected it, and the other women would do everything imaginable for five American dollars, boom-boom. Billy was getting decidedly unrelaxed, and was considering having the second joint, when the sound of hands clapping sharply, once, twice, intruded on the perfect silence of the little room. Nga got up quickly and darted through the dirty beaded curtain that separated the room from the main house.

Damn Ah Loan, thought Billy, reaching inside his trousers to straighten out his semihard penis.

Billy heard the sounds of argument from beyond the curtain—Ah Loan's gruff singsong and Nga's softer replies. What does the old dickhead want now, thought Billy, fully awake and pissed off. Nga came back into the room, her head bowed, and knelt beside Billy. He could see she was crying. "What is it, my lady moon?"

"Ah Loan say time up, you must go, Bi-lee."

"Why? What's the hurry, Nga?"

"Ah Loan say, you no smoke, you no drink, you no make

boom-boom, he lose too muchee monee, Bi-lee.'' She put her arms around his neck and gave him one of her dry kisses. He brushed her tears away gently with his calloused fingers.

Here comes the squeeze, thought Billy. ''Tell Ah Loan I want to speak with him, Nga.''

''He angry, Bi-lee.''

''Tell him to come in, please, Nga.''

''Yes, Bi-lee. Bi-lee, you not leave Nga, please?''

Billy's heart rolled over. I can't possibly be in love with this Asian child, but I am. ''No, Nga, I won't leave you.'' She was crying again. ''I will speak with Ah Loan.'' Nga got up and left the room. There was another noisy conversation, and Ah Loan entered the small room, his face set in theatrical anger.

Billy decided to wait until the other man spoke. Ah Loan seemed to have the same expectation, so for a moment the two men studied each other as Ah Loan arranged himself carefully on the mattress across the room. Billy decided it would be polite to begin. ''Your daughter says I have offended your house, Thich Loan.''

Ah Loan's set visage softened slightly at Billy's use of the wholly inappropriate honorific, which meant ''venerable.'' ''Sergeant! You spend all time with youngest daughta, not take pipe, not take muchee drink, no make boom-boom otha daughta! Ah Loan you friend, all time, but must have business!'' Once again he twisted his face into an exaggerated scowl.

Hunter said, ''Why don't you charge me a fee for the time I spend here?'' He had suggested this before.

''No good! Otha marine, they no come, they know all time youngest daughta with Sergeant Hunta. *No* come, *no* spend money! Old Loan, old wife, all daughta all starve.'' Ah Loan leaned forward, with a big, sad frown, and spread his hands like a supplicant. The greedy bastard must have millions, thought Billy.

''So you don't want me to come any more.''

''Not if no can spend money, enjoy *all* hospitality of Ah Loan.''

''I couldn't spend so much money every time I come. A sergeant doesn't get much.'' I'll bet he knows to the penny what my pay comes to, thought Hunter.

''Maybe sergeant can get mo' money.'' Once again Ah Loan leaned forward, but this time his expression was pure greed. ''Maybe Ah Loan can help.''

I shouldn't even listen to this, thought Billy. There has to be a way I can keep seeing Nga, but I can't have anything to do with this old thief. ''How might that be, Ah Loan?''

Ah Loan grinned, revealing his prized gold teeth. "Ah Loan thinking, Sergeant, this place of Ah Loan special. Only fliends of Ah Loan can come, people tlusted, no bad tlouble from camp. But Ah Loan know many marine smoke glass, one, two joint." Billy knew that was true. The stuff was everywhere, and as long as nobody used too much, or used it on duty or in the field, nobody said anything. "Maybe Ah Loan get mo' glass, not so good as Ah Loan have here, this place. Maybe sergeant can sell to marines."

"I couldn't do that, Ah Loan." I wonder if I could, thought Hunter.

"Make muchee money, come all time see youngest daughta."

They get it somewhere, thought Hunter, so where's the harm? Still, I don't want to be a pusher for this old crook. "How much would I have to sell?"

Ah Loan shrugged. "Start slow, careful. No muchee."

No muchee, thought Billy. That's where it *starts*. There has to be another way. He stood up, and put on his shapeless jungle hat. "Maybe I'll think about it."

"Maybe make enough money buy Nga virgin price."

"I'll think about it, Ah Loan." I am in a box, thought Hunter.

Ah Loan rose, rubbed stiffness from his legs. "Take time, think *here*, have one mo' smoke, guest of Ah Loan. Sit, fliend Sergeant Hunta, I send youngest daughta." Before Billy could answer, Ah Loan slipped through the curtain. Billy sat.

Nga reappeared with the joint and a teakettle full of hot rice wine. She looked radiantly happy. She chattered and rubbed the tense muscles of Billy's neck while he smoked. Billy relaxed. How bad could it be, he thought. If I do it carefully, nobody gets hurt, and I can be with Nga. If Ah Loan ups the ante, I can get out. I'd lose Nga, but I lose her anyway if I don't go along. But it is dealing.

Nga took the roach from his fingers before it could burn him, then pushed him onto his back. She crawled on top of him and kissed him on the lips, a slightly more adult kiss, her mouth partly open. Billy touched her lips with his tongue. She moaned a little, and shifted her body on top of his, and gently nibbled his tongue with her lips. Billy's penis straightened out and swelled, pushing against Nga's thigh. When her hand found his engorged member through his trousers, Billy knew it was no accident. Her mouth opened and engulfed his tongue.

Billy found himself fighting against the effects of the joint. Part of him wanted to make love to Nga; part of him wanted to preserve her chastity. He felt too weak to do either. Nga took her sweet lips from his. He realized she was unbuttoning his trousers. A protest arose in his mind and died in his throat.

Slowly, awkwardly, Nga unbuttoned his fly and jerked his penis free. If he had been wearing underwear, she never would have managed it. Billy lay back, and covered his eyes with his left arm, torn between ecstasy and remorse. Nga began to jerk him off, not the way he would have done it himself, holding his dick in a fist, but with her hand on top of it, fingers downward, like a spider caressing the very tip of it. Billy squirmed with pleasure and pain. Her other hand grasped his shaft around its base while the fingers floated and danced at the tip, teasing, caressing. She leaned across his chest and kissed his neck. "Bi-lee."

"Yes, my lady moon," rasped Hunter.

"Bi-lee, I love you. I want to give you my virginity."

Hunter came, explosively. The juice sprayed everywhere, on his face, and hers. Gently, she let his penis fall from her hands, leaving it wilting on his stomach. She took the towel from the tray, and gently dabbed at his face, then hers, then at his uniform. "Bi-lee, I love you."

Billy's head was clearing rapidly. He put his arm around Nga's neck and drew her to him, gently. She kissed him on the lips, and once again, he explored her soft mouth with his tongue. "Nga, I love you too." He held her in his arms until the dope and the spell receded, and then he dressed, went through the curtain, and told Ah Loan that he would deal marijuana.

3 March 1967   Camp Seven

Sergeant Hunter led his patrol squad out of the camp in the early afternoon. They still hadn't replaced Rains, the second lieutenant who had gotten killed. Hunter could hardly remember what he looked like. Replacements had come in for the two riflemen killed in the same action, but Sergeant Nigroni's billet was still empty, so they were only nine leaving camp, heading for the foggy hills and jungle-choked creek beds of the dead marine zone.

The men of the LRRPs considered themselves special, different from the troops who moved in the light. Hunter watched as the men took up single-file patrol alignment, without any spoken commands. Trace took the point, with the M-60 machine gun. Once in the jungle, he would watch the ground in front of him for trip wires and other booby traps. The second man, Capiello, looked up, for wires in the trees. The third man, Phillips, one of the cherries, looked right, and Stevens, behind him, looked left. Hunter walked fifth, with Jonas, the other replacement, behind him, humping the radio. Seventh, Stinson, looked right, and eighth, Da Silva, looked left. Smith, the drag man, the marine with the most experience in the LRRPs after Trace, walked backward much of the time, watching their rear. Each man except Trace carried the clumsy fourteen-pound M-14 rifle and two bandoliers of ammunition magazines. The Army had the new, lighter M-16, but the marines still humped the fourteen. More accurate, the old-timers said. Still, Hunter would have liked the extra firepower of the newer weapon, with its lighter ammo and higher rate of fire.

Each man carried a light battle pack, which weighed about half the standard infantry pack at thirty pounds, and two big canteens of water. Jonas was additionally burdened with the bulky PRC-10 radio, but the other guys divided up most of his extra ammo, and Stinson carried the radio's extra battery. Each man other than Jonas carried a Claymore mine and either a machete or an entrenching tool, a small spade that could be set at an angle to its shaft and used like a pick. Phillips carried detonators, both screw-type and claquers. Da Silva carried the hundred-fifty-foot roll of detonation cord, a kind of linear plastic explosive, and a roll of insulated wire nearly half a mile long, which could be used to make both trip wires and detonation connectors. The top of Stevens's pack held eight wrapped one-pound bricks of C-4 plastic explosive. Fragmentation and smoke grenades rounded out the outfit.

Hunter found it ironic that his nightcrawlers carried less gear than the marines who moved by day, and who could expect to be resupplied in the field by helicopter, usually no less often than every other day. The main force marines would carry four or even more bulky one-quart canteens, because they didn't trust the water in the streams. The LRRPs didn't trust the water either, but since they couldn't possibly carry enough to last an entire mission, they drank stream water heavily salted with water-purification pills, and resigned themselves to having the shits. Similarly, the nightcrawlers preferred dried rations, most of which had to be cooked, to the heavier, bulkier canned C-rations the others carried.

The LRRPs looked like normal marines, except for two small differences. The LRRPs had been issued the new canvas-sided jungle boots, while the rest of the battalion still wore leather, which turned sodden and rotted in the jungle. In addition, the nightcrawlers wore shapeless hats of green camouflage cloth, eschewing the protection of the steel helmet because it was thought the harsh outline was too easy to see in the jungle, even with leaves stuck in the fabric helmet cover. Before going out, Trace checked every man's gear, even Hunter's, for anything that could rattle or clank as the men moved.

Hunter didn't like walking the middle. The officer should be there, next to the radio, and the VC knew it, so the radio antenna made a popular aiming point during an ambush. By rights,

Hunter should have been back with the drag man. Hunter didn't like talking on the radio. Hunter didn't like having the responsibility of command.

The men walked in silence. As soon as they passed out of the cleared zone outside the camp's barbed wire perimeter, they were in territory claimed by the enemy and, at least at night, patrolled by him.

Hunter thought about the mission. The first night they were to set up an ambush at the intersection of two trails the intelligence types said had been getting a lot of traffic. Both trails led south from North Vietnam, and were used by the 219th NVA Division to support and resupply the Viet Cong units that operated in the area near the strong points of the Leatherneck Square. The nightcrawlers would mine the crossing with Claymores, and observe as best they could. The unit was too small and too lightly armed to get into a firefight even with a supply column.

The second part of the mission was more tricky. If activity was detected on the first night, the patrol was to follow the most promising of the two trails, to determine where it crossed the river and how. Hunter had been told that the NVA built packed gravel roads on the bottom of the shallow, slow-moving Ben Hai, but he had never seen one. Rumor control even alleged that the NVA had tanks that could cross over these bridges to attack the marines in their camps. Hunter, who had crossed the area many times, scoffed at this; the jungle trails were passable at best for a bicycle. Moss, the grizzled lifer topkick up at Headquarters Company, said that the RAMF experts had made the same judgment about the Ardennes Forest at the beginning of War Two.

If the patrol located a significant crossing, they were to conceal special devices at either end. The briefing officer had told Hunter that the devices would just sit there until activated by a radio signal from an air force B-52, after which they would signal the precise location of the bridge, which was otherwise invisible from above. The need to mark both ends meant that the unit, or at least part of it, would have to cross the river into North Vietnam. Hunter hoped they wouldn't find any bridges.

The men walked deeper into the damp jungle in silence, spacing themselves two meters apart, watching where they stepped. There was plenty of time; their first objective was only five kilometers from the camp, and most of the walking was downhill. They reached the first of the trails at 1545, and followed it north to an intersection with what looked to be a much larger trail. They had followed the smaller trail south on previous patrols,

but they had never been this far north, and they hadn't seen the
larger trail before. The men dropped their packs by the side of
the road, and fanned out cautiously. The larger trail was about
ten feet wide and well packed down. Maybe a track for a jeep,
if not a tank, thought Hunter. There were marks of recent clearing on the trees and creepers. Looking up, Hunter could see that
in some places branches from trees on opposite sides of the trail
had been pulled together and tied, adding to the difficulty of
spotting the trail from the air. Hunter heard a low whistle, and
turned to find Phillips pointing at something beside the road with
his rifle. Hunter squatted and looked, pleased that even the
cherry knew not to touch anything found in the bush. The object
was a rubber sandal, the kind worn by VC and peasants alike,
but there was no reason for a peasant to be anywhere near this
place.

"Trace," whispered Hunter. The machine-gunner joined him.

"VC shoe," said Trace.

"They don't leave them around."

Trace circled the rubber sandal with his machete. "No wire
that I can find."

"No? What do you think?"

Trace looked at Hunter, then at the jungle surrounding them.
It was still early afternoon, yet the light level was dropping.
"Trap. They left this for us to find."

"Do you think the VC know we're here, Trace?" asked Phillips, his face taut.

"Sure they do. We know they're here, they gotta know we're
around. Whaddya think, Sergeant?"

Hunter drew in a breath, then let it out slowly. He wasn't
afraid of command; he just felt he had never been prepared for
it. "I say we change the plan. For some reason, the VC have
left us a sign that they've been here. They never do that, except
to set a trap."

"So what do we do?" asked Phillips.

Hunter fought back a mild anger. In time, the cherry would
learn not to ask. "We move the ambush." He looked at his
watch. "We have at least two and a half hours of daylight. Let's
follow the big trail north, find a better place."

"We gonna stay on the road?" asked Trace.

"No, we'll slide through the bush, and follow the ridge line
and the stream that shapes this track. What we do best, nightcrawlers."

Trace grinned, "Aye, aye, *Sergeant*!" Trace hated roads.

Hunter smiled. Trace always guided him, but never obviously.
How I wish for some nice young officer for me to guide, then

leave to him the awful decisions. "Move out, quietly, men. Let's get up near that ridge line, without showing ourselves." The unit moved off with silence restored, Da Silva now at point. Trace had moved back to fourth, in front of Hunter. Hunter spoke in a whisper that wouldn't carry. "Trace we need a straight stretch, with a turn, so we can observe. This is a heavy-duty trail."

"Yeah. Basic chicken-leg ambush. What do you think we might catch?"

"No idea. I keep thinking about old Moss. Vehicles, at least light ones, could move down this trail."

"Maybe we should just mark that crossing with those air force doodads, and di-di-mau back to camp."

Hunter thought about it for only a moment. "No. We're good, Trace. We can set up a mechanical ambush, and watch what goes through. If need be, we can slip out." Trace looked proud and skeptical at the same time. "We can, Trace."

The patrol slipped slowly through the thickening jungle. Only by moving slowly could the men move in silence. They stayed well below the crest of the ridge. They were able to see the road through the jungle only occasionally, but they could see enough to follow it. It was important not to leave any sign of their presence on the road itself to alert the enemy.

After nearly an hour of snail-like progress, they reached a sharp bend in the trail, dictated by a rocky outcropping that had shifted the course of the small stream's flow toward the Ben Hai. The patrol carefully glided from the jungle back to the edge of the road.

"Almost perfect," said Trace.

"Yeah. We can set it up a hundred meters away, on the bend, and watch it from the straight," counseled Smith.

"Trace, take two men, and chart our routes of escape, if we have to pull back into the jungle," whispered Hunter. "Smith, scout the ambush site, and if it looks OK, rig it."

Trace pointed at Phillips and Capiello, and disappeared noiselessly into the damp jungle. Smith took the rest of the patrol save Jonas and Da Silva, and headed for the ambush site one hundred meters away. His detachment kept well away from the trail itself. Hunter, Da Silva, and Jonas waited fully ten minutes before they could see Smith cross the road with a Claymore in his hand, trailing, then burying, wire. Stevens crossed quickly, carrying the det cord. Smith wired the charges, then scored the packed earth surface of the road, and buried a second wire. Hunter watched through his night binoculars, admiring the way the ambush was planned, even though he could not see everything that Smith was doing.

Smith had chosen a place on the trail where it bent as the stream bent. Above the curving streambed and next to the trail was a large tree, which had prominent roots standing out from its base. Smith wedged a Claymore in the cleft between two roots, about knee-high, where it wouldn't be seen by anyone coming down the trail until he was directly in front of the mine. Without seeing it done, Hunter knew that the other four Claymores Smith had collected would be arranged on the opposite side of the trail, around the outside of the same curve, and would be on a separate detonator circuit. The det cord, on a third circuit, would be laid in the streambed behind the big tree. Hunter watched through the binoculars as Smith and the others completed the layout, and swept up every trace of their activity with branches they had cut from trees growing well away from the trail.

Trace returned to Hunter's side. "We can get up and out of here due west, Billy," he whispered. "There's a shallow cave just up the back, here. We can see the road and shoot it, if we want."

"Show me," said Hunter.

Trace picked up the M-60 and turned back into the jungle, with Hunter following. Soon they reached the cave, some ten meters back and three meters above the road. The path could be easily seen, and commanded from the cave, while the vegetation would partially mask much of the patrol's muzzle flashes, even at night. "Pretty nice, hey, Sarge?"

Hunter liked it. The jungle behind the cave was thick; they could lose themselves quickly if pursued, and the machine gun could drive anyone off the trail. The dinks couldn't really have tanks, he thought. "Set up the machine gun here, Trace."

Trace smiled. "Aye, Billy."

Trace, Phillips, and Capiello, with some help from Da Silva, set about making up the night defensive position, or NDP. They broke out entrenching tools and dug a shallow pit at the entrance to the cave, to hide their gear. Nightcrawlers stood their night watches light and ready to move. They built earth barriers to hide and protect the machine gun, and they filled canteens from the green, decay-smelling stream. Jonas answered a call from the company headquarters for a position report with a single press click on the microphone switch, which meant the patrol was on its night position. Which isn't entirely true, thought Hunter.

Smith, whistling softly to announce his approach, entered the NDP. "Ambush is all laid out, Sergeant, good and proper, as the Aussies say."

"You walk it around, Smith?"

"Yeah, Sarge, me an' the kids walked the whole perimeter; no less than a hundred meters from the road, around the ambush, and this position. Reckon we oughta put out our remaining Claymores in front of the NDP, pointed toward the road?"

"Done," murmured Trace from the lowest point in the dug-in position, where supper was being organized.

Smith grinned, and deferred to Trace, "Sorry, pardner, didn't mean to step in."

"The sergeant is drivin', Smith." Trace and Smith exchanged a glance. The two men had different feelings about cherry sergeants.

Billy spoke. "Let's get supper on. Nearly fully dark. Trace, set a perimeter watch."

"Aye, Sergeant." Trace motioned to Da Silva and Jonas. Jonas unloaded the heavy radio gratefully, picked up his M-14, and followed Da Silva to the mouth of the cave, the edge of the falling darkness.

Capiello had become, by consensus, the cook for the team. From all the men's packs he assembled the basics for a meal—dry spaghetti, canned tomato paste, dried cheese, and dried peas. He boiled water from a canteen in the patrol's one cooking pot. The men would drink the fetid jungle water, but they wouldn't eat food prepared in it. The fire was made of shavings carefully carved from a block of C-4 explosive; it burned quickly but very hot, with an acrid chemical smell that dissipated rapidly but with no smoke. In five minutes Capiello had the spaghetti cooking in rapidly boiling water, with the cans of tomato paste resting in the water above the softening spaghetti. At the right moment, he tossed the dried peas into the water with the spaghetti, and shortly after, added the cheese to the bubbling tomato paste. "Um, um," said Capiello, tasting, "that's Italian." The meal was doled out reverently into the men's mess kits, and consumed in silence.

"Damn good, Cap," said Hunter. The others murmured praise. The men finished quickly, and washed their utensils and the cooking pot in creek sand, and rinsed with water. The night watches were set as darkness closed on the jungle like a shroud.

Trace awakened Hunter from a doze. "Sergeant, Smith thinks he sees some activity near the ambush."

Hunter was instantly alert. "Coming down from the north?"

"He says they came from the south. Says they're just sitting there, under our tree."

Hunter stood up quietly, and picked up his night binoculars and his M-14. "Let's go have a look."

Trace and Hunter joined Smith at the machine gun. The rest of the men in camp awakened and silently checked their equipment. Hunter steadied his night glasses on the earthwork next to the machine gun, and trained the glasses slowly back and forth across the road. The darkness was inky, and at first he could see nothing. Then he saw a flicker of movement, slightly grayish, and as his eyes completed their adjustment of the darkness, he could see a group of men squatting just off the trail. "Jesus, they're right on top of the first Claymore."

"Yeah," said Smith. "A trained man might find it, if he was lookin', but it's pretty well hidden by the cleft between the roots, and we dumped a lotta leaves and shit all over it." Smith moved closer to Hunter as Trace took over the M-60. "Do we blow it, Sarge?"

Hunter continued to peer through the big eyes. "You say these gooks came from the south?"

Smith whispered, "They couldn't have come from the north, Sarge, they would have had to pass right in front of me. Really, it seemed to me that they just appeared there."

"Coolies?" offered Trace.

"Probably," said Hunter. "Waiting for a load of something to come down from the north." He put the binoculars aside. "Smith, take me through the ambush plan once more."

Smith slid over to the right of the machine gun where the detonators were laid out in a neat row. "OK, Sarge. Me, I always do them right to left. The first one blows the Claymore at the base of the tree. The second blows four Claymores laid out on the other side of the road at about seven-meter intervals, except there's a gap about twice that wide across the field of the first Claymore."

"Good," said Hunter, "Pick up a whole section with that, if they bunch." Which they won't, he continued the thought. Still, if all five mines fired when pulled, the whole road would become a killing zone for a distance of thirty to forty meters on either side of the tree.

"Yeah, thanks, Sarge. I figure we should be ready for a big force. We get a coupla guys only, we just blow the first Clay, an' we can dig up the rest in the morning."

"Yeah, maybe. Let's see who else shows up. What more you got?"

"Well," resumed Smith, "we packed the gap between two o'

the roots on the other side of the tree with C-four, and rolled a rotted log on top of it. That's on the same circuit as the four Clays on this side of the road. I figure the tree should fall right across the road, dividing whatever force is out there in two.''

Clever, though Hunter, taking another look through the night glasses. The coolies, if that's who they were, had not moved. "You sure that big tree will fall on the road, Smith?''

"I couldn't say for sure, Sarge. If'n I had a coupla sandbags, then for sure, but the log is just kinda wedged on top of the plastic. Lotta blast might just go straight up.''

Hunter digested that. It would be nice to be sure of the tree, especially if vehicles did appear, but he knew Smith was as good at making shaped charges in the field as anybody in the battalion. "What about the det cord?''

"Third screwgee, Sarge,'' said Smith. Screwgee was a nickname for the screw detonators. "There's det cord laid out continuously from twenty meters the other side o' the tree, a good forty meters this side. Any gook the Clays don't get who jumps down into that creek is history.''

Blown to catsup, mused Hunter. Blown to bits and pieces no bigger than a hand. The thought made him feel slightly queasy. "And the fourth detonator?''

"That's Trace's,'' said Smith.

"I got two Clays facing north, about ten meters up the trail from the bend we're looking at. I got one more facing east, back toward Smith's setup, on a claquer,'' whispered Trace.

"So, we wait,'' said Hunter. And *they* wait, and patrol, and some of them are waiting for us, and looking for us, and if we wait too long, they will find us.

"Sarge,'' whispered Capiello, "Trace says come up.''

"Right,'' whispered Hunter, looking at his watch—0200, my turn to watch. Moving quickly but quietly, he slid to his belly beside the machine gun. He was about to adjust the night glasses when Trace placed his hand on his, pushing the glasses down quietly. Trace pointed straight ahead.

Hunter's heart stopped, then began to race. Not ten feet away, between their position and the road, was a man, silhouetted in the dim light. The shape disappeared and was immediately replaced by another. Like the first, the second man held the distinctive shape of an AK-47 at the ready. As did the third man, and the fourth. They followed each other with a curious swaying motion, which Hunter thought must make it possible for them to avoid scraping against branches. Hunter's straining ears could pick up no sound, other than the roaring of his own breathing. The column ended as the last man disappeared from view.

On their heads, the apparitions wore the shapes of pith helmets with narrow brims. Hunter looked at Trace, who looked back. Trace mouthed the letters, NVA. Hunter nodded. The VC wore flatter, conical straw hats, or no hats at all. These men were regular troops of the North Vietnamese Army. Hunter gave Trace the hand sign that meant how many. Trace opened and closed his free hand six times, then held up two fingers. Thirty-two, and doubtless not alone, thought Hunter.

Minutes passed that seemed like hours. Hunter consulted his watch twice before 0210. Just as Hunter felt he was getting his breathing under control, he heard a squeaking sound, as a squad of soldiers moved down the road, pushing a heavily laden cart that looked like it could float like a barge. These soldiers were on the road surface, and were not being at all quiet. I wonder how far ahead the NVA patrol is, thought Hunter. He looked through the binoculars without raising them from the earthwork. He didn't see the soldiers, but he could see that the coolies had abandoned their positions next to the tree, and were standing in the middle of the road. He could also see that they weren't all coolies. Jesus, he thought, whatever deal is going down, it is going to happen right under my tree. Then he heard a sound from up the road that was unmistakably the noise of a vehicle grinding in low gear. Holy shit, not a tank, prayed Hunter, not a fucking tank.

Trace gripped his arm. His face looked pinched with fear. "What the fuck we gonna do, Billy? We can't blow it, there's hundreds o' the fuckers comin' down the road!"

"We wait, Trace. I hear a vehicle, but I think only one. Hang on." Hunter felt Trace's grip relax, and the corporal turned back to the machine gun. Through the leaves in front of them, Hunter could make out a truck about the size of a marine six by six, with a star painted on the near door. In the darkness, the star looked black against the gray truck body, but Billy felt sure it was red. The truck labored under a heavy load of what looked like crates. Billy could see stacks of 82mm mortars on the tailgate of the vehicle, tubes on one side, base plates on the other.

The truck labored past, moving at the same speed as the slow-walking soldiers beside it, and stopped right in front of the tree. Men swarmed over it to begin to off-load. A soldier lit a dim lantern to assist the identification of the various crates. "Blow it," whispered Sergeant Hunter. Smith twisted the first detonator, and an ear-splitting explosion shattered the darkness and silence of the night.

The initial explosion seemed to freeze the action in its brilliant flash of light. The truck rocked as it took the impact of the shrapnel, and the man who had been on top of the load flew away in an odd cartwheeling motion. The truck's fuel tank blew up just as Smith twisted off the second detonator. Hunter was blinded as the four Claymores poured white-hot shrapnel into the mass of the working party. The tree fell forward across the road, striking the front of the burning truck, knocking it back toward the LRRPs. Hunter's head rang as he struggled up the face of the earthwork with the night binoculars.

"Sarge," asked Smith, "OK to blow the det cord?"

"Go ahead, I sure don't see anyone moving around up there." There was a flat report and a pale flash in the trees beyond the road as the det cord detonated. For the first time, Hunter heard a man scream.

"We gotta di-di, Hunter," said Trace, urgently.

"No shit. Can you rig the last Claymores to trip wires?"

"Already done. Smith, can you shift the leads from my Clays? Put the taped ones on the battery box."

"Gotcha covered."

From north, up the road, came more vehicle sounds, and sounds of men running and shouting. The enemy soldiers began pouring thick bursts of automatic weapons fire into the jungle on both sides of the road. Hunter turned to count his men. "We got time to pick up our extra gear, Sarge?" whispered Capiello.

Hunter heard a distant pop and heard the breathy whistle of a mortar round. He held his breath. There was a loud crash as the mortar round landed in behind their position. "Just weapons and canteens. Get moving. Trace, take point. Smith, take the M-sixty and the drag and cover our asses. Nobody fires unless we're spotted." Heavy machine gun fire raked overhead, causing a fine rain of wet vegetation. "*Go*, Trace!"

The patrol moved off swiftly along the route Trace had scouted earlier. Silence was no longer necessary, but the nightcrawlers still made far less noise than a normal column. Hunter had to admire the way his men kept going, not tripping despite the darkness. Every hazard found by a man was pointed out to the man behind him as the column flowed, feeling its way, but rapidly leaving the sound of machine gun firing behind them. There was a sharp double bang as two of Trace's Claymores were tripped, and followed immediately by much heavier firing, now far behind them.

As they marched, Hunter got on the radio and called their control in the camp. They were supposed to be radio silent during the mission, but Hunter figured the enemy knew for sure about where they were by now. He gave the grid coordinates of the ambush site, as well as the location of the crossroads where they had found the VC shoe, and asked for some night artillery or naval gunfire to be sent up. He then explained that his patrol had no more Claymores or detonators, and had had to abandon their food and equipment. Control agreed they should come on in.

Trace led them nearly due west from the ambush site, until they cut another trail heading south. This was a much narrower track, and bore no signs of recent use. The patrol crouched in silence for twenty minutes in a hollow some ten meters off the trail before Trace, once again carrying the machine gun, crept out and took a look. Seeing and hearing nothing, Trace signaled the men up, and they began walking down the darkest edge of the trail, spaced five meters apart, pressed into the shadows. The five kilometers back to camp took them two and a half hours. When they reached the cleared perimeter, Hunter radioed their position, and waited for the guard tower to confirm their recognition by the nightwatch light signal. The patrol walked cautiously up to the camp and through the gap the guards had pulled in the concertina wire just as the thin clouds overhead went pink with dawn.

The patrol was stood down, but without any indication from the captain as to when they would be going out again. The other probes in the area had reported no unusual enemy movements during the previous night, and were continuing to patrol. It seemed likely that they might have to go up again, and finish backtrailing the road to the river. Hunter suggested in his report that it might be a good idea to send a somewhat larger reconnaissance force. The captain read the report and smiled his wintry smile. "Rebuild your field packs, Sergeant Hunter, then rest your men."

"Aye, aye, sir."

Hunter joined Trace and the others in the two twelve-man tents pitched on a raised wooden platform that was their home. He was pleased to see every man in a clean pair of trousers and T-shirt, each man with his new gear unpacked and spread out before him, checking each item, replacing what had been expended or abandoned before rebuilding the pack, ready to go. The M-14s were stacked by their swivels, clean and shiny with oil. The last thing the men would do before moving out would be to rub down the weapons with an old T-shirt with talc on it, to remove the shine.

"You learn anything, Sarge?" asked Phillips.

"Not really. The artillery guys on the rockpile pounded the shit outa the ambush site with one-oh-fives half the night. Captain was kinda disappointed we didn't get a body count." Marines sniggered.

"Hey, how in the fuck could we have gone out there and counted?" asked Phillips, incredulous.

"It's a joke, cherry," said Smith.

"Oh, sorry," said Phillips.

"We goin' up tonight?" asked Trace, reassembling the M-60.

"He wouldn't say. Do your packs up, men, then get some rest."

Hunter showered carefully after chow, and put on another clean uniform. The heat of the day had gone quickly, and the chilly dampness returned. He had been up to see the captain just before chow. The captain told him it had been decided that the artillery would fire harassment and interdiction (H and I) fire into the areas described by Hunter's patrol all night, so they would be stood down until morning.

"Good," said Hunter, and immediately regretted it.

The captain looked up from the papers on his desk. "You tired of LRRPs, Sergeant Hunter?"

"No, sir! I just think the men will be better off with a bit more rest. None of us ever saw that many of the enemy before, sir."

"Of course, Sergeant," smiled the captain. "But the Air Force will still want that bridge marked, so be ready to go tomorrow."

"Aye, aye, sir." Asshole makes it sound like we didn't try hard enough, thought Hunter.

Hunter had reported the news to the men at chow. The men took it without emotion. Some drifted off to the sandbagged hootch that served as an EM club, some went to write letters. Capiello went to chapel.

Trace walked into the curtained-off corner of the tent that was Hunter's tiny bit of privacy. "What you gettin' dressed up for, Billy?"

"I'm going to see Nga for a while."

"Hey, no, man! We're goin' out tomorrow! You and me, we got a rule, remember?"

"I'm not going to smoke. I just want to spend some time with Nga."

Trace put his hand on Hunter's forearm. The grip wasn't threatening, but it was firm. "Man, Ah Loan won't let you fool around with Nga unless you smoke, and smoke plenty. We both know that."

"Ah Loan and I have reached a different understanding, Trace. I won't be smoking."

"Yeah. Well, maybe I heard about that different understanding. Do you want to talk about that?"

"No, Trace, I don't." Trace let go of Hunter's arm, and Billy left the tent.

I be waiting up for you, man, thought Trace.

Hunter's patrol returned to the scene of the ambush the following afternoon, just as the light was going. Even the NVA hadn't been able to clean up the site completely. Swarms of fat, black flies covered broad areas of bloodstains, and the whole area stank of rotting flesh. Bits of charred metal and rubber were spread around where the truck had been, but no pieces big enough to be of any use in identifying the vehicle or any of its former cargo. No bodies were found, but when Capiello turned over a fly-covered piece of rubber with his machete, it turned out to be a human hand. Phillips promptly threw up.

The road was badly cratered from the artillery barrages, and more trees were down. "It will take those assholes a week with a bulldozer before they can roll trucks through here again," commented Da Silva.

They inspected their NDP from the previous night, and found that their extra gear and rations were gone, except for one shiny red object. "Hey, they missed my Swiss army knife," said Phillips. When he reached for it, he found his arm clamped in Trace's viselike grip. Phillips's face faded to the color of ashes as he looked at Trace. "Wired?"

"Of course," said Trace. "Look." Trace reached out with his machete and carefully lifted the branch that partially concealed the knife. A fine black wire led from the knife's ring away into the bushes.

"What do we do?" asked Phillips.

"We leave it. You'll have to get another pocket knife."

Phillips stared at the pocket knife. It was a gift from his mother, and he had carried it since Cub Scouts. "But, shouldn't we cut it off? Some other marine might find it."

"We can't cut it off, Phillips; we have no idea how it's set up. And if we blow it up, we give away our own AO. No, we just leave it."

"But what if another marine finds it?"

"Just hope he ain't a cherry."

Phillips reddened, but said nothing further.

* * *

Taking great care to give wide berth to the areas where he had set up his own trip wires the previous day, Trace led the patrol through the jungle parallel to the trail as it headed due north. They found a high point, fairly well concealed by the intersecting trunks of two fallen trees, and once again set up the night defensive position and the ambush, and scouted escape routes. Hunter guessed they were no more than a klick from the Ben Hai River itself. We will plant the Air Force's toys in the morning, he thought, if we are still here.

The men passed the night from watch to watch. Shells from the marine fire base at the rockpile rumbled in south of their position at irregular intervals, sounding like distant trains until they exploded. The boom of the explosions was muffled by the intervening jungle. Trace, Hunter, and Smith rotated the watch in three sections, one noncom, one gunner, and one observer in each section. They detected no movement along the trail. Rain, fine and cold, began about 0300, and continued until dawn. It was so foggy at dawn that Hunter decided to risk a C-4 fire for coffee and instant oatmeal. Capiello had a can of C-ration peaches, which he shared. Split nine ways it wasn't much but the syrup helped the flavorless cereal.

The men policed the area, disconnected and dug up their Claymores, and rebuilt their packs. Hunter dug up one Claymore himself with a piece of thin bamboo that Trace had made for him when he had first reported to the LRRPs. At Pathfinder School, they had been trained to dig the things up with bayonets, but Trace had told him that the VC had learned to defeat that by trailing bits of wire off the contacts on the back of the mine. The bamboo was strong, springy, and nonconductive. Hunter hated digging up mines, even when he knew the detonators had been disconnected, but he made himself stay in practice.

By 0600, they were on the march, moving slowly and quietly through the bush. At 0815 by Hunter's watch, the patrol was concealed in the bush, twenty meters off the trail and five meters from the muddy, sluggish waters of the Ben Hai. The men regarded the southern border of North Vietnam with curiosity and awe. And fear, thought Hunter, as though seeing the borders of hell.

Trace and Smith were opening up the green plastic cylinders that contained the air force remote-activated position repeaters, called RAPS. Each was about ten inches high and three inches in diameter. On the bottom was a sharp spike, and on the top, a quartet of stubby antennas.

"How these mothafuckas work, Trace?" asked Smith.

"Says on the side. Just stick it in the ground where it won't be seen. Twist the top collar a half turn to the right; that activates it. Antenna part got to be at least five inches outa the ground." Trace held the camouflage-painted cylinder aloft. Piece of shit, he said to himself. "What's the plan, Sarge?"

Hunter looked at the repeater. Hope these fuckers work, he thought; lotta risk to get them here. "Well, they gave us four of them, so I guess they want two on each side of the river."

Everybody peered through the undergrowth at the Ben Hai. "How wide is it, you reckon?" whispered Da Silva.

"Gotta be half a mile," said Capiello.

"Less," said Smith, "Maybe five, six hundred meters. So who feels like a morning swim?"

Nobody volunteered. Hunter spoke softly, "Let's do this side first, in case we get chased away."

"Chased away or just plain fucked up," whispered Smith.

"We just have to wade in. If there really is a road, the water won't be more than chest deep. If there ain't no road, then fuck it, we go home." Hunter watched as the men looked at each other and at him. They knew there had to be a road; they had all seen the truck go down the trail three nights before.

Trace and Smith placed a repeater on either side of the road. It was a quick job, with nothing to wire. When Trace crossed the road, the birds and the monkeys fell silent, always an eerie sensation. Everyone looked expectantly at Hunter, who held the last two repeaters in his hands. Gradually the animals returned to their calling. The day was becoming hot. Leadership time, thought Hunter. "I guess I'll run these doodads over myself. Trace, tie the end of the wire reel to my belt."

Trace looked uneasy. "I'll go, Sergeant, 'sides, we got the climbing rope."

"Nowhere near long enough. Just hoop me up, there isn't much current, anyway." Hunter had shucked his boots and socks, and his shirt and T-shirt.

"Hell, Sergeant, wading across will take forever," spoke up Phillips, a little too loudly. "Let me swim those things across."

"Attaboy, Phillips," said Trace quickly.

Hunter held his green T-shirt in front of him, uncertain as to whether to take the cherry up on his offer. "You swim good, Phillips?"

Phillips grinned. "I grew up in Santa Cruz, California, Sarge. All we did as kids was surf. And I was on the swimming team at college."

"What college?" asked Hunter.

"San Jose State. I, ah, only did two years."

"You can make it OK?"

"Hey, no sweat! Be back in fifteen minutes!" Phillips stripped to his trousers. Trace went over the arming procedure with him, and helped him secure the repeaters around his waist.

"Be careful, kid," said Smith, bringing up the wire.

"Forget the wire, Smith," said Phillips, confidently, "I'd rather have my legs free." Smith looked at Hunter, a question on his face. Hunter nodded.

"Phillips, every fifty meters or so, let your legs down. See if there's a road surface, and if so, what it feels like."

"OK, Sarge," grinned Phillips.

"Don't stand up, just let your legs down." Phillips gave a mock salute, and lowered himself into the brown water. Soon he was pulling himself into midstream with powerful, graceful, silent strokes.

"Cherry's gonna make history, Bro," said Smith to Trace, quietly. "First American gyrene to visit the North."

The patrol watched as Phillips stroked across the river, stopping from time to time to probe the bottom with his feet. The birds were calling in sharp notes that seemed like warnings. The monkeys began screeching in a new tone, then dropped their voices in a low chatter. Hunter watched through the night binoculars, whose big objectives gave the water a bright, coppery sheen. He was thinking of snakes and crocodiles beneath the surface. *If I were out there now, I'd be scared shitless.*

Phillips reached the shadow of the trees on the opposite bank before he reached the bank itself, and for ten anxious minutes, he was out of sight. Trace listened intently for a shot, or a cry from the opposite bank. *I wonder how we go after the kid if he gets in trouble,* he thought.

Phillips finally emerged into the sunlit river, stroking strongly. He apparently thought he had done enough surveying of the road, for he did not stop. Nevertheless, his progress seemed slow, as though an unseen current were dragging him back. *Come on, kid,* thought Hunter, staring at Phillips's swiveling head and stroking arms. "Come on, Phillips," whispered Smith, out loud.

Now all the men were up, inching toward the bank. "Come *on*, man!"

Phillips reached the bank in the middle of the road, and strode slowly out of the water. He did not seem winded, and he was still grinning. Smith waded in up to the tops of his boots, and put his arm around Phillips's shoulder, pulling him back to the others. "Good job, kid."

Phillips just nodded, and Hunter could see that he was winded, after all. "Strip him down, Smith, and check him for leeches. What did you find, Phillips?"

"Road feels like gravel, about three feet underwater, all the way across. On the other side, there are a lot of tire marks, right down to the riverbank." Smith had Phillips's trousers down and was toweling him off.

"Well, Phillips," said Hunter with a smile, very glad Phillips was back on the near side of the river, "I guess the gooks never figured a mad marine killing machine would ever have the balls to swim over and take a look. Well done, Marine."

"Thank you, Sarge—ah-YAOOW!"

"What the fuck?" said Hunter, seeing Phillips double over and clutch his groin. Smith held up a black and white leech easily three inches long. "He had this ol' leech right next to his dick, Sergeant. I couldn't be sure, so I just ripped off the smaller of the two." Smith held the fat leech under its bloody mouth, and gestured for Phillips to take it. At first Phillips recoiled, then he reached for the leech, threw it on the ground, and crushed it under his bare heel. Smith held Phillips by both cheeks and they grinned at each other. "Welcome to the LRRPs, Marine."

"OK," said Hunter, "get some ointment on the bite, and let's clear out of here."

The patrol withdrew along the opposite side of the trail from the one they had come up, looking for signs of the enemy's traffic. They detected nothing of value until they were nearly back to the site of the ambush, where they found a body, already badly decomposed. He had wounds on his legs and back, Hunter guessed from the Claymores.

"Fucker crawled a long way," commented Smith.

Hunter took papers from the man's tunic to give to intelligence. "He must have crawled so far the others couldn't find him. They never leave bodies unless they're driven off."

"Them papers make him NVA?" asked Da Silva.

"I don't know. Gotta picture, probably so. Let's go."

They drew up beneath the shattered trunk of the tree that had been the focal point of the ambush. "Let's just take one more look at the blast site," said Hunter, quietly. Trace nodded, then crept to the edge of the trail, lying still and listening. Satisfied that there was no enemy near, he hand-signed the men forward. One by one, the men emerged and fanned out. Hunter looked around in disbelief. The big tree had been cut up and the logs removed to the sides of the trail. Smaller trees and branches knocked down by the artillery had also been cleaned up, and more impressively, shell craters, which had been full of dirty water when they had passed by eighteen hours before, had been filled with packed earth. The area where the truck had blown up was covered with new earth as well.

"The place looks like it's been fuckin' *raked*!" spat Smith.

"How did they get by us last night?" asked Capiello.

"They might have come from the south of here. Local VC, like the coolies the other night," said Trace.

"Hey, look!" called Phillips, pointing at the jagged stump of the downed tree. Stuck into the stump about two feet above the ground was Phillips's Swiss army knife. "How the fuck did that get here?"

"Didn't walk," remarked Trace, dryly.

Hunter's throat was tight. He could almost feel the eyes of the men who had cleaned up the ambush and left the knife pressing into his back. The men moved in a loose circle, looking outward. "It's a signal, that's for sure. Says they know it's us, know we're here."

"What it says is 'Fuck you, LRRPs,' " put in Trace. "You gonna take it, Phillips?"

Phillips took a step closer. "Watch your feet, Phillips," said Hunter.

Phillips stopped, and looked down. "Could it still be booby-trapped?"

"I don't see how, but it could."

Smith took out a lined pad he carried in his pack, and a marking pen. He often drew cartoons for the guys, and sometimes he sketched flowers. "Leave it, kid; I'll get you a real knife." Smith drew a series of characters across the page. They looked like a string of x's and n's with no tops and long tails. The last character was an exclamation point. Smith tore the page from the book, and cut a hook in the top with his razor-sharp spring-steel knife. Holding the paper on the point of the knife, he reached out and hooked it over the Swiss army knife. "Now at least it says 'Fuck you' in Vietnamese as well."

"Let's di-di," said Trace. "This place give me the shits." Without waiting for any acknowledgment, he led off into the bush. The patrol followed, and they kept well off the road until they once again cut the small trail that intersected the big one. They followed the small trail south, and were back in the camp by 1500.

27 March 1967   Camp Seven

Hunter hadn't really found dealing for Ah Loan difficult, once he started. He never pushed anyone, just let it be known to a few trusted friends that if they wanted a smoke, he could help them. Ah Loan himself, to do him credit, was not anxious to make waves; he did occasionally try to convince Billy to move up-market, at least to five-sixths, but when Billy declined, Ah Loan smiled his gold-toothed smile, and let it go. Billy was able to see Nga nearly every night when his patrol squad was stood down, which made him happy. She had never quite reached the level of boldness she had the night of Ah Loan's proposal, but Billy was content to think she had frightened herself as she had frightened him, and besides, he liked her fine as his chaste and happy lady moon.

Billy was just setting out to see Nga after three days in the bush when a jeep stopped in front of him, blocking his path. The driver was a scowling coal-black corporal in pressed utilities. Next to him sat a small, elegant, very light-skinned black man with a pencil mustache and conked reddish hair, with the insignia of a first sergeant on his crisply pressed collar points. Billy stopped dead. He had never seen the man, but recognized him immediately from the stories he had heard. He was the

Topkick of Headquarters Company, 1st of the 9th Marines, Henry "Whitenigger" Johnson. In the back seat of the jeep sat the ugliest man Hunter had ever seen, easily six feet five inches tall, if his legs lived up to his torso, and fat, with his coarse features broken by angry red sores. He had thick, wet lips, and one of those mouths that just hangs open. Next to him, pinned under his thick fleshy elbow, was a thin marine named Johanssen from Hunter's own company. The first sergeant spoke quietly, around a cigarette, which dangled theatrically from the corner of his mouth.

"Sarn't Hunta!" The voice was between a whistle and a rasp. "A word."

Hunter stepped to the jeep. He had sold a couple of joints to Johanssen just that morning. Here it goes, he thought, his heart cold.

"Sarn't Hunta, thiss man, thiss ma-*rine* tells me he bo't some maryjuana fom yo. I, pee-sonally, be sorry to think such be true." Whitenigger looked sad, and happy, and insincere, all at the same time.

Billy looked at the scared face of Johanssen, then back at the sergeant. "What do you want, Sergeant?"

"Selling, *dealing*, drugs is highly illegal, *Sarn't*."

Shit, thought Hunter, I'm busted. It all seemed so easy. "I was just helping out a few friends, Sergeant."

"Illegally."

"Perhaps. So what?" What can they do to me, thought Billy, send me to Nam?

Whitenigger looked interested. "I think it better, Sarn't Hunter, if we had an informal, *unofficial* talk. My office?" Whitenigger gestured Hunter to climb into the jeep. At the same signal, the ugly mountain in the back seat released the skinny marine, making room for Hunter. Johanssen fled. Hunter thought about it, and very slowly climbed into the jeep.

"Very *sensible*, Sarn't," hissed Whitenigger.

"Where we goin'?"

"Just 'cross the way, to our encampment, Billy. May I call you Billy?"

"Suit yourself," said Billy, his voice reflecting his surly despair.

"Ex'lent."

The jeep sped through the open gate of Camp Seven, across the kilometer separating it from the next concertina wire-encircled camp, Camp Five, where the 2d Company, 1st of the 9th Marines, as well as the Headquarters and Headquarters Company and a transport company were billeted. The jeep stopped in a cloud of grit and fine dust before a sturdily built hootch, canvas over wood, on a raised wooden platform. "Here, Sarn't," said Johnson. Billy Hunter got down, and entered without a word. The silent black corporal and the ugly monster followed.

The hootch had the look of a home more than an office. There was a bunk, neatly made up, on the left side, and several beat-up soft chairs. There was even a rug on the floor. The back wall of the hootch was covered with neat bookshelves, filled with books with lurid covers.

First Sergeant Johnson sat down behind an elaborate brass-bound camp desk of dark, polished wood, and motioned to Hunter to take a seat in front of the desk. The black corporal and the wet-lipped giant stood behind Billy, unseen. Billy could hear the labored breathing of the fat man. Be calm, he told his racing heart. Johnson unbuttoned a pocket on his shirt and withdrew a tightly rolled joint, which he placed in the center of the desk. He rebuttoned the pocket, and smoothed the flap. He put his thin, carefully maintained hands on the desk, making a steeple with his fingers behind the joint. "This the joint yo' sol' that ma-rine, Sarn't Hunta? This the one?"

Billy said nothing. What would be the point?

"Say he pay you fitty cents."

Billy looked into Johnson's yellowish eyes. The pupils were light brown, flat, and dead.

"That's a problem, for yo' *and* for me, Sarn't."

Billy sighed. Let's get on with it, he thought. "Why is it a problem for you, Sergeant?"

"This is a small marketplace, Sarn't. Need *discipline*. No *room* for com-pe-ti-shun!"

"Even *small-time* competition," growled the corporal behind Billy's ear.

"Guy like yo', Sarn't, coming in, sellin' who-know-what kinda shit, way off *market* price, makes the whole thing *dangerous* for the people who rightly *maintain* and *control* the market-place." Whitenigger spread his fine hands on the desk top, palms up. His palms were a sandy-pink color.

So this isn't a bust, thought Billy. "What do you want from me, Sergeant?"

"Co-operation," said Johnson, with a slight smile.

"Respect," growled the corporal. Billy could actually feel the man's breath on the back of his neck. The giant giggled.

Billy sighed again. "I don't want trouble with you, Sergeant."

Whitenigger's hands made the steeple again. "Of *coss* not. Let's do bid-ness, then?"

"I asked you, Sergeant, what do you want?"

"Yo wanna sell dope, you sell dope. My dope."

"And we'll need to know where you bin gettin' your shit," growled the corporal, from inches behind Billy's ear. Billy felt the skin on the back of his neck crawl.

This is worse than getting busted, thought Billy. "What if I just stop, ah, doing it?"

Whitenigger shrugged, "No reason yo' should, Sarn't. Long as yo' co-operate."

"We *still* need to talk to your supplier, dude," breathed the corporal.

Billy got up quickly, turned, and placed his hand flat on the corporal's chest, shoving him backward. The man lost his balance, regained it, and lowered himself into a martial-arts crouch, his teeth bared. Billy tried very hard to stare the corporal down.

"Now, *gennlemen*!" purred Whitenigger, "this a *bid-ness* meetin'!"

"I don't need this asshole breathing down my neck," said Hunter, firmly.

"You don' need *none* of the trouble I got for you, white meat," spat the corporal through his clenched teeth.

Billy turned, very slowly and half expecting an attack from behind, to face Johnson, who was now standing behind the spotless desk. Whitenigger smiled pleasantly. Billy spoke softly, holding Whitenigger's flat eyes. "Perhaps we could continue this *discussion* one on one, *Sergeant*?" Billy felt his anger rising, and decided to show it. Whitenigger did not seem impressed.

"Why not? That seems *very* sensible, Sarn't! Crow, Zits, go get a beer, then bring back a couple for me and the sarn't here." Billy turned, and watched the other two slide out of the office. The corporal's hate-filled eyes never left Billy until the door closed.

Johnson sat. "So what do yo' pro-*pose*, Sarn't Hunta?" Johnson picked up the joint from the desk, gestured with it in Hunter's face, then lit it, pulling a deep toke into his lungs. He hoisted his feet onto the desk, and smiled.

"Look, Sergeant—"

"Call me Whitenigga."

Hunter choked. Why would anyone want such a name?

"Bothers yo', don't it, fa'mboy?"

"No. Fine, Whitenigger, if you like. It's just this. I heard of you. I know you got, well, influence—"

"Power," said Whitenigger, drawing Ah Loan's smoke deep into his lungs, "power."

Hunter chose his words carefully. My ass is on the line, he

thought, and so is my ability to see and to protect Nga. "Thing is, Sergeant, ah, Whitenigger, I don't want trouble from you. Hell, I'm not even doing this to make any money."

Whitenigger offered the joint to Billy. He waved it off. "Lak, no shit, Hunta, at fitty cents a J, you ain't goin' to make none."

Hunter smiled ruefully. "You think I'm dumb."

"Yep," said Whitenigger, exhaling a great cloud of pungent smoke.

"Well," said Billy, "fact is, I kinda love this girl. So her father, he wants money for me just to be with her, see?"

"Happens," said Whitenigger, without inflection.

"So he asked me to sell dope. Just a little."

"A little too much, Sarn't Billy."

"OK. OK, Whitenigger," the name stuck in Billy's throat. "I gotta buy the guy's dope, and I can't afford to throw it away. So how about I sell it to you, like at my cost?"

Whitenigger offered the joint again. Billy thought it best to take it, a sign of bargain. The smoke was much rougher than the stuff Billy had smoked at Ah Loan's, but it was good. "I don' *know*, Billy, that would make yo' almos' a partner."

"I don't want nothing, man, just to see the girl."

Whitenigger leaned forward. "Yo gonna tell me who is this supplier?"

"I can't, man."

"Hard, *hard* do bidness, wit'out trust," said Whitenigger, leaning back.

Billy frowned, "Look, I just want protection, for me, and for my girl."

"And yo' *will* stop dealing?"

Billy hated the word "dealing." "Yeah."

Whitenigger smiled his insincere half smile. His eyelids drooped. "I am sure we will work something out. Trust me, Billy."

Billy smiled, "Yeah, well, I want to. Just keep that corporal away from me, OK, Sergeant?"

"He could take you."

"Maybe." Billy's smile evaporated.

"If things didn't go well."

"But they will, won't they, Whitenigger?"

"Of coss-ss." Whitenigger's voice had all the menace of a snake's hiss.

Billy got up. "OK, then, we'll work it out."

Whitenigger smiled. Billy could see his eyes were still dead. "Stay for a beer."

"No, thanks, Sergeant. I'm late for an appointment. I'll just get back by myself."

Whitenigger spread his hands, "As you wish, Billy."

Hunter threw a half salute with a smile, and left. Now, that didn't go half badly, he thought, relieved to be out of Whitenigger's office with a whole skin.

In the office, First Sergeant Johnson seethed with rage. Fucking patronizing asshole racist cracker, he thought. First I'm going to let you live, and then I'm going to fill that life with pain.

Crow reentered the office, almost silently, carrying a paper sack full of cold beers. He looked quickly around the office, saw Hunter had gone, and came forward, setting the sack on Whitenigger's desk. Wordlessly, he took two cans of beer from the sack, and opened them. They each drank. Whitenigger extended his soft hand, and Crow took it in both of his. "Find out what slope-head chick our read'-mix sarn't is fucking, Crow. Find out! That will lead us to his supply."

Crow kissed the tapered fingers slowly, stood, and withdrew.

Whitenigger took another joint from the desk, and lit it. God, I hate these cocky white bastards, he whispered to the joint.

Hunter's Pathfinder unit was split between two marine corps CH-34 helicopters, skimming over the treetops on the way back to Camp Seven. The entire battalion had been involved in an operation called Jackstay II, joined by two other battalions of I Corps marines and a battalion landing team from the amphibious squadron offshore. The operation was a sweep, intended to force the enemy to retreat from his bases in the many jungle valleys west of the Leatherneck Square. Hunter's company had been picked up by helicopters seven days previously and lifted to a nondescript hilltop called Landing Zone Stud, where they formed a blocking force for the mobile units from the BLT. Hunter and the other nightcrawlers felt like fish out of water in the big, company-sized actions, with helicopters, artillery, air strikes, resupply, noise, and daylight movement. The Pathfinder unit was operated as a rifle squad, and the whole operation seemed so conspicuous and so noisy that the nightcrawlers were confident that the enemy would be nowhere in evidence.

The operation ground through the week in the growing heat of the early southeast monsoon season. The men got wet and stayed wet, and stank and cursed. Insect repellent was a major item on each resupply list. Leeches were a problem, especially when the men tried to sleep. There was a rumor that one of the men from the 1/9 had a leech crawl halfway up his cock.

Hunter's company came under a night mortar attack, which

was terrifying even though no one was hurt. Hunter watched as the company commander called in artillery on the opposite wall of the little valley to suppress the mortars, and admired his coolness. The men got more tired and more irritable, and many VC sightings were cause for thousands of rounds of ammunition to be loosed into the jungle, but no bodies were found. Supply caches were found, and the rice dumped out or contaminated with aviation gasoline. A tunnel complex with a hospital and several tons of rice was uncovered, and dynamited after many pictures were taken. The colonel commanding the operation made a speech to a small group of correspondents on the pad at LZ Stud, while marines, including the nightcrawlers, maintained a double perimeter. The colonel listed the accomplishments of the operation in terms of tons of rice and rounds of ammunition found and destroyed, individual and crew-served weapons captured, kilometers marched, and square kilometers denied the enemy. American casualties were two KIA, both due to mines, and fourteen WIA. Enemy casualties were put preliminarily at twenty KIA. Hunter didn't know where those enemy kills had occurred, and he hadn't heard about them from anybody else. The colonel counted the operation a success. The marines withdrew to the strong points, and from there, the BLT flew back to the ships. Hunter's company, holding the perimeter at LZ Stud, was among the last flown out.

The helicopters banked in and landed, four at a time, in the middle of Camp Seven. The men humped their gear off, and headed for their hootches. Billy went off to a final debrief with the other senior NCOs and the officers at the captain's office.

The debrief was short, with each unit leader giving a quick comment on the performance of men and equipment under his control. The captain took it all in, and his company personnel sergeant took minutes. At the close, the captain signaled for silence. The tired men were pleased to comply. "Men, while we were out, there was an incident here, at our camp. The ville beyond the wire was attacked by VC infiltrators."

The ville? thought Hunter. Oh, my God, no.

"The ville's headman, old Loan, and his family, were killed."

Jesus, Mary, and Joseph, prayed Hunter. It cannot be. "What about the sentries in the towers?" asked a voice. Hunter belatedly recognized it as his own.

"They saw nothing, Hunter, heard nothing. To those of you who knew those simple people, I'm sorry. Dis-missed." The captain left the tight circle of officers and NCOs.

Hunter turned and hurried toward the Pathfinder's hootch, his mind racing and his guts burning. "Trace. TRACE!"

Trace appeared at the flap of the tent, jumped down, and grabbed Hunter by the shoulders. "You heard."

"Jesus, yeah! Let's get up there!"

"It's cordoned off. It's off-limits."

Hunter shook free. "Let's *go*, dammit!" He ran, and Trace followed.

Trace and Hunter walked around the little hut village, followed by frightened eyes in every doorway. Every doorway except the doorways of Ah Loan, his ancient crippled wife, and the "daughters." Yellow plastic military police ribbons encircled the hootches, but Hunter was not deterred. There were no military personnel in the ville. The sentries in the nearest tower watched them without interest. Hunter knelt in the trampled mud, and picked up a fake tortoise-shell comb. He recognized it; he had given it to Nga. There was glossy black hair on the comb, and blood on the hair. Billy held the comb in both hands, then slipped it into his shirt pocket.

"Let's *go*, man!" whispered Trace.

Billy shook a tear from his eye, "Wait, man. Wait."

Trace took Hunter's arm. "Man, everybody is *looking at us*!"

Hunter shook free. "Look around you, Trace! VC don't leave a place like this!"

Trace looked. The hootches hadn't been stripped. The blood spoor was not in a neat execution row. "Look, man, who the fuck else coulda done this? And why?"

"I don't know. But look. Blood is all over the hootches, like someone came in cutting, slashing. You know the VC would have taken everyone out, then executed them. Maybe mutilated the bodies, *pour encourager les autres*, like the French taught them. We've seen that, but the execution would have been in the usual form, to set an example. You know that, Trace."

Trace looked around. It *was* too messy. "Maybe they had to do it quick, because of the sentries in the towers."

"The *sentries*! The ones who heard nothing, saw nothing! Trace, you *know* this wasn't done quietly! You *know*!"

Hunter let Trace hustle him back to the hootch. Hunter's face was hot, and he felt the aches in his back and legs that heralded a malaria attack. His mind was racing, filled alternately with grief and rage. He forced himself through the routine tasks of the stand down, stripping his pack and his weapon, organizing his dirty clothes, showering thoroughly through seven days of sweat and jungle slime, delousing his head and his crotch, showering again.

He tried to focus on the scene in Ah Loan's little compound.

A thousand things that seemed out of place shrieked through his mind, yet when he tried to list them, he could not. He saw Trace watching him intently as he dressed. *Trace thinks I'm crazy. Trace knows I'm not crazy. But who would kill Ah Loan and—the others.* Billy knew he was fighting admitting to himself that Nga herself could be dead.

"Let's go eat, Billy," said Trace, eyeing him gravely.

"OK." Billy forced a smile.

They ate in silence. Most of the marines in the mess tent were wolfing down their first decent meal in a week, so the silence wasn't conspicuous. Billy tried to eat; he felt hungry, but he was just too distracted. Images of Nga, her child's body broken and twisted, forced their way into his brain, and he tried to squeeze them out. *Too much to do, too much to find out, before he could grieve for Nga. He hoped she would understand.*

Trace finished, and they got up to go back to their hootch. *He's watching me like a hawk,* thought Hunter, with a twinge of irritation. "Hey, Trace, why are you looking at me like I have leprosy?"

"You don't look well, Bro. You're flushed, and you're sweating. You better get some lie-down."

Hunter shook his head, and increased his pace. Trace kept up. "I gotta find out, man. I gotta talk to people, find out what really happened."

Trace stopped him just inside the tent and spun him around. His voice was hard and even, though very quiet. "Now *listen*, Sergeant! The *VC* killed those people! The fucking *VC!* That's what happened, and that's all!"

Hunter looked at his friend. Trace looked more scared than angry. "Trace, I know you want to protect me from any association with Ah Loan and drugs, but you saw that mess. The VC don't leave a site like that."

"We *don't know* that, man! For all we know, the MPs messed up the site, or just curious guys."

"I just want to ask around. Find those so-called sentries, for one thing."

"Well, you ain't a-gonna, Billy Hunter, because you're *sick*, and your head is on crooked. You go to bed before you do something stupid."

Hunter bowed his head. He squeezed his eyes shut against his own tears and against a picture of Nga, frightened, being attacked with a machete. A groan escaped his mouth, and he shook his head.

"You gotta get a grip on yourself, man." Trace's voice was gentle, comforting. He led Hunter toward his little enclosure,

holding him tightly around his shaking shoulders. "You go to
bed, get the fever down. I'll, ah, ask around."

"Pro-promise," rasped Hunter, allowing himself to be lowered into his cot.

"Yeah. I will. Sleep."

"Thanks, Trace."

Trace pulled off Hunter's boots, and pulled the blanket up
under his chin. Poor fucker, he thought; he really loved that little
girl.

Hunter slept fitfully, the fever distorting the images in his
brain. A corpsman, sent by Trace, came in and took Hunter's
temperature, then made him drink a canteen full of water and
gave him three aspirin. Sleep and water, said the corpsman.
Hunter nodded and drifted off again. The incident at Ah Loan's
place slipped away from him, and his fevered brain slept.

Billy took a long shower and returned to his quarters, and
dressed. His temperature was almost down to normal, but he
felt weak as a kitten. He felt hunger, but the thought of food
made his stomach churn. He sat on the bunk and shook his head
to clear it. Trace walked in, with Smith. "How you doin'
Hunter?" asked Smith. He looked concerned.

"I'm OK. Little weak. Few hours sleep took care of it."

"You bin out more'n twenty-four hours, man," said Trace.

Jesus, thought Hunter, that never happened before. "Wow."

"Corpsman came by coupla times, made sure your temperature didn't stay too high for too long, fry your brain," continued
Trace. "He said it ain't that unusual, you bein' tired from seven
days in the bush."

Hunter shook his head again. It wouldn't clear. "Twenty-four
hours! Hey, Trace, did you find out—" He stopped, and looked
uncertainly at Smith. Smith had never been admitted as one of
Ah Loan's "friends."

"Yeah. Some. I tole Smith what you were thinkin'. We trust
Smith." It was a flat statement. Trace was taking charge. "Figured we'd both talk to you."

Hunter leaned back. "So what did you find out?"

Neither Trace nor Smith would look him in the eye. "Billy,
this is from the heart. I know how you felt about little Nga, but
you got to promise me and Smith, *promise*, that you won't do
anything stupid."

Billy felt chilled to the bone. A last lick of malaria, he thought.
"Trace, what did you find out?"

"Promise. I mean it, man, promise."

Billy's throat was dry and his vision was blurring. "I promise."

Trace took a deep breath, and let it out. "Billy, you was right. VC never hit that place."

"Who?" rasped Billy. Trace sat down beside him on the cot. "Who?"

"A guy named Crow and another they call Zits. They're close to Whitenigger Johnson."

Oh, my God, thought Hunter, clutching himself around the elbows. "What happened to the sentries? That near tower isn't ten meters away from—"

"Who knows? With the combat units in the field, probably just clerks up there anyway. Or maybe bribed. You know Whitenigger draws a lot of water, Billy."

They figured out my supply came from Ah Loan. And they killed him, and—his family, even though I said I would go along, they killed them, *all*. Billy fought the pain, but gave in to the tears. "Are you sure, Trace?"

"Yeah. But remember, you promised not to try anything. There is nothing you can do."

"Bu-but it's murder! We-we can't j-just let it go!"

"Billy, what are you going to do? Turn them in? There are no witnesses, and the investigation will probably find out about your dealin' for Ah Loan." He doesn't know the worst of it, thought Hunter. "I warned you about that dealin', Billy."

Billy straightened himself up on the cot. "How do you know this, Trace?"

"Smith did some nosin' around in Camp Five. Nobody knows him over there. Heard that guy, Zits, bragging about it."

Hunter looked at Smith. "What did you hear, Smith?"

Smith grimaced and looked at Trace. "Like Trace said, Sarge. We was in the latrine, but Zits couldn't see me. He said him and Crow wasted this old drug dealer."

Billy took a deep breath. "Di-did he mention Nga?"

Smith squirmed. He looked at Trace, not at Hunter, "Hey, Sarge, you don't want to hear it all. Prob'ly not even true, anyway."

"I want to hear. I want to know." Hunter heard his own voice full of pain, but resolute.

"Billy, it won't bring her back," whispered Trace, putting his arm across Billy's shoulders.

"I have a right. I want to know. What did he say about Nga?"

Smith's face contorted with real pain, and he closed his eyes. "He said that Crow held the little gook for him, but he couldn't fuck her; she was just too small. So he made her suck his cock before he smashed her skull with h-his machete.'' It all came out in a rush.

Hunter just stared at Smith in horror. Very slowly, and without a sound, Hunter doubled over, clutching his gut tightly. Burning bile from his stomach rose in his mouth, and dribbled out onto his knees. He couldn't breathe; his solar plexus was paralyzed as from a physical blow. Still holding Hunter around his shoulders, Trace gestured with his head to Smith, who went out and returned with the corpsman, who dabbed alcohol on Billy's clenched elbow and injected the tranquilizer he had prepared. He watched anxiously as Billy resumed breathing, then slid to the floor.

Trace and Smith pulled him back onto the cot, and the corpsman checked him over. ''He'll sleep again, but we better take him over to the sick bay.''

''Jesus, he made me tell him,'' whispered Smith.

''I know, Bro,'' said Trace. ''But it was better he heard it from you and me than some other way later on.''

''But what a thing to have to know.''

''He'll make it, he's strong. We'll have to help him. Anyway, let's get him over to sick bay. Pick up that end of the cot.''

Hunter swam underwater for the longest time. He could see the surface of the pool, dotted with lily pads, just above him. He did not come up to breathe, but he felt no shortness of breath. He swam on, the grasses and sunken branches tugging at his body, frightening him. Terror stared at him with glowing eyes behind the swaying grasses. Yet the water was warm, and the sensation of swimming pleasant. And in the back of his mind, he knew far greater horrors waited above the surface.

He was vaguely aware of being in a hospital, and of people moving around, and stopping to look at him. They were hard to make out above the water's surface. He couldn't move his left arm. He knew there was a tube stuck in at the elbow, even though he couldn't really feel it. He did feel straps across his legs and chest. He supposed they were for safety. He vaguely recalled falling out of his own bed some time ago.

Nga swam up to meet him from among the waving leaves of grass. She smiled her joyful smile and extended her arms toward him. Billy felt happy as he enfolded her in his right arm. She drifted close to him, almost touching his face. He stroked her shiny black hair, but it was sticky and warm on the back of her head. He looked at his hand, and saw blood and brain tissue. Nga continued to smile at him, but her eyes were open in terror. He realized she was dead. He opened his mouth to scream, but his mouth filled with water and he choked. Nga drifted away, spinning weightless in the current.

It was nighttime in the hospital. It was dark around Billy's bed, and fewer people were moving around. Billy's head rang with fever, but he was beginning to see more clearly. A corpsman with a clipboard came to the side of Billy's bed, and looked at him, grinning. It was Crow, and he was saying something Billy couldn't hear, and laughing. Billy recoiled, tried to sink into the mattress. Crow bent over, his face becoming huge, and kissed Billy on the forehead, laughing all the while. Billy struggled to cry out, but his lungs were empty, and he couldn't get a breath. Crow's head withdrew, and Billy could see the bloated, blistered face of Zits, who leaned over from the other side of the bed. Zits unbuttoned his fly and pulled out his cock, pointing it at Billy. It was dripping with blood. Billy twisted against the restraints of the bed, and managed a low cry of "nu-un-unh!" He opened his eyes, and Crow and Zits had gone.

Nga sat beside him on the bed. He reached out to her, but she was too far away for him to touch. When he beckoned to her, she shook her head, and frowned. The frown cut through Billy like a knife. "Come, my love."

"I can't, Bi-lee. Otha ma-rine ruin Nga."

"No, child, come to me."

"Otha ma-rine, he take Nga's virginity. Now Nga cannot give to Bi-lee."

"That doesn't matter, Nga."

"Yes it does. All man want virgin. Now Nga cannot have love of Bi-lee." She stood up and walked away. He called after her, but the words stuck in his throat.

Nga drifted in and out of his vision the rest of the long night, but she wouldn't come to him. He could see she thought he had failed her, and he knew that he had. He should have gotten her away from Ah Loan. She was raped and killed because he had failed. Toward morning there was only her voice, as musical and sad as a wind chime, "Help me, Bi-lee. Help me to rest."

Hunter was wide awake and his mind was clear when the lights came on in the sick bay at 0600. He knew with perfect clarity what he had to do.

2 March 1967   Balboa Island, Newport Beach, California

Lieutenant (jg) William McGowen Stuart stood at attention at the foot of the garden, squinting into the sun setting over the gold-dappled Pacific. He was sweating slightly from the sun, and from nerves. The high collar of his starched dress-white uniform pulled his neck like a noose, and he wished he could raise a hand and give it a tug to loosen it, but he did not. Lieutenant Hooper stood next to him, and Lieutenants (jg) Buck Thomas, Gordy Mason, and David Epstein, and Ensign Barry Fiedler stood in a curving line beyond, facing five very pretty bridesmaids in a curve on the other side of the priest. Everybody waited for the bride to make her entry. Karen and her father should appear at any moment, but the moments dragged. We're on stage, thought Stuart. We are the main event. Let the show begin; let's get this done.

The garden, and the sprawling house behind the wedding party, sat on a low bluff overlooking Balboa Island and the Newport Breakwater. It belonged to Karen's Aunt Liz, her mother's sister. Karen and her parents had decided to have the wedding on the west coast to allow more of William's friends to be present, and because Karen had made many friends since beginning her job with the Bank of America. Karen's maid of honor and one of her bridesmaids had flown out from the east, as had

Karen's parents and her two brothers. William's parents had made a visit to San Francisco, and then had driven down from Palo Alto with William's sister and her husband. The total number of guests was about one hundred and fifty. Dinner and dancing would follow the ceremony.

"So where is the lovely Karen, William? My thirst grows to dangerous proportions," rasped Hooper out of the corner of his mouth.

"Quiet, Hoop. We're on stage here," whispered Stuart through his fixed smile. A drink would not be amiss in my too-tight guts, he thought.

"Look at Epstein! He's positively drooling! There's going to be some serious womanizing after you two lovebirds fly off tonight," continued Hooper, not to be quieted.

"Shut *up*, man!" Stuart suppressed a grin. David Epstein was definitely in full mating display.

"I think ole Gordy diddled the maid of h last night, after your fine speech at the rehearsal dinner."

Stuart fought back a guffaw. He turned a bit toward his tormentor, who was grinning his wolfish best, just as a long chord swelled from the electric organ on the porch behind them, and Karen and her father emerged from the guest house across the lawn. They marched slowly together down the aisle between the rows of smiling guests. Stuart's mind blanked to all sensation except the sight of Karen, truly glowing with color as she glided along beside her father's measured tread, in time to the march William could no longer hear. He was aware that she was wearing a dress of heavy silk, the color of thick cream, and a diamond cross around her neck, and a tiara holding a veil, and that she was carrying a long bouquet of orchids. The rest was—just Karen, more beautiful than he had ever seen her.

William turned and took Karen's arm as her father, his eyes misty, stepped back and sat beside his wife. The priest began the ceremony, and William and Karen made the responses on cue, William as if from a deep trance. The only thing he noticed as the ceremony progressed, and the only thing he would remember, was the ring, borne by Aunt Liz's youngest son in a crystal dish. The kid was so nervous that the ring clattered and danced in the dish, until the priest took it up and handed it to William, who slipped it onto Karen's poised finger. She certainly is taking this all in stride, thought William, feeling proud to be so close to this magnificent woman. Jesus, I'm marrying her, *right now*! He felt a twinge of panic. The priest told him he could kiss the bride, and Karen tilted her head up to him, eyes half closed, lips slightly parted. William drew her to him, lifted the gossamer veil, and kissed her. The electric organ began to play again, and Karen gently turned William toward the multitude. William took one step forward, and felt his dress sword catch in Karen's dress. He reached down and freed it, and they marched slowly down the lawn toward the gleaming harbor, to the stirring strains of Handel. William was vaguely aware of the ushers and bridesmaids forming up behind them as they walked down to the guest house from which Karen had emerged with her father about ten minutes ago. They stepped into the cool darkness, and William really kissed the bride.

Karen giggled and pushed him away slightly. "My, aren't you the bursting groom!" She stroked his crotch teasingly through the tight cloth of his white trousers.

William held her wrist. "Do-do you suppose we could, ah, slip away for a few moments?"

"And loosen our garments?"

"Ah, as the saying goes, yes."

Karen put her hands on his cheeks and kissed him lightly. "There's nothing I'd like better, my husband, but I think the standard response is that we have a lifetime to be doing that."

William smiled, beginning to feel somewhat in control. His heart slowed to a medium jackhammer inside his chest. "Still, you know, these Catholic marriages have to be consummated, or they don't count."

Karen pushed him away playfully. "I think we're expected to go and greet our guests, William, dear."

"We have to do that, huh?"

"It's traditional," said Karen, with mock aloofness.

"Then let's get her done," said William, smiling and once again offering his arm.

5 April 1967   USS *Valley Forge*, in port, Long Beach, California

"Come on, man!" Mendoza's voice had taken on a wheedling tone. "This is a great opportunity!"

Moser wiped the gun oil from his hands on a big red rag, then stuffed it back into his pocket. He replaced the M-1 in its rack, cleaned and greased, and picked up the next one. These old guns sure do rust up, if you don't stay on them, he thought. "Juan, I tole you, I tole you in the Philippines, an' I'm tellin' you here, I don' want *nothin'* to do with no drugs."

Mendoza hopped off the stool, and spun around in frustration.

"It ain't real drugs, Moser, just marijuana! Grass! The guys all smoke a little, even some of the officers!"

Moser sprung the bolt out of the second M-1 and dropped it in the bath of nitro-powder solvent. He removed the wooden stock and set it aside, then took the gas-pressure tube off the barrel, and dropped both in the bath. "You do as you like, Juan; jest leave me out of it."

"Hey, Moser! There's money, big money, to be made. You're my buddy, and the armory locker is the perfect place to store it, since you got the only key." The armory is nice, but what I really need the big dummy for is muscle if anybody tries to move in on the traffic. "So I'm doing you a favor, letting you in as a partner." For ten percent, that is, but he don't need to know that.

"Lieutenant Stuart has a key, Juan; so's the chief," said Moser, slowly running a wire brush through the barrel of the rifle in front of him.

"Yeah, but those dickheads never look in the lockers, man; you're the only one."

What yer sayin' Juan, is that they trust me, thought Moser. "No, Juan, no dope in my armory. Ferget it."

"OK, OK, we'll find some other place. Look, just come in with me, help me handle the, ah, buying and selling."

"How come you need me fer that?"

"Well, look, Moser, OK, you're a big man. Everybody, well, knows you can handle yourself in a fight."

"I don' wanna fight nobody."

"Hey, I know, but with you in, nobody will fuck with me. With us. And look, man, don' you wanna make some cash? What with sendin' money off to your mother, and to that court-house, you can't even buy a beer most nights."

"I manage."

"Yeah, sure, you think I don' know? This isn't like bein' at sea, man. You can go ashore three nights outa every four, and these are stateside prices. It takes money." Juan backed off to let that sink in.

Moser replaced the wire brush on the cleaning rod with a slotted tip, threaded in a patch, and swabbed out the bore of the M-1. He was broke, and Juan knew it. Everybody knew it. Guys laughed at him because he had no civvies, and the chief was on him to buy some decent uniforms. He didn't do anything expensive, but Juan was right, a guy had a lot more ways to spend money in Long Beach than at sea. He would be OK, but he was still paying off the front window of the store back home, and the windshield of the police car. And his mother had written she was feeling poorly, so Moser had made a small allotment of his pay out to her, too.

"It's easy money, Moser. You don' even have to touch the stuff if you don't want to."

Moser held up the barrel of the rifle and looked through it directly at the light on the overhead. The old barrel was pitted, but no amount of swabbing was going to change that. Better let it soak some more, he thought, dropping it back into the cleaning bath. "Bet 'at ole gun kilt Japs, or Germans, in War Two, Juan."

"Yeah, sure. Look, man, I need you on this. You're the only one I trust to watch my back."

I don't need money that bad, decided Moser. The decision felt right, now that it was made. "No, Juan, I ain't gonna be involved in no drug dealin', no way."

Mendoza stormed out of the armory without another word, seething with anger. That's what you think, asshole.

Lieutenant and Mrs. Stuart fell easily into the routine of married life in the apartment Karen had rented in Long Beach. William liked the feel of "Lieutenant and Mrs. Stuart," and used it with Karen, who laughed at him.

Karen had continued success in selling the BankAmericard to merchants, and she bubbled with energy. Most evenings she cooked their dinner, full of enthusiasm from the results of her day. When her days went less well, William barbecued, or they went out. William's own work on the ship was increasingly boring; the division had off-loaded all its ammunition in a short visit to Seal Beach, and the long yard period had begun, which meant the guns were being retrofitted, and that William had to write endless reports. The hardest times for both of them were the nights, every fourth night, when William had to stay on board the *Valley*, as part of the duty section.

"I'm sorry you're bored on the ship, darling, but after all you've been through, it must be a relief."

William had said nothing about the run up the Cua Viet River, convinced that Karen would worry without need. He had given a sparse account of the helicopter crash, only enough to explain the Purple Heart and Silver Star he had been awarded, and made light of the decorations themselves. Even so, Karen had seemed frightened, and they had not spoken of the matter since. "I'm just glad to be here, my love. Being with you almost every evening of my life makes all boring aspects of this man's Navy easily tolerated."

Karen flew into his arms, upsetting his drink. "Oh, my love, you really will never leave me again. Say it, please!"

Stuart held her close, tight. "I can't see how, love. By the time the *Valley* finishes her yard and the fleet refresher training, I'll be too short to deploy." Just let me train the boots, then off the ship before she heads west again, he prayed. I never want to be apart from my love again.

Karen nuzzled his neck. "Then champagne, my love, and then do the steaks. Gordy Mason and his boring Nebraska wife will be here in half an hour. I'm so glad she wasn't at our wedding."

So was Gordy, thought William, with an inward smirk. He gently lifted his wife aside, and went out to the patio to light the charcoal grill.

Moser lay in his bunk, thinking. Mendoza had been strutting around the G Division berthing space, resplendent in his third new set of dress whites, waiting for liberty call. He had a new watch, and even a gold chain around his neck, long enough to be concealed beneath the collar and kerchief of his blouse. Mendoza had been bragging about his vast success with the chicks, as usual. Moser didn't care about Juan's bragging; bragging came as natural to Juan as breathing, but Moser felt every day his own poverty, and the temptation to get into the easy money Mendoza was making supplying marijuana to the guys. Yet he still resisted. Maybe if I can make second class, I can get out of this hole, he thought.

"Goin' ashore, Moser?" Mendoza leaned over his bunk.

"Nah. I think I'll jest stay aboard, maybe watch the movie."

Mendoza smiled, "Hey, look, man, come on over to the Blue Girl. I'm buyin'."

What the hell, thought Moser. I could use a beer. "Thanks, Juan, I will."

Mendoza reached down and slapped the big man's shoulder. "Way to be, man, let's go."

Moser returned to the ship after accepting two beers from Mendoza, along with a pitch from Juan once again to get into the dope business. Moser's head hurt from the conflict within; it wasn't easy to be without money while the ship lay in dry dock, but he still refused Mendoza's entreaties to join in the dealing. He was beginning to wonder why he struggled against sin. Hell, nobody really cared about grass.

Mendoza continued cruising, pleased with himself. Moser would be in his pocket before too much longer. How the hump can live with no money is beyond me, he thought idly. The business was going well, but Mendoza knew he would feel a lot better with Moser along for backup. Moser was *big* backup.

Mendoza strolled from bar to bar, always being the big man, standing drinks, sometimes making appointments to score dope for some *Valley* sailor. He was careful; he sold to no one he didn't know, unless the new person was introduced and vouched for by someone he did know. As Mendoza sometimes sold on credit, his clients were eager to find new buyers; Mendoza gave back a little on the debt for each new pigeon. It was so easy.

Mendoza tired of the bar scene around 2300, and took a cab back to the base. As he walked through the gate, two petty officers fell into step with him, one on either side. Both wore shore patrol arm bands. "Mendoza, Juan E.?" said the first class on his right, taking Mendoza's arm.

Mendoza shook his arm free, feeling sick with fear. "What the fuck, man?"

The first class took his arm again, more firmly, and the third class on his other side did likewise. "Step over here, to the gatehouse, Mendoza. A little talk."

Mendoza was hustled inside, his knees going to water. The civilian security guards who should have been in the gatehouse were nowhere in evidence. The third class pushed Mendoza down into a hard chair, and stood behind him. The first class sat on the desk, looking down at Mendoza, with his nightstick across his knees. Mendoza fought to hold his voice steady, "Hey, man, I mean, what the fuck—"

"Stow it, asshole," said the first class, quietly. "We want to talk to you about dope."

"Hey, man! I ain't got no dope! Search me!"

The first class smiled, tapping the nightstick rhythmically against his palm. "No need. We ain't concerned with what you might be carryin'."

Mendoza relaxed. This is about business, then. "So what, then?"

The first class hitched himself higher on the desk. "You dealin' dope on the *Valley*, Juan E., and we on the master-at-arms." The first class paused, and Mendoza said nothing. "The *Valley*, and its good order and discipline, are my responsibility."

Mendoza couldn't suppress a smirk. Amateurs, he thought. "I don' know what you sayin', man."

"Of course not, Juan E. But we figure an operation as large as *yours*," the first class reached down and ripped the gold chain from Mendoza's neck, "needs protection." Mendoza felt him-

self flush with anger. The chain disappeared into the first class's
pocket.

"You don' *know*, man," Mendoza hissed. "I ain't in this
alone!"

"So what?" asked the first class, real quick.

"So, *man*, you fuck with me, maybe *your* ass get kicked."

The first class laughed, loudly. Behind him, Mendoza heard
the third class ho-hoing as well. The first class tapped his nightstick on Mendoza's shoulder hard enough to make him wince.
"You Messican cocksucker, you ain't got nothing wit' which to
kick *no* ass! You meat to me, *anytime!*" he finished with a final
bark of laughter.

"Sure, man," said Mendoza, pushing the nightstick away with
more confidence than he felt, "you got you, and I got Moser."

The first class put the butt of the nightstick in the center of
Mendoza's forehead and pushed. Juan twisted away. "Word we
have is Moser is nowhere near this thing of yours, Juan E."

"That's because he ain't been needed before now, man."

The first class was thinking about that. Mendoza watched his
mind grinding through low gear. The quiet lasted a full two
minutes. Juan rose from the chair. Neither man stopped him, so
he stepped toward the door. "Jest one minute, Juan E.," said
the first class, softly, but with an edge of meanness in his voice.
"It seems to me you might still need some supplemental protection."

Mendoza snickered, "More'n Moser? I don't think so."

"Yeah, well, maybe he's in, maybe not. My offer is twenny
percent, full cover on *Valley*, and cooperation on other ships in
Long Beach."

Mendoza stood in the doorway, feeling in complete control.
"And just how much you reckon twenty percent is, cowboy?"

The first class smiled, slowly, "About three hundred dollars
a month, more or less."

"Shit, man, that's more like sixty percent," said Mendoza,
smiling back. Actually, he knew that the figure was almost exactly twenty percent, and he wondered how the master-at-arms
had figured it out.

"Anyways, we can talk about details—" the first class offered.

"Anyways, fuck you, asshole," said Mendoza, as he left the
gatehouse and strode back toward the ship, his balls clanking.
His rush of triumph faded as he climbed the after-brow onto the
ship. Now I really better get the big guy, he thought.

William joined the going-away party for Buck Thomas at the
Long Beach Officers' Club, which was already in full swing.

Buck had received his orders to return to Nam as the officer in charge—the skipper, really—of a PCF, or swift boat. He was scheduled to leave for San Diego in the morning for training on the boats, then off to the patrol squadron based in Vung Tau, at the mouth of the Saigon River.

Most of the ship's junior officers and quite a few seniors were gathered in a knot at the end of the bar, drinking at happy hour prices. The men were boisterous, and Buck Thomas was enjoying the attention.

"Congratulations, Buck! I know you wanted this," said Stuart, raising his beer glass to his friend.

"Hey, William! Shit, *anything* to get away from this filthy, boring shipyard! Did you hear, Gordy is leaving too!"

"No! Where are you going, Gordy?"

"Pensacola! Flight School, William, gonna fly the jet. Just got my orders today!"

William was nonplussed. "Didn't you have to extend to get that?"

"Yeah, two years, but what the hell; I'm probably going to stay in, anyway."

Jesus, I'm going to be the only one left if this keeps up, thought William, as he half listened to Buck talking about doing river patrols in the forty-foot swift boats, taking the war to the enemy with the boat's twin .50-caliber machine guns and other weapons. Buck was really excited and he made it sound like an enormous lark. Good for Buck, thought William. Of course, he doesn't have a wife to consider. Imagine Gordy, though, adding two years to his commitment, and going aviation!

"So what do you think, William? Why not come and join me? With your jacket, you could get a boat, easy!" Buck slapped him on the shoulder.

"Gee, maybe I would, Buck, if I didn't think my wife would cut my balls off if I asked for orders." There was a chorus of jeers, and laughter. "Besides, staying here and getting short is a dirty job, but somebody has to do it." Stuart refilled his beer glass and forced himself to join the fun of the party.

21 April 1967

The XO stopped Stuart as he was leaving the wardroom after breakfast. "A word, William."

"Yes, sir."

"My cabin, ten minutes."

"Yes, sir." I wonder what that's about, thought Stuart. He

walked up to the hangar deck, and took the morning report from the chief and the division. All present or accounted for, sir. Fine, mused Stuart. Every day the same. The men looked good, all except Mendoza, who managed insolence even when standing at attention. Stuart looked at Mendoza's dungarees, tailored like all his uniforms, skintight to the thighs, flaring widely to the bell bottoms. "Chief?"

"Yessir."

"Get Mendoza into a proper working uniform of the United States Navy."

"Yessir." The chief allowed himself a half smile. Mendoza's eyes smoldered with hatred, and a few snickers could be heard from the men. Stuart turned away from the men, and spoke to the chief alone. "I want that man out of this division, Chief Everson."

"Workin' on it, sir," said the chief, barely moving his lips. "Without him, we got a good division."

"Right, Chief." Stuart strode from the hangar deck to the XO's stateroom.

The door to the XO's stateroom was closed, so Stuart knocked and waited. After perhaps thirty seconds, Commander Simon barked "enter," and Stuart did. Stuart realized that this was the first time he had been into the executive officer's quarters since the day some eleven months before when he had received his assignment to G Division. It seemed a very long time ago. "Commander?"

The XO smiled his tiny smile. "Sit, William. This will be brief. The captain wants to see you in his cabin, at ten-hundred hours, exactly."

William felt a jolt of electricity. The captain rarely bothered with junior officers. "May I ask what the captain wants, Commander?"

The commander arched his brows, indicating the question was inappropriate. "The captain will enlighten you, at ten-hundred, William."

"Yes, sir. Sorry, sir."

The XO granted Stuart a wintry smile. "Until ten, then William? Close the door as you leave, please."

That man hates the entire world, thought William, closing the door behind himself. A shiver ran down his spine.

Mendoza caught Moser putting his shaving gear into his locker. Moser shaved morning and evening, even when he wasn't going ashore. Even freshly shaven, his big cheeks were blue.

"Hey, Moser, goin' ashore tonight?" Mendoza makes it sound like a taunt, thought Moser; he knows I'm broker than ever.

"No, Juan, I'm takin' duty for Harada. His girlfrin' is sick."

"Sick, my ass, she's preg. Bet he paid you five bucks to take his duty," smirked Mendoza.

Ten, actually, thought Moser, bleakly. "I gotta get to the armory, Juan."

"I'm still keeping a place for you in the deal, man."

Moser sighed. I sure could use it. "No, Juan, but thanks."

"Hey, man, I understand. I'll be here, if you change your mind."

"Thanks, Juan."

Mendoza started to walk away, then came back. "Hey, man, my momma sent me *another* box a' cookies, an' I got no room in my locker. Could you keep it for me?"

Moser took the box and put it in the bottom of his nearly empty locker. "No sweat, man. Jest tell me when you want it."

"Thanks, man. Catch you later."

"Yeah. Hey, take care, Juan."

Mendoza walked to the ladder that would carry him to the hangar deck, then to mount 52, grinning broadly. You in the drug business now, asshole buddy of mine.

Stuart busied himself with yet another sitrep, a report on the status of the after-port-side mount, called mount 58. The old gun continued to have more problems than all of the others put together, but Stuart felt a certain affection for it. When he had first become assistant division officer of G Division, mount 58 had been his general quarters station. She was now Gunner's Mate Third Class Gretz's mount, and he and his crew labored to keep her spotless and shining, but stack gas had eaten into every crack and seam for twenty years, and the gun got worse despite the effort. Nonetheless, when the *Valley* had taken her practice fire at the towed target sled off Okinawa, fifty-eight alone had direct hits under visual spot. Stuart looked at his watch continuously as he labored over the boring report form, until finally it was 0950. He locked away the file, climbed out of the division office, and made his way to the captain's in-port cabin.

Stuart was admitted by a uniformed Filipino steward, who gave him coffee from a silver pot, and withdrew. The in-port cabin was like a house, or at least a big apartment, suspended below the flight deck. The living room, Stuart couldn't think of any other words to describe it, was twenty feet by thirty, and furnished with leather chairs and sofas, a rich deep blue carpet, and oil paintings of naval battles on the bulkheads. Stuart had been in the room only once before, the day a month ago when he had been promoted to lieutenant, junior grade, and the captain and the commander had snapped into place his new shoulder boards with a stripe and a half. Seated on a leather sofa, peering at a painting of the USS *Wasp*, a revolutionary war sloop of war engaging the HMS *Frolic*, Stuart wondered what the rest of the in-port cabin contained, though he never expected to see it.

A door opened in the bulkhead to Stuart's right, and the captain walked in, followed by the XO. Stuart rose to attention, and was invited to sit down. The captain was carrying a thin folder, which he placed on the coffee table in front of Stuart. The captain congratulated Stuart on his marriage and repeated his apologies at being unable to attend, then got down to business.

"William, I'm sure you know this old warrior lady will be in dry dock for some months, and I know you're bored at the prospect."

"I'll see her through and back to sea, Captain."

The captain put on his half-lens reading glasses. "Thank you, William, that's the right thing to say. But luckily for you, you will not." The captain tapped the folder on the table in front of him. "This folder contains new orders for you, William. You're to be spared the drudgery of the rest of the yard period."

William swallowed, half elated, half panicked. "Orders, sir?" he croaked.

"Yes," smiled the captain. "You are to report to the Naval Demolition Training School at San Diego, then a quickie course in battlefield casualty management—read first aid—then to the Seventh Air and Naval Liaison Company—Seventh ANGLICO—in Danang."

Stuart felt as though he had been kicked in the solar plexus. He was totally breathless, and had to wait until he could get some air before he replied. "Whe-when does this happen, sir?"

"The first of the schools begins in three weeks."

Stuart sat silent. Karen is going to go crazy, he thought.

"It's a great opportunity, William. This assignment will launch your career." The captain seemed hurt that Stuart wasn't jumping for joy.

Stuart regained his composure. Of course it would, he thought, and I really don't want to spend six months in the yard. "Captain, I just got married," he blurted.

"I know, and the little lady may not love the idea that her officer is going back overseas so soon, but it really will be good for you. For both of you."

"Yes, sir, but I'm a reserve. I just—I know it's an honor, sir, but I had kind of wanted to spend some time with my wife" I shouldn't be saying this, he thought, but Karen—

The captain took off his reading glasses, and dropped them on top of the orders. He suddenly looked tired. "William, you are a serving officer in the United States Navy. You have received the top fitness reports from the weapons officer, and from me. Please don't embarrass us."

"No, sir," said William, quickly.

"It's a volunteer assignment, six months only. You know we want you to consider staying in the Navy. We know you like the Navy more than you admit."

"Yes, sir." William knew he did like the Navy, and he felt small for putting his own preference before his duty. "I understand, Captain."

"My wife, and the other *Valley* wives, will look after Karen. In six months, you will have a jacket the envy of any jaygee in the Navy. If you want to get out, fine. If you want to stay in, go regular Navy; you will be well placed."

Stuart felt miserable. He wanted to please the captain, and he realized he wanted to go back to Nam, where it was happening. But he loved his wife, and his marriage, and his little apartment in Long Beach. "Yes, sir. Thank you, sir."

"Talk to your wife, then come and see me tomorrow, William."

"Yes, sir. Sir, I'm proud to be selected for an ANGLICO." Stuart was only vaguely aware of what an ANGLICO did, but he had heard it was both elite and highly visible.

"Talk to your wife, William, and decide. It's a volunteer assignment."

"Yes, sir, I will. What time should I report to you tomorrow, sir?"

"Ten-hundred would be fine, William."

"Yes, sir." And I have seven hours to figure out what to say to Karen, he thought, as he walked from the captain's cabin in a daze.

"Goddammit, William, why in the fuck does it have to be you?" William was shocked by the tone and vehemence of Karen's outburst. He had never heard such harsh language from her, or ever expected to. He was stunned enough to remain silent as she paced the room from one side to the other. "How can you just sit there, damn you? Why *you*?"

"Karen—" William felt his voice weak, pleading.

"Just tell me, William! You went to Vietnam! You were

wounded! You even brought back a *fucking medal*! Haven't you had enough? Haven't *they* had enough?''

"Karen, it's a six months tour, and that's it, stateside shore duty until I get out—"

"Damn you! You were missing from my life, except for a week in Manhattan Beach, from February of last year to January of this year! *Another* six months is OK with you?''

"Karen, I'm a naval officer. I have to go where they tell me; you know that.'' William tried to embrace his wife, but she shook herself free and walked away from him. She felt a deep hurt, mixed with anger. Karen turned to look at him, her face screwed up with rage. She was almost ugly. Suddenly she burst into tears, and ran to him, throwing her arms around him and sobbing like a widow at a graveside.

William closed his eyes as he held her, holding back his own tears. He had to go, he knew, even though the captain had left open the door by saying it was a volunteer assignment. William knew for certain that his navy career would be ruined if he went back and said he wouldn't go. He also knew he had to go for something inside himself. No man need seek danger, William's ancestor had written during the Civil War, but none could run from it once it was at hand. Danger in war was an honor unto itself.

Yet is that a selfish position? he asked himself, as Karen keened softly in his arms, and he rocked her gently. Hell, the truth is, I want to go back, at least to get close to the fight. But do I have a right to put an ancient male honor and the ethics of the armed service ahead of Karen's happiness? He knew what the captain would say, or Bill Donald, or even Hoop. Other women have made greater sacrifices. I'm just being sent to some headquarters type of job for six months; Karen will be all right. He nuzzled her hair and she raised her face, red from crying and wrinkled from pressing into his shirt. She kissed him, hard, deeply, then pushed him backward, into the tiny bedroom and onto the bed.

Their lovemaking was urgent, almost violent, as Karen took complete control. She seemed to be able to go places in her passion where he could not follow, though she tried to draw him after her into the scary night where passion became total abandon. She thrashed wildly, giving voice to harsh cries that could mean pleasure or pain or savage anger. She pressed him onto his back and rode his penis mercilessly, painfully, as if to break it. He winced as her nails pulled skin from his chest in angry, parallel lines. He was enchanted, and he was afraid. Finally she came with a shudder, and a long, low cry, and collapsed on his chest. They were soaked with sweat. William felt his penis soften while still inside her, though he had not come. Karen rolled off him, and lay quietly, looking at him. He looked at her, and then at the ceiling, then back at her. "I love you, Karen." She didn't reply, but turned her face to the pillow, and began to cry again, softly. William got up and went into the shower.

"William, did you know about these orders back to Vietnam before we were married?" The question had come across the small room like a missile, and William had almost ducked. They had prepared and eaten dinner in virtual silence, then washed the dishes, and now they sat across the room from each other, staring at the flickering image on Karen's tiny black and white television.

"No, of course not, love. I only found out today."

"Would you have still wanted to get married if you had known?"

"Of course," he paused, but Karen sat silent. "Wouldn't you have?"

Karen looked at William across the room. She seemed to be far away. "Why would you want to marry me, and then go back to Vietnam? Marriage means *together*, it means *sharing*, and *loving*. I love you, your bright spirit, William, but I also need what your body gives me. Sometimes I think I'm only truly me when I'm loving you. While you were gone, I wasn't really sure *who* I was, Karen the bank trainee, Karen of Long Beach and the Bank of America, but not Karen the *woman*. Since you've been back, all those Karens have become one again, William, and I've been so *happy*—" the word came out like a sob "—and now you want to go away again!"

William got up quickly, crossed the room, and sat beside his wife, hugging her as she began to cry, rubbing her eyes with her knuckles like a little girl. There was a lump in his throat, and William felt overwhelmed with the enormity of his love for her. For a moment he just held her, awkwardly, as she sat stiffly. He wanted to do anything that would make it right for her. "Karen, the last thing, the very last thing I want on this earth is to be separated from you, ever. But suppose, just suppose, I were to go to the Navy, and say I've done enough for you, for the country, and now I just want to stay home. What would you think of me, as a man?"

"I would still love you, and I would still have you."

"I'd never feel worthy of you, ever again, if I did that."

"But why? What do you care about most? Loving me, or some medieval code? You already have a goddamn medal."

"Karen, there's a war on. The armed forces have to fight when called. Men have to go when called."

"Oh, William! Don't you read the newspapers? Don't you watch television? Nobody wants this war, *nobody*! Every day, people protest, march, demonstrate!"

"Students, perhaps afraid to go themselves—"

"William! Students, and grandmothers, and everyone! People either oppose the war, or simply don't care!" Karen bent forward, pressing her face to her knees, and put her hands over her ears.

William sat silently, his arms folded across his chest. His breathing was rapid and shallow, as his mind raced from the adrenaline of fear and anger and confusion. "Karen, I care about the war. Men I work with, men I respect care about winning the war, and ending it, and coming home. But we have to fight and win; we can't just turn our backs."

"Why, *why* do you have to care?" said Karen to her knees.

William fought the fear, and the anger, and the overriding confusion. He had never really tried to analyze the war. He just went, because—dammit, because the country had called. "Maybe I do it for you. For us, Karen. To be your man, I have to be a man, to myself. That isn't medieval."

Karen dropped her hands, and looked at him, suddenly dry-eyed. It was a look of pure contempt. She shook off his arm and stood up. "You won't be satisfied until you come home in a goddamned box." She turned and strode into the bedroom, and slammed the door.

William sat in the G Division office, drinking coffee and smoking. He couldn't decided which tasted worse, the coffee or the cigarettes. His head pounded as he thought about the awful fight with Karen and what it might mean to his marriage.

After Karen had gone into the bedroom and closed the door, he sat quietly for a while, drinking Scotch and smoking, staring at the television set with no idea what he was watching. After an hour, he got up, shut off the TV, and brushed his teeth. When he went to the bedroom, he found the door was locked. He had knocked gently, then more loudly. Karen had called through the doorway for him to go away. He pleaded, but she didn't answer. He went into the kitchen and got the whiskey bottle, and quietly finished it, along with another ten cigarettes. He found himself weeping with frustration and rage, so he brushed his teeth again, and pounded on the bedroom door, demanding to be let in. Karen had shouted hateful things at him, suggesting, among other things, that since he loved the Navy more than his wife, he could go sleep on his ship. William would have done that, he was angry enough, but he knew he had drunk far too much either to drive or be seen on the ship. Finally, he gave up, and slept on the old, too-short couch in the living room, in his clothes. It was no wonder he felt awful.

Karen and he had both apologized in the morning, but her manner had been distant. She announced that her Aunt Liz had invited them down to Balboa for the weekend, and she hoped they could drive down after she got home from work.

"Ah, Karen, I have the duty on Saturday. I'll drive down Sunday, early."

Karen had smiled sweetly and said that would be fine. She would, therefore, go directly from work. It meant he would sleep alone for the next two nights at least, he thought bleakly.

Stuart crushed out the cigarette. He could not be in a worse humor, and he hoped nothing else would happen today. He heard the clatter as a sailor came down the ladder into the division office, and winced as the sound reverberated inside his head. It was Simmons, one of the new replacements.

"Sir," began Simmons, breathlessly, "the chief sent me. He wants you to come to the ammo handling room under mount 53, right away, sir."

Stuart closed his eyes, then opened them, slowly. His silent wish had not been granted, and Simmons was still there. "What's the trouble, Simmons?"

"He just said to get you, sir; said he had to wait right there."

Stuart pushed himself out of the chair and stood. He was dizzy, and he wanted to throw up the greasy breakfast he had eaten. Pull yourself together, man, he thought. He picked up his cap, and followed Simmons through ladders and passageways up to the flight deck, then to mount 53, just forward of the bridge, and down into the ammunition handling room directly below the mount. In the dim light of the handling room, Stuart could see the chief standing over a scared-looking Juan Mendoza.

"Caught this man smokin' a Mary-juana cigarette, Mr. Stuart, an' I think I foun' his stash."

Stuart pressed his fingers to his throbbing temples as nausea and rage fought for control.

Mendoza felt cornered, trapped between the bulk of the chief and the ammunition hoist inside which he had stashed a shoebox full of cleaned, cured grass, the twin of the one in Moser's locker. He had figured no one would be going in and out of the ammo handling space since the ship had off-loaded all of her ammo in Seal Beach weeks before. Harada was supposed to clean the space, but Mendoza was sure he never opened the hoist itself, and besides, Harada was smart enough to be afraid of Mendoza. Everything would have been fine if I hadn't come in here for a quick toke to make the morning go, thought Mendoza. The fucking chief must have been following me around, because no sooner did I get it rolled and lit up, the fucking hump came charging in and clouted me. My fucking head still rings.

Mendoza was afraid of the chief. He was a big man, and he was quick with his fists when no officer was looking. Mendoza had never been able to con the chief, or to buy him off. For this reason, he was glad to see the division officer step into the ammo handling room, and to see his expression of disgust. This is a man who can be had, thought Mendoza, though Stuart had proved less of a patsy than most of these college-boy assholes. Nevertheless, at least his being here will keep the chief from doing a tap dance on my skull.

Stuart finished rubbing his eyes, pushing the rage back deep in his brain. His mouth was dry, and he still wanted to throw up. Make yourself think, William, he thought. This is a serious problem, but if we handle it just right, old Mendoza is gonzo. "Where is the marijuana cigarette, chief?"

"There, sir." The chief pointed to a stamped-out butt on the steel deck between his own feet.

Stuart took his little spiral notebook from his shirt pocket, tore out a clean page, and knelt and swept the butt and the surrounding ashes onto the paper. He lifted the paper carefully, and set it on the flat surface of the ready ammo box near the hatch. "That's evidence, chief. You'll have to write down where you first saw it, and how you observed it continuously until I took control of it."

"I know, sir, I bin there."

"Good." Stuart stood up, and his head reeled. "So, where's the stash?"

"In the hoist, sir." The chief twisted open the bronze dogs, then lifted the lid. Stuart could see a shoebox.

"You look inside?"

"No, sir," said the chief with a grin. "Figured I'd best wait for you."

"Good, we'll get the master-at-arms to remove it, presently."

Mendoza snorted. It was the first sound he had made since Stuart had entered the space.

"This is funny, Mendoza?" asked Stuart.

"I was just thinkin', sir, if that shoebox is what you think it is, you give it to the M-As, they just gonna steal it.''Mendoza was working up his courage, getting some defiance into his voice.

"Do you have anything else to say, Mendoza?"

"Yes, sir! Only that this is a crock. I'm in here, so maybe havin' a smoke, whatever, and the fuckin'—sorry sir—the *chief*, sir, comes bustin' in, and belts me, an' there he, you know, *finds* this box he says is Jane. I don' know *what* is in that box.''

"This isn't your property?"

"Hell, no, sir!"

"Then whose do you suppose it is?"

Mendoza smiled. Dumb fucking officer, always trying to be fair. "Maybe the chief's. Like he says, he found it."

The chief started forward, his big fists balled. A gesture from the Lieutenant stopped him. William felt his hangover and his frustration drain away, like the water after a cold shower. The bright, ice-hard sharpness of anger swept over his mind, and he looked at Mendoza. What manner of creature is this? He tears at the very fabric of discipline, of honor, of duty. "So you, Mendoza, say that you're innocent, no *persecuted*, in this matter?"

Mendoza couldn't decipher the taut expression on the Lieutenant's face, and that cost him some of his confidence. "Well, yeah, uh, yes, sir. You know the chief always has it in for me."

Stuart heard a growl from the chief, behind him, and again held up his hand. "And, Mendoza, what will you say if we can *prove, prove* that this box is yours?" Stuart pointed at the open hoist, his gesture abrupt. He expected Mendoza to show fear in his eyes, and Mendoza did. "There will be fingerprints all over it, and the chief has told us he didn't touch it." Stuart knew that the chances of lifting a readable print from a cardboard box were minimal, but he doubted Mendoza would know that.

Mendoza's anger, like that of a cornered rat, overcame his fear. "You still could do nothing, *Mister* Stuart, because maybe the box belongs to your war-hero buddy, *Moser*!"

Stuart was taken aback, but fought not to show it. So the little weasel has baited a trap.

"Sir," growled the chief, on the edge of losing control, "maybe I asked you to come up here, ah, prematurely. Let me *talk* to Mendoza—"

"He already whupped me once. I got rights—"

"Shut UP!" bellowed Stuart. He paused, forcing a veneer of calm over his anger. He spoke softly. "Mendoza, you've made accusations, serious accusations. Are you sure that you wish to say these things, for the record?"

Mendoza felt good. Fuck you, asshole, he thought, as he

worked his face into an insolent smile. "I don't know nothin' sir; I'm just tired of bein' dumped on for nothin'."

Stuart turned, slowly, and confronted the chief. "Chief, I want you to go down to the armory, and ask, *ask* Moser for his permission to search his locker. If he refuses, confiscate his locker key, and report to me in the division office. If he agrees, and if you find anything he can't explain, lock his locker, and wait for me. Clear?"

"Yes, sir," said the chief, visibly angry. "What about Mendoza?"

Stuart tried to make his face blank. "Chief, Mendoza has made serious allegations, which must be heard."

The chief shifted his bulk. His face was knotted with rage. "Sir, with due respect, such a *hearing* is usually taken by a *chief* in this man's Navy!"

Stuart smiled. Only the chief could see the smile. "I understand, chief, but given the extent of Mendoza's allegations, I think it better if I talk to him."

The chief caught Stuart's expression, and allowed his face to relax. "I understand, sir; I'm sure you'll handle it best." He turned and left the handling room.

Mendoza calmed himself. Now I have the asshole officer to myself, he thought. Let him make the first move.

Stuart propped his left foot against the hoist, and pulled up his sock. What kind of a pussy wears long socks, thought Mendoza, gaining confidence. "So, Juan, what do we really have here? Surely you don't think the chief and your friend Moser are setting you up?"

"I don't have nothin' more to say, sir."

Stuart gestured casually toward the joint, resting on the sheet of notebook paper on the ready box. "You were smoking a joint, at the very least."

Mendoza moved cat quick, and swept the joint off the ready box onto the deck, then scattered it with his boot. "What *fucking* evidence, *sir*? You got no shit, an' if you get me, your pal Moser goes down, and maybe the chief!"

Stuart moved forward and struck Mendoza on the ear with an open hand. The force of the blow sent Mendoza skidding on his ass across the deck and into the bulkhead. Mendoza sat silently and smiled, then rubbed the ear. "You can't do that, man. They court-martial you for hitting me."

"Why, Mendoza? What happened?" Stuart smiled, but his eyes were ugly.

Mendoza began to feel afraid. Better deal, he thought, getting slowly to his feet. "OK, Mister Stuart, I—" The second blow rang his head, and he slipped to his knees. "Hey, officers can't just hit enlisted men! We can't hit back!"

Stuart circled, watching the downed man. He unbuttoned his shirt, and tossed it toward the bulkhead, then tossed his cap after it. "Officer, Juan? I don't have any insignia, and lots of civilian yardbirds wear khaki pants, just like these. There isn't a lot of light in here; I could be anyone."

Definitely crazy, thought Mendoza. "You sayin' I should hit you back?"

Stuart stood, casual, relaxed. The indifference of the pose infuriated Mendoza. "You make accusations against your friends—my friends, too, Juan. Surely you're not afraid to back them up?"

Mendoza shifted himself, ready to spring. Stuart just stood there. Mendoza spoke, very softly, "Esta bien, culo," then he rushed. In one motion, Stuart slipped off his shoe, and kicked Mendoza's flying body in the solar plexus. Mendoza's lungs emptied in a pained gasp, and he crashed to the steel deck, flat on his back. Stuart stood smiling faintly as Mendoza caught his breath. It took a long time. Mendoza gasped, "You fucker, you'll never get away with this! I'll just sho-show these bruises to the Captain, and you'll be permanently fucked—"

Stuart's second kick caught Mendoza in the throat, choking off the sound. Mendoza's harsh breathing had a sickening clicking sound. Stuart kicked again, striking under the last rib, and Mendoza curled into a ball and began to whimper.

"There won't be any bruises, Juan, other than those you might have gotten from a fall down a ladder." Stuart paused as Mendoza continued to gasp and whimper. "But then, if you did show marks from a fight, who would know who did it? You have a lot of enemies." Stuart slowly raised his leg in the crane posture. Mendoza cringed back into the corner between the deck and the bulkhead.

"OK, what do you want?" Mendoza's plea barely registered on Stuart's rage.

Stuart lowered the threatening leg. "Do you wish to reconsider your story about whose box of dope this is in the hoist?"

Mendoza battled his terror, but could not overcome it. "It's mine," he rasped.

"And the stash we're sure to find in Moser's locker?"

"Mine," said Mendoza, miserably.

"And the chief. Do you still wish to say he was involved?"

"No." Mendoza rolled to a kneeling position, holding his battered ribs.

Stuart knelt on the deck in front of Mendoza. "And, Juan,

you will remember your story, when you go before the captain?''
His face was inches from Mendoza's, and he could smell the
other man's fear.

"Yes. Yes, sir," Mendoza blubbered.

Stuart struck Mendoza sharply on his other ear with an open
hand, and Mendoza cried out. "And, Juan, you aren't going to
suggest, even on the mess decks, you were beaten by a mere
college-boy officer, are you?"

"No, sir, just stop; you're killing me."

Stuart sat back on his haunches, smiling his awful smile.
"Hardly, Juan. Are we agreed the lesson has been learned?"

"Yes, sir." Oh, God, get me out of here, thought Mendoza.

Stuart jumped up, and kicked Mendoza again, in precisely the
same spot as the previous kick under the ribs. Mendoza
screamed. "We'll just *reinforce* the lesson, Juan." Stuart kicked
him again, in the same spot, and Mendoza waited and crawled
behind the hoist. "Wait here, Mendoza, for the chief, or the
master-at-arms. Do you understand?"

"Yes, sir," sobbed Mendoza.

"Understand *everything*?"

"Yes, *sir*!"

Stuart stood, and retrieved his shoe, then his shirt and cap,
and put them on. "So be it."

14 May 1967   USS *Valley Forge*, in port, Long Beach

Stuart walked into the ship's armory and found Moser working on the action of a .50-caliber machine gun.

"You wanted to see me, Moser?"

"Um, yessir." The big man looked up, then continued prying the delicate return spring from the mechanism.

Stuart marveled at the deftness of Moser's blunt fingers, and at his concentration on the work, but he felt antsy, and wanted to take care of Moser's problem, and get on with his own. "The chief said you wanted to see me privately, and in here. What is it we couldn't deal with in the division office?" Stuart winced at the irritation in his voice, but couldn't think of a reason to be cross with Moser.

"Uh, yes, sir. I jes' thought we'd be better off in private. I won't keep you long."

Stuart felt his irritation rising again. He had gotten used to Moser's slow speech, but just now he wished the big man would come to the point. Moser was filing the edge of some part of the disassembled machine gun, something that looked like a cam. His absorption in the task was complete, and Stuart felt Moser had completely forgotten his presence. "Moser, please, what is it you wanted to say?"

Moser gave the cam one final careful stroke with the jeweler's

292

file, then took the part from the vise and dropped it back into the solvent bath. "There she be. Well, Mister Stuart, I'm real concerned about Juan."

Fucking Mendoza, thought Stuart, always trouble, and always dragging Moser into his schemes. Well, no more. "What about Mendoza, Moser?"

"Well, you know, sir, he was my friend, all the way from San Diego."

The irritation flickered low in Stuart's brain. "Moser, it's not my business to pick your friends, but you have to know that Mendoza took advantage of your friendship many times." Including setting you up to take his drug bust, thought Stuart, though it will do no good to say so.

"Yeah, I know. Juan thought I was dumb, an' maybe I am." Moser looked sad, even sorry.

"Well, you're a third class gunner's mate in a good division, and Mendoza is busted back to seaman recruit and on his way to the brig in San Diego to do two years hard time, so who looks dumb now?"

"Oh, I know, sir. I know Juan got me into trouble, fightin' and all. And I figured he tried to set me up with his dope stash in my locker."

There's hope for you yet, thought Stuart. "Then why do you still think of him as your friend?"

Moser turned from the work in front of him and looked fully at Stuart. His rugged face held a look of puzzlement, even sorrow. "I ain't got no frinds, sir. At least Juan, he needed me." Stuart eased himself into the stool next to Moser's workbench, fighting the impatience inside him. He thought briefly of all the paperwork he had to get through before he turned over the division in four days. Relax, he told himself. It's your job, and besides, you owe it to the kid to talk to him; he really has no one else. "I almos' wish I could go with him."

"Moser, Juan was a fuck-up, from the day he came onto this ship, and probably will be all his life. You have all the makings of a good sailor, and you're never going the route Mendoza has chosen."

"When does he actually go to the big brig, sir?"

"In a few days, as soon as the verdict of the special court-martial is confirmed."

Moser extracted another tiny part of the machine gun in front of him and dropped it into the cleaning pan. Stuart waited. "Sir, I know Juan stole, an' cheated at cards, an' I guess I know he was dealin' marijuana. For a long time, I wouldn't believe what folks said, but I know. Juan got me into things, sure, but he always came to me. The other guys don't even talk to me.''

"Moser, I talk to you.'' For another week, then what? I wonder if I should tell him I'm leaving? ''And the chief talks to you. All Mendoza ever did was get you into trouble.''

"You talk to me, sir, when you're not busy, an' I know you're busy now, gettin' ready to leave, and all. The chief, well mostly he jest yells.''

"What about me leaving, Moser?''

"I heard you bin transferred off the *Valley*, to some unit back over in Nam. Ain't it true, sir?'' Moser seemed to cheer up a little.

"It's true, Moser, but nobody is supposed to know until a new division officer is named.''

"That's OK, sir. I won't say nothin'. Sir? Do you like me, sir?''

"Sure, I like you, Moser.'' Stuart smiled. He did like big Moser.

"I know, sir.'' Moser seemed suddenly happy. ''Then, kin I go with you in country?''

Stuart felt surprised, amused, and flattered. ''Well, Moser, that's nice of you, but you have an important job here, and the war's a little dangerous.''

"I don't care, sir! You see, I like you, too.''

"Well, Moser, I—''

"You 'member, Lieutenant, when you took that convoy of mike boats up the Cua Viet, an' you took me along, me an' the long-barreled fifty? An' I shot them gooks on the riverbank?''

"Well, sure, but—''

"This here's the same gun!'' said Moser, pointing to the parts in the tray. ''And 'member when we got back, you asked me ta volunteer if'n yo' ever agin needed someone to guard your back? Well, sir, you're goin' in harm's way, and I'm volunteerin'!''

Stuart was moved. He shook his head, and smiled at the big man. ''Moser, now all that's true, and I sure appreciate what you've done for me, but why in hell would you want to go into the shit with me?''

"Well, sir, I've thought about it. I don' like 'at many people. You always stood up fer me when I got into trouble.'' Moser actually looked eager.

"OK, Moser.''

" 'Sides, somebody got to cover your back, Lieutenant.''

"OK, but I don't think I can take you with me, Moser.'' Moser looked a little hurt. Damn.

"Sir, I'd really like to go with you.'' The big man's voice was soft, but insistent. Well, why not, thought Stuart. The guy did save my life; I had almost forgotten. I can at least try.

"OK, Moser. I'll talk to the people."

---

18 May 1967   Camp Seven

Billy sat on his bunk, the parts of his M-14 spread out in front of him. Smith lay dozing across from him on Trace's bunk. Trace and Smith rarely left Hunter alone anymore; Billy knew they were watching him, but he didn't mind. He rather liked the company. "What's the rumor of the day, Smith?"

Smith sat up. "Hey, Sarge. You feelin' better?"

Billy smiled. It's important to put my friends' minds at ease. "Yeah, better each day. I just keep eating and sleeping good, I'll be one hundred percent in a coupla more days. So what have I missed?"

"Not much. You gave us a scare, blacking out like that."

Billy remembered everything that had happened before he went into sick bay. "Yeah. Oh malaria really took me for a turn."

"You, ah, remember much about that day, when you blacked out?"

"Not really. A few things, but fuzzy." Sure, I remember it all, Smith; who could ever forget such horror? But I have it locked away in a tiny part of my brain, knowledge waiting to be used. "I just remember you and Trace helping me."

Smith looked relieved. "Hey, Sarge, don' mean nothing. Man's gotta look after his buddies." Smith smiled happily. Billy smiled back, completing reassembly of his weapon. Be relieved, Smith, you did the right thing.

Trace came in and sat. "You lookin' a little better, Billy."

"Yeah, stronger every day. The captain got any work for us, Trace?"

Trace grinned. "You anxious to nightcrawl, Bro?"

Billy shrugged. "Yeah, I guess I am. Sit around camp, you think too much, right?" Billy waited to see how they would take that one.

Trace frowned. Smith looked at Trace, and then down at his feet. Trace spoke softly, "Guess there's a lot you still don't want to think about, Bro."

Billy played his face. He hoped he looked manly and grieving at the same time. Trace and Smith must be made to feel at ease. "Well, of course. But I want to put all that behind me. A little walk in the darkness might be just the thing to make me feel better." Billy chuckled inside his mind. It was funny how almost anything you said had a double meaning when you had a secret.

Trace seemed to relax a little. "Yeah, we've all been in camp too long. Anyway, we're still at max readiness, bags packed and canteens full, but the captain doesn't have anything down for us for today or tomorrow."

"Anybody in the squad got any problems—other than me?" Another gentle probe.

Trace stood up. "Nothing getting at you you can't handle, Sergeant Hunter. You a marine and a nightcrawler. You tough enough."

Hunter stood and slapped Trace's shoulder. He made his face gentle. "I got to thank you two for helping me through it. I think I'll just go see the captain and volunteer us for Vinh Linh."

Trace and Smith laughed nervously at the old joke. When the Marine Corps had first moved into northeastern I Corps, some gung-ho second lieutenant had written a staff memo declaring the market town of Vinh Linh, some seven kilometers inside North Vietnam, to be an ideal target for a commando raid. LRRPs all tossed occasionally in their sleep fearing some rear-area idiot might actually order such an operation.

Hunter left the hootch and strolled over to the wood and corrugated steel building that housed the company office. He could see Trace and Smith follow ten paces behind, then Smith put his hand on Trace's shoulder, and they veered off toward the EM club.

Hunter found the captain in his office talking to a young black second lieutenant. "Sorry to interrupt, sir, I'll come back."

"No, come in, Sergeant. This is Second Lieutenant Edward Brown. He just reported in, and I'm putting him in charge of your patrol squad." Lieutenant Brown jumped up and wrung Hunter's hand.

Strange, thought Billy, for weeks I have wanted an officer to take some of the load, yet now I'm not so sure. "Welcome to LRRPs, sir."

"Thank you, Sergeant, Hunter, isn't it? Captain Rodriguez has nothing but praise for the way you've run your squad. I only hope I won't get in the way." The lieutenant smiled winningly; the captain looked sour.

The captain stood. "I think we're through here, Lieutenant. Why don't you take a walk with Hunter, look around? Hunter, you could drop the lieutenant by the officers' mess when you're finished."

"Aye, aye, sir. Ah, sir? A question?"

"Go ahead."

"Sir, the guys are kind of curious about why it's so quiet. We going up any time soon?"

The captain managed his sardonic half smile. "I didn't know your men were such fire-eaters, Sergeant Hunter. No, nothing is imminent, but I take note of your zeal."

"Ah, yes, sir. The men are just restless, that's all." Hunter thought of adding a salute, but decided that would be way overdoing it. Once again, he heard the chuckle inside his brain.

The captain regarded him skeptically. "You're feeling better, Hunter?"

"Yes, sir! Ready to go."

"Hunter had a bit of a malaria problem last week," said the captain in answer to Lieutenant Brown's unspoken question. "You were sick enough that the doc wanted to send you home, Sergeant."

Hunter remembered that. The news that would have delighted any marine in Vietnam had left him near panic. He had assured the navy doctor that he was fit to return to duty, and the doctor had reluctantly agreed to send him back to his unit. "It was just malaria, Captain. Everybody has malaria." It's just Nam, he wanted to say, and I'm not done with Nam, yet.

The captain smiled. "Well, anyway, I'm glad you're feeling good. You're too good a man to lose. Until later, then, Lieutenant Brown?"

Hunter walked out into the fading twilight, with Brown following.

19 May 1967

Hunter flagged a passing six-by truck and rode over to Camp Five. He got down by the little commissary and bought a pack of cigarettes. He then strolled in the general direction of Whitenigger's hootch, taking in details of the surrounding area. Camp Five was larger than Camp Seven, but laid out in much the same way, with offices, machine shops, mess halls, and the parade ground/LZ in the middle, living hootches and tents in rings surrounding the central area, and the wire with guard towers beyond. Whitenigger's sturdily constructed hootch was in the inner ring, a preferred spot, near the earthwork-revetted vehicle park. It was a nice location, and a nice hootch, built on a platform about eighteen inches above the damp earth on columns of cinder blocks. It even had a metal roof instead of the tent-canvas roof usual for sleeping hootches. Very snug indeed, thought Hunter, walking slowly around, smoking his pack of Camels one by one. He looked at paths, and alleys between buildings, and at the guard towers. Lines and shadows, he thought.

A hand grasped his left wrist lightly. He jumped; he hadn't heard or felt anyone approach. He looking into the scowling face of Corporal Crow.

Hunter worked his face into a smile, suppressing alarms from the special corner of his brain. "Hello, Crow. I was just coming to see First Sergeant Johnson."

"He send for you, white boy?" Crow seemed to sweat bands of hatred.

"No, but we got business."

"What kinda bid-ness?"

"Same's we talked. Dealing."

"What about you' own source?"

Stupid men should never try to act clever, thought Hunter, deep in his brain. Still, I want him to think, and then to doubt. "Got blown away. I was getting it from the old dink in the ville near our wire. VC got 'em, you musta heard."

Crow looked at Hunter with hooded eyes. "I *heard*, white boy."

"Sergeant White Boy to you, Corporal," said Hunter, amiably.

Crow seethed. He looks like a rattlesnake ready to strike, thought Hunter. He willed himself to stay loose. "*Forget* that rank shit, Sergeant *Asshole*! Where *Whitenigga* involved, *Crow* beat out any damn mothafucka sergeant!"

Good, get angry, Crow, thought Hunter. "Well, anyway, let's go see First Sergeant Johnson."

"He ain't heah."

"How do you know that, Crow?"

"Cause it my *bid-ness* to know when he is an' when he ain't, white boy. Now, scat."

Billy took a step backward, held his hands up, palms forward. "Hey, no sweat, I'll come back."

"You take ma *ad-vice*, white boy, you come when *he* call you. He don' call you, you don' got *no bid-ness* here."

"I'll keep it in mind, Corporal," said Hunter, turning. He walked back to the gate, and once again caught a passing truck, and returned to Camp Seven. That should play just about right, he thought, rubbing at the constant, sharp pain in his temples. Three more days, he thought; in three days there would be no moon, and the dead would rise.

21 May 1987

"So, what do you think, Smith?" said Trace, urgently.

Smith shrugged. "He seems OK, man."

"Not different?" Trace pressed.

"OK, he is different. He seems almost old. What do you think?"

Trace paced inside the narrow hootch. "He looks at me like he's very sad about something. Not angry, just sad."

"Like it might be the last time he ever does see you."

Trace whirled, and pointed his finger at Smith, "Exactly! Like you was already dead, or he was!"

Smith nodded, "Like he's trying to be extraspecial kind."

"Yeah," said Trace, pounding his fist into his hand. "He's sure right about one thing. If we could get him out in the field, then we'd know."

Smith sipped his beer. Taps would sound in another twenty minutes. "He's in his bunk, right?"

"Yeah. Still claims he needs the extra sleep."

Smith shifted his weight in the uncomfortable chair. "You bin sayin' he was all right, Trace. Why you so uptight tonight?"

Trace slugged down the last of his Budweiser. "I don't *know*, man. Just something about the dude! Like, he's just different!" Trace again pounded his fist into his hand in frustration. "Shit, man, I don't fuckin' know! Maybe it's just the night, the night and the moon."

Smith laughed, "Us darkies always get strange in the dark o' the moon, Trace."

"Fuck you, nigger." Trace fought back a twinge of anger.

"Hoo, hoo," laughed Smith.

"I'm goin' to bed."

"Hey, Trace my man, I really think he's OK. Real sad, but cool."

"Good night, Smith."

"Good night, man. If you need me, I'll be close."

Hunter heard Trace come into the hootch, and he felt his friend bending over his bed. Still not quite sure, are you, my good friend? Trace went to bed across the passageway. Hunter listened until his breathing became regular, then he looked at his watch, 2210. Another hour, a bit less. He would need the time in hand, once it began. He felt hot; beneath the sheet he was dressed in uniform trousers in addition to his T-shirt. He would feel better once he began to move.

Hunter drifted into light sleep, waking every twenty minutes or so to check the luminous dial. At 2305, he declared it a go. Like a snake descending a rock pile, Hunter slithered down from his bed onto the wood floor. He made contact with the floor first with his fingertips, then his palms, then his elbows, chest, knees, and finally his bare feet. His ears were tuned up for the slightest sound, either from his own movement, or from Trace. Flat on the floor, he crawled silently from the hootch, caressing his boots to him as he went.

Once outside in the silent camp, Hunter pulled on his boots. The rest of his gear was in a small pouch the marines called a kangaroo, originally designed to carry battle dressings, which Hunter had hidden earlier in the space under the hootch. Out of the kangaroo Hunter took a pair of green socks, which he put on over his boots to stifle the crunch of gravel. He left the wire cutters, a short spool of wire, his spring-steel knife, and two frag grenades in the pouch, which he now secured around his waist. He put a length of flat bamboo into his left boot.

Hunter took a jar of camouflage face paint from under the hootch, and daubed his face, neck, and arms below the sleeves of his T-shirt in the dim light of the floods by the wire. In five minutes he was ready, and walking, slowly and deliberately, toward the wire.

The best spot to cross the wire was through the shallow ravine that ran out to the creek and the ville, because it had shadows of its own, even in the bright floods that illuminated the cleared zone on both sides of the wire. Hunter reached the back of the hootch closest to the wire in slow, silent steps. Standing in the deep shadow of the hootch, he studied the guard tower, watching the movement of the two sentries, who took turns peering out at the jungle. He examined the ground between the shadows he was in, inch by inch, even though he had walked over it two evenings before. He felt the texture of the night, the color of the shadows. In fifteen minutes he was once again ready to move.

Hunter felt he could probably rush to the little ravine, but decided against it. He dropped to the ground silently, and began to move in what the infiltration instructors had called the lizard. Moving first an arm, then the opposite leg, then the other arm, then the other leg, and with intervals of stillness, Hunter emerged from the shadow and became a shadow himself. Moving smoothly, sinuously, Hunter willed himself to be like a drop of dark oil flowing slowly across a smooth, shiny surface. He slipped over the top of the ravine and disappeared into it without even the smallest sound. Flowing oil is silent, he told himself, repeating it like a mantra. Flowing blood is silent.

The chain-link fence around the camp was well dug in, and Hunter slipped the cutters from the pouch and made eight careful cuts, six horizontal and two vertical. He lay against the wire, perfectly still, and then flowed through. He pulled the cut pieces together, and fastened them at the corners with short lengths of wire.

Outside the wire, the floodlights were brighter than inside, and the sentries had movable searchlights to supplement the fixed illumination. And, naturally, the sentries looked outward. Hunter took a deep breath to slow his heart, and began to move again. He crawled along the outer edge of the wire, using the lizard. He paused frequently, and finally stopped under the shadow of the guard tower itself, resting, and waiting.

Hunter heard the creak of the bamboo ladder as the relieving sentries started up. They laughed and talked. When they reached the top, a conversation began among the two sentries going off watch and the two coming on. As they chatted, discussing the night and the watch, Hunter made his slow, very slow, and painful passage through the concertina wire outside the fence. Lifting himself on fingers and toes, he flowed over the lowest wire, under the higher, changing direction as the coils of wire changed. When he came to a trip flare, he gently supported it with one hand; the fuses of the flare were mercury switches, triggered by the acceleration of a fall. Once supported, they were easily cut off and laid down on the ground, harmless. Hunter flowed through, as smooth as oil, but even still, his face and arms ran with fresh blood from the wire. He reached the outer edge of the concertina, and paused, listening. A bark of laughter burst from the tower, and Hunter heard the sounds of the off-watch sentries descending.

Hunter launched himself into the darkness, sprawling like a lizard, flowing like oil. I am invisible, he chanted. Once the searchlight swept across his body, and he froze, suspended on fingertips, one knee, and the toes of one foot. I am a shadow, he thought. The light swept on without pause. Hunter crawled, arm, leg, pause; arm, leg, pause. He entered the deep shadow of the trees.

Hunter relaxed, taking deep, measured breaths, examining the layout of Camp Seven's defenses, refiguring his way back, for he for sure was going to come back. The shadows all pointed out to the jungle. How easy for an infiltrator, he thought. Satisfied after ten minutes of study, he was up and running through the trees, toward the lights of Camp Five. When he reached the point in the shadows of the trees nearest his selected point of entry, he stopped once again, and studied the night.

A light rain had started, adding a white noise to the background. The fine drops diffused the lights of Camp Five. The shadow of Billy Hunter crept into the lighted area, in a sinuous, snake-lizard line, making for the guard tower nearest the hootch of Whitenigger Johnson. Hunter's mind suffused his being into the lizard, silent, intent on scented prey.

Whitenigger Johnson sat in his big chair behind his desk, stacking money in neat piles. Tonight was payday for his little group, and he was satisfied. Drugs had proven a much more dependable source of revenue than the petty graft he had organized in exchange for contracts for booze, food, and entertainment for the officers', sergeants', and EM clubs, and since the elimination of the old gook's drug push by Camp Seven, the monopoly was total. He had been disturbed by Crow's report of Sergeant Hunter's showing up near his hootch two days before, but Crow worried a lot, and Hunter hadn't been back.

Hunter reached the wire of Camp Five, and started through, keeping to the dark shadow of the guard tower. I am the snake, the snake with legs, the fire lizard. The twenty feet of concertina took him two minutes to pass, an arm, then a leg. The trip flares, backlit by the camp's floodlights, were cut off, and laid down. Billy probed ahead of his advance for Claymores with his flat piece of bamboo; he found only one. He pulled the cap and the detonator wires. He slid on, snake-self, till he was flat against the fence.

* * *

From under his bunk Whitenigger pulled the rucksack full of
dope that had been taken from the old gook's hootches. He realized the potential of the haul, even if Crow and Zits had not.
Four blocks of pure opium, and stacks of tightly rolled joints
much too fragrant to be marijuana. If he had known what the
old fool had, Whitenigger would have done business with the
gook rather than kill him. Still, he had this, and as a reward, it
would please Crow and Zits.

Hunter was satisfied that the camp was free of alarm. The
tower above him was quiet, except for a low murmur of voices.
He cut through the chain link, repeating his actions at the fence
at Camp Five, except that he did not wire the corners. He picked
up his lines from his earlier study, and slid-crawled from light
into shadow, to the first building, where he paused, then on
through the silent camp to the revetted vehicle park. Once again,
he stopped, pressed into the shadow of the earthwork. He saw a
figure moving behind him, and pressed himself into the ground,
breathing suspended. As the figure entered the light in front of
Whitenigger's hootch, Hunter recognized it as Crow. Billy
waited, listening to Crow's boots grinding in the gravel, and his
labored breathing. Billy smiled, and the voices inside his brain
cheered. Crow climbed the steps to Whitenigger's hootch, and
slipped inside. Stay awhile, willed Hunter's brain. Hunter stood
up, and slipped into the vehicle park, passing within three feet
of a half-awake sentry.

In the darkened park Hunter found a jeep with a steel gasoline
can fastened to its tailboard with web straps. He pressed his
body tightly against the can to muffle any sound, released the
clasps, then lifted the can out of its holder onto the ground.
Shaking the can gently, he determined that it was almost full.
Half full was what he needed, so he carried the can deeper into
the vehicle park, looking for a spot to dump some gas where the
smell wouldn't immediately carry back to the sentry. He found
a row of empty cans, and poured about half the contents of his
can, then returned to the front of the park. The sentry hadn't
stirred. Hunter made his way from the park to a machine shop,
which had an overhanging roof, and sat in the deep shadow,
studying the approach to Whitenigger's hootch. He felt a little
sick wave of fever wash up from his stomach and into his aching
head, but it passed, leaving an intense chill. They deserve to
die, said a voice in his brain.

Hunter started forward, holding the can just above the ground,
gliding it, so the contents wouldn't slosh. He moved from shadow

to shadow. The only lighted part of the passage was just before the back of the hootch. Hunter crossed the lighted patch in a crab crawl, dragging the can beside him, and flowed between the cinder blocks and under the hootch. He listened to the muffled voices above him, then pulled the can on its side to the place where the voices were loudest. He took off the kangaroo, and got out the spring-steel knife. He traced the can with the knife in the dirt, moved the can aside, then began removing the soft earth from within the trace marks.

Crow sat across from Whitenigger at the desk. They both had their feet up and were drinking beer, ignoring, for the moment, the piles of money between them. Crow was holding one of the tightly rolled joints he had taken from the hootch of the old dink by Camp Seven, turning it over, inspecting it. "So yo think this shit special, Whitenigga?"

"Yeah. Soon's Zits get heah, we gonna smoke us a couple. Toast our good frien' Sarn't Hunta!" Whitenigger laughed, a wheezing, unpleasant sound.

Hunter heard footsteps approaching the hootch. He froze, directing all his attention to his ears. The footsteps reached the front of the hootch, and rasped up the cinder-block steps. The man stepped inside, and the plywood floor groaned under his weight. He sat along the wall, and the hootch shook, then settled. A third voice was added to the muffled conversation.

Zits! thought Hunter.

Hurry! said the voice inside his brain.

Hunter pulled the gasoline can into the shallow depression, and shaped the loose earth around it, packing it tight right up to the edge of the can. He held his knife down close to the point, where there was a can-opening hook. He pressed the point into the metal, gradually increasing the pressure, until the point broke through with a tiny searing sound. He stopped and listened, then began cutting through the side of the can, using the wire cutters and the knife.

Whitenigger passed out the bonus money to Crow and Zits, and they each had a beer. Zits started to get up, but Whitenigger stopped him. "I suggest, gennle-men, that we all try some a t'is special shit y'all brought back from yo' little *raid!*"

Zits giggled nervously. He liked to think about that raid.

Crow lit the first joint, and placed it between Whitenigger's lips. He lit one for himself, then tossed the third and the matchbook to Zits. The hootch filled with sweet gray smoke. "Hoo, wow," said Zits. Conversation ceased.

Below, Hunter struggled to cut the can. It was proving far more difficult than he had figured. He smelled the dope, and smiled. Have another joint, he prayed.

Hurry! said the voice inside his brain.

Whitenigger finished his joint first. He found himself grinning. This shit is *heavy*! I am *sailing*! He looked across at Crow, who was smiling, eyes closed, trying to get the last of the roach. Whitenigger plucked the roach from Crow's fingers, and handed him another joint. "We got *plenty*, Babe!"

Crow opened his eyes. "Wow, huh," he giggled, "wow." He took the fresh joint, and carefully lit it. He and Whitenigger shared it, passing it back and forth. On the other side of the room, Zits rolled against the wall, and began to snore.

Crow kicked his legs down from the desk and stood up. The room took an agreeable roll, then steadied. Crow strolled around the desk, and sat on it, next to Whitenigger's legs. He placed his hand lightly on Whitenigger's thigh, then began to massage his crotch. He could feel Whitenigger's sex stirring inside his uniform. Whitenigger closed his eyes, and sighed a slow, hissing sound. Crow took the joint from Whitenigger's delicate, tapered fingers, and set it in the ashtray. With slow fingers, he unbuttoned Whitenigger's trousers and freed his sex. He bent his head over Whitenigger's crotch.

"You want your daddy, Crow?" breathed Whitenigger. Crow nodded. "Show me, Crow, sweet baby."

Crow got up slowly, unbuckled his trousers, and let them fall, then climbed up onto the cot on his knees.

Hunter had the hole in the gasoline can complete enough that he could bend the inner piece up and away like the lid of a tin can. He was soaking wet and shivering from the exertion and the fever. The odor of gasoline was strong in the confined space, and he hoped the men in the hootch would not smell it and come to find its source. He laid two frag grenades, their spoons taped to their bodies with surgical tape, next to the can, then pulled himself to the back of the hootch to look around. He looked and listened for five minutes; the camp was silent and deserted. He crawled back in, picked up the first grenade and pulled the pin, and dropped it into the gasoline. He pulled the second grenade's pin, and dropped it in alongside the first. He knew the surgical tape would hold the spoons down, and thus the grenades harm-

less, until the gasoline dissolved the adhesive, but he had no
firm idea how long that might take. He crawled out from under
the hootch, and started back down his lines and shadows toward
the wire.

Whitenigger knelt behind Crow, admiring his smooth, mus-
cular black ass. He massaged the rippling muscles of Crow's
back and shoulders and pressed his body against the much darker
man's, admiring the contrast in their color. Against the wall,
Zits snored like a buzz saw.

Hunter was through the wire and the concertina when he heard
a sharp crack of explosion, followed by a whoosh of flame.
Knowing that the sentries in the towers would look inward, he
jumped up and sprinted for the trees, following his own dancing
shadow. Once in the trees, he turned and looked back. The
flames were rising fifty, maybe seventy feet high behind the rows
of hootches that shielded the center of the camp from view. Men
running toward the flames cast long, jumping shadows, radiating
out all the way to the trees. Hunter looked for a full minute,
etching the picture permanently into his brain, then ran for Camp
Seven.

Twenty minutes later, Hunter snaked back through the wire at
Camp Seven, and slipped into the head. He was still shivering
and sweating, but he could feel his fever dropping. He showered
thoroughly, and dressed in the clean uniform he had stashed in
the head. He dropped the dirty uniform in the laundry bag, except for the socks he had worn over his boots, which he put in
the waste bin, under the paper towels. Carrying his boots, he
crossed the quiet camp to his hootch, and crawled along the floor
to his bunk. He snake-climbed in, and drew the blanket up to
his chin. "Rest in peace, Nga," he whispered.

Thank you, Bi-lee, she said. Hunter was instantly sound
asleep.

Across the tent, Trace looked at his watch, 0210. Whatever
Billy had to do, it's done.

21 May 1967   Quang Ngai, with the 197th Light Infantry Brigade

Bobby Coles dropped his seabag outside the hootch that served as the field office of the ANGLICO detachment attached to the 197th Light Infantry Brigade. The office was a rude wooden structure, made out of the sides of large packing crates resting on a raised platform of planks. The peaked roof was made of tent canvas. Someone had built a railing along the front of the floor where it jutted out three feet beyond the front of the building, which gave the air of a little balcony. The whole structure couldn't have measured more than twelve by fifteen feet.

Coles was tired from his long journey, from California via Hawaii and Guam to Okinawa, where he had undergone a refresher in night exercises and small-unit tactics. He had then gone on to Danang, where he reported to the commanding officer of the 7th ANGLICO, a marine corps major named MacIntyre, who seemed a pretty decent type. He expected to be able to rest and get oriented to the company and its mission while in Danang, but the platoon sergeant of the detachment with the 197th had become very ill with malaria, and was evacuated to the naval hospital in Honolulu, so Coles was sent right down.

Coles straightened his uniform prior to entering the office, where he was to report to the detachment's commander, a navy lieutenant (junior grade) named Robinson. Major MacIntyre had told him nothing of Robinson, other than he was a good officer. Coles felt nervous and ill-prepared to step right into a combat assignment, but he also felt a strange sense of relief that he was finally *here*. From here, one could begin to think of going home. Coles rapped on the door, and a quiet voice said "Enter," without inflection. Coles pushed open the door, and went in.

Coles came to attention and saluted. The officer waved him to a chair, and smiled. "You must be Sergeant Coles."

"Yes, sir, reporting as ordered." Coles's mood jumped a notch. Lieutenant Robinson was black! A black officer in an elite unit was a very good start, he thought.

Robinson was a short man, not more than five-feet-six. He had a smooth, intelligent face, and looked rather scholarly. Robinson moved a few papers around his tiny desk, apparently without purpose. He's nervous, thought Coles, as he waited.

"Well, then, Sergeant Coles, welcome to the ANGLICO."

"Glad to be here, sir, hope I can be of use."

The lieutenant beamed, "I'm sure you can. Sergeant Macon was good, very good, but, I must confess, I found him at times difficult."

Coles was on his guard. "In what sense, sir?"

"He was white, Sergeant," said Robinson, dryly, "and he tried to compensate for what he viewed as my, ah, inexperience. I'm sure you know what I mean."

Coles thought he did. "Yes, sir."

"Good, good, Coles. Have you met the men?"

"Not yet, sir, but I'm anxious to."

Lieutenant Robinson took off his steel-rimmed glasses. "They're good men, Sergeant, though green. But you'll like them."

This conversation is not what I expected, thought Coles. The lieutenant is preoccupied with something else. "Shall I go and meet them, sir?"

Lieutenant Robinson smiled, "Yes, of course. You'll find them in a twelve-man tent, on the end of the second rank, that way, near the motor pool." The lieutenant gestured absently. "I've reviewed your record, Sergeant Coles; I'm convinced you'll be a real asset."

"Sir," said Bobby, leaving the dark office. There ain't *nothing* in my record, he thought.

Coles found the men of Lieutenant Robinson's detachment in their twelve-man tent, most taking their ease, getting ready for chow. They seemed an easy group of guys, friendly. Maybe a little too friendly, thought Coles; I am the sergeant here, and they don't know me. Take it easy, he told himself. "Tell me who you are, men."

"Adams, Sergeant, rifleman. Radio talker, now." He was a tall, confident-looking white man, with a faintly midwestern accent.

"From Chicago," guessed Coles, trying to project friendship.

"Close, Sergeant," the man grinned easily, "Evanston, Illinois."

"I'm Lancey Watts, Sergeant," said a light-skinned black man with conked hair, "New Orleans."

Sergeant Coles nodded, and looked at the next man, a skinny black kid who was cleaning an M-16 between his knees.

"Mo-rice Jackson, Sergeant! The men call me Monkey!"

"OK, Monkey." He looked at the next man.

"Morgan, Sergeant," said the big man, black, and restless, his voice pure New York.

"Walker, Sarge, New Jersey." Another black man, who looked proud. "M-sixty light machine gun."

"Cardenas, Sergeant, Los Angeles. Medical, and radioman." A dark-skinned Mexican who sounded educated. Coles nodded.

"Staples, radioman, Sergeant." A heavy-set white man with an earnest expression. Coles looked at his hands. "Now, tell me what we do here. I'm anxious to learn."

The unit received orders into the field on the following day. The lieutenant, visibly agitated, came down to the hootch himself to tell them to build their rucks and be ready to move out at 1400. The army scout teams had cut some fresh trails in the paddy country to the north, along the banks of the Song Tra Khuc. Song meant river, the first Vietnamese word Coles had learned. The Army had decided to let a navy destroyer, which was lying off the coast waiting to give gunfire support to the brigade's coastal operations, take the mission. The Army, Coles had been told, was a little skeptical about the navy's ability to deliver supporting fire with precision, so the Army preferred to limit the destroyers to harassment and interdiction—H and I—fire missions, like the ones against these newfound trails. Precision fire, close to the troops, was kept to the brigade's own artillery. Nevertheless, the ship would need a spot, and it was a chance for the unit to prove its worth. The men seemed anxious to go, to try it on.

"You mean you guys haven't ever made a real spot before?" asked Coles.

"That's *right*, Sergeant Brotha!" said Monkey, lifting his pack. The little man couldn't really be expected to hump a thirty-pound radio, so he was designated as a runner. Staples, Adams, Morgan, and Cardenas carried the unit's four radios.

"We go out with de grunts, we come back. So far, we only bin wid dese humps six weeks," added Morgan.

Coles's mind reeled. I'm in charge of these men, and neither they nor I have any experience whatsoever in real conditions. "How about the lieutenant? He been there?" asked Coles, almost dreading the answer.

Cardenas spoke softly, "He's been to school, Sergeant. Didn't nobody tell you this was a green outfit?"

They told me it was an elite outfit, thought Bobby, feeling angry. Well, we'll just have to make it one. "We'll get old quickly enough, Cardenas."

The unit was formed up and loaded into big twin-rotored CH-47 helos at the pad in the middle of the huge encampment. They were going up with an infantry company to do a sweep and map the trails.

This was Coles's first experience with helicopters in Vietnam. He had been trained in them in California, but they always landed on concrete pads; he was unprepared for the volume of dirt and grit that was blown into his eyes, ears, nose, and mouth, as well as practically filling the shirt of his uniform. When he finally got on board the aircraft, he noted that his men had buttoned their uniforms all the way to the neck, and had covered their faces with bandannas or small green army-issue towels. Monkey removed his black kerchief and grinned impishly, leaning close and shouting above the engine noise as the helo took off. "Don't worry 'bout us bein' green, Sarge. Wait'll you see some of the things the army fucks up."

Coles grinned, suddenly. Of course. Relax, let it flow. This is Vietnam. He gave Monkey a thumbs-up sign, and Monkey and Adams and Morgan all gave it back to him. The rest of the unit was with Lieutenant Robinson in another helo.

The infantry company swept slowly through the AO. The evidence of Viet Cong passage was tenuous at best, but it was there—footprints and faint wheel marks, all one ever expected to find.

The jungle was thick near the river bottom. Above the banks, the land was cultivated into paddy; the spring rice had already been transplanted, and had grown to a height of two feet. The peasants who tended the crops had faded away from the helicopters and the tramping soldiers. All the villages were empty and silent.

Coles joined his men with the lieutenant's group, and followed, as the infantry led them to the crossing paths that had been discovered. The unit moved the destroyer *Morton* into position to fire. The infantry company commander cleared his soldiers well back, and Lieutenant Robinson called for the first shot.

The theory of H and I fire was to force the enemy to abandon his carefully prepared trails. Lieutenant Robinson would spot for the destroyer, and then the soldiers would pull back. The destroyer would calibrate and store the coordinates of their target, and probably several others called in by other spotters, in her gunfire-control computer, then return at night to lob shells onto the crossroad at irregular intervals. As a spotting mission, it wasn't very challenging, but it was a mission.

Coles watched the lieutenant; he looked excited, and his fingers tapped the gunfire plotting board he held on his knees, waiting for the shot to fall in. The infantry commander, an army captain, watched with a smirk that angered Coles. Get it right, dammit, he thought, looking hard at Robinson's back.

The spotting round landed with a flat report and a burst of orange smoke well beyond and to the right of the crossing paths. Robinson spun the board, and called the spot back to Adams, who put it on the radio to the destroyer. The next shot was still beyond the silent target, and even farther to the right. Robinson was beginning to sweat. He adjusted the board again, and shouted back to Adams. The third shot faded into the jungle, almost too far away to see.

"Fuckin' Navy," snorted the company commander, behind Coles. Coles heard other laughter, and he crawled forward to Robinson. He looked at the board on Robinson's knees, then at the lieutenant. Robinson was near panic. The destroyer's call for spot was crackling in Adams's radio. Robinson looked at Coles without speaking.

"Lieutenant, the solution is wrong. You, ah, didn't adjust line of sight to the gun-target line."

The lieutenant didn't move; he seemed frozen. Gently, Coles took the plotting board from Robinson's unresisting fingers, and adjusted it with the aid of his hand compass. "Adams, spot. Left, two mils, to me. Drop five hundred."

The five-inch shell landed on the crossroad, spraying dust and belching orange smoke. "Ok, Adams, tell 'em they're on."

"Yes, Sergeant," said Adams, obviously relieved.

"We're done here, sir," said Coles, softly.

"Right," said Lieutenant Robinson. "Quite. Spot is in, for tonight, Captain James."

"Thanks, Navy," said the company commander, with exaggerated courtesy. Coles looked at him with hatred, and was pleased to see the captain look away. We're all just learning, thought Coles, looking anger at the army captain's back.

The infantry continued its assigned sweep, found nothing and saw no one other than a scrawny Vietnamese peasant with two small children, all riding on a water buffalo. Buffalo were too valuable to be left alone, even when threatened by Viet Cong or Americans. I wonder who the old guy fears most, mused Coles. The company set up a perimeter around the dry field that had been designated the landing zone for the helos. Most of the men lounged around, smoking and eating C-rations. Nobody seemed to be taking this war too seriously, thought Coles.

The helos came, and they piled into the one with their letter taped to the door, passing the door-gunner, who at least looked watchful as he scanned the trees along the riverbank. The helicopter took off with a jerk, and in ten minutes they were back on the ground inside the big base camp. The infantry company was formed up to hear some kind of announcement from their CO. The ANGLICO marines just kind of wandered off in the direction of their hootch. This unit is *fucked up*, thought Coles to himself, his face burning. And that is going to change.

He quickened his step and caught up with the men in the hootch. Most were picking up shower kits, and Monkey was snapping his towel at Cardenas's rump just as Coles entered. There was laughter, and it deepened Coles's anger. "Ten-HUT!" he said, just loudly enough so that there could be no doubt that he meant it. The men fell silent, and assumed the posture of attention, looking faintly ridiculous, holding towels, bars of soap, pieces of uniform. Coles paced back and forth in the confined space, and scowled his worst street face, heated with genuine anger. Most of the men looked the blank look every marine learns in boot camp; don't notice me, the look said. Monkey was unable to control a smirk. Coles looked Monkey full in the face for ten seconds before the little man swallowed the smirk with a bobbing of his prominent Adam's apple.

Coles began speaking, very softly, but with an edge of iron in his voice. "Where were you men going? Staples?"

"Ta—ta the head, sir—Sergeant," Staples replied, keeping his eyes blank and exactly straight ahead.

Coles looked at Staples for half a minute, then walked down the line of totally silent men. They didn't seem to breathe. "Do

I take that to mean that every one of you men has already cleaned his personal weapon? *Jackson!*'' Coles pushed his face to within an inch of Monkey's as he spoke his name, and the little man jumped.

"No, Sergeant. But none of us even fired our weapons today."

"But they got dirty, didn't they, men? The dust on the LZ alone will have gotten them dirty."

"Gee, Sarge," said Adams, "you just put a rubber over the end of the barrel; it keeps the dirt out. We shoulda told you—"

"What?" snapped Coles, his eyes inches from Adams's. The rest of Adams's sentence died in his throat.

"Sergeant," began Walker. Coles rounded on him, but Walker kept on speaking, with a slow, firm voice. I want this man on my side fast, thought Coles. "We may be a little sloppy. We are sloppy. But with due respect, Sergeant, this is Vietnam. It's different here."

Coles moved close to Walker, and studied his smooth black face. Coles's own face lost its anger. He had their attention, now he had to win them over. He turned away from Walker, then turned back to address the group as a whole. "Men, I know this is Vietnam. Let me tell you what little else I know. This is the United States Marine Corps, and we have ways to do things. The fact that we are in the middle of a bunch of sad-ass draftee soldiers makes it all the more important we remember, every minute, that we are *marines*. If the Army wants to put condoms over the muzzles of their weapons rather than clean them, that's their lookout, but we will clean our weapons, and oil them, and inspect our ammunition. Men, the unit I saw in front of me in the field today was *fucked up*, and I, Coles, *Sergeant Coles*—" Bobby jabbed his chest with his thumb, and looked at each man in turn "—does not ride with any fucked-up outfit." Coles walked to his bunk and picked up his M-16, locked the action open, and reached into his ruck for the rifle cleaning kit. Without a word, the men began cleaning and oiling their weapons. Coles heard a few whispered complaints, caught the word "ballbuster," and ignored it. Bobby cleaned his weapon slowly, watching as the men did likewise. He sensed none of them wanted to be satisfied before he was.

Bobby finished cleaning the weapon, then popped the ammo out of the magazine and wiped off each round. The M-16 was prone to jam; some said it was just too precise a weapon to be used in the normal, dirty conditions of combat. Bobby put seventeen cartridges back into the twenty-round clip, and locked the weapon away. He looked at the men, and smiled slightly. "Probably just time for a shower before chow, hey, Marines?"

There was a little banter as the men went off to shower, but very little. It felt to Bobby as though an embarrassing truth had been revealed to them all, and they weren't quite sure how to deal with it. The awkward silence and nervousness persisted through the evening meal. When the men returned to the hootch, Bobby took a walk. Let them work it out themselves. They don't have to like it, or like me, but they are going to be marines, and they are going to learn gunfire and air spotting. The commandant at Pendleton told me I was going to have an elite unit, and I shall.

Bobby walked around the camp for more than an hour, gradually cooling off, and thinking about what he was going to do next to build his unit. As he approached the tent, he still had no clear idea. A figure rose from a seat on the wooden floor of the tent, and walked toward him. Coles recognized Walker in the dim light. "Walk a bit farther, Sergeant?"

"Sure, Walker."

They walked in silence, back along the row of tents, out to the big parade ground in the center of the camp. After a silent minute, Walker spoke. "I guess you felt you had to say those things, Sergeant."

"I guess I did."

"And I guess I'm the man responsible for the way things are. Were. I'm a corporal, was acting sergeant until you came in."

"It wasn't my point to fix blame, Walker. As far as I'm concerned, we've started over, as of today. I want a good unit, that's all."

"Fine, Sergeant, and I'll help, if you'll let me."

Coles looked at Walker. He was the same height as Coles, and he returned Coles's look. "I appreciate that, Walker. I think the men will be fine."

"They're OK, Sergeant, but right now they're angry."

Coles stopped. "Angry because I told them to shape up?"

"The way they look at it, Sergeant, you yelled at them because you couldn't yell at the lieutenant."

"I don't follow you, Walker."

"It was the Lieutenant who fucked up the spot, not the men."

Coles shrugged. "I just thought he was green. It isn't hard to get one of those solutions backwards."

Walker nodded, and they started walking again. "I figured you might think that, which is why I came out to speak to you, privately. You see, this isn't just one incident. The men just don't trust Lieutenant Robinson."

"Why not?" Coles saw nothing wrong with the man; a little nervous, perhaps, but he was green, too.

"Just what you saw. He panics. He freezes. The men like him, but they're afraid he's a coward."

"Come on, Walker! You guys haven't seen enough real combat to make that kind of judgment. Besides, we owe him our loyalty. He's our leader, and besides, he's black; he's a brother."

Walker stopped Coles with a hand on his shoulder. Coles tried to read Walker's face, but it was completely in shadow. "Sergeant Coles, let me try to help you understand the real world, which for you, like the rest of us, is Vietnam. Lieutenant Robinson is not a brother. Officers are neither black nor white, in *Vietnam*, Sergeant. They are army-issue olive drab. The men don't trust the Lieutenant, and that's the problem. Good night, Sergeant."

Walker turned and walked rapidly away, leaving Bobby standing by himself in the tepid darkness.

29 May 1967   DMZ, West of the Rockpile

Hunter's patrol walked north in the darkening evening, following a narrow footpath that diverged from the large trail they had mined and ambushed several times. It wasn't really Hunter's patrol anymore; Lieutenant Brown had been an assertive leader and, Hunter was quite pleased to acknowledge, a competent one. Among Brown's priorities was cross-training, and he especially wanted everyone to learn to walk point. Hunter was in charge of the training, and for the most part he walked slack, right behind the point man. Phillips had the point.

Hunter didn't mind slack, and he didn't mind the training duty. At least it kept him concentrating, focused. Hunter was finding it harder and harder to stay focused, and he knew that inattention could easily get men killed. But Hunter found himself drifting nonetheless.

He had thought that after the incident at Camp Five (his brain never wanted him to put a name to it) he would have been able to return to as near normal an existence as anyone in the Marine Corps in I Corps could have, but it hadn't happened. Somehow the incident had left him empty; what was to have put his world into some sad but comprehensible balance had left it overturned. The taste of revenge was ashes. Hunter stopped as Phillips stopped, holding up his hand. He moved forward to join Phillips while the rest of the patrol crouched and waited. Phillips pointed to a freshly disturbed line on the surface of the trail, like a tiny trench, maybe two inches wide.

"Mine wire?" whispered Phillips.

Hunter shrugged, and knelt down. He pulled his thin piece of flat bamboo out of his boot, and followed the trench out of sight on each side of the trail. On the right side, a black wire emerged from the trench among thick roots, and led farther up the hill. "Get Trace," whispered Hunter. Phillips crept back to the next man, and passed the word.

Perhaps the thing that had most changed in Hunter's life since the incident was the loss of Trace as a friend and confidant. Hunter was sure Trace knew what really happened to White-nigger Johnson and Crow and Zits, although he never mentioned it. The morning the trio had died, the captain paraded the company, and, in the context of giving a lecture on the need to improve camp security against enemy sappers, gave some detail about the incident, especially the condition of the bodies, burned beyond all recognition, flesh melted away, bones shrunken and dried. The largest of the three bodies was only about three feet long. Hunter watched Trace through the captain's whole speech, but Trace never looked at him. Hunter and Trace could not talk about the incident, and in time they found they could not talk about anything else, either.

Trace moved up quietly beside Hunter at the point. "What do we have, Sergeant?"

Trace won't even call me by name anymore, thought Hunter, sadly. "Wire, Trace. Leads out to the right."

Trace knelt down beside the wire, and probed under the foliage at the right, as Hunter had done. "It's buried. Why is it buried?"

"I dunno, Trace. Maybe it's spring-loaded?"

"It's too thin to be det cord. At least I think it is."

"So what do you think, Trace?"

"I dunno, Sergeant. Step over it, drive on. We ain't comin' back this way, anyway." Trace stood up, and looked at Hunter. He looked sad.

"OK. Step back and wait. I'm going forward a ways to see if there's anything else. When I signal, send Phillips back up."

"OK, Sergeant." Trace moved back. Hunter looked the trench over once again, then mentally holding his ears, he stepped over it, and moved up the narrow foot track. Nothing happened, and his close examination of the trail and the sides of the trail, and of the overhanging branches, revealed nothing. Moving carefully back to where Phillips could see him, he hand-signed the patrol forward, pointing at the trench, and gesturing to Phillips that he should step over. Phillips nodded, stepped over, then pointed out the trench to the next man. Hunter whispered to Phillips to keep a wary eye, but to try to pick up the pace. They were still half a klick from their prepared NDP, and it was nearly dark.

The trail widened as they moved forward. If this really was a gook trail, they could very well have mined it if it wasn't active, but clearly they couldn't mine it and use it at the same time unless they left markers around the triggers their own men could see. The nightcrawlers were adept at finding these markers, and often they would use the markers to avoid the trap, then remove the markers and leave the trap intact for the enemy.

This was the last night of the mission, and Hunter was tired. He felt little inklings of fever, and knew his malaria was hiding inside, waiting to burn him again, but he didn't care much about that, either. What he really wanted was to be someplace where he could really rest, really forget, really sleep, free of the horror that he had caused, or allowed to happen, or actually done. He sighed. He wished his malaria would get really bad again; he was sure if any doctor wanted to send him home again, he would gladly go.

The night defensive position was just ahead, on the edge of the larger trail, concealed in the trees. It was at the southwestern end of the patrols' range from Camps Five and Seven, no more than three kilometers from the wire of Camp Seven. The other side of the road was a large open hilltop that had once been cultivated in rice, but now was dry and deserted. The patrol approached the NDP carefully, wary of infiltrators. The NDP had been abandoned all day. First they watched it, concealed in the bush, and then they walked around it. Lieutenant Brown and Hunter were satisfied that it was deserted, and Phillips led the unit in. Just as he stepped over a branch that helped to conceal the entrance, Phillips stumbled, nearly falling, and reached out to steady himself on the branch. Hunter heard the sound of sni-ick! ding! and time seemed to freeze. Phillip's face twisted in terror as he tried to push himself back from the branch. Hunter's body was turning, frantically trying to pull away from the mine. He saw the men behind him backing away in very slow motion. His mouth opened to shout a warning as the mine blew. He felt a thunderous blow on the top of his head, and he flew forward toward the jungle floor. His brain granted him one phrase before it winked out like a candle. The phrase was "I love you, Bi-lee," and the voice in his brain was Nga's, clear as a wind chime.

Lieutenant Brown walked among the men of the patrol, taking a quick assessment of the damage. He held the jungle hat against a deep gash on his forehead, which was pouring blood into his left eye. He felt dizzy and afraid. "Trace!"

"Here, sir." Trace was straightening Hunter's body on the path, probing gently at his injuries.

Lieutenant Brown squatted. "What do we have?"

Trace shrugged, fighting tears. "Billy's hit bad, Lieutenant, back of the head. He's alive, but unconscious. I don't know, but I think his skull is busted."

Lieutenant Brown wiped his face, and shook the blood from his hat. "Did you put your hand behind his head?"

"Yes. It feels soft, sir."

"Let me see your hand." Brown took the hand and held it up to the thin moonlight, running a finger through the mess. "Blood, no brain tissue. Give him first aid as best you can, Trace; he may make it."

"He needs a hospital, sir."

Lieutenant Brown looked around, at the jungle and the night, taking stock, fighting fear. Phillips had been literally blown in half. Sergeant Hunter was critical at best. Capiello had a sucking chest wound, and he himself had a bad bleeder in the head. "Sure he does, Trace, and we're going to get him there. Stabilize him as best you can."

"Aye, aye, sir." Feeling relieved, Trace moved quickly, gathering dressings from several men's packs for Billy's multiple wounds. The worst, on his head, he bandaged with two large field dressings. Oh, God, he thought, I wish I could have at least shook his hand and said good-bye. Hunter had shrapnel wounds all over his back, and Trace worked, and worked.

Lieutenant Brown moved back to the frightened group of men that constituted the rest of his patrol. Everything had changed; nightcrawlers, masters of the darkness and the soggy trails, had reverted to frightened nineteen- and twenty-year-old kids. "Jonas, call control. Break silence."

"Control is on, sir," said Jonas, handing him the radio handset.

"Control, Alpha Blue, we need a dust-off, over."

"Roger, A-B," said the RTO, far in the rear. "Hard to get at night."

"Get it, damn you," spat Lieutenant Brown into the handset. "Get it."

"Grid coords," said the talker, now taut and professional.

Brown gave them. Shit, he thought, three fucking klicks from the fucking wire. "I got serious wounded, control. Serious. I want *helos*, for my wounded, and then for the rest."

There was a long pause. Brown was just about to press the mike button again when the RTO came back. "OK, man, we got helos from the *Princeton*, inbound. You'll have to illuminate."

When they get here, thought Brown. "Helos enough for all of us?" he asked.

"Un-huh, Bro."

Brown hated RAMFs, especially the black ones. "Trace?"

"Sir." Trace surprised Brown by being right beside him.

"We're going to be picked up. Set the men to make a hot perimeter enough for the fuckhead helo jockeys to land." Trace smiled. Somehow the unaccustomed profanity of the lieutenant calmed him.

Trace took the M-60 and Smith and set out onto the dry paddy, securing a point that would define the outer edge of the landing zone. There wasn't time to dig in, and the men, used to concealment, felt terribly exposed. Smith ran around a thirty-meter circle, laying flares. Da Silva followed, laying wire from the reel, then Smith went back and connected up all the flares. When he sets that off, I'll be nicely backlit, thought Trace, lying flat behind the machine gun. The nightcrawlers faded back into the jungle, and Smith returned to Trace's side. "Here they come, man," said Smith. The wop-wopping sound of helos, three H-34s of HMM-362 from the *Princeton*, shattered what was left of the night silence. Smith detonated his flares.

The helos flew in a circle, blazing the jungle night with their door-guns. Trace felt that the noise and the lights the lead helo now turned on to land emphasized the failure, the defeat of the nightcrawlers. Their darkness, their silence was shattered, given away, because Phillips had missed a wire.

Smith lay prone beside Trace, handling the belt for the machine gun. Trace looked away from the flares and landing lights behind him as the first chopper landed. He peered at the jungle, trying to maintain at least some of his night vision. Smith contributed a running description, as the helicopter crew threw off two basket-stretchers for Hunter and Capiello. Smith's voice dropped as he described the loading of a body bag, which he guessed contained the remains of Phillips. The helo lifted off, with a downdraft that blew grit and bits of dry vegetation against Trace's neck. He hunched lower, willing the second helo to hurry and pick them up. "Looked like Stinson made it out in the medevac bird, man," said Smith.

The second helo landed, as Trace continued to stare into the jungle. The tracer fire from the third bird as it poured machine gun fire into the jungle destroyed what was left of his night vision, but he continued to look out as best he could. He felt the blast of dirt and fragments as the second chopper touched down. "Lieutenant's waving us in, man," said Smith, reaching up to grasp Trace's collar. Trace struggled to his feet, cradling the heavy M-60, and walked backward, while Smith led him toward the helo. When they reached the door, Smith jumped up beside Jonas, Da Silva, and Stevens, and took the machine gun from Trace, who followed. Lieutenant Brown, standing with one foot on the wheel, was the last to board. The helo rose immediately.

Trace crawled to Lieutenant Brown's side and shouted above the noise of the helicopter. "Hunter? How was he, sir?"

Brown turned and shouted into Trace's ear, "Alive, Trace. When they loaded him up, he was alive."

Trace hunched in the corner of the helicopter and silently prayed for Hunter, whether he was alive, or dead.

---

4 June 1967   Monterey, California

William lay back in the lawn chair, with Karen cuddling next to him. He drifted, gently stroking her fair hair, as they watched the sun fall slowly, grandly, toward the Pacific. Karen and William had pretty much gotten back to normal, but there was still a distance between them, a holdover from the fight after William had told her of his orders back to Vietnam. William was sure of their love, but he feared Karen's anger; when she rejected him, wouldn't let him touch her, he felt he was standing on the edge of a precipice, paralyzed. She could pull him back with her love, or hurl him over with her anger. He could not help himself.

William had spent quite a bit of his time in schools since his orders had arrived. Battlefield medicine in San Diego, special weapons and demolition at Camp Pendleton, aircraft ordnance spotting in the desert near Twentynine Palms, and finally, naval gunfire spotting, partially at San Diego and partially on the island of San Clemente off the coast of California, where the trainee officers and noncoms crawled through bunkers and controlled the fire of destroyers at targets of junked cars. Real bullets, the lieutenant commander who headed the course had called it. Stuart had gotten pretty good at calculating solutions on the circular plotting board, and he caused the death of a lot of rusty Fords and Chevys in his five days and nights of exercises. He shot well, the Commander said. Stuart felt good about himself, confident, ready. He just wished Karen could give him more support.

She was cheerful, and loving, especially physically, and even more so as the time for his departure grew close. The school schedule had given him time at home, including every weekend but one since his orders had arrived—really a lot better deal than shipboard life. Karen and he had spent a lot of time walking, and driving around southern California. After the rainy season they had weekends on the beach at Aunt Liz's house in Newport Beach. William guessed that Karen had decided to live with the notion that he would soon be going back overseas—by unspoken mutual consent, they both said overseas and not Vietnam—but she still hated it. He wished she could be a little bit proud of him, but there was no sign of it.

The sun touched its bottom edge to the Pacific horizon, and rapidly sank to its waist. Karen stirred on William's chest, and said something he didn't hear. The sun blazed red, and slipped into the sea. William always expected to hear a gigantic hiss.

Karen's head blocked out the sunset as she kissed him. "Hey, lover man, are you in there?"

William came back to the present with a start. "Sorry, love, what did you say?"

Karen climbed out of the chair. "I said it's getting cold, and I'd like a drink before dinner." She reached out her hands for him, "Come along, sailor."

William got up and followed. It was chilly in the sea breeze. Fog tomorrow, he thought absently.

When William's movement orders had arrived two weeks before, Karen suggested that they take a few days and drive up the coast to Travis, stopping along the way. They spent a night in Santa Barbara with a friend of Karen's, then drove up the coast highway admiring the craggy headlands and giant redwood trees of Big Sur country, and stopped at the Mark Thomas Inn in Monterey. They wandered around Carmel, window-shopping, and ate fresh fish and shellfish along Cannery Row.

William followed Karen into their room and put on his one sport jacket. "Where do you want to eat, love?" asked Karen, putting her arms around his neck.

William kissed his wife tenderly, drinking in her beauty, storing it up for the long separation to come. "Let's try that fancy place in town, Galletin's, something like that."

"OK. I guess I'll put on a dress, and you'd better find a tie." Karen disappeared into the bathroom.

The restaurant was crowded and a little noisy, and they were lucky to be seated without a reservation. William had fresh scallops in a creamy wine sauce, and Karen had an abalone dish. They tasted each other's meals and enjoyed both. They drank a bottle of Grey Riesling, and lingered over espresso. Karen talked about her job, and her new sales territory. William mostly listened, filling his memory with sight and sound.

On the way back to the hotel, Karen fell silent. It has just caught up with her, thought William. Tomorrow we'll drive up to San Francisco, and the next day, to Travis.

William presented his orders to the air force sergeant, got his boarding plaque, and checked his B-4 and seabag. The plane would leave in two hours, at 1000. William walked back to the waiting room, crowded with servicemen and their families gathered in tight knots. Travis seemed to him a haunted place, as he remembered the last time Karen had left him at its gates. On one side, the lovely and sane hills of northern California, on the other, the steaming, deadly jungles of Vietnam. Damn this waiting, he thought.

He found Karen talking to a USO lady by a huge coffee urn. Karen looked small, and a little frightened, and she had a bright spot of color on each cheek. She handed William a paper cup of coffee, and offered him a doughnut. She had powdered sugar on her nose, and he playfully kissed it away. "How are you feeling, Babe?"

"OK. Maybe a little shaky. I think I drank too much wine last night."

"Well, getting up at 6 A.M. was never one of your favorites, either." William put his arm around her shoulders, and led her away from the coffee counter. There was no place in the crowded waiting room where they could be alone, but William figured no one would notice them whatever they did, any more than he cared what anyone else was doing. He found two chairs, between a black family with three small children and a marine sergeant father, and a sailor who looked about sixteen necking frantically with his weeping girlfriend. Karen and he sat. "You'll be fine, Babe. Six months is nothing. Six months ago, we were just pulling into Long Beach. That seems to me like yesterday."

"Six months, you promise."

"I'll be counting the days. From today, let's see, December sixth. December sixth is the day."

Karen's eyes brimmed with tears, but she fought against them. "William, I love you so much; I'm sorry I haven't been a better wife."

William touched her cheek. "You are a wonderful wife, Karen. I love you."

"I mean, I should be more supportive, more dutiful. I should be proud of your navy career, but I just hate the thought of all this *loneliness*!" The tears were coming now, and William kissed them as they fell, savoring the salty essence of his wife. "But I'll be loyal, and I'll wait for you, like the good navy wife I wish I could be."

"I'll think of you, every day, especially at sunrise, my love."

"And I'll concentrate hard at sunset, to try to reach you. It worked before."

"Yes, love, I think it did."

They sat in silence, William watching the big twenty-four-hour clock on the far wall over Karen's shoulder. Karen touched his face, the way a blind person might. She's trying to remember, thought William. There was so much he ought to say, but he felt the silence was better, more healing. Karen is trying to understand. I must be worthy of her.

At 0930, the flight was called over the public address system. Stuart jumped up. Karen looked up from the chair, her face a mixture of surprise and pain. She rose slowly, and he took her in his arms. She put her cheek against his chest, and with her finger, she traced the campaign ribbons on his jacket, tapping the Silver Star and the Purple Heart. "Don't do anything foolish, William. No more medals," she said softly.

The flight was called again. William tilted her head up, and kissed her lightly. She closed her eyes and drove her tongue between his lips with passion, and pressed her body to his urgently. William felt his penis stirring, and he reddened with embarrassment. Karen pushed him away, gently. "I want you back, all in one piece, on December sixth."

Stuart smiled, a lump in his throat, and whispered, "December sixth. I love you."

"I love you, too, sailor."

William turned and walked through the gate and across the concrete to the big passenger jet.

15 June 1967   Camp Tien Shaw

It was midmorning when Stuart reached Camp Tien Shaw, by way of Hawaii, Guam, Clark Air Base in the Philippines, Ton Son Nhut near Saigon, and finally Danang. He had been in an airplane seat or in a transit lounge for thirty-three hours. He felt dirty and tired and thoroughly disoriented by the nine-hour time change from California. What I need is a shave and a shower and about twelve hours' sleep, he thought, and then I will be able to get on with the war. The only way he was going to get the shower and the sleep was to report for duty, and get quarters assigned to him.

Stuart had a little difficulty finding the offices of the 7th Air and Naval Gunfire Liaison Company. For something with such an imposing name, few seemed to have heard of it. He eventually found the office in a row of hootches with tin roofs. Other hootches in the row contained a chaplain's office, a public affairs office, and the Red Cross. Good martial company we keep, thought Stuart, pushing open the door marked Headquarters, 7th ANGLICO. He dropped his seabag and his B-4, and approached the marine corporal who was pounding a typewriter in the corner. Behind him was a closed door with a stencil, in black, of an oak leaf. The marine looked up from his typing at the khaki-uniformed officer. "Yes, sir?"

"Lieutenant jay gee William Stuart, reporting, Corporal." Stuart dropped the dog-eared copies of his orders on the table.

The man stood up, smiling courteously. "I'll tell the major you're here, sir."

"Thank you." Stuart wanted a cigarette, but decided against it. Better get the formal part of this out of the way. The corporal backed out of the office with the oak leaf on the door, and beckoned to Stuart. Leaving his luggage where he had dropped it, Stuart pulled himself to attention, and strode through the door. A major in pressed fatigues sat behind a metal desk, and a major with a face Stuart had never expected to see again. Stuart stopped dead, and he felt his jaw drop.

"Come in and sit, Shit-Spattered Dog," said Major Mac-Intyre, amiably.

Stuart sat, and managed to close his mouth. "I *will* be damned! The Di-wee!"

The major grinned broadly, and spoke with his accent from the camp. "*Dai-uy* no more. *Thieu ta*—major—now." He got up and poured two cups of coffee from the thermos behind him, and offered cigarettes. Stuart tasted the coffee, which was surprisingly good, and lit a cigarette.

"So, Lieutenant Stuart, how does it feel to be back in the grip of the beast of the red camp?"

"Jesus, I don't know, Major. When I walked in here, I actually thought I was hallucinating from the jet lag. How did you get here? And congratulations on your promotion."

"Congratulations on yours. I volunteered for this, to set it up. The Seventh was established, on paper, only sixth months ago, and we are not yet up to full strength. The outfit is a little raggedy, but we will make it better. You will lead the fourth and last platoon we establish, as soon as we have the marines to make up the unit."

"What made you want this duty, Major?"

"Call me Mac. It's good duty, William—or do you prefer Bill?"

"William, sir, if you please."

"This duty is high profile. If this unit can be made to perform well, it will be good for all of us."

"Is it dangerous?"

Major MacIntyre shrugged. "It's war. It *is* combat. For the most part you'll be working very close to the action. I would doubt that it's as dangerous as the job of a line rifleman, but yes, it's dangerous."

No guts, no navy cross. The boot-camp cheer echoed hollowly in Stuart's brain. "Did you know I was coming out here?"

"Indeed I did! When I saw your name on a list of junior naval officers possibly available, and saw you were languishing in some shipyard, I asked for you."

Oh, Lord, thought Stuart, and to think I never was supposed to take that SERE course. But what do you say? "Thank you, sir."

"I figured you'd like it. You have the right background in naval gunnery, and I liked the way you handled yourself in SERE."

If Karen ever finds out about that turn of events, she will go completely crazy, thought Stuart. Still, if I was listed as available, somebody would have picked me up. Shit. "Well, Mac, where do I start?"

"Corporal Ramirez will get you into quarters, then I suggest you clean up and get some rest. You will need to draw uniforms and boots, and a weapon, but Ramirez will organize that while you sleep. Come back here at seventeen-hundred, and we will talk over dinner. I think I will put you with Lieutenant Wilkes until your own team is formed. The other two are deployed with army units."

Stuart stood. Mention of rest had made him suddenly aware of his fatigue. Yet, despite it all, he felt excited. "Until seventeen-hundred, then, Major."

"Welcome aboard, William."

Corporal Ramirez led Stuart to his quarters, a comfortable four-man hootch two streets back from the main grinder in the center of the camp. Ramirez dropped Stuart's seabag on the bunk, then pulled a notebook out of his side pocket and quickly noted Stuart's sizes for uniforms and boots. "What kinda weapon you want, sir? Forty-five, or M-sixteen?"

Stuart looked at his seabag, feeling a little guilty. "I have a Stoner carbine, Corporal, broken down in my seabag." Stuart waited to see how the corporal would note the breach of regulations.

"Hey, they're supposed to be good, better than the sixteen. I'll just draw bulk ammo, then."

No questions asked, thought Stuart. Welcome back to Nam. "Thanks, Corporal."

"Get some rest, sir. I'll bring the stuff by about sixteen-hundred."

William told the major about Moser during dinner. MacIntyre had seen Moser's orders weeks before, and had initially been skeptical about taking a sailor into a marine combat unit, but the accompanying letter from Stuart, addressed to Commanding Officer, 7th ANGLICO, which said that Moser was steady, and good with weapons, and wanted to be there, had swayed him. God knows he needed men to fill out the company.

To the south some sixty miles, Bobby Coles followed Lieutenant Robinson as he led the ANGLICO detachment up the coastal road. They were attached to an infantry company and the cavalry platoon moving up the coast to look over an area north of the Tra Khuc. The area was paddy, which made it difficult to move trucks and artillery, so a destroyer was detailed to follow them up the coast, like a distant shadow, to provide gunfire if needed. Bobby hoped for a real fire mission.

The unit and the soldiers of the infantry had been heloed up to the dry paddy fields just north of the river three days before. The cavalry, in ACAVs and M-48 tanks, were confined to the road, Highway One. They crawled to keep pace with the infantry, which struggled through flooded paddy and jungle. Everyone was soaked, and leeches attached themselves to uniforms and crawled toward exposed flesh. The men plucked them off matter-of-factly, but Bobby pulled them off and threw them away from him in horror. The soldiers plodded on, stopping each afternoon to dig night defensive positions in the sodden, rotten jungle, and trading with each other and especially with the drier cavalry for dry socks and insect repellent.

By the morning of the fourth day, the men of the ANGLICO were into a routine, as they walked with the headquarters and weapons platoons of the infantry company, usually closest to the inland side of the coastal highway. Little sign of the enemy was found, and there was no fighting. Some of the men groused that the brigade commander was just running these sweeps as exercises, that the enemy had no serious presence in the area, and would surely never attack a company-strength unit. The operation had two more days to run.

Adams and Cardenas were both on the spot net with the destroyer *Turner Joy*. Morgan was on tac net, with the infantry and the cavalry, and Staples was on command, with the staff in the rear. The whole outfit moved slowly across the difficult terrain. Coles was drifting, fighting heat and fatigue and boredom, when the first mortar round struck in front of them, followed immediately by a B-40 rocket in the trees behind them. Coles flattened himself on the spongelike earth, knowing immediately they couldn't dig in, as a second and a third round crashed through the trees and exploded in their midst. Coles heard screaming, and saw Adams clutching at a shattered leg. Coles crawled forward, without thinking, and pressed a dressing into the wound on Adam's thigh. He looked up, and realized that the screaming came from farther down the trail. Lieutenant Robinson was holding Monkey to his body, keening like a woman. Coles could see Monkey's head had been blown clean off.

Coles patted Adams on the shoulder, and inched toward the lieutenant. He heard the light crackle of M-16s as the soldiers returned fire at a wooded hillside that overlooked the road. The tanks on the road behind them had joined the battle, pumping high-explosive and white phosphorous rounds into the hillside. Bobby remembered his briefing about VC ambushes; they never lasted long. Well, he thought, as another group of B-40 rockets screamed in, this one can end as soon as it likes. I'm terrified, he thought, but I am still thinking.

He turned when he heard a dull whump of exploding fuel, and saw one of the ACAVs on the road behind him overturned and blazing. He reached the lieutenant, who was still cradling the grotesque, headless body of Monkey Jackson. The lieutenant wept and mumbled something Bobby couldn't make out. Bobby felt saddened by Robinson's grief, and frightened by his apparent collapse. "Sir, give me the man. You got to spot."

The lieutenant looked at Coles without seeing him, and continued to blubber. Bobby was struck in the back by the shoulder of the army captain who commanded the infantry, who had slid down into the shallow depression where Coles and the officer and Jackson were. "Navy! Fuckin' A! We need that tin can, for fire! The rockets are coming from the other side of the hill, up there, and the tanks can't fire in defilade!"

Robinson continued to cuddle Monkey's body and moan. Coles felt he had to act. "What, Captain, is defilade?" he tried to make his voice firm.

"Jesus, Sergeant! It means tanks can't elevate their guns enough to drop plunging shot on the other side of the hill. Our artillery is too far back to do it effectively, but the destroyer ought to be able to."

"OK. What do we aim for?"

"Just shred the back of that hill. Anything you guys carry that will make big bangs and splinters. You don't even have to be accurate."

"OK. Just lemme get my second radioman down, Captain, and we're on it."

"What's the maximum elevation of that can's guns?"

Five-inch fifty-fours, thought Coles. "Eighty-five degrees," he said, from memory.

"Christ! You can fire like mortars! What's the matter with the lieutenant?"

"Head wound," said Coles, evenly, "not serious, but he can't see well. The other man is dead."

The captain started to scramble up out of the hollow. "Well, you will get her done, eh, Sergeant?"

"Count on it, Captain." Without knowing why, Coles grinned. The infantry officer disappeared, apparently satisfied. The rocket and mortar barrage had moved away from the center, at least temporarily, and Coles hand-signed Morgan forward, got him onto the spot net, and shouted to Cardenas to shift to tac net as he slid into the hollow beside Morgan. Coles took the telephonelike transceiver from Morgan's radio, and talked directly to the *Turner Joy*. Within twenty seconds, she had shots in the air.

The first rounds surged in, purposely laid into the top of the hill by Coles. They came like noisy freight trains, clearly audible above the noise of the VC mortars and rockets, and the small arms, mortars, and tank cannons of the 197th. Bobby gave the destroyer a spot to add one hundred yards, then to shoot a box pattern two hundred yards beyond that line, and through three mils, either side. The *Turner Joy* was firing at her maximum rate of three guns, forty rounds per minute per gun. The earth shook, and the air hummed. Enemy rockets slackened, and then ceased. Coles was told by the infantry commander to cease firing, as an air strike was imminent.

The infantry moved carefully out of the jungle and onto the hillside. There was no further enemy firing, but the Army waited until the air strike from Danang came over and incinerated the back of the hill with high explosive and napalm before they moved cautiously forward to assess whatever the enemy had left behind.

Coles stood up, stiffly. He looked at his watch, and noted the action had taken only about fifteen minutes. He looked at the crumpled figure of Lieutenant Robinson below him, and realized he had completely forgotten about the officer. Robinson had set aside Monkey's stiffening body, and was absently stroking at the stain of blood and brains that completely covered his shirt and lap. "Sergeant, are the rest of the men, er, all right?"

Coles looked at the man, more in sorrow than anger. He had tried. "Adams will have to be choppered out, sir; I think it might be best if you went, too." Bobby said it with as much compassion as he could.

The lieutenant looked startled; his eyes seemed to plead for mercy, or understanding, then his head fell on his bloody chest. "Perhaps that's for the best, Sergeant," he whispered.

"Sir," said Coles, and helped the deeply hurt man up and toward the road where the medevac helos were landing to pick up wounded and dead. Walker and Staples carried Adams, and Morgan followed, cradling the tiny body of what had been the cheerful, boisterous little man called Monkey.

Adam's wound was bad enough to get him out priority, but the lieutenant and Monkey Jackson would wait. The infantry captain who had first ordered the naval gunfire found Coles and told him to get his unit back down with the headquarters platoon, as the company was ready to move. A UH-1E slick banked in and landed just behind the medevac helos, and a short, stocky black man dressed in perfectly pressed, starched fatigues jumped out. He gestured to the medics to load wounded onto his bird, then walked to where Lieutenant Robinson sat on the ground, his head slumped on his bloody chest. The newcomer said something to Robinson, who shook his head without looking up. Bobby felt deeply ashamed, and turned away. He found Walker standing beside him, and the men of the ANGLICO detachment gathered and ready to go. Their expressions told them they were apprehensive, even scared. "Let's go, men," said Bobby, in what he hoped was a firm and confident tone of voice.

"Yo, Bobby," said Walker, just above a whisper, "you want us a black role model, there he is."

Bobby looked back at the stocky man in the pressed greens. He wore no rank devices, but he seemed very much in charge. "Who is he, Walker?"

"The brigade commander, man, Colonel Blackjack Beaurive.'

Bobby looked back once again at the small man, standing with his arms akimbo talking to the infantry captain and another officer. Bobby straightened his posture, and hand-signed his unit forward. Now I know we have to hack it, he thought, and we will.

Major MacIntyre was waiting for Stuart when he entered the ANGLICO office. He was red in the face, and he waved Stuart brusquely into his office and slammed the door behind him. "William, sit. Smoke. We have a problem."

William fitted a Dunhill, one of his last from the duty-free in Guam, into his black holder, and lit it. MacIntyre paced.

"William, one of my platoons, my detachments, is with the One-Ninety-Seventh Light Infantry Brigade, a very prominent unit trying to prove the Army can fight big battles with their mobile techniques. Who knows if it can work; God knows the Marine Corps doesn't think so, but anyway, it's high profile, and the unit's commander is a very high-profile colonel named Blackjack Beaurive. OK, well, I just got a call from this Colonel Beaurive, and he says, in his lilting southern drawl, that he has 'lost confidence with my officer's judgment in the field,' and wants him out of there. William, I want you to take over that unit."

Stuart paused. He felt a thrill of excitement and a dash of fear. "I'd like to take Moser, sir."

"No problem. I'll arrange that. The detachment had one wounded, and one killed in its last action."

Stuart felt a chill as something unseen walked across his grave.

17 June 1967   Quang Ngai

Stuart crouched on the helo pad, instinctively cringing away from the rotors of the CH-47 helicopter, which spun and screamed six feet above his head. His face and hands were shot with stinging sand thrown up by the rotor blast as the rest of the men disembarked, then finally the crew chief of the helo, his own face shielded behind the black plastic visor of his flight helmet, reached behind him for Stuart's seabag, and threw it onto the pad. Stuart picked it up in his left hand, slung his Stoner over his right shoulder, and scuttled away, still bent over, as the big helo powered up and took off.

Stuart brushed the grit from his eyes, nose, ears, and mouth as best he could. His ears were still ringing from the forty-five-minute ride from Danang to Quang Ngai. At the edge of the pad was a jeep with a slim black soldier driving. The army major who had ridden down with Stuart in the helo beckoned from the front seat. Stuart threw his seabag into the back seat and climbed in after it. The jeep moved off with a jerk.

"We'll take you over to the one-niner-seven, get you squared away, Lieutenant," said the major, whose name was Danby. "I'm the operations officer of the brigade, by the way, so you might as well give me your orders."

"Thank you, sir," said Stuart, shaking his head and swallowing, trying to get his hearing back. "Do you happen to know where the ANGLICO detachment is billeted?"

"Not exactly, but it will be somewhere near the staff. ANGLICO meshes tightly with brigade staff."

"So I'll be working with you, Major," said Stuart, with a smile.

"For planning, yes, but during operations, you'll be up front. You can't spot from the rear."

The jeep skidded to a stop in front of a large, sandbagged metal building, with a carefully painted sign in front. The sign read "Headquarters, 197th Light Infantry Brigade, Freedom's Swift Sword," and below, in smaller letters, "Hubert O. Beaurive, Colonel, Infantry USA, Commanding."

"Come on in, Stuart," said Major Danby. "We'll get you checked in, and then the colonel will want to see you." Stuart picked up his seabag, shouldered his carbine, and followed the major into the building.

Stuart introduced himself to several officers from the staff. They seemed glad to see him, glad when he told them he had been in country before. Fortunately, no one asked whether he had ever spotted naval gunfire in a live situation. After an hour of standing around and drinking coffee, Major Danby came and got him and took him to the colonel's office.

Colonel Hubert O. Beaurive stood behind his polished camp desk to receive Lieutenant (jg) William Stuart. The colonel was short, perhaps five-foot-seven, but he exuded an aura of energy that made him seem larger. He had smooth, very dark skin, and large, intelligent eyes. His hair was cropped so short it almost appeared his head was shaved, and the hairline had receded to the top of his skull. He was dressed in the sharpest-creased, most heavily starched greens Stuart had ever seen, greens that had been subjected to many hours of hand tailoring. The colonel smiled broadly and held out his hand in response to Stuart's salute. Stuart took the hand, and was guided to a chair away from the desk. The colonel poured coffee from a pot on an electric ring on a table behind him, handed a cup to Stuart, and took one himself. The colonel drew up a chair facing Stuart, and looked at him carefully. Stuart felt himself being examined, and it made him a little nervous. Suddenly the colonel leaned back, apparently satisfied, pulled a cigar from a leather case on the desk, and lit it. Stuart felt his tension ease away as the room filled with thick, acrid smoke. "Cigar, Lieutenant Stuart?" The colonel's first words since "good afternoon, come in" and "thank you, Major Danby" caught Stuart somewhat by surprise, as though he had never expected the colonel to speak.

"Thank you, Colonel. I'll have a cigarette, if you please." Stuart dug his pack of Pall Malls from his pocket, along with the holder, and lit up.

"Stuart—I'm going to call you William—let me add my welcome to that of Major Danby. I have but a few things to say to you, and then I'll let you get on to your men."

"Thank you, sir."

"Hm," said the colonel, to his cigar. "First, let me tell you that I believe in the ANGLICO concept. I believe that this war will ultimately be won by large American ground forces confronting and defeating large enemy ground forces. Because this country is long and narrow, our forces will have the advantage of naval gunfire support in most of our operations. Many of my officers, William, especially the younger ones, are skeptical of the navy's ability to deliver precision fire. I remember Korea, William, and I especially remember the USS *Missouri* peeling a Chinese regiment off my face at Dong Hah."

The colonel paused, and examined the wet end of his cigar. He looked at Stuart, apparently expecting some sort of response, so William said, "Yes, sir."

"Good, good," said the colonel, beaming his engaging smile. "So I need you to prove to my officers, and to the entire United States Army, that naval gunfire is a major asset to our operations, and indeed may be the single thing that makes large-unit actions in this jungle war truly feasible."

A tall order, thought Stuart. "Yes, sir."

The colonel relit the cigar. The smell and the smog grew worse. Stuart lit another cigarette in self-defense. "Now, William, having said all that, the excellent Major MacIntyre will have told you about our little problem with the ANGLICO, here."

"He said only that there was a problem with the previous officer in charge of the unit, sir."

The colonel studied Stuart again, for a moment. "Right, Lieutenant Robinson was a good man, a very good man. Perhaps, as Churchill once said of one of his ministers, too good a man for this grisly business. In any event, I need a tough commander to make this work, and Mac says you are that tough commander. Is the major right, Lieutenant?"

Stuart swallowed, "I hope so, sir."

"Good, good. Your marines seem like good men, and I'm sure they will help you get the job done, if you help them." The colonel paused, and once again seemed to examine Stuart, looking for some flaw. "Your platoon leader is a Sergeant Coles, about whom I've heard good things. A little hard-nosed, I'm told, but solid. He provided a very nice piece of work, spotting gunfire in the unit's last action, and probably prevented the enemy from inflicting heavy casualties on my men."

Thank God I have an experienced sergeant, thought Stuart. "I'm glad to hear that, Colonel."

The colonel grinned again. "Did you volunteer for this duty, William?"

The question caught Stuart off-guard. "No, sir, not exactly."

The colonel frowned, leaned closer, "But you do want to be here?"

"Yes, sir," said Stuart, automatically, and then he felt that he did. "I hope to make a contribution, Colonel."

The colonel stood up, and held his hand out again. William took it, and returned the colonel's smile. "Good, good, William. Go find your men, cheer them up, harden them up, and then we will go out together and destroy the enemy."

William saluted, and left the colonel's office. How well the man can say such grandiloquent things and make you believe them, he thought as he emerged from the headquarters into the hot afternoon, and hailed a jeep to take him to his unit.

15 June 1967   Quang Ngai Town

Bobby Coles had been trying all morning to finish a letter to his brother. He wanted to tell Simon about his last mission, but he didn't want to worry him. The unit had been off the line for two days, and Bobby had nothing but time to think about the enemy ambush, the death of Jackson and the wounding of Adams, and the collapse of Lieutenant Robinson. Coles heard nothing of what had happened to the lieutenant.

Rumors were out that the brigade would soon abandon its defensive position around the several strategic hamlets that made up the western fringe of Quang Ngai Town and sweep inland through the Elephant Valley. Bobby thought that would be just fine; as soon as the Army was out of naval gun range, the 7th ANGLICO would be released back to the relative sanity of headquarters, 3d Marine Amphibious Force, in Danang.

A jeep pulled up outside the hootch. Staples stuck his head in. "Hey, Sergeant, the new CO is here, and wants you in the command tent."

Bobby grimaced. The command tent. These army assholes had such heavy titles for everything. A village empty of military-age men, wrapped in barbed wire and lighted all night, was a strategic hamlet. A headlong rout last month had been described as a strategic redeployment. Sergeant Coles jammed on his leather helmet and headed for the command tent.

Coles knocked on the rickety half door.

"Come."

"Coles, sir. Second Platoon." Bobby saluted.

"At ease, Sergeant," said the seated officer, "I'll be with you in a moment." Soft Southern accent. The navy lieutenant junior grade did not look up from the map he was studying.

At ease! thought Coles. Nobody had talked about ease since the unit came onto the line. Next we will be setting up the "We Salute with Pride" signs out by the wire.

Coles studied the new lieutenant. Ugly. Long features, fine blond hair, pale honky skin with a flush of pink sunburn. The whitest white man Bobby had ever seen. The lieutenant seemed to feel Bobby's stare and looked up. Blue eyes, hard, under straw-colored lashes. He put both hands on the table, and slowly stood to a relaxed posture of attention. At six-foot-one, the officer was about an inch shorter than Coles, and Bobby stretched to make that count. Man looks fit, Bobby thought. About 180 pounds, muscles hard and flat under the green T-shirt. But so white!

"Sergeant Coles, I am Lieutenant Junior Grade Stuart. I am the new officer in charge."

They shook hands awkwardly, without moving close enough to each other to do it and maintain erect posture. Bobby felt a pang of anger as he realized he had sort of bowed to take the lieutenant's hand.

"You'll have to bring me up to speed, Sergeant. Lieutenant Robinson's departure and my assignment here were somewhat sudden."

"What happened to Lieutenant Robinson, sir?" asked Coles.

Stuart looked at him with the hard blue eyes. "What have you been told?"

Coles almost looked down, stopped himself. "Nothing really. That he had to fly to Danang, something with Third MAF. Two days later we were notified that you would be taking over."

"Sit down, Sergeant." The lieutenant sat behind the table with the map. There wasn't another chair in the hootch, only kind of a low bench.

"That's OK, sir, I'm easier standing."

Stuart swung a boot up onto the table, leaned back. "I was told that Lieutenant Robinson asked to be relieved."

"Asked to be?"

"Yes."

Bobby let that sink in. "He had to give a reason."

Stuart swung the boot down, sat up, and leaned forward. Bobby decided he liked the new lieutenant's stare. Powerful. *Almost* badass. "I was told Lieutenant Robinson said his . . . nerves were shot."

Bobby felt himself getting hot. "You saying he was a coward, sir?" The sir came out just a little too loud.

"I'm not saying anything, Sergeant. It's what he said of himself. I never met the man, and make no judgment."

The right answer, thought Coles. He stood silent.

Stuart swung the boot back up to the table, and smiled just a little. "Was Robinson a popular officer, Sergeant?"

Robinson. No more Lieutenant Robinson. The honky had made *his* judgment.

"The men liked him." Bobby knew they hadn't. "I liked him. He did the job." Well, at least he tried, Bobby thought.

"What was it about him you particularly liked?"

Bobby felt the heat behind his face. So how come you liked the *coward*, boy? "Well, *sir*," said Bobby, keeping all expression out of his voice, "for one thing, he was a nice, rich, chocolatey shade of *black*."

The lieutenant swung the boot down and got up quickly. "I see. Well, Sergeant, loyalty between an officer and men is important, very important. Affection, too, can make the difficult things we are asked to do easier." The lieutenant paced the tiny room in two strides, then turned and leaned across the desk. "I hope in time you may come to feel loyal to me, and even like me. In the meantime, and even in the unhappy event that you may never come to like me, I'm sure you will continue to perform your military duty."

"*Military* duty, sir? Perhaps you would like the men on parade?" Coles tried to build a smile on that one, to take the edge off.

Stuart looked at him thoughtfully. "That's a good suggestion, Sergeant. You may parade the men. In ten minutes." Stuart sat. "On second thought, best make that in an hour. Your men will want time to see to their gear."

"Yes, sir." Coles felt his throat constrict.

The lieutenant watched him a full minute in silence. "That's all, Sergeant."

Coles hadn't realized he had been standing at attention.

15 June 1967
Dear Brother Simon,
     We have had us quite a day. The new officer arrived to take

Jack Robinson's place, and he had the strangest effect. He is an aristocratic type from Virginia, dead pale white like you have never seen in California. He called me in when he arrived, and told me a little more about why Robinson was canned, but I just couldn't help but be rude to him! You know that's not like me, brother, and I just can't explain it. In the end he told me that he hoped that I might learn to like him, but if I didn't, he was sure I would do my *military* duty. I asked him if he wanted the men out on parade! Here in the field! I should have lost my stripes right there, but he just said yes, good suggestion, and gave me an hour to get the troops ready. Well, then the fun really began. Since Adams was still in the hospital, and we hadn't gotten a replacement for Jackson, who was killed in the action north of the Tra Khuc, there were only six of us to muster. I got them together, and told them to get as clean as they could, because I figured this lieutenant—his name is Stuart—for a real ball-buster. The guys were *not* pleased; they weren't all that rested from the last six days of burning Vietnam with Blackjack, but I told them. They were at attention, but not at *full* attention (you know how a marine can be barely at attention and say fuck you with his posture at the same time), when this snowflake walks out on the little covered platform in front of the hootch we use for an office. He comes out, and looks at each of the men. He has an almost badass look, very blue eyes, like pure ice. I'm standing on the left end of the line, so I can see the guys, and I can see he is getting under their skin, just like he got to me earlier on.

After what seemed like five minutes, he begins to speak, real softly, but loud enough to be heard by every man. He has this deep Southern accent, like the Confederate colonel in a Civil War movie; it's a voice you have to listen to. He starts out by saying he didn't know any of us, but he would tell us what he had been told about us—that we were a new unit with good personnel, but our morale was low.

He said that low morale, low *spirit*, did not belong in a marine unit. He said that marines in small units relied on no one else to accomplish their missions, relied only on their buddies to keep them alive or bring them back in honor if they died.

It wasn't anything he actually said, but the strength, the insistence in the voice, and the command in those icy eyes, that made it seem like a very important speech I could see the guys tightening up, getting taller, you know, getting that fuck you right out of their attention.

At the end of his speech, he said that we were marines attached to an army unit, and that while the U.S. Army was the finest in the world, we were marines, and better yet. It was boot camp shit, but it got the guys. He stopped his pacing on the tiny platform, and asked the guys whether they were proud marines, and there we were, screaming, "Yes Sir!" I think I screamed the loudest.

Chow now. I'll finish this later.

Stuart looked out at the faces of the six men, returned Coles's salute, and watched the men dismiss. "Sergeant Coles, remain with me a moment." He stepped into the hootch and sat down.

Coles stepped through the door, his face a mask. He stood easily, still impressed with the power in the lieutenant's eyes. Stuart did not ask him to sit down this time. Coles felt strangely relaxed, awaiting the dressing down he felt was both inevitable and deserved.

"Sergeant Coles, I understand that as topkick of this unit, you have to push a new officer a little to assert your position. I'm sure you understand as well that I can't let you get away with it. Now so far this afternoon we've both been a little foolish, but we haven't hurt each other. Would you agree with that?"

"Yes sir!"

"Good, very good." Stuart reached behind him and produced a sealed bottle of Jack Daniels whiskey. He pointed at two not-very-clean coffee cups on the dented file cabinet to Coles's left. "Now, I'd like you to have a drink with me and tell me about the men."

Good my lady wife,

My first day commanding this detachment from the AN-GLICO was something never to be forgotten. The sergeant is a man of about my own age, very intense, and very black. I didn't realize, never having met the man, that the previous officer in charge of this unit was black as well, and Sergeant Coles evidently thought a lot of him. At the end of a very frigid interview, Coles suggested sarcastically that the men be paraded. You must know how inappropriate it would be to parade combat veterans in the field to greet a lieutenant jg, but I saw it as defiance, and I was so angry I told the sergeant to have the men ready in an hour.

That hour may have been the longest of my short naval career. When the men were assembled, I walked out and faced them. Six men only; the detachment is four short. Four blacks, one white, and one Spanish name, I believe Mexican. The

hostility was palpable. Marines have a way of showing contempt in their very posture, and I was sure I had made a
dreadful mistake in letting this parade go forward. I looked at
them for a couple of minutes, then got together sufficient courage to speak. On the whole, they looked like pretty good men.

I made a poor little speech about pride, and the need to
take care of one another, and the need to show the soldiers
the pride of marines. I think it helped break through some of
the hostility at least; the men seemed more relaxed when it
was over. When the sergeant saluted to end the drama, I of course
should have come to full attention to return the salute, but I returned it still leaning on the railing in front of the tent, because, Karen dear, I was afraid my legs would shake if I stood
straight up. Anyway, the sergeant and I made a sort of truce after the parade, and I do hope he will support me with the men.

I'm glad to hear your job is getting even bigger, and better.
Please write when you can, you know how I depend on your
strength.

Your loving William

"Sergeant, I'm glad we've had this little talk," said Stuart,
pouring a little more of the Jack Daniels into each coffee cup.
He balanced the bottle in his hand, noted it about half gone.

"I appreciate your not taking offense of what I said earlier,
sir."

"None taken. Now, you've told me about the men—Staples,
Watts, let's see, Walker, Morgan, Cardenas—one missing." Stuart tilted back in the rickety chair.

"That's all, sir, save Adams, and I don't think they'll send
him back to the unit."

Stuart sipped the mash slowly. He felt a trace too relaxed, but
he felt good. "There's Coles, Robert R., Sergeant, USMC."

Bobby rolled the mash off his tongue. "That's hard, sir."

"I'm sure. But you're the most important man in this thin
outfit, Sergeant, and I have to know you."

"If I tell you what I can, will you tell me about Stuart, William M., Lieutenant jg, USNR? Sir?"

"Of course. You need to know about me, too."

I'm back, Simon. Chow was good tonight; the Army takes
good care of itself when it's off the line. There's a lot of talk
in the sergeants' mess that Blackjack has asked for a sweep up
the Elephant Valley. They say he has asked for this before,
but MACV won't let him go without supporting troops to cover
the ridges while we sweep. I hope they're right, because the

Elephant punches right through to Laos, and the enemy would
love to catch us in that valley, after all the shit the 197th has
heaped on him. At the same time, if a good rousing fight
proved Blackjack right, and those MACV pussies wrong, I
think the men would want that. Especially the black soldiers,
but really all the men. The press calls the colonel the Black
Patton, which apparently drives George S. the III, down in II
Corps, to distraction.

Anyway, I have to finish telling you about this new lieutenant. After the parade, the guys fell out, and I think they felt
better about themselves. I remember thinking I should have
done that for them. So the lieutenant calls me into the hootch,
and was I expecting to get my ass reamed! I just hoped he
wouldn't can me out of the unit. Can you imagine me not
wanting to leave the ill-starred Seventh? But I didn't, not then.

He sat me down, and gave me a drink from a bottle of Jack
Daniels he had brought from Danang. He gave me no shit,
but none. He asked me about each of the guys, a lot of detail;
he said that he and I had to know what each man would do in
any situation. It's amazing how good Jack Daniels tastes from
a dirty coffee cup. Simon, I believe this Stuart cares about
men. He is not phony gung-ho, but he wants to get it done. I
almost think I could like the guy.

Do you think I am growing up, big brother?

Taps. I'll mail this and get some sleep.

Love to you and Becky, when you write,
Bobby

17 June 1967   Quang Ngai Town

Stuart handed Coles a navy personnel jacket, which he described as the "Life and Times of Douglas MacArthur Moser,"
a sailor Stuart said had been sent along with him to join the
Seventh.

"But what's he gonna do, sir?" asked Coles, leafing through
the jacket, noting quickly the nonjudicial punishment for fighting.

"The platoon is short one heavy machine-gunner," said the
Lieutenant, blowing cigarette smoke at the ceiling.

"We don't have any allowance in the Table of Organization
for a heavy machine-gunner, sir."

Stuart had leaned back, screwed a fresh cigarette into a black
holder, and lit it. "Precisely my point, Sergeant."

"I assume you want me to run the guys, sir?"

"Quite right, Sergeant. If Moser can't hack it with you, I will find somewhere else for him. But he's a good man, and I feel I owe him." Long drag of the cigarette. "I ask you to try to fit him in."

"Yessir." Not such a bad thing to start off with this honcho in my debt, as long as I really can get rid of Moser if he's a fuck-up. I wonder why Stuart owes him? "When will we have him?"

"Tomorrow, I expect, in the afternoon. Sergeant, Moser, like me, is from the South, but he's no cracker. His main weakness of spirit is his temper, but he's very loyal where loyalty is deserved."

"Yessir?"

"He's also a man of very few words. Please don't mistake that for rudeness."

Coles sat in the little office tent with Moser's file before him. Not much. Just the one disciplinary action for fighting. Good evaluations apart from that. Promoted to gunner's mate third class last year.

A knock at the door of the hootch; Coles said "Come," and grinned to himself at the unconscious mimic of the lieutenant. Suddenly he was looking at the man himself.

"Moser, Sergeant. Third class gunner's mate."

Coles had trouble seeing the man who completely filled the doorway and stooped to do that. He blocked virtually all the light from outside the hootch. Coles reached very slowly right and lit the night lantern.

Literally, thought Coles, a man who darks the sun.

"Welcome to the second of the Seventh ANGLICO, Moser. Lieutenant Stuart speaks highly of you."

"Hm. Thank you, Sergeant."

"Sit down." Moser engulfed the tiny bench. "What do people call you, Douglas? Doug?"

"Just Moser, ah, Sergeant. It's the navy way, if you please."

At least the giant is benevolent, thought Coles. "OK, Moser. Now, we're going to talk a bit about this unit, and how we operate, but first, the lieutenant said you were to be our heavy machine-gunner."

"I can do that, Sergeant." The man looked positively eager.

"We never had a heavy mg."

"No?"

"Neither does any other ANGLICO unit."

"Well, I'm here if'n you want me."

"I'm sure we do want you, Moser. We're supposed to do our

job under the protection of the soldiers for whom we spot bombs and gunfire, but we very often do not get much protection.''

"This ain't a good outfit?''

"It's good, but it's thin. So a bit more firepower couldn't hurt.'' Coles looked down at the file, and closed it. "Now the question is where can we scrounge an extra M-sixty?''

"Uh, M-sixty not really *heavy*, Sergeant.''

Curious. "What do you mean? It's what they use hereabouts.''

"Light gun. Seven-point-six-two NATO round. Not good in heavy brush. Not good against vee-hicles.''

Vehicles! What have we here?''

"We need a fifty, Sergeant.''

"Where are we going to find a fifty?''

Moser got up, went out, and returned with a navy seabag. "I got a Browning M-Two air-cooled fifty here, Sergeant, tookin' down.'' The big man grinned. "Fires a round as big as this finger!'' Moser showed Coles a finger that had to be at least .80 caliber.

Moser opened the seabag at its end and withdrew the machine gun, wrapped in towels and in many pieces. Faster than Coles could have spoken the steps of the weapon's assembly, Moser had it in one piece, and mounted on its swivel tripod on the table in front of Coles. It shone with care and oil.

Bobby looked at the gun carefully. The thing was enormous, nearly five feet long from the twin handles at the back to the tip of the solid barrel. "I've never seen a tripod like that.''

"I built it, Sergeant. I rebuilt the whole gun.''

"How old is it?''

"War Two, most likely. It's a real early Mark.''

"Looks powerful. I haven't seen one of these since basic.''

"Powerful and accurate! I hit what I aims at at eight hundred yards, single fire.''

"How, ah, Moser, did you come by this weapon?''

Moser looked down, then touched the gun, gently. "Well, Sergeant, the *Valley* had this one listed as unrepairable, because it was broke till I rebuilt it, so the chief, well, he wrote it off lost, and he give it to me, like, when I was leavin' the ship. He tole me protect the lieutenant, like I done in the boats.''

Now that is interesting. Maybe the lieutenant has Been There, and Moser with him. The unit could use some experienced people. "I'll want to hear about that, Moser. You think highly of this lieutenant?'' That's not a fair question, or a wise one, thought Coles, too late.

"He's a good officer, Sergeant. I've known good and bad, and real bad. He's good.''

Coles smiled, and nodded slowly. "Only one little problem, Moser. With the infantry using M-sixties, where will we get ammo for the fifty?"

Moser grinned. "The tankers. This outfit's got a battalion of old M-forty-eight-A-three tanks and they got fifties. The cavalry platoon has the modified M-thirteens the troopers call ACAVs. They each mount a fifty as well as two M-sixties."

"You have talked to them?"

"I rode over from headquarters with the cav platoon sergeant. He a Southern man like me. He'll trade."

"Trade for what?"

"Ammo belts, parts if'n I need 'em, for I fix his guns."

Coles grinned back at Moser. "Let's get you settled in, Moser."

I like this man, thought Coles.

16 July 1967   Oak Knoll Naval Hospital, Oakland, California

Billy Hunter swam toward the surface of the shallow river, never breaking through to the air above. He knew the stream; it was the branch of the Ouachita River in Arkansas that wound through his home, the stream he and his brothers had played in as kids. He wondered, absently, why he couldn't get through the surface, but it had been that way for days, maybe weeks.

Slowly Billy's body rolled over, and he shot to the surface. He felt the cooling wind on his body, but he could see nothing. He tried to swim toward the sandy shore, but he could not move his limbs. Billy opened his eyes. He caught a glimpse of a woman with a white hat looking at him. She got up, and ran away from him as he closed his eyes against the fierce glare of the sun.

That wasn't Nga, he thought. Where am I?

Billy heard people moving around him. Nothing seemed to fit. He had no sensation of the river at all; the air, and his body, were dry and cool. Billy opened his eyes in a squint. The light was still very bright, but gradually it became tolerable. He opened his eyes and saw a man in a white coat leaning over him. He felt several people touching him—his arms, his face, his eyelids. Where am I?

"Nurse, get Doctor Barnes!" said the white-coated man, in a voice that seemed to roll from him in a deep, slow bass. Billy looked around, and realized that he was in a hospital. I'm alive, he thought, though that didn't seem to have meaning, or importance.

Another white coat entered his field of vision, and repeated the touching of Billy's arms, and face, and especially, his eyelids. "How—are—you—feeling—son?"

Billy winced. The voice was so loud. "I, I don't feel, anything." It came out as a croak. Billy said it again, more clearly, he thought.

The man smiled. His face seemed huge, and blurry. "That's OK, son, now just relax." Billy was glad the man had stopped shouting. "Now, I'm Dr. Barnes, and you're in the Oak Knoll Naval Hospital. Can you tell me your name?"

Of course, thought Billy. "William Hunter, sir, Sergeant, USMC."

The man beamed. "That's good, William! I'm so relieved you're really awake!"

"Have I been asleep—long, sir?"

"You've been with us here nearly two months, in a deep coma. You have awakened before, but never before have you been able to tell me your name."

Jesus, thought Hunter, how could that be? He tried to remember what had happened, but could not. "What, what happened to me, sir?"

"You had a severe head would, in Vietnam, son." The room was filling with men and women, all dressed in white. Head wound? thought William, I don't remember that. "Just where am I, sir? In the world?"

The doctor didn't rightly understand the question, but he answered it. "You're in Oakland, California, son. Near San Francisco. How do you feel?"

California! thought Billy, "Tired, sir, I feel tired, and confused."

"That will pass. Rest now, son. We've all been praying for you."

Praying for me? thought Billy, as his consciousness faded. California? Where is Nga?

4 August 1967   Quang Ngai Town

Stuart dropped off the jeep as it rolled past the command tent. "Sergeant Coles!"

Bobby stepped off the low platform in front of the office. "Yes, sir!"

"Get the men ready, Sergeant. There's a warning order; we're going out." Stuart reached the sergeant's side and spoke more softly. "Colonel Beaurive has gotten MACV to approve his sweep up the Elephant Valley, Sergeant. Details and the op order, back here, in ten minutes."

It doesn't sound like we are getting sent back to Danang any time soon, thought Coles.

"Sergeant, it shapes up like this." Stuart spread the Task Force Organization section of the mimeographed ops order on the desk. The brigade was comprised of three infantry battalions, the 1st of the 39th, the 2d of the 48th, and the 4th of the 63d. There was one tank battalion, 1st of the 33d Armor, and a cavalry platoon, 1st of Bravo Troop of 2d Squadron, 5th Cavalry. Separate units of field artillery, signals, heavy transport, and the many headquarters-attached units filled the double sheet of paper with their reporting lines and call signs. Coles saw that AN-GLICO was attached to Headquarters and Headquarters Company of the brigade. "The sixty-third is staying here to provide security in and around Quang Ngai. The other two battalions sweep the valley up to twenty kilometers, one on either side of the river. The cavalry platoon, without its tanks, will be up front on the track that follows the south side of the river."

"Why leave the tanks?"

"They don't figure the road will hold them. They figure the ACAVs will be OK if they stay on the road, but the tanks will just get stuck and hold up the advance."

"I have always found the presence of tanks comforting in an operation. For one thing, the noise they make tends to drive the VC back into the hills."

Stuart grinned. My fearsome sergeant has a humorous streak. "Then you can cheer up, Sergeant. Two platoons from the tank battalion and the artillery battalion will be following the grunts, back with the reserve infantry and the rest of the Headquarters Company, to provide a stiff center should Charlie get rough."

"To come thundering up the road after the infantry stamps it dry," Coles smiled back. Lieutenant Stuart is as scared as I am, he thought. And he deals with it in the same way.

"Hm. Well said. There will also be a platoon of tanks on each ridge flanking the valley north and south, accompanied by infantry platoons."

"Why does all this remind me of an enormous chessboard?"

"Tried and true, Sergeant. If the enemy is foolish enough to tangle with us, we will crush him sixteen ways. If not, we will have demonstrated the U.S. Army's ability to penetrate enemy-held territory in force, causing the enemy to flee in terror."

I hope they flee in terror, thought Coles. Dear God I hope the bastards run away.

"What do we do?"

"We go with the point infantry units and the flanking tanks on the south ridge. Colonel Beaurive figures the fog will blow off the valley from south to north, with the monsoon, so we will be able to see to spot air cover."

"Navy?"

"Most likely Air Force. From Thailand. Have you guys pulled the Air Force before?"

"No, sir. We've never handled air. Twice, destroyers for gunfire."

"Well, can't be that different. We'll learn quickly."

"Sir, have you ever spotted Air Force?"

"No, but we spent some time on air force doctrine in school, in California."

California, thought Bobby. Great.

* * *

The sweep ground through its second day. Rumor control had given the operation its special name, the convoy up the con voi. *Con voi* meant elephant, and Bobby added the word to his growing vocabulary of Vietnamese words.

The rain fell in sheets. On the bottom of the valley, it came down finely but continuously through the canopy of dense forest, the top of which was nearly two hundred feet up, drenching the troops with a constant clatter. On the ridges, it fell in thick showers, fat drops, sticky like ripe tropical fruits, each drop expressing its own insult to the men. The water invaded every part of a man's uniform, his body, his boots, his eyes. There had been no sign of the Viet Cong other than the flooded tunnels and abandoned caches of food and ammunition, mostly empty.

Along with the soaking rain, the soldiers who were walking fell victim to immersion foot and several varieties of fungus. All the men were beset with insects of all types, hungry or just plain mean. Mosquitoes, midges, fat red spiders as big across as a man's hand, and scorpions infested the overhanging branches and the rotting forest floor. Leeches added to the misery, crawling up pant legs and around buttons. One man from Charlie Company of the 1st of the 39th was bitten by a green bamboo snake, and had to be evacuated by chopper during a comparatively clear spell in the weather.

The tankers and the infantrymen riding on the vehicles had their own problems. Because of the hazard of land mines, the men rode on top of the M113 armored personnel carriers rather than inside. The antennas of the vehicles swept nests of red ants out of the trees and onto the men. The ants bit fiercely, and had to be killed and taken off each man one by one.

The deep rumble of the diesel engines of the M48A3 tanks seemed to infuriate bees, which came in swarms. Every tank crew had several aerosol cannisters in the tank, but sometimes the bees attacked anyway, and the tanks had to shroud themselves in green smoke from grenades. Men receiving multiple stings became very ill.

In early afternoon, the whole brigade halted and established a perimeter, defended by infantry dug into night defensive positions and by the tanks and armored personnel carriers. Infantry patrols were sent out just before dark to select and spot fire from the artillery batteries, set up in the center of the valley. Most of the targets were trails or narrow places through which the enemy might be expected to come on night attack. The howitzers dropped shells on the targets at irregular intervals all night.

The ANGLICO unit slept with the armor on the south ridge.

The men slept on groundsheets in the center of the circle of tanks. Outside the circle the tankers erected a ring of cyclone fencing attached to engineer stakes, to detonate any incoming rocket-propelled grenade (RPG) rounds before they could reach the tanks. Tank machine guns were manned all night.

Coles wrapped the groundsheet tightly around himself, trying to keep dry and avoid the ubiquitous leeches. Up on the ridge the leeches weren't that numerous except near the many streams running into the valley, and near the large puddles left by the rain. Coles heard many horror stories about the leeches in the valley, including one of a grunt waking up with his mouth open and finding a leech eating his tongue.

The enemy made his first presence felt on the 7th day of August, three days in. A T-shaped ambush stopped the point cav platoon. The lead ACAV ran over an antitank mine, which blew off the carrier's right track and caused it to block the road. The outriding infantry came up quickly, and came under fierce mortar and rocket fire from both ridges of the narrowing valley. The artillery batteries unhitched their 105s on a piece of slightly higher ground and fired as best they could to the cavalry lieutenant's adjustment, but the thickness of the canopy made the fire difficult to concentrate. The tanks on both flanks sprayed the jungle ahead of the cavalry, firing their 90mm cannons and their .50-caliber machine guns. Stuart, Coles, and the rest of the ANGLICO detachment screwed themselves into the ground and held their ears against the sharp bark of the tank cannons and the urgent rattle of the machine guns.

I like this, thought Coles, big guns firing, infantry staying down. Keep the casualties down that way. Not like the Marine Corps, where it seemed that doctrine required each VC to be killed by a rifleman, or the rifleman himself to be killed.

The enemy fire subsided after about five minutes. The damaged ACAV was pushed off the track. Four wounded, none seriously, were treated and sent back to Headquarters Company to await evacuation by helicopter when flying was possible. The advance resumed. The troops moved up cautiously to the places from which the enemy fire had come, watching for trip wires and booby traps. They found shell casings, mortar round increments, and cigarette butts—as usual nothing useful. The 2d of the 48th reported some blood and torn clothing. They didn't find any bodies. They had known they wouldn't find any bodies. The advance continued.

By early afternoon, the point was eighteen kilometers from the line of departure just west of Quang Ngai. The monsoon clouds were boiling just above the trees, making precise air strikes impossible. The APCs and the ACAVs slewed around in the sticky pink clay. The men rotted in the rain. Fearing a larger ambush, Colonel Beaurive ordered a greater number of soldiers up along the ridge lines on both sides of the valley. The NDPs were set up early.

8 August 1967   Officers' Call, 0600

Colonel Beaurive took the baton from the S-3 major. "Men, I am not liking this. I am smelling a rat."

Silence. Fidgeting.

"The Cong are flowing away from us like a bow wave. They have to be going someplace; I suspect they're backing up onto the ridges." Further silence.

"Meteorology gives us better weather tomorrow, and for two days. We could withdraw away from any trap, and let the flyboys protect that withdrawal."

Stuart thought the fidgeting had become almost noisy.

"Or we could advance, and provoke the attack, to occur in the same good weather window. Comments?"

Don't these guys ever talk? thought Stuart.

"May I take your silence to mean you place your tender butts confidently in my hands?" The famous grin. Nervous laughter in response.

"Lieutenant Stuart, you look thoughtful. How about a fresh perspective from a navy–marine corps point of view?"

Stuart might have thought he was being ragged, since he was certainly the least experienced officer in the brigade with respect to infantry problems. But when Blackjack asked for an opinion, that was exactly what he expected.

Stuart went to the front of the tent and looked at the large-scale map, which showed about ten square kilometers of the valley and surrounding terrain. "The colonel is aware that my only experience is in small-unit tactics."

"To be sure. Proceed." The colonel lit a cigar.

"The colonel is also aware that, as a spotter, I have to consider this pretty much as a supporting-arms problem."

"Your excuses are duly noted, Lieutenant. Get on with it." The colonel was still smiling. Stuart pressed on, hoping only not to embarrass himself and his men.

"Aye, aye, sir." The colonel's grin broadened. What message is he trying to send his own officers? "Colonel, you've already thinned out the center, the troops advancing up the valley. I would respectfully suggest you thin them even further, to the point where there will be just enough men to make enough noise to be a believable sweep, and few enough to get back quickly to the tanks and guns should the enemy attack in the valley.''

Colonel Beaurive blew out a foul-smelling cloud of cigar smoke. Anyone who can smoke that thing at 6 A.M. on an empty stomach *must* be tough, thought Stuart. ''Where do I concentrate my men, Lieutenant?''

''Mostly on the ridges, I think, sir. Thicken up both columns, so they can move out farther from the valley. Get some tanks up there, where they can move more rapidly and see better.''

''What does this formation look like, Lieutenant?'' The colonel placed a piece of chalk firmly in Stuart's hand.

Stuart took the chalk and sketched rapidly. ''Like a box, with strong sides and bottom and a thin paper lid. The light forces in the valley are the lid.''

''Good. So you're set up. How do you fight with this formation?''

''I'm assuming we won't find the enemy unless and until he attacks. Depending on the perceived shape of the attack, we can respond in a variety of ways.''

Blackjack examined his cigar, and appeared to find it amusing. ''Continue.''

''If the enemy hits the point, like he did yesterday, the light forces fall back on the Headquarters Company and the infantry and armor reserves, and form a blocking force. Then you can use tanks from both ridges and guns with the main body in the valley to contain and kill the enemy.''

''Wouldn't the tanks and cavalry on the ridges be shooting at each other?''

Whoops! thought Stuart. ''The artillery would be shooting into the valley beyond your forward positions, to break up enemy concentrations. The tanks could roll up and shoot downhill.''

''But if the enemy enters the valley in strength, he splits my force. What's good about that?''

''Well, sir, I'm thinking about this form from my own discipline. With the clouds this low, any air cover we get cannot be precisely spotted, but we can still use it.''

''Continue. This is interesting.''

Is it? thought Stuart. I am getting way out on a limb. ''Once we're sure the valley is populated by the enemy and only the enemy, we can bring the Air Force in above the clouds. We give them a bombing bearing that basically follows the river. We bring them from behind us, and we can call the drop from each pair by the sound of their engines as they pass overhead.''

''Whew!'' Colonel Beaurive gave a little bark of laughter.

Several of the other officers chuckled. Stuart's ears burned. "Your ears are that good, Lieutenant?"

"Well, it won't be precise bombing, Colonel, which is why we will need to clear the whole valley, but we will get a lot of bombs down."

"OK, assuming you can really spot that close. Assuming that for the moment, what happens if the enemy hits either column from the uphill side?"

"The engaged side collapses into a triangle with the rear and the other columns as sides. We bomb away from the line of contact, or let the tanks and supporting infantry from the unengaged side run around the end."

"And if they attack from all sides?" The colonel was grinning again. Please, God, don't let me make a fool of myself, thought Stuart.

"I'm assuming that the enemy could not have a force in this valley large enough to attack this brigade from all sides without our intelligence knowing about it."

"That is, I believe, what General Custer *assumed*." Light laughter, but not unfriendly. Colonel Beaurive went back to the map. "Where would you expect this attack to occur?"

"About six klicks farther along, sir, by that round turn in the river. The valley narrows just there."

Colonel Beaurive ran his finger up the river and tapped at the narrow spot. "You could be right." He turned back to the officers. "We will do that, then. The hill that pinches the river, hill five-six-seven, is our objective, gentlemen. If we get up there without major contact, we will think about it again."

Stuart backed away from the map with a feeling of relief. His suggestion was both obvious and consistent with what changes Blackjack had already made, but he guessed the colonel had wanted someone else to introduce it.

"Oh, Lieutenant," grinned the colonel, "are you *confident* your men can time the bomb release by the sound of the aircraft engines? *Confident?*"

"We've been trained, Colonel. You listen for the change in pitch. The, ah, Doppler effect."

"The Doppler effect! Amazing. Have you ever actually used the, ah, *Doppler effect* to spot a bomb fall, in what, perhaps even later today, Lieutenant, we might be forced to call a *live battle problem*?" The grin masks everything, thought Stuart.

"I have not personally, Colonel, no, sir. But engaged marines did it twice in Khe Sanh, last April, when their positions were nearly overrun. We did study the technique in the desert, back home." Stuart felt this last comment came out a little lamely.

"Good, OK, thank you, Lieutenant. Major Danby?"

"Sir!"

"Get out a warning order ASAP, Major, and then a full op plan to me for approval not later than oh-seven-hundred, so we can get it to all subordinate commanders by oh-seven-thirty. I want to move as soon as the troops finish breakfast. Lieutenant Stuart, you come with me."

Stuart followed Colonel Beaurive into his command tent. "You asked to see me yesterday, William, sit down." The colonel sat on one side of his polished brassbound campaign desk, and Stuart sat facing him.

Leather sling chairs, Stuart noted. How does he keep them clean in the jungle? he wondered. I guess someone else worries about that.

The colonel looked at Stuart carefully while lighting a fresh cigar. He rapped on the table and a corporal appeared with a silver coffee pot and two china cups, which he filled, then left the pot and departed. The colonel dropped the match in a large brass ashtray.

"William, I know what you want to see me about, and I don't want to hear it."

"Sir."

"I don't want to hear what you'll say, although of course I will. But before we get to your business, I should like to say I liked your solution to our little tactical problem."

Stuart screwed a cigarette into his black holder and lit it. He didn't ordinarily smoke before noon, but he needed some defense from the reeking cigar. "Fairly conventional, Colonel."

"All solutions are, William, after everyone finally sees them. I'm sure you're wondering why I singled you out to arrive at that solution?"

"Ah, yes sir."

"This operation was entirely planned by my officers. The men in the briefing. And me. And the operation is going wrong. Instead of killing the enemy, we're simply displacing him. We've lost the initiative; we must get it back. So I really did want you to come up with a fresh idea, a fresh perspective. Only you, William, of my officers, had no part in the planning, and therefore no vested interest in our preconceptions." The colonel sat back and sipped his coffee.

Stuart sipped his. It was excellent.

"On the whole, William, you performed well. Your fresh idea, conventional to be sure, allowed me to scrap elements of my own plan without embarrassing either myself or my officers."

So that was his game. And I never saw it, thought Stuart.

"And now, William, what can *I* do for *you*?"

Stuart cleared his throat. "My orders from Third MAF were to support your brigade while it maneuvered in the coastal plain."

"Indeed."

"And to return to Danang when you left the range of naval gunfire."

"Go on, finish it."

"We are, sir, outside the range of naval gunfire, and the nearest aircraft carrier is on Yankee Station, around five hundred miles from here."

"There is the Air Force."

"Captain Collins on your staff is better trained to call Air Force than I am, Colonel. Air force doctrine is quite different from navy air. Besides, all of your unit commanders are fully trained in calling and spotting air strikes."

The colonel leaned forward and looked upward into Stuart's eyes. "My officers can spot a target for an aircraft that can see it, William." The grin turned impish. "But they don't know about the Doppler effect."

"Sir—"

The colonel stood up and began to pace. "Let us not spar with each other, Lieutenant. You want to pull your unit back. I want to keep you here."

"There's little we can do for you here, sir."

"William, I have been twenty-one years in the United States Army. We are the finest large fighting force in the world. But I have the greatest respect for the marines. And Navy."

"Thank you, sir."

"I smell a big fight out there, William."

"Yes, sir. I know."

"I have a sixth sense. Learned it in Korea. Learned it again when I served with the British in Malaya. I sense the presence of the enemy, Lieutenant. Not just a few skinny Viet Cong." Blackjack expelled a large cloud of gray smoke, nearly filling the tent. Stuart sipped coffee and drew on his cigarette. He could barely taste it. "But a large and organized enemy force, which is withdrawing before us only to choose the best place."

"Then why go on? You've proved you could move a big force through this valley, and drive the enemy out."

Blackjack stubbed out the cigar in the brass ashtray. "Because, Lieutenant, one does not withdraw an intact force from an enemy of no evident superior strength." The voice was even. Blackjack paused. "No, that's unfair. You're asking a very valid question. I guess the best answer is that we've been trying to prove to the desk soldiers in the rear, especially at MACV, that we can maneuver large units in this country, to kill the enemy and drive him from concealment. If we can get these bastards to stand and fight, we can destroy them not only with our superior *valor*, William, and our superior *purpose*, but also with our superior goddamn *firepower!*'' Blackjack slammed his fist on the desk and Stuart jumped.

Colonel Beaurive lit another terrible cigar. ''We cannot lead brave men away from a fight, Lieutenant. Certainly not because of the maidenly hunches of an eccentric old campaigner.''

''I'm sorry, Colonel. I shouldn't have asked.''

The colonel turned to face Stuart, face now serious, even sad. ''No, William. Ask, always ask, because others will; no matter what happens up there, others will ask.''

''Yes, sir.''

The grin returned. ''William, do you not think my staff holds me somewhat too much in awe?''

''Ah—'' Stuart choked on a bit of coffee in his windpipe.

''Quite,'' beamed Blackjack. ''Now, I was telling you I want to keep your spotting detachment.''

''Yes, Colonel.'' Stuart helped himself to more coffee, and surprised himself by lighting another cigarette. He'll have me smoking his stogies in another week.

''A lot of these soldiers are very green, William. If for nothing else, I want you as a fire team. A marine fire team.''

''Yes, sir.'' He is trying to make me feel guilty, and he's succeeding.

''I think you're pretty good, William. And Sergeant Coles is absolutely first rate, wouldn't you agree?''

''Yes, sir.''

''I need your men, William. I need all the men I can get. Do your men want to miss this fight?''

''No, sir, they're game enough.''

''Do you?''

''No, sir!'' It was a lie, but one anyone would tell. Screw it, Blackjack knew either way.

''If you force me to ask Third MAF to extend you, I have to tell him where I am. He knows anyway, of course. He'll demand your return, to get you spotting H and I fire in I Corps.''

''Yes, sir.''

''My need is greater, Lieutenant.''

''Sir.''

''So, William, I am asking you not to remind me of your orders. I would otherwise forget.''

"Sir."

"See this thing through with me, William."

"Yes, sir."

Blackjack sat back. The tension that had been growing in the tent seemed to evaporate. Blackjack smiled, and seemed genuinely relieved. "Good man. Now, about your conventional solution. The box with the paper top. Two strong columns connected by blocking force but not really tied together in the van is not all that conventional. But I believe it fits this situation. Did you think it up all by yourself?"

"Ah, no sir, it's based on something we studied in ROTC."

"Who?"

"Admiral Jellicoe, sir, the battle of Jutland."

Blackjack threw back his head and gave a great laugh of pure delight. "Of course! The fast dreadnoughts in one line, the battle cruisers in the other, the light cruisers in the van, and the old battleships as the blocking force between the columns."

What an amazing man, thought Stuart.

The rain stopped, and the jungle steamed. The monsoon clouds continued to boil overhead with very few breaks, and the tops of the higher hills were shrouded in cloud above 300 meters. The river was swollen, but there were many fords, and the sweep force, now composed of only the cavalry platoon and one company of infantry from each battalion, moved more easily as the road and surrounding countryside dried. The valley narrowed as the brigade approached the big turn in the river, which itself narrowed and became deep and swift, effectively cutting the force in two. The cover was thinner, due to most of the forest having been cleared and planted with rice. The advancing soldiers saw neither people nor animals in the fields. The rice was green, and high enough to require weeding and transplanting, but the peasants were nowhere in evidence.

The attack, when it came, was like a violent thunderstorm. A curtain of mortar fire fell without warning on the lead ACAVs. Rifle and heavy machine gun fire from ahead and from the left forced the soldiers down and off the road. Two of the ACAVs caught fire, and the troops coiled out. Second Lieutenant Dent, the platoon leader, ordered his drivers and gunners back to the three serviceable ACAVs, which were maneuvered into the tree and brush cover to give what protection they could to the infantry. They were Dent's only heavy machine guns. The mortar fire continued, and light artillery and heavy B-40 rockets roared overhead to crash into the jungle behind the cav, along their intended path of withdrawal.

On the north ridge, the leading platoon of tanks came under heavy and accurate cannon and small-arms fire. The ridge was split at this point by a creek entering the valley, and the tanks stopped, reporting that they would have to advance slowly to cross the creek, with enemy fire coming not only from ahead, but from the center of the creek ravine as well. One tank could not protect another.

At the Headquarters Company, the staff rapidly collected information from the unit commanders over the command radio net. From these reports, they would build a picture of the attack, and coordinate a response.

How truly beautiful it is, thought Colonel Beaurive. Every movement of every man purposive, economic. The radio traffic was heavy, but the men's voices were calm. My God, this is a fine group of men. Blackjack spoke quietly. "All right, two and three, tell me about it." The S-2 was Major Phipps, the intelligence officer. The S-3 was Major Danby. Danby spoke first.

"In the van, the cavalry and the infantry are pinned down flat, under heavy mortar fire. The cav commander says he can't see anyone, so he's laying down only light rifle fire, to conserve his ammo. He says there's heavy rocket fire and some artillery falling in behind him."

"The infantry?"

"Alpha Company of the thirty-ninth is linked up with the cav. Bravo Company of the forty-eighth must have lost its command net radio. but their point platoon is talking to Alpha Company of the thirty-ninth on a reserve net. Pinned down by mortars and heavy rockets from positions they can't see through the mist but OK for now."

"So Alpha Company commander is in command forward," said Colonel Beaurive, putting it together in his mind. The Alpha Company commander was Captain Martinelli, regular Army and very solid. "What does he want to do?"

"He says he can't do anything until the mortars stop. He figures the VC never go very long with their mortars; they don't carry much ammo. He expects that when the mortars stop, the VC will charge out from positions about a hundred meters to his left front. Alpha Company is mortaring those positions now. He says he'll have to take that charge before he can start moving back toward us."

"What about the artillery and the rockets falling behind him?" asked the colonel.

"Martinelli can't tell where they're coming from. Dent thinks they're firing from the front or the top of hill five-six-seven, from above the clouds. If we can, Alpha Company would like them knocked out before they have to move back.''

"Artillery?"

"Our gunners on both ridges are putting some high-explosive rounds into that hilltop, but Lieutenant Dent can't spot any fire-fall because of the cloud covering the hilltop."

That's something we should have considered, thought Colonel Beaurive. "Air? What says our navy friend?"

"Recommends we try to pop the hilltop and the closest face."

"Tell him to phone Thailand and get on with it. Now tell me about my formations on the ridges.''

"The forty-eighth's commander is up front in an APC with the tanks. His day code is Lion Six. He says he can see pretty well what's shaping up in the valley, and he could get down there if he had to to stop a major VC charge. Right now he's pulled the tanks and his M-one-thirteens back below the military crest because he's taking antitank fire from across this creek, here, Colonel." Major Phipps indicated the position of the 48th commander and the creek. Phipps had taken up the briefing; he and Danby had divided their responsibilities along the battalion boundary that followed the river.

"What kind of fire?"

"He thinks eighty-two millimeter, probably some of those Russian B-ten recoilless rifles that are mounted on a kind of handcart."

"And he can't take them out?" Blackjack heard impatience in his own voice. We have to get this going, he thought.

"He's mortaring, sir, but he figures there will be guns covering the streambed, to get his tanks as they cross. It's narrow, and he can only get one tank through at a time, so he can't maneuver to give his own forces supporting fire." Major Phipps paused, and listened to the urgent talk on the radio beside him. "He says he'll go through if he has to, but he doesn't want to lose a tank if he can get those eighty-twos another way."

"So?" demanded the colonel, starting to pace. Come *on*, he thought.

"He's trying to flank with infantry. Get close and use a flame-thrower, or if they can squirm into that creek bed, a light anti-tank rocket."

Beaurive had the instinctive suspicion of an infantry soldier for armor. Why have the damn tanks at all if you had to get infantrymen killed to get them past a couple of dinky recoillers rifles?

"Tell Lion Six to stand by on that for now, unless he's pressed. Dandy, what's happening on the left?"

"No contact of their own, Colonel. There's a steep scarp just there, almost a cliff. The CO of the thirty-ninth, Leopard Six, says he can't get vehicles over the ridge and down, unless he comes back about three hundred meters to a shallower slope."

"Tell him to stand by."

"Yes, sir. They're digging in."

Beaurive rubbed his chin. "Assessments, gentlemen?"

The two majors looked at each other. Phipps spoke, "This attack was planned by one brilliant son of a bitch, Colonel."

"Not, you're suggesting, some half-trained Communist zealot in black pajamas?"

"No, sir."

"Sir?" said Kelley, the radio telephone operator answering for Alpha Company commander.

"Yes, Kelley?"

"Leopard One-Six says the mortar barrage is stopping, and he can see people coming through the trees."

"What about the rockets and artillery?" asked Colonel Beaurive.

Kelley spoke into his lip microphone, and got a response. "Still falling in behind him, sir."

Damn! thought Beaurive. If we don't get some help down there, Martinelli is going to be making his whites-of-the-eyes speech very soon. Damn! I should have seen this! "All right, men, here it is. Get the artillery to concentrate fire in the trees on Alpha Company's adjustment. I want tanks on the right ridge ready to go down there if needed, so they better get busy finding accesses of approach, and a river ford upstream." If we can't knock out the guns on the mountain, thought Beaurive, those guns will kill my tanks. "Tell Leopard Six to hold in place, and try to get some forward observers over the ridge for artillery. Tell Lion Six to cross that goddamn creek. And tell Lieutenant Stuart to get us some goddamn Air Force!"

Yo, Blackjack, thought Danby, and swung back to his charts and his radios.

An ANGLICO detachment fights its battles with radios. Of the nine men in the unit, five wore radio backpacks. The unit had to be in continuous contact with command, at brigade HQ, but it also guarded battalion net, and sometimes individual company nets to talk to the forward commanders for spotting and evaluation of strikes. Another radio was needed to talk on the air and naval gun support frequencies; once spotting began, those frequencies had to be continuously open. When spotting, both

Coles and Stuart had to be on spot net, so that Coles could carry on if Stuart went down.

Morgan carried the radio for Stuart, and changed the frequencies at Stuart's command. Cardenas and Watts watched Morgan, and made sure they were on whatever frequencies were not being guarded by Morgan. Staples was Coles's operator, supposed, like the sergeant himself, to stay far enough away from the others to avoid getting killed by the same bomb or shell. Walker carried the reserve set, always on command net unless one of the other radios went down. The rest of the men were trained to replace radio operators, or to act as runners, and to protect the team. Moser and the new men, Morris and Cataldo, organized themselves as security for the unit around Moser's heavy machine gun.

From their position with the point platoon of tanks on the south ridge, the ANGLICO detachment could see the cloud-covered hill 567. Coles was plotting bombing lines and flight and distances to targets from their own position. Stuart told Morgan to switch to the spot net.

"High Ground, this is Whiskey Delta Orange." Stuart checked his call sign. Navy spotting units got their call signs not from the army op order but by code each morning over spot net from the commodore, who controlled all naval gun and air in the south. The call signs were always two letters, followed by a color that gave the general direction of the spotter's movement. Orange meant northeast today.

"High Ground, roger." The air-mission assignment control in Nakhon Phanom, Thailand, answered immediately.

"We are urgent priority one to break up attacking heavy forces, artillery, and rocket launchers on a hilltop."

"Target coordinates."

Coles handed Stuart the work sheet and Stuart read out the coordinates.

"Coordinates of closest friendly forces to target."

Stuart read them off. High Ground then asked for the clear-of-target line, the danger close lines on the various elements of the brigade, and the local weather conditions.

"Whiskey Delta, we'll have to drop through the clouds. It's light and broken above two thousand feet. Your call."

"Roger, High Ground."

"I'm giving you two flights. Bluebell is closest. Polaris will be up in four minutes."

"Roger, High Ground, Bluebell and Polaris. Thank you, over."

"We will monitor. Good luck. High Ground out."

"Bluebell, Whiskey Delta Orange."

"This here is Bluebell, Whiskey Delta. We'll be on your line and overhead in thirty-two secs."

"Units and payload?"

"Flight of four. Thuds. Rockets, high explosive, and napalm."

"We will need to call you down by sound. We won't be able to use the rockets."

"We will pickle 'em off after we drop. Might get something. Dangerous to land with the damn things, anyway."

"We need your bombing altitude and airspeed."

"Figure two-five-hundred feet and one-niner-zero knots. These birds are too heavy to go any lower or slower."

"Roger, Bluebell. Confirm two-five-zero-zero and one-niner-zero. I will take one pair, then the other."

"Roger, good buddy. We drop on your hack. You should hear us in about sixteen secs."

Stuart put the altitude and speed numbers on his work sheet. "What is the distance to that hilltop, Sergeant?"

"Make it two thousand three hundred twenty meters."

No hesitation. Excellent, thought Stuart. He computed the solution on his circular slide rule and wrote it in the box. He and Coles compared solutions, and nodded at each other. Thank God the solutions agree, thought Stuart, because if they hadn't, doctrine said Stuart's would be used, and any awful mistake would be his alone to bear. "Command net?"

"Sir!" Watts answered.

"Tell Six we're bombing hill five-six-seven on this run, repeat, on this run."

Watts spoke into his microphone, then listened. "Six rogers, sir!"

Over the crackling and booming of the fight, Stuart heard the whine of Bluebell's jet engines. Pray that solution is right. When the pitch of the engines suddenly rose to a scream, Stuart punched his stopwatch, and watched Coles do the same. The planes roared overhead and on up the valley. When the stopwatch read 24.1 seconds, the solution from the work sheet, Stuart pressed the microphone button as hard as he could and said "Hack!"

In the lead F-105, Capt. Carter Peters, USAF, pulled the toggles that released the high-explosive bombs and napalm cannisters. The aircraft bucked and rose as the weight of the payload fell away. He could see that his wingman had dropped his as well. He tipped the nose of the fighter-bomber sharply downward and fired all eighteen 2.75-inch rockets into the seething clouds, then rose with his wingman into a wide turn. Looking behind his aircraft as it rose, Peters thumbed the microphone button. "Bombs away, good buddy."

Stuart looked at Cardenas. "Can Alpha Company give me a spot?"

Cardenas shook his head while still speaking into his microphone. "No, sir, but they heard the impact."

Shit, thought Stuart. "Bluebell Three, Whiskey Delta."

"Bluebell Three, roger."

"We want you on the same line, but maybe fifty meters to the left of Bluebell's track."

"Whiskey Delta, this is Bluebell Leader. There is flame and heavy smoke coming up through the clouds where we dropped. Major secondary explosions. Recommend Bluebell Three and Four gain altitude, then dive-bomb the smoke."

"Roger, Bluebell Leader! Excellent!"

"Bluebell Three from Leader. Pull 'em up and bomb the smoke, Chuckie."

Cardenas jumped up. "Sir! Sir! It's Leopard One-Six. It's Alpha Company, sir! The guns have stopped! We got 'em!"

In the command tent, Colonel Beaurive heard the same report. "Danby! We'll commit the reserves. Get the tank company started up the road. And get us mounted with their second platoon." When I see Stuart again, I am going to kiss his Doppler effect.

9 August 1967   Elephant Valley

The lead tank on the northern flank roared up over the shallow crest of the ridge and down into the creek bed. The tank commander had the turret trained out ninety degrees to the right of his path ready to shoot at the antitank gun they all were sure they would find in the cleft that disgorged the creek itself. His gunner manned the .50-caliber machine gun above and behind him, and was firing short bursts into the undergrowth even before the tank was fully into the creek bed. The tank commander saw a flash and heard a cannon shell scream overhead. He aimed and fired the 90mm main gun with one motion. With a roar of its engine and a clash of gears, the lead tank was through the creek and out.

The 48th commander monitored the spot report from the lead tank to the rest of his platoon. "Looks like a cave up there, about thirty meters from where you have to go down into the water. When you hit the water, it will be at about two o'clock, maybe ten-twelve degrees up from horizontal." The other three tanks acknowledged. Lieutenant Colonel Fairbrother pressed the microphone talk button. "Boomer Leader, this is Lion Six."

"Go ahead, Lion Six," answered the platoon leader in the lead tank.

"I'd like Boomer Two to go across with the squad from combat support shielded behind him. I'd like him to stand and suppress antitank fire with main battery and machine gun fire *unless he comes under fire from more than one source*, in which case he'll proceed through and link up with you.''

"Roger, Six. Boomer Leader to Boomer Two, you copy?''

"Yo, Leader.'' Boomer 2 rumbled over the ridge and turned left toward the creek. The squad from combat support walked along the left side of the tank, crouched low, protected from gunners to the right. The tank commander swung the turret to preset the main gun at the two o'clock, twelve degrees of elevation spot given by Boomer Leader. The .50-caliber machine gun raked the trees as the tank tilted down into the creek bed. The tank commander saw the cave at once, thinking fleetingly the bastards could have camouflaged it. He stood with his head and shoulders outside the hatch, trained the cannon onto the target, and barked into his intercom mike to the gunner below to adjust and fire. The 90mm cannon cracked and the mouth of the cave blossomed in a brief white-orange flower. The tank commander heard the empty shell casing ring on the floor of the tank, and the cannon cracked again, and again.

"Boomer Two to Boomer Leader. Three in the cave, no response.''

"Roger. Hold the slopes down with your fifty-cal and get the combat support guys up. I want you outa there ASAP.''

"Yo, Leader.'' Boomer 2 gave a hand sign to the troops below. Go right, go left, it said.

The squad from combat support flowed around the skirts of the tank, crouching below the invisible ceiling made by the tank's still-firing machine guns. The first four men formed a wedge, with the M-60 in the middle, and advanced into the cleft, firing as they went, keeping a jerky, side-to-side movement under the light enemy fire. The flamethrower operator slid in behind them, like a shadow, made slow and clumsy by the tanks on his back. The squad worked up the little creek valley in short runs. Boomer 2 crouched down into the turret, watching, his hand on his gunner's shoulder. "Load Willy Peter,'' he shouted. The 90mm gun was still trained into the cave. At ten meters from the cave, the flamethrower operator aimed the nozzle, and with the igniter on the off position, directed a stream of thick black oil up and into the cave, then dropped to the ground.

Seconds passed. Smart bastard, thought Boomer 2. Let it soak into the limestone.

The flamethrower operator triggered the ignitor, and directed a fat plume of flame into the mouth of the cave. There was a dull boom and a spout of red flame and black greasy smoke from the cave mouth. For good measure, the flamethrower operator aimed thick streams of burning oil at both banks of the cleft, then the squad backed up to re-form behind the tank. Boomer 2 advanced out of the cleft and joined Boomer Leader. The remaining tanks splashed across the creek, with their supporting infantry crouched beside their left flanks.

"Lion Six, we are over," radioed Boomer Leader.

"Roger, Boomer Leader. Is there a seat in Boomer Two?"

"Yessir."

"I want it," said Colonel Fairbrother.

In the valley, the two infantry companies, with the cavalry between them, watched the enemy's advance with increasing concern. Men in gray, black, and green uniforms, in teams of three to six, advanced in short three-meter rushes, diving into the tall elephant grass of the dry field at every concerted fire from the Americans. Martinelli figured a company at least, spread out over a front 100 to 150 meters wide. Each time the cav's heavy machine guns fired, a light rocket slammed into their vicinity. The first five missed; the sixth took out the point M113, and killed most of a squad.

The tanks descending from the north ridge found their way to the river blocked by a string of flooded rice paddies, separated by lines of tall palm trees. There was a narrow, packed road about twelve feet wide between two paddies. The road looked firm enough to support the tanks, but they would have to go single file, vulnerable to enemy guns. Because there was thick forest just along the river, they could do no good until they crossed to the same side as Alpha Company and the cavalry. The topographical map of the valley showed a shallow pool above rapids two hundred meters farther upstream. Colonel Fairbrother weighed it. If that pool is a good ford, the enemy will have it prespotted for his mortars. Still, we have to get down there. We will have to rely on our artillery and air to knock out the enemy artillery.

Colonel Fairbrother called on command net, "Request permission to leave my infantry on the ridge and advance to flank the enemy. I cannot protect the infantry—" His transmission was interrupted by the rolling crash of the air force bombs falling on hill 567.

"Stand by," said Major Phipps. "OK, the bombers may have given you room. Go."

Fairbrother called Boomer Leader to move up. Boomer Leader told his three following tanks to follow at 100-meter intervals, guns trained right, buttoned up. Boomer Leader accelerated across the narrow and crumbly track.

"Danby, what of my left? Has Stevens found a way to get down into the valley?"

"Negative, Colonel. The steep ridge is apparently continuous for quite a ways. The map does not reflect that. Neither Stevens nor the ANGLICO can see down, or get down."

"Damn! Those bastards really knew this spot!"

"I should have anticipated this, sir," said Phipps.

"Fuck the blame, Major! We can still win this thing! We must! What does Stevens suggest?"

"A reconnaissance in force, Colonel. His tank platoon, and two platoons of mounted infantry. Try to find a way down, or at least a place from which to lend supporting fire."

"That would really stretch us out."

"Yes, sir. I told him to hold."

Stevens is too good a commander to be held, thought Beaurive. Fuck it, I'm damned either way. "Move him up a thousand meters, Major. We have to relieve the point."

Major Danby tore off his headset. "Colonel!"

Blackjack whirled. "Yes?"

"It's Dent, the cav platoon leader, sir. He wants an air strike. Says he is not able to hold them off."

Beaurive snatched a headset connected to the command net frequency. "Cobra Leader, this is Six. What is your situation?"

"Peeling back, sir! We cannot hold!" screamed Dent.

"Where is Captain Martinelli?"

"Dead, sir, along with most of Alpha. The Charlies are turning us. We need air support!"

"Remain calm, Lieutenant Dent," said Blackjack evenly, feeling far from calm himself. "Tanks from the right flank are coming to you."

"They didn't make it, Colonel! They were rocketed from the trees! They are four Roman candles out there, in the river ford! We cannot hold!"

Jesus, Mary, and Joseph, thought Beaurive. "Dent, get Whiskey Delta, that is, Stuart, on battalion net." He put the headset down. "Danby! Get us mounted on the reserve tanks!"

Stuart had turned his attention to Polaris, now circling above. Coles had run the first flight of two aircraft over their position on bombing bearing in a dry run, and was passing the corrections, this time to move the line left 100 meters, to Polaris Leader. Stuart told Morgan to shift to command net after an urgent signal from Watts.

"Six, Whiskey Delta. We have a second strike for the mountain."

"Negative! Negative!" Danby's voice had risen in pitch. "We need close support in front of the point!"

Stuart took a deep breath, and hand-signed Coles to hook into command, "Major, we can't do anything close. We can't see our Forward. We can't see the aircraft. We can only do area."

"Stuart, Goddammit! This is Cobra Leader! Dent, at the point! We're getting killed! Give us a goddamn strike!"

"Dent, you have no idea what you're asking!" Stuart's throat was constricted.

"We die either way, Stuart! We're being overrun!"

Stuart tapped Morgan's headset, the sign for him to monitor. "Sergeant Coles! Can we?"

Coles was ashen, his teeth clenched and his lips compressed. "Not according to doctrine, sir. Too close even if we *could* see. And we're not close enough to the cav to time it."

"Try to figure it out." Coles plugged his headset back into Morgan's radio. "Cobra Leader, we can't, we simply can't call it. We can't solve it from this far back."

"Jesus, you navy bastard! Do it anyway! Please!"

"Whiskey Delta! This is Six!" In a lower voice, but insistent, "William, this is Colonel Beaurive! Do it as carefully as you can, but *do it!*"

"Polaris Leader, Whiskey Delta. Danger close; repeat, danger close. We have a troop concentration advancing against the friendly front edge. We have no choice but to call you by sound-timed drop."

"Jesus, cowboy, you better be plenty desperate and plenty good." Polaris Leader's voice crackled from the handset.

"We'll need your left-hand aircraft on the line described as overhead our spot," said Stuart. "Spread your aircraft at twenty-five meter, repeat twenty-five-meter intervals, in line abeam."

"Roger, turning and forming now. We'll drop from twenty-five-hundred feet. We would like an extra twenty knots airspeed to help us maintain formation."

"Roger, two-hundred-ten knots." Stuart worked through the solution. "I'll give you a hack at drop. First drop the napalm, then give me one-and-a-half seconds delay, then the H-E."

"Are you saying we're dropping close enough in to the friendlies to blow our own napalm back?"

"Polaris, the point forces are being overrun. Overrun." Stuart felt his voice shaking.

"OK, kid. We're lined up, all pilots on your net. Napalm on

hack, H-E one-point-five secs after. Twelve secs to overhead. God help you, either way.''

''Roger, Polaris.'' Stuart dropped the mike. ''Cardenas! Watts! Tell Six and Cobra Leader we're bombing now! Ten seconds!''

Stuart finished his solution—2.10 seconds; he held it up to Coles, who had 2.90. ''Jesus, Bobby! That's nearly ninety meters difference in depth.'' If I use his and I'm right, the strike falls behind the enemy. If I use mine and he's right, I drop right on top of Dent. But I have to use mine. Doctrine defeats doubt, mumbled Stuart to himself, swallowing the coppery taste of fear.

Overhead, the tone of the jet engines rose sharply, then fell, and Stuart punched the stopwatch, his eyes on Coles. Coles looked up from his calculation, and pointed at Stuart with his index finger, the thumb up. The stopwatch said 2.1 seconds and Stuart, his microphone switch already pressed in, said, ''Hack!'' Then he closed his eyes.

The ANGLICO team could hear the scream of the bombs over the heavy noise of gunfire, then the soft, fat, growing whoosh as the napalm ignited and consumed all the oxygen in the immediate area. Red and orange flames surged out from the many points of impact, which the men could not see because of the steep ridge in front of them, and rolled and splashed for a hundred yards or more, right up to the tree line that had concealed the enemy assault force's initial position. The ANGLICO marines heard the sharper explosions of the high-explosive bombs crashing into the trees themselves, then could see nothing but flame and billowing smoke. The blast wave and the heat from 250 meters away struck their faces like a hot slap, and they sank back into their shelters.

Stuart sat with his head in his hands, his forehead resting on the radio pack on Morgan's back. Morgan was on command net. Come on, Dent! Report! Please be able to report! The stopwatch in Stuart's fist now showed nine seconds.

Coles put a hand on the lieutenant's shoulder. ''It was a good drop, sir. Your solution was right. I forgot to change the airspeed up to two-ten.''

''Thanks, Sergeant.'' Twelve seconds.

''Cobra Leader, this is Six, over.'' Fourteen seconds. ''Dent, answer Six on command net, over.'' Six himself. The voice was Blackjack's.

''Six, this is Cobra Leader, Dent, sir, over.'' There was a sharp and audible crackle of flames in the background.

''Report the effect of the air strike, Cobra Leader, over.''

Very crisp, Colonel, thought Stuart, fighting his racing heart; just find out who is alive and who isn't.

"Jesus, Colonel, you can't describe this." Dent's voice was soft, almost reverent, and lower pitched than before. "All the men here and forward are a little singed, you know, on the helmet covers, like that. But we are OK. The enemy is just . . . gone." Thank God, thought Stuart. How shocked Dent sounds.

"No sign of the enemy?"

"Well, we can't see more than a few yards because of the flames and smoke. The closest slope got to about ten meters away. I think he had a satchel charge. The napalm set him afire, and he jumped up and Mason shot him. We can't see any others, alive or dead."

"OK, Dent. Well done up there. Sit tight."

"Do we pull back now, sir?"

"Stay there. Tend to your casualties. Improve your position. We are coming up to you."

"Roger, Six. Hey, Stuart? Stuart? I forget your call sign."

"Whiskey Delta. I'm here, Dent."

"You shoulda *seen* it! It was dead solid perfect."

"Just thank God it worked, Dent."

"Yeah. And thank *you*!"

"Get off the command net, you two." Blackjack sounded hoarse. "Well done, Whiskey Delta."

The battle for hill 567 continued another two and a half hours, but the enemy did not mount another attack. When the fires had burned out and the smoke had cleared in the valley, the casualties were taken to a landing zone in the blackened area that had been the battlefield. Helicopters from Quang Ngai and Chu Lai shuttled the wounded and dead back to the hospital, as the southeast wind cleared the clouds and bore away the stench of burnt gasoline, vegetation, and flesh. The tanks and infantry of the reserve force advanced cautiously to and through the tree line from which the infantry charge had come; they found nothing and pulled back. Lieutenant Stuart directed two more flights of F-105s to bomb hill 567, a task made easier by the clearing weather. Lieutenant Colonel Stevens's force surprised an enemy relief column and shot up twelve trucks, without suffering any casualties. Swarms of helicopters brought two fresh companies of infantry from Chu Lai. An engineer company covered by helicopter gunships climbed hill 567, and blew up what remained after the air strikes of what proved to be a major enemy forward base.

Stuart reported to Colonel Beaurive, who was lying on a

stretcher, being bandaged over his right eye. The colonel joked
with the nervous medic about his war wound, actually a cut from
a branch received as the tank on which he had been riding raced
through the jungle to relieve the point. Blackjack placed his hand
gently on the medic's as he finished taping, and pushed him back
and stood up.

"William."

"Sir."

"We are together on this field of glory, William."

"Yes, sir."

"It was a brilliant, boiling battle, William."

"Yes, sir."

"That was a fine piece of miracle, that last spot, William."

"It was much too close, sir."

"Dent doesn't think so, and neither do I."

"How is Dent, sir?"

"A bad shoulder wound. I would guess he is going home."

"A brave man."

"He will be decorated. As will you."

"I was never in danger, sir."

"You were. In your soul. That is the hardest."

Toward evening, the 197th Light Infantry Brigade turned over
its positions to the relieving forces. The trucks started back along
the track they had cut, some towing their howitzers, and the
APCs and tanks followed, protecting the rear of the column.
The exhausted grunts boarded trucks and helicopters to follow
their wounded and dead back to Quang Ngai.

   10 August 1967
   Quang Ngai
   After-action Report
   Section III, Commander's Remarks

I have little to add to the remarks of my acting operations
officer as to the way the battle was waged, except to second
his view that the men in all units performed brilliantly, in the
aggressive, attacking tradition of this brigade. As to the significance of the action, I submit that the destruction of at least
a regiment of the North Vietnamese Army, its Viet Cong light
forces, and a major base camp must be held as a success. That
we hold no new territory is of course true, but our mission
was originally described as to seek out the enemy in force,
and destroy him. This mission should be viewed as a large-

scale raid, as Merrill raided in Burma in 1943, or Sheridan in Virginia in 1864.

In his intelligence summary, Major Phipps cites our failure to anticipate the enemy's near-perfect use of terrain to divide our previously closely linked formation into three parts. We had been advancing through a broad, shallow valley and along contiguous ridges, the force divided by a sluggish and easily forded river. At the exact point of the enemy's attack, the river narrowed and became swift, forcing a barrier at the battalion boundary, and the left ridge became a cliff, preventing the tanks and troops from rendering immediate assistance to the point cavalry and infantry. The enemy was thus able to concentrate his firepower and infantry on a single infantry company and the cav platoon. We should have anticipated such a prospect, but it is noted that the topographical maps of the valley suggest neither the confinement of the river nor the cliff to the south.

Major Phipps also notes that the enemy was able to conceal his artillery above the cloud cover, and that his shelling of the area between the point units and the central main body prevented us in the early stages of the battle from either strengthening or withdrawing our comparatively light leading units. It is true we expected better weather, but the responsibility for pressing our advance despite weather that made the precise use of supporting air strikes impossible was entirely mine. I do submit that if the brigade had waited for a sunny day, and had marched behind a flock of gunships, we would not have found the enemy in force, but only his litter.

Our casualties were heavy, not in proportion to the losses of the enemy, whose counted losses exceeded our total casualties by more than eleven to one, but because every one of ours was a crack soldier and a beloved comrade. The losses among company and field grade officers were particularly grave. The brigade will miss and mourn Lieutenant Colonel Fairbrother, commander of the 2d Battalion, 48th Infantry, killed after personally taking charge of a tank column advancing under enemy guns in a gallant effort to relieve the infantry and cavalry pinned down in the valley; Captain Martinelli and First Lieutenant Morse, both of Alpha Company, 1st of the 39th Infantry, killed in the spirited and lonely defense of the center. Of special pain was the loss of Major Danby, the S-3, who volunteered to ride with the lead tank of the relief column, and who was killed by a sniper's bullet just as the battlefield was being secured.

There was much heroism on that glorious, blackened battlefield. All of the men who gave their lives did so unselfishly and bravely. A full list of recommendations for decorations, for the dead and for the living, will be forwarded separately. I mention here but two young men, whose separate but connected courage turned the battle at a critical moment—Second Lieutenant Dent, who continued to lead his men and Alpha Company's as well in resisting an attack of at least ten times his strength, and Lieutenant jg Stuart, U.S. Navy, who guided the fire of the Air Force down through the dark clouds that had provided the enemy's shield.

Blackjack took up his pen, thought to delete the last florid phrase, hesitated. Fuck it, he thought. That's how I feel, and one bombastic (his critics would say ''in character'') phrase more or less won't change how this one gets evaluated by the rear-echelon mothers who decided winners and losers.

Blackjack signed Hubert O. Beaurive, Colonel, Infantry, Commanding.

They are going to give me a big damn medal for this one, thought Blackjack, or they are going to fry my black ass to a crisp.

12 August 1967   Quang Ngai

Stuart and Coles decided to let the men rest and recuperate from the six days in the field before getting them packed up to move back to Danang. The 197th was off the line, and its place was being taken by two brigades, which made all the troops, from Colonel Beaurive to the last private soldier, immensely proud. The new brigades were fresh in country, and they had assigned to them a team from 1st ANGLICO in Long Binh.

Coles observed the men do what men always did when they came out of action in Vietnam. First, they cleaned their weapons because it was expected of them. Then they took overly long showers and put on their cleanest uniforms over clean underwear, often underwear freshly purchased from the PX for the occasion, socks and T-shirts, all in military green. Then they lounged around for a while, wrote letters, drank beer, and told lies in the enlisted men's club, and ate everything they could find. After a period, the lounging just ended. The period varied in length after each action, but Coles had observed that in good, close-knit units, the lounging ended for all the troops at the same time. Coles knew that when the men cleaned their weapons for a *second* time, and really cleaned them, it was time to put them to work.

The adjustment time had ended the day before, so Coles had

the men pack their gear. They would fly up to Danang that afternoon by transport helicopter.

Coles decided to go over to the sergeants' mess for a last lunch. He hadn't been with the 197th long enough to have made many close friends, but there were some NCOs he wanted to say good-bye to. His earlier opinion that the Army needed too much equipment to do anything, and was generally less aggressive and less able than the marines, had been completely erased in the Elephant Valley.

Bobby stepped into the cool of the club to find a cheering mass of sergeants crowding the bar, slapping each other on the back and the palms of their hands.

"Hey, guys, who just won what? Or are we going home?" asked Bobby.

Bates, the big black master sergeant who did maintenance on the tanks, poured Bobby a beer from the pitcher on the bar. "Next best thing, gyrene Sergeant Coles. We've just been informed through the sergeant's telegraph that Blackjack Ballbuster Beaurive has been selected for brigadier general!"

Bobby's jaw dropped, and he let out a whoop of joy. He was pulled into the backslapping, beer-spilling melee. Why does that make me feel *so good*? thought Bobby. Sure, he's our colonel, and sure he's black, and I should feel good, but *this* good? Maybe I'm glad to be alive. Imagine, in Nam and glad to be alive. Bobby drained his beer, and got a sloppy refill from the pitcher. Forget the heavy thinking, Bobby, he thought. This must be celebrated. "When does the promotion take effect, Bates?"

"I dunno," said the tank maintenance sergeant. "I think a promotion to general has to be confirmed by Congress. But the whole brigade is on parade tomorrow to cheer the old bastard deaf."

"Tomorrow! Jesus, our unit's being flown up to Third MAF this afternoon!"

"Well, Bobby, you're just going to have to get your orders cancelled. You do not want to miss Blackjack's triumph," said Bates.

"Shit, no! But my lieutenant has gotten us places on a supply bird this afternoon."

"Or miss *our* party afterward."

"I believe he had to call some friend of his to get us squeezed in today."

"So get him to cancel, or be a real sergeant and assume responsibility. Cancel it yourself." Bates refilled his glass, then threw an arm around Coles's shoulders. "Come on, Bobby. Blackjack is important to all of us, but especially us blacks."

"I'm not sure that argument will impress my lieutenant," said Bobby. For the first time in a week, Bobby thought of Lieutenant Stuart as a white man.

"Bullshit!" growled Bates. "And besides, the contribution of your little group to our recent victory over the hated Cong has not gone unnoticed in this man's Army, son. The men of the One-ninety-seventh Light will want you there."

"I don't know. Jesus. I'd *hate* to miss this."

"Well, if you won't seize the initiative like an *army* sergeant, at least go talk to the man."

Coles found Stuart writing a letter to his wife. Coles knew the lieutenant hated to be disturbed when he wrote to his wife. He hesitated.

"Something urgent, Sergeant?" The ice-blue eyes held Coles.

"Sir, I guess you heard they made Black—, er, Colonel Beaurive up to brigadier."

"Of course. Wonderful news. We can all be very proud."

"Sir, the brigade is going to parade tomorrow, to honor him. I think we should be there, sir."

"The men would want that?"

"Yes, sir! Even the fucking *Army* wants us there, sir! I've just come from the sergeants' mess."

Lieutenant Stuart put down his pen and rubbed his eyes. "I had to promise Captain Bishop a case of Jack Daniels to get us on that flight. He had to move a lot of priority loads around."

Damn, thought Coles. "I, ah, guess it would be pretty embarrassing to ask him to change it."

"Oh, indeed it was, Sergeant! Now I owe the bastard two cases of JD." A smile started across Stuart's face.

"You changed it? We'll be here?"

"Until the day after tomorrow."

"Ah, thank you, sir."

"Come off it, Bobby. Of course we'll parade with the brigade." Stuart was grinning. "We shouldn't miss this for anything in the world."

13 August 1967   Quang Ngai

Lieutenant Colonel Stevens had the brigade on parade by 1145 hours, waiting for their commander to arrive at noon. There was really no way for the men to look individually sharp in the baggy green nylon uniforms, but one could easily see that the effort had been made. Stuart thought they looked as they should: jungle fighters knew that a sharp edge often drew a bullet.

My guys look good, thought Stuart. Coles gets them to try harder. The ANGLICO marines and Navy were dressed in the tighter green utilities still in use by the marines, even though the Army had abandoned them in favor of a lighter, cooler, and faster-drying uniform. The marine corps uniform was definitely hotter, thought Stuart, but it looked sharper.

Lieutenant Colonel Stevens knows these men and trusts them, thought Coles. Any other ball-busting executive officer would have had the men out here at least an hour before the general was due to arrive, so he could do a little preinspection and aligning of formations. The men would have been half dead from heat stroke by noon, but the XO would have been covered. Lieutenant Colonel Stevens had told his officers to have the men in place by 1145, the officers told the NCOs, and it was done.

Coles was impressed by the size of the brigade. He had never seen it all in one place before. The three infantry battalions and Headquarters Company were lined up with the ten-man fronts for each company, and seemed to stretch back fifty or sixty meters. The cav platoon was to the right of the infantry, and the armor battalion's tanks were lined up spindle to spindle behind the grunts, four tanks in a rank six ranks deep. The guns and the armored personnel carriers were precisely positioned alongside the tanks with the brigade's trucks behind all. As he had marched his detachment up and into its assigned position with Headquarters Company, Stuart marveled at how clean the vehicles had been made.

Blackjack rolled up in an unmarked jeep at exactly 1200. As he stepped from the jeep, Lieutenant Colonel Stevens bawled, " 'Gade, ten-HUT! Pre-sent HARMS!" With a crash, the brigade presented arms, the riflemen holding their glossy black M-16s smartly in front of their chests, the tank and vehicle drivers holding hand salutes. The ANGLICO men with their .45s strapped on also hand saluted. Colonel Stevens did a smart about-face, and saluted the newly minted general. Blackjack returned the salute with equal crispness, and mounted the platform in front of the troops, to see and be seen.

"Put the men at ease, Colonel," said Blackjack.

"Yes, sir!" Stevens did another about-face, and shouted loud enough for the men way in the back to hear, "Order-r-r HARMS!" Another orderly crash as weapons were grounded beside the men. The hand salutes were completed, and hands snapped back at the men's sides. "At HEASE!" As was customary, the men did not stand at ease, but at parade rest, a posture showing greater respect, but hardly more comfortable than attention.

Stuart could see that Blackjack had screwed one new silver star right through the black sewn-on colonel's eagle patch on his right collar point. The left collar point still displayed the infantry patch. Stuart smiled. He had read that Patton never bothered to wait for congressional approval of his promotions, either.

Blackjack leaned forward on the railing of the platform and grinned the grin. He seemed to look at each man in turn. There's art in that, thought Coles. What a credit this man is to black people. To all people popped into his mind, surprising him.

"I hear you men wanted to see me." Blackjack's voice, rich, deep, and clear, extended like a drumroll out over the brigade. There was some laughter, and a few scattered shouts of "yes, sir," a rising murmur.

"DID YOU MEN WISH TO SEE ME?" Like a thunderclap.

This time the men knew their cue, and bellowed with one voice, "YES, SIR!"

"Well, and now you do see me. Colonel Stevens suggests you men want to hear me give a little speech. Do you men really want to stand in the noonday sun to hear me speak?"

"YES, SIR!"

"Very well," smiled Blackjack, his eyes sweeping the crowd. "I humbly acquiesce. But first some *important* business." Blackjack beamed. "Some of you may have heard that the Army has seen fit to raise this unworthy to the rank of brigadier general."

"YES, SIR!" Laughter.

"How news does travel through an army. Well, it's true. And while my *friends* at MACV inform me that it must have been in the works for some time, I choose to celebrate it with you as a result of our great victory in the Elephant Valley! All right?"

"YES SIR!"

"Good. That victory has produced and will produce many honors for the gallant men of this brigade. Because of the complexity of command in the *modern* army, a commander has to have his commendations *approved*!" Blackjack paused for the laughter, and got it. Blackjack's contempt for the bureaucracy was too well known. "So those of you most deserving will have to wait. But before celebrating my promotion, it is only fitting we honor others who will also be promoted, for without the men who stand with him, and *fight* for him, and correct his *mistakes*," another pause, laughter and cheering, "a commander would be *nothing*!" prolonged cheering, "and a colonel would

never become a general.'' Cheering growing louder, then sub-
siding.

"So, honor with me, men, those of your comrades whose
promotions should rightly precede my own.'' Blackjack read a
list of eighteen names. Stuart was surprised to hear the second-
to-last name was Coles.

And the last was his own.

Blackjack quickly came down the line of stiff-legged men. He
knew how hot the men would get. The new operations officer,
Major Dominelli, scuttled alongside like a gangly terrier. As the
general stopped at each man being promoted, Dominelli whispered something as he handed him the certificate, along with
the new rank devices. Stuart observed this sidelong, and wondered what the major was saying that caused Blackjack's grin to
take on an irritated rictus.

That major should be careful, thought Stuart. Blackjack still
grieves for Major Danby.

Stuart didn't know all the men in the line, but he was able to
identify those nearest to him. Master Sergeant Gomez, who had
commanded the Boomer 2 tank in the Elephant, received a direct
commission to second lieutenant. Gomez had been one of only
five survivors of the ill-fated tank column from Boomer, and he
had led the others, including two badly wounded, back through
to 2d Battalion lines before the second air strike had burned the
battlefield.

Next to Gomez was First Lieutenant Hawkins of the 33d Cav,
who had led the relief column up the center, promoted to captain. Next to Hawkins was Sergeant Coles. Now Stuart could
hear what the major was whispering to Blackjack. "Sergeant
Coles, sir, USMC. To staff sergeant.''

Jesus, thought Stuart, didn't anybody tell this turkey that
Blackjack took pride in the fact that he knew nearly all his men,
and for certain all his officers and NCOs, by sight and name?
No wonder the general was seething.

Stuart was standing at rigid attention, with the general so close.
He wished he could see how proud Bobby must look, but he
kept his eyes front.

"Sergeant Coles, you and your team have become a part of
this brigade. An integral part.''

"Thank you, *General!*''

"Thank you, Bobby. Your team's part in the Elephant will be
recorded in the history of this outfit. Now, you are hereby promoted to staff sergeant.''

"Thank you, General. I don't deserve it, but thank you." No soldier knighted by his king was ever prouder, thought Stuart.

"It is far less than we owe you, Staff Sergeant Coles. I think you will find this is the correct collar device. Marine insignia are hard to find in Quang Ngai, but Major, er, Dominelli has been very resourceful."

"Thank you, sir. It is quite correct."

"Keep well, Bobby. If I could, I would keep you with me always." That was for my ears, thought Stuart.

Blackjack stood before Stuart. His strained grin filled Stuart's field of vision.

"Lieutenant junior grade Stuart, sir—" said Dominelli.

"Hello, William," grinned Blackjack.

"Good afternoon, General," replied Stuart, answering as best he could, grin for grin.

"William, as I told you on the field of glory, in the valley, you will be decorated for the brilliance and the courage of your spotting on that day. But my rear-echelon *colleagues* have to approve of my *recommendation*. They will, in due course."

"Thank you, sir."

"In the meantime, I have deemed it only fitting to recognize your impressive maturity and grace under fire by promoting you to captain."

"Thank—"

"Uh, General?" whispered Major Dominelli, urgently. "Not to captain, sir. Lieutenant."

Blackjack's face twisted in anger. "What did you *say*?"

Stuart closed his eyes. Oh, Major Dominelli, you poor, dumb son of a bitch!

"Well, the general overlooks. Stuart is a naval officer, and the navy equivalent of army captain is lieutenant, sir."

"Do you actually think I don't know that?" Blackjack's voice was a strangled hiss. Stuart had never seen him so angry.

"No, of course not, sir, I just thought—"

"You thought! You didn't think! Am I, *Major* Dominelli, a brigadier general in the United States Army?" The general's grin was shaking, but it held. The grin was cutting Dominelli like a can opener.

"Yes, sir!"

"Then I *can* promote this officer, who is of my command, *Major*?"

"Yes, sir! I only wished to remind the general—"

"That the naval rank equivalent to army captain is lieutenant. Thank you, Major."

Beaurive and Dominelli faced each other, inches from Stuart's nose. Dominelli has guts, and Blackjack will recognize that, Major, thought Stuart, and eventually he may accept you.

Blackjack spoke again, now in full control. "Understand me, Major. When he serves with me, Stuart is a *soldier*! Oh, he may wear a navy uniform, but he is a *soldier*. And I don't feel I honor him enough if I call him lieutenant!"

"Yes, sir." Very crisp. Thank God, you are learning, thought Stuart.

Blackjack turned back to Stuart. The grin was back rightly now, the anger and tension gone. "And therefore, I congratulate you, *Captain* Stuart." The general handed Stuart the double silver bars that were the common rank device of an army captain and a navy lieutenant.

Stuart grinned, relieved that the scene was over. "Thank you, General."

"Major Dominelli, return the forward party to their units." General Beaurive strode back to the platform.

"Yes, sir!"

General Beaurive looked out at the sea of proud faces. Good men, all kinds, all races, all accents. I feel genuinely unworthy to lead them on this day, he thought. What on earth should I say to them? He took a deep breath, and relaxed into his famous grin.

"Men of the One-ninety-seventh Light Infantry Brigade, I am honored to command you, and to have shared your great victory in the Elephant Valley." There was not a sound from the brigade. "There is little I can say beyond that." There was some scattered cheering. "I suppose you men's heads should be sufficiently soft-boiled under those steel pots, you will cheer for anything I say, as long as I don't go on too long about it." Laughter, and more widespread cheering.

"That you are a fine outfit with superior fighting spirit is I am sure a fact that no man of this brigade could ever doubt." More cheering. "But it has come to my attention that there is a thing that some of you have indeed come to doubt." The men fell totally silent.

"When we came back here to the rear after our victory, one of the first bits of *home* I encountered, aside from welcome letters, was a week-old edition of a national news magazine. I have seen many copies of that same magazine being passed among you. There is an article, quite a long one, in which the editors, and many *civilian* experts, question whether we should be fighting this war. There is also a story of soldiers in an action south of here who refused the orders of their officers and noncoms to move up and fight, and of *their* general who had to go up in his helicopter and *urge* his men forward. The magazine suggests that these soldiers are opposed to the war on *moral grounds!*"

The brigade remained completely silent, waiting as Blackjack swept the men's faces with his eyes. Stuart shivered despite the heat, chilled by Blackjack's fearsome power.

"Now, men," continued Blackjack, "you and I know it is the constitutional right of the editors of this or any other magazine, or of *civilian* experts, to hold any view about this war they may see fit. We soldiers have fought and died to preserve those rights since the Revolution! But I am *angered* that they would impugn the honor of this Army in which *we* serve because a few *cowards* refused to obey a lawful order to move up, refused an order on *moral grounds!*" Blackjack paused, and gathered his men with his gaze and his erect posture. "So I felt I should say a few words to this brigade about *moral grounds.*" The colonel paused again, and looked at the upturned faces. In all the vast brigade, not a man coughed, not a piece of gear clanked.

I love these men, he thought, and I believe in them and they in me. I speak to them as a father to his strong, proud sons.

"Our *mission* as soldiers is to go anywhere our country sends us, fight her battles, and defeat her enemies. Our *purpose* is to accomplish our *mission*, and to protect each other by moving as one under our officers and noncoms. Our *moral ground* is the battlefield secure and under our boots at day's end. And our reward is *glory!*"

The men roared, as though a dam of pent-up emotion had suddenly burst. A football stadium full of rabid fans could not make so much noise, thought Coles. His own throat burned with the force of his cheering, and he could taste his tears in the back of his throat.

"That is what a career army officer says," continued Blackjack, as soon as he could be heard. "Do you men, you *soldiers*, agree with me?"

"YES, SIR!" roared the brigade.

"Good, good. Then I will *never* have to *personally* come to any unit in my brigade and *urge* the men of that unit to *fight!* Will I?"

"NO, SIR!" The men were almost cheered out, but from the rear ranks rose a chant, which swelled till it came from every corner of the formation:

"Black JACK!"

"Black JACK!"

"Black JACK!"

Beaurive held up his arms, and the chant subsided. "You are kind to cheer me on, with my sorry little speech about a soldier's honor. You men teach me more about a soldier's honor every day I serve with you. Now I would like you to cheer yourselves. You are a riotous, righteous bunch of warriors! You are the One-ninety-seventh Light Infantry Brigade, and I salute you!" General Beaurive stood stiffly at attention and snapped his right hand crisply to his helmet brim. The cheering rose and held until he finished his salute and turned to Lieutenant Colonel Stevens.

"Thank you, Colonel." Blackjack's throat was tight. "Now let us get these brave men into the shade."

Lieutenant Colonel Stevens stepped to the platform, "Ten-HUT! Battalion commanders, take charge!"

Stuart listened as the commands flowed along, a sound he found musical every time he heard it, like a chant from an ancient temple.

"First Battalion, company commanders, take charge!"

"Yes, sir!"

"Alpha Company, platoon leaders, take charge!"

And on it went, as the units marched from the parade ground in close order, like big many-legged machines.

A music as old as armies.

16 August 1967
Headquarters, 3d MAF, Danang
Dear Brother Simon,

Well, didn't we have some kind of time of it in the sweep up the Elephant Valley! I told you when I last wrote that Colonel Beaurive—Blackjack—had been pressing the army brass to release the 197th for a deep raid in force up the valley, and damned if he didn't get it. I won't give you all the details, but the advance up that rain-soaked and jungle-choked valley was near to hell, not to mention the main enemy action when it came.

I told you I thought this Virginia gentleman Lieutenant Stuart was probably all right; well, Simon, he is more than all right. He called down air force bombers *through the clouds, man*, in close support of the troops! I couldn't believe it, but he just did it. I guess it's fair to say that our little navy–marine corps ANGLICO saved the army's ass, and I hear and I believe that Blackjack is going to decorate Lieutenant Stuart well and proper, as indeed he should.

What amazed me most, I guess, was the way Stuart just stood in there, computed his solution, and dropped his bombs, without a single doubt. He was maybe a little shaky waiting for the forward units to report that the strike had hit the enemy and not our guys, but that was *after*. The man has ice water in his veins; in fact, the black troops—not just the ANGLICO guys, but all the blacks in the brigade, because *everybody* knows about this cat now—have named him Ice, as in cool.

When we finally got out of that valley and back to Quang Ngai, I noticed a real difference in the army sergeants. We, that is, 7th ANGLICO, are serious fighters in the eyes of these guys, not some trivial appendage like before. Ice did that, with his precision wipeout of the enemy unit that was about to break our center. Lieutenant Robinson, who I still respect, never was more than staff—you know, something extra to the fighting thrust of the brigade, and we, the marines in the ANGLICO, were *rear echelon*! I mean, an army combat trooper can hardly say anything more demeaning than *rear echelon* about anyone, but after the Elephant, we are *line* as in *up front*, with the *men*! I know it sounds chickenshit, but my guys are walking taller. Me, too.

It all felt different back in Quang Ngai. Then we get the incredible news that old Blackjack is to get a star! Brigadier General! A black General! But we were due to leave the brigade the same day, for Danang, and would have missed the brigade formation to celebrate! Well, brother, I knew the lieutenant had pulled a few strings to get the ANGLICO on a helo back to Danang, but I went right up to him, and said we should stay. At first I thought he'd get pissed, but he agreed. I think he's beginning to trust me more than he lets on. So we stayed for the ceremony.

Well, it's a good thing we did (hey, look, brother, I know what you're thinking; so he knew. OK, probably. I'm just feeling good!). The General walks out in front of the whole brigade (and all together, the brigade is a *big* and *Bad* looking fighting force!), and he calls a bunch of names, Stuart's and mine among them. And he gives me a Rocker; I'm a Staff Sergeant now. And he bucks Stuart up to full lieutenant (actually, Blackjack called Stuart Captain, like Army Captain, and some new whitebread Major corrected Blackjack, who in turn removed all the major's skin). So, Brother, I have to think we did good.

So, after The Blackjack finishes promoting maybe twenty guys, he gets up on this little platform and gives a short speech. He talked about the honor and duty of soldiers, and he related it to the battle in the Elephant. The men cheered him deaf, as one of the army sergeants had told me earlier that they would. I have to tell you, Simon, I cheered my throat out. I couldn't have stopped. I was crying like a baby, but I didn't feel ashamed; I felt proud just to be there, with those men, with that great man to speak to us. One of the army Sergeants later on, when we were drinking to Blackjack—*General* Beaurive's health—said we would gladly follow the man to hell, but that we had done that in the Elephant, so we would now have to follow him even farther. And we would. I would.

Simon, I still don't know about this war, I really don't. But now I want to serve, and to be the best Marine that men like Blackjack, and Lieutenant Stuart, could ever see. My anger is giving way, and changing into pride.

We flew up to Danang yesterday, and aren't doing much. I Corps is quiet. It will be nice to take showers and drink beers for a while.

Your loving brother,
Bobby

Dear Momma,

I got three letters from you when we landed back in Quang Ngai. I like it you write so much and I guess I should write more myself, but it's real hard to put a lot of the things I see out here in words. Somethin happens to people here, they get bigger than real. Like actors shoutin down a stage. The people here, they all seem grander than real people. The L.T. has his cool reserve, the stiff military way of the sargint—even more the general that commanded the army brigade we was with, who made fightin men go crazy cheerin stuff he said about honor and duty. These men are like one-eyed Jacks, Momma, and you never even *expeck* to see the other side of their faces. So, Momma, what I am sayin is that I am puzzled about what is goin on. And about what I think about it. I am not sure who I really am or who any one else is. I really thot I knew the L.T., but I am not even sure about that. It is like when you are walkin in the hills at nite and feelin like there is somethin followin you, and bein afraid to turn round and look. I think all these guys, even that general, are afraid to turn round and look. So Momma, I jest go along and try to do what the others do. And I hope if it ever gets rough for me that whatever happens, I do right like the brave men who never turn around.

Love to you,
Douglas

Dear Karen,

We arrived back at headquarters, 3d MAF in Danang last

night. The ANGLICO, including Mac MacIntyre and the other teams, have all moved over here from Camp Tien Shaw now, and the quarters are bigger and better. My detachment had been on the march with the 197th Light Infantry Brigade since June, and the men are due some rest. I've only been with them about eight weeks, but it feels like six months. The soldiers call it military tired, the fatigue that reaches every part of the body and every part of the mind, the final washing away of all the accumulated adrenaline that comes from being afraid even when there is no obvious danger present. I am convinced that one of the greatest fears men have in war is that they may do badly under fire, that the fear they secretly harbor will come out where their comrades can see it. It is the fear that creates true bravery; any damn fool can be brave when his heart is pure and his reward is in heaven. The bravest men I have seen did their duty and beyond with their knees locked rigid to prevent the trembling, and their bowels turning to water.

We did have one major action while we were in the 197th Light. Prior to my arrival, the ANGLICO detachment under its previous CO had been in a couple of sharp fights supporting the company-sized formations from the brigade, but this time the entire brigade marched up the Elephant Valley, which leads from the coast of Vietnam west many miles into enemy-controlled Laos, and had been a major infiltration route for the enemy not only into our area but into the Central Highlands as well. Our mission was to seek out and engage the enemy in force if he chose to fight, and find and destroy his bases if he retreated. In the best Viet Cong manner, he did a little of both.

I won't bore you with details of battle, which I know you find disturbing. I will tell you one more thing I learned about myself, and to do that, I will describe briefly one part of the action.

The brigade was in a formation that seemed to fit the terrain and what we believed to be the enemy's size and disposition. When the enemy's attack came, however, it became apparent that the formation we were using played very much into his hands, and our light center forces were too weak to hold off the enemy, and too far up to be easily reinforced. So I was forced to call in close air support under very difficult conditions, such that if I erred in one direction, I might miss the enemy, and if I erred in the other, I could hit our own troops. Well, the air strike was successful, thank God, and the forward units were relieved, and after that, the battle was pretty much in our hands. But what I want to tell you is that after the bombs were dropped, there was a delay of a few seconds before we knew whether the bombs had hit the enemy and or struck our own people. During those seconds a thousand thoughts ran through my head, but the strongest was the least appropriate: I worried what the others would think of me if I hit our guys instead of the enemy. I felt concern for the guys pinned down, and genuine fear of the enemy, but the strongest silent prayer was for God not to let me screw up. And when the commander up forward finally called in to say he was OK, I was glad he was alive, *for him*, but also *for me*.

I don't know what I am becoming.

Which brings me to your letter. I don't tell you about these fears of mine to depress or frighten you, or, certainly, to deny you the right to live your life as normally as possible. But I *need* to tell you, my love, my anchor in the world of sanity, what I *feel*. There is no one here who can discuss these things, because they are living the same fears. So please try to understand. Only you know me well enough. I need your help.

My love,
William

18 August 1967   Danang

Major MacIntyre looked up from his work, and smiled. He pointed to the one folding chair in the tiny office, and Stuart sat. Mac signed his name to three different documents, then threw them into his out tray with a look of disgust. "Fucking papers, Stuart, not the work of men of war."

"Aye, sir," said Stuart, with a grin. "Believe me, we lowly spotters regret hogging the fun."

"Seventh ANGLICO is on the map, William, and thanks."

"The guys were good, and we were lucky, Mac."

"Hm," said MacIntyre, leaning back. "Ever the modest warrior, eh, William? I have talked to General Beaurive; I know you did good."

"Yeah, we did, Mac, but I have to tell you, it was a very near thing."

MacIntyre lit a cigarette and threw the pack to Stuart. "Shit, I believe you, but my experience tells me that a lot less of this game is luck than we might think. You did good, and that is it. By the way, you are out of uniform, Troop."

Instinctively Stuart looked down. "What, Mac?"

"Blackjack tells me you're a lieutenant now, or, as he put it, a 'fucking captain, by God and the U.S. government.' "

Stuart thumbed his jaygee bars on his collar points. "I wasn't sure that was serious."

"You didn't think *Blackjack* was *serious*?"

"Well, you know, Mac, I figured if he really wanted to make me up, it would have to go through channels, all that."

MacIntyre dropped his feet off the desk, picked a piece of paper from the litter on his desk, and handed it to Stuart. "I am going to do you a favor, lad, and never tell Blackjack that you doubted his intent for even one second. Here's his letter to CINCPACFLEET, with details. Keep it, but for Blackjack and for me, lad, you are *dai-uy* now."

Stuart took the order, and read it. "Thanks, Mac. I really don't think I deserve this."

"If you live long enough, Troop, you will learn to accept whatever praise you get; there will never be much. Blackjack is tough, and if he says it, I certainly believe it."

"I'll go over to the navy exchange and get some navy railroad tracks," said Stuart, still finding the idea of the promotion strange.

"No need, lad, take mine." MacIntyre took his own captain's rank devices from the top drawer of his desk, and placed them before Stuart. "I would be happy if you wore them."

Stuart looked at Major MacIntyre. He felt his throat tighten. "Thanks, Mac, I'd be honored."

MacIntyre lit another cigarette, and brushed at his eyes to clear the smoke. "So it goes, kid."

18 August 1967   Oak Knoll Naval Hospital

The middle-aged nurse Billy called Miss Cora came in and cleared away Billy's breakfast dishes. As usual, she had brought him in double rations, and Billy had eaten it all, although his appetite still wasn't good. He was anxious to regain his strength, and get going.

"You have a visitor, Billy," said Miss Cora, with a smile. Billy was a favorite of all the floor nurses, with his cheery smile, and gentle, courteous ways. "Your brother Joseph, all the way from Arkansas."

Billy smiled. He had written to his mother when he was first able, about three weeks ago. In reply he had received a letter from Joseph, saying little except he would get up and visit as soon as he could. The nurse walked out of the room with the breakfast tray, and Joseph walked in, his sunburned face creased with a pained smile. Joseph reached across the bed and grasped Billy's hand, then grabbed the only chair in the room and pulled it close to the bed.

"How are you feeling, Big Brother?"

"Better every day, Joseph. I still get awful headaches, but I guess that's to be expected. How's Momma? Tell me everything from home."

Joseph's face lapsed into a look of grief. "News isn't good, Billy. Momma died. Six weeks ago, Billy. I'm sorry."

Billy was still holding his brother's hand, and he squeezed it, and closed his eyes tightly. He couldn't imagine that Rose Ellen could possibly be dead. "Why didn't anyone tell me? I didn't even know she was sick."

"You were still in your coma. She had a stroke. It, ah, was quick; she didn't suffer."

In my coma, thought Billy. So much happened while I slept, and I'm not sure what is real. "Oh, Joseph!"

"Henry and I came to visit you when they brought you here, last May, Billy, and again when Momma passed away. Henry sat right here, and told you, and you seemed to cry, so we thought you understood, but the doctor told us you couldn't possibly hear us."

Jesus, thought Billy. What have I left behind in Nam, and what have I come back to? He felt his dream in the corner of his brain, saw the images underwater. What is real? He opened his eyes, and looked at his kid brother. Joseph's eyes were wet, and he looked frightened. "She's been buried, then?" Of course she had, he thought.

"Right next to Daddy," said Joseph.

Billy's mind raced. I just can't believe any of this. A sickening feeling of pure fear almost stopped him from asking any more questions. He wished he could descend back into his dream. It was almost as though he feared losing it. "Where's Henry?"

"Henry got drafted, Billy. He's in the Army, at Fort Benning. He just got out of basic."

Billy closed his eyes. He saw an image of Henry in green fatigues marching into a wet, choking Vietnamese jungle. He tasted the coppery bitterness of his own fear. "I hope they don't take you, Joseph, there'd be no one to look after the ranch."

"They won't; I'm the last Hunter on the land. I'm exempt."

Well, that's a little good news. Billy looked at his baby brother, and felt a wave of pure love. "Ranch runnin' good, then?"

"Fine. Stock prices bin good, and we got some new wells in. You'll see, soon's we get you home."

Home? thought Billy, am I going home? "Gosh, I miss it, Joseph. I miss home."

I miss Momma, he thought, the grief striking suddenly and with great force. His head began to pound beneath the tight bandages. A sob rose in his chest, and he heaved it out.

Joseph hitched himself onto the side of the bed, and put his left hand on Billy's shoulder. It was awkward, because Billy was still gripping his right hand tightly. "You'll be comin' home, Brother, just as soon as you get better."

I don't know, I just don't know anything, thought Billy. He opened his eyes, and let go of Joseph's hand. "I had no idea I was out for so long, Joseph. They never told me. I didn't know I was even that badly hurt."

"They didn't even know, when Henry and I were here, if you'd live. So I gotta tell you, you look awfully good, as bad as you really look!" Joseph tried to smile, and almost made it.

Billy ran his hands down his chest, and felt how thin he was under the gray blanket. "Yeah. But I gotta get stronger. They let me walk, some, with a nurse to help me if I feel weak. Come on, I'll show you. I can lean on you."

Joseph stood up and stepped back, and Billy pushed the covers off, and swung his legs over the side of the high hospital bed. He took Joseph's arm and stood, fighting the dizziness. "Just a little way down the corridor."

The two brothers walked in silence. Joseph was pleased to see Billy didn't need much help. Billy's mind was a little clearer, and the grief filled in. So much has happened while I was in the dream. "Joseph, do you know what unit Henry is in? I'll write to him."

"I'll write it down for you when we get back to your room. From the look of the nurse who's following us, we'd better go back right away."

Billy held his brother's arm tightly, willing away the dizziness and the sadness. "No, a little longer. You lie in bed so long, your muscles just disappear. But I'm feeling better, Joseph."

"That's good."

"Henry reckon he'll get sent to Nam?"

"He thinks his unit is going to Germany."

God, please, I hope so. One Hunter killed in Vietnam was sure enough. He pulled up short, and looked at his little brother. Why did I think that? I'm not dead.

"You look tired, Big Brother, and kinda confused. Let's get you back to bed."

Billy nodded, and allowed himself to be led back to his room.

The following morning, Billy asked to see the doctor. Billy waited until 1000, his brain boiling. When the doctor entered, all crisp and white-coated, Billy bombarded him with questions about his illness, and his present condition. Doctor Barnes answered the questions carefully, and, Billy thought, honestly. "Doctor, when will I be well enough to leave here?"

The doctor frowned. "Honestly, that's difficult to say, Billy,

You're a strong young man, but you took a hell of a knock. Your brain function is good, but we have to let the healing progress. The headaches you get are because the brain gives off fluid as the tissue heals, and the fluid causes pressure. We hope the fluid will eventually be absorbed and carried away in the bloodstream, but these things are very difficult to predict.''

Billy smiled, waiting for the doctor to continue. When he didn't, Billy asked, "Best guess, Doc?"

"It's really a guess, Billy. Three to six months, if we're lucky."

Three to six months! I'll go crazy long before that. "Let's try for the three, hey, Doc?"

"Sure, we will try, Billy, you know that." The doctor rose to leave.

"One more thing, Doc. I gotta get my body back in some kinda shape. I want to start physical therapy."

"I don't think you're ready."

"Please, Doc. Just some light stuff at first, but let me try."

"I don't know, Billy, it does no good to rush these things."

"Please, Doc, I'll be careful."

"I'll talk to the chief therapist. Maybe I'll ask her to come and see you."

Billy grinned, "Thanks, Doc."

The head nurse met the doctor just outside the door to Billy's room, and led him silently to the nurses' station. "Doctor Barnes," she said, her tone severe, "you don't honestly believe we're going to be able to release that boy in three to six months?"

The doctor turned and faced the head nurse. "Cora, I had to give him something. Some hope."

Miss Cora watched the doctor's back as he walked away, his shoulders slumped.

15 September 1967   Oak Knoll Naval Hospital

Billy lay in his bed, sweating. The headache was ferocious, but he didn't ring for a painkiller. He had been telling the doctor and nurses that the headaches hardly bothered him anymore; he felt he had to do that to have any hope of getting out of the hospital. Billy lifted his arm, which felt unbearably heavy, and looked at his watch, a new one, with a date, which Joseph had sent him. September 15th, 0130. He reached up and rubbed his temples. The pain made him weep. He groaned softly and wished for the dream, but without painkillers even the dream wouldn't come.

Since Joseph's visit four weeks ago, Billy had thrown himself into physical therapy, and his body was rebuilding, albeit with agonizing slowness. The chief therapist, a gentle, pretty black woman named Marie Toussaint, watched him, and helped him, but this afternoon she made him stop when she saw the veins in his temples throbbing and felt the unnatural heat of his body. She commanded him to bed, and canceled tomorrow's session as well.

Billy felt a gentle pressure on the edge of his bed, and opened his eyes. The night nurse, a quiet, plain redhead named Rose, sat on the bed, a glass of water in one hand, and a paper cup with a pill in it in the other. Billy recognized the codeine pill, and longed for the release it would give. He shook his head.

"I know you need this, Billy."

"No, thanks, Rose, I'm fine." Billy smiled as best he could.

Rose put the pill between his lips, and tilted the glass of water to his mouth, holding the back of his neck. Billy swallowed. "I know you're trying to get released, Billy; I know how unhappy you are here. I won't tell the doctor."

Billy smiled, and lay back against the pillow, waiting for the drug to work. Rose leaned forward, kissed him lightly on the lips, and left the room without another word.

Rose, thought Billy. Rose. Rose Ellen. Rose. He fell into a deep sleep.

Billy continued to press himself on the machines, but he learned to pace himself, so that Marie wouldn't cut his sessions short. He also learned that the pain in his head wasn't nearly as bad if he took it a little easy, but he still needed the pill most nights in order to sleep. Rose came to him every night when she was on duty; and the nights before she was to be off, she gave him two, one of which he hid in the ammo can in which he kept his few personal belongings. Some nights, when the pain was hardly there at all, he would roll the pill under his tongue while she kissed him, and then add it to his supply in the can. His vision got better, and he could read, but not for very long. He was allowed to watch television, and he watched the NFL games on Sundays, but usually his vision became blurry after about an hour, so he would pick one game, and watch only the second half. His muscles gradually responded, and began to fill out. His balance was almost normal. On the 20th of October, he asked Marie if he could skip the machines and go outside, and try to run.

Marie studied him, a look of indecision on her smooth, kind face. Billy cranked up his winning smile. "Are you sure, Billy?" she asked, "Bouncing that banged-up head of yours might be very painful, and might reinjure the tissue inside."

"I'll be OK, Marie, I'll go slow, but I want to try."

She got up from the bench. The look of concern and doubt had not left her. "Do the machines today, Billy. I'll ask the doctor."

Doctor Barnes examined Billy every other day, usually spending most of his time shining lights into Billy's eyes, which hurt. He gave Billy an electroencephalogram once a week. He didn't like the idea of Billy running, but he didn't like to discourage someone who so clearly wanted to get better, and he really didn't think a little jogging could do damage. Anyway, the pain will make him stop, he thought. "OK, Billy, run a little, but only with Marie or one of the other therapists. And promise me you will stop at once if your head begins to throb."

"I promise I'll be careful, Commander." Billy had learned that the doctor was more likely to permit something if he was given his naval rank. He was really a lieutenant commander, and should more properly have been addressed as Doctor or Mister. Whatever gets it done, thought Billy.

Marie led him out of the hospital herself. Billy was thrilled to see the sky and feel the fresh air. The day was warm and sunny, and Marie walked with him to a grassy area. "Now, Billy, let's just try a few steps at a time, nice and easy."

Billy felt newly alive as he began to jog. He yearned to sprint, to run a forty-yard dash, or maybe an out pattern. Wouldn't it be great to have a football, he thought. He trotted about forty yards, and stopped when Marie called to him. He felt a little dizzy, but good. My ankles are weak, and my knees feel creaky, he thought. I'll have to take this slowly. He trotted back to Marie, a little breathless.

"How does it feel, Billy?" asked Marie, taking his head in her hands.

"Good, great! I've got to get my wind back!"

"No dizziness, no pain?"

"No," Billy lied. Marie looked a little blurry, and Billy's stomach was churning. There was a hot, liquid pool of pain on the top of his head where he imagined the fluid the doc talked about must be.

"OK, then, let's go back." Marie took his arm.

"Marie! I feel fine! One more time?"

Marie looked at him closely. She doesn't believe me, thought Billy. "OK, one more tiny run, and then the whirlpool."

Great, thought Billy, fighting the pain. He ran the forty-yard hook pattern he had loved at Arkansas a hundred years ago, and he felt his balance was actually a little better, but the pain was definitely getting worse. Marie led him back to the whirlpool, and he sat in it with his eyes closed as the pain rolled around inside his skull like fiery liquid sloshing in a spinning bowl. As soon as he was alone back in his bed, he liberated one of the cached codeine bombers from his ammo can and swallowed it, then gritted his teeth and wept silently until it worked. I am going to continue running until I am strong. I will continue. I will leave this place. He fell into a shallow, dreamy doze, until he was awakened by Miss Cora with his dinner tray.

Billy lay in darkness, feeling oddly peaceful and ready to enter the dream. His head was much quieter, and he felt he could sleep through the night with just the sleeping pill everybody got. When Rose slipped in and closed the door behind her, he smiled. She kissed him, and put the pill into his mouth. He rolled it under his tongue. She kissed him more urgently, and ran her hands under the covers, inside his hospital gown, kneading his chest. "I hear you ran today, Billy."

"Yes, Rose, just a little."

Rose's fingers traced his emerging muscles, on his chest, and down his abdomen. "You're getting stronger every day, Billy."

"Slowly, slowly. Got to get better, Rose."

Her questing hands caressed his stomach, then played with the thick hair patch below his navel. She bent and kissed him again. Billy felt an intense thrill, as he sensed his erection. He could not remember the last time he had felt the tightness of sexual arousal in his groin.

Rose pulled the covers off him, very slowly, and climbed into the bed, above him. She picked up the hem of his gown, and stroked his aching member with both long-fingered, gentle hands. Billy wanted to say something, do something, but he couldn't remove any of his sense from his organ. Slowly, unbelievably slowly, Rose lowered her head over his sex, and kissed it, then slid her mouth over its entire length. Her hair, like fine-spun copper, spread over his stomach and thighs as she gently sucked and tongued his penis. "Rose," he moaned softly. "Rose."

Billy felt his climax approaching, beyond control. He felt he should say something, to warn Rose, but he was utterly paralyzed. He came in long, thick spurts, praying she wouldn't choke, praying she wouldn't hate him.

Billy writhed, his face twisted into a grimace of pleasure contesting pain. He covered his eyes with his arm, pushing the dim light in the room far away. "Nga, Nga!" he cried. Rose released his twitching, shrinking penis, and laid her face next to his, pushing his arm away.

"Who is Nga, Billy?" said Rose, playfully.

"A woman. A girl I knew in Vietnam," said Billy, feeling helpless.

Rose's heart fell. "A girl you loved?"

"Y-yes." Poor Rose, he thought, she deserves better than this.

Rose lay silent, cradling Billy's face. He watched her, then pulled her close, and kissed her. He tasted the salty, slick taste in her mouth.

"That is why you are doing this, killing yourself to get out of here. You want to go back there, and find her."

"No, Rose. She is dead. But I do have to go back, to find some answers."

The young nurse felt hope rise again in her rapidly beating heart. "Why, Billy? What kind of answers?"

I don't really know, thought Billy, "I don't really know, Rose, but I know I must."

A loud, insistent buzz came from the nurses' station across the corridor. Rose jumped up. "I love you, Billy!" she said, in a loud whisper.

"I love you too, Rose." She smiled brilliantly, kissed him quickly, and darted from his room to answer the buzzer. Who knows, thought Billy, maybe I do. He felt a bitter, acrid taste in his throat, and realized he had swallowed the painkiller. He reached for his glass of water, and washed it down, then lay back and waited for deep sleep. Rose. Rose Ellen. Nga, my poor Nga.

20 October 1967   Danang

Moser sat in the darkness in front of the tarp-draped doorway to the hootch in which the lieutenant lay thrashing through his dream. He listened to the low moans coming from the officer, some short, some longer; insistent, pain-filled but never loud. Lieutenant Stuart never actually cried out; Moser took that as a sign of strength.

Coles stepped out of the shadows and squatted next to Moser. "He's having the dream again?"

"Yair, Sarn't. A bad one. Long."

Bobby Coles lit two cigarettes from a limp pack and passed

one to Moser. "You think it's the same dream he told us about in the Elephant Valley?"

"I dunno. I guess."

Coles shivered in the heat. "People say it's bad luck when a dream repeats."

Moser smoked. "He's had 'at dream many times."

"Before the Elephant?"

"Way before. Tole me oncet he had it even on the ship." A sound like a large sigh floated through the doorway.

"We should wake him."

"Hell, no. That's why I'm here, see nobody goes in. He gets real crazy if he wakes afore it finishes."

"Well, shit, what about the other officers billeted in there?"

"He was asleep when they came back from chow. I tole 'em find som'other place fer a while."

"They went?"

"Shit. Yair. I tole 'em he real sick. They left."

Coles shifted his weight and stubbed out his cigarette. "Maybe you shouldn't have said that."

"Hell, Coles, he is sick. He never dreams like this 'cept in a fever from the malaria he got."

"Hm."

Another low sound, halfway between a moan and a cough, came from the hootch.

Coles stood up. "Moser, I'm going over to liberate a beer from the sergeants' mess in motor transport. You want to come?"

"Brang me one here. And one fer the L-T. He'll be awake when you get back, and powerful thirsty."

Stuart emerged from the tent, rubbing himself with a large green towel and shaking his head to clear it. "Moser! You waiting for me for something?"

"Jes' setting." The big man looked at his boots.

Stuart sat beside him, clutching the big towel around his shoulders.

"You sweatin' a lot, sir."

"It'll pass quickly now, Moser. So you're here covering my back like always."

"Yessir. Ah, sir? Was it the same dream? The fire 'n' all?"

Stuart reached into the narrow hootch and took out his shirt, which he pulled on slowly, wincing at the pain in his shoulders. "The same. The dreadful fire dream, Moser."

"Hm."

"But, you know, the ending was different this time."

"How?"

"Well, at the end, when the burning faded away, but before I felt my fever break, I could look out through the shimmering of the heat and see three figures."

Moser looked away. "People?"

"Well, you know, they were just shapes behind the flames, but I think they were people. The one in the middle seemed to carry a long pole over his shoulder."

"Were you scared a' the people?" Moser felt uneasy talking about the Lieutenant's dream.

"No. I felt very serene. Peaceful."

"Who did you think they were, sir?"

"I suppose the obvious symbol is Death, Moser. Maybe here in Nam the only peace is death." He got up. "Don't worry about it, Moser. It's a dream, nothing more. I'm going to the O club. You needn't wait here any more, my friend."

Bobby Coles returned with three cold but warming beers.

"Lieutenant's gone," said Moser.

"Where? How'd he look?"

"To the officers' club. He looked shaky, you know, sweatin', but all right."

"So, he had the dream, right?"

Moser stood up and stretched his stiff legs. "He says the dream got a new endin'. He reckons he saw Death."

"Jesus, that's creepy. How did he feel about that?"

"Says he felt nice. Peaceful." Moser sat back, and opened one of the beers.

"You look sore troubled, Moser."

"Had me a uncle, in Georgia. Real hill man, some said witch-man." Moser finished the beer. "Him, he said, man dream about seein' Death, it gonna come."

"You believe that?"

"Hm. Don't know. Maybe a little."

"Did you say this to the lieutenant?"

"Couldn't. Anyway, no need."

"No need?"

Moser rose again. "Nope. Uncle said, man what dream it, he ain't the one to die. Someone close to 'im, but not the dreamer."

12 November 1967   Danang

Stuart stepped into the ANGLICO office. "You sent for me, Major?"

Major MacIntyre looked up, and smiled. "Yes, William. Good news! Your orders have arrived." He handed the stack of mimeographed sheets across his desk. William scanned them greedily, looking for the key sentence.

> . . . when relieved, proceed military air transport CONUS, then by civilian carrier under voucher, report Commanding Officer, Naval Investigative Service, Washington, D.C.

William sat down, and read the rest of the order. It only ran one page; the rest were copies. He read it again. Finally, and Washington! "What does 'when relieved' mean, Mac?"

The major lit his pipe. William started a cigarette. "It means that as soon as I can get a replacement for you, and you can break him in, you can go back to the World."

William frowned, "How long do you think that might be?"

MacIntyre shrugged. "Kid's orders are cut. His name is Malvern, a jay-gee. Presuming he has thirty days permanent-change-of-station leave, just as you do, and he has his schools, he should be here in late December. Later, of course, if he still has to go

397

through training for the job. Then, you break him in, which shouldn't take too long, if your unit is in the field.''

"Jesus, Mac! I don't want to bitch, but this was supposed to be a six-month assignment! I have a very impatient and unhappy wife back home.''

MacIntyre looked up from his papers, and frowned. ''We all do, Lieutenant. And remember, some of us have been here longer than you have, and indeed will remain after you depart.''

Stuart felt ashamed of himself. ''I'm sorry, Mac, what I said was way out of line.''

"That's OK, William. Some day I'd like to meet that wife of yours; she sounds terrific. Look, I'll do the best I can, but I have to have a trained officer to run your unit. Surely you understand that you and I owe that to your men.''

"Of course.'' Stuart felt miserable. Karen would go crazy, but he did owe the men a properly qualified commander in the field. ''So what do you think, Mac?''

"Realistically?''

"Please.''

"The end of January, if we're lucky. But be prepared for delays, William, and prepare your wife. This is still the Navy.''

The end of January. That won't be so bad. I just hope Karen will understand. ''Thanks, Mac.''

"Good man, William.''

William walked quickly back to his hootch. Washington! Karen will love Washington. He decided to send her the good news right away, and see how she reacted, then tell her about the delay afterward. Since the mail turnaround was ten to twelve days, by the time she knew he would be a couple of months late, it would be about December sixth, and hopefully the magic of moving to Washington would make up for the failure of the Navy to make good on its promise of six months.

He dashed through the letter, painting the naval, political, and social life of Washington in lavish tones, and hinting gently that though his relief had been ordered in, he might be a little late. Just let her get used to the idea of Washington, and then he could explain the two-month delay. Hell, two months was nothing, and the war was quiet. He finished the letter, and took it across to the post office to drop it. He then went to the Stone Elephant for happy hour, and found Hooper, who whooped for joy and embraced him when he heard the news.

The days dragged as Stuart waited for Karen's reply. The unit spent three days operating out of Gio Linh and LZ Stud, but the VC were quiet, apparently tired of chewing at the tough hide of the marines. On the twenty-fourth of November, Moser came by Stuart's hootch as he worked on an after-action report. "Letter, sir," said Moser. He dropped the envelope on Stuart's tiny field desk, and withdrew.

Stuart tore open the envelope, having recognized instantly Karen's handwriting. It was a long letter, and it seemed to be written in blank verse. Stuart smiled, willing himself to read it slowly.

Think of me as a princess riding in a carriage of silver, studded with pearls,
Think of me at sunset, and moonrise, yours and not yours, mine and not mine,

Fine images, thought William, and despite himself, he sped on, looking for her reaction to Washington. Midway through the second page, the letter became simple prose. His eye found the word Washington, and he read the sentence around it.

When you go to Washington, I will not be going with you. William, please don't hate me, but I have a life here, a life I don't want to leave. My life with you was an idyll, a dream of wonder, a love of uncommon strength. I love you, but I could not go into a good navy wife's cocoon, to watch at the headlands for her hero to return. I am sure Washington will be good for you, and the career you love. And you have grown used to missing me.

William read the entire letter, and read it again, and a third time. The awful paragraph would not go away. William's heart pounded and he began to sweat, a deep aching feeling rising in his chest. He closed his eyes, and rolled onto his bunk into the fetal position. A great moan of despair burst from within him.

Stuart was waiting for Major MacIntyre when he came to open his office the following morning. MacIntyre could tell from Stuart's expression of agitation that something was very wrong. MacIntyre unlocked the door of the office, and beckoned Stuart inside. MacIntyre's yeoman handed him a cup of coffee and his overnight messages, then turned and poured a cup for Stuart. Stuart followed MacIntyre into his tiny office, and closed the door. "You don't look well, William." MacIntyre sat behind the desk. Stuart sat down, but got up immediately and began to pace. "What is it, William?"

"Sir, Mac, I really don't know how to say this. I got a letter back from Karen, my wife. She says she doesn't want to go to Washington with me.''

"What? Why not? Washington is very good duty."

"I know. I appreciate that. But, she, well, she wants to just continue with her life in LA."

MacIntyre brooded. "What do you want me to do, William?" Poor kid, he thought, thinking briefly of his own very loyal wife, and their three-year-old son, back in Oceanside, near Camp Pendleton.

Stuart turned, and placed his hands on MacIntyre's desk. "Is there some way I could get some kind of emergency leave, sir? Just fly back there, explain things, talk things out?''

We all think our problems are special, thought Major MacIntyre, bleakly. Imagine if we gave emergency leave to everyone who got a shitty letter from his wife. "I wish I could do that, William, but I can't. Emergency leave can be granted only in the case of a death, or impending death, in the immediate family."

Stuart sank into the chair, suddenly very tired. "But that doesn't seem fair, Mac! A guy can fly home to bury someone who can't possibly benefit from the act, but a guy can't fly home to try to save a marriage, a lifetime?"

MacIntyre sat silent. There was nothing to say.

"A week. Ordinary leave, Mac. Get me down to Ton Son Nhut, or over to Subic, and I'll just catch a civilian airliner," Stuart's voice was a whisper.

MacIntyre was torn. Stuart was his best field commander, and MacIntyre thought of him as a friend. "You know I can't, William."

He looks miserable, but he will pull through. Stuart is tough; he is just young. Poor bastard, thought MacIntyre.

Stuart slumped in the chair, his chin on his chest. "I know, Mac. Please don't think less of me for asking."

MacIntyre reached across the desk and placed a hand on Stuart's shoulder. "Hell, no, William. It's rough, believe me; I've seen too much of it."

"Vietnam," whispered Stuart.

"Yeah, Vietnam," replied Macintyre. Fucking Vietnam, a war with no battle lines and no home front. "Look, William, I'll take you off the duty roster for a few days. Go over to the air force area. There's a MARS hookup there; call your wife. Maybe that could help."

Stuart got up slowly. He smiled faintly at MacIntyre. "I'll try. Thanks, Mac." Stuart turned and left the office.

Poor rat-fucked back-stabbed brave bastard, thought Mac-

Intyre, suddenly very angry. How could any woman do that to her man?

Stuart first tried to place his call at 1000, which would be 6 P.M. in California. He waited two hours for the call to go through, pacing and smoking in the tiny office. The air force radio operator has heard it all before, thought Stuart. His conversation with Karen would be shared with the bored kid, and indeed anyone else who had a shortwave radio and cared to tune in. MARS was a radio-telephone hookup with the States that depended on ham radio operators to make the transoceanic link. Once you got through to a ham in the States who had a phone link, he would then place a collect call for you.

"Lieutenant Stuart? Ringing, sir," said the radioman, without expression. Stuart leapt from his seat, and entered the cramped booth. Envious eyes from the many servicemen trying to call home followed him. Stuart glanced at his watch, 1215, 8:15 P.M. in California. At least she'll be home from work. He adjusted the headset, and held the mike, ready to key in as soon as she answered and accepted the call and the radioman gave him a hand sign through the glass. He heard the phone ringing, half the world away. Pick it up, my love, he willed, pick it up. The phone rang and rang, and Stuart massaged his temples. There was a distant click, and a tinny voice came on. "No answer, Danang."

Much louder, Stuart heard the radioman on the other side of the glass, "Roger, kilo-niner-six-hotel-bravo-India. Try once more, please?"

Once again, clicking sounds, and the mournful, endless sound of a phone ringing in an empty apartment. In Minneapolis, K96-HBI stood by, waiting for the next call. The radioman was already reading the next phone number off his sheet when Stuart got to his desk. When he finished, Stuart asked, "When can you try it again, Airman?"

"Hard to say, sir, this crowd. Gotta say two hours, sir. My suggestion, sir, go get some lunch, an' come back around fourteen-hundred."

Stuart smiled. "OK, Airman, thanks."

"Yo, sir."

Stuart walked out into the cloudy, steamy afternoon. Lunch, he thought, stifling his anger at Karen; where the hell was she at 8 P.M. on a Tuesday? Across the dusty street was the air force officers' club, the Danang Officers' Open Mess. The sign says it all, thought Stuart, the DOOM Club. Stuart walked in, and found the bar. It was well populated with aviators. Stuart found a relatively quiet place near the end of the bar. He ordered a beer, and asked what was for lunch. Hamburgers, of course. Stuart had never been in an air force club that offered anything else.

Two hours, thought Stuart, glancing at his watch. Where could she be? Terrible thoughts forced themselves into Stuart's mind, but he rejected them. He had to; he loved his wife, and the only good news in her letter was that she still loved him, or said so. I cannot doubt her, he thought, and thought. She just doesn't understand.

Stuart ate the tasteless hamburger, then another, and drank beer, as the time crawled. The aviators, drinking boisterously even at midday, ignored him. The Vietnamese barman was solicitous, and Stuart drank steadily, if slowly. At 1345, he paid his bill, and walked back to the MARS office. As he walked through the hot sun, he felt a decided buzz in his head.

"Yo, Lieutenant, you're next," said the radioman, with a wink. I wonder if he has had any lunch, thought Stuart. He had barely sat down when the radioman hand-signed him to the booth. Stuart jammed the headset onto his head, and soon the ringing sound began. Stuart looked at his watch, and calculated. Shit! Ten o'clock at night, and where is this wife of mine? After the tenth ring, he slammed down the headset, and emerged from the booth.

"I know, Airman, two hours," he threw at the radioman as he stalked out. "Thanks, I'll be back."

The radioman smiled. Stupid fuck, he thought.

The 1600 call was midnight in California, and the 1830 call was two-fucking-thirty in the morning. Stuart's strategy of drinking slowly but steadily between his returns to the MARS station was wearing thin, and his throat and gut were sour with beer and greasy hamburgers and too many cigarettes as he listened to the steady, mocking ringing at 1830. There was a new operator on since 1600, so Stuart's embarrassment was not that well known. The phone rang on at 2020, oh-four-twenty in the morning. Stuart set down the headset, and wearily walked out into the humid blanket of Vietnam in dying autumn. After he took the bus back to the marine base and his quarters, he dug out a bottle of Scotch he had been saving, and drank from it until he couldn't think.

The next morning he was back at MARS early, trying to catch Karen at her office. No answer. He worked his way through the day, calling, and drinking at the DOOM Club. By afternoon, the off-duty airdales were talking to him. Still the phone only rang. Stuart took himself home after midnight, angry, befuddled, and alone.

"We have to do something, guys!" said Coles, looking at Moser in the twelve-man tent they shared with the rest of the detachment. "We *know* Ice!"

"Leave him be. He got a lot ridin' with 'at woman," said Moser.

"He's killing himself, and we have to think of the unit! He's falling apart," insisted Coles, pacing the wooden floor of the tent.

"You never bin in love, S'arnt?" asked Moser, quietly. Bobby stopped, turned. In fact, I never have, he thought. Women, sure, but school and football always kept love away. "Let 'im work it out," said Moser.

Coles continued to pace. He recognized the scent of fear, his own. This man had led them through the battle of the Elephant, and several smaller actions where the gunfire was nearer. He was legend. He simply could not collapse and leave them to some young and incompetent officer! Bobby felt guilty as he remembered Lieutenant Robinson. I told my men to trust him, not because he was good, but because he was black. Now I know what having a good officer means. "Look, Moser. You care about him; so do I. Don't you think we should try to help?"

"When he asks, S'arnt," said Moser, very softly. "This is Nam, man, things git fucked up all the time."

"Jesus! We're due for a call, man! He will have to lead us into the field! And he has been drunk for two days!" Moser's face was tight with anger. Coles turned away to think thoughts at the blank green wall of the tent.

"Give it a lil' mo' time, Sarn't; he's a strong man." Moser looked at Coles with the hatred in his eyes of a hound protecting an injured man against wolves. At that moment, Coles decided he had to go and find Lieutenant Hooper.

Major MacIntyre sat alone in his office in the cool of early morning. He had wanted to ignore Stuart's misconduct for a few days, let him work through his anger and grief, but Stuart just seemed to sink further. He had watched him stumble from his hootch an hour before, bleary-eyed and pale, his uniform wrinkled and dirty, and go to the bus station to catch the shuttle to the MARS station. Maybe that was a bad suggestion, thought MacIntyre. Maybe she just flat up and went, and the kid is clinging to that phone line as he slowly drowns himself. That fine young man is becoming a blasted, empty husk, to be filled up only with booze.

I'll let him have till tomorrow, thought MacIntyre, then I will get him out on a medical.

Lieutenant Hooper pulled up beside Stuart and beeped the horn of the jeep. The claxon sent waves of pain through Stuart's head, and he grimaced, ready to shout at the asshole driver, until he recognized Hooper.

"You are moving early, Lieutenant," said Hooper.

"Yeah. Going over to the M—, to air force, Hoop. Ah, how you been?"

"Better 'n you. I only bin fighting a war." Hooper's voice had a twist of disgust.

Stuart had to squint into the rays of the rising sun to see Hooper at all. "What is that supposed to mean?" Stuart knew what it meant, but it angered him anyway.

"You look like you bin sleeping in a stable. Smell like it too. You had breakfast?"

"I don't think I want to have breakfast with you, Lieutenant, but thank you for your consideration." Stuart started walking toward the shaded bus stop. Hooper popped the clutch of the jeep, and the vehicle jerked forward, blocking Stuart's path. "Get *in*, asshole," Hooper growled, pointing at the passenger seat.

Hooper and Stuart sat at a table at the far end of the mess tent. The tent was just beginning to fill up. Hooper had heaped Stuart's tray with pancakes, eggs, sausage, bacon, juice, and coffee. Stuart could barely carry the thing, and the combined smells made him gag. "Why we sitting way over here, Hoop?"

"Because, dear William, while I do want to talk to you, I *do not* want to be seen with you. You look like you have been in the bush for a week, which I know you haven't."

"Maybe something worse, Hoop," said William, feeling the sadness well up behind his eyes.

"I heard. Your wife left you."

Just like that, bang, like a slap in the face. Stuart's eyes cleared, and he looked at Hooper, who was looking at him while stuffing his face.

"And you've been acting like an asshole ever since," continued Hooper matter-of-factly, around a mouthful of bacon.

"I appreciate the sympathy," said Stuart, hot with instant anger. He put a fork full of pancakes into his mouth, and found he was moderately hungry.

"You don't need sympathy, Troop, you need a kick in the ass." Hooper drank some coffee and dabbed his lips.

"If Major MacIntyre wants to fire me, he can do it himself."

"I didn't hear this from the good major."

"Where, then?"

"Doesn't matter, just tells you there must be a lot of folks talking about you."

"Well, it's none of their fucking business!" said Stuart, hotly.

"Is," said Hooper, around another mouthful of breakfast. "Definitely is. You're a serving officer in the United States Navy. You have duties, responsibilities."

"Fuck it, Hoop, we are stood down."

"There is a war on, sonny. We are never *that* stood down."

"Shit, Hoop! You and me been drunk before—"

Hooper poked a finger into Stuart's chest, pushing him back and causing him to spill coffee on his leg. "Stop right there, asshole, and think. We drink, but we drink as gentlemen. We hoot and holler, but we never really get drunk when the war is close. Did you ever feel that you couldn't take a deep breath and then function as an officer after any of our outings? Think!"

Stuart backed away from the jabbing finger. Hooper was right, they always kept enough control so they could go to work. Still, under the circumstances . . .

"Do you feel competent to lead your good men in battle this morning, Lieutenant?"

Stuart shook his head. No, he didn't.

"I'm telling you this, Troop, because what you do about your wife is your business, but she's yesterday's problem, or maybe tomorrow's. Today's problem is your job, and mine. Do you remember the First General Order?"

Stuart looked at Hooper. His expression was bordering on rage. "Of course. 'Accomplish the mission.' "

"And the second?"

" 'Take care of the men.' "

"Good." Hooper stood up abruptly. "Now, you want to go to the air base, I'll drop you."

Stuart ran a hand over his jaw, and realized he had missed patches of his beard in his hasty shave. "No, thanks, Hoop. I think I will finish this breakfast. I have things to think about."

"So be it. I have a place to go; be back in about three days, at which time I will come looking for you. I hope to find you feeling better at that time, Lieutenant." Hooper smiled slightly.

"Fuck you, Hooper." Stuart tried to be angry, but he couldn't.

Hooper's smile expanded into a grin. "I'm glad we had this little chat, Lieutenant."

Stuart just waved him away, and addressed himself to the cold eggs. MARS could wait.

He finished his breakfast, slowly. *Fucking Hooper, making me recite those General Orders like a fucking cadet. Accomplish the Mission, Take Care of the Men.* Most people said to turn them around; take care of the men and the mission got done.

Stuart felt suddenly hot with shame. *What Hooper is telling me is there's nothing there about taking care of one's own feelings. Nothing at all.* He felt angry and disgusted, and he got up and left the mess tent quickly, and started walking back toward the bus stop.

He walked about fifty meters, and stopped. *Nothing in there about being a drunken bum, either.* Hooper was right about that, too. The way Hooper and he partied *was* different. They had fun, but they *cared* about themselves, and the men they commanded. Stuart walked on, putting some snap into his stride. *It's my business, dammit! My rage! My pain! But Hooper was right! Damn* him!

To reach the bus stop, Stuart had to pass the grinder in the center of the camp that was occasionally used as a drill field. A corporal was putting some cherries from a replacement battalion through close order drill. As they passed, they sang out a cadence with which marines always greeted new arrivals:

> Ain't no need to hurry *home*!
> Jody's took your girl and *gone*!

Stuart stopped dead in his tracks. His anger was joined with a sensation of paralyzing awareness. *Of course. That's what Hooper saw. "Your wife left you."* Karen's words, burning in his brain, echoed: "I love you, but I could not go into a good navy wife's cocoon, to watch at the headlands for her hero to return."

How sordid, he thought, watching the men wheel and march away across the grinder. *How banal.* He turned once again, and headed for Major MacIntyre's office. *I have to make this right.*

Once again he stopped. He rubbed his chin, feeling the stubble. He smelled himself, and was revolted by the stale smells of beer and sweat. He got himself moving again, this time toward his hootch.

He gathered his shaving gear and a clean, pressed uniform. He marched to the latrine, and shaved, carefully, staring back at his angry face in the cracked mirror. He showered thoroughly, and dressed. He carried his douche kit and the filthy clothes back to his hootch, dumped the uniform, and left the douche kit. He marched to the major's office, and told the orderly that he had urgent business. MacIntyre admitted him at once.

"Sir—" William began without preamble.

"Sit down, Lieutenant." The major had not looked up; when he did, he was pleased to see Stuart had apparently pulled himself together. "What news from the home front?"

"None, sir, I never got through."

"Will you keep on trying?"

"No, sir, I think not. I will, of course, write. Mac, I have to say I'm ashamed of my conduct over the past three days."

MacIntyre looked at Stuart, carefully. "And?"

Stuart sat straight. "That's all, sir."

Major Macintyre smiled. Thank Christ, he thought. He bent his head to his paperwork. "Good. Then carry on, Lieutenant."

"Aye, aye, sir." Stuart stood, and left.

MacIntyre felt immensely pleased. He's a hell of a good kid.

"Sergeant Coles?" Stuart pulled the tent flap aside.

"Yes, sir," said Bobby, getting up from the bunk.

"Sergeant, if you please, you and the other noncoms, my office, in fifteen minutes." The flap fell closed.

He sounds better, thought Coles, and went to hunt up Walker and Moser.

"Well, men," said Stuart, from behind the desk, "any new business for the unit?"

"Reports are all caught up, sir. No assignments. Rumors, of course," said Coles, looking carefully at the lieutenant. He looks sober, maybe a little flushed. Probably hung over.

"Well, that's good, I guess. Thank you for covering for me, Sergeant."

"Sir."

Stuart stood up. There weren't chairs enough for all three noncoms to sit, so it's better I stand, he thought. "Men, what I have to say is very difficult, so I ask you to bear with me if I say it badly. We all know there are no secrets in a camp, and I'm sure you know my wife has told me she won't be going with me when I go on to Washington."

"You shoulda gone home," blurted Moser, who then reddened with embarrassment.

"Perhaps. Maybe that would have helped," the cadence call from the grinder echoed in his mind, "maybe not. But that's for another day. What is important here is that we all have a job to do, and for the last several days, I haven't been doing mine. I haven't been worthy of you men, and the others, and I apologize.''

The three stood silent for a moment. Moser said softly, ''No need, sir. Losing a good woman tear anybody up.''

''I know, Moser, I've been hurt, and I'll be hurting for a long time. But with your help, I will do my job until you have a new unit commander.''

Another awkward silence. What do they really think? wondered Stuart. A man whose woman leaves him is what? A wimp? A cuckold? The words rattled around inside his skull. Moser looks protective; Walker impassive. Coles, as usual, is difficult to read. I am going to have to prove it to him all over again. ''Well, that's all, men. Thank you.'' The three men nodded, and shuffled out.

''He's fine, man. He had a right to go a li'l crazy,'' said Moser, as the three walked back to their tent.

''He's all right *today*!'' shot back Coles. ''We don't know how much that really took out of him.''

''He done enough for the fuckin' military. They shoulda let him go home, see to that woman.'' Moser thought of his own mother, so often alone.

Coles stopped and turned. Moser's loyalty shamed his own doubts. ''You sure you can trust him still?''

''He'll be fine, S'arnt. He knows, now, what too few learn,'' said Moser, filled with a sadness he couldn't understand. ''Nam is everything, and everything is Nam.''

Coles snorted. ''You sound like you expect to spend the rest of your life here, Moser.''

Moser smiled. He was short, down to twenty-two days and a wake-up, and then he was going home. ''Yair, S'arnt, I guess I do.''

12 November 1967   Oak Knoll Naval Hospital

"He demands to be released," began Dr. Barnes, after the meeting had come to order in the hospital's small conference room. Present, in addition to Dr. Barnes, were the chief of neurosurgery, Commander White; the chief of surgery, Captain Freinberg; the head of physiotherapy, Marie Toussaint; and Nurse Cora Wright. "He says he is well, and he wants to go back to normal duty."

"Just like that," grunted Captain Freinberg, loading his pipe.

"Not exactly, Captain," said Mrs. Toussaint. "He's been working very hard, and the recovery of his body from the effects of the coma and confinement to bed has been truly remarkable."

"You would account him physically fit, Marie?" asked Captain Freinberg, putting a match to the mass of shag in the bowl of his pipe.

"Well, Captain, yes, I would. I am sure he is not as strong as he was before he was hurt, and I have to admit I would like to keep him a little longer, but he is in better shape than most men his age, even most servicemen."

"I remember you came to me about six weeks ago, Marie, to ask me if he could get out and run a little," said Doctor Barnes. "Did anything come of that?"

"He's now running two to three miles, every other day."

409

"Two to three *miles*?" interjected the chief of surgery. "This is the same marine who lay in a coma for two months?"

"Yes, Captain," said Mrs. Toussaint.

"Well, then," said the captain, once again relighting his pipe, "so his body is fit. Doctor White, what about his mind?"

Commander White spread his fine hands on the tabletop, then made a steeple of his fingers. "That's always hard to say, Doctor. As you know, most men who come in here with head wounds that grave are *never* released, unless it is to some Veterans' Administration hospital for permanent care. The surgeons in Vietnam did a competent job of cleaning the wound, removing bone fragments and foreign matter, and managing the blood and fluid loss, but there was massive damage over a large area of the right posterior cortex. Usually we just plug up the hole, and wait to see which functions return, and which do not. In Sergeant Hunter's case, no conscious functions at all returned for nearly two months."

"He has a plate in his skull."

"Yes, Captain, a small one. Bone regrowth has been quite good."

"And his brain remained active while he was comatose?"

"Oh, yes, indeed. His brain-wave activity was completely normal for an unconscious man."

"And then he just woke up," said the captain.

"Essentially, yes."

"What is your prognosis, then?"

"Well, there are several good signs. His vision has improved to near normal, and his balance is good. The wild card is the edema in the brain itself, which is very hard to measure except through the patient's own evidence."

"His pain, you mean."

"Yes, sir. The pain is normally excruciating. Therefore, we have to take the fact that he seems to be in little pain as a good sign."

"He's not taking painkillers?" asked the captain.

Doctor White looked at Nurse Wright, who shook her head. "Not at all, sir, for, how long, Cora?"

"He started refusing them about the first of September, Doctor, and I don't see any administration of codeine at all since the fifteenth of that month." Nurse Wright closed her chart.

"Would you release him, Commander?"

"No, sir, I really would not. It's just too soon."

"Thank you. Now, Dr. Barnes, you've been the attending physician throughout this man's care, have you not?"

"Yes, Captain."

"Tell us about him."

"I would say he's a young man of remarkable courage and determination. He is fairly, but not overly, intelligent, was apparently a good marine in all respects."

"In other words, Barnes, a nice all-American kid."

"Precisely, sir," said Dr. Barnes, and smiled.

"Would *you* release him, then, Doctor?"

"Well, we medical men always like to hedge, don't we? I'm with Marie; I'd like to keep him a little bit longer, but I really can't give you a hard reason as to why. I would release him."

"Cora?"

Nurse Wright drew herself up straight and faced the captain. She knew the chief would take her views very seriously, and she had been listening carefully to what each of the others had said. What they wanted from her was a picture of the man himself, beyond the medical. "He is a lovely boy, Captain, always cheerful, always patient and polite. He never complained about the pain of the injury, and he has endured the pain of rehabilitation. He has so much courage! All the nurses love him so, we'd all like to keep him forever."

"But would you let him go, Cora?" the captain smiled at her, a look of deep affection.

"Yes, Captain, I would, and I will tell you why. You doctors know better than I that he could fall, or he could overexert and have a stroke, but that boy would be happier if he fell down dead tomorrow in the middle of a sunny meadow than if he lived a hundred years in a hospital bed."

"Thank you, Cora," said the chief of surgery. The captain looked around the table, searching each face in turn, weighing what each had said. "What will the Marine Corps do with him if we do give him back to them?"

"Probably light duty, Captain," said Dr. White, "some sort of desk job, until the end of his enlistment. Or they might just give him a medical discharge."

Doctor Freinberg stood up, his decision made. "Run him through a complete physical, Doctor Barnes. Test *everything*. If nothing turns up, release him."

"Yes, sir." The meeting broke up quickly, and the staff dispersed back to their duties.

"Sergeant Hunter?" A marine captain walked into Hunter's room, and found him on the floor, doing sit-ups.

Hunter sprang to his feet, to attention. "Yes, sir!"

"At ease, Sergeant. I'm Captain Willis, from the Pacific Fleet

Marine Force Personnel Command. I was asked to come up and talk to you about your next assignment. How are you feeling?''

"Well, sir! Rarin' to go.''

"Well, sit down, Sergeant, and let's talk about your options.''

Ain't none, thought Billy. No options. "Only one thing I want, Captain. Combat. Vietnam.''

The captain looked at Hunter thoughtfully. "You were badly wounded, Sergeant. I would have thought you'd had enough of Vietnam.''

"Have you been over there, sir?'' Billy knew the captain hadn't, because he wore neither the yellow and red Vietnam service ribbon, nor the green and white Vietnamese campaign one. He had the look of a RAMF right down to his plastic name tag and his national service ribbon.

"No, Sergeant, I haven't yet had the privilege.''

Some privilege, thought Billy, bitterly. "Well, sir, I was only there a few months, and I left some things undone.''

"What kind of things, Sergeant?''

"Live gooks, Captain,'' said Billy, leaning forward, and grinning his best boot-camp crazed marine grin. "My personal MOS is killing gooks.'' Billy hated himself for saying these things, just as he had been disgusted by marines in Vietnam who boasted of wasting gooks, or worse, taking heads, but he knew that RAMFs, especially RAMF officers, stood in awe of the men who *could* boast of personally killing the enemy.

"Well, Sergeant, it's commendable, of course, for a marine to volunteer for combat,'' he opened Hunter's medical record on his lap. "This says you are fit for duty, but recommends light duty.''

"Damn, sir! These doctors don't know everything! They've never seen anyone come back so fast from a head wound! And they don't know what it's like to be a *marine*! I'll bet you're busting to get in on the fight, eh, sir?''

Captain Willis continued to stare at the record, hiding his expression. Come on, RAMF! thought Billy, urgently. He calmed himself as best he could, around the searing headache. I have to be careful, not lay it on too thick. Keen but not crazy is the impression I have to give.

Captain Willis looked up from Billy's medical record. "You have listed as next of kin two brothers, one in Arkansas, and one a soldier at Fort Bragg. The Defense Department has a policy of not allowing two brothers to be in Vietnam in combat assignments at the same time.''

"My brother Henry says he is going to Germany.''

"I think the Army tells them all that,'' said the captain, with

some heat. "Still, if, and it's a big if, I can get you back to
Vietnam, if that is really what you want?" The captain paused,
and looked up. Billy nodded emphatically. "Then I'll make sure
that your assignment is noted in your brother's records; maybe
then they really will send him to Germany."

Now you're cooking, RAMF, thought Billy. "I'm sure Henry
would like Germany, sir."

The captain looked distressed. Something is bothering him,
thought Billy. Softly, softly, almost there. "Sergeant, in fairness,
maybe you should stay in the U.S. You have done enough for
your country."

"Sir, we both know a marine can never do enough. I really
want to go back, sir." Please, dammit, Billy finished the thought.

Captain Willis stood up. "Well, Sergeant Hunter, I'm going
to try. In these days when long-haired, pampered college kids
are chanting slogans and fleeing to Canada to avoid their country's service, I'm not going to stand in the way of a man proud
and anxious to serve in combat."

"Thank you, sir," said Billy, trying to look manly and hum-
ble.

"And I want to say, Sergeant, you make me proud, proud as
an American, and as a marine. I'd like to shake your hand."

Billy stood up and gave the captain a firm handshake. Semper
fi, thought Billy, and almost said it. That would be laying it on
too thick.

"Semper fi, Sergeant," said Captain Willis.

"Yes, sir," replied Billy, a choking feeling in his throat.

"I could only get you five more pills, Billy," said Rose, and
she hugged his naked chest. "That's all I can put on other patients' charts before the drug control inventory is checked tomorrow morning."

"You shouldn't take chances for me, Rose; you know I'll be
all right." Billy had built his cache up to seven pills over the
preceding six weeks. Some nights his head hardly ached at all.

"You know you need them to sleep."

That was true, usually, but Billy also knew that once he got
to Pendleton, codeine would be no harder to get than any other
drug known to man, and when he got back to Nam, it wouldn't
even be expensive. "I'll get by, Baby. Don't take any more."

Rose frowned, and touched Billy's lips with a finger. "Do you
really have to go, Billy?"

She asked that question often. Billy hated lying to her; she
was so sweet, and so vulnerable. "For a little while, Rose. I
was only there part of my allotted tour."

"But you were so badly wounded, surely—"

"Rose, please, we've been over this. I have to go back. I want to go back."

Rose gripped him tightly, and Billy felt her tears on his chest. He lifted her gently, and kissed her, as she fumbled urgently to take off her panties from under her stiff white skirt.

Their lovemaking was always quick, always urgent. Rose couldn't be away from the night nurses' station for long, and they never knew when the buzzer would sound. Rose dug her nails into Billy's shoulders and shuddered as they came together, then collapsed on his chest, breathing deeply. "I love you, Billy. Promise you'll come back."

"I love you too, Rose," he said automatically, gently stroking her red-gold hair. He felt a stirring in his chest, a feeling he thought had died. It isn't a lie anymore, he thought, as Rose pulled herself free and adjusted her uniform. "I will come back, when I can."

Rose bent and kissed him, and ran for the buzzer.

The day after Thanksgiving, Sgt. Billy Hunter reported to Alpha Company, 3d Replacement Battalion, attached to Headquarters, 3d Marine Division, at Camp Pendleton. He spent his days taking refreshers in rifle marksmanship and special weapons and demolitions. He attended lectures on topics like The Role of the United States in projecting Ideals of Freedom in Southeast Asia, which he found silly. At night, he sat around the sergeants' mess, listening to war stories and catching up on news. He phoned Joseph, and talked to him for a long time. He spoke to Henry at Fort Benning, who seemed not to be liking the Army at all, although he enjoyed jump school. Henry was going to get a four-day pass at Christmas, to go home. Billy told neither brother he was shipping out to Danang on the second of January.

Billy decided to take a week's leave, and to go home for Christmas. He felt good, and the headaches really came on only when he got overly tired, and then one codeine bomber took care of it. Christmas would be soon enough to tell his brothers that he had to go back, or anyway, that he was going back.

26 December 1967   Sparkman, Arkansas

The three brothers sat in the dining room, smoking and drinking beer. The dinner dishes lay in front of them. They had all remarked how strange it seemed to be together in the big house, without either of their parents. Billy had noted with unspoken amusement how naturally Joseph, the youngest, had taken the chair at the head of the table that had been their father's for so many years, and after his death, their mother's.

Billy was sipping his beer; he had discovered at Pendleton that even a small amount of alcohol made his head pound. He had just finished telling his brothers about Nga. He had not spoken about the drugs, just about the girl, and about how he had loved her, and that she had been killed—by the Viet Cong. Henry and Joseph had sat through the narrative in silence.

Henry popped open another can of Lone Star. He spoke softly, "I'm real sorry, Billy."

"Yeah, well I thought you boys should know, because—"

"Would you really have brought her back here, if you could've?" interjected Joseph.

"Yes, I sure would have."

"I wonder how the good people of Sparkman, Arkansas, would have felt about a Vietnamese bride?"

"How would you have felt, Little Brother?" said Billy, evenly.

Joseph looked at Billy, embarrassed and hurt. "Hey, Billy, she would have been family. I'm sorry, I spoke without thinking."

They sat in silence. Billy leaned back, enjoying the kinship, the alikeness of these two men. Here at least he could still feel love unsullied by guilt. "I had to tell you about Nga, because you have to understand something else. You won't really understand, but you must try. I'm going back to Vietnam."

Joseph set down his beer bottle abruptly. The dishes on the table rattled, then fell silent. "No! Why? You just got out of the hospital! Christ, Billy, you almost died!"

Billy looked at his kid brother with fondness. "I'm all right now. But there are things I did, and things I ought to have done, that make me want to go back. For a short while. Please trust me." Billy's head was throbbing violently, and his vision was blurring. He raised his napkin to dab his lips, and sucked the codeine pill from behind the curled little finger of his right hand as he did so. He washed the pill down with a swallow of beer. It was his second pill of the day, but it had been a long day.

Again, the brothers fell silent, and this time it lasted longer, as each retreated into his private thoughts. *I wish I could tell them that it's best for everyone I love that I do this,* thought Billy, *but some of what I did can never be told.*

"Billy," said Henry, "this has something to do with Daddy."

Billy looked up from his reverie. "No, it doesn't. What do you mean?"

Henry reached across the table, and put his hand on Billy's forearm. "You know. You fought with Daddy, about us playing contact sports, and getting low grades, and about other things. You always protected me and Joseph. You know."

"That's all past. Daddy's gone, God rest him."

"But you're still fighting with him, and still protecting us."

Billy got up, and brought three beers from the refrigerator. "You're grown now, brothers; that's past us."

Joseph looked up from his clenched hands. "Why are you doing this to us, Billy? You belong here, on the farm."

"Shit, Joseph! You know I never wanted to be a farmer! I just don't have it. The place is better run now than it ever has been."

Henry tightened his grip on Billy's forearm. "So why do you have to go back to Vietnam? I know the Marine Corps wouldn't send you, unless you volunteered."

Billy pulled his arm free. "What do you know, Boot? Why do you question me? Do your duty in Germany."

"And leave you alone, is that it?" said Henry, angered and hurt.

Billy rubbed his temples. The codeine was taking its own sweet time. "Yes."

The three brothers sat for a while, in a tension that none of them understood. Billy stood. "I'm going to bed. I'm sorry, gentlemen, but I have to ask you, though I *shouldn't* have to, not to doubt me! I'm doing what I must. I am going back to Nam, and that is it."

"You sound like Daddy, at his worst," said Joseph.

"You're protecting us, Big Brother, and you're wrong not to at least talk to us about it," said Henry.

Billy scowled at his brothers. How much I love you, he thought, as he went up the stairs to his childhood room and to bed.

2 January 1968   Headquarters, 3d Marine Amphibious Force, Danang

Staff Sergeant Coles had spent his entire morning at a meeting being told about new restrictions on off-duty movement of personnel in the Danang area, and he felt decidedly parched. He walked into the cool darkness of the sergeants' mess, sat at the bar and ordered a beer. Bobby heard a voice, soft and Southern, from directly behind him.

"Hello, Bobby Coles."

Coles turned and saw a tall, thin marine in pressed greens, with black metal sergeant's stripes on his collar points. The man's face was split with a lopsided grin, crinkly around the eyes. His white skin was very pale; he was obviously new in country. "Well, I will be damned! Billy Hunter! Step up, and get a beer!"

Hunter and Coles took their beers to a small table, and each gave the other a brief rundown of what they had done since they had separated at Pendleton a hundred years ago. Neither dwelled on the military aspects and neither asked many questions. Billy made short reference to a head wound that had gotten him some stateside hospital time, and Bobby just kind of nodded. Bobby felt very pleased to see his friend; it seemed a good omen, especially since Billy seemed so relaxed and mellow, compared to the intense young marine of less than a year ago.

417

Bobby finished his tale of the unit, including a spare account of the great battle of the Elephant Valley. "Well, so that's the ANGLICO, Billy. What outfit are you with now?"

"I just got here, Bobby; I gotta find a new outfit. I'm attached to the replacement battalion at Third MAF."

"You aren't going back to the LRRPs?"

"Not if I can help it!" Billy saw and smelled the dank, night-time trails in his mind. "That war just gets worse. Maybe I can find something nice and tranquil, like you're doing."

They laughed together. The only war story Bobby had told concerned the blind spot in the Elephant Valley that had broken the VC charge.

"Shit, Bro, that would be great, if you could jump on with us. We're a couple of men below rated strength, but I know we don't rate another sergeant."

"Maybe we can do a deal, somehow. I would really like to— be with friends, this tour."

Bobby looked at Billy's eyes, and saw the ache of some deep loss, just for a moment, and then Billy's eyes became kind of blank. It startled Bobby, but he decided to let it pass. "Do you want me to talk to my lieutenant?"

"Can't hurt. I don't want to lounge around the repple depple any longer than necessary."

"I'll talk to him this afternoon. Come by the sergeants' and petty officers' club at Camp Tien Shaw for happy hour, at seventeen-hundred, and I'll tell you what he says."

"I'll be there, Bobby, and thanks."

Coles walked out into the bright sunshine, feeling strangely excited. I wonder what happened to Hunter that caused that fleet-ing look of profound grief? I guess he'll tell me when and if he wants to, thought Bobby. I have to find Ice. It would be great to have Hunter in the unit.

Stuart sat back with his feet on his little desk, smoking. The door was propped open to catch any breeze, but the hootch was hot. I wish we could scrounge a fan, he thought idly. He looked across the desk at Coles, who had just finished telling him about his friend.

"Sergeant, if he's as good as you say he is, I'd love to talk to him, and I'm sure I'd want him in the unit, but sergeants with combat experience are very hard to come by, and a line unit will surely snap him up."

"I know, sir, but we still don't have an NCO to replace Walker, and I think Hunter really wants to come with us. He said he would ask for us, if you'll ask for him. He's on a voluntary second tour, and he thinks he'll get a pretty fair hearing."

"I just can't think how we can rationalize a second sergeant."

"We gotta think of something, sir. Let me bring him over to meet you, this evening. You'll see he's worth calling in a few favors." Bobby's grin was conspiratorial.

"Why, Sergeant," said Stuart, with mock disapproval, "to think that you or I would go outside normal channels! But bring him over, if you like. What's his full name?"

"William Hunter, sir."

"William Hunter. I know that name," said Stuart, thinking back. Hunter! "Is he a big guy, your size, maybe an inch taller, blond, country-boy type?"

"That sounds like him, sir, but all you white people look alike," replied Coles, with a grin.

"If it's the same guy, he was at SERE training with me. He even engineered my escape."

"That's him! He was at SERE back east, just before he came to Pendleton! He told me he escaped with an officer!"

Stuart swung his boots to the floor. "Billy Hunter! If it is the same man, we definitely want him, Bobby, and better yet, so will the major!"

"I'll have him here at seventeen-thirty, at the latest, sir."

"Good, good, do that, Sergeant!" Now I have to find Major MacIntyre; we'll have to move fast. It couldn't be coincidence: Billy Hunter taught me more about being an officer than all the schools I ever went to, and much about being a man.

Coles left, and Stuart went across to the ANGLICO office. The major was not there, but his clerk said he expected him back about 1700. Stuart left a message that he would return about 1800 to take the major to dinner at the Stone Elephant if he was free; he had something urgent to discuss.

"He has a similar note from Lieutenant Jay-gee Fox, sir, but I'll put yours on top," said the corporal, with a slow smile.

Stuart grinned. Fox was one of those officers who insisted on treating enlisted men like servants, and it cost him more than he knew. "Thanks, Corporal Ramirez."

"Sure, I remember Hunter," said Major MacIntyre, around his martini. "You and he gave me fits. I still remember when he threatened to kill me, just before you escaped."

Stuart smiled. It seemed a very long time ago. "You made it pretty rough on both of us, sir."

"I know, I hated that duty, but I have to tell you, I really believed in that program, and I still do. But you know, William, a guy like Hunter would have tried to resist, but I could have broken him, except that for some reason he attached himself to you. My guess is that he somehow influenced you to be tough, and he therefore thought it necessary for him to carry on.''

''I really think I would have withdrawn without him. He was so sure I would resist, I just had to carry on.''

''Yeah, I worried about that eye of yours, but the doc told me it was just conjunctivitis, and told me what to look for if your vision was really threatened. And we were loading your food with antibiotics.''

''I never knew that.''

''That's why the program was so good, in my opinion. The illusion was complete, yet you men were really never in danger.''

''I sensed that. Hell, I *knew* that, but I couldn't convince most of the others.''

''Imagine what a real prison camp would be like.''

William shuddered. He touched his thigh pocket under the table, felt the 7.65mm Walther PPK he had bought from an ARVN captain in Quang Ngai. He had sworn to himself he would never be captured. ''Do you think you could resist, Mac?''

The major sighed. ''I doubt it, William. I would try. But between you and me, I hope I would have the guts to put a bullet through my brain before allowing myself to be taken. My nightmare is to be knocked unconscious, then taken.''

Stuart smiled, and signaled the hovering barman for another round. ''Mine, too, Mac.''

The men shared a silent moment. Fear of dishonor was for both of them greater than the fear of pain and death. ''But what are we going to do about Hunter, William?''

''We have to get him.''

''You already have two good noncoms. Do you think Moser will pass the second-class exam?''

''Yes. He's not the brightest guy in the outfit, but everybody is helping him.''

''Is he steady in the field?''

''Excellent, but he's here on a six-month assignment, so he's short. If he does make second class, we'll have to give him back to the fleet. And don't forget we just sent Walker back to the World, Mac.''

''OK, so we shift Walker's replacement to Lieutenant James; he's still building and training his unit, and then I go for Hunter.'' MacIntyre paused, thinking. ''I'll bid for Hunter as an eventual replacement for Moser.''

Stuart remembered that he himself had been short only a few

months before, but now was on indefinite extension. He could not put aside the rush of sadness, thinking of Karen's decision to leave him, which had caused him to decide to stay on in Nam, at least for a while. He looked up at Major MacIntyre, and could tell the major knew his thoughts. "Right, Mac," he said, taking a pull on his Scotch, and smiling. "But can you do it?"

"I believe so. I have some markers, and if I run out, I can always use some of yours."

Stuart smiled. "Let's go in to dinner, Mac."

Coles met Hunter at the sergeants' mess in Danang. "It's done, Bro. The major pulled strings; you're in the ANGLICO."

Hunter smiled, and seemed relieved. "It will be great serving with you and Lieutenant Stuart, even thought you're both getting short."

Coles grinned. "We'll get you settled, Bro. Ice is extended, month to month, and I'll be here until April, maybe longer. The Marine Corps doesn't like anybody green dropping bombs and shells over their heads."

Hunter closed his eyes, and fought the pain. I'm finally back in the only reality that matches my pain. In Nam at least the pain makes sense. "Bobby, you can't know how glad I am to have found you, and Lieutenant Stuart."

"We're glad to have you, Bro. Welcome."

7 January 1968   Stone Elephant Officers' Club, Camp Tien Shaw

Stuart looked at his friend Lieutenant Hooper. Hooper was agitated, and taking it out on the bottle. Since their earliest association on the *Valley Forge*, Hooper and Stuart had drunk champagne when together; Veuve Clicquot Ponsardin, when they could find it.

Hooper drained his glass. "Something very disturbing happened in Quang Tri Province yesterday, William. Something I can't quite grip."

Stuart let the dry, sparkling wine go slowly down his throat. He refilled his and Hooper's glasses. "What?"

Hooper drained his glass. "Someone, presumably someone in his own platoon, fragged a second lieutenant named Hoffmeyer last night. At Gio Linh. My Sealies were attached."

"Fragged him?"

Hooper picked the bottle out of the plastic ice bucket, emptied it into the two glasses, and signaled the Vietnamese waiter for another. "I wonder if they stock this stuff here for anyone but us? Doesn't matter; we don't let it spoil in the heat. Yeah, fragged him. Some fuck took a fragmentation grenade, pulled the pin, and rolled it under the raised floor of Hoffmeyer's hootch. Splinters went right up through the plywood and through Hoffmeyer. I guess he never felt a thing." Hooper took the bottle from the waiter, who wanted him to taste it in a new glass, and poured both glasses full.

Stuart rolled the champagne off his tongue. He knew a connoisseur would say it was too chilled, but it was delicious. Nothing in Vietnam could ever be too cold. "I heard the Army lost some officers that way. Drug cases, crazy. But never in the Marine Corps."

"This was marines, little buddy."

Stuart couldn't really get into it. "You worried about your SEALs, Hoop?"

Hooper laughed, but not his normal hearty laugh. He paused, and stared at the glass. "Only the ones that owe me money. Look, Stuart, don't you see it? Something is getting to the men. OK, so the Army is fucked up, drafting every swinging dick who's not already in jail. But the marines have always held their discipline and morale. Now the grunts want to kill their officers. What do we represent to them, that they would want our blood? Aren't we in the same fight?"

Stuart shrugged. "Was this Hoffmeyer a good officer?"

Hooper threw up his hands, and twisted in his seat. "I dunno. Average. Tried to be a disciplinarian, but you know, nothing out of the ordinary. The thing is, some fuck just killed him. It almost doesn't matter how good or bad he was. An American, a *marine*, killed the hump. Jesus."

Stuart sipped the icy champagne slowly. "What do you think it means, Hoop?"

Hooper refilled glasses. "I'm afraid, my good friend, it means we are losing the hearts and minds of our own people, our own *marines*, for Christ's sake! Which means we could lose the war."

Stuart sighed. "You specialty troops have too much time on your hands. We're going to have to send you back north."

"Hey, man, I am serious! Do you know what these guys hear from home? What they read? That everybody at home is demonstrating, and burning the flag, and jeering at men in uniform, while the chumps over here fight the heat and the mud and the Cong, and for what?"

"Why do you think there's so much opposition to the war, then, Hoop?"

"I'll tell you. It's because Johnson didn't want to rouse the people, get them behind the troops, behind the war. The government pretended that the war wasn't a big deal, so they didn't need to get the nation pumped up. Johnson figured that if the people really wanted to win this war, they would insist he get on with it, give the lads what they need, *now*! Bye, bye, Great Society.''

Hooper paused and sipped his champagne. ''What I'm saying is that the government never went to the people and said we had to win this war, for good and high-minded reasons. In War Two, the people *hated* the Germans and the Japanese, and demanded they be crushed! Without that kind of public support, what we do here just looks like killing, William, killing in cold blood.''

''Maybe it *is* the wrong war, Hoop.''

''You don't think we should fight these bastards, beat them?''

Stuart sipped a bit. ''Yes. I do. But you have to see, Hoop, as much as *you* want to kick ass, the feeling generally is who cares? Do you think the brass is behind the purpose? Bullshit! So the troops die, and they blame us.''

Hooper scowled. ''Is that treason, or do I just imagine it?''

Stuart spread his hands. ''Look, man, haven't you ever had an inkling that Westmoreland, maybe even fucking *Johnson*, doesn't really care as much as you do?''

Hooper shrugged, spread his hands on the table, and fell silent. Stuart realized he had never really asked himself how he felt. He just joined up and fought the war because it was there. Wasn't that what a citizen should do? A flicker of Karen's angry face rose in his mind, and he shook his head and gulped his champagne. This has to be right; we are all hurting so much.

Hooper broke his silence. ''I saw Westmoreland again, last week.'' Stuart laughed, and Hooper held up a hand. ''OK, so I screwed up again, and ended up someplace where an inspection was going down. By the way, I have to tell you, some dickhead must have spent *six fucking hours* starching and ironing the general's uniform.'' Hooper pulled at the floppy pocket of his decidedly unstarched uniform. ''You would not have believed how even these fucking pockets were pressed. Anyway, after boosting the troops, like he always does, he has an officers' call, like he always does, and I ask him, just like I did at Phu Bai, when we were both stuck in that parade, when we could expect the Joint Chiefs, read the president, read the fucking politicians, to let us win this chicken-shit war.'' Hooper drained and refilled his glass.

Stuart drank, and accepted the refill. ''And you got the same answer.''

''Word for word. 'I believe the American fighting man has the support of the president, and the Congress, and the American people.' Shee-ut, William, if you believe that, you can believe a stiff cock has a conscience.'' Hooper again lapsed into silence.

Stuart let the silence go a few minutes. ''So, fraggings?''

Hooper sighed. ''You're remarkably slow sometimes, Willie. Look, they don't believe Johnson, they don't believe Westy, so why should they believe you? *Newsweek* informs them that the citizens of their own country hate the war. So why shouldn't they hate you? What's the difference?''

Stuart swallowed his mouthful of champagne. ''But murder?''

Hooper refilled the glasses. ''The demonstrators say we murder people every day, son.''

At 2130, they were drinking coffee in near silence. A marine second lieutenant, recently attached to 7th ANGLICO, approached their corner table, and, without being invited, sat.

Hooper regarded the interloper with malice. ''Interrogative the fuck your presence, junior?''

The kid blanched. ''The major wants to see you, Lieutenant Stuart, ah, now.''

Hooper made a sweeping gesture with his left hand, which threatened the bottle of Jameson's that accompanied their coffee. ''Tell him to fuck off, Willie. We have serious business.''

Stuart looked at the kid, who looked back, steadily. ''So what is it?''

''What is it? Fuck it! Piss off, shavetail,'' demanded Hooper. ''We're men off-duty! Can't you see this officer is *drinking*?''

''Leave it, Hoop.'' Stuart poured a glass full of whiskey for the kid, who was now showing white at the corners of his mouth. ''What is it?''

''Your unit is to fly down to Quang Ngai. To spot for an army operation.''

Stuart felt an anger of his own. ''My men, Lieutenant, are off-line. They are due an R and R. Why are we sent out again, when the other platoons rest?''

The butter-bar rose. ''You were requested, *by name, sir*! What shall I tell the major, *sir*?''

''Who requested us?''

''The One-hundred ninety-seventh Light Infantry Brigade, *sir*.''

Hooper paid the bill. ''Come on, William. Do what you have to, but I prefer the smell of combat soldiers.''

Blackjack wants us back, thought Stuart. Is that a compliment?

"What do I tell the major, sir?" rasped the kid, veins standing out on his neck.

Stuart looked at the kid a long time. "What time at the helicopter pad, sonny?" Why am I beating up on this kid? thought Stuart. The messenger with the bad news? Even if the boot is taking himself awfully seriously, for one so newly come.

The kid stiffened, struggling with his humiliation and anger. Well, serves him right, thought Stuart. He should have waited for me by my hootch, never have come to the club. That's enough. Stuart stood up carefully, and followed Hooper out of the Stone Elephant.

"Oh-five-hundred, sir. Sir? I had hoped to accompany you on the mission."

Stuart stopped, and stood looking at the kid with arms akimbo. "You're not ready to go with my unit, kid."

Hooper roared up with his jeep. Stuart got in. The kid looked back with hatred. Fuck you, thought Stuart. Hooper floored the jeep, and slewed around a muddy corner, toward their quarters.

I hate everyone tonight, thought Stuart. I don't want to go back out there.

8 January 1968   Quang Ngai

The two army HU-1E helicopters pulled their noses up sharply and landed hard at the pad in front of Blackjack's command tent. Coles led half the ANGLICO platoon out of one bird while Stuart and the rest of the men coiled out of the other. They ran low, in full battle dress with packs, radios, and weapons, through the stinging dust kicked up by the departing Hueys. When the men reached the line of mess tents to the left of the command tent, they dropped their packs and sat in the shade.

Coles looked cautiously at Lieutenant Stuart. The lieutenant looked tired and a little pallid; Bobby had heard that he had been drinking with Lieutenant Hooper the night before. Still, Stuart looked sharp and alert, a far cry from his appearance right after he got the Dear John. We will soon know if he is back in top form, thought Coles.

Stuart drank a swallow of water from his canteen, then poured a few drops in his palm and rubbed his eyes. He set his pack next to Coles's.

"How are you feeling, sir?"

"Capital, Sergeant. Never better." Stuart closed his eyes against the glare.

"Want me to organize some coffee, sir?"

Stuart's empty stomach rose at the thought of coffee. "Try for something sweet, Sergeant. Juice. Donuts. Then coffee."

Coles sent Moser and Cardenas into the nearby mess tent. They returned rapidly with juice, rolls, and coffee. Stuart ate a roll and drank the juice rapidly. A hint of color returned to his cheeks. He took a sip of the coffee, then another. "Thank you, men. Very resourceful."

"You feel better, sir?" asked Moser.

"Much, thank you. Helicopters on an empty stomach are not to my liking." Stuart rose as Major Dominelli emerged from the command tent, and beckoned. "Come on, Sergeant. You had better be briefed with me."

Stuart and Coles saluted Major Dominelli, who looked harried. Lucky to be still alive, thought Stuart, remembering the first time he had seen Dominelli after the Elephant. "Hello, Major."

"Come on in, Stuart. We're just starting the intelligence and ops briefings. You want your sergeant, too? Good, good, come on."

They stepped inside, and found the tent surprisingly cool, though smoky and close. Officers and noncoms were milling around as the junior staff officers put up maps and organizational charts for the operations and intelligence briefings that were about to begin. Major Phipps is still S-2, noted Stuart, as the man pinned up a large-scale map of a piece of the Vietnamese coast that was unfamiliar to Stuart. A sign above the maps read "Operation Storm Cloud."

Coles saw Blackjack seated at a low table in the front of the tent, and pointed him out to Stuart. Stuart went forward and stood at attention until he caught the general's eye. Stuart saluted. "Seventh ANGLICO detachment, General, reporting as ordered."

Blackjack rose, grinned, and held out his hand. "William, *finally* we have you back!"

Stuart couldn't keep his own grin from spreading. "They told us in Danang you had work for us here, sir."

"Indeed. Sit down and we'll tell you about it. Hello, Staff Sergeant Coles!"

"Hello, General." Bobby was proud to be recognized.

They sat, and Phipps and Dominelli began the briefing.

"The large-scale map is the coast, along Highway One, between the market towns of Duc Pho and Sa Huynh," began Major Phipps. "This area is just south of here, with Duc Pho at twenty-two klicks from the Quang Ngai perimeter. As background, the marines fought heavy concentrations of VC in the jungles around Duc Pho in '65 and '66, and air cav units have been in and out since, but the area has never been classified as cleared or pacified.'' Phipps shifted to a larger area map. "Beginning a week ago, we have had intelligence reports of large VC units operating north from Binh Dinh, here.'' Phipps indicated a somewhat larger town on the smaller scale map, about forty klicks from the southern end of the large-scale chart. "In the last week, the ARVNs have driven north out of Binh Dinh some thirty-five klicks, and have cleared the highway. The ARVNs and, better yet, most of the 3d Infantry Division, hold Duc Pho and a line fifteen klicks south of Duc Pho, along the southern bank of the Ve River, which empties here in Quang Ngai, but which tends southwest to its headwaters.''

The men began to murmur as Phipps changed to the other side of the easel. It's a near-perfect box, thought Coles.

"Here, just north of the village at Sa Huynh, is a hill, ah, hill three-oh-four,'' Phipps indicated with his pointer. "It's the only significant high ground in the area, and it commands the entire battlefield, in good weather. It's an incursion of rocky, badly decomposed granite, while most of the surrounding countryside lies on porous limestone. Gentlemen, we will take that mountain before lunch, but Major Dominelli will elaborate on that. Questions on the situation?''

There were no questions. These staff officers do a lot more than I guessed, thought Coles.

"Good, good,'' said Phipps. Stuart was amused at how these officers picked up Blackjack's mannerisms. Phipps picked up the pointer, and continued. "We estimate enemy strength to be no more than two battalions, with perhaps some light forces accompanying. Mortars and rockets, probably no artillery pieces. As of this morning, we have reports that the ARVN lost contact during the night, but are now moving into position to block the southern part of the road just to the north and south of the hill, er, three-oh-four, which is called by the Vietnamese Dau Con Ngua Nui, Horsehead Mountain.''

Stuart shifted in his seat, and smiled at Coles, who looked really interested. Stuart screwed a cigarette into the black holder and lit it. The bitter smoke tickled the fur on his tongue.

Phipps tapped the map, "Lastly, weather. We expect broken clouds and some sun today, but more southeast monsoon rain tomorrow, with low clouds. Therefore we cannot count on much air support. We're lucky, however, in that the entire plain is within easy range of naval gunfire, and we're pleased to see Lieutenant Stuart and the Seventh ANGLICO back with us.'' Heads and bodies turned, and Stuart acknowledged waves and thumbs-ups from many officers he recognized from the tour last August. "For those of you new to us, Stuart and his marines helped us defeat the enemy in the Elephant Valley last August." The men gave a soft, friendly cheer, and Stuart waved and smiled. Stuart felt very good to be back with these men, and wondered about his sour fear of last evening. Maybe I am a fire-eater, he thought. Still a fighter, my Karen, among fighters. He dismissed the thought as Phipps sat down and Dominelli began.

"Let's get right to mission. What we have to do is fairly straightforward, and like most good plans, it follows the dictates of the terrain. If the ARVN thrust is broad enough along its front," Dominelli swept the pointer from the sea inland several kilometers, "then the enemy eventually will be canalized between the 3d Division, with ARVNs, holding both sides of the Ve River, and the coast. Now, there are approximately twenty-four klicks of flat, slightly rolling country in the box formed by the Ve River to the north and west, the coast to the east, and the ARVNs on the road and inland to the south. Since the enemy broke off contact with the ARVNs last night, and *unless* he slipped through this narrow gap—" Dominelli pointed at the broken country between the 3d Infantry Division and the advancing ARVNs, "then he is in this box." Dominelli slowly traced the perimeter of the box with the pointer. "Gentlemen, the one-niner-seven has been asked to enter the box, and kill the enemy."

There were a lot of questions. Was the enemy really in such a trap? Intelligence believes so. Were there friendly civilians in the area? No, it was virtually deserted, a free-fire zone. Would the bloody ARVNs hold the cork in the bottle long enough? Phipps stood up and raised his hands. "Gentlemen, this operation has been on the general's mind for some weeks. General?"

Blackjack stood, and faced the men in the crowded tent. He looks thin and tired, thought Stuart. But Blackjack's grin, and his rolling command voice, brought a hitch to Stuart's throat. "Now, I'm not going to let my staff get away with letting their commander do this briefing, but I do want to answer the last question. Captain Bigelow, Captain Black? Come up here, please, and confirm the positions of your units."

The two marine captains stood, and moved forward to stand beside the general. Beaurive handed the pointer to Bigelow, the nearest, a sandy-haired plug of a man in a crisp, starched uniform. Captain Black was a baleful looking black man, a few inches shorter, with an expression as fixed as obsidian. Bigelow pointed to Horsehead Mountain, and the area around it. "I have the Fourth Vietnamese Marine Battalion, here, just south of the mountain. Black has the Two-oh-eighth ARVN, lined out west, and the Two-oh-third is west of them, with First Lieutenant Stanton and his advisory unit. They are moving slowly, clearing, but they are all in communications, and they are *moving*.''

Why all that emphasis, wondered Stuart. Is he saying something else?

Lieutenant Colonel Stevens, the commander of the 1st Battalion, 39th Infantry, asked, ''Captain Bigelow, Captain Black, we mean no disrespect, but for this to work, we have to rely on the units you advise to drive the enemy into Major Dominelli's fine box, and hold him in. How good are your troops? Can they do it?''

Bigelow and Black looked at each other, then Black spoke, his voice a surprising deep bass from his small body. ''Colonel, they're as good as we can make them. They will never be a fast-maneuver, attacking force like this, but they will damn sure hold ground. We will close the door, and keep it closed.''

General Beaurive nodded enthusiastically. ''Thank you, gentlemen, and Godspeed back to your units.'' The two advisers saluted and left, boarding a waiting Huey. ''Now, Major Dominelli, tell us what we're going to do.'' Blackjack sat, and Dominelli retrieved his pointer and continued.

''We will rely on the Third Division to hold the river and the northern and western perimeters. We will send our cav and our armor in a broad line over these low hills on the western edge, with the first of the thirty-ninth accompanying, on a measured advance through to Highway One, which hereabouts is right on the coastal escarpment. The second of the forty-eighth and fourth of the sixty-third will be in reserve, able to move laterally behind the tanks and APCs as needed. The enemy must either stand, or be driven down to the beach. If the enemy's resistance is strong either way, we have a commitment for two navy destroyers to supply whatever firepower is necessary to break the enemy's concentrations. Naval gunfire will be spotted from hill three-oh-four, if it is needed.''

The men in the tent chattered enthusiastically. It looks good on paper, thought Stuart.

Best-laid plans, thought Bobby Coles. Still, it's the general's plan.

The briefing droned on for another two hours, rich with detail about troop positioning, radio call signs, plans for interunit support. Timetables were set forth and argued, and the op plan was completed. The officers and noncoms, grinning and backslapping, left the tent. I am glad I have seen this, thought Bobby. He saw Blackjack draw Lieutenant Stuart aside as he left the tent. Bobby went on back to the ANGLICO, and briefed the men.

Stuart was drawn back to the maps, with Majors Dominelli and Phipps, Colonel Stevens, and General Beaurive.

Phipps spoke. "What do you think, Stuart? Feel free; it's not your plan."

Stuart stood before the large-scale map. "You want us to hit the enemy with naval gun over about twenty-four klicks of ground."

"Yes, more like twenty in all, but we expect to find most of the enemy facing the ARVNs within a few klicks of hill three-oh-four," said Phipps. "You should be able to see well, if we have a decent ceiling under the clouds. Our own officers will be able to refine your spots." Blackjack grinned. "Since the Elephant, we have worked on that."

"We could get fog."

"If we do, we won't go. Fog isn't likely this time of year, according to the met people," said Dominelli.

"OK, I have to say I like it. We're going in today?"

"Right," said Colonel Phipps. "You will have Bravo Company of Colonel Richmond's forty-eighth with you, and the ARVNs around the base of the mountain. The main attack, by the armor and the cavalry platoon, will begin to enter the plain at thirteen-thirty, to get the best chance of clear weather."

Blackjack slammed his hand on the leather desktop. "Then make it *so*, gentlemen!" The remaining officers left the command tent. Blackjack walked out with Stuart. "You find no flaw, William?"

"No, sir, I wish I could," said Stuart.

"So do I, William." Blackjack looked deep into Stuart's eyes, his own face thoughtful. Then he grinned. "Glad to be back, William? You, your men?"

Stuart grinned, "Yes, General. We're here, and glad to be."

"Good, good," said Blackjack.

Stuart returned to ready his men. Coles had gotten them into their packs and weapons. They loped down the track toward the line of screaming helicopters, already loading infantry for the assault on Horsehead Mountain.

The vertical assault on hill 304 began as scheduled at 0900. The Huey and the larger CH-47 Chinook helicopters landed three at a time at a gently sloping landing zone on the broad plateau at the top of the hill, which, from the valley, did look like the head of a horse. The first troops to land were infantry, 2d Platoon of Bravo Company, 2d Battalion, 48th Infantry, along with

the weapons platoon from the same company. The soldiers
fanned out in a manner well practiced, and secured the perimeter. For once, thought Second Lieutenant Greenglass, leader of
the 2d Platoon, intelligence has gotten it right, and there is no
enemy presence.

More helicopters brought in the ANGLICO detachment, and
the forward artillery observers for the brigade. There was a fes-
tive air as the men unloaded their gear. Rumors of the huge trap
for the VC had infected the men. Coles bantered with the first
sergeant attached to the forward observers about who would
shoot the first of the VC flushed by the 197th's assault into the
box.

The rest of Bravo Company landed on the plain below, in a
landing zone now under the guns of the soldiers on the hill.
They were to climb to a row of clefts about a third of the way
up the mountain on both sides, dig in, and link up with the
ARVNs who should be coming in from the south and west at
any moment.

Coles set up the unit on the end of the plateau nearest the sea,
almost to the horse's nose. The artillery observer sergeant took
a slightly higher position some fifty meters back inland. They
could see nothing of the sea itself, half a klick to the east, as
the monsoon clouds had rolled in thick and wet some hundred
meters above them, and fog clung to the shoreline. The jungle
thickets on the plain below had pockets of fog caught in their
branches, and even on the hilltop, water condensed instantly on
all metal surfaces.

Coles watched as the men fell to improving their positions
without being told. The guys are more a unit all the time, and
having Hunter, a second experienced sergeant, helps, he thought.
First, the men dug a trench four feet deep and twelve feet long
in the loose, flinty soil, which would protect the radiomen and
the spotters. Then, at the seaward end of the trench, they dug a
shallower foxhole with the excess dirt, forming a wall for Moser
and his machine gun, plus Cardenas, Moser's favorite ammo
handler. Moser set the big fifty-cal on its tripod; then Moser and
Cardenas filled the bags they had brought with earth to weigh
down and steady the tripod.

"Hey, Moser," joked Coles. "How come you got that cannon
facing south? The VC are supposed to be north of here."

Moser packed yet another sandbag under the long-barreled
gun. "S'arnt, I know at least some a' the folks comin' from the
north, an' 'ats the fuckin' Army. I don' know *who* might come
up from the south."

Coles felt a dent form in his good humor. He walked back to

where Hunter and the radio operators were settling in and checking frequencies. "Billy, get on battalion net and see if Bravo
Company down on the plain has linked up with the ARVNs
yet."

Hunter spoke softly, listened, spoke again. "No, Bobby, no
linkup, and so far, no contact."

Coles looked back at Moser's position with unease.

Stuart was talking with Captain Watson, commanding the elements of Bravo Company digging into the rocky hillside below.
Watson had been unable to contact the ARVNs on the agreed
frequency, but had reached the ARVN brigade in Binh Dinh,
who assured him the drive was on schedule. Even though on
schedule should have meant that the ARVNs were already here,
Watson seemed unconcerned. ARVN time was not U.S. Army
time, Watson reminded Stuart. He knows better than I, thought
Stuart, and began reviewing the day codes and assignment codes
for the naval gunfire net.

On the plain between Duc Pho and Horsehead Mountain, the
troops had been getting into position before daybreak, sent by
the general's op order even before the briefing had begun back
in Quang Ngai. Trucks and tanks and armored personnel carriers had ground slowly south from the forward positions of the
3d Division on the southern bank of the Ve, down muddy, fog-
shrouded country lanes between flooded rice paddies. First
Lieutenant Rufus Loonfeather sat on top of his M-48 tank as it
picked its way around the worst of the mudholes. Lieutenant
Loonfeather commanded the cavalry platoon from Bravo troop,
2d of the 5th Cavalry. His tanks, APCs, and ACAV scout vehicles had the point. They would have the southernmost position
on the line when the whole formation wheeled to the east and
assaulted the broad plain the men were calling Blackjack's box.

Rufus Loonfeather was a full-blooded Dakota Indian, the tribe
the white men called the Sioux. He had grown up in a little town
in the upper peninsula of Michigan, but his grandfather claimed
descent from the Nation of West Rivers, and from the war chiefs,
including Red Cloud and Sitting Bull, who had routed the 7th
U.S. Cavalry at Little Big Horn in 1876. When Loonfeather had
told his grandfather he was being assigned to the 5th Cavalry
after he had completed armor school, his grandfather's reaction
had been short.

"Good. Your blood can teach them something."

Sergeant Elkins, the tank commander, rose through the hatch,
lit a cigarette, and handed one to Loonfeather. "What do you
think, Lieutenant?"

Loonfeather sucked on the cigarette. "They aren't here, Sergeant."

"Not yet, but we'll catch 'em on the plain, hey?"

"No, they're gone."

"Injun magic, Lieutenant?"

I know the spirits of this place, thought Loonfeather. I feel the spirits of the rocks, the rain, the mud, the trees. The VC are gone. "Heap big medicine, Elkins. Nobody home in the general's box. I just feel it."

It began to rain, softly. Loonfeather looked at his watch: 1130. In two hours they had to be another ten klicks south, to turn southeast toward the coast. From positions astride Highway One they would advance toward the blocking force at Horsehead Mountain. The assault line would be almost eight klicks wide. Thin, but the reserves would fill the gaps, if they were in position.

The rain increased. Elkins threw away his cigarette and dropped back into the tank. He emerged a minute later with his rain parka, and Loonfeather's.

"You goin' to sit up here, in the rain, Lieutenant?"

"Yep. Got to feel the place, Sergeant."

Elkins sat next to Loonfeather on the turret. "You really believe that spirit shit, ah, Lieutenant?"

Loonfeather looked carefully at Elkins's dark eyes. Elkins was a slender black man from Chicago, streetwise and contemptuous. Loonfeather knew the sergeant disliked him intensely. "Yep, sure do. It's too bad you have lost touch with your own roots." Loonfeather smiled thinly.

Elkins smiled back, his eyes dead. Crazy redskin bastard, he thought.

Coles sat in the trench with all of the ANGLICO except Cardenas, who stood watch beside the .50, with binoculars. The sea breeze had died, and the clouds, though higher, seemed more oppressive as they hung motionless and dripped. Coles listened to the soft talk of the men as they ate C-rations and waited.

Stuart was writing in an exercise book he always carried. I wonder if he writes to his wife, thought Coles. He used to talk a lot about her, and when he did, his eyes shone. Stuart had not spoken a word about his wife since his explanation to his NCOs six weeks ago.

Stuart was in fact writing notes on the action, but he was thinking of Karen, of how he would like to describe the magnificent way all these men and machines could be organized to

act as one huge engine of war. But while he had not fully accepted her rejection of him as final, he knew she didn't care for
his reflections on the war.

Stuart closed his book, and looked at his watch. The assault
has been going on two hours. He leaned over to Roland, who
dozed on the command net. "Any news from the armor? Any
contact, Roland?"

Roland came awake with a start, and licked his lips. "Ah,
no, sir, no contact. The tankers are moving faster than they
thought they would, but they ain't seen Charlie."

"OK, Roland, keep listening."

"Yessir."

Stuart looked down the slope to the south. Bravo Company
was well dug in, waiting for something to happen. I wonder
where the fuck the ARVN is, thought Stuart. Those two marine
captains seemed sure of them, at the briefing. Stuart wiped his
face. The briefing seemed hours ago. Was hours ago.

To the north on the plain, the assault ground forward with
sand-table precision. The tanks rolled forward at a walking pace,
machine-gunning thickets and ravines. The troops called it recon
by fire. The infantry, both in M113s and on foot, checked farm
hootches and other places an enemy might conceal himself. They
found some discarded supplies, and a few tunnels, but no enemy. The civilian population had long since been relocated, or
simply disappeared.

Lieutenant Loonfeather continued to ride on top of his lead
tank, sweeping the terrain with binoculars. They always know
we're coming, he thought. Elkins had made some pointed remarks about snipers, but Loonfeather knew the enemy had gone.

In the command tent, which had been flown with the staff by
helicopter to a cleared LZ on the plain south of Duc Pho, near
the northern pivot of the assault, Phipps and Dominelli gathered
information from the unit commanders, and soldiers marked each
unit's progress on the large-scale map. The line looked neat and
regular, with the northernmost elements already on the highway,
and the whole line closing on the strong point around Horsehead
Mountain.

Blackjack sat and smoked a cigar. I don't like this. It was too
good from the beginning. Too pat. The bastards knew we were
coming, and they have withdrawn. But where? He looked at the
gap between the last reported position of the ARVN battalions,
now more than four hours old, and the advancing line of his own
troops. I just don't believe they could have figured me out enough
to have gotten through there. Besides, we have gunships searching, and they could not have missed a large-scale troop move-

ment. General Beaurive sat back and blew out a long gray cloud of smoke. On the other hand, we have helicopters looking for our shy friends, the ARVNs, and they have found nothing, except elements of the 203d, on the west end of the line. The helo had gone in low, and one of the slopes had held up a radio, and made a cross over it with his hand. Maybe one unit could lose a radio, but not all.

"General?" It was Phipps, a handset to his ear.

"Yes, Major?"

"The forward observer on hill three-oh-four reports troops in sight south of their position, advancing in strength up the highway."

"ARVNs?"

"He isn't sure. No radio contact. The troops are mounted in trucks and APCs, but he says they don't look right."

Damn! "Get a helicopter down close. Tell Captain Watson to challenge, with caution. Tell him to treat the force as unfriendly until he's *sure*."

"Yes, sir!" said Phipps. Blackjack looked a question at his S-2. "I completely concur, General. It doesn't feel right."

Damn, thought Blackjack.

Coles jumped down into the trench with the radio talkers, who were now all standing up, watching the advancing column. Stuart trained his 7×50 spotter's binoculars on the approaching vehicles. The tall teak and mahogany trees gave him a dappled, diffused view. The lead vehicle was a jeep, with ARVN markings, but without the yellow- and red-striped flag of the Republic of Vietnam flying from the antenna. The jeep mounted a 106mm recoilless rifle, and Stuart studied the gunner standing in the back of the jeep, holding onto the 106. His uniform was light blue, and he wore a strange conical helmet. Stuart could see the trucks beyond, most with their canvas off. The road gave off shimmers of heat, and Stuart couldn't really be sure, but all the uniforms looked blue.

Our Viets wear green, like we do. The VC wear black, or black and white. The NVA wear dark green Chinese uniforms; so who in the hell are these guys?

Coles heard a sharp pop as Bravo Company fired its first warning shot at the front of the advancing column with an 81mm mortar. It landed, a green flare, today's day color, a hundred meters in front of the column. Coles, making himself believe that the guys driving up the road in American trucks and jeeps and APCs just *had* to be the missing ARVNs, watched with growing horror as the lead jeep rolled over the smoking flare without stopping. Bravo Company fired a second warning. Bobby screwed his eyes into the binoculars. The flare landed just to the right of the highway, as the trucks slowed and soldiers in blue uniforms spilled out. Jesus, thought Bobby, we're going to get fucking *hit*. He turned as Stuart tapped him on the head and dove for his radio.

"Lieutenant! Permission to commence fire, sir!" yelled Moser, a grin splitting his big face. Cardenas looked a little scared, but he held the belt of linked ammo steady as he looked back at Stuart.

"Fire when the Army fires, Moser. Kill with every round; there are a lot of them," said Stuart, still looking through the binoculars.

"Aye, aye, sir!" Moser pulled back the bolt and chambered the first round. Stuart bent over the radio, his arm on Coles's shoulder. Coles looked up as Bravo Company began firing, down below and around the plateau at the top of the mountain. Coles looked at Moser, as the big man sighted over the long-barreled .50 and began firing single rounds. There was a whoosh, and a sharp crack above them, and they were showered with stone splinters. That must be that recoilless, thought Coles.

Stuart pointed to the code book in front of Coles, who nodded while tightening his chin strap. The world has suddenly gotten very loud, thought Stuart, cupping his handset. "Seafire, Seafire, Seafire, this is Foxtrot Lima Red, for immediate fire, over."

The only quiet place in the world is this fucking radio, thought Stuart, as another recoilless round cracked into the mountain over his head. "We on the right freq, Hunter?"

Another 106 round banged in behind them, and Hunter heard a man wail. "Yes, sir."

"Seafire, Seafire, Seafire, this is Foxtrot Lima Red. Come in, Seafire."

Seafire was the coordinator of all naval gunfire from the DMZ to Qui Nhon, far to the south, and should have answered the first call. Stuart was about to try one of the other radios, when his handset crackled. "Foxtrot Lima Red, this is Conqueror, over."

Conqueror! Neither Coles nor Stuart had to look that one up. Conqueror was the USS *St. Paul*, the only all-eight-inch-gun cruiser left in the Pacific Fleet. Coles and Stuart grinned at each other. "Conqueror, Foxtrot Lima. We're at point Delta Golf four-four-five-five. You copy?" I hope to hell they have our op plan, he thought.

"Foxtrot Lima, Conqueror. Authenticate Quebec Whiskey."

Coles had the day code pub open on his lap. He checked the

date and time sector, correct. He ran the cardboard template down the page to QW. The slot in the left side of the template offered two solutions. He took the first, and shouted at Stuart, "Bravo Zulu!"

Stuart repeated the code into the handset. Conqueror came back with a second authenticate, this time Mike Romeo. Coles had the solution in less than a second. The cruiser came back up, "Roger, Foxtrot Lima, we know where you are and what you are doing. What is our target?"

Stuart was concentrating so hard he could hear the talk on the ship's bridge, behind the radio operator. "Right standard rudder. All engines ahead flank!"

"Ah, Conqueror, your target is troops and vehicles, south of our position, advancing. We are engaging with small arms. They are a vastly superior force, so appreciate your earliest assistance."

"Roger, roger, Foxtrot Lima. We are a little south of you, but should be able to fire our forward guns for spot in about fourteen minutes."

"Roger, Conqueror. We will stay on this net."

Roland, one of the new replacements, tapped Coles's shoulder. He was on command net. "The general *himself* wants to know what we have up, Sergeant!"

Coles grinned at Roland. "Tell him we have a heavy, coming up from the south, firing in fourteen minutes."

There was a strange sound above them, like huge, heavy birds whiffling through the air, then a mighty crash on the mountain about eighty meters beyond their position. Every man on the mountain got as low as he could, or as far below ground as he could, as the earth shook. Coles looked at Stuart, and was shocked to see fear in his eyes. Bobby looked a question, and Stuart nodded. The enemy had artillery.

Conqueror better hurry, thought Coles.

8 January 1968   Headquarters, 197th Light Infantry Bridge, South of Duc Pho

All the radios in the command tent were crackling. Order was being maintained, the frantic reports were being reduced to a situation description by the staff, yet the urgency was beginning to fray the fabric of discipline. Majors Phipps and Dominelli gathered information, and watched as other officers updated the maps, and placed colored markers indicating the dispositions of friendly and enemy forces.

Blackjack put down his dead cigar. The situation grew worse with each report. The assault force in the plain had no contact, although elements of the 1st Battalion, 39th Infantry had been slowed by antivehicle mines, recently placed.

This is a trap, all right, thought Blackjack, but whose? "Major Phipps, Major Dominelli, give me what you have."

Dominelli spun the large-scale chart toward the general. "We have no ARVNs, General. We have no idea where they are. Bravo Company of the forty-eighth is dug in well, but they're taking moderate artillery fire, mostly on top of the hill, where the spotters are."

"Those spotters dug in?"

"Reasonably well, sir. Navy says they expect to start handling a cruiser in, oh, ten minutes, sir. We have no artillery of our own near—''

"What's the caliber of the incoming artillery?"

Phipps spoke up. "Lieutenant Greenglass doesn't know. He, ah, has never been under artillery fire before."

Jesus, that's true, thought Blackjack. Probably none of those boys have. "He sound all right?"

"Yes, OK, General. Scared, but OK."

I guess he's scared. "Ask First Sergeant McCloskey, with the forward observers, about the caliber. Now, what does Thunderbolt Two-Six tell us about the enemy force?"

"Captain Watson thinks at least a battalion, though maybe more, since there was no way to see the length of the column. He says they have deployed off the highway, and maybe two hundred meters to the west of it. There is good cover, and they can't see the vehicles, but Watson figures the vehicles may come up and cover a charge, as soon as the enemy figures out Bravo has no artillery support. Watson says, ah, the terrain is good vehicle country."

Which is why we chose the bloody place, thought Blackjack—easy for the ARVNs to find. "OK, get Lieutenant Stuart."

Dominelli pointed to the Spec 4 radio telephone operator assigned to command net, who spoke into his handset. "He's talking to his asset, sir, to the ship. Sergeant Coles is on."

"Ask him his situation. Are they still receiving artillery fire?"

The RTO spoke, and nodded. "He says the artillery is pretty bad. He says the ship is going to fire colored smoke, to get spotted, so they can stay down as much as possible. One of the army RTOs is down."

"How long for effective fire?"

There was another delay while the questions were asked and answered. "He says the cruiser has the spotter's position in its gunfire control computer, from the op plan, and Lieutenant Stuart has given a prespot. He says they expect the first spotting round in under eight minutes. Stuart says he'll have effective less than a minute later, if the prespot works."

"Tell him 'good lad.' "

"Yes, sir."

Blackjack looked sullenly at the map, with its thick enemy arrow so close to Bravo Company on hill 304. How in the name of Christ did an enemy force larger than a battalion spring up in an area controlled only this morning by the ARVNs? And where the hell had the ARVNs gone? "Well, gentlemen, here's where we earn our money. Those guys on Horsehead are in deep shit.

We have to get down there. Who's commanding the point tanks?''

"First Lieutenant Loonfeather, sir, the cav platoon commander. He has his cav and a mechanized infantry platoon.''

"Good man?'' Blackjack remembered the name from the role of replacements, but couldn't put a face to it.

"Been with us only since September, General. Joined after the Elephant,'' said Major Phipps. "Good training record.''

Blackjack remembered reading the record. "He is an Indian, isn't he?''

"Yessir,'' said Phipps. "Sioux.''

General Sheridan wrote that the Plains Indians were the finest light cavalry in the world. I hope he was right, thought Blackjack. Damn me! I have got to decide! "How far is Loonfeather from the highway?''

"About one and a half klicks, sir, though he's paralleling it, at this point,'' said Dominelli.

"Get him up on that road. Fast. Where are the rest of my tanks?''

"In the middle of the advance, sir, maybe, ah three klicks behind the cav, but they're on the road.''

Blackjack took a deep breath. "Major Phipps, tell Lieutenant Loonfeather to turn, and advance to the road. Tell him to *charge* to the road! If he encounters resistance, tell him to cut through and keep going. Tell our armor to hustle down the road to link up with the cavalry, then all the tanks and all the mounted infantry that reach the linkup in time are to sprint south for Horsehead Mountain, and get in the game with those enemy vehicles.''

"Yes, sir!'' said Dominelli, who started working out the communications. His first order went out to Lieutenant Loonfeather. The rest had to be worked out.

Phipps stood at the general's side. "The whole nine yards, eh, General?''

"Yeah. Fucked either way, I'm afraid.''

"Even if those tanks get there, sir, they're going to have a much larger force, with artillery, to contend with.''

"We have to assume, have to *believe*, that the Navy will deal with those guns. And cut into the enemy's numbers.''

"Well, we know Stuart is good.''

"Would you do it differently, Major?''

Phipps lit a cigarette. "I honestly don't know. In a sense, you risk all. But once again the enemy has matched strength against our weakness. You're rolling the dice.''

"Napoleon said, 'Always have two plans; leave something to chance.' ''

Phipps smiled, and lit the general's cigar. "You're betting on the Navy, General."

Blackjack puffed the cigar. "A tiger strikes with the paw that proved the fastest when last he killed, Major."

"Who said that?"

"Blackjack Beaurive." The general's grin brightened. "Let's get this done."

"Yessir. What about the rest of the infantry, and the guns?"

"As many as make the linkup, go south, lickety-split. The rest will have to fall back on the lines of the Third Division. Colonel Richmond will have to accomplish that, though let's wait till we get up there to decide."

"We're going up?"

Blackjack's grin widened again. "To hell or glory, Phipps. If I don't win this battle, I had rather not survive it."

The old man means that, thought Phipps. "It's not your fault, General. This situation, the attack coming from the south, couldn't have been predicted from the information we had."

General Beaurive fingered the silver star on his collar point. "It's my fault, son. Now, get us a helicopter or two. We will land here." He indicated a spot just to the rear of where the tanks and mounted troops were to rendezvous before going into the battle. "We will meet Colonel Stevens here, and decide."

"Yes, sir." Phipps turned away, and began helping Major Dominelli formulate what was essentially a whole new plan.

Blackjack stood, and felt the sharp pain in the middle of his back that had been nagging him. "Major Phipps?"

"Sir?"

"When we get in the helicopter, I want every man on this staff to have a weapon. A rifle."

Phipps grinned. "Yes, sir!"

Highway One, Eight Kilometers North of Horsehead Mountain

First Lieutenant Loonfeather switched his radio frequency to the cav platoon net from command. He whistled as the order from command sank in. He was to charge to the road, join with the lead armor platoon, then *lead* the tanks and APCs right down the enemy's neck.

His tank crew had heard the orders come over the radio. Elkins and the driver, Lopez, grinned tightly at Loonfeather, their faces sweating in the oily heat of the idling M-48. Loonfeather chuckled low in his throat. "We're going to *hit out*, men! Wind this fucker up!"

"Just like in the cowboy movies, eh, Lieutenant?" said Elkins, with an uncertain sneer.

"Right, Sergeant," replied Loonfeather, holding his gaze. "But this time the colored guys got the *cavalry*!"

Elkins let out a bark of laughter. Loonfeather thumbed the radio handset. "Dogfight, this is Dogfight Leader. Wheel left, form in double line, tanks up, then scouts and APCs. Advance on my order to the road. We will *charge* to the road, tanks first. APCs, remount your infantry, and follow. Acknowledge by units."

The two other tanks and the four ACAVs and three M113 armored personnel carriers acknowledged, and the units formed up. Loonfeather flipped back the hatch and sat on it. His mind reached back to Sitting Bull. Old Ones, help me, he prayed.

Lopez had the tank bucking along at fifteen miles an hour, bouncing over bumps and tearing through paddy. The ground was nice and firm despite the rain.

The tanks made a rise, and dropped over. Normally a spot to stop and take a look, but the general wants us on the *road*, so Loonfeather shouted at Lopez to keep cranking.

Before them on the faint track was a small village, with paddy to the left, and a thick stand of trees around a small pond to the right. The woods twinkled with small-arms fire, and bullets zinged off the turret. Loonfeather slipped below and closed the hatch.

"Elkins, load beehive." Loonfeather slewed the main gun to the right. "Cut away that brush next to the pond."

"You wanna stop, and form up the tanks, sir?"

"No, keep going. It's a few snipers. Shoot, Sergeant."

Crazy fucking Indian, thought Elkins. Still, this is fun. The cannon crashed and the beehive round went out. The beehive was like a giant shotgun round. Loonfeather peered through the periscope, and watched a large section of brush beneath the trees tear away.

"Another, Sergeant, a little to the left."

"Yessir," said Elkins, and the cannon roared again.

The rattle of light machine guns ran down the hull of the tank as they sped past the village at twenty miles per hour. Loonfeather radioed to the M113s behind to keep the troops' heads down. They popped over a small ridge, and Loonfeather squinted through the thick plastic vision blocks, and could see the highway. To the north, he saw a dust cloud, closing. Must be the rest of *my* attack force, he thought, elated. He shifted his radio to battalion net. "Thrasher Leader, this is Dogfight Leader."

"This is Thrasher Leader. We see you, Injun. Get your vehicles on the road, and we'll go and get her done."

"Roger, Thrasher Leader," said Loonfeather.

Yeah, thought Elkins! Yeah!

Eight Kilometers North of Hill 304

Lieutenant Colonel Stevens cupped his ear against the roar and whine of helicopters overhead and landing behind him on the road. He was trying to organize the remaining elements of his task force for the race south along Highway One. His tanks were now separated from the infantry by four full kilometers, he decided, and told the forces already formed up to kick off. The task force would be all over the highway, but reports from the south indicated the lifespan of the company and support troops on Horsehead was short without swift relief. But if the enemy force was as large as described, he thought bleakly, the tanks alone could not much change the outcome.

General Beaurive sat well back from the map-strewn camp desk, watching the staff hurriedly set up the headquarters and command functions. He felt very tired. He took one of the pills the doctor had reluctantly given him. He watched as Dominelli tried to organize and collect more helicopters. Phipps continued to monitor the swirling battle around Horsehead Mountain, a battle none of them had anticipated, or prepared for.

"Major Phipps, what can you tell me?"

Phipps put down the handset. "I can barely hear Watson, with the forward elements of Bravo Company. He says the enemy is just on the other side of the LZ they cleared earlier for their own landing. He expects the enemy to use his tracked vehicles to cover an infantry charge across the LZ and up the hill to their position."

"What's the slope in front of him? Can those vehicles climb to him?"

Phipps listened to the faint transmission from Captain Watson, and acknowledged. "He says they can get up. He has his mortars and heavy machine guns up the hill, behind him."

"What's his ammo status?"

Phipps shook his head. "He has used most of his small-arms ammo. He has enough to knock back one strong probe of infantry."

"But no antitank weapons."

"A couple of LAWs, General."

"Tell him not to waste those. Where are my tanks?"

"The cavalry has just reached the highway. The tank platoon is at the rendezvous; they should be ready to proceed shortly."

Blackjack stood, and leaned over the map-covered table. "*Shortly*, Major?"

Phipps blanched. "I have impressed upon Lieutenant Loonfeather the urgency of the mission. And I will remind him."

Blackjack sat, his face relaxing. I am showing too much tension. I need fresh minds. "Get me Lieutenant Stuart."

Phipps nodded, then nodded to the RTO on the command net, who called. Once the call was acknowledged by Walker, the RTO passed the handset to the general.

"Storm Cloud Six, Foxtrot Lima, over."

"Six up. Hello, William."

"Ah, yes, sir, Six."

"Tell me what it looks like to you."

He's asking me to be his eyes inward, thought Stuart, just like before the battle in the Elephant. And I was wrong then. "What, exactly, sir?"

"Nothing exactly. What does it look like?"

Stuart took a deep breath, and motioned Sergeant Coles to switch into the net and listen. "Yes, sir. A coordinated, large-scale enemy attack at this position. No surprise, no deception. Somehow they outmaneuvered the ARVNs, more likely overran them."

"Big enough unit to overrun two battalions, William?"

"Well, sir, they're here, and we haven't heard from the ARVNs."

"You figure they're mounted in the ARVN's vehicles?"

"Yessir."

"You figure they're VC?"

"No, sir. Hunter, ah, Sergeant Hunter, sir, mine, was at Lang Vhe during the battle for Khe Sanh, when the NVA attacked every night for a week with Russian-built light tanks—PT76's. He says he recognizes the light blue uniform. He says they're NVA, main force, tankers, maybe motorized infantry."

Blackjack bowed his head and rubbed his eyes. "William, can you, or you and your Sergeant Hunter, tell me what in the bloody hell a major force of tank-trained troops is doing attacking me on *the bloody coast*? Where did they come from, and more important, William, *what the fuck is their objective*?"

Stuart thought about that. He sensed the general's question was rhetorical, and asked out of frustration, but he thought about it nonetheless. Who are these guys and why are they here? "No answer, sir. If the general has no urgent need of me, I have a difficult spot to plan." That is true, thought Stuart; it is also evasive. The general's uncharacteristic outburst nicked Stuart's confidence; still, he thought, I am glad he is the general, and all I have is a difficult spot to plan.

"William, can you stop them, if they come up the hill?"

"We need about three minutes, maybe a bit less to get set up and spotted in. I don't think the enemy can get here in that time. We pretty much know where he is, and we have plenty of fire-power."

"If you have time enough."

"Yes, sir."

"If you have time enough, you will break him up, and hold him *off* until we can get reinforcements down to you? For sure, you to me?" Blackjack heard the strain in his own voice, and fought it back.

Stuart grinned at Coles, who grinned back. We are talking *Conqueror*! thought Coles. "If we have time, Six, we will de-stroy the enemy force in front of this hill. Utterly." Coles stuck his palm out and Stuart slapped it lightly.

Blackjack laughed. Phipps, monitoring the net, laughed too, as did the RTO. Tension lifted in the noisy, confused command tent, as all eyes turned to the general. "That *exceeds* your mis-sion plan for today, Lieutenant, which was to *support* this bri-gade! But you have my permission to *do so*! Six *out*!" Blackjack handed the handset back to the RTO. He believes it, and maybe, so do I. "Major Dominelli!"

"Sir!"

"As soon as Colonel Stevens is rolling, and Colonel Rich-mond is able to advise us as to disposition of the remaining forces we have, I'll want you to prepare to get us back on the helicopters, and up to hill three-oh-four."

"Yes, sir!"

Good, good, thought Blackjack. To hell or glory.

Loonfeather pulled his three tanks onto the road. The scout vehicles and troop carriers waited until the tanks from the armor platoon pulled into line, then filed in behind. Eight additional M113s from various units, all at the leading edge of the advance, had formed up as well.

Loonfeather conferred briefly with Thrasher Leader, Second Lieutenant Cox, probably the only officer in the brigade junior to Loonfeather himself who was commanding anything. He called back to headquarters, and spoke to Major Phipps. Lieu-tenant Colonel Stevens would command the advancing infantry and artillery as soon as they became a coherent force. Loonfeather was to leave his infantry, and advance with the eight tanks and four scout vehicles, advance to engage the enemy at Horsehead Mountain, and not stop unless stopped! Loonfeather acknowledged, and grinned at his nervous crew. "We're the point tank, Elkins. Load high explosive, and train the tube straight out, and low. Shoot anything that looks back at you."

Crazy Indian motherfucker is too dumb to be scared, thought Elkins, ramming the H-E round into the main gun. Loonfeather was up on top of the turret again. He looked back to the fourth tank in line, and saw Cox holding his thumb up, ready. Loonfeather made a fist with his left hand, and pumped it up and down three times in the air, meaning let's go! Loonfeather shouted down to Elkins, and the tank lurched forward and accelerated ponderously up to its best speed of close to thirty miles per hour. Loonfeather saw the tanks draw into line, tubes alternately trained out right and left, herringbone fashion, and close up as each tank reached speed. I wish I had a fucking *saber*, he thought, Here comes Task Force *Loonfeather*!

Exactly twelve minutes and thirty seconds after Stuart had authenticated for the *St. Paul*, the gunnery officer came up on spot net. "Foxtrot Lima, Conqueror, we'd like to spot at extreme range."

"Conqueror, go ahead. The enemy is closer, and getting thicker on the ground. We are expecting a charge."

"OK, Fox Lima, we are on it. This fire will probably fall about a thousand yards short. Two rounds, in the air, *now*, one from each forward turret, time of flight, 25.5 seconds."

Stuart adjusted his spotting table. One of the frustrations of spotters was the fact that the Navy persisted in measuring distance in yards, while the Army and Marine Corps used meters. At gun ranges, the difference was important.

Jesus, thought Coles, staring at his watch, the ship is still nearly seventeen miles away.

Stuart looked at his stopwatch, and at Coles. At twenty-three seconds, he stuck his helmet up above the trench and rested his nose on the edge. An enemy shell landed some twenty meters down slope and showered his face with grit. Through the trees that concealed the enemy, he saw a flash, then another, followed by plumes of orange and white smoke. He ducked down, wiped the grit from his eyes and nose, and thumbed the handset. "Conqueror, Foxtrot Lima. You are back at least a thousand yards, more than fifteen hundred, but your line is good."

"Not to worry, Fox Lima, we have covered most of that distance in the time the shells took to arrive. We can give you six guns in thirty seconds, with really no spread, and nine guns plus the five-inch battery in six minutes, when we hit station."

"Good, Conqueror. Remember we are on the edge of your gun-target line. Danger close, on the end of the gun-target line."

"Roger, Fox Lima, roger. We will walk to you. How close is the enemy to your forward position?"

Hunter had crawled to Stuart's side and was yelling something to Coles. Coles popped his head up, and down, as the artillery barrage slowly died. "Stand by one, Conqueror. What is it, Sergeant?"

Coles's lips were drawn tight, but his voice held steady. "The grunts down below, sir, they see the enemy vehicles coming through the trees."

Damn! thought Stuart, I need one more minute to get this halfway safe. "Conqueror, Foxtrot Lima. The enemy is three hundred yards away, and charging. You are going to have to peel him right off our faces."

"Roger, Fox Lima. You will *have* to spot. We'll fire rapid, not salvo, OK? Keep the bastards' heads down."

"Roger, Conqueror, let's go with it." Over his head, Stuart heard Moser's machine gun open up in long, thick bursts.

"Fox Lima. Conqueror. Firing now, six guns. H-E, point detonating, for effect. Say twenty secs. Spot and spot. Recommend you tell your infantry to loosen chin straps, and get as low as they can. We're going to shake the earth."

"Roger, Conqueror. Shake the earth." Stuart nodded to Coles, who informed the infantry of the incoming rounds. Stuart watched the stopwatch tick down, then stuck his head up and pressed the binoculars to his eyes. He heard a low-pitched rattling roar, like many freight trains, which rose in pitch and volume to a deafening surge, drowning the small-arms fire. Six eight-inch shells, each weighing more than three hundred pounds, detonated in the front of the tree line, just as the enemy troops and vehicles emerged from cover.

Lieutenant Loonfeather stood in the tank commander's hatch in the lead tank and swept the trees, paddies, and occasional farm buildings on both sides of the road with his binoculars. The enemy is near, he thought.

The road surface was cracked, but good. Some of the larger creeks had bridges down, which happened so often that wide, clearly marked fords had taken their places. The tanks rolled onward.

There was such a ford just ahead, with broad stands of tropical oak, red teak, and other hardwoods shielded by thick undergrowth on an island in the middle of the creek and on the near shore. Maybe here, thought Loonfeather, and he dropped back inside the tank. "Watch those trees, Elkins. Go wide in the ford."

Elkins squinted through the periscope as Loonfeather radioed the column to slow slightly, and passed his concerns about the place to the other vehicles. "What do you reckon we gonna find, sir?"

Loonfeather shrugged, and replaced Elkins at the periscope. "You have to figure the enemy knows we're here, and where we're headed. They have to try to stop us at some point. The situation is good for an ambush, and I figure that once we pass this ford, and get up over the next rise, we'll be able to see Horsehead Mountain."

Elkins trained the gun out right, then back in. "What'll they throw at us?"

"Well, mines, if they had time to dig them in. Rockets, light antitank guns, RPGs, whatever they have." Loonfeather smiled quizzically at his sergeant. Doesn't this powdery city spade like a fight?

This crazy fucking redskin makes me squirm, thought Elkins. Why doesn't the asshole ride in his scout vehicle where he is supposed to, and leave me to run my tank?

The lead tank was just emerging from the ford when the first three tanks came under fire from the trees on the gravel island in midstream. Heavy machine gun fire raked the vehicles, and a B-40 rocket smashed into the road in front of the lead tank, cratering the road and shaking the fifty-two-ton tank as if it were a Volkswagen. Elkins trained the 90mm gun at the trees, and fired. The other tanks fired when they saw his shell flash brightly at the base of a two-hundred-foot-tall oak.

Lopez slewed the tank around the deepest part of the crater, and climbed it to the top of the bank. Loonfeather continued to shout over the radio to the other vehicles as Cuervo loaded, and Elkins trained and fired the gun. The first three tanks of the armor platoon swiveled right and splashed up the river toward the trees and thick brush that concealed the enemy. The other two tanks held the near bank, and added supporting fire to that of the tanks advancing. Elkins squinted through his periscope and fired. "Load me a Willy Peter round, Cuervo," he shouted.

He saw the first of the ACAVs enter the river, and immediately receive a rocket square in front. The vehicle began to burn fiercely, as Elkins fired again. He was able to see four of the five crewmen of the scout vehicle get down into the river, then the vehicle exploded. I guess that's why the crazy lieutenant sits in my tank instead of roaring around in a scout, he thought.

A heavy thud struck the side of Elkins's tank, followed by a choking explosion. Dust and hot gas flooded the turret. The engine screamed and gears clanked as the right track broke, and wound off in a neat, straight line behind the tank. The tank swerved right as the engine continued to drive the left track forward, then the engine died. The interior of the tank was suddenly quiet, the battle sounds outside were muffled.

Loonfeather thumbed the handset. Dead. "Sergeant, get the hatch open. Take a look."

Elkins pushed up the armored hatch on top of the turret. No enemy fire was coming at them. Elkins reckoned that any enemy left in the ambush would be concentrating fire on the advancing tanks pouring high explosive and white phosphorous fire into the wooded island, but he doubted any VC would be dumb enough to hold ground. He leaned far out of the turret, knowing the lieutenant would be watching, and saw small flames licking along the starboard side of the tank. Probably just lube oil, he thought, but serious nonetheless. Unlike the M113s and the ACAVs, the tank had a diesel engine and the fuel would not normally explode.

"No hostile fire here, sir. But we're burning a bit on the right underside."

Loonfeather climbed out behind Elkins, pushing the sergeant out through the narrow opening. "OK, Sergeant, get your men out, and get back to one of the scouts. Tell 'em to make room. I'm shifting to the next tank."

"What do we do now, sir?"

"Re-form. Haul ass. We still have to relieve the grunts at hill three-oh-four."

Loonfeather climbed up onto the turret of the second tank, which was idling behind the crippled point. He had the radio handset passed up to him, and got reports. No one was receiving fire from the enemy. Loonfeather set about re-forming the column. The only casualties were the point tank and the scout vehicle and its unlucky driver. The scout was burning too intensely to allow recovery of the remains of the driver, so Loonfeather radioed back to battalion and asked them to recover the body.

The column resumed its crossing of the river, passed the still slowly burning point tank, and climbed the low rise to the highway. As they resumed best speed, Lieutenant Loonfeather could see the shape of Horsehead Mountain rising above the coastal plain, and an oily black cloud blowing over the top of it. Charge, he thought, charge!

* * *

The six-gun salvo of eight-inch shells knocked Stuart to his knees inside the trench, and tore off his helmet. The earth rocked in waves. Stuart felt a stinging sensation on his right cheek. His hand probed a deep cut. He flung the blood on his hand away impatiently as Coles handed him his helmet. He saw the camouflage cloth cover had been shredded.

Stuart got to his feet slowly, and looked over the lip of the trench with the powerful spotting binoculars. The radio crackled. Hunter handed him the handset. Stuart pressed it to his ear without taking his eyes from the terrain below.

Small-arms fire from both sides of the line had been snuffed out by the eight-inch shells. As Stuart looked out, firing began again, and quickly intensified. The enemy APCs and the light blue–uniformed men who were bunched tightly behind the vehicles pressed forward. Bravo Company on the plain and the weapons platoon above poured out rifle and machine gun fire.

"Fox Lima, this is Conqueror, we *must* have your spot!"

Stuart swallowed, with no moisture in his throat. Behind the advancing troops, where the shells had landed, trees had been uprooted, and others simply shattered. Stuart could see two of the captured M113s had been blown off the highway. One was on its side, and the other was upside down. Both were burning brightly through the haze.

"Fox Lima, Conqueror." Sergeant Coles tugged urgently at Stuart's sleeve.

Stuart's eye sockets ached from the binoculars being rammed into his face by the blast. When he spoke, his voice sounded thick and unfamiliar. "Orj—" he cleared the fear from his throat. "Orange, forward edge, add one hundred. No, correction: add one hundred *fifty*. White, add fifty, spread left, *your* left, two hundred. Shoot a box pattern a thousand yards back from the forward edge, but do the front up first, over."

"This is Conqueror, roger. Spot corrected, firing, *now*, T.O.F. eighteen, rapid and continuous, forward then back. Good luck and stay down, Fox Lima."

Eighteen seconds later, the shells began landing, and the ground shook and shook. Stuart found himself on the floor of the trench, on his knees, his face full of sand and stone fragments. The ground boomed and cracked. He tried to stand, but could not. He knelt, face to face with Coles, whose face blurred with the vibrations. Dirt from the walls of the trench streamed down and covered their bent legs to the thighs. Stuart could not rise. The first salvo had been more powerful, due to the cumulative effect of six shells arriving simultaneously, but at least the noise and the sickening lurching motion of the ground around them had subsided. With each shell now arriving irregularly, but no less frequently than every four to five seconds, the ground rolled continuously. Coles spoke, but the noise overwhelmed his speech, and the vibration made lipreading impossible.

We have to get a look, thought Stuart. Those shells are landing practically on top of us! With improvised sign language and single shouted words, Stuart indicated to Coles that he intended to stand up, and that Coles should stand behind him and brace him against the crumbling wall of the trench with his body. He had to see what the enemy was doing, and make sure the cruiser was keeping the shot in front of the friendly troops as the ship hurtled straight at them at thirty-three knots.

Hunter knelt next to Coles, his handset pressed against ear and mouth, his other hand tight against his ear, talking to Captain Watson dug in with the infantry below. Watson had asked Stuart to take a look, saying smoke and dust had reduced his own visibility to zero. Stuart was relieved to hear the infantry was apparently safe for the moment both from the enemy's charge and from the awful weight of the cruiser's shell fire.

Stuart timed the fall of two shells. Four seconds apart. As the second hit, he half stood, half sprawled against the front edge of the trench. Coles grabbed him from behind in a bear hug and pressed him strongly into the dirt face.

Stuart pushed himself as near upright as he could against the rolling motion of the earth. He could see a huge, boiling cloud of dust and smoke spreading from the bluff to the left of the highway almost 400 yards inland, and rising in the light breeze about 1,500 feet before blowing off to the northeast. Shells landed irregularly along the base of the cloud, and their explosions, plus the flames from many separate fires, lifted the cloud to the point where Stuart could see the battlefield reasonably well. Sweeping his eyes rapidly back and forth, he tried to memorize everything of importance, then he tapped Coles's forearm rapidly as they had agreed. The bear hug loosened, and both men dropped to their knees on the floor of the trench.

"Hunter, switch to spot net and tell Conqueror to drop fifty, then get me Two-Six," said Stuart, wiping his face. Coles handed him a canteen, and he drank. Now that I've seen where those shells are *really* falling, it's not nearly so terrifying.

Hunter gave a thumbs-up and bent over the radio. "Conqueror acknowledges spot, sir. I have Captain Watson. Conqueror wants to talk to you, sir."

"As soon as I speak to Captain Watson."

Hunter grinned. "I told 'em, sir."

Stuart took the handset. This trench seems a lot less tense. It even seems quieter. What was it Blackjack said about battlefields? "Fear puts the volume up."

"Two-Six, this is Foxtrot Lima."

"Go ahead, Foxtrot Lima."

"OK. What I could see down there is this. There are four knocked-out armored personnel carriers about seventy meters in front of you, near the road. There are two more APCs halted all the way out by the seaward end of this hill, apparently undamaged, but beyond the fall of shot from the ship. We might try to get a shot at them from up here, or maybe you can. Right now, they're not moving. From the intensity of the fire, and the damage to the trees, I would guess neither men nor equipment survive in a zone at least a thousand meters back from the forward edge. I observed no enemy artillery landing, but I'd like to walk some of the guns back along the road, to knock out any artillery, or reserves, if he has any, behind the main body."

"Well, let's just be sure. Could you see any enemy infantry?"

"There appear to be two lines of infantry lying in the mud between the base of the hill in front of you and ahead of the forward edge of shot fall. I don't know if they're dead, wounded, or just pinned down."

"I'd like to get a look, Foxtrot Lima."

"I've called the shot fall back fifty yards. That should mean the nearest shells will be falling in about three-hundred-fifty meters from your position."

"They seem closer."

"They sure do. I was afraid I'd been a little, ah, aggressive, with my spot."

Watson laughed, high-pitched. Stuart could feel the strain. Watson continued, "In this brigade, you have that reputation, son. Stand by one, I'll try to get a look."

"Standing by." Stuart rested the handset on his knee. The noise and ground heaving had lessened appreciably since the shotfall had been moved back. Men from the weapons platoon crawled out of their holes just below the ANGLICO, and began mortaring the lines of prone enemy soldiers below. "Hunter, get me Conqueror. Sergeant, hold onto Two-Six." He gave Bobby the handset.

"I got Conqueror, Lieutenant." Hunter handed Stuart the other handset.

Stuart thumbed the handset. "This is Foxtrot Lima."

"Fox Lima, Conqueror. We're nearly on station and turning to unmask number three turret. We will be able to fire the secondary battery in about one minute."

"Roger, Conqueror. There is too much smoke for a decent spot. Spread the number three turret back along the highway, say between one thousand and three thousand yards back from the forward edge of the current shotfall. Concentrate the five inch in the same area, training back and forth. Will the computer do that?"

"Roger, Fox Lima, no sweat. Only enemy south of you, along the highway, right?"

"Roger, Conqueror." Stuart certainly no longer expected the ARVNs.

"Roger, Fox Lima. We have nine guns firing, rapid and continuous. If you can, spot color for number three."

Stuart flinched as Coles swabbed the cut on his cheek with alcohol. Bobby took Stuart's hand and placed it over the dressing on his cheek. "You hold this, Lieutenant. My turn to get the spot." Stuart grinned, and handed Bobby the binoculars.

Coles peered over the edge of the trench, which was continuing to disintegrate from the rhythmic vibration that shook the world. The falling eight-inch shells were tearing up trees and bush, exposing vehicles, and destroying them. The enemy infantrymen who could crawled away from the mortar and small-arms fire, but most died where they lay, as the explosions tossed the blue-uniformed men and tore them. Coles could see two M113s still on the road, moving north, away from the terrible naval gunfire. Then he saw a faint green smudge, landing inland.

"Conqueror, Fox Lima, on the *green*, drop two hundred. Right four hundred. I can't give you a mil spot."

"Rog, Fox Lima. Corrected. We are *here*, man! Call my secondary, four shots, *now*!"

"Roger." Bobby waited. There was no more small-arms fire from either side. Four shells, obviously lighter than the eight inch, landed together, all red, about a mile away to the south.

"Red," said Bobby, "all together. Good, good. Spread them your left, fire for effect."

The din increased as the eight five-inch guns that could bear joined the nine eight-inch guns, pouring hot metal onto the pinned enemy. Bobby slid down into the hole and grinned at Stuart, as the *St. Paul* turned the battleground to hell.

8 January 1968   Horsehead Mountain

As Loonfeather's formation approached hill 304, he took optical ranges on the heat-shimmered images of two armored personnel carriers. They looked U.S., but he still saw them as targets. Loonfeather squeezed down inside the turret, and slammed the hatch over his head.

"Thunderbolt Two-Six, Dogfight Leader, over." Loonfeather used the Thunderbolt prefix because he had not previously talked to the 2d of the 48th, Bravo Company commander.

"Dogfight Leader, this is Thunderbolt Two-Six. We have been expecting you, over."

"We see two APCs, out east of the hill. Friendlies, over?"

"Negative, negative, Dogfight Leader, we have no friendly vehicles."

"Roger, Two-Six. What other opposition will we encounter as we come up?"

"Not much, Dogfight Leader. Scattered infantry. Advance no farther than the southern base of the hill; the Navy is still shelling. Acknowledge."

"Roger, Two-Six, we will hit these APCs and advance on the road to the southern base, over."

"This is Two-Six, good hunting, out."

Loonfeather deployed his first four tanks in a line—his own

on the road, two on the right shoulder, the fourth on the left. The line and the remaining vehicles behind it slowed to ten miles an hour, as the tankers looked into the tall grass and scrub vegetation for further signs of the enemy. Loonfeather could see the two armored personnel carriers in the grass next to the east face of the hill, motionless, seeming to cringe against the granite cliff, as the range between them and the advancing tanks steadily decreased. Beyond the APCs, and beyond the mountain, Loonfeather could see smoke and flames boiling higher, and he could hear the steady drumming of the shell fire. He was aware that the tank was bouncing and swaying under him as it advanced.

The range to the APCs dropped to 2,000 meters. Loonfeather divided the targets among his four tanks. He knew he should stay inside the buttoned-up tank, but he couldn't resist popping up for a better look. The tank commander shook his head as Loonfeather opened the hatch. Fuck him, thought Loonfeather, adjusting the binoculars braced on the top of the turret. He could see forty or fifty enemy infantrymen in light blue uniforms moving out from around the APCs, spreading and concealing themselves in the high grass. Better do this from here, he thought. Don't get too close before tearing things up a bit. Don't want to get my Injun ass barbecued by an RPG. At 1,500 meters, Loonfeather stopped the advance, and ordered the line of tanks to open fire. His tank bucked under him as it fired, and Loonfeather observed antitank shells bursting around the APCs. One of the enemy vehicles had started up and was crossing the road, with infantry behind it. Loonfeather watched as his tank and the one on the left shoulder trained their guns to follow, and adjusted for their first shot. Both cannons cracked at once, and at least one shell struck the APC in the left track and halted it. Loonfeather trained his binoculars at the stalled vehicle, and saw it was gamely answering fire with its .50-caliber machine gun. Loonfeather slid down inside the tank as its cannon cracked again.

Cardenas dropped into the trench beside Stuart. "Sir, Moser 'n' me, we can see the tanks. They're fightin' down on the road, with a couple APCs."

"What can you see down in front, to the south?"

"Jeez, nothin' sir. Just smoke and flames."

"I'll come up. Bobby, tell Two-Six we want to lift fire soon. Hunter, shift to spot, and follow me." Coles grinned and turned back to the blackened battlefield. Earth and trees and men and machines continued to be thrown and tossed by the exploding shells.

From Moser's machine gun position, Stuart saw the end of the sharp action on the road just to the north. A line formation of M-48 tanks advanced slowly toward the mountain, firing at targets too close to the foot of the mountain to be seen from the summit. Must be those two APCs that got out ahead of the shell fire, he thought.

Moser shook his shoulder roughly. "There she *is*, sir!"

I *will* be damned, thought Stuart. The clouds had broken, and on the sun-brightened sea, maybe four miles away, was the *St. Paul*. Stuart raised his spotting binoculars to his eyes. The eight-inch guns were firing at point-blank range, elevated only enough to lift the shot over the coastal bluffs and onto the road. Great tongues of yellow flames shot from the big guns in an irregular cadence. The water alongside the ship was whipped to froth by the continuous concussions. The five-inch guns, in contrast, were elevated past forty-five degrees, throwing shells high into the sky to plunge miles through the air before rending the battlefield below. Nothing could stand before such a destructive barrage, thought Stuart. She is both beautiful and profoundly terrifying.

Stuart handed the binoculars to Moser. "Take a look, Gunner. That's a gunner's mate's heaven. Hunter, to go battalion net, get Two-Six."

"Aye, sir," said Hunter, shifting frequencies and then talking. "He's on, sir."

"Two-Six, Foxtrot Lima. Recommend we cease fire. We can't see any life down there in front of you."

"Roger, Foxtrot Lima, I guess we ought to go on down there and do our job, though I don't mind telling you we appreciated what little you could do to help."

Stuart smiled. The fear was gone, the residue was bravado, but bravado understood by all who shared the experience. We can all pretend we weren't afraid because we know we were all afraid. "Happy to do what we could, Two-Six. Don't pick your tails up before I tell you the ship has cleared her guns."

"What does that mean, Foxtrot Lima?"

"After I tell him to cease firing, he will want to fire all the guns that are loaded. You can't leave a naval gun loaded, especially not a hot one."

"Roger, OK; let us know."

"Roger, out. Hunter, spot net, get Conqueror."

Hunter handed Stuart the handset. "Conqueror, Foxtrot Lima. Cease fire, and stand by."

"This is Conqueror, roger, cease fire! May I clear my guns?"

"Roger, clear and advise." Stuart stood behind Moser and watched as the last rounds were fired by the five- and eight-inch guns. There was a pause of perhaps a minute, during which time Moser and Stuart knew the gunnery officer would be verifying that all guns were indeed clear.

"Foxtrot Lima, Conqueror. My guns are clear and I will stand by. The Captain would like to know if we did you any good."

"Please tell him you destroyed the entire enemy column, as near as we can tell. We were way overmatched here on the ground. The commander forward has already expressed his appreciation."

"Very good, Foxtrot Lima. Conqueror standing by."

"Foxtrot Lima out." Stuart slid back down into the trench, and picked up Morgan's handset, on battalion net. "Two-Six, Foxtrot Lima, ship reports clear guns; it's safe to come out now."

Watson's laugh was distorted over the radio. "OK, hotshot, we are moving. That ship of yours isn't leaving yet, is it?"

"Negative, Two-Six, we will be here and they will be here. Careful, old man." The last was by no means a joke.

"OK, Foxtrot Lima, watch and cover as we go. Two-Six out."

Moser grabbed Cardenas by the shoulder. "C'mere, gyrene, I'm gonna let you see what saved the grunts today. Look out thar at 'at lady. They got the bosun's mates out on deck coolin' down the guns with fire hoses."

Loonfeather had the tanks advancing at a fast walking pace. I wish we had infantry behind us, he thought. Both enemy APCs were burning hulks, popping and zinging as their ammo exploded. The tanks were firing beehive rounds into the grass, and machine guns swept and probed for the enemy. Loonfeather could see some small groups of enemy standing by the cliff behind them. Many appeared to be unarmed, but as they made no sign of surrender, Loonfeather kept the tanks firing, and the men fell. Enemy small-arms fire slowly died away.

Loonfeather opened the turret and pulled himself out cautiously. The loader was manning the machine gun on the Chrysler mount behind him, firing short bursts into the grass. "Cease fire," he said to the loader, then he said it again into his microphone. He gave the cavalry hand-sign commands for forward in a column, then repeated the order into the radio. His tank lurched forward and took the point. They rolled past the gutted APCs and on around the seaward point of hill 304, just as the rumble and crack of the naval shelling died away. They topped a slight rise, and the driver of the point tank braked to a sudden stop. Loonfeather looked over the rise at the plain south of the mountain, and his jaw dropped. The entire plain as far as he could see was blackened and flickering with low fires. The trees were shattered and the ground was cratered like a picture of the moon. Loonfeather shivered. It was a vision of hell.

The driver popped his head out of his own hatch, forward. "There ain't no more road, sir."

The flight of Huey helicopters carrying General Beaurive and his senior staff officers wop-wopped down onto the LZ on top of Horsehead Mountain. Blackjack emerged stiffly from the lead bird, and acknowledged the deferential nods from Lieutenant Greenglass and Lieutenant Stuart. A salute in a battle area could have pointed the general out to a sniper as a prime target.

Blackjack strode to the forward edge of the flinty plateau and looked at the blasted battlefield. In the foreground on the plain below, Captain Watson's B Company held positions around the landing zone at the base of the mountain. Helicopters were landing and taking off, bringing reinforcements from Lieutenant Colonel Richmond's force. The general walked out toward the eastern scarp of the hill, where he could see the main force forming up.

Lieutenant Colonel Stevens and the main body of APC- and truck-borne infantry and artillery were visible moving down the highway from the north. First elements had already linked up with the tanks of Loonfeather's task force, and the rest of the column stretched back into the haze for more than two kilometers.

The tanks and M113 Scout vehicles were lined up neatly across the gap between the east face of Horsehead Mountain and the coastal bluffs. Beyond them, some four miles at sea, the *St. Paul* shimmered in the bright slanting sunlight of late afternoon. Beaurive noted that her big guns were neatly trained fore and aft.

The general turned back to the battlefield itself. A few fires still burned in the downed trees and underbrush, and wispy smoke obscured the road to the south. Within the zone of naval bombardment there was no trace of the highway. The blackened surface of the plain was pockmarked with literally hundreds of overlapping craters, some forty or more feet in diameter. The shells had gone deep enough in most to enter the limestone subsoil before exploding, and the surface of those craters was covered with light gray powder. There was nothing that could be identified as a military vehicle. The two rows of blue-clad bodies that had been cleared from the LZ down below were the only visible remnant of the enemy force.

Who were these men who came from nowhere? wondered Blackjack. Who commanded them, what was their mission? Their blood and bones are mixed forever in this savaged ground.

The general thought of the brashness of Lieutenant Stuart on the radio, scarcely one hour before. "We will destroy the enemy utterly." Just like that. One naval officer, one sailor, eight marines, and that silent, deadly gray shape out there, haloed in the light of the sinking sun. Just like that. Twice, twice now, the enemy has had me in his grasp. Twice we celebrate a victory we earned, but maybe don't deserve.

Blackjack felt the strange reverie pass from him. He turned away from the battlefield, and walked to the spot where the men of the ANGLICO detachment were packing their gear. He motioned Stuart to follow him, then walked to the place where Moser had set up his machine gun. Moser, Cardenas, and the gun were gone. The general swept aside a pile of spent cartridge cases with his boot, and watched them rattle down the slope to join many others. "How many belts did Moser fire, William?"

Stuart took a drink from his canteen. His throat was still sore from yelling into radio mikes. "Couldn't say, General. Looks like a lot of brass down there."

"It must have been hot up here."

"Yes, sir, it surely was. There had to be three hundred men in that enemy advance, coming fast behind the APCs, and those were only the ones we could see."

"But you stopped them."

"Well, I think the grunts would have held that first rush with small arms and mortars. I was kind of surprised the enemy didn't shell us longer with his own artillery."

Blackjack smiled at Stuart. He looks so young to be standing here. "You're beginning to think like an infantry officer, son. You really should stay with me permanently."

Stuart blushed. Blackjack was taken aback. This kid who just called heavy fire practically in his own lap actually blushed. "Thank you, General, but I like the Navy."

Blackjack stared out to sea. "That ship can sure throw metal."

"The *St. Paul*, sir. She's the only all-big-gun cruiser in the Pacific Fleet." Stuart smiled broadly.

Blackjack moved his face close to Stuart's and matched the grin. "You're goddamn proud of your Navy, aren't you, William?"

"Sure am, General. We did a job today."

Blackjack's grin faded a bit. I wish I could say the same for myself. Still, in a war with very few good breaks, you took the ones you got. Never complain, never explain. The REMFs in Long Binh, Bien Hoa, and Saigon did enough of both. "That you did, William, and I thank you."

"Thank you, sir. Would the General like to thank the ship, personally? They're still on net."

Blackjack's grin went back up to full power. "Good, good! Let's go and do that!"

Beaurive and Stuart walked back to the rest of the detachment. Hunter had the spot net. "Sir, I have Conqueror. They would like permission to depart gun station."

Stuart took the handset. "Conqueror, this is Foxtrot Lima. I have Storm Cloud, code seven, requesting Conqueror himself."

"Stand by."

Stuart passed the handset to General Beaurive.

"This is Conqueror himself. Hello, General."

"Hello, Captain. Permission is granted for you to depart. You leave a grateful Army behind you."

"Thank you, General. We appreciate your taking time to say so. My gunnery officer says much credit should be given to your spotters."

Blackjack looked for Stuart, but he was out of earshot. "I am glad to hear that. He is a fine naval officer with a fine marine corps team."

"Well, thank you again, General. We'll be going now. Good luck."

"Captain, my name is Beaurive."

"Mine's Hunnicutt."

"Godspeed, Captain Hunnicutt. Storm Cloud out."

Blackjack climbed back up to the point of the mountaintop. He watched alone as the water boiled under the cruiser's stern as the ship gathered speed. Across the water, clear though softened by the distance, he heard the whoop, whoop of the ship's siren. The cruiser executed a broad, foaming turn, then headed south at a high speed. Blackjack watched her out of sight.

13 January 1968
Quang Ngai
After-action Report
Section III, Commander's Comments (Excerpt)

During the day of 9 January 1968, and the morning of the following day, elements of this brigade swept the scarred battlefield south of Horsehead Mountain (hill 304). First Lieutenant Loonfeather, with his cavalry platoon reconstituted following his heroic advance, led, followed by B Company, under Captain Watson. This force swept south seven kilometers, and found nothing remaining of an enemy concentration. They did find a vast network of tunnels collapsed by the naval gunfire, but revealing a supply cache of unparalleled proportions. It is with regret that I confirm Major Phipps's report that they also found the shattered remains of the two ARVN battalions upon whose help we had waited in vain. It must be said that the configuration of the bodies—Captain Black, Captain Bigelow, and the senior Vietnamese officers, including Major Tranh and Colonel Minh—that were found, dead and mutilated, but in star formation just south of the battle area, requires us to believe and report that they fought valiantly before their deaths.

My opinion is that the tunnels we found both north and south of hill 304 were connected, and that the force we expected to contain within the area of the Storm Cloud operation went south through the tunnels in its entirety during the night and early morning. The enemy then surprised and annihilated the ARVNs, probably attacking in daylight from within the ARVNs' own laagers. This same force then mounted itself in captured ARVN vehicles, and attacked our forward observers from the south.

Our casualties were extremely light. Four were killed—one of the cavalry's ACAV drivers and three of 2d Platoon, B Company, 2d Battalion, 48th Infantry, whose position on the side of hill 304 received a direct hit from an enemy artillery shell. Twenty-one men were wounded, mainly by shrapnel during the enemy's brief artillery barrage, others by stones and other debris thrown by the naval gunfire.

The enemy's casualties can only be estimated. Two hundred forty bodies were counted in the battle area south of the hill, while the cavalry accounted for thirty-six more in the action described at the eastern foot of the hill. No enemy wounded were found, and no prisoners were taken. In the area of concentrated naval bombardment, about 400 meters wide and more than 3,000 meters deep, where we believe the bulk of the enemy force had concentrated for his assault, numerous fragments of bodies, bits of uniforms, weapons, and other equipment were found. We believe the enemy must have lost many more inside this vast beaten zone than outside it. The earth was literally plowed and turned over on itself, and only a complete excavation could allow an accurate count. The S-2's estimate, elsewhere in this report, of four hundred casualties *over and above* the bodies counted is, in my view, conservative.

Recommendations for decorations will follow. Worthy of special mention here are Lieutenant Colonel Stevens, who organized and led the march southward, First Lieutenant Loonfeather, who fought his tanks through three separate actions on his way to relieve the units trapped on hill 304, and Lieutenant Stuart, of the 2d Platoon, 7th ANGLICO, who spotted the naval gunfire that broke and destroyed the enemy's attack utterly. I would like as well to be permitted to decorate the commanding officer and the gunnery officer of the USS *St. Paul*, CA 73, for their providing supporting fire of inestimable worth.

* * *

My own opinion of the significance of this action is controversial even among my own staff. I believe the question is *why was such a major force of NVA deployed in an area so remote from their strong points in North Vietnam or in Laos?* I am convinced that no sense can be made of such a disposition *unless* a major enemy operation is planned, to occur *soon*, with any *or all* major U.S. and ARVN positions targeted. I therefore *urgently* suggest that MACV consider the possibility of a *major* enemy attack, *imminently*, upon all of our forces.

(signed) Hubert O. Beaurive, Brigadier General, USA, Commanding

DATD: 01-19-68 0444Z
SECRET
PRIORITY

FM: COMUSMACV
TO: 197 LT BRGD, BGEN BEAURIVE, COMDNG.
REURS: HILL 304 ENGMT 8 JAN 68
 MANY THNKS GENL INTEL REPTS NO RPT NO
LIKELY ENEMY INFORCE ATTK IMMINENT. ROGERS
MGEN INTELLIGENCE.

Those desk jockeys are *wrong*! thought Blackjack, in Quang
Ngai.
That black prima donna will do anything to cover his ass,
thought Major General Rogers, in Saigon.

20 Jan 1968 Danang

Dear Simon,
 We just finished a fantastic action to the south of here. We
were called up by General Beaurive, who still commands the
197th, the unit we went up the Elephant Valley with last August. The general asked for our unit *by name*! Damn, I was
proud. The brigade was glad to have us back, especially since
the operation was to be right on the coast, and fine for naval
gunfire.
 Well, the enemy foxed us, just like in the Elephant, and
came at us from the south, while the whole damn brigade
was supposed to be catching them on the plain north of us,
or at least pushing them toward us and two battalions of
ARVNs, who were supposed to be with us. We, that is the
ANGLICO and some army artillery spotters, were just there
to spot. Fortunately, Blackjack gave us a rifle company to
protect us and maybe stiffen the ARVNs, but instead of the
friendly Vietnamese we are expecting, suddenly this NVA
unit comes rolling up the road in the ARVNs' vehicles, and
we were at war with an enemy force maybe five times our
size.
 Well, Brother, the good news is that we were ready. Lieutenant Stuart had been in a real bad state, and talking to no
one, since his wife told him she was leaving him, and that
was six weeks ago. He finally sobered up after about three
days, but it was obvious to us that he could feel nothing but
pain. I have been worried, Moser more than me, that he wasn't
going to make it. I have never seen a man so changed, all
confidence gone, all purpose gone. Moser and I and my buddy
Hunter have been taking turns watching him, thinking he might
eat his gun. Simon, I really felt for the guy, but more than

that, I was scared for the platoon, and for me. An officer goes that wrong, and the guys start getting killed. I almost wished the major would get him replaced, and you know I really like him.

But as soon as the lieutenant walked into Blackjack's briefing, he changed. His head came up, and he looked like he had some of his old spirit back. He was easy with the army types, and got right into the op order. But the real change was when we were set up and dug in on the hill the Army called Horsehead Mountain, and the enemy was coming down the road, with nothing but murder in *his* op order.

The enemy starts up our hill, man, in the hundreds, protected by the ARVN ACPs they took away from the suckers who were supposed to be protecting *us*. Stuart is talking extreme-range solutions with this giant cruiser, the *St. Paul*, nine eight-inch guns. So, they fire, and the first salvo knocks us flat—imagine what it does to the slopes! So Stuart just corrects it a bit, calm as you please, and the Navy just does rock and roll on the whole battlefield for about twelve minutes, which seems like hours. The ground is shaking so bad, Stuart tells me he has to get a look. I'm thinking the next shell is right down our necks, and my knees are weak, but I say OK, let's go. He stands up and sticks his head up, and I grab him from behind, to hold him from falling. My heart is trying to break out of my *chest*! But I am holding him, and I can feel his heart, like it is beating *not at all*!

Well, so Ice is Ice again. But I am glad, Brother, and relieved. Your officer goes crook, and your chances of living go way down. That wife of his must be some bitch to fuck him up like she did, but I know he is OK. Moser knows too. We will be safe with him. He is still almighty sad, but he will still be the best fighting officer we could have.

What a long letter! I just got two of yours. And thanks for the Bible to replace the one I gave to Hunter.

Your loving brother.

Robert

Dear Karen,

I had hoped to find a letter from you in reply to mine of January 2. I don't know what I can give up, or concede, that might make you change your mind. We've had so little time together, yet we loved so well, we dreamed too much together.

We just returned from a great battle on the coast near a place called Sa Huynh. We were successful in destroying an enemy force many times our size, with virtually no casualties of our own. My naval gunfire team played a small role in driving the enemy off.

Karen, I just do not understand your wanting to *give up* so easily! Why can't you give me a small measure of support, or at least take an *interest* in me and my hopes and fears? Must you be only concerned with your *own* needs? Are we not pledged to each other, *married* to each other? Is not my crisis *important* to you?

Oh, my love, disregard that. Come with me to Washington, in a few short months. There are jobs for you in Washington, and friends, and interesting things to see and do. When I get out of the Navy in July of 1969, we'll go back to California, if it's what you wish. Please think about it.

Your loving husband,
William

Stuart wiped his eyes. It's time to find Hooper, he thought. He pulled on his shirt, then picked up his sidearm. Fuck this, he thought, and locked the .45 in his footlocker, and picked up his Stoner and a canvas bandolier of magazines. We're supposed to be armed on this base, he thought; I might as well be really armed. He pushed aside the flap of his hootch and stepped into the damp evening. Coles was standing in front of the hootch.

"Evening, Lieutenant. Want me to mail that?" Coles reached out for the letter in Stuart's hand.

Stuart drew the letter back quickly, "No, thanks, ah, Bobby. I may add a few more thoughts."

"OK, sir. Enjoy your evening."

"Thanks, Sergeant." Stuart caught a ride over to Camp Tien Shaw, then walked slowly toward the Stone Elephant. On his way, he passed along the deep drainage ditch, its bottom littered with garbage. Slowly, he crumpled the letter into a tight ball, and just before entering the officers' club, threw it into the ditch.

Dear Momma,
I have tole you a lot about things out here that are not like

back home. Tonite I want to tell you about the feelin I have about bein in the Navy, and bein a gunfire spotter. I hope this ain't borin but I got to tell you. I saw one of the most beautiful sights of my life a week back or so. And that was a Navy Ship, the cruiser, *St. Paul*.

We were in this fearsom fix, settin atop of a little hill, sposed to be watching for our own Slopes to come up to help us block for the Army comin South drivin the VC before them. I kinda knowed it wasn't goin to work that way, and set my machine gun lookin south but I never dreamed what was goin to happen. This big ole force of Dinks comes boilin up the road to our position. We were on top of this little hill, and they was comin from the south. At first I thot they were the friendlies who were sposed to be blockin the road and the ground to the west, but these boys had no doubt about who we were, and they fell rite to attacking without so much as takin a breth to look us over. We opened up with rifles and machine guns and a few mortars but then they started firin at us with artillery and the Army's own big guns was miles away.

So the L.T. calls for fire, and up comes this big ole cruiser. At first we coulden see the ship cause clouds and rain hid it, but she jest pored in shells and broke the enemys rush. Dinks just disappeared. But then the clouds broke and we seen the cruiser out there four-five miles, spoutin fire and wrapped aroun with her own gunsmoke. 8-inch and 5-inch all goin at once. I pointed the ship out to this army spotter settin next to me and he jest shook his head. Momma, I was so proud to be a gunner's mate in the U.S. Navy, I'd ashipped over another tour on the spot.

Gotta go to chow now. Glad you bin gettin the alotment checks ok.

 Your son,
 Douglas

Dear Joseph,

I didn't get dragged back to Nam, I came here volunteer, and if you think I am crazy to come back, you won't be alone. I just kept thinking about Momma dying that way, while I was in the hospital and didn't even know, and I just couldn't stay home.

It is never going to be easy for you and Henry to understand, but I am here because I want to be, and because I should be. Don't think on it, it is just so.

Don't worry, little brother. Look after things like you always have. We can talk about the farm when I get back.

Sorry, kid. Take care.
Billy

TET

30 January 1968   Camp Tien Shaw

Moser and Hunter and Coles walked to the large EM club near the helicopter pad at Camp Tien Shaw just after 1600. The club was crowded, as many units had come in from the bush for rest due to the truce declared by the enemy in observance of Tet, the Vietnamese lunar new year.

The club was buzzing with rumors of heavy enemy attacks at many points throughout South Vietnam, and the men wondered whether the truce would take effect, or whether the combat troops among them would soon be recalled to the fire bases and strong points they had so recently left.

The ANGLICO team had been inactive since returning to Danang after the Horsehead Mountain action, going out only twice on daylight missions to spot destroyers onto crossroads and trails for nighttime H and I fire. Walker's numerical replacement, a boyish Irishman named Leary, had arrived that afternoon, and Morgan and Cardenas had taken him into Danang, along with the other new men, Roland, Cataldo, and Morris, to the Broken Hand Bar on Da Lat Street to get them properly initiated. Staples and Watts had gone home after the Horsehead Mountain battle, and Morgan himself was down to twenty days and a wake-up, then he would be gone. The three NCOs had said they might join the others later. Stuart reached the bar at

471

the Stone Elephant Officers' Club at 1700, just in time for happy hour. He found Hooper already at the bar, talking to a marine major with black cloth RAMF rank devices sewn to the collar of his starched fatigues. As Stuart joined them and was introduced, the major looked at his watch and finished his drink, said he had to catch the 1730 helo to Monkey Mountain, and departed. Hooper picked up his bottle of Veuve Clicquot Ponsardin in its plastic ice bucket, and headed for a corner table. Stuart picked up two clean glasses and followed.

"Fuckin' major is on Third MAF staff. Going to Monkey Mountain, and he thinks he's going into the bush," said Hooper, pouring the champagne.

"Didn't think you talked to RAMFs, Hoop," said Stuart, as they clinked glasses.

"I don't, normally, but the hump bought the bottle. He could see by my somewhat disheveled appearance that I was a number one strack warrior, and he wanted some pointers about dealing death to the hated Cong."

"I hope you set him straight."

"Nah! Lied to him. He did tell me, however, that intelligence is feeling some strange, *major* inklings that Tet may not be the quiet period we had been expecting." Hooper drank deeply, and refilled his glass. Stuart had taken only one small sip.

"I heard this morning that Khe Sanh had gone quiet.'

"Not so. The NVA has been working that shithole over for ten days, and the marines tell me it's even hotter than the first Khe Sanh battle last spring."

Stuart drank a little more. I am losing my taste for this stuff, he thought. "Where else is getting hit?"

"According to the good major, enemy probes, heavy ones, have been reported in the Quang Tri area and up in the Leatherneck Square, and at Pleiku and Kontum in the highlands, *and* in the delta, not too many klicks from Saigon."

Stuart waved to a passing waiter and ordered a gin and tonic. When it came, he found he didn't like the taste of it either. "What is the major going to do about all this enemy activity?"

Hooper emptied his glass, and shrugged. "Didn't say. Officially it's just probes, with no real evidence of coordination. Officially the truce is being observed, albeit unofficially, of course."

Stuart smiled, and nodded. Every year the VC announce a truce, and every year the U.S. and the government of Vietnam refuse to acknowledge the truce, yet it had generally been observed by both sides.

"Hoop, you think something's up?"

Hooper drank. "Yep, ole Hoop think something up, Bro." Hooper talked an imitation of black talk when he felt philosophical. "Hoop think a ton o' excrement be very close to the air-conditioning."

"Do he?" replied Stuart.

"Yep. My Sealies are in town fornicating, Bro me, but they're armed, and been told to go easy on drink, and no smoke. They can watch, but stay together. Yours?"

Stuart shifted in the seat. "Not so well deployed, I'm afraid. Some in the Broken Hand, some here."

Hooper lit a Dunhill cigarette, and passed the pack to Stuart, who screwed one into his holder and lit it. "Shit go down, Willie, I'll get the ones in the Broken Hand, and make 'em into SEALs." Hooper laughed. He turned toward the bar to yell for another bottle when the phone behind the bar cut through the din of the drinkers with its loud, shrill ring. Old Minh, the senior Vietnamese boy, answered, and put the phone down. The noise died away as Minh approached a gray-haired marine colonel at the bar, and motioned him to the phone. The colonel listened, and hung up, then raised his voice. "Listen up, you men. LISTEN UP! Danang perimeter is under attack, so is Monkey Mountain, so is Chu Lai and Phu Bai. Return to your units and listen to Third MAF net. We are undergoing large-scale attack. Move out!"

There was a noise like a freight train, but rising in pitch and volume, from outside the club building, followed by an enormous crash and echo. Windows blew into the club, and dust and smoke choked the air. Stuart was thrown backward in his chair and onto his back on the floor. A sharp pain stung the back of his skull. Hooper stood up as another crash erupted on the other side of the club. Everyone not already down hit the deck.

Hooper knelt quickly next to Stuart. "Those were one-twenty-two-millimeter rockets, buddy buck. We are under serious attack."

Stuart levered himself up to a sitting position, and rubbed his neck. "No shit. We got to get moving."

Hooper grinned. "They comin' into the open, Troop. Plenty kill-kill for our side."

Stuart got to his feet. He felt a bit dizzy from the blow. "But the fuckers are inside the perimeter of *fucking Danang!* This place is supposed to be rear of the rear!"

Hooper's grin was mean and wolfish. "I'm going after my Sealies. *Plenty* kill-kill. You want to come?"

Stuart shook his head. He and Hooper were the only ones standing in the crowded club. More rockets landed and rocked the building. "I'll get my men here. We'll be needed to bring down guns and bombs."

Hooper shoved a magazine into his Stoner. "Good luck, Bro." He slipped out the front door of the club, on the run.

My men will come here, thought Stuart; that's our doctrine. At least Coles, and Moser, and Hunter if they haven't gone into the ville. He inserted a magazine into his own Stoner, eased the selector to stitch, and stepped outside. The night sky was bright with flares, and over toward Danang, heavy artillery and rockets. Holy shit, they are really in our faces.

Coles, Moser, and Hunter departed the darkened EM club on a dead run. We got to get Ice from the O club, thought Bobby. We got to get to the lieutenant, and to our radios. The sky is falling.

Billy Hunter sprinted through the darkened alleys of the camp, avoiding the areas brightly lit by many fires. He had been detailed as a runner by Stuart to try to reach the emergency command post at the military police barracks behind the line of warehouses that split the camp roughly in half, and was now on his way back. The first VC rocket barrage to hit the area earlier in the evening had knocked out electrical power and the camp's telephone system, and Stuart, Moser, and Coles, along with a mixed bag of cooks, bartenders, and patrons, were pinned down without a battlefield radio in the Stone Elephant Officers' Club just across the main square of the camp from Hunter's present position.

Billy ducked into a doorway as a short burst of light machine gun fire swept up the alley and away to the right. With no light other than the fires and the sudden and sporadic flashes of gunfire, there was no way of knowing whether the gunfire was friendly or not. As confused as things were, Hunter reckoned he stood as good a chance of being cut down by his own people as by the enemy. No one, either at the Stone Elephant or at the military police barracks, knew how many enemy soldiers had penetrated the camp, and the Americans were jittery and trigger-happy after the rocket attacks.

Hunter shifted quickly out of the doorway and zig-zagged another forty yards to dive behind an overturned and smouldering jeep. Not much cover. Machine-gun bullets rent the metal siding of the building behind him, and he flattened himself yet further into the gritty concrete.

The news he was bringing back from the military police barracks wasn't good. The enemy seemed to be everywhere. The colonel directing what remained of camp defenses from the military police headquarters had reports of heavy damage done to the airfields in Danang, and of attacks all the way down Highway One to Saigon. There were even rumors that the American embassy had been breached, and worse, that main force NVA units had overrun parts of the army's huge bases at Bien Hoa and Long Binh. The colonel could offer no relief to Stuart and the others, telling them through Hunter that they should gather all men carrying weapons and work their way down to help *him*.

The ground before Hunter was open now, about seventy yards across the square, to the front of the Stone Elephant, which he had left only forty minutes before. It was too far to do in one sprint. There was a blackened truck, still burning slightly, in the middle of the square that had shielded him on his way out. The square was quiet, but in the middle distance bullets and shells from many different types of weapons cracked, rattled, and roared. Billy couldn't guess the direction of any of the fire because of the continuous noise.

A breeze from the southeast, wet with light rain, was blowing the guttering flames on the truck away from Hunter, so that the side of the truck closest to him was in darkness. He decided to chance a stop at the truck.

Billy Hunter launched himself from behind the jeep and was quickly at full speed. He ran crouched through the darkness, putting on every move he had ever learned playing football, and prayed he wouldn't trip over something unseen. Ten yards from the burning truck he heard a machine gun open up from ahead, and saw the tracers flashing over his head like darts of fire. He dove headlong for the ground behind the truck. The bullet struck him in the right side of his abdomen with such force that it lifted him in a somersault and drove him backward onto his knees.

Almost immediately after Stuart had sent Hunter to the command post, he and his pickup squad of cooks, bartenders, and three rather drunk supply officers had been driven from the refuge of the Stone Elephant. It was as strong a building as existed at Tien Shaw, and was sandbagged outside up to six feet off the ground. The rocket barrage intensified and the building began to shake and crumble from accurate fire from the south and west, from the area around Monkey Mountain. Stuart decided their chances were decidedly better out in the streets.

He now had ten men; only Coles, Moser, and he had combat experience. They had a total of eleven weapons, all .45-caliber military-issue automatic pistols except Moser's .50-caliber machine gun, Coles's M-16, Stuart's Stoner, and Stuart's backup

7.65mm Walther automatic. He formed the men into a rough squad with Moser leading on point and Coles herding stragglers from the rear. He wished to hell Hunter would get back to stiffen up the middle.

Stuart decided to follow a deep drainage ditch that led around from behind the officers' club to the end of the line of warehouses and barracks that separated them from the military police barracks. He thought it likely that VC sappers would have infiltrated into the ditch, perhaps mining it or at least leaving punji stakes at the bottom. He discussed this with the men, and instructed them to use only the upper lip of the ditch as cover should they come under fire. There was a path about a foot below the top of the ditch that should be easy for the men to follow and would afford some protection to a prone man. Stuart could see that his noncombatants were thoroughly frightened, but at least they were calm. Moser led the squad out the side door and onto the path inside the ditch.

There were no fires next to the Stone Elephant, but a lot of dense smoke. The men made good progress through the darkness, and the path proved smooth. They reached a point directly behind the warehouse at the end of the long line that split the camp. Coles got the men down on their bellies and crept them forward, while Moser crossed the alley in a silent rush. Moser waited a full two minutes before giving a hand sign for a cautious advance. Stuart stepped forward along one wall of the alley, keeping pace with Moser on the other. Coles got the others up and started along in two columns. The second man in each column was just stepping over the edge of the ditch when the night was hacked open with blinding and deafening force by a four-inch searchlight and the roar and clank of an armored vehicle advancing into the alley, followed half a heartbeat later by the clatter and boom of the vehicle's machine guns.

Stuart and Moser compressed themselves into the horizontal corners between the sidewalks and walls on opposite sides of the alley. Coles dropped back onto the path and immediately opened fire at the searchlight. The first four men up behind Coles froze and were cut to pieces by the machine gun fire. The three men behind them were suddenly covered in the blood and flesh of the men who had been right in front of them; as one, they recoiled in horror, stepped back, and tumbled into the ditch. A flat report and a blast of heat from the bottom of the ditch told Coles that an antivehicle mine left by the VC had blown them to hamburger. Coles fired again and the light shattered and died.

With the searchlight gone, Stuart could identify the vehicle as an American ACAV, but the excited squeals from the crew told him it was no longer in American hands. Moser had the big fifty working across the alley, and Stuart took cover behind a long burst to cross and join him, just as Stuart knew Moser expected him to do. They had some protection from behind a badly bent dumpster. Stuart could hear the sharp cracking of Coles's rifle, but no other firing behind him.

Hunter felt paralyzed as he looked up at the thick clouds above, pushed along by the southeast monsoon. The bullet wound was first felt as a stunning blow, not sharp, not acutely painful, but numbing his entire torso. Then he sensed he could feel the bullet's passage through his body, but very slowly, like a thin rod of white-hot iron thrust into his right side just below the ribs, then straight through his diaphragm and lung and to his back, and out. But the track of the bullet began to scream as the iron rod burned. He tried to rise, but he could not feel his legs. In time he realized they were bent beneath him at the knees. He listened for a while to the quiet square, then carefully rolled over toward the burning truck. The pain rolled through his body in waves. He knew that the wound would have left an exit wound in his back far larger than the iron rod he could feel, and he thought vaguely that he should try to stop the bleeding until help arrived. He felt sleepy. It was hard to concentrate on anything in the face of the pain. He heard a fuzzy clatter of automatic weapons fire to his right and behind him—nearby but how near? The noise grew to an angry buzz and he lost consciousness.

The captured scout had stopped firing. Stuart thought he had seen a man at the machine gun on the top of the vehicle go down just as the light went out. Moser stopped firing, and inserted his last belt. Coles had come up to join the other two behind the dumpster. Minutes passed with no sound other than the revving of the carrier's engine and the clanking of gears, punctuated by the random single round harassing fire from Moser's machine gun. Twenty minutes passed, then an hour.

"Coles."

"Yessir?"

"The others?"

"All down. Dead. The last three went down into the ditch and tripped a mine."

"Jesus."

"You tried, sir."

"Yeah, but what a mess. The poor bastards."

"Sir, do you think we oughta rush it?" asked Moser, quietly.

"The vehicle? No. The machine guns aren't manned, near as I can see, but there may be infantry behind the vehicle."

"They seem to be having trouble running the thing," said Coles.

"Moser, you got any grenades?" asked Stuart.

"Just two frags. That track's thirty yards off."

"Give one to Bobby. Bobby, try to arch it high. I'll give you covering fire. Moser, get set to pick off anything that sticks a head out."

Coles rose from his belly to his knees, and pulled himself to a crouch behind the dumpster. Stuart fired the Stoner on full auto—a burst at the top of the scout, then two short bursts around the tracks to discourage any infantry who might be hiding around the vehicle's skirts. Coles came to full standing quickly and hurled the grenade like a baseball, just the way you are taught not to do it. The clank of the grenade hitting the roof of the scout and the explosion came almost together. Screams and more frantic clanking of gears, then the ACAV lurched into reverse and banged into the left alley wall, caromed, and backed off another thirty yards before stopping with the rear of the track against the right alley wall. Four soldiers in green uniforms jumped out of the way as the carrier backed up, and the fifty barked twice.

"Got two, sir," said Moser.

The carrier had been motionless, engine idling, for an hour. Stuart, Coles, and Moser had ceased to fire, mindful of a dwindling supply of ammunition. Stuart suspected the Vietnamese had the same concern.

"What do we do now, sir?" asked Coles.

"We wait, and they wait. By dawn, either our people will get here, or theirs will."

Coles turned his luminous watch dial cautiously toward him. "I make dawn in about two hours."

"You guys take ten-minute turns closing your eyes."

Billy Hunter felt and smelled the dawn before he could see it. He had drifted in and out of consciousness but his eyes remained closed. He could smell smoke from burning fuel and rubber, and from gunfire. He could hear distant gunfire, and nearer, an idling engine. He could taste only thirst. He could feel dampness on his face and neck, and that feeling was dawn. He knew he was dying.

"Bi-lee!" the voice was soft, musical, like the belling of a wind chime. "Bi-lee!"

Nga, thought Billy. He spoke her name inside his head.

"Bi-lee, you came back! You did! You are so close, now. Let go, come to Nga."

Billy gritted his teeth and shut his eyes tight against the pain. I gotta get to the guys.

The gray light of first dawn turned the armored vehicle into a more distinct shape. The engine coughed twice and died. The pink-pink of the cooling radiator made the only sounds, and then the insects and birds began.

"They must've gone, sir," whispered Moser.

"Somebody shut off that engine," said Coles, sighting his rifle on the empty driver's hatch.

"Maybe outa gas."

"There's not a sound. No firing. They might have pulled back," said Stuart.

"I'll go up and look," said Coles.

"You left, me right. Moser, kill anything that moves on or near that thing, and watch behind you."

"Yessir."

"Give Bobby that last grenade."

Coles slid more than walked along the left alley wall, his rifle cradled in his left elbow. Stuart walked just far enough off the right wall to allow him to train the Stoner fully. At twenty feet from the scout, both stopped, and Stuart gave Bobby a thumbs-up. Coles ran up five more feet and lobbed the grenade into the open hatch of the scout. Both men hit the ground as the grenade exploded with a dull clang inside the vehicle. The insects and birds stopped, then started again. Stuart ran to the right of the scout and checked behind and underneath. Coles jumped up and thrust his rifle into the still-smoking open hatch. He stepped back quickly.

"Strawberry jam, sir. But I think they were already dead."

"There are four dead behind the scout, one of them crushed by the track," replied Stuart.

"Jesus, that's over!"

"Moser! Let's move out! We'll backtrack Hunter, then try to find some American forces!"

Billy Hunter heard a grenade explode nearby and forced his eyes open. The flames from the truck were low now, more smoke than fire. He closed his eyes again and rejoined the shimmering vision of Nga. She held her tiny hands out to him, inches away, and smiled her beautiful, sad smile.

"It's all right, Bi-lee, you come back, we will be together at last. Let go, Bi-lee, Nga will catch you."

"Nga, I gotta get back to my unit. I gotta tell 'em where to go."

Nga smiled, flickered, and faded. Don't leave me! thought Billy. "That's all right, Bi-lee. Soon, all your friends dead, then we all be together. Let go, Bi-lee!" Her arms beckoned.

Billy forced his eyes open. Advancing very slowly through the smoke and guttering flames Billy could see what appeared to be three figures, and the tall one in the middle carried over his shoulder what looked to be a cross.

Billy Hunter let go.

Coles and Moser lifted Billy Hunter's body gently onto a crude stretcher they had fashioned from a wooden door that had been blown off its hinges. Coles took off his shirt and covered Hunter's face and chest. Coles felt the death of Hunter as actual physical pain in his abdomen, and he had to steel himself against a whimper that lay trapped in his throat. Moser laid his big machine gun carefully next to the body, and took the front end of the door. Coles slung his M-16, and took the rear.

With Lieutenant Stuart taking the point, the three men walked carefully through the deserted camp down toward the military police barracks. What had been an unattainable objective on the previous night would now be a ten-minute walk. Stuart watched for booby traps and pointed out unexploded grenades and shells to Moser and Coles. Shell casings were everywhere along with other debris of war, bits of clothing, and trash. There were very few bodies, mostly those of Vietnamese nationals who had worked in the camp. Stuart knew he should check the bodies, but he didn't. Stuart guessed that American casualties had been light, because the camp had been nearly empty. Tien Shaw was a transient camp, and most of the transients were elsewhere for the holiday occasioned by the Tet cease-fire.

Coles is really cut up about Hunter, thought Stuart. They knew each other since way back. What do I feel? Hunter was the first real military comrade I had, back at Camp Pettigrew, a hundred years ago in the world. Hunter is the first man under my direct command to be killed. Even though he wasn't with the AN-GLICO long, he had fit in. A strangely private man, despite the aw-shucks, good-ole-boy demeanor. Always a volunteer, always helpful, and last night it got him killed.

Or did I get him killed? thought Stuart. Maybe the mission was just too risky. Maybe I should have kept the guys together. But what the hell do I know, I was never trained for this infantry shit. I should have kept the guys together. How lonely Hunter must have felt, dying out there all those hours, bravely trying to block the massive exit wound in his back with his cloth cap in his hand. I wonder if he was in great pain. He must have been in pain.

Coles carried his end of the door with his wrists flexed, trying to cushion any jolts. Why am I doing that? he thought. Billy can't feel anything anymore. Moser took a long step over a crater left by a mortar round, and the door jounced. Instinctively Coles flexed his wrists and dampened the impact.

I got Billy into the unit, thought Coles. Pulled strings, I did, conned the lieutenant into requesting him from the replacement pool. Billy and I figured he'd be a hell of a lot safer with us spotting gunfire than going back to the DMZ. Why did he come back here at all? Surely he didn't have to, but he begged me to get him into the ANGLICO, and I did. So back here, safe in the rear with us, death catches him on the first pass.

Moser kept his eyes on the ground ahead, watching for things not to step on, and nodding when the lieutenant pointed something out. Moser felt sad abut Hunter dying back there, but he couldn't focus on the sadness. Anger boiled in his mind, anger at the ambush and the results. These bastards just kill, they don't fight, thought Moser. Killers, not soldiers. Just came into the camp in the middle of their own cease-fire, and killed people. Those seven guys from the Stone Elephant weren't killed in a fair fight, they were just shot down by these bastards while holding onto guns they didn't know how to use.

We shouldn't have stayed pinned down by that ACAV, thought Coles. We were waiting it out safe, long after the firing stopped, while Billy lay dying not twenty meters away.

The military police barracks was surrounded by men in all variations of uniform—some in full battle dress, some in skivvies, some in various states in between. There was even a man in a flannel bathrobe; Stuart recognized him as a chaplain who had been with the *Dubuque*. His arm was crudely bandaged and slinged, but he moved among the wounded and the merely stunned.

There was a big tent with the sides rolled up set up as an aid station next to the barracks. Men lay on stretchers in long rows. Many had sheets or blankets covering them. Casualties not so light after all, thought Stuart.

"Coles, Moser, take Hunter's—take Billy over there, guys. I'll go and report us in."

"Aye, sir," said Moser. Coles just nodded. God, he feels the pain, thought Stuart.

Inside the barracks, men and officers sat around looking like shocked victims of a great disaster. Many were bandaged. Stuart saw that the somewhat fussy MP captain who had run the military police had been replaced at the commander's desk by a crisp, flinty-looking marine lieutenant colonel. Stuart stood until he was noticed, then saluted.

"Stuart, Colonel. Seventh ANGLICO, with two men."

The colonel returned the salute without rising. "Sit down, Stuart. Where are the rest of your men?"

"One killed in action last night, sir. Trying to bring word back to us from here. The other six were all on liberty in Danang when it hit." Stuart sat.

The colonel looked at Stuart, and noted the dark rings under his eyes, the smoke smudges smeared with sweat. "Your men will be gathered, Lieutenant. The enemy has pulled back from Danang." The colonel looked closely, "Can your two men and you move up? We may well need navy gun."

"Yes, sir!" Better to fight just now than think, thought Stuart.

"Very well. The enemy has cut the road north in a few places between here and Phu Loc, but we'll clear that, Lieutenant. Danang is safe, for the moment. We're gathering all available forces to go and aid the marines who will retake Hue, where the enemy is holed up in strength."

Hue! thought Stuart. The enemy holds the old capital! Incredible!

"Your men will be needed, Lieutenant," continued the colonel, his voice very even.

Stuart realized he had been drifting. "We are ready to go, Colonel, if we can get back to our HQ on the marine base and pick up our radios and spotting gear."

"Sergeant Moran will send someone. Give him the location. Rest your men, get them fed. It is oh-six-hundred now, we will move at oh-nine-hundred. Use the three hours well, Stuart."

"Aye, aye, sir." Once again Stuart saluted, and left the barracks.

Moser and Coles waited just outside. "Is Billy, ah, all right?"

"Yes, sir," said Coles. "They said just put him down. Moser and I found a place in the shade."

"OK, Coles. Moser. Let's go and get some breakfast. I want to talk to you both."

The men sat down on the scrubby grass near the field kitchen, plates piled high with pancakes, scrambled eggs, and sausages. Stuart felt sick and without appetite, but his first bite changed that, and he ate hungrily. He watched as Coles and Moser did the same. They finished the meal in silence, drank coffee, and smoked.

"We have three hours. Do you men feel like sleeping?"

"Ah, no, sir," said Moser.

"Maybe after awhile, sir," said Coles.

"OK. Now, this is irregular, but I have to ask you this, as men, as fighters, not as enlisted men to an officer. Was I wrong to send Billy out to get down here, and back to us?"

Coles and Moser looked puzzled at the question. This isn't really fair, thought Stuart. I am trying to share my responsibility.

Coles put down the plastic coffee cup. "No, sir. We had to report. Hunter had the best legs, and he volunteered." Coles stopped, thought. "It never occurred to me you shouldn't have sent him, sir."

"He could run like the wind, sir," said Moser.

"I just hate to think how he was cut down so close to us, and we didn't know," said Stuart.

"Sir, if we had known he was there, we would have charged that ACAV, wouldn't we?" said Coles.

"Jesus, yes! We would have *gone*!" Stuart looked thoughtfully at the pained expressions on the two men's faces. "Maybe we should have charged it anyway."

"No," said Moser, firmly. "We didn't have any idea where he was at. If'n we had, you'd led us, and we'da follered."

"That's right, sir," said Coles. "You would've been the first to help a downed marine, especially one of yours. And you know you would never have had to look around to see if we were following."

Thank you, thank you. But the hurt remains. "We take care of each other, men. We have, and we will."

"Yes, sir!" Coles and Moser together, smiling through the pain. If they are this courageous, thought Stuart, then I must try to be.

"You're right, men. So, look. At oh-nine-hundred we and the rest of this pickup team are going up north to help relieve Hue. So see to your gear, and try to get some rest."

"Yes, sir!"

"Good."

"Sir?"

"Yes, Moser?"

"We are the Seventh ANGLICO, sir."

"That we are, Troop. And we have a job to do, and a score to settle." Stuart got up from the little conference, and walked back to the mess tent.

Moser looked at Coles, and saw the pain and fear in the sergeant's eyes. "We gonna be fine, Bobby. We bin there, we're good."

Coles managed a smile at the big man. "On to hell, Moser, or to glory."

Dear Simon,

We are about to go into action to counterattack the enemy, who hit U.S. bases all up and down Vietnam during his Tet cease-fire. You will have heard all about it on the news long before you get this letter.

We are supposed to be resting now, but none of us can sleep. None of us! There are only three of the ten-man ANGLICO unit left—Stuart, Moser, and me. Most of the rest of the guys were on liberty in Danang town when the enemy struck, so we don't know where they are or if they are o k, and won't be able to find out until this operation is over. But Billy Hunter, my friend from Pendleton, was killed last night while trying to run a message for us.

My heart is so sore, Simon. That is why I have to write. I have seen people hurt and killed since nearly the first day I got over here, even guys right next to me, but it never felt so personal, so close to *me*. So there are some things I have felt that you should know about.

Hunter and I were friends, and we were made close by the shared experience of early military training. We did a lot of stuff together at Pendleton, but lost touch afterward. Billy went to Nam before me, and we never saw each other in the eight months or so I have been in country. Billy was hurt bad in his last night operation up near the DMZ, and spent nearly five months in the naval hospital in Oakland, then just showed up one day with a group of replacements in Danang. He didn't have to come back; he volunteered, and he never told me why he volunteered, but it seemed important to him to be here. I got him into our outfit because we both figured he would be safe with us. I know I have told you about some fairly hairy things the ANGLICO has seen and done, but we are not *supposed* to be front-line troops, and none of our guys has gotten killed since Jackson, way back before Lt. Stuart took over.

Well, Brother, all this history is to tell you that I have very complex feelings about Billy Hunter's death. First I felt guilty because I got him into the unit. I already know that's silly. Then I felt real sad and angry that I had been deprived of such a good friend, but as you can see from the above, we weren't really that close, even though it feels like we were. And then

I felt a little envious because Billy died the best of military deaths, that of the unselfish hero. I think that the major fear of a lot of the guys is that they will buy it by stepping on a land mine while walking into the bush to take a piss. But I reject that, too, because I want to be alive.

So now I really don't know what I think. I still feel the pain, but less. I guess that pain is really for me, and not for Billy. I am suddenly very afraid of dying, and not only of dying, but of dying badly, because Billy died so well, so bravely, and we all saw it. And, Brother, I also know that if losing Billy hurts this bad, losing Stuart or Moser would be crippling to me.

So I still hurt, and I guess I will for a while. But I am calmer and less scared; talking to you always helped me to know myself, even, as now, when I don't hear your answers. I will be ready to do the job when we go, and right now I am ready for an hour's sleep.

Your loving brother,
Robert

Dear Momma,

We are setting in the shade, drinkin coffee and tryin to unnerstand what hurts in each one of us. Billy Hunter, a new sargint and a friend of the L.T. and Sargint Coles, got hisself kilt last nite. He got kilt when he was doin' a run back to try to get us some help while the L.T. and Sargint Coles and me was fightin our way down a back trail with the enemy bangin away from all sides and at the last, from in front. We broke them Momma, but Im still angry. We had with us a handful of cooks and clerks and like that, military but not real soljers, and the L.T. thot they would be safer with us than alone, but they all got kilt, ever sorry one.

I never really hated til las nite. I allus figgered that in war you could mebbe cheat a little bit but the enemy tole us, tole all the Americans and even our own Vetmanese that they needed a cease fire to pray to there ancestors and visit with there dead. So in the first hour of the nite, the first nite of the cease fire, they attackd our men in there beds. Many died. The L.T. led us out of it but we had all those dead. Not men I knew, and not fighters, but Americans. And then we lost Sargint Hunter.

I never really got to know this Billy Hunter, Momma, he sassed me a lot about bein big, and carrin a big gun. He sassed everbody; I guess it was jest his way. But I cry for him. He was one of us.

The L.T. hurts real bad. He was allus real proud he never lost anyone. Not at least kilt. Now he has, I kin see him, ten feet from me, writing. I know he is writing about this. I wisht I could tell him I know it was never his fault.

In an hour or so we be goin north, up Highway 1. We have to crack the slopes out of this place Hue, the ole imperiel city. Otherwise the protestors will say we got beat.

I guess this is as good a time as any to tell you Momma. I shipped over. Im goin to stay in the Navy and one day I will be a CHIEF. When I signed the papers for another 4 years, they give me six more months in country, so I will be here til the L.T. goes home, lessen he extends agin, in which case I will. I wisht I could do more for the L.T., he is a good man. And for the sargint. I never partickly cottoned on to the blacks, but Coles is fair, and a good Marine.

Ill get home soon, Momma. Dont you fret.

Your son,
Douglas

Dear Henry and Joseph,

By now you will have been informed of the sad news of your brother William's death in action in Vietnam. I had the honor of being Billy's last commander, and I wish to assure you, he died bravely, as befitted a proud Marine. I realize you may find in that little comfort, but I believe bravery and honor meant a great deal to your brother. His bravery and his spirit meant more to me than I can ever explain.

Sergeant Hunter was always ready to volunteer for any dangerous assignment, and he consistently placed the welfare of his comrades above his own. Last night we were separated from main units by an enemy attack, and William volunteered to go back to headquarters with word of our condition. While returning to us through enemy lines, he was killed.

William was a brave man and a good comrade. His other friends and I share your grief and send our condolences.

With deepest sympathy,
William M. Stuart
Lieutenant, USNR

I thought I would feel better after I wrote that, thought Stuart, but I sure don't. The truth is, Henry and Joseph, that I sent your brother on a mission that was just too dangerous, and he died in great pain because I didn't want to rush a scout vehicle manned by soldiers already dead. I wonder how combat commanders deal with the guilt. One mistake, and good men die. Maybe that explains why Blackjack Beaurive was so cut up about Major Danby. What was a staff major doing riding on a lead tank?

Stuart sealed the letter, and got to his feet. Coles was sprawled out on the ground fast asleep. Stuart saw an envelope addressed to Coles's brother in Los Angeles, and gently plucked it off Bobby's chest. Moser got up from his place by a banyan tree and stepped in front of Stuart.

"I'll take the letters, sir. I'm goin' ta get me a col' drink."

"Ok, Moser, thanks. Get me one too, if you find anything."

"What do you want, sir?"

"Anything cold." Stuart sat down next to Moser's tree and dozed. He opened his eyes with a start and saw Moser had returned. Almost hidden in one huge hand were three cans of San Miguel beer.

"Where did you find beer at seven o'clock in the morning, Moser?"

"Sailor kin always find what he needs around gyrenes, sir."

In other words, don't ask, thought Stuart. Beer did taste good, though. "That third can for Coles?"

"Well, if'n he wakes up, hit shore is. If'n he keeps on a'sleepin, and it starts to get warm, why, I'll jest drink it for him, and tell him how good it tasted when he wakes up." Moser grinned at Stuart.

He is trying to cheer me up, thought Stuart, and grinned back. He tilted up the beer can and poured the remainder of the wonderful drink down his throat, savoring the last mouthful with his eyes closed. He was instantly asleep.

31 January 1968   Danang

Coles, Stuart, and Moser stood in a circle, looking outward from the four-foot-deep fighting hole in the middle of the makeshift NDP. All around them, the ragtag force of pickups—soldiers, sailors, marines, airmen, mostly from noncombat specialties—dug and swore and chattered excitedly in the quickly falling darkness. Low monsoon clouds scudded up from the southeast, driven by a warm wind, alternately black and translucent to the sliver of the new moon, spraying the camp with fine drizzle and torrential downpours.

Harried officers walked to and fro, checking weapons and ammunition, trying to quiet the men. They were going up Highway One in the morning, to aid and stiffen the marines investing the citadel of the old imperial capital of Hue, to do what they could. The officers were trying to put the night defensive position into some sense of order. It was well within what had previously been considered a secure perimeter, but the enemy had been driven out of Danang and Camp Tien Shaw and the surrounding bases only twelve hours before, leaving heavy casualties. No one knew the enemy's intentions, and the officers assigned to lead this group of disparate and largely inexperienced men didn't want to risk anything, so they tried to form the encampment into something approaching a field NDP.

"At least we know what the fuck we're doing," commented Coles, quietly.

Stuart screwed a cigarette into his black holder and lit it carefully, shielding the flame behind his hand and below the rim of the foxhole. He slumped onto the bottom of the hole to smoke. The other men moved to make room. "Coles, Moser, I want to talk about Billy Hunter."

"Morale talk, sir?" asked Coles, as he stared into the night. At least we are away from the main body of these cooks and clerks, if their noise and light draws a rocket, he thought.

"No, Bobby, I'm all out of morale. Just talk."

Coles shifted down the slope of the hole and sat beside Stuart. He looked for expression on the lieutenant's face, but the light was too dim. Moser continued to man the fifty, sandbagged in, at the lip of the hole. "What you thinking, man?"

Stuart blew a cloud of smoke skyward. "I think Billy's dying like that, with us so close and not knowing, well, I think it closed a chapter for me."

They sat in silence. Coles broke in. "He was special to all of us."

"Because we knew him, before, in the World. He seemed to be the best of us," said Stuart. He looked at Coles, almost invisible beside him. "Yeah. I never told you. At SERE, a hundred years ago, he was simply the best. The toughest, the most resourceful, the best." Stuart took a long drag on his cigarette. "Just that. He had hope. We had hope. We felt we were fighting for something important."

"Or maybe we just told ourselves that, sir."

"Maybe you're right. Maybe we've been painting a picture around our motives. Ourselves."

Stuart and Coles lapsed into silence again. Both stared at the big, dark shape of Moser's back. Moser had worked closer to Billy than either of them since he had come into the ANGLICO, but neither Coles nor Stuart knew just how Moser felt. He was always so reluctant to speak. Moser stared into the night.

"You know, man," said Coles, slowly, "I wish we had a

bottle of wine, or even a joint, something to share in communion, about Billy.'' Moser's big shoulders seemed to shake, just a little.

''Good idea. Yes. Hey Moser. Moser?''

''Sir.''

''You always got a beer or two in your pack.'' Softly, softly, thought Stuart.

''Slide down here, man,'' said Coles. ''VC will make some noise before they get this far in.''

Moser waited a full minute, then turned and scrunched down into the hole. There was so little space, the three men found themselves touching each other, shoulder to shoulder, thighs to thighs. Each was aware of the warmth of the other in the chill of the tropic winter night, and the smells—dirt and sweat, and warmth.

''Only one,'' said Moser.

''Drink it yourself, man,'' said Coles, very softly. ''Your big body runs on beer.''

''No, Sergeant, let's share it out, like the lieutenant said.''

Stuart handed his box of cigarettes to Coles. ''Let's just take one, Lieutenant, pass it around; Moser and I don't really smoke, anyway,'' said Bobby, pulling one smoke from the box and handing it back.

Moser opened the beer carefully with his C-rat can opener. ''Take a sip, Bobby, an' pass it.''

Each man took a sip. The cigarette followed the can around, cupped hand to cupped hand. ''We mourn for Billy Hunter, comrade and friend,'' said Stuart. It sounded stilted, but it felt right.

''Yo,'' said Coles.

''Fuckin' A,'' said Moser, barely audible. They finished the cigarette, and nursed the only beer.

''You know, guys, when my wife sent me that letter, I thought I just wanted to die.''

''You shoulda left sir,'' said Moser, with a hint of passion.

''I wanted to, at first. But not to go back there; I guess I knew it was finished. But I wanted to leave because I felt unworthy of you guys.''

''Why, man?'' said Coles, rolling a tiny sip of beer around his tongue.

''I felt unmanned. We spend a lot of energy, here, being men, men of honor. I felt she took that.''

Another silence. Coles passed the beer. Nobody was really drinking it, so he guessed they all wanted to talk. ''Why do you think you came out here, sir? I mean, what do you think it meant to you?''

Stuart lit another cigarette. "I didn't think about it, really, not until tonight. I think I came out here because I wanted to prove something about myself—that I'm a man, and better. It sounds really stupid, even to me; and worse, it sounds selfish. I think I wanted to be a hero of some sort."

Coles chewed on that. "Not just for yourself. For your wife."

"No, man! She hates this shit! It's why she, ah, left me."

"No, it ain't, man. Somethin' like this ain't why a woman leaves. Strays, maybe, but not leaves."

Stuart was glad the inky darkness hid his face, which was hot with anger, and shame. "How do you mean that, Bobby?"

"I wanted to say this to you before, when you got the Dear John, sir, but I just couldn't. Maybe I should just shut up and say I'm sorry, sir."

"No, I want to hear. I do." I think I do, thought Stuart.

Coles sighed, and shifted a cramped leg. "Lieutenant, you had that woman so high on a pedestal, you couldn't see. You hadda be bigger than life for her, regardless of what she thought. You would have rather gone home dead with a Medal of Honor than alive as a failure."

Stuart closed his eyes and thought. "Jesus. She said almost the same thing to me, once."

"Yeah," said Coles, and passed the tepid beer back to Stuart. "You know, Lieutenant, you're a strange man, in some ways. Most guys trying to look like heroes, they're assholes. But not you. You really tried, for the men under you. You still do." Bobby paused; this is hard to say, he thought, but why? "I respect you, sir, and I guess I'm sorry I didn't always show that, at least at first. You are the best, and I hate that woman for bringin' you down."

"Thanks, man, I guess," said Stuart. I can't hate her, he thought. We share the guilt.

"No, sir, I mean it. When you started coming apart, after that letter, I was afraid. So was Moser, hey Moser? I always knew you would never use us up, just to look good, like some officers we have seen." Bobby was appalled at what he had just said.

Stuart spoke softly. "Thanks, Bobby. Why didn't you tell me? It would have helped in a difficult time."

"Sir—"

"Leave off the 'sir' please. I want to feel close with you two, and with Billy."

"Sir, OK. But I don't feel right, calling you by your first name. Let me call you what the men—your men—call you, sir, with affection and pride."

"What's that?"

"Ice. We call you Ice, as in cool, at least the black dudes do."

Stuart chuckled. "Blackjack told me that, once. I never believed it."

"Nobody believed what you did, with the air spot in the Elephant, Ice."

Stuart laughed, softly. "Ice. OK, Ice. So why didn't you tell me?"

Coles sipped the warm beer, just a drop, and passed it to Moser, who sat in dark silence. "Maybe now you're asking about me."

"Maybe."

Coles looked up at the pale moon above thin clouds. "OK, for Billy. I couldn't approach you; you were going crazy. I went to Lieutenant Hooper. I'm sorry, sir, but, I just couldn't say it."

"It's OK. Someone had to straighten me out."

"So now you're still here, instead of being back in the World."

Stuart chuckled, sipping the beer. He looked at Coles, and at the silent, set face of Moser. "My man Moser always says it doesn't matter, everything is Nam. I'm all right here, now, but why was that hard for you to say to me?"

Coles blew out his breath. "I guess I came here to prove something to myself, too, and maybe not just to myself. When you showed up, took over from Lieutenant Robinson, I hated you. You were white, and you never showed fear. Lieutenant Robinson was black, and afraid. Bobby Coles is black, and afraid."

Stuart thought, and absorbed. He felt almost drunk with the sense of sharing in the close space. "Surely you don't think I wasn't afraid, Bobby?"

"No, sir, not *now*! But shit, you shoulda heard me brag about your cool after the Elephant, and after the Horsehead! The other sergeants, the *black* sergeants, they all envied me such an officer! And we all had Blackjack to worship, but still they would talk about Ice!" The beer can was empty. Wordlessly, Bobby set it aside, and pulled another cigarette from Stuart's pack, lit it, and passed it to the still-silent Moser. "I knew you were afraid, Ice, scared shitless just like me, but you never showed it. I tried to copy you, but I felt shame because I had insulted you, the first day. But I gotta say, the black noncoms, back down with the one-niner-seven, envied me my Ice."

"I'm a better actor than I thought. And I remember looking at you, in the Elephant, when we had to make that impossible spot, and you looked so confident, so professional. Shit, I figured, if Coles thinks I'm about to fuck this up, he'll just stop me.''

Bobby guffawed. ''My fucking knees were water! I couldn't even read my stopwatch right!''

Stuart laughed with him. ''Yeah, Bro, but we were *good* that day! We shattered the enemy, and stunned the fucking U.S. Army!'' Stuart held out his palm. Bobby could barely see it, but he slapped it accurately.

Once again, they sat in silence, but it was easy silence. Stuart mused, drifted. ''So what did you come here to prove, then, Bobby?''

Bobby blew smoke up into the night, and stubbed out the cigarette. He felt very free, very relaxed, as though the cigarette had been a joint. ''I joined the marines for all the wrong reasons. My brother Simon had a friend, a topkick at Pendleton. He said I would get better training in the corps, be better off. Then I get to Pendleton for AIT, and I find they have a football team, and that the camp commandant would keep good players from going overseas just to play. So I went out, and made the team, and when my unit—Billy's unit, too—was sent to Nam, I stayed and played. I didn't see Nam as anything to do with me, and I figured I had a right to try to save my pro career. But as soon as I decided to stay at Pendleton, I started to feel bad, because all those gung-ho assholes who couldn't wait to get killed wouldn't even hate me for sliding out. But still I slid out, until finally the team was disbanded. But then I had to prove I was as good or better than any marine, so I took the ANGLICO, because I thought it sounded like a small, up-front unit. But I wanted to fight, to be brave, *black* and brave. I have to say that when you moved us up during the Elephant, and then blew away the enemy attack, that was the first day I felt brave, and proud, even though I fucked up the time solution.''

Stuart dragged on the cigarette, feeling the lightness of the box in his pocket. It will be scrounges tomorrow, he thought. ''You been brave enough, Bobby. You know that.''

Bobby smiled, aware no one could see it. ''Yes, *sir*! I believe I have. But you showed me how.''

Stuart shook his head in the darkness. ''I'm amazed. When I first saw you, towering above me—''

''Hey, Ice! One inch.''

''Seemed like ten. You looked so strong, and so angry, I was petrified.''

''Hah,'' barked Bobby. ''My badass stare worked, and I never even knew it!''

Stuart laughed softly. "So all in all, it sounds like you wanted to be a bit of a hero, too, my friend."

Coles paused. "Yeah. Sure I did. But what you got to know, sir, is that no one wants to be a hero for himself. Heroism is public. I wanted it for my brother, for all my black brothers, and, after awhile, even for you."

Stuart smiled in the warm darkness. How we learn without knowing. "Maybe that need to be strong, even heroic, for one's brothers is part of what Blackjack meant by glory."

"Yes, sir, I think it is." Coles nodded to himself. I know it is.

Moser got up silently. "You OK, Moser?" said Stuart.

"Ah, good, sir. You know I listen better than I talk. Can I go an' scrounge a couple more beers?"

What the hell, thought Stuart. The NDP is still noisy, and the VC are late, if they are coming at all. "Go ahead. Be back quick."

"Yo." The big man disappeared up over the rim of the hole.

Bobby watched Moser go over the rim, fluid, careful. By God, Moser is a rock, he thought. He let the silence concentrate around him. This is wonderful, and scary at the same time. I wish Billy could see what he has done. "Sir, ah, Ice?"

"Ice, aye," said Stuart. What a strange compliment, Ice, he thought.

"You ever think about dying?"

Stuart thought about it, lighting another cigarette. Two left in the pack, shit. He passed the cigarette to Bobby. "No. No! Not since I was in that helo that went down near Danang, a hundred years ago. I guess that scared all the thought of dying out of me. You think about it, Bobby?"

"Yeah, Bro. I have—" Bobby struggled with the thought, "—a premonition. Probably don' mean nothing. I think I'm going to get it."

"Shit, man, grunts get it, H and H guys like us don't get it. We'll get through." I wonder what life here without Bobby and Moser would be like, he thought.

"What about last night? You can't get much farther into the rear than an officers' club."

Stuart shifted his weight against the side of the cramped bunker, Coles adjusted his position. Stuart felt a loss of the closeness, and regretted it. "I have to think that won't happen again."

"But it could."

"Sure, but so what? I just don't feel I'm going down. Why should you?"

Bobby shrugged to himself in the darkness. "So it's stupid, I know that. But I want to ask you something."

"Go," said Stuart, feeling good, feeling near to the night, and unafraid, with good friends.

Bobby leaned close to Stuart, close enough to see his white face in the dim ambient light. "If I go, I want you to go see my brother Simon and tell him what this was. What we were."

Stuart was proud of Coles's confidence. "Sure. Absolutely. But you and I travel together, man; if you get it, I probably will too, at the same time."

"That's not what my premonition tells me, Ice."

Stuart felt a chill. What do premonitions mean? "I'd go tell him. But we're both short; never happen."

"Promise you will go see him."

"Hey, I said sure. I promise." Stuart felt the closeness, the understanding."

"What would you want me to do if you bought it, sir?"

Stuart sat, silent. He was trying to figure out how he would approach Bobby's fearsome brother. Bobby's offer just didn't fit with the Bobby he knew, but this night was different, hanging, as it did, on this soldier's wake for Billy Hunter. Stuart felt he had nothing to ask.

"I'd want to go see your wife, Ice."

The thought startled Stuart. He rolled the thought of Bobby meeting Karen through his mind, and fought down the impossibility of the thing. "You couldn't do that, man, if you hated her."

Bobby chuckled, low and lethal. "I wouldn't hate her. But I'd tell her that you were the *best*. She'd go crazy, she see my Shine charm."

William giggled, and then he laughed. "Yes, she would. Yes. Good, good, go see her, Bobby." He felt the chill of death again. Crazy Bobby's premonitions. "But gently, gently."

"You still love her. Why, man?"

"I just love her, man. I just do."

They sat in silence, watching the moon break through the clouds. It would be hot in the morning.

Moser slid quietly over the bank of the foxhole and down to the bottom. "Three beers, sir, an' two packs of English smokes. Not yer usual, sorry."

Stuart looked at the cigarettes as Moser opened the first of the beers. "Player's Navy Cut, how well done, Moser."

Moser smiled. There was enough moonlight to see it. "Tanker I know, his lieutenant smokes 'em. Took awhile to find the hump."

"Well thank you," said Stuart, lighting the second-to-last Dunhill, and sipping the beer as it passed.

"You're welcome, sir."

"Moser, we been talking near an hour," said Coles. "We knew Billy, a hundred years ago, in the World, but you really knew him better, since we been out here."

Moser took a big slug of the beer. How hard it must have been for him to sip before, thought Coles. He supported the communion for Billy by holding back. Moser looked, first at the lieutenant, then at Bobby. He looked thoughtful and sad, thought Stuart. "I liked Sergeant Hunter, I guess. He taught me things, like you two done. But he never had no hope, like y'all talked about, earlier."

Stuart listened, but couldn't believe. "Shit, Moser, Billy was always helpful, cheerful. He had more hope than anyone."

Coles nodded. "From the moment he joined us, he did everything for the unit."

Moser opened the second beer. "You guys knew him in the World; I didn't. I'm just a country boy. Maybe y'all didn't see nothin' change in him?"

Coles thought. "He was quieter, maybe, but still Hunter."

"He was quieter, sure, but still the fighter," said Stuart.

"Y'all never looked at his eyes," said Moser, very softly. "Did y'all?"

Coles looked at Stuart in th moonlight. Stuart shook his head. "What do you mean? What did you see, Moser?"

Moser shuddered, fighting off the image of pain. "His eyes were dead, sir. Sergeant. Somethin' musta happened to him on his first tour, though he would never say, but it killed his soul. He never had no hope in him, long as I knew him. He came back here to find his death, where he had left it off, I reckon. Now he has. Sir."

Coles covered his face in his hands, grieving, and praying silently for Billy, and for himself. Stuart stared at the moon, and wondered. The spell of the wake was broken, and the night felt cool. Moser got up and manned his machine gun.

6 February 1968   Hue

Stuart, Moser, and Coles were screwed to the ground on a narrow ridge south of the Perfume River, in the old French colonial quarter of Hue. The neighborhood was made up of small Mediterranean-looking houses and shops, all deserted. The NVA had held the old imperial capital for a week, since assaulting it and overrunning the headquarters of the 1st Division of the Army of the Republic of Vietnam on the night of January 31. Thick clouds boiled overhead about four thousand feet above the terrain, pushed along by the southeast monsoon dropping intermittent, soaking showers on the dug-in marines.

The citadel, just north of the river, was shrouded in manmade clouds of thick, greasy black smoke, boiling with flame. Marine F-4s from Danang circled above, then dove in and bombed the ancient walled town. The marines felt and heard the scream of engines followed by ear-popping pressure waves and heavy thuds as the bombs exploded. Navy F-4s and A-4s waited their turn just out over the sea. When the magnitude of the enemy's Tet offensive had become clear, MACV called for the carriers on Yankee Station off North Vietnam to come south to render close air support for the many battles in progress. The carrier battle groups with more than 150 combat aircraft of all types now maneuvered in the haze and rain five miles offshore, while their aircraft flew close support along the coastal battlefronts, and interdiction raids deep inland. Soldiers and marines were on the move everywhere to catch the VC and main force NVA units before they could withdraw to Laos and disperse.

The bombing aircraft over Hue were being controlled by a marine officer on the outskirts of the citadel itself. Stuart and Coles were on the naval gunfire net, talking to the cruiser USS *Boston* and the Australian destroyer HMAS *Hobart*, both waiting close inshore. Once the air attacks had broken the enemy's strength inside the citadel, it was thought, the eight-inch guns on the *Boston* would be used to try to breach the walls. Really a job for a battleship, thought Coles. Every navy and marine spotting team in Vietnam wanted to be the first to handle the *New Jersey* with her nine sixteen-inch fifties, the biggest naval guns on any ship afloat, but the big guy wasn't due in the South China Sea until summer.

Stuart adjusted his binoculars and tried to peer through the smoke. The ANGLICO detachment was with the Headquarters Company of the 2d Battalion, 26th Marines, which was waiting to go into the fight. By all one could learn by monitoring radio traffic, the fighting in the citadel was fierce and sometimes hand to hand.

Stuart could hear that the marine spotter was working the air support very close to his own position, which he was marking before each bombing flight with colored smoke grenades.

"Sir! Lieutenant!" called Hansford, one of the marines from 2/26 that the S-3 had lent the ANGLICO to man the unit's radios. "It's division, on command net."

Stuart took the handset. "This is Papa Delta Green."

"OK, Papa Delta, we are patching you through to Mike Oscar Blue." Mike Oscar Blue was the marine spotter working close.

"Papa Delta Green, this is Mike Oscar Blue."

"This is Papa Delta. Go ahead."

"Hiya, Spotter. You got naval gun lined up?"

"Roger. I have one light and one heavy in close, ready to pass over to you for spot."

"Ah, no, son. You will have to spot them in from there, unless you can cross over the river and do it from here."

"Surely, Mike Oscar, you can get it in closer from down there." This guy sounds like he's drifting away, thought Stuart.

"Time was, Papa D, but the medic just finished bandaging my eyes. Little bitty piece of shrapnel."

"Mike Oscar, I hear you. What of the rest of your team?"

"Ain't been no *team* since yesterday, Papa Delta."

"Stand by." Stuart motioned to Coles, who squirmed over to his side. "Bobby, raise Battalion. Tell them we are urgently requested to cross the river and take up the forward spot from Mike Oscar Blue, who is down. Ask them if there's any way they can get us down there." Coles nodded and wormed back to his hole and his RTO.

"Mike Oscar, Papa Delta. Do you have any information about the river crossings on this side?"

"Roger, Papa Delta. The Truong Tien. The old French bridge is in the care of our finest green marines. Span's blown, and the arches are down, but barges and pontoons are laced to the piers with cable. No vehicle passage, but men can cross. Pay to keep heads down while they do it." The voice was weaker, and the speaker sounded detached, even amused. "Y'all comin' over?"

"Soon as we hear from Battalion. Tell me why you want gunfire."

"Right! I should bring you up to speed, in case, ah, I'm not *here* when you arrive!" Stuart could hear a little giggle over the radio. Pain or morphine, or both, he thought. "The VC have barricaded two narrow streets on either side of the Palace of Harmony. They will be roads fourteen and seventeen-A on your street plan. You got a street plan?"

"Negative, Mike Oscar." Stuart tapped Bobby's shoulder. "Sergeant, ask Battalion if they have a Hue street plan." Coles nodded, pressing the handset to his ear.

"Well, anyway, the slopes have filled in these two little streets with rubble and have hidden men and mortars behind. Most of the bombs I called in struck the walls of the palace, or the walls of the old keep behind. We can't get enough explosive down to break up those rubble barricades.'' Stuart was relieved to hear a measure of crispness and control returning to Mike Oscar's voice. ''Are you Navy or Marine, Papa Delta?''

''Navy, Mike Oscar.''

''Good. You'll handle Gun better than I would, anyway. If you can get your assets lined up, it's a rifle shot. We have to clear those alleys or the bastards will keep dumping rocket sand mortars on us till kingdom come.''

''Can you give me a compass bearing line into the blocked streets?''

''Well, only from memory, son. I had the aviators dropping on line to target of two-eighty magnetic.''

Stuart shifted to the gun net and gave the ships the coordinates of the targets and the approximate gun-target line. The ships acknowledged, and began to maneuver to give themselves a straight shot in enfilade, down the alleys and into the rubble barricades. Stuart shifted back to the air net and Mike Oscar. ''Mike Oscar, I had better pick up your air.''

''Roger, son, you got 'em. Marine is Idaho Five and Seven. They are back in Phu Bai to rearm. Navy callup is War Eagle Strike. Flights standing by are Blue and Yellow. Yellow is the A-fours with seven-hundred-fifty-pound H-E. Blue is F-fours with lighter H-E and rockets. Willy Peter and nails.''

Stuart called the navy flights. Since he would have to lift the aircraft before commencing naval gunfire, he told the yellow flight to go in on Mike Oscar's line to target and drop over the citadel, away from the marine positions. The F-4s had tanks and could loiter; he might need them before the gunfire was established. He would have to get in close before he could make use of the white phosphorous and the shotgunlike flechette rockets, which the troops called nails.

The delta-winged A-4s came in in two fights each of two aircraft, and shook the earth with their heavy drops on the old city. Nothing was visible but boiling smoke and dust reaching out across the river toward the ANGLICO and the 2/26 Marines.

''Lieutenant, battalion wants you on command net,'' said Hansford.

Stuart took the handset. ''Papa Delta.''

''Papa Delta, this is Two-Six. This battalion is going to deliver you personal to where you are needed. Get your boys down to Alpha Company, who will lead. They will get you up to where you can crack those barricades ASAP. Alpha Company is right in front of you. You hear?''

''Roger, Six. We copy. We are on our way down to Alpha.'' Going in with the point troops! thought Stuart.

"Good. Move out. And don't get your asses killed before you clear those barricaded streets for the grunts."

"Roger, Six." And a hearty fuck you, thought Stuart. He felt strangely excited. Moser and Coles watched him; Coles looked worried and Moser looked angry and determined. He grinned at them. "Men of the Seventh ANGLICO, we're going up with the leading company. We'll bring the *Boston* and the *Hobart* in for close!"

Both Coles and Moser grinned back. They're as crazy as I am, thought Stuart.

Crossing the Perfume River was an experience Coles would not forget. There were two marine M48A3 tanks at the south end, firing into the citadel with cannons and machine guns, trying to suppress the constant small-arms fire that rattled against the twisted girders of the old French-built bridge. The marines of Alpha Company advanced in two columns along each edge of the line of pontoons and barges cabled under the bridge itself. The ANGLICO detachment was at the rear of the first platoon, radio antennas flapping as they advanced in short rushes from girder to girder.

Coles felt like he was in a movie. He began to understand why infantry soldiers and marines had a special feeling about themselves. Out in front with zero protection, they felt superior to tankers, artillerymen, and certainly to gunfire spotters, who normally sat well back. The tank cannon fire cracked and screamed overhead.

When they reached the north end of the bridge, they found a marine fire team emplaced behind sandbags, also popping away at enemy positions and calling spots back to the tanks on the south shore. Stuart called the two ships, Mauler *(Boston)* and Royal Purple *(Hobart)*, and found they were on station to Mike Oscar's gun-target line.

The grand avenue of Hue connected with the French bridge, and had carried the emperors and their courts and followers across the river during the new year's celebrations in years past. The marines used what protection they could find in the narrow alleys that led into the avenue. The second lieutenant leading the point platoon was talking to the marines up front with Mike Oscar; Stuart stayed on the gunfire net with the ships. ANGLICO was ready to shoot as soon as they could see their targets.

As the point platoon crept closer to the action, they passed hundreds of marines crowded in the alleys of old Vietnamese stone houses. An entire assault force is set to finish off the VC and NVA in the old city, thought Stuart, if we and the air can break the enemy's fortifications.

The men continued forward to a battalion command post in a partially destroyed building. The roof was down, but the walls were of stone. There was also a casualty concentration point within the walls. Alpha Company commander, a red-faced Georgia captain, and the point lieutenant went to get more information about the enemy formations they would soon attack. Stuart sought out Mike Oscar. His head was completely swathed in bandages above his nose, and he was sedated, but he had a spotter's sense of sound, and recognized Stuart's voice as soon as he spoke.

"You're Papa Delta. You gonna take care of those little barricades?"

"No sweat, Mike Oscar. You just rest."

"Mike, Oscar, shit. You gotta *real* name, boy?" Mike Oscar was a marine captain who had obviously seen many years of enlisted service before being commissioned. Stuart felt he could hardly object to the "boy."

"William Stuart, Lieutenant, navy type. Yours?"

"Jimmy Parish, Captain, USMC, for my sins. You done gunfire before?"

"Roger, we been there. We'll get your barricades."

"Yo, fucker. Clean 'em *out*! We'll wait ten years for the airdales to get accurate enough." Parish shifted a little, and drew a sharp breath of pain. "I told these fuckers I wanted to stay right here till you came up and did it. Do it now, navy-type lieutenant; them mud marines are getting chopped as we chatter."

Stuart felt a hand on his shoulder, and looked up. It was the Alpha Company captain. He hand-signed "forward." Stuart rose, and patted the marine spotter on his shoulder. "We're going now, Parish."

"Good. I'll just rest here a spell till you get back and tell me you broke through. You *will* come back and tell me, William?"

"For certain, Captain."

The lead platoon of marines, with the ANGLICO, crossed the last transverse street and reached the forward position of the assault force, in a shallow basement of a bombed-out stone house. The Palace of Harmony and the barricaded alleys were clearly visible on the far side of a broad plaza. Coles could see that the infantry could not possibly get across that plaza until the enemy had been driven from positions around the ornate palace.

Rockets soared overhead, and some fell close in, with the characteristic thump-and-hail sound of an exploding shrapnel-loaded B-40 rocket. The heavy, low-toned bark of AK-47s and heavier automatic weapons erased the silence between the rocket rounds, and the zip! pling! of bullets kicked dust and sharp bits of stone into men's faces and rattled off helmets.

We are really *up front*, thought Coles.

Stuart picked up his handset, and signed the RTO to gunfire net.

"Mauler, Mauler, this is Papa Delta Blue, for fire now."

"Roger, Papa Delta. Have you now Blue. Go ahead."

"Mauler, I have two targets, both loose stone and rubble fortifications with troops behind. Will bring you down first on left target. Can you do two separate solutions?"

"We can strong-arm it at the computer, Papa Delta. We only have one surface director, since they took off number three turret and gave us the useless missiles aft."

Spoken like a true gunner, thought Stuart. "OK. Grid coordinates I gave you are still good. Gun-target line is two-eight-five mag. Stand by for single-shot smoke round, as soon as I clear my aircraft."

"Mauler standing by, over."

Stuart caught Coles's eye. Coles was on the air net. "Sergeant, tell the airdales to clear out, and report clear."

Coles gave Stuart a thumbs-up acknowledgment. Moments later, a hand-flat, palm-down-sweeping hand sign indicating the aircraft were cleared away from the target area, and clear of the airspace between the ships' guns and the target.

"Mauler, Papa Delta. Area clear, ready for spot."

"Roger, Papa Delta." Stuart listened for the count. "Shot away, Papa Delta. Time of flight 5.2 secs."

Stuart had popped his stopwatch at the word "shot." He heard the shell coming in overhead, booming in with a sound between the rising roar of an oncoming freight train and the prolonged cra-a-a-ack! of a thunderclap. Stuart had never heard one go right over his head before, and instinctively he screwed his body tighter to the ground. He looked up at the flat crack of the smoke round, and saw the column of red smoke rising from the keep behind the palace. "Smoke is red, Mauler."

"That's a roge."

Stuart set aside the rotating table. Gun-target and spotter-target lines were the same. "Left four mils, drop two hundred."

"Spot corrected. Shot away, 5.2 secs."

The second round crashed through the atmosphere over Stuart's head and landed just behind the left-hand barricade. Stuart squinted through the dust and smoke, estimating distance. He noticed that small arms on both sides had largely fallen silent.

The show begins, he thought. "Line is good, Mauler. Drop one hundred minus. One gun, H-E, to correct."

"Shot away, 5.1 secs."

Stuart knew it had to be his imagination, but he felt this last shot coming in lower and louder. He was relieved when the shell landed just in front of the barricade and exploded with a brilliant, almost smokeless flash. Boulders started to rumble down the front of the rock-and-rubble wall from the near miss.

"Mauler, Papa Delta. Add twenty. Two-zero yards. Fire for effect, salvo, mixture of H-E and armor piercing. Three guns."

"Roger, Papa Delta." The officer on *Boston* left his microphone open, and Stuart could hear the spot passed to the director, and the instructions for the turret to alternate salvos of three guns at a time with high explosive and armor-piercing rounds mixed to break up the barricades and blow the rocks back into the enemy concentrations. In less than two heartbeats, the director reported ready, and Stuart heard the command: "Turret two, commence firing!" and then the roar, strangely flattened and muted by the radio. "First salvo's up, Papa Delta. Evaluate, then expect salvos four to the minute."

"Roger," said Stuart. He gave a handsign to his own men to stay down, and saw at once that it was a needless gesture. The sound of the shells overhead was at least three times as loud as the single shots had been, thought Stuart, and then the shells landed about a third of the way up the face of the barricade. The center of the barricade slumped about ten feet, and the front of the rubble slid away in an avalanche. Boulders the size of small cars crashed to earth in the square between the marines and the barricaded streets.

"Spot on, Mauler. Give me two more salvos, then add thirty and give me two more."

"Roger. Now, can you estimate for turret one the right deflection to the second target?"

The second salvo screamed overhead, and the barricade slumped further. The marines began to cheer. "Roger, Mauler. Looks like fifty or sixty mils to me. Try your two mils to the right."

"Roger. What is in between the two fortifications?"

"A temple, or a palace." Stuart turned to the Alpha Company commander, and pointed across the plaza. The captain showed Stuart his street guide. "The Palace of Harmony," said Stuart, into the handset. What a name for a target, he thought.

There was a pause. "Ah, Papa Delta, captain says the op order requires we limit where possible destruction of historically significant structures."

Jesus *CHRIST*! thought Stuart, these RAMF op-worker writers get crazier at every turn! "The palace is an empty strong point, Mauler, and probably an ammunition dump."

"Roger, Papa Delta! Just checking for the log. Shot away, 5.1 secs, call smoke."

Better, thought Stuart. He never heard the shot, which came in with the third salvo on the left-hand barricade, but he saw the smoke round carom off the right side of the palace.

"Smoke is green!"

"Roger. Adjust."

"Right your one mil. Hold the range. Fire for effect, salvos, three guns, same mix of H-E and A-P." Stuart observed the third salvo on the left-hand blockage. The rubble wall was nearly gone, and the leftmost wall around the palace collapsed in smoke and dust.

"Roger, Papa Delta. We aim to please. Call us when you're done."

The first salvo on the right barricade landed, and the palace took most of it. So much for historic structures, thought Stuart.

"Mauler, Papa Delta. Jig it right a trace, can you?"

"Roge. Right one-half mil."

Stuart turned and saw the assault marines filling the alley behind him. Give me time, guys, and you can walk in. Impatiently, and futilely, he hand-signed the marines back. Salvos landed on both targets at once.

"Papa Delta, this is Roy'l Purple. Can we get in the hunt, mate?"

Why not, thought Stuart, in the spirit of international cooperation. "Glad to have you, Aussies! I'd like two guns up over Mauler's firefall, falling shot, mix of VT frag and able-able common!" VT frag and able-able common were antiaircraft shells designed to fragment and chew up airplanes, but both made excellent shrapnel rounds. "Add three hundred to Mauler's spot, and fire for effect. Spread of two mils. No friendlies behind."

"Can do, Yank. No spot?"

"Not if you're on, Royal Purple; we won't see through Mauler's smoke. If you fire short, you will for sure hear from me." I hope these Aussies are good, thought Stuart. I hope my adrenaline is not affecting my reason.

" 'Strines are *nevah* short, Yank. Shots are in the air."

Salvos fell a split-second apart on both barricades. The marines crowded forward, cheering every explosion, stamping and shaking their weapons at the unseen enemy.

Up in those rocks brave men are dying, thought Coles, and stopped cheering.

26 February 1968   Highway One, South of Quang Tri City

The marines of 1st Platoon, Bravo Company of the 2/26, moved cautiously into the little village of Ca Tin. The few shacks seemed deserted, and the sparse belongings of the people who had lived there lay about in the road. A little rice had been spilled by the retreating NVA when they looted the peasants' stock. The head of a small pig that had been crudely butchered lay partially buried in the muddy soup created by the unrelenting monsoon rain. The marines fanned out in squads and checked each hootch. All were deserted. The men remounted the M113s, and the advance continued.

The citadel of Hue had been secured on February 24th. The 2/26 had been in reserve during the final assault, and there had been no opportunity for the ANGLICO to call air or gun as the fighting during the last week had been street by street inside the citadel, and finally hand to hand. Rumors of enormous casualties spread through the battalion as the operation wound down.

Since the battalion had been "resting" in reserve, they had been headed up Highway One to clear it of enemy stragglers as soon as they were relieved. A day later, the 2/26, along with marines landing by helicopter from the ships offshore, had been organized into a task force to seek out and destroy the main force VC and NVA units that were now withdrawing toward their bases in North Vietnam and Laos.

The advance was slow, because every village had to be checked. Most were deserted and looted, and the countryside was oddly quiet. The rain blurred sounds and images. The APCs clanked along at the pace of a walk, and the men stank and rotted. No one had been dry in days.

Stuart, Coles, and Moser, along with most of 2d Platoon with whom they had been riding, dismounted from the M113s when the company moved on from Ca Tin. The troops were encouraged to walk part of the time to keep their wet muscles from cramping, and to relieve the crushing boredom of the slow advance. Stuart daydreamed about hot food and hot showers as he walked. His reverie ended abruptly by a stinging slash across the back of his neck, punctuated by the crack of an AK-47. The grunts hit the deck at the sound, then squirmed behind the cover of the APCs. Stuart clapped his hand to his neck, then looked at the handful of blood. I'm hit, he thought, staring stupidly at the hand.

"GEDDOWN, SIR!" bellowed Moser, rising from behind the nearest M113 and running to grab the lieutenant. Moser twisted and started back for the shelter of the carrier's skirts. The rifle cracked again, and Moser felt the round strike his hip like the kick of a mule. Pushing Stuart ahead of him, Moser sprawled behind the vehicle and let out a curse.

Stuart realized where he was and what was happening just as Moser grabbed him. After Moser had pushed him face down on the pavement, he rolled over quickly. His ribs hurt sharply where he had landed on his rifle. He saw Moser dragging himself closer to the APC, his right leg stiff behind him and spurting blood. Stuart pulled several sterile dressings from his pack and crawled rapidly to Moser's side. Up on top, the machine-gunners in the APCs sprayed the trees with fire, but they could not locate the sniper.

Stuart put his hand gently on Moser's broad back. Moser's face was screwed up with pain, and he was crying soundlessly. "Stop crawling, Moser. Let me take care of the wound."

"My leg is numb, sir, but the hip is on fire."

"OK, Moser. Just hold still."

Coles crawled over, removed Moser's helmet, and held his head still. "Easy big guy." Stuart noticed the gentleness of Coles's touch, almost caressing.

Stuart took a pair of tape scissors from the battle aid kit and cut rapidly through the wet fabric of Moser's uniform to expose the wound. The neat hole was just below the hip joint, and the blood oozed out thickly with the slight pumping motion that indicated the rupture of a minor artery. The flesh for six inches around the wound was already turning to black bruise from the shock of the bullet's impact. Probably struck the bone, thought Stuart; that's why the leg is numb below. Pray it didn't sever the sciatic nerve.

This is my fault, thought Stuart; if only I'd been dumb enough to fall on my face and crawl six feet, this man would not be down. This is my bullet in Moser's leg.

Since the wound was pushing out blood, Stuart could assume it was clean. He broke an alcohol ampule and poured the fluid on a sterile dressing, then swabbed the wound and the surrounding area. He was relieved to see the bleeding had slowed. He opened a tube of penicillin ointment and smeared a generous amount on a second sterile dressing. Coles moved up beside him and held the dressing by both ends tightly over the wound while Stuart taped. Finally Stuart took a morphine Syrette and injected its contents into Moser's other hip. "You're OK, Moser. Hey, thanks for pulling me down. I don't know where I was, but you covered me once again."

"You was hit, sir. That's all."

So I was! I had forgotten, thought Stuart, and he was suddenly aware of the sharp, razorlike pain on the back of his neck as Coles swabbed his wound with alcohol. Stuart forced himself to hold still.

Stuart squeezed some penicillin ointment on another dressing and Coles slapped it on the wound. Stuart held the dressing from the front while Coles taped.

"You want morphine, Lieutenant?"

"No, thank you, Bobby," said Stuart, moving his head carefully. "I'm quite stupid enough today without it."

The machine-gunners still fired short bursts into the trees. During the next silence, the rifle cracked again, and the platoon leader standing behind the nearest APC spun to the ground. His helmet, with a neat, new crease in it, rolled away from him.

"I know where that sniper is, sir," said Moser.

"Where?" said Stuart.

Moser was peering intently around the front of the APC's track. "Right there, near the base of that big ole tree with the broken branch in front. He down *low*, the yeller possum. Gyrenes all looking *up*." The sniper's rifle cracked again. "Right *there*! You can see the smoke wisp, plain as day."

Stuart looked at Coles. Both shrugged.

"Hey Coles, get me my ole gun." Coles crawled to the spot

where Moser had left the .50 when he had gone after Stuart, and dragged it back.

"Moser, you're wounded, buddy," said Stuart, "your war is over."

"Bullshit, ah, sir. Just a scratch on my big ole ass, and it feels real fine already. Coles, put that iron in front of me."

"Is the tripod in the APC?" asked Coles.

"Yair. Fuck it. Sling your pack on the ground under the gun."

Stuart crawled to the side of the platoon leader, who was propped against the track of the APC, talking on the radio. He was still without a helmet, but fortunately unhurt. Stuart took a quick look at his scalp.

"Old steel pot worked today, Stuart," grinned the second lieutenant.

"Yeah, Reilly. How's the head?"

"Feels like a regular navy hangover. I'm trying to get some artillery up to deal with that sniper. How's your man?"

"Bad enough so we ought to get him out. Shot in the hip. Bullet's still in there; probably hit the bone."

"If it hit the bone, it broke it."

"Most likely. Look, Reilly, Moser thinks he can see the sniper. He'd like a shot."

"Tell him to go right ahead."

"He'd like the machine-gunners to let up for a while; he wants to be sure he sees the enemy's fire and not one of our tracers."

Reilly looked skeptical. He rubbed the stubble of his hair and winced. "You really think he sees anything?"

"His eyesight, and his marksmanship, are somewhat famous."

Reilly shrugged. "What the hell. We'll be all day waiting on line for artillery. Sergeant Brooks! Cease firing up there! Moser wants to have a try at our sniper."

Moser rested the machine gun on Coles's pack. The long-barreled .50 was so low to the ground Moser's chin was in the grit of the road surface. Stuart rested his 7.5×50 spotter's binoculars on the track just above Moser. He centered the cross hairs on the fallen branch behind which Moser claimed to see the sniper. Stuart could see nothing. Then he saw a glint of brown metal, and a tiny dart of flame. Stuart opened his mouth to speak when he heard Moser's .50-caliber machine gun crack once. Stuart screwed his eyes into the binoculars. Moser's round was a tracer, and Stuart saw it arch like a firefly over the fallen branch. Something appeared on the top of the log. It teetered, then slowly slid down the face of the log. As it fell, Stuart recognized the familiar shape of an AK-47 rifle, topped with an odd-looking telescopic sight.

Holy shit, thought Stuart. Using the mil markings on the cross hairs of his binoculars, Stuart made a rough estimate of the distance to the target. About four hundred meters. Moser made that shot with an open iron sight and an eight-four-pound gun. "Nice shot, Moser," said Stuart. What else do you say?

Stuart saw that Coles had removed the machine gun from in front of Moser, and was resting Moser's head on the pack. Moser had passed out.

"Reilly, he did it. I saw the rifle fall," said Stuart, still not quite believing it.

"Yeah. Sergeant Brooks, have your machine-gunners pour a couple of belts into that spot, then get a squad down there real carefully to check it out. Stuart, I'm calling a medevac helo for your man."

The marine H-46 landed on the highway. Its flight mate hovered two hundred feet above to supply fire support if needed. The squad that Sergeant Brooks sent down had encountered no enemy force, and returned with the AK-47. Stuart looked at the weapon; it showed much more care than these crude weapons usually displayed. Moser would have appreciated that, he thought.

It took four marines to position Moser in the helo's litter. He woke up, protesting. "Hey, Lieutenant, I'm OK. Just a scratch. Don't wanna go back."

"Easy, Moser. You need hospital. You will be back in no time."

"I always took care of your back, sir."

"Yes, but you go get that round taken out. We'll be OK."

"Hey, Coles? You watch him real good."

"Sure, Moser, I will." Coles helped lift the big man into the helo. The crew chief was clearly anxious to depart.

"You be sure, Sergeant."

"Right on, big guy. Have a couple beers for us."

Moser gripped Coles's neck with uncomfortable force. "Promise me."

Coles bent close, under the whipping downdraft of the helo's rotors. "I promise. I love him, too, Moser."

Moser released his grip and Coles stepped back. "An' take care a' my goddamn gun!"

Coles waved and smiled as the helo tilted forward and clawed its way airborne, blowing dust and grit in his face.

"Good buddy, heh?" said Sergeant Brooks.

"The best. You know, I feel my, well, my personal danger is greater now that he's not here."

"Real good buddy. OK, Marine, let's get mounted."

Stuart got into the APC beside Reilly as the company resumed its advance.

"Your young sailor now has his own legend in the two-twenty-six, Stuart."

"It was quite a shot, from this distance."

"True. I suppose there might have been a little luck, but the squad I sent down there told me the sniper was shot exactly between the eyes."

Moser lay strapped tightly in the wire-basket stretcher inside the helicopter. The aircraft stooped again, just over a ridge, and another litter in which an unconscious black marine was strapped was heaved aboard and secured above Moser. The engines whined as the helo rose, filling Moser's mind with the agonizing sound of giant insects. His wound didn't hurt, and he resented the way Bobby Coles and the jarheads had bundled him off from the war for such a trifle.

Moser raised his head, fighting the morphine, and looked at the door-gunner of the big helo. The man was just a black silhouette in the bright glare of the open door. These CH-46s were now equipped with Browning air-cooled .50-caliber machine guns, unlike the older marine birds with the pissant thirties. A big gun, like Ole Betsy, except that the ones on the helos were the new mark and had a shorter barrel with a cooling jacket around it. Less accurate, thought Moser, as he watched the gunner's shoulders shake as he poured streams of fire into the jungle below. Works nice and smooth, he thought.

Moser lay back. It just don't *feel* right, leaving the lieutenant down there. I been covering his back how long now? Must be near a year, no more, since the boats. It's what I do, and what I want to do.

The helicopter bucked violently, and shuddered. The pitch of the noisy engines rose to a scream. Moser raised his head and saw the door-gunner's head drop onto his right shoulder as the helicopter pitched to the right and down. The door-gunner slid slowly to his knees, letting the gun hang in its swivel mount, and then the gunner fell sideways out of the aircraft. Moser could see the green jungle rushing up toward the open door as the helicopter slewed back and forth. Oh, baby Jesus, thought Moser, look after Momma, and the lieutenant, and the sergeant. Oh baby Jesus.

The helicopter hit the ground hard, and Moser was catapulted through the door, still strapped in his litter. He fetched up against a tree as the helo bounced, then crashed again, and exploded. Moser felt the heat and saw drops of burning fuel land around him, igniting patches of dry grass. The pain in his head rose with the heat as he struggled in vain against the straps. He closed his eyes and prayed. He had a sensation that he was being lifted in the litter. Take me home, he prayed, and then his world went black.

Stuart was dozing inside the well of the slow-moving APC. Coles crawled in, and sat across from him, touching his knees. "Lieutenant, wake up. Moser's dead."

Stuart rubbed his burning temples. "What? Bobby?"

"Moser is dead."

"He couldn't be! That wasn't a bad wound!" Stuart felt acid rising in his throat. No! his mind screamed.

"We just heard. That helo he was in was shot down. It never even made it out over water."

"Jesus, I am sorry," said Stuart.

Bobby swallowed. "I know you and Moser go back a long way, sir."

Stuart shook his head, rejecting the report. "Jesus, the poor, good-hearted, brave bastard. Are you sure, Bobby?"

"The grunts just got it over the radio, sir. Basset Force was near the crash site and checked it out. It was the same bird. They found the body of a door-gunner two hundred meters short of the crash site, and five bodies in the helo, all burned beyond recognition, including the one in the litter."

Stuart looked at Bobby Coles, concentrating on his smooth features. "It's just us, now, Bobby."

"Yes, sir." Tears streamed down Coles's cheeks. "Everything is coming apart. God, I'm so scared!"

Stuart sat up and put his hands on Bobby's knees. "Take it easy, Bobby."

"No, man! You don't understand! Moser thought he had witching powers; said a lot of his family had them. He understood that dream of yours. He said people around you were marked!"

"Bobby, it's just a dream. A malaria dream. That's superstitious nonsense."

"Fine! I *know* that! But you had the dream, and Billy bought it, at Tien Shaw. And again, and Moser's gone. Jesus, sir, I just *know* I'm next!"

"Pull yourself together, Sergeant," said Stuart, aware that his voice lacked conviction. "We're all scared, but don't let it grow." Stuart's hands tightened on Bobby's knees.

Bobby rubbed his streaming eyes, and leaned back, breathing deeply through his mouth. "OK, OK. I'm sorry, Lieutenant. But you know, I kind of feel the gooks know it was us, at the Elephant, and Horsehead, and all the places where we killed them from a long way off, and they couldn't get us. Well, now they can. I know I'm next."

"Easy, Bobby, easy. This operation will be over in a couple of days, and we'll be back in Danang." He took Bobby's face in his hands, and looked into his eyes.

Bobby wiped his face again as the tears stopped. "Don't forget, you promised to go see Simon."

Stuart felt the fear coursing from Bobby's cheeks into his hands, like a chill. He fought it down. "I'm going to get you back, and anyway, we are always together, so we will go together, and I have no premonition."

"Moser said that too, that the man who dreams will not see death. You have to go back, because of us, because of *this*." Bobby made a broad sweep of his arm, encompassing, Stuart supposed, all of Nam, and therefore everything.

"Sergeant, we are going to make it. I am as afraid as you are, but that's because we're still sane. You know that. It's the way, here."

Bobby pulled himself back, letting Stuart's hands fall. "OK, I'm all right now. I'm sorry, sir. But if, well, if, you won't fail to go see my brother?"

"Guaranteed, Sergeant. Now, let's get out and walk awhile; I'm getting stiff." Stuart patted Coles on his shoulder as he crawled out into the glaring sunlight, and Coles followed him.

27 February 1968   Highway One, Quang Tri Province

The advance of the 2/26 ground northward up the deserted highway. The rain had become scattered heavy showers, and still nothing dried. The wind from the sea brought a chill to the dampness, and the men shivered and scratched. Hot chow was fast becoming a memory. Most ominous to the marines was the continued absence of civilians in the many villages and towns along the highway. If the enemy had gone, the farmers would have come back.

The sun burned a hole through the gray monsoon clouds, and the day warmed. Stuart popped his shoulders against his pack in the well of the APC and dozed. Coles sat on his pack eating peaches from a C-ration can. He listened to the faint murmurings on the commando radio net, with the detached alertness that allowed his brain to disregard any sounds that did not contain his call sign. He looked up sharply at the radio pack, whose operator was sound asleep as Coles had suggested he be.

"Bulldog Two-Six, Kilo Quebec, this is Jackhammer, over."

Bulldog 2-6 was Bravo Company, 2/26's commander. Kilo Quebec was the ANGLICO detachment's day call. Jackhammer was Major General Willis, commander of the entire coastal operation.

"Roger, Jackhammer, this is Bulldog Two-Six." Captain Prescot's voice crackled in Coles's handset.

"Jackhammer, Kilo Quebec Red, over." Coles added the orientation code to the day code. Might's well tell them we're still walking north, he thought.

"This is Jackhammer. We will be sending helos to move you up. Get your vehicles off the road and laagered up just south of the ville marked Ky Lai Three on your map. Leave the drivers and gunners with a rifle squad for security. Acknowledge."

"Roger, Jackhammer. What's happening? Bulldog Two-Six, over."

"Boxer and Basset have trapped an enemy force they estimate as battalion or larger near Binh Thout, about six miles inland from Quang Tri. They need help containing them. Kilo Quebec?"

"Kilo Quebec, roger," said Coles. Stuart had come up beside him and picked up the extra handset.

"We're picking you up in the lead bird. They will need air and maybe naval gun to break the enemy formations. You will go in with lead elements of Borzoi coming up from Chu Lai."

"Roger, Jackhammer. How long?" asked Coles. Coles grinned at Stuart, who looked through the summary op order to find that Borzoi was the 1st Battalion, 19th Marines. General Willis's penchant for code-naming his fighting units after pet and game animals was a source of amusement among the troops. It seemed every commander had to have some idiosyncrasy.

"Have your unit dressed and ready to go in one-five minutes, Kilo Quebec."

"Roger, Jackhammer. Kilo Quebec, out."

The flight of eight CH-34 helicopters wop-wopped overhead. The lead aircraft made a wide circle to the left and landed on the highway. Coles and the two drafted radiomen from 2/26 ran to the helo and climbed in.

Stuart shook hands with Reilly. "See you, buddy. Wear your steel pot."

"Mow 'em down, Navy. We'll be right behind you."

"Roger, gyrene."

Reilly embraced Stuart. "Go with God, Stuart."

Stuart climbed aboard the helo, which lifted immediately.

Coles looked at his two RTOs, who looked thoroughly frightened. "Easy, guys. We been there. You'll be OK." He felt very strongly the foreboding that had taken him when Hunter had gone down, and then Moser, but he held his comforting grin. No need to let these poor, green kids think the sergeant is scared.

Stuart shouted into the radio, cupping the microphone against the noise of the helicopter. He was lining up his naval gunfire assets. Two destroyers, firing, if they did, at near maximum range. Where were the cruisers when you most needed them? thought Coles, carefully pushing his fear back into a corner of his brain.

The country below them was rolling and many shades of green rice fields separated by narrow lines of tall trees. The clouds were thick gray-black, swollen with rain, but broken. The mixture of clouds and clear spots created turbulence that rolled and shook the helicopter.

The landing zone was on a gravel bank on the edge of a stream. Alpha Company of the 2d Battalion, 6th Marines (Boxer), had secured the area immediately surrounding the LZ, but was reporting sporadic fire from the tree lines ahead and to the right. The bank was long enough to take three helos at a time. Stuart and Coles squinted past the door-gunner as the helo, followed by two others, began its wide turn into the wind for landing. The other five birds hovered at 1,000 feet of altitude, downwind.

I don't like this place, thought Coles. Three H-34s is only twenty-seven guys, max. An awfully small force until the other five get down. If the VC have heavy machine guns in the trees above the river, they could burn our helos and block the LZ for the rest. Those grunts down there might have a perimeter, but they're not going to know what Charlie has in those trees. An almost perfect trap. Suddenly he shivered. Moser had been good value in a fight, and good luck. Until yesterday.

Stuart called the two destroyers, waiting seven miles away in the South China Sea. He read out grid coordinates of a solid clump of two-hundred-foot-high trees as an initial spot. He didn't like the looks of those trees. Thick enough to hide a regiment, and maybe just waiting for us to land. He turned and motioned his men to get ready, as the second lieutenant leading the first platoon of the Borzois did the same.

The helo came in fast, pulled up into a nose-high attitude ten feet off the ground to stop its forward motion, and landed hard. The door-gunner moved out of the door to let the troops jump out. The second lieutenant and his five marines went first, sprinted to the shallow trench the marines on the ground had dug, and dropped in. The trench was cut where the gravel bank adjoined the thick elephant grass that bordered a rice field, which in turn stretched some seventy meters to the dense growth of trees. Stuart and his detachment followed, running crouched, Stuart and Coles with their rifles ready, the two radiomen bouncing along under the heavy packs and not able to use their .45s. The second and third helos landed, and their troops had just started out the doors when the enemy opened fire with light rockets and heavy .51-caliber machine guns from the tree line ahead. The first helo, airborne six feet off the ground, took a hail of .51, slumped forward, and crashed nose down, bursting immediately into orange flame. The second helo pulled full collective and rose rapidly above the trees, leaving two marines on the ground who were cut down by machine gun fire. The rest of the troops stayed in the bird. The third helo was struck forward by a rocket, and had the entire engine blown off.

Stuart and Coles made the shallow trench with one of the RTOs. The other radioman caught a .51 round in the face while Coles had a hand on his shoulder, pulling him down. He died instantly, and his blood and brains splashed as a pink and gray foam into Coles's nose and mouth. Coles let go and dove into the trench beside Stuart, and was violently sick.

DiNapoli, the second lieutenant who had come on the helicopter with the ANGLICO, was working his radio on the command net, reporting his position and the heavy fire. Other unit commanders along the stream reported fire from other positions in the tree lines. The five remaining helos of the flight were diverted to another LZ some half kilometer to the rear. The heavy enemy fire continued from the tree line in front and from the one on the right as well. Marines from Alpha Company began retreating from positions on both sides of the river. Survivors from the third helo, including its copilot, clattered down the embankment into the shallow trench. A mortar round landed on the gravel bank behind the men, then another, spraying the shallow depression with gravel and steel splinters.

Stuart was on spot net. He directed the two destroyers to begin continuous fire immediately on the coordinates he had given them from the helicopter, telling them he would spot if he could. The first salvos were widely split, and over. Stuart stuck his head up quickly at the sound of the exploding shells, deeper and louder than the sounds of friendly and enemy small arms and rockets. He was able to see the colored smoke of the spot rounds.

"Redwing, Goshawk, this is Kilo Quebec. Yellow for spot."

"This is Goshawk. Yellow is ours."

"Roger, Goshawk. Right twelve mils, drop three hundred. Continuous fire, for effect. Orange is Redwing?" Wrong procedure, thought Stuart. I cannot fuck this up.

"Redwing, roger."

"Left three mils, drop three-fifty. Continuous fire, for effect. Urgent, urgent, danger close." Stuart gave the danger bearing and range from the target.

"Roger, Kilo Quebec. Firing now. Redwing over."

"This is Goshawk. Firing and standing by on the net."

Coles heard the sweet scream of the five-inch shells overhead, then heard the explosions crashing in a steady stream in the trees. It was his turn to risk a peek over the embankment for spot. He was up and down in less than a second. The enemy's fire was drowned out in volume by the navy fire, which was close enough to shake the ground under him, but the volume of bullets and rockets singing and popping overhead seemed undiminished.

"Let's drop fifty, sir; get the fire closer to the front of the trees," suggested Coles, looking through binoculars.

Stuart looked at the sergeant, surprised at his icy-calm voice. He nodded. "Goshawk, Redwing, drop fifty. I say again, drop fifty."

"Goshawk roger."

"Redwing roger."

DiNapoli crawled to Stuart's side. "Navy, we're pulling back along the streambed. Bravo is dug in about two hundred meters downstream, and the rest of the heliborne force has landed about a klick back."

Marines from DiNapoli's group had dug in an M-60 machine gun under a hollow tree stump on the top edge of the bank. One of the troopers bellowed down, "Lieutenant!"

"Yes, Grossbeck," answered DiNapoli.

"The gooks are coming out, sir! Zillions of 'em." The M-60

began firing in long bursts at the advancing enemy. The gun suddenly stopped firing, slewed around sixty degrees to the right, and resumed long bursts. "Sir! They're already down in the fuckin' streambed!"

"Stuart, we'd best be going. Go ahead, we'll follow. Try to walk that fire back as we go."

"Roger, Lieutenant. Coles, Hansford, let's hop it. Hansford first, me last." He thumbed the handset on the radio pack, "Goshawk, Redwing, drop fifty more." He didn't wait for an acknowledgment.

Hansford, the surviving RTO, shouldered the pack and ran crouching out of the shallow shelter into the streambed. As Coles stood up to pass Stuart, he saw a green-uniformed soldier stick his head and rifle into the opposite end of the trench. Bobby fired by instinct at the same instant as the enemy. The enemy's first bullet hit Bobby in the left shoulder and spun him around. The next bullet hit him in the middle of the back and exited through his abdomen. He was propelled to the gravel next to Stuart. Stuart fired his Stoner on full auto and the enemy disappeared, immediately to be replaced by another, who threw up his arms and fell back as Stuart's rounds hit him. Holding the Stoner in his right hand, Stuart grabbed Coles by the collar and dragged him toward the stream. Bobby felt surprisingly light. DiNapoli and his two living marines ran out of the hollow and downstream, moving backward and firing as they went. The M-60 had fallen silent.

Stuart had dragged Coles to the edge of the stream. He turned to lift Bobby down into the water. A bullet struck him from his left side, passing through one thigh and into the other. His lungs emptied in a scream and he fell into the water. Coles slid over the edge and fell in beside him.

Coles came to, choking, his mouth and nose full of water. He rolled onto his back and choked again, then breathed deeply. There was a strange, cold burning in his gut, and he tasted bile in his throat. He had no feeling in his left shoulder. He knew he had been shot. He looked up and saw Lieutenant DiNapoli firing on the bank above him, covering another marine as they fell back. He saw the other man fall, then DiNapoli turned and ran down the streambed, fell forward, his head in the water. Bobby felt an arm around his neck and heard a voice. He couldn't make out words, but he recognized the voice as Stuart's. He passed out.

Stuart said, "Come on, Bobby. We've got to get downstream." Stuart pulled with his right arm, his left holding Coles's head above the water in a cross-chest carry. Stuart was half swimming, half pulling along the reed-choked bottom of the swollen stream. The current took them swiftly around the end of the gravel bank and into a deep pool. Stuart saw a turn in the stream bank, which had been undercut by the current. The cut was overhung with reeds and elephant grass. He made the bank, and pulled Bobby in as far as he could with his arms. His legs were lost to him.

Bobby lay on his back on the gravel, his legs still partly in the water. Stuart rolled out of his pack. He got the battle-dressing kit out and opened it. The kit contained four sterile dressings. Stuart opened Bobby's shirt and looked at the oozing exit wound. If Bobby's not in a hospital in an hour, he's not going to make it, thought Stuart. The thought made him infinitely sad, and he began to cry. He pulled himself against Bobby, and carefully touched the wound. The flesh was pulpy and slimy. Bobby's breathing was raspy and shallow. Stuart squeezed penicillin ointment on a sterile dressing, and pressed it gently into the wound, then taped it as best he could with clumsy, sleepy fingers.

Three dressings left. If Bobby is going to die anyway, I should use them on my legs. But I have to try. Marines are only a klick away.

Stuart tried to roll Bobby onto his side to get at the entry wound, but found he couldn't. He was on his stomach and could only push with his arms. He tried to get to his knees but the pain nearly blinded him. I must not pass out, he thought. As the pain in his legs receded, he took a dressing, smeared it with ointment, and laid it on Bobby's chest. With his left hand, Stuart probed beneath Bobby's shirt and found the wound on his back. He forced the dressing in under the shirt and against the wound.

Stuart heard only sporadic firing nearby, as the battle moved downstream. He and Coles were fairly well concealed, and Stuart could see little. He took the tape scissors from the aid kit and slit open both his trouser legs. He rolled onto his back and waited out the surge of pain, then finished the cuts. He had an entry wound and an exit wound in his left leg, and an entry wound on the inside of his right thigh. The bullet had passed through the heavy muscle in both legs. Probably not too bad if it doesn't go septic, thought Stuart.

He was startled by a shout and a splash from directly across the stream. Through the reed and the grass he could see a Vietnamese soldier lifting a body up onto the embankment. Stuart crawled backward into the water to his chest. Gently he pulled Bobby further into the water. Bobby coughed and moaned. Stuart put his hand on Bobby's mouth as softly as he could, and whispered, "Quiet, Sergeant. The NVA are just here."

"I'm hit. Hit bad." Stuart closed his hand tightly over Bobby's mouth.

When the soldier had lifted the body of the marine up onto the opposite bank, an officer with red collar tabs carrying a long-barreled automatic pistol bent over and looked for signs of life. Apparently he found none, for he barked an order at the soldier, who promptly rolled the body back into the stream. Through the grass, Stuart saw another soldier pointing and jabbering in the tall grass. The officer walked to the spot, and kicked at something in the grass. Stuart heard a scream of pain, then another as the officer kicked again. The officer took a step back, and fired a single shot from his pistol. The scream died in a gurgle.

Jesus, Bobby, be quiet. Stuart opened his fingers a little so Bobby could get more air, but the hand was tensed to close again at the first sound.

The enemy patrol worked the area methodically, searching for the downed marines and shooting the ones they found alive. Stuart's heart stopped at each single shot. He unbuttoned his thigh pocket and removed the small automatic pistol, and laid it on the gravel in front of him. Several times a soldier would peer at the undercut where Stuart and Coles lay, and once the officer seemed to be looking right into Stuart's eyes. After minutes that seemed hours, the patrol moved on.

Night was falling rapidly. Stuart rolled onto his back and pulled himself backward out of the water. The pain was much less, and he found he could sit up, and he quickly applied a sterile dressing to the jagged exit wound on the inside of his left thigh. He examined the other two holes, decided the entry wound on the left leg looked worse, and dressed it. He had no more sterile dressings. He took off the towel he wore around his neck, rinsed it in the stream, and wrung it out. He squeezed the last of the penicillin ointment onto the towel, and tied it and taped it to the wound on his right leg.

He considered the morphine. Plenty of that left. Bobby was sleeping, and sure to be in shock, so morphine was out of the question for him. Stuart decided he had better try to stay alert, though the temptation to take a nice drugged sleep was almost irresistible.

Stuart noted with a start that it was fully dark. He looked at his watch. 1900! Where the fuck was that relief column?

Are those bastards going to leave us out here all night? Suddenly he was very afraid. He knew that Vietnam, and especially its streams like the one he had been in for some hours, contained every nasty germ known to man, enriched as they were by runoff from rice fields fertilized with human excrement. If I lie here all night, I could die from the infections in the wounds; septic shock. Even if they pick me up tomorrow, I could likely have enough gangrene to cost me both my legs.

Stuart felt rage boiling through his fear. Those bastards! Marines pride themselves on getting back their wounded, even their dead! We've been here since 1400, and they were supposed to be coming up from a lousy klick away. "Damn you, damn you!" Stuart whispered aloud.

"Sir?" It was Coles. His voice was soft, and very clear.

Stuart forced the panic to recede. "Bobby. You OK?" Inane question, thought Stuart.

"Yes, sir. You hit bad?"

"Not too bad, in the legs." Stuart could almost feel the microbes crawling beneath his bandages. Especially the filthy towel.

"I'm cold, sir."

Bobby's in shock for sure, thought Stuart. He himself was beginning to burn with fever as the Vietnamese shit germs raced through his blood. "I'll give you my shirt, Bobby." He unbuttoned the shirt and pulled it off, tucked the collar under Bobby's chin, and spread the shirt over his chest. He could feel Bobby shivering. "Take it easy, Bobby."

"I am dying." Bobby's voice had a serene quality.

We're both dying, thought Stuart. Suddenly the anger slipped away. What does it matter. "You're hurt bad, but you're strong, Bobby. We can make it."

"No, sir. I'm sure. I can't feel anything but the cold."

Stuart moved his body close to Coles, and put his arm across his chest above the wound. Maybe my fever will help him.

"Sir, remember your promise. Remember you promised to go see Simon."

"We'll go see him together, Sergeant. Just hang on."

"Don't even call before you go, 'cause he might not want to see you. But you have to go, sir. You have to tell him—what will you tell him?"

"I'll tell him you were a good marine, and a good friend," said William, trying to swallow a sob.

"Simon won't believe I was all good, sir."

William struggled against his grief. He no longer felt the need to pretend for Bobby's sake. ''Maybe I'll add you were a bit of a handful, at first. But you were for sure a good marine, and my friend.''

''Thank you, sir. He'll believe the part about the handful. But you have to tell him about all of this, and about the way we felt, here.''

''Tell me what you feel, Bobby.''

''Pain, sorrow, anger. But most of all, pride, sir.'' Bobby's voice seemed incredibly gentle.

''Pride? How so, man?''

''Pride in me. Pride in us, pride in the corps. I finally understand Blackjack's words, though I always knew what he meant.''

''Honor and duty, Bobby?'' Stuart felt fear, and anger at the marines who hadn't come back for them.

''Yes. And glory.''

Stuart hugged Bobby gently. ''Just hang on, Bobby, I'm going to get you home.''

Bobby laughed, a single low note. ''OK, sir, but if I die, go tell Simon how it was.''

''Look, Bobby, of course I'll go. But let's not give up yet.''

''Thank you, sir. I'm going to sleep, now.''

Stuart felt the pulse, strong and rapid, through his shirt. Stuart choked back a sob. Hunter, Moser, Coles, and me. How good we were together! How *alive*.

Stuart heard the wop-wop of helicopters from a long way off. He screwed his eyes open and squinted in the glare of the tropical dawn. He saw men moving along the stream bank, weapons ready. Marines! He opened his mouth to call them, but the only sound was like the mew of a kitten. He tried again and no sound came. Fear rose up in him and brought him fully awake. Christ, he thought, the NVA never found us; now our own people won't. He pulled himself a few feet up the bank, and was aware of shooting pains in his legs. I must call them. I *must*. He dug his hands into the gravel, and pulled himself up to his knees. The pain boiled up to his skull and at last the scream came. He collapsed onto the gravel and screamed again. A marine splashed across the stream and parted the reeds and grass with his rifle.

''Two guys in here, Lieutenant!''

Lieutenant Reilly of the 2/26 crawled into the undercut. ''Jesus, Mary, and Joseph, it's Stuart, and Coles!''

Marines lifted Stuart out of the hollow and carried him quickly across the stream. Medics jumped from the idling helo and put him in a litter. He held up his hand. "Reilly, Bobby's alive. He's gut shot. Get him out."

Reilly wiped the tears and grime from Stuart's face with gentle fingers. Tears flowed freely down his own face. "Bobby didn't make it, William. He's gone."

Stuart felt the litter pulled into the helo, which tilted forward and jerked into the air.

THE WORLD

3 March 1968   Danang

Stuart drifted in the dream, detached as never before. The fire burned, his flesh and bones cooked and boiled, but the terror was completely absent. He could feel pain only as a memory, almost as a long-known enemy who had become a friend. When the dream ended, the three figures stood silent behind the dying flames, and Stuart knew the figures at last, but it was too late, and somehow it didn't matter anymore. He drifted toward consciousness, and there was no scream, or any need of one.

Stuart felt very far away from his body, and he knew that was the effect of painkillers coursing through his brain. He forced concentration to push the drugs aside. He felt the deliciously cool texture of smooth, dry sheets. He smelled air-conditioning, sharp and mechanical. His hands reached in front of him and pulled up the thin blanket. He knew he was in a hospital bed, and he remembered his wounds. Cautiously he opened his eyes.

Stuart could see his legs had been propped up under the calves. His bare feet stuck out at the end of the bed, seemingly yards away. He felt the pain in his thighs, dull and throbbing. He wiggled his toes, first the right foot, then the left. The pain increased, but he did it again. Glad to see you, feet, he thought. He put his hands under the sheets, and ran them over and under his thighs. Through the thick bandages he could feel the plastic drains. Good, he thought, draining away the infection. Almost as an afterthought, he ran his hands over his genitals. One cock, two balls, intact. Present and correct.

His next sensation was the distantly familiar itch of an IV. I hope that is pure antibiotics, he thought.

A black man in a white garment leaned into his vision. "Ba-bobby?" rasped Stuart, his throat sore and swollen.

"Dawson, sir. Medical corpsman third class. Need anything?"

Stuart felt a crushing weight upon his heart. Bobby Coles is dead. "No, no."

Dawson smiled. "Doctor will want to see you, now's you're awake. OK to leave you alone?"

"Sure. Give me some water first."

"It's right there by the bed. Every time you wake, you ask for water." Dawson left.

I have no recollection of having been awake since I came here, thought Stuart.

The doctor came in with the smiling Dawson. "Good afternoon, Lieutenant. I'm Doctor Marcus. Do you remember me?"

"I'm embarrassed to say I do not, sir. Have you been treating me?"

"Yes, and I did once before, for burns on your left leg." The doctor consulted his chart. "Almost a year ago. You don't go easy on your legs. How do you feel?"

"Kind of spaced out. Painkillers?"

"Indeed, but we've reduced the dosage, as of this morning. Pain?"

"Not much. How, ah, are my legs?"

"You were lucky. The bullet did extensive damage to the muscle tissue in both thighs, but whoever applied the field dressings got enough penicillin into the wounds so the infection isn't too bad. The wounds are draining nicely, and the antibiotics are gaining all the time. You'll be with us for a while, but you will walk out of here."

"Here in Danang?"

"Yes. Dawson here tells me you ask that all the time. Do you remember Dawson?"

"Only from a few minutes ago. I guess I've been discourteous."

"You've had a severe trauma, and a high fever. The fever is down now to a mere hundred and one degrees. You'll feel better every day."

"Thank you, sir. Thank you, Dawson."

The doctor smiled, and departed. Dawson said, "I'll be here, sir. It's a pleasure to take care of a genuine hero."

"Why do you think I'm a hero?" asked Stuart. Why indeed, he wondered.

"The general told me, sir. He asks for you every day."

What general, thought Stuart. How is a man a hero who loses his entire command?

"You be OK for a visitor, Lieutenant?" asked Dawson.

"Why not, Dawson. But first, you got anything to eat around here?"

"Comin' right up. Better be nothing fancy, though. All the antibiotics I bin pourin' into you, your digestion won't be too good."

Dawson brought some thick soup, fragrant with chicken and thick with potatoes, and some fresh buttered rye bread. Stuart ate it slowly, with great relish, washing it down with large glasses of cold water. As soon as Dawson took away the tray, Stuart fell into a dreamless sleep.

When he awakened, Dawson brought him orange juice and scrambled eggs. That must make it morning, thought Stuart. Once again, Stuart marveled at the flavor and texture of the simple food. His request for coffee was gently denied. Once again Stuart dozed.

Stuart yawned and hitched himself up in the bed. In the corner of the room, attired in a dark purple silk bathrobe, sat Gen. Blackjack Beaurive.

Stuart hitched further upright. The pain in his thighs throbbed, and the flesh itched deep inside.

"General Beaurive. Hello!"

Blackjack grinned the grin. "Hello, William. I see you're better."

"Gaining, I think, General. It's good of you to come and visit." Blackjack wheeled his chair to the edge of the bed. "Are you wounded, sir?"

"No, William, regrettably my incarceration here is not a result of gallant wounds. But how are you?"

"Better, sir. The doc says my legs are going to be OK. But why are you here?"

"A liver ailment. The medical experts want to send me back to the States for some, ah, tests. I am of course resisting. My work is here."

He sounds sad, thought Stuart. "How is the one-niner-seventh, sir?"

"Well, William, and safely under the command of Colonel Stevens. I insisted on that, and after a struggle, I won."

"Do you have a new command, General?"

Blackjack sighed. "At present, only this awful chair. But that will change."

They sat for a minute in silence, looking at each other. Blackjack looks thin and tired, thought Stuart.

This boy nearly died, thought Beaurive. "I have some trifles for you, William. From a grateful nation." He produced a manila envelope from his lap. "The Bronze Star, with Combat V, for your good works in saving my ass in the Elephant Valley." Blackjack laid the medal lightly on Stuart's chest. "And another Purple Heart for whatever it was you just got shot up doing with the marines up north. Presumably they can be relied upon to give you some serious commendation for what I'm told was a couple of fair pieces of spotting."

Stuart looked at the two colorful medals on the blanket in front of him. Gaudy badges. He felt slightly sick, thinking of the cost. "I don't deserve these, General. You know I lost all my men. I lost Sergeant Coles."

"I know."

"I don't feel a commander who loses all his men should be honored, sir."

Blackjack sighed. "Will you allow me to advise you, Lieutenant?"

"Of course, sir." Stuart felt deeply embarrassed. What a thing to say to Blackjack.

"William, I have sent beautiful, proud young men to their deaths, and led them to their deaths, in numbers greater than you can count. I almost believe, though it is surely vanity, that I remember each one, and suffer with and *for* each one. But I also believe that each of those brave men is in a better place, for having given his life for country and glory."

Stuart started to speak, anger reddening his face. Blackjack held up his hand. "Allow me to finish, William. Glory is not an empty word, as you're thinking. Nor is Bobby Coles better dead for glory than alive had he escaped. I don't mean that, and I'm not doling out a speech. You, William, are a hero, whether you like it or not. Coles was killed by the enemy because he was up front fighting. He died because he was a fighter in a soldier's war, and not because you couldn't save him. And everyone in this hospital, and more importantly, every marine in I Corps, knows you tried to save him. He lived almost through that long night because you took the best care of him you could, and because he believed in you."

Blackjack paused, looking into Stuart's eyes with force. He leaned forward. "You will believe and accept these things as facts, Lieutenant. At first, perhaps just because I say so, but eventually because you will know them as truth. We will talk again, in a little while." Blackjack turned his wheelchair toward the door.

"General," said Stuart, very softly, "how did you really feel when Major Danby went down in the Elephant?"

Blackjack whirled the chair, and propelled himself back to the bedside. His face was grim, and hard. "Bloody awful, Lieutenant, just as you do. And for a long time, Lieutenant. But do you *really* think, that men, *heroes*, like Danby and Coles didn't know the risks of battle? Didn't *want* those risks? We mourn these men, William. We cannot ever *forget* these men, but we go on. Do you disagree, Lieutenant?"

Stuart said nothing. He felt his anger slip away into confusion.

"I thought not," said Blackjack, who turned the wheelchair again and left the room.

I wonder, thought Stuart. I just wonder.

7 March 1968

Stuart was allowed to get out of bed for the first time. His legs hurt, and felt weak, but he could stand. His first real pleasure was to walk to the head and take a piss. He hated the bedpans the nurses or the corpsmen had given him previously. The day of his first walk to the head, the rather pretty red-headed navy nurse held his arm all the way to the urinal, then placed his forearm on the top of the urinal and turned away, apparently without interest or shame. Stuart felt a little let down.

Stuart walked along the corridor, very slowly arm in arm with the nurse, whose name was Rogers. Nurse Rogers. No apparent first name. She did hold his arm nice and tight. Maybe if I wear my medals on my robe, Stuart thought. The walking was making him giddy. Nurse Rogers guided him around a corner, and they came face to face with General Beaurive, leaning on the arm of the red-faced senior nurse they all called Beast.

"Ah, William. I was just making my way to your cell." The general's grin was strained through tight skin. Stuart realized the general was very ill.

Beaurive disengaged his arm from the beefy senior nurse, who seemed reluctant to let him go. She scowled at Stuart.

"Good morning, General, how are you feeling?"

"Well enough, lad. Come and let us walk a bit." Blackjack

took Stuart's arm tightly. His hand felt hot and dry. "You will let us soldiers walk together, and please excuse us, ladies?" The big nurse continued to scowl menacingly. Rogers looked sad, and concerned. They fell back a couple of paces, but remained close to the two men.

"William, I've been reviewing in my mind our conversations of the past two days."

"Yes, so have I, General." How frail he is, thought Stuart.

"Please call me Blackjack, William. We are far from the battlefield, now."

"Yes, sir. Thank you, Blackjack."

"There's a part of this I have perhaps not seen, or seen and ignored. Purposefully."

Stuart knew his anger at the war had offended the general. "I've perhaps spoken rather too freely, sir, the, ah, pain of losing my people so quickly."

"You have spoken well, William. You have spoken honestly. I still do not agree with your indictment of this campaign as wasteful, or at least, not as only wasteful."

His voice is sad, thought Stuart. I have hurt him. I have hurt a man of such valor.

"Nonetheless, I do have some good news, William. Of your men of the Seventh ANGLICO, and your friend you asked me to find out about."

"Good, thank you, sir! What did you learn?"

"The six men who were on liberty in Danang when the Tet offensive began are all fine, and have been assigned to different elements of the ANGLICO, as needed."

Stuart felt relieved, and saddened. "So our old unit, Second Platoon of the Seventh, is disbanded." Somehow that didn't seem fair to Billy and Moser and Bobby.

"I'm confident that it will be reactivated as soon as Major MacIntyre can get the people in and trained. I told you long ago, William, that I believed in the ANGLICO program, and the Army has finally begun to take a fraction of my advice. ANGLICOs will become ever more important."

"How so, General?"

Blackjack smiled. "MACV has finally agreed with me to give I Corps to the Army, and move the marines to the south. Marines are magnificent fighters, William, but only the Army has the weight, the equipment, and the numbers to fight the campaign in I Corps as it must be fought, over control of every inch of ground. And air and especially naval gunfire will be indispensable for the big maneuvering divisions."

Divisions! thought Stuart. "Will there be divisions maneuvering in I Corps, General?'' They are going to have to knock down a *lot* of jungle before that happens, he thought.

"Not maneuvering as divisions, but holding, and fortifying, and improving strong points, and driving the enemy away or killing him. Big divisions, William, the First, the One-Hundred-and-First, the Americal.'' Blackjack's eyes shone, though William couldn't tell whether it was excitement at having his ideas finally find support, or fatigue.

"Might you get command of one of those big units, General?''

Blackjack smiled, but it was sad. "How I would love that, William. But enough of this. You asked me to find out about a naval lieutenant named Hooper?''

"Yes, sir.'' Stuart couldn't help but feel apprehensive, thinking back to Hooper's sortie from the Stone Elephant the first night of Tet.

Blackjack beamed. "He was wounded, but he's recovering nicely. He was put in for a Navy Cross for his spirited leadership of a small unit of his SEALs and others—'' Blackjack pulled reading glasses from the pocket of his robe, along with a yellow military communique ''—for extraordinary heroism in action against a superior enemy force.'' Blackjack put the paper away. "It seems your friend attacked a whole *company* of NVA, and left them rather the worse for it.''

William laughed, and enjoyed laughing. Good old crazy Hoop. "Where is he, General?''

"He was taken directly from the field where he was wounded to the *Valley Forge*. I believe that was his old ship, and yours.''

"Yes, sir, it was.''

"He's recovering nicely, and will be shipped home soon. At least he has friends on that ship.''

"Yes, sir.'' Since the yard overhaul, neither he nor I would know anyone on the *Valley*. "Are his wounds bad, sir?''

"No. He'll be fine.'' They reached Stuart's room and turned in. Blackjack sank gratefully into the wheelchair in the corner. The Beast took the blanket from Stuart's bed and arranged it across the general's knees, scowled at Stuart once more for good measure, and left. Rogers caught Stuart's eye, signed caution, then withdrew. They think I'm tiring him, he thought. What is this wasting liver ailment?

The general appeared to be composing himself. Stuart sat on the edge of the bed, and waited in silence.

"William, the fact that we have watched, personally watched, too many brave men die in this war does not make us evil for having lived, does it?''

Stuart was puzzled. "No, sir."

"Have you ever felt, William, even fleetingly, that you would rather have died yourself, than see your men die next to you?"

Stuart swallowed hard. "Well, yes, General, maybe fleetingly. But, well, only for a second, I mean, I wanted to get my men back, but I wanted to get back, too. I—"

The general held up his hand. "I know. Of course you were glad to live, even as they did not. Every soldier has felt that. William, I want to tell you a little more about heroism. Not just from my view, or perhaps what I might excuse as my public view, but from yours. And, more importantly, from the view of one Bobby Coles, Staff Sergeant, USMC."

Blackjack paused, and gave a little cough. Stuart poured water from the pitcher by the bed into the only glass, and handed it to the general. "General, I don't understand."

Blackjack raised his hand in the familiar gesture for silence. "That overprotective nurse will come for me soon, William. I ask you to listen to me, as a commander, but more as a friend. I want to tell you about yourself. While there is time for both of us to understand what we are."

"I'm listening, Blackjack."

The general sipped water from Stuart's glass, and looked into Stuart's eyes. His sad expression dissolved into one of resolve, and he straightened himself in the chair. "William, you're aware that Bobby was no lover of the white race."

"Yes, sir. He as much as told me the first day we met."

"The officer who preceded you in command of the ANGLICO detachment was a black man, and Bobby was very anxious to build an elite unit under him, nearly all black. That officer, I regret to say, did not live up to expectations, neither mine nor Sergeant Coles's. Yet when Lieutenant Robinson was relieved of his command, at his request and with my consent, Bobby came to me and asked that I find another black officer. I of course sympathized with him, and his manly black pride, but I refused. I told him I would ask I Corps for the best officer they could send, because I knew then I would eventually find the enemy in strength, and engage him, and, William, we both know the light brigade was indeed light on supporting arms. That is precisely what I asked from my commander, and you were the officer they sent to me, and to Sergeant Coles.

Blackjack paused, the gaze unwavering, and a hint of a smile flickered around his lips. A thousand images of Bobby Coles buzzed around Stuart's brain, as if they wished to speak their own piece.

Blackjack continued, "As you know, William, Bobby was a

thorough professional, and he soon came to respect you for your abilities, and your capacity as a leader. But he tried to hold himself aloof, because as competent an officer as he could see you were, you remained unalterably white.'' Blackjack gentled his irony with a smile.

"I believe he began to view my race as less important, with time, sir."

"And so he did. In time, indeed, William, he came to feel something akin to love for you, and that was a very confusing thing. You see, it is hard to hate the white race and yet love a white man. Many white people must experience the same sort of thing when they get to know blacks as people beyond their stereotypes, but that does not concern us here. The important thing is that Bobby's racism, which, ironically, had been a major source of strength and pride, had to go, or if not, his feelings toward you had to be repressed."

"Did Coles write to you, General?"

"Often. Do you not think I was violating my own chain of command, William; the letters were entirely personal. Bobby needed a black role model, and I was available. But the surprising thing, William, is that while I lectured him tirelessly to put aside racism as a passion that could only distract him and limit his own achievements, it was his experience with you, in a very few months, that finally caused him to examine the issue, and in the end, begin to change his mind."

"I'm glad of that at least, General." That really does make me feel good, thought Stuart. The images of Bobby in his brain smiled.

"William, you are aware that I asked the commanding general of the Third MAF to allow me to offer transfers to you and to Bobby into the Army, and indeed I wanted to give Bobby a direct commission as a second lieutenant."

"Yes, sir. I took him the news. He was immensely proud. I don't think he had ever before considered staying in the armed forces, but he was sure thinking about it when—'' When he died, thought Stuart.

"Yes, he was. He wrote me a letter, his, ah, last, presumably, about his thoughts. He wrote it on the thirty-first of January, and it reached me here the same day you were brought in. I would like to read to you a brief excerpt." Blackjack reached into the pocket of the elegant silk robe and produced a letter and his reading glasses. "All right?"

Stuart hitched himself a little more upright on the bed. "If you think he would have wanted it, sir."

"He would. First he says how proud he is that I should offer him a commission in what he calls *my* Army." Blackjack smiled softly at the letter. "He goes on to say he is really thinking about it." Blackjack placed one page behind the rest, and looked at Stuart over the glasses. "He says you encouraged him to accept."

"I did. He would have made an excellent officer."

"Indeed he would have. This is the passage I want to read. 'Before I can decide what I want to do, General, I have to finish something with Lieutenant Stuart. He's the finest officer I've ever known, and the reason I say that is that his care for his men is without reservation. We lost one of our men last night in a sharp action just up the road, and I can see Lieutenant Stuart ten feet away writing a letter as I write this, and I know that letter is to Hunter's brothers. When Moser, the big guy who lugs around a Browning long-barrel .50 as a personal weapon, first came to the ANGLICO, I asked him why he volunteered, and he said he just wanted to serve with Stuart, and to protect his back. After awhile, I came to understand. Moser and I now have a pact, an agreement to keep this man who has always been there for us from harm. So I want to stay with the ANGLICO until Stuart's tour ends, which won't be long now. When he goes home, I'll give you my answer.' " Blackjack paused and looked up.

Stuart felt a hot lump in his throat. "That makes me proud, sir, and even more ashamed that I got him—I lost him, sir." Stuart felt his eyes brimming, and the first tear slid down his cheek. He wiped his eyes with his sleeve.

"There is just a little bit more, William. On the last page. 'Moser and I have often discussed what we would do if Stuart were to go down and we were forced to pull back. Moser says he would stay with the lieutenant no matter what, and I believe him. I only hope I'd have the courage to do the same, General, because I know for a certainty that if I ever get wounded, Stuart would never leave me.' "

Stuart held his head in his hands and sobbed aloud. Blackjack put the letter in his pocket, and the glasses. He motioned to the big nurse, who had been waiting just outside the door. She entered, wiping her eyes, and helped the general to his feet. Blackjack walked to the edge of the bed, barely controlling his own tears, and placed his head gently on Stuart's bowed neck. He spoke at barely a whisper.

"Now you know another kind of glory, William. When I die, I could desire no finer epitaph than 'he earned the love of soldiers.' " Stuart placed a tear-soaked hand on top of the general's, looked up, and nodded. He couldn't speak. The big nurse led Blackjack gently to the wheelchair, and pushed him from the room.

Stuart felt keenly alert. I must remember this conversation forever. It must be with me even as I continue to doubt.

8 March 1968   Danang

Stuart lay sweating in his room, completely exhausted. He had just completed the first session of physical rehabilitation for his legs on the hospital's weight machines. Nurse Rogers had called him a baby and said fifteen minutes was too short a period even for a first session. Stuart would have betted the session had lasted at least three hours.

Stuart's battle medical training had told him what to expect from therapy—sharp and continuing pain as the adhesions between muscles and ligaments tore and re-formed themselves along their proper lines. Nurse Rogers had smiled, stroked, cajoled, and bullied, but the pain had made Stuart gasp. He finally had to stop, and convinced the nurse to let him stop, when his face turned dark red and his pulse threatened to split the veins on his forehead.

He had not seen Blackjack all day. He had been told that the general was undergoing a new course of medication. He hoped it would make the man stronger, but deep inside, he couldn't shake an image of the general's thinning face and flagging energy.

Dawson came in with his hourly glass of fruit juice. Stuart had never known how boring and genuinely distasteful fruit juice could be.

"Dawson, tell me something, how sick is General Beaurive?"

Dawson stiffened, frowning. His normally expressive face became a mask. "The general has a liver disease, sir."

"Fine, Dawson, but he doesn't seem to get better. What is it?"

"Can't say, sir." Dawson shifted his feet, and Stuart came upright on the bed.

"Look, Dawson, the general and I are comrades. Friends." Stuart felt himself using the general's words. "He would want me to know."

"He doesn't, sir; please don't ask me." Dawson turned and left before Stuart could ask again.

Maybe hepatitis, thought Stuart; lot of that out here, and it does take a long time to heal.

Stuart pressed the buzzer clipped to his pillow to call Dawson back. Nurse Rogers responded.

"Yes?"

"Ah, Lieutenant Rogers, can I go and visit General Beaurive?"

"No, not today."

"Why not?" Stuart felt the sharpness in his voice.

Rogers's face froze. "The general is in therapy."

"He told me tests."

"Therapy."

"Why can't I see him?"

"His wishes."

"His wishes or yours, Nurse?" Stuart felt odd, detached. The edge on his voice distressed him. Not her fault, he thought.

Nurse Lieutenant Rogers burst into tears and fled. Stuart sank into his pillows, closing his eyes against the dread. Everyone around me dies. But it isn't possible. He's a young man and had always appeared full of energy and strength.

10 March 1968

Doctor Marcus strode into Stuart's room, with Nurse Rogers in tow. "And how are we feeling today, Lieutenant?"

Who is we? thought Stuart. My ass hurts like hell. "Better, Doctor. How is General Beaurive? I'd like to see him."

Doctor Marcus frowned. "General Beaurive is not my patient, Lieutenant. His treatment is difficult. How are your legs?"

"Why, Doctor, will no one tell me about the condition of my good friend, the general?"

Doctor Marcus busied himself with Stuart's chart, whispering notations to the hovering nurse. "The general is one of those people, Lieutenant, who feels unmanned by disease. He has forbidden any of us on the hospital staff to discuss his case, outside of professional requirements. As you know the general, you will appreciate he can be very forceful, in, ah, his *requests*. Do I make myself, and by proxy, the general, clear, Lieutenant?"

Stuart sighed. "He's my friend, sir. Can I just go see him in his room?"

Doctor Marcus finished his examination and condemned Stuart to more rigorous physical therapy. "I'll inquire, Lieutenant. Now do as Nurse Rogers directs."

Stuart finished the thirty-minute workout, and really felt much better. His legs still felt weak, but so much stronger than the day before.

Nurse Rogers took him to the central ward to have his dressings changed. Stuart felt sharp pangs of pain and guilt as he walked past the silent rows of serious casualties. He thought of Bobby Coles and Moser and Billy Hunter, who never even made it this far, and of Hoop mending on the *Valley Forge*.

Doctor Marcus removed the last of the drains and cleaned and inspected the wound. He told Stuart to go and take a shower before having the wounds redressed. Stuart stood in the shower and luxuriated in the steam and soap until his legs once again grew tired. His wounds were dressed in light bandages, and Nurse Rogers (who did have a first name; it was Amy, but Stuart persisted in calling her Rogers) took him back to his room, where he fell instantly asleep.

When Stuart awakened, it was dark outside. He felt heavy, almost drugged. *A little physical therapy and a hot shower and I'm wiped out. I'm going to have to get a lot stronger than this.*

Dawson entered quietly, then smiled and came to the bedside as he realized Stuart was awake. "What you like for supper, sir? The beef is an appetizing shade of gray."

Stuart smiled, "Whatever the chef recommends, Dawson."

Dawson leaned close to Stuart and whispered. "The general isn't supposed to have visitors, but he bin asking for you. I could get you down there and bring your tray along after."

Stuart swung his legs down to the floor. "Good. Let's go."

"Wait till I get a wheelchair. No one around here ever looks at a man in a wheelchair." Dawson slipped out the door.

Dawson had sat Stuart in a wheelchair and wrapped his legs in a blanket, then wheeled him down the long corridor to the elevator. Down one floor, then another long corridor. *I wonder why they moved him,* thought Stuart. They found the general sitting up in bed. *He looks better,* thought Stuart. *His color is healthier.* The general's voice had an odd whistle as he greeted Stuart, and Stuart noticed the tube leading into Blackjack's nose. Dawson returned with a tray for Stuart. The general apparently was not eating.

"How are you feeling, Blackjack?"

The general sighed. "Not bad, really, though this prison's cuisine is even worse when they pump it into you through a tube."

"Why are they doing that, sir?"

"I was losing weight. Anyway, it seems to be working. I've begun to gain it back."

"Have they figured out what's wrong?"

"Oh, I think they know." There was a twinkle in Blackjack's eyes, and his head had lost some of its previous skull-like appearance. He definitely looks better, thought Stuart. "They tell me you're coming along very nicely, William. How are your legs?"

"Stronger, sir. Really not much of a wound, once the infection was arrested." Stuart felt carried back to his night of terror on the stream bank, and felt ashamed. Bobby died so bravely. William could still imagine the sensation of the infection crawling into his blood.

The general smiled. "I'm truly glad. You're going home very soon, you know."

"I am? My last extension was through April." I'm not ready, he thought.

"You'll go to the Naval Intelligence Command early. You wouldn't be ready to go back to the war before May, anyway, though we both know that's what you would wish."

He is joshing me. He knows I am afraid. He doesn't know about Karen. Maybe he does. Stuart grinned. "The general is looking much better, sir."

" 'The general.' You enjoy playing the courtly Southerner with me, William. Yes, I feel better. Perhaps these quacks will soon let me return to my work."

Stuart felt a chill. For a heartbeat, the general's skull face had returned. Blackjack seemed to set his jaw against a bolt of pain, which passed slowly. For a moment, neither man spoke.

Stuart broke the frozen silence as Blackjack's face softened. "General, can you tell me why it is you feel so, well, *close* to this war? Why it must be *your* work? With respect, sir, I'm well saddened by all I have seen, which is far less than you have seen."

Blackjack folded his thin fingers on his chest. He looked at Stuart with an expression of calm thoughtfulness. He started to speak, stopped, closed his eyes, and then opened them, slowly. He smiled, toward a grin, but soft, so soft. Stuart felt tears welling.

"I will try to answer that question, Lieutenant."

"Yessir." Stuart felt miserable.

"Two months ago the answer would have been very difficult." I know, thought Stuart.

"Two months ago, I would have said that a man of my training needed only his directive: Kill the enemy, take the battlefield, win the glory."

"Yessir."

"Now my perspective has been altered. I am an old soldier with time to think, William."

"Blackjack, OK, I'm deeply sorry. I know your convictions."

"My convictions haven't changed, William. It is my perspective. When I led you, did you ever doubt my convictions?"

"No, sir."

"William, when I was a commander in the field, I felt that if I only led my men well, and if the mission was both important, and *prudent*, that I was doing the right thing. Did you sense that?"

"Yes, Blackjack, I did." Now I understand why we pushed on up the Elephant Valley.

"Recently, I have had, ah, the *luxury* of time to think of this conflict in a somewhat larger perspective." A shadow of the famous grin fleeted across the general's shrunken face.

"Yes, General, me too. I almost regret that luxury."

Blackjack pushed himself slightly more upright in the bed. His eyes grew penetrating. "William, I still believe in the rightness of our purpose in this war."

"Of course, sir." Stuart found himself trying to sit up straight.

"And I still believe that those self-styled antiwar people who defile and insult our fighting men do a great wrong."

"Yes, sir."

The general slumped back, and looked at the ceiling. "You must let me rest, William, I tire. Thank you for your visit. And thank the brave Dawson." He closed his eyes.

Stuart started to wheel the chair around. "Thank you, sir."

Blackjack opened his eyes. "William?"

"Sir?"

"Do you still think that some of those men, some of *our* men, were wasted?"

"Ah, some, sir, yes, I do, but—"

"So do I, William." The general closed his eyes.

12 March 1968

Nurse Rogers came in at morning rounds, happy and sad and confused. She told Stuart that he would be released the following day. She kissed Stuart furtively, as the door to his room was open and there was heavy traffic in the adjacent corridor. Stuart swung his legs out of the bed. Rogers offered the wheelchair to take him to physiotherapy, but as he had on the past three mornings, Stuart insisted on walking. Walking to the scaffold, he called it.

The therapy itself was hard work, and still very painful. Stuart could feel it working, however. His legs hurt all the time, but although the therapy made him very tired, he soon recovered.

Stuart was often up and around the corridors, walking and talking to the other patients in the surrounding wards, despite the continual scoldings of the harried floor nurses. He used the wheelchair only for his nightly visit to the general, assisted in his disguise by Dawson.

During Stuart's afternoon exam, Dr. Marcus had confirmed his probable transfer the following morning, and, if air transport could be quickly arranged, Stuart would be in Hawaii or California by the end of the week, due thirty days convalescent leave, plus thirty more days to get moved to Washington and his new assignment.

"A fine chance to get reacquainted with your wife, hey, Lieutenant?" said Dr. Marcus as he looked at the red but healing scars.

"Yes, sir," said William, dreading the confrontation with Karen, and hoping that, whatever came of it, it wouldn't last sixty days.

"Well, William," continued Dr. Marcus, rubbing vitamin E ointment into the scars. "We all here envy your going back to your happy wife and home, though we're all damned sure you've earned the privilege."

William forced himself to smile. "Thank you, Doctor. All the doctors and staff have been very kind."

Doctor Marcus smiled, and turned to his next patient. Rogers took Stuart to the dressing station, where a light support bandage was wrapped around each thigh. The corpsman handed Stuart several extra rolls. "I hear you'll be changing your own from now on, Lieutenant. Congratulations." He extended his hand, and Stuart shook it.

Blackjack seemed restless, distracted. He watched Stuart eat his dinner slowly from the tray on his lap. Stuart had the impression that the general was impatient for him to finish, impatient to begin the evening's conversation. He set the tray aside rather than prolong the general's fidgeting.

"The general seems agitated," offered Stuart.

Blackjack sat suddenly quiet. "Do I? Well, maybe I am. I'm feeling strangely, William. I think the drugs the quacks are pouring into me are affecting my mind." The expression was questioning, bordering on anxious.

"I'm sure the doctors know best how to treat you, sir." Stuart felt himself trying to reassure. But I'm well and going home and he's ill and will remain. I feel false even as I say these words.

"To be sure. Yet I cannot concentrate. I dream, and the images are strange. I see myself walking away, with my back to myself, over and over, walking away.''

"Have you told the docs?"

"No. What would be the point?"

If Blackjack Beaurive could be afraid, this is how he would look, thought Stuart. He had nothing to say, so he waited for the general, who sat slowly kneading the skin over his closed eyes.

"Within a week, William, you will be home, back to the World, as the soldiers say. Have you thought about what that will be like?"

I guess I really haven't, thought Stuart. I guess my problems with Karen have caused me to push away all other thoughts of the World. "Not really, sir. I reckon I've been wondering how long I'll have to be there, what I'll have to do before my painful memories of, well, all we've seen here will soften. Once Nam really feels like the past, then I'll go forward." Stuart listened to himself. It seemed an odd little speech, and he had no idea where it came from.

Blackjack dropped his hands back onto the blanket and opened his eyes. Stuart saw the eyes were steady now, fully in control. The realization allowed Stuart himself to relax. "You won't have the luxury of time to contemplate the whys and wherefores, William. The World will rush upon you. You must decide how you will face it."

"I'm not sure I understand, Blackjack. The World won't even notice me. I go to Washington, I serve out my time."

"I have a letter from my son. He doesn't write often, though he is a good son. From what he tells me, the people march and chant and curse the soldiers. They insult and revile the very President of the United States."

"But why? Surely they know we're fighting for them?"

"They say it is for imperialism. They say we kill for no reason. They say the enemy's great victory during Tet proves we cannot win."

"But we kicked their asses during and after Tet! The casualties we inflicted—"

Blackjack held up his hand, and William stopped.

"The facts as we know them are of no importance in the World. William, in War Two, even after Korea, the boys *marched* home, in regiments, with flags and bands, and the civilians cheered. Now the men, the men of *honor*, *slink* home, time served, but the war not won, and the people sneer."

Stuart felt himself getting angry, and he also felt a little frightened. "I don't think I'm up for much in the way of sneering, General."

"The politicians who sent us here to fight are joining the rabble, William. This is the beginning of a betrayal of our fighting soldiers without precedent in the history of the nation. Men like you, William, *fighting* men, must tell them, tell them all, that we fight this war with honor!" Blackjack gripped William's arm in his bony hand.

"Yes, sir," said William.

Blackjack rushed on. "If we fail to show the citizenry that we were true to our ancient code, we risk *destruction* of that which we hold most dear, William." Blackjack's voice had sunk to an insistent rasp.

"The *nation*, sir?" William looked at the general's flushed, anguished face.

"That, and the nearer love, which defends the nation, indeed makes nationhood possible. My Army, your Navy." Blackjack released William's arm and fell back against his pillows, exhausted. "The antiwar people, William, especially the young ones, of your own age, will want you to set aside the glory you have earned here, to *deny* it!" Once again, Stuart saw the mask of pain. "You must think about how you will respond, William."

Oh, Jesus, thought Stuart, choking. "What does the general suggest?"

Suddenly the general grinned with a portion of his old vitality, "With dignity and honor, Lieutenant. And never lose sight of how hard you worked to get that way."

I'll remember, Blackjack, thought Stuart. Why can't I just go home and disappear?

"You will never put down the honor of the uniform, William, even long after you have taken it off for the last time."

As usual, the general reads my mind, thought Stuart. "General, I didn't know you had a son."

Blackjack brightened. "Yes, Jefferson, but his friends call him Beau. Medical student at Johns Hopkins. I have, ah, requested that he call on you once you get settled."

Stuart smiled, considering what a "request" from father Blackjack to a son must be like. I'll bet it would be damn all right, he decided.

Dawson appeared, greeted the general, and put his hands on the push handles of Stuart's wheelchair.

"William, if I don't see you again before you go home, I want to tell you I have enjoyed talking with you, and soldiering with you, as with few men."

Stuart swallowed the lump in his throat painfully. "You've been an inspiration to me, General, and a friend."

"Thank you for that, William, and thank you for being what you were in the Elephant and at Horsehead Mountain. I will never forget your courage and your skill on those two glorious days. But if Dawson will give me but one more minute, I want you to have something of mine, to remember me. I have worn this with pride, and it has meant more to me than all of the decorations I have received in three wars." The general's skeletal hands brought the badge from beneath his covers, a blue rectangle with a flintlock rifle surrounded by a silver wreath, the badge of a combat infantryman. "I put a letter in your jacket, William. Major MacIntyre has a copy. Wear this over your ribbons."

William held the simple badge in his hands, and he felt deeply honored. "Thank you, sir, but you'll need this when you get out of here."

"I have several others, William. I just wanted you to have one I had worn, as a link between us."

Stuart stood up out of the wheelchair, and shook the general's hand. "I am honored to have served under your command, General." He saluted crisply.

Blackjack returned the salute, and smiled, but fatigue marred the grin. "Remember old Blackjack, William."

"Yes, sir! Yes, Blackjack. But I'll see you before I go."

Blackjack's eyes were closing despite himself. "Good night William."

"Good night, Blackjack."

Dawson put a hand on Stuart's shoulder, gently guiding him back into the wheelchair, and wheeled him to his room.

13 March 1968

Stuart awoke with a start, and looked at his watch, 0835. Never in the hospital had he been allowed to sleep so late. He rolled out of bed, and without thinking, made his own way to the head. Nurses and orderlies scurried about, without taking any apparent notice. Some he barely recognized; most he didn't. Where is Dawson, where is Amy Rogers?

he did his morning washup, shaved, and returned to his room. No Dawson, and no breakfast appeared. Stuart puzzled. It's as though I've already been discharged, he thought. I'm no longer here.

The evening before, Rogers had brought him a fresh set of

greens, starched by the hospital laundry, new underwear and socks, and the boots he had come in with. Stuart dressed quickly. In the drawer by the bed he found his lieutenant's bars, and screwed them to the collar of the uniform. Bending over to lace the boots was painful, but he got it done. He carefully wrapped the Combat Infantry Badge in toilet paper, and put it and the medals Blackjack had given him in a pocket and buttoned it. Then he sat down to wait, listening to his stomach growl.

An orderly with a first class corpsman's crow on his arm arrived at 0930, with a clipboard. "I'm here to check you out, sir. Back to the BOQ at Tien Shaw, and in a few days, home."

Stuart nodded. He emptied the drawer, and shoved his few possessions into a plastic AWOL bag Rogers had provided. He wondered vaguely what had happened to his field gear, especially the little Walther pistol. He stood, and spoke to the corpsman. "Where's Rogers, and Dawson? All the people I've come to know here?"

"Couldn't tell you, sir. This is my first day of duty here, from stateside."

Stuart studied the man. Short, black, taciturn. "Well, Corpsman, let's get her done."

"Right, sir."

Stuart spent the better part of an hour signing papers and picking up temporary and permanent change-of-station orders. His assignment to NIS in Washington had been moved up, and it was just a matter of transport. He finished all the paperwork, but as he was confronted by the open front door of the hospital, he stopped. "I would like, Corpsman, to say good-bye to General Beaurive."

The corpsman frowned. "Give me a minute, sir; I'd best take you to Dr. Broderick."

The corpsman took him back to the floor where Blackjack had his room, into an office, and left him. In a few minutes, a doctor with commander's insignia appeared and closed the door.

"You're Lieutenant Stuart. I'm Doctor Broderick; I treated General Beaurive."

Treated? thought Stuart.

"The general died during the night. We realize you were close to him, and we're sorry."

Stuart sagged into a chair, his lungs empty. When he didn't speak, the doctor continued.

"The general asked me to answer any question you might ask."

Stuart shook himself. His lungs stayed empty, as after a blow to the solar plexus. He sensed his mouth gaping, like a stranded fish. The doctor looked at him with apparent concern, and leaned forward. "Are you all right, Lieutenant?"

Stuart forced himself upright in the low chair, fought to control his breathing. The light-headedness, the panic, receded. "Commander, the general is *dead*?"

"Yes. He died last night." The commander paused; Stuart did not speak. The commander continued, "General Beaurive asked me to answer any questions if you asked them, Lieutenant."

Stuart gasped, recovered. "What killed him, Commander? He told me he had some liver disease, and was here just for tests."

The doctor shifted uneasily, then sat behind the desk. "The general had inoperable liver cancer, Lieutenant."

Oh, my god, thought Stuart. "Why didn't he tell me?"

"He never told anyone. He refused to speak of it."

"How long did he know?"

The commander looked at the record. "He was told seven months ago. He was told to go back to the States, for chemotherapy that might have arrested the spread of the cancer. He refused. He insisted on staying with his brigade." The commander lifted a single sheet from the medical file. "He signed a specific release. Four weeks ago, he collapsed in the field, and he was brought here. There was little we could do, other than make him as comfortable as we could."

"But, in the last few days, he seemed better. Didn't the medication work?"

Commander Broderick sighed. "There was no medication, Lieutenant, just painkillers and vitamin supplements. We started feeding him through a tube because he couldn't keep solid food in him."

Jesus, thought Stuart, sweet Jesus. "Did he have much pain?"

The commander stood and turned his back on Stuart. "Son, he told me not to lie to you, though I would dearly like to. He felt very close to you. Yes, Lieutenant Stuart, yes, he felt excruciating pain, all the time. Every evening, before those visits you paid to him, which we weren't supposed to know about, he *refused* his painkiller." The doctor turned to face Stuart, his face stiff. "He endured, Lieutenant, he suffered to give you some message. I hope you know what that message was."

Stuart looked at his hands. How slowly the mind accepts, he thought. How finely the pain and the message of pain is etched. "I believe I do, Commander."

Once again the commander sat behind the chipped gray steel desk. "I shouldn't be hard on you, son. It just seemed to a lot of us who tried to care for that wonderful man that he kept living just to tell you something.''

Stuart looked the commander in the eye. ''I believe he did, sir, though right now I couldn't explain it. It was something he had to pass on. Has his family been told?''

''His wife died two years ago. He has a son, at Johns Hopkins. They were apparently estranged.''

''Estranged?''

''The boy opposed the war. Opposes the war.''

So, thought Stuart. We all, in the end, suffer and die alone. ''Where will he be buried, sir?''

''At Arlington. It's all arranged.''

''I would like to escort the body there, sir.''

The doctor separated an envelope from the medical record. ''He expressly forbade it, Lieutenant. He let me read this letter, meant for you after he died.'' The doctor handed the slim envelope across the desk. Stuart took a deep breath, and withdrew a single sheet of paper.

Dear William,

If you are reading this, you know I have had to ride on ahead. So be it. I know you will want to bury me, but I forbid that. The Brigade will attend to the mortal remains; I want you to think of me always as I was alive. My last preaching to you is at least short. Don't grieve; grow. Bobby and I expect a lot of you.

We won two glorious battles. They were the best in my life.

Go with God,

Blackjack

Stuart felt the tears run freely down his cheeks. He sighed, and rubbed his eyes, but they wouldn't clear. He looked at the doctor, who looked back, no more able to speak than Stuart. Stuart folded the sheet of paper and put it carefully in his left shirt pocket. ''I know what he wanted to tell me, Commander.''

''Good, son. Then it was worth it for him.'' The commander got slowly to his feet. ''Stay here awhile, son, until you feel better.''

''Thank you, Commander. Ah, Commander, how old was the general?''

The doctor looked again at the record in front of him. ''Forty-eight, Lieutenant. Would have been forty-nine in ten days.'' The doctor gathered the record and left the room.

Stuart sat in the hard chair for about half an hour until he felt composed. He felt calm and numb. He left the hospital and was enveloped by the Vietnamese heat. He hitched a ride to Tien Shaw, to the Stone Elephant, and got slowly and miserably drunk, alone.

---

18 March 1968   Between Honolulu and San Francisco

Stuart sat on the aisle of the chartered Braniff Airways DC-8, dozing in spite of the dull ache in his thighs. He reached up and loosened the tie of his class A khaki uniform. The plane had taken off from Danang the previous day, rising into the sunrise bright above heavy monsoon clouds, encouraged out of Vietnamese airspace by the cheers of its passengers. The flight carried 220 other returning servicemen. The plane made the short hop to Clark Air Base near Manila, then flew on through the day and evening to Hickham in Hawaii. The passengers, many of them walking wounded, had mostly been drinking steadily on the flight, spending the last of their military payment certificates, and Stuart felt the sour stomach and desiccated mouth that signaled a regular navy hangover.

The plane took on a new crew in Hawaii while the men emptied the bars at Hickham Field. At 0200 Hawaiian time Braniff took off again on the last leg to San Francisco International Airport. Stuart thought about what he would say to Karen if she met his flight, as she had promised, and his stomach tightened. He wondered if any of the other passengers had less to look

forward to going home than he did. He suspected many probably
had.

Stuart sat up and licked his dry lips with his furry tongue. A
stewardess stopped, then perched on one hip on the armrest of
Stuart's seat. "You look a bit rough, Lieutenant," she said, with
a double arch of eyebrows.

The woman looked about thirty, tautly pretty. She was dressed
in a garish orangy pink bubble-shaped skirt, tight around her
narrow waist, and pulled tight above her pretty knees. Above
the silly-looking skirt, she wore a blouse of fawn-colored material that looked like silk but probably wasn't, which swelled
nicely over her breasts. Her hair was done in a stiff bubble-
shaped cut. "Hello, Bubbles," Stuart grinned thickly, and immediately regretted the remark.

The woman smiled thinly. "My name is Laurel. I didn't
choose the costume." Laurel had a pen and clipboard in her
hands. "Care for a little brightener before lunch, Lieutenant?"

"Um. Thanks, ah, Laurel. Perhaps a beer might help."

Laurel wrote on her clipboard. The dress was gathered around
her nice thighs by something that looked like elastic. Laurel
inserted the plastic ballpoint pen inside the elastic, and scratched
the inside of her thigh. Stuart grinned, and felt aroused, and
then foolish. "This outfit is not only funny looking, Lieutenant,
it's hot. What about your buddies?"

Stuart looked across at the marine sergeant next to him, and
the army corporal by the window. Both snored loudly. It seemed
pointless to wake them.

"Uh, dead of wounds, ma'am, I reckon."

Laurel pushed herself up from the armrest, and adjusted the
skirt of her uniform with a slow left hand. "Be right back with
the first one of the day, blue eyes." She smiled brightly.

Stuart closed his eyes, and concentrated on the slow beat inside his head. So this is the World, he thought.

Stuart drank beer slowly as the plane flew over the blue, cloud-
dotted Pacific. He had had two Michelobs, decided they tasted
sweet, then tried two Coors. No better. The plane banked, and
Stuart looked across the two drowsy men to the view outside the
window, and saw the Golden Gate.

In a few more minutes they landed, at 0830, Pacific Standard
Time, more or less on schedule. Everybody got up at once, and
bumped into each other for a few minutes; then the doors
opened, and the men, laden with all kinds of gear, trooped slowly
off the plane. Laurel smiled brightly, and reminded Stuart he

had promised to call. Stuart grinned a bit lopsidedly, and patted his shirt pocket where he had put her number.

Customs had been cleared in Honolulu, so the men walked raggedly into the main terminal. Most would be loaded on buses to go to some military base or other, but since Stuart had orders to Washington, and leave papers, he could pretty much do as he liked. He walked slowly, willing the stiffness to leave his legs. Men, anxious to be met by loved ones, surged past him in the narrow corridor.

Inside the main terminal building, a small group of people in scruffy clothes stood across the passageway, watched without much interest by a couple of airport cops. The carried signs like the ones Stuart and the other servicemen had previously seen in *Time* and *Newsweek*. End the War, Bring the War Home, read the nice ones. Baby Killers, Heroes of Death, read the others. Stuart heard a low growl from the protestors at the same time he heard a sigh from the servicemen.

Stuart walked beside the marine sergeant with whom he had ridden across the Pacific. They both wore masks of indifference, determined to stride past the demonstrators without comment or expression. The demonstrators began a chant.

"Hey, hey, LBJ, how many kids did you kill today?"

A young woman, really a girl, stepped forward quickly and threw a can of red fluid at the approaching servicemen. Stuart ducked his head instinctively, and the bulk of the slop hit the sergeant. The sergeant cried out, dropped his seabag, and pawed at his eyes. The woman screamed something about blood on all of you, and ran. The marine bellowed, and charged the crowd. Stuart brought him down with a leg tackle, and held him. The police scattered the remaining demonstrators.

Stuart released the marine, and cleared his eyes with his handkerchief. "Easy, sergeant, easy. We can't react to this shit."

The sergeant's eyes were tearing from the red fluid, but he calmed quickly. "Jesus, Lieutenant, what the fuck did *we* do?"

"I don't know, Sergeant. Let's go find the head, and clean this stuff off."

Whatever the red stuff was, it wasn't blood, for it came easily out of the sergeant's gabardines. Stuart's shirt was stained, so he replaced it with a fresh one from his B-4 bag, after a sink wash-up. The starched cotton felt good, so he shaved and felt even better. The marine had thanked him, and departed. Stuart looked at his watch, and decided to find another beer.

Welcome home, all, he thought.

* * *

Stuart phoned Karen from the cocktail lounge. She said she was sorry she had not been able to come up to San Francisco to meet his plane. She was anxious to see him, to hold him, to talk. Had she changed her mind about coming to Washington with him? Well, no, but she wanted to explain to him where her head was, and why a temporary separation was best.

Temporary separation? The last nine months hadn't been enough? thought Stuart. He decided that the reunion with Karen could definitely wait; he just wasn't ready for it, or for much of anything else. His beer had no taste, so he asked the barman for a Jack Daniels straight up.

"Little early for that, isn't it, son?"

"I'm still on Vietnam time; late evening for me." Son, indeed. I'm a naval officer in uniform and this asshole calls me son. Great being back in the World.

Stuart next called his sister in Palo Alto. "Hello, Carole Ann? It's William."

"William! You're here! We were sorry we couldn't come up and meet you at the airport, but . . ."

"Not to worry. Airport's got its own welcomers. You and Dan OK? Kids?"

"Everybody's fine. Ah, how's Karen?"

"Sounds OK over the phone."

"Oh, she didn't get there either. How sad, after all you've been through."

Stuart banged his glass aggressively on the bar and glared at the bartender, who was too busy with his newspaper to attend to his one customer. The bartender ambled over and very slowly rebuilt the drink.

"William? Are you still there?"

"Yep." Sipping.

"Are you going to Long Beach to see her?"

"Well, yes. I have to pack up my stuff, and, I guess, say good-bye."

"I really don't know why she's doing this to you."

No one ever understands why somebody else does it to you. "She has reason enough, I suppose."

"When will you go down?"

"I don't know. I don't have to report to navy intelligence for nearly eight weeks. Maybe I'll wander around San Francisco for a few days."

"Come down here."

"Thanks, but I'd just be in the way. I'm not real good company just now."

"That's just jet lag, William." Jet lag my ass, thought William; more like war lag, love lag, hurt lag. He sipped his drink, not knowing what to say. "You should be with family, William; come on down, be with us."

She sounded like she meant it. "OK, big sister, I'll rent a car and drive down."

"It'll be so good to see you safe at home, brother."

Stuart left what he could guess was above five cents over the exact price of two drinks on the bar, picked up his gear, and left. The bartender didn't look up from his newspaper.

"I thought we were just going to be family."

"It's just a few friends for cocktails. They'll be gone by eight, and then we'll just be us."

"You didn't mention it on the phone."

"I was afraid you might not come if I did."

Right again, big sister. "Who are these people?"

"Mostly young lecturers and professors, friends of Dan's from the university."

Oh, Judas! "Sister, I've been shouted at and spat at and someone threw blood or something made to look like blood on me and a marine this very morning. The best I've been able to get back from my fellow man during the rest of this day has been hostile indifference. Now you want me to exchange banter with a bunch of left-wing professors? I really think I should maybe take a drive over and look at the ocean. Or sleep off my jet lag."

"William, I'd like you to be there. I'd like to show you off! And I'm sure Dan's friends will be polite and respectful to you as befits a veteran, no matter what they may think of your war."

My war! What has happened in this country?

Stuart took a long shower, then climbed into the bunk bed above that of his nephew, Toby, who was out with friends. He slept deeply for a few hours, his head filled with the sounds of the airplane, and was jolted awake by a brief dream of walking down a narrow tunnel and being soaked in blood. He rolled out of bed feeling even worse that when he had gotten in it.

Stuart shaved carefully, and took another shower. He selected a fresh shirt, and transferred his rank devices to the collar points. He looked at the uniform he had worn on the flight, decided it was just too shabby, got out his only other uniform, and stretched it out on Toby's bed. He unpinned the ribbons and the Combat Infantry Badge from the soiled blouse and laid them on the clean blouse above the left breast pocket. Maybe I better leave these off, he thought. I really don't want to be asked what they mean by Dan's professor friends. Still, they are part of the uniform.

Stuart sat on the bed, next to the fresh uniform, and looked at the ribbons. These aren't supposed to mean much to me, but they do. Each one brings back a memory, and some of the memories are good.

The first time he was put in for a medal was when he had been a boat officer, taking the marines and their armor up the Cua Viet. He had never been decorated for that, but Moser had gotten a Bronze Star for his part, on the basis of Stuart's strong recommendation. Stuart touched his own Bronze Star, which Blackjack had given him for the Elephant Valley, and thought about big Moser and his deadly big machine gun, and he smiled. His fingers moved to the Silver Star, which the CO of the *Valley* had gotten for him, with the endorsement of the marine special landing force commander, for his conspicuous gallantry when the ship's helicopter was shot down on the way to Danang. Stuart had always thought the citation overblown and the award too great, but captains of ships didn't get many chances to decorate their own, so they took the ones they got. Touching the ribbon reminded him of the recommendation he had written in the hospital in Danang for a posthumous award of the Silver Star to Bobby Coles, with the general making suggestions for the wording. How convincingly the general could speak and write of gallantry! He had written a citation for the same award for Billy Hunter, and he was fairly sure both would go through. He had already made sure that the men's Purple Hearts had been sent to their brothers, and Moser's to his mother.

Stuart's eyes misted as he thought of his fallen friends. He had won his first Purple Heart for the burns on his leg in the helo crash, and his second for the bullet in his thighs, so the ribbon had a gold star in the center. The Purple Heart seemed to represent all the hurt of the war—not gallantry, not honor and glory, just hurt. Fuck it, thought William, these ribbons mean everything to me, and they belong on the uniform.

The ribbons on the bottom row were the three "show-up" awards, including the red and yellow National Service Medal, which everybody got for joining up. Maybe, thought William, as he aligned the block of ribbons above the pocket of his jacket, that ribbon says the most, here in the World. The red, yellow, and green Vietnamese Service Medal followed, and then the green and white Vietnamese Campaign Ribbon, with its metal tab, which said, enigmatically, "1960–." I was there, thought Stuart, pinning the ribbons in place.

Stuart pinned the Combat Infantryman's Badge above the ribbons, in the place of honor. This badge will always remind me of Blackjack, the greatest and bravest man I've ever known.

William secured the pins, and felt a flash of shame and anger that he had even considered not wearing his decorations. They were part of the uniform.

Stuart stood in the corner of the small living room of Carole Ann and Dan's house off University Avenue. It was hot in the room, and most of the men had taken off their jackets. Stuart would have liked to at least unbutton his uniform jacket and loosen his tie, but he wasn't about to let these pukes see him out of uniform.

So far nothing truly awful had happened. Wintry smiles and firm, dry handshakes from the men (see, soldier, I'm a man, too), and rather more engaging looks and touches from the wives and girlfriends (is it true about the Oriental women? . . .). No one had called him a baby killer, and no one had even thrown blood, and it was nearing eight o'clock. The crowd was thinning, and Stuart was mellowing out on his third Jack Daniels.

"William, I'm Professor Kraft, history, and this is my colleague, Dr. Bruce."

"William Stuart, sir. At your service."

"Yes, ah, very nice. First, of course, we would like to add our welcome home to those of the others."

"Everyone has been most kind."

"We were curious, however, as to why you would attend a party in this place in uniform—that is, after so long in Vietnam, one would think you would be glad to get into civilian clothes."

"My civilian clothes are all in transit, or in southern California waiting to be packed. But I feel perfectly comfortable in uniform." Because it sets me apart, thought Stuart, and it should.

"My friend Bruce, here, and some of the younger lecturers thought you might have worn your uniform as a provocation."

Stuart turned to the younger man, who only grinned. "You find the sight of an American uniform provocative?"

"I believe I do," said Bruce. He had a smooth, urbane voice, "given the feelings of this university community about the war in Vietnam."

"Surely any political hostility you may feel about the war does not cause you to condemn this country's men at arms?" Stuart felt his awareness increasing and realized the rest of the room's conversations had ceased. He was on stage, and he wondered whether he had not indeed been waiting for the opportunity to draw the hostility to a head and lance it.

"Not as individuals, no, of course not," smoothed Bruce, "but the symbolic effect of your uniform on, or at least near, a university in these times might, ah, be construed as an intrusion into the freedom of expression at that university.''

''Don't you think that's a bit broad?''

''Well, no, actually, especially as your particular uniform shows obvious and direct symbolic support for the war in Vietnam.'' Bruce placed a long-fingered hand lightly on the group of ribbons on Stuart's left breast. Stuart stiffened, and the hand was quickly withdrawn.

Dan Pierce, Carole Ann's husband, appeared at Stuart's shoulder. ''Hey, old buddy, I brought you a refill.'' Dan pried the empty glass from Stuart's tight fist and inserted a new one. He glanced nervously at Bruce and Stuart. ''You've been standing too long in this corner.''

These people think they can feel the force of great rage, thought Stuart. They think they see a beast within. How little they really do see. ''I was trying not to be noticed. I guess the uniform gave me away.'' Stuart said evenly. He felt pleased to be back in control. He made sure his eyes never left Bruce's eyes. Bruce was getting pale around the mouth, but his grin still held. He'll try one more smart remark, thought Stuart.

Professor Kraft interceded, and tried to pick off Stuart's stare. ''I say, you have rather a lot of ribbons. The end one on top, that's a Silver Star, is it not? For gallantry, I believe?''

''Yep.'' Stuart sipped his drink, feeling the high of adrenaline in control.

''Yes! I recognize it from my service in World War Two.'' Avuncular.

Here comes junior, thought Stuart.

Bruce was screwing up his courage behind the grin. ''How many men did you have to kill to get that medal?'' Manly, jocular.

''Fuck you.'' It came out softly, with an edge of steel. Stuart thought Bruce would faint.

''What did you say?'' The question came from Kraft. Stuart held Bruce in his stare, and slowly placed his glass on the table to his left. Stuart put a hand into his pocket and withdrew a cigarette. Bruce opened his mouth to breathe, and took a half step backward. Stuart put his hand in the same pocket, and withdrew his black cigarette holder and his silver lighter. The hump thinks I'm going to pull a gun and blow him away, Stuart thought.

Stuart screwed the cigarette into the holder, and lit it carefully. ''Fuck you. I said 'fuck you.' ''

Professor Kraft tried to cut through the tension with bluff. Stuart was determined to keep the heat all the way up.

''I say, that's a bit rude for an officer in mixed company.''

"I said it to him. He is not obviously mixed company."

Bruce flushed. Kraft spoke. "Now—"

"I suppose you did not find the question rude? Quite possibly even insulting to a man of my position, *in my uniform*?"

"Well, I, yes, I—"

"I suppose your *colleague* felt he was exercising *restraint* in that he did not ask me how many *babies* I had to kill to get his ribbon?" Nice and measured. If it's hate you want, I've had all day to get ready, thought Stuart.

"I'm sorry. And I'm sure Dr. Bruce meant no offense." Kraft turned to Bruce, whose head bobbed like one of those spring-necked toys people put in car windows. "The fact is that the uniform you wear has come to be a symbol of all our government is doing—"

"Professor, spare me the speech. To the extent you have any right to treat *this* uniform that I wear with pride as a *symbol*, which you do *not*, you should recognize it as a symbol of protection for your right to ponder ideologies in your secure ivory tower. The military does not govern in this country; it never has. The young men fighting and dying in Vietnam have no say in foreign policy; indeed, they have far less influence than do you. If you mean to oppose this war effectively, you will try to reach the politicians who run this mess. How much to you really accomplish by encouraging bullies to sully the uniforms of ROTC cadets?"

"Well, not a lot, I admit." Kraft suddenly reddened with genuine passion. "But dammit, man! Surely you must grant that intelligent men, men of good will, oppose the war as evil and immoral?"

"I grant nothing. You may of course oppose the war for any reason you please. You may hate the war and protest against it and the political leaders who got us into it and who keep us in it. But to the extent you protest by reviling the brave men who fight that war on this nation's behalf, *you do great wrong*."

There was a silence. Stuart felt a sense of release, as at the end of a dramatic play. He felt his face soften, and saw the hostility disappearing from the faces of the guests across the room. He wished he could see more understanding.

Professor Kraft looked sad, and somehow older. His voice had lost its patronizing crispness. "I'm gratified that at least you show some sympathy for the antiwar movement."

"Don't put words in my mouth, Professor. As a serving officer in the armed forces, I can have no opinion about the merits of this or any other war I may be asked to fight."

" 'My country, right or wrong?' " The voice was Bruce's, but the smoothness had been replaced by a raspy whistle.

"As I recall it, it runs 'My country, *may she ever be right,* but right or wrong, my country.' Patriotism is not required to be without doubt, Dr. Bruce. We in the armed forces of the United States protect your right to question, to doubt."

"But as a soldier, you're not free to doubt."

"On the battlefield, Doctor, doubt is the precursor of disaster."

Stuart smiled despite himself, finished his drink, then went across to the bar to make another. While his back was turned, the cocktail party ended.

19 March 1968   Palo Alto, California

The atmosphere at breakfast, Stuart thought, was mildly tense. He felt sorry for disturbing his sister's hospitality and home, but not of what he had said and done.

"How long can you stay with us, William?" said Carole Ann.

"Oh, sister, I'd best go on today. I don't wish to embarrass you further."

"You didn't. You don't. You should stay and heal."

"I am healing. Besides, I think I should deal with my own problems, with Karen and all. This morning I feel like I want to start a new life without further delay. Might's well get on to Washington and start."

Dan poured William another cup of coffee. "William, you took ole Frank Bruce down pretty hard."

"Dan, I'm truly sorry if I offended your house, but he was way out of line, what he said."

"He's a good scholar, and not normally an incautious man."

"Are you saying you really think I provoked him?"

"No, he made his own, but you sure seemed ready to answer."

Stuart dabbed his lips with his napkin. "Well, brother, in my business, a man learns to get ready very quickly. I'll just pack up and make the ten-fifteen PSA flight from San Jose to Long Beach."

"Dan, I'm worried about him."

"About him?"

"My own baby brother, and he frightens me."

"He's all right."

"He doesn't frighten you? The way he crushed Frank Bruce last night, without moving a muscle?"

"No. What frightens me is that assholes like Frank Bruce will teach the students and eventually write the histories that seek to explain your brother and his war in terms he could never accept.''

''But you yourself oppose the war.''

''I do. But I oppose even more strongly the Frank Bruces who advocate violence against this nation's institutions. And last night I couldn't help thinking that for Frank the antiwar sentiment may be something to be used to gain a wider revolution.''

''It hurts me that William wants to get away from us.''

''Like he said, he has to get on with his life. Imagine all that happening to him his first day back from that horror.''

Carole Ann was crying. ''I wish we had made time to fetch him from the airport.''

Dan put his arm around his wife's shoulders and kissed the tears. ''You know, it frightens me the more because I know that your brother is a gentle and intelligent man.''

''Dan?''

''I mean the ones that come home after him won't all be wise and gentle. And this country doesn't yet know how to receive them.''

Stuart was relieved to find no spitting protesters at the Long Beach Airport. There was a lot of Navy in Long Beach, and a healthy portion of the people passing through the airport were in uniform. He considered taking a cab to his apartment, but thought of the probable need to depart quickly, and decided to rent another car.

Money burning a hole in my pocket, he thought.

He phoned Karen from the rental car counter, and asked if he could come by in half an hour. She said to come right away. Stuart wanted to think he was just being polite, but he knew he wanted to be sure she was alone. A lot of married servicemen phoned home before they went home, and they joked about it, but they did it to avoid hurt. Servicemen understood loneliness perhaps before all other emotions, and they understood it in their wives as well.

Karen opened the door. Stuart was struck by her beauty as though he were seeing her for the first time, and his sense of loss knocked the wind out of him. She smiled with joy and threw her arms around his neck.

''Oh my God, William, you're back, you're here!''

Still he could not speak. He felt his knees turn to water. She dragged him inside the apartment. He staggered, and she sat him on the couch.

''You look so handsome!'' She traced the new ribbons on his

breast, and frowned. He kissed her forehead. She kissed his mouth. The pain increased in waves.

"I'm so sorry, William, that I—, well, that I wasn't able—. God, I don't know. I feel so miserable. When you phoned from the airport, I suddenly felt I just should have *made* myself wait! But I guess there's just no point in saying that, now." She tilted her face up, and he kissed the end of her nose, feeling drawn to her, and yet repelled. I should never have come, he thought, as his heart ached. "Please try not to hate me, William, or at least try not to let it show. I know that isn't even fair, but you were always the strong one."

"Karen, I don't want to talk about it now. Coming back here, to you, is overwhelming. Just let me sit for a while. Sit here with me."

So they sat with her head on his shoulder and his arms around her until the day slid away to darkness. Then Karen led him into their bedroom and they made love. With great tenderness, Stuart thought. Somewhat awkwardly, Karen would later complain.

The three days that Stuart stayed with Karen were so filled with emotion that Stuart would have trouble remembering them clearly. They almost never left the apartment. They argued, Karen trying to explain how she needed to grow up as her own person before she could do justice to their marriage, William saying he could forgive anything or accept anything except further separation from her. They cried together. Karen told stories of her work and they laughed. William told about the men he had led, and how he had lost them, and they cried. They made love a lot, or as the new and worldly Karen preferred it, they did a lot of sex. William drank a lot of bourbon and Karen smoked a lot of grass, and they cried and laughed and cried and argued and made love and did sex.

"Oh *William*," said Karen, like a teacher, he thought, with a particularly difficult pupil. "Can't you see that I was never a real person to you? I wasn't *Karen*, I was just some extension of you—the perfect love, the perfect wife. You put me on a pedestal, and worshipped me, and dammit, William, it felt *so* good! But when you went away, the *first* time, and I was alone, I realized that I had no idea who I was when you weren't around to tell me."

"Baby, there's no need for this."

"There *is*, dammit! You *must* understand me! You loved me so much, you protected me, but then you went away! Can't you see that I couldn't be your perfect goddess, described by you, defined by you, and *protected* by you, once you went away?"

"I always believed you could take care of—"

"Of *course* I could! But 'taking care of' *changed* me, William. I began to see myself as Karen the *person*! Loving of you, but not merely a *part* of you. Karen the *woman*, confident and strong, able to do things for herself, things that would have made you proud—" Her voice broke, and she pounded his chest softly with her fists.

"Karen, I'm proud of you. I always—"

"But I couldn't do what *you* wanted! What *you* needed! Dammit, William, can't you see my road was in some ways as hard as yours?"

"Of course, baby, I—"

"No, you can't." She got out of bed and went into the bathroom. William heard the shower start. He got up and walked into the kitchen and mixed himself a drink. I guess I really didn't see. He remembered a night in an NDP, and a conversation with Bobby. The awful thing is she's right, and so was Bobby. And even though I finally know that, even if I *could* accept it, it makes no difference. Nam is everything, he thought, feeling immensely sad.

By the third afternoon the emotions seemed largely spent. Karen had held firm against going with William to Washington, and William had packed his clothes and his few belongings. Karen's Aunt Liz had called and invited them to come down to her home in Newport Beach for Easter. William said he really had to be getting east. Karen protested, but William could sense her relief.

In the morning, Karen found William making coffee in the kitchen. He was once again in his dress khaki uniform."

"Where are you going in uniform?"

"A thing I have to do before I go to the airport."

"So you are really leaving today?"

"Yes. It's time."

"You don't have to be in Washington for weeks."

"It's time, Karen. We both have lives to lead."

"I just wish you would stay a few more days."

"It hurts too much. I may never get over losing you, but I have to try."

Karen nodded, and poured coffee for both of them. "Where are you going before the airport?"

"To Los Angeles. I promised one of my marines I would go and see his brother."

They washed the dishes together in silence. Why are we prolonging this? he thought. Go. Go now.

William packed the last of his gear in his rental car, then went

back to the apartment to say his last good-bye. Karen was crying, but somewhat surprisingly, he was not. They held each other
in silence.

"Please forgive me, William. I'm not worth your grief." Kar-
en's voice was very small.

"I love you, Karen. That's all I know how to do just now."

"I love you, too."

Karen walked him to his car. "Which man's brother are you
going to see?"

"Bobby Coles."

"The black man? The sergeant?"

"Yes."

"Does his brother know you are coming?"

"No, his phone is out of order." William opened the door of
the car.

Karen held his arm. "You could get hurt wandering around
the black parts of L.A. in that uniform."

"I'll be all right." William gently took his arm from his wife,
and got into the car.

"Why do you have to go up there?" She sounded really worried.

"Because I promised I would." Go. Go.

"Please be careful."

"Don't worry." Would she really care if Simon Coles tore
me in half? Would I?

She kissed him through the open window of the car. He
smiled. " 'Bye, babe."

"Good-bye."

24 March 1968   Los Angeles

Stuart followed the Harbor Freeway north, to Manchester Avenue, and then took the surface streets to Watts. He had listed as a standby on a TWA flight to Washington that would depart at 1600. He found Hickory Avenue, and turned in. The neighborhood was mostly neat one-story houses, mostly well kept if a little faded, not the way he imagined a ghetto would look. Some businesses, especially gas stations and liquor stores, were burned out, but the damage seemed old, and there was evidence of much rebuilding and refurbishing. He remembered that the riots had occurred only two and a half years ago.

There were for sure no white people around. Stuart felt a strange feeling of dread; he had lived among black people all his life, but the ones on these roadsides were different—hostile, their eyes penetrating as they tracked him in the car. Stuart held his breath at each stop sign on the length of Hickory Avenue, till he reached the 9400 block, and finally, number 9410.

The house was neat and unassuming, painted recently, the tiny lawn in front cut short. No one was around in the street except three young boys, maybe twelve years old, who drifted like smoke in the heat toward the spot on the curb where Stuart carefully parked the rented Ford. Stuart turned off the ignition, stepped out of the car, and locked it, under the dead-eyed gaze of the three boys who wore shields of hostility over their non-descript clothing.

The biggest boy stepped forward, between Stuart and the house at 9410 Hickory Avenue. "You *lost*, honkie?"

Stuart smiled, "Just going to see the man in this house, boys."

"Boys. Whyn't you just call us *niggers*, asshole?"

The boys formed a crude line. I don't need this, thought Stuart, but then again, I really don't know why I'm here, and maybe I shouldn't be.

The lead boy stopped three feet away from Stuart, which seemed very close. He smiled his street-battle smile. "Why you lock your car, honkie? You don't like the neighborhood?"

Stuart felt a bit of dread and a bit of anger. He controlled his voice. "I'm going up there to that house to see a man. I ask you to stand aside."

The boy shrugged. "Don't care, man, who you think you gotta see. More interested in all your shit, in the car. Why don't you open it, so we don't have to work up a sweat bustin' windows?" The boy on the right of the spokesman produced a tire iron from the back of his trousers in one fluid motion. The leader smiled with satisfaction, and with sinuous smoothness made a half turn to his right, and turned back, a six-inch switchblade knife showing in his hand.

Stuart took a step back and dropped into a fighting crouch. The quickness of his move startled the boys, and they paused, uncertain. They quietly counted odds, and once more began to crowd.

This is it, warrior, thought Stuart, bitterly, more in sadness than in anger. The choice. Kill one or more black children, or die in a gutter in Watts.

"HEY YOU DAMN KIDS, GET THE HELL AWAY." Stuart cocked an eye to the sound. A squat black man had stepped across the porch of the house at 9410, and strode toward the confrontation. The boys shrank back two paces, and the switchblade was folded and disappeared into the lead boy's jacket.

Stuart eased himself back a step toward the car, and upright. He looked carefully at the advancing man. Maybe five-feet-ten, maybe 230 pounds. Face scarred around the eyes, cheekbones, and nose. Strong stride, muscles evident under the cotton shirt and pants. Gut projecting over his belt, small and hard. This must be Simon Coles. The man stopped ten feet away, his gaze hard, but more questioning than hostile. The boys continued to slide silently backward.

The man spoke, carefully. "Who are you? No, I know, you are Robert's officer, Lieutenant Stuart."

"Yes, sir, William Stuart. And you are Simon Coles."

"Don't be sirrin' me. I was a staff sergeant, like my Robert was to you."

"Yes."

Simon spoke to the boys in a low, sibilant voice, almost a dialect, "Willie, Nicky, Paul, I am take this man i'side. You be *guard* the man's car till I say you don'!"

The boys nodded solemnly, and stood very still.

Simon took another pace toward Stuart. "What for you come here?"

"Bobby, ah, Robert, asked me to come and see you, when I got home."

Simon nodded. "You come inside with me. Boys'll watch the car." He turned and strode toward the simple house. Stuart followed.

Simon led Stuart into a parlor, dark, cool, and sparsely furnished. Simon nodded Stuart to a chair. Stuart noted it was the only comfortable one, and passed it to sit in an old sprung wicker peacock chair. Simon regarded him quizzically, then sat himself in the comfortable chair.

"You shoulda telephoned, Lieutenant. I would have prepared a bit, and made sure of the street for you."

"Bobby, ah, Robert—"

"Bobby is all right."

"OK. Bobby said I should just come. Said if I telephoned, you might not wish to see me. It was, ah, important to Bobby that I come." Stuart's heart was still pounding from the street confrontation. I want to get this over with and *leave,* he thought.

Simon fooled around with a pipe for a while, then set it down. He shook his head. "That Robert. Of course I'd have wanted to see you. Every letter I had from that boy for five, six months talked about you."

Stuart felt the stiffness in his body slowly slipping away, and his heartbeat slowed. He leaned back into the creaking wicker chair and breathed deeply. "He was the finest marine I knew. I liked him. Did he really write about me?"

"Did. Very much. The war, and the Marine Corps, changed for him, with you. Did you know that?"

Stuart smiled. "I think I did."

"You know, Lieutenant—"

"Please, make it William. I'd like to call you Simon."

Simon smiled, quickly, fleetingly. Stuart was painfully reminded of Bobby. "Only name for me, with friends. You know, of course you know, William, that my younger brother had a big kind of problem with his race, and yours."

"Yes. He never really wanted to discuss it, but I think he got away from it, or from part of it."

Simon's face was hard to read in the dim light of the parlor. "He always felt the white man held the black man down. I always tried to tell him thoughts like that did him no good. He listened, but he hated still."

Stuart stretched his legs, but nonetheless felt some tension returning. "Much wrong has been done."

"And more will be done. But after you became his commander, his attitude changed, William, gradually at first, then quickly."

"I'm glad, Simon, but I don't know why."

Simon laughed. "I know why! Shit, William, he wrote it all! You wouldn't be a jive ass honkie oppressor, and you wouldn't be a patronizing *liberal*! You were to him a better man! But my brother finally learned that a good man is just that, whatever his born color."

Stuart sat quiet, and relaxed again.

Simon pushed himself to his feet. "How 'bout a little taste, Lieutenant?"

Stuart glanced at his watch, 1305. A bit early, he thought, then thought better of it. "I'd like that, Simon."

Simon brought an unopened fifth of Virginia Gentleman bourbon from the kitchen, along with two chipped glasses and a small bowl of ice. He poured a careful measure into each glass, added ice, and handed one glass to Stuart as he sat back down in the overstuffed chair. Stuart raised his glass; Simon raised his.

"To Bobby, rest in peace."

"To Robert Richmond Coles, amen."

Stuart took a small, thoughtful sip. I thought this would be really hard, coming here, but it is really all right. In some way I belong here, like I didn't belong in Palo Alto or in Long Beach.

The two men sat without speaking, looking steadily at each other across the narrow room. Having this man here makes me see Robert again, but Robert at peace, thought Simon. This man was Robert's teacher, and his friend. From the letter he had received from Major MacIntyre of the ANGLICO, Simon knew that Stuart had been with Robert all the night he died.

There is so much we should be saying to each other, thought Stuart, yet the silence is very comforting. We just sit and think of the man we lost, bound together by the love of the man gone. Bobby loved me, thought Stuart. His throat caught, and he took another small sip. Stuart saw that his glass had a pattern of daisies painted on it, as he slowly turned it in his hands.

"You want to talk about Robert?" asked Simon. His voice was warm. He wants me to talk, thought William, but if I said no, he would accept that.

"Sure, Simon. I came here to tell you what I could. Bobby wanted it."

"Did you find it hard to come here?"

"Before I came, yes. But I feel better here with you than I have felt in a long time."

Simon chuckled. "Bobby probably told you I was one fierce nigger."

Stuart grinned, "He did."

"Tear your head off, he say."

"Yes, he did."

Simon smiled. "Bet he tried to stare you off, first time you met, big badass stare."

Stuart smiled, "Yes, and it damn near worked. He told me you could look a man so bad he would wet himself."

Simon cackled. "He loved to try and copy that, but how could he? I had raised him from a baby."

Simon really did most of the talking, and continued to serve out the Virginia Gentleman. He talked about Robert growing up, about his sister Becky, now living in France, about Robert's athletic scholarship to USC, about his plans to be a lawyer.

Simon gradually got William talking, first about Bobby as warrior—his calm, his precision under fire, and his careful leadership of the team—then more about Bobby at play, his humor. They compared impressions of various things and people and events. Simon from Robert's letters, which he had fetched in a shoe box from his study, William from memory. Stuart was surprised that Bobby had thought him, William, fearless. Simon was pleased to hear that Robert had been a source of William's courage.

Bobby's letters mentioned Moser and Hunter, and Simon and William talked about those men as well. Simon had a lot of questions about Gen. Blackjack Beaurive, and seemed surprised to learn he was not at least eight feet tall. Simon leaned forward, rapt and deeply saddened, to hear of Blackjack's last days and death in Danang.

Tears were shared, but more laughter. The two men seemed held together by the dead, and the loving that sprang from the dead. The conversation and the Virginia Gentleman flowed, as natural and unforced as the lengthening shadows from the sun shining through the parlor window.

Stuart sat up with a start, and looked at his watch. "Damn, Simon, it's three-fifteen! I have to catch a plane at four o'clock!"

Simon sat bolt upright. The spell was broken. He looked hurt, even a little angry. "You have to leave now, William?"

William stood, and Simon stood. "I have a four o'clock flight to Washington. I have orders to a new assignment there." The new assignment suddenly seemed very far away, and very insignificant.

Simon smiled, a little crookedly, and held out his hand. Stuart took it firmly. There was formality between them, and for the first time, an unshared sadness. "Thank you for coming to see me, Lieutenant. Thank you for what you did for my Robert."

What I did was get him killed, thought Stuart, the first guilt he had felt in this house. He turned toward the door, thinking of the drive to the airport, guessing he could make it. Instantly, he felt angry with himself, selfish, and stupid. He turned quickly back to Simon, who was looking at the thin rug on the floor. "Simon, my orders, that is, my orders to Washington, fact is, I have plenty of time. We could talk some more. I want to talk some more."

Simon looked up and into the taller man's eyes. "That's OK, William. You did right, you kept your promise. You go get your plane."

Stuart felt the flush of anger in his cheeks. "Simon, I'm asking you. For me. I can get a plane tomorrow."

Simon reached for Stuart's hand; now he gripped it. "You sure?"

"Yes, Simon. We're not done here, are we?"

Simon's fearsome face softened into a grin. "You stay, you stay for supper, all right?"

"Yes, sure. I have about fifty days to get where I have to be."

"Good, then, William, sit." Simon picked up the bottle, about half gone, and filled both glasses. Without bothering about the ice, he handed Stuart his. They raised the glasses and drank, and this time the toast was unspoken. "I had a feelin' you weren't ready to go, William."

They sat back, and the warmth, the kinship, returned. "I'm sorry about the airplane, Simon. I completely lost sight of what was important. Too long taking orders, I guess."

They sat for a while, each man feeding on the comfort of the other. "William, if it ain't presumptuous, we have talked about all the men who Robert felt touched by over there, save one."

"Well, I don't know any others, really."

"Sure you do." Simon held up Bobby's letters. "You yourself." Simon perched his half glasses on his nose. "Lieutenant William McGowen Stuart."

* * *

Stuart awakened slowly, as though coming up from a deep dive. His head was cottony and his temples pounded. His tongue tasted like a stable, and felt worse. He wished he could spit it out.

His memory of the last hours of the previous evening was not precise, but he remembered the empty bottle of Virginia Gentleman being replaced by a six-pack of Coors at about 11 P.M. He hadn't felt drunk, though he must have been. He felt protected, and most important, not alone, as Simon and he talked and talked.

Stuart had begun to talk about himself, first in the context of Bobby, but then just about himself. He told Simon of his fears in combat, his fears he might fail his men. He told him how he had really felt the night in the riverbank undercut while Bobby lay dying, about his thoughts for himself, and about the last sterile dressings in the pack, which he had wanted to put on his own wounds, even though Bobby needed it more. Simon hugged him, and they cried.

He talked about the general, how Bobby worshipped him, and how maybe Stuart worshipped him more. He talked about his own anxiety. He told about the crowd at the airport in San Francisco, and Simon got angry. He talked about the smug professor at Carole Ann's cocktail party, and Simon had raged around the room, then come back and hugged William again, and they agreed Bobby would have hated such a homecoming. Simon said that Bobby would have been home here, and that he, Simon, would have made it right. His words stuck firmly in Stuart's fuzzy brain.

"He'd be here, and I'd love him. You here now, needin', as he would. It is right you should be here, and I am glad. I wish you could have come here together."

Would that I could have brought him with me. Would to God, thought Stuart.

Stuart smelled brewing coffee, and cooking bacon. The rich smells made him feel slightly sick. The bed he was lying on was soft, the room dark. He could make out a couple of banners tacked to a wall, and some athletic trophies on a low bureau. With a start he realized he was lying in Bobby's bed.

Stuart lay back, and looked at the ceiling. His mind kicked back again to the evening before. The two men had taken their drinks, and the bottle that symbolized the sharing, into the kitchen around six o'clock, and Simon had cut up and fried a chicken and steamed some fresh string beans from his own tiny backyard garden. The chicken was stiff with crisp batter and fragrant with herbs, and between them they ate the whole bird, washing it down with whiskey and laughter as first Simon and then William told stories of the funnier sides of military life. They washed the dishes together, then returned to the parlor, and the talking went on. The bottle emptied, and the tongues thickened, but the talk continued.

Stuart couldn't quite remember how it began, but he remembered telling Simon about his marriage, the love and hope between Karen and himself, and then about the gradual tearing apart as their lives separated and their selves grew separately. Simon told him about his only real love, who had drifted away while Simon was in jail, years ago. By midnight, Stuart felt drained. He had exposed every hurtful thing that weighed upon him, and Simon's quiet encouragement kept him talking. All that hurt was still there, now in the morning, but it seemed deeper within. He could think about any of it now without the tightness in his throat or the stinging in the eyes. Stuart felt himself once again in control, and ready for something new.

Stuart swung his legs out of bed, and his head spun. He held on, then got up and found the bathroom. Without thinking, he used Simon's razor for a quick shave, then showered and rubbed his teeth with a washcloth. Back in Bobby's room, he found his B-4 that Simon had brought from the car, so he dug out his toothbrush, went back to the bathroom, and did the job properly. He also helped himself to two aspirin, though the shower had mostly cleared his head. He wrapped the Ace bandages around his itching thighs, dressed quickly in fresh khaki, and joined Simon in the kitchen.

Simon was draining bacon, and preparing to start frying eggs in the grease. Stuart's stomach rolled, then calmed. "Good morning, Simon."

Simon turned, grinned. "Good morning to you, William. Feeling well?"

Stuart laughed. "Don't tell me you're not the least bit hung over."

Simon handed William a steaming mug of coffee, and started cracking eggs into the grease, where they sizzled noisily. Simon turned down the gas. William took a tentative sip of coffee, and waited for a rebellion from his stomach. When none occurred, he drank some more. It was excellent, flavored with chicory.

"Well, William, I might have felt a bit peaked when I got up, but I am fine now. I let you sleep."

Stuart looked at his watch, 0800. "You couldn't have slept much."

Simon put thick slabs of cooked bacon on two plates, then three eggs on each. The eggs were crisped on the edge from the grease, and the yolks barely cooked, the way Stuart liked them. A far cry from the leathery, fish-belly-white bull's-eyes the military served up. Both men ate greedily, pausing to sip the rich coffee.

"William, just before you went to bed, you remember how we prayed?"

William had almost forgotten, but the image came rushing back—kneeling side by side on the thin rug, the big black man with his tattered Bible in his hands, reading slowly, then handing the book to William, who found some verses he liked and read them aloud. They had passed the Bible back and forth several times, then said the Lord's Prayer for Bobby. Finally, William read the passage the Navy had long ago adopted as its own: *And the seas shall give up their dead.*

"After we prayed, William, I couldn't sleep. My mind was filled with Robert, almost like he was here."

"Maybe he was here," said Stuart. It seemed like merely a comforting remark, but Stuart wasn't sure. There had been a presence in his dreams as well. Stuart regretted the alcohol that had suppressed the dreams and lost the presence.

Simon got up and fetched the coffee pot. "Have some more of this, and go call your airline." He smiled as he poured. "I'm sure glad you stayed."

Stuart drank deeply of the cooling coffee. "So am I, Simon. I thank you for everything."

Simon beamed, and started rinsing the dishes.

The girl at the standby desk at TWA told William that he had a good chance to get on the 10:30 A.M. flight to Washington if he came right out to the airport. She said he sounded nice, so she was going to put his name down right away, but he should be sure to bring her a copy of his orders as soon as possible. Stuart thanked her, and hung up. He helped Simon dry the dishes, then packed his kit and knotted his tie. Simon walked with him out to the porch.

"Piece of advice, William."

"Sure."

"Forget what you can, what you should, but cherish the rest."

"I know, Simon, I'll try. I think I can do that, now. Yesterday morning, I wasn't so sure."

Simon beamed, and threw his big arms around William. William hugged him back. "You find you a pure fine woman, as quick as you can. That'll help."

"Thanks, Simon. You don't know how you have helped me."

"William, you are a good man, like that ornery, proud Robert found out. I know, more than anything, you wanted to bring him back to me. And I know that you tried, right to the end. You tried, but you couldn't, and Robert is dead. But you brought me back my brother yesterday, in a very special way. Through you, I could see the *big* man the angry boy I raised had become.''

Stuart felt the tightness in his throat, but it was love, not grief. Simon released the bear hug, and stepped back, holding Stuart's shoulders in his powerful hands. ''This is why Robert sent you here, William.''

''And I think he also knew that I'd need you, Simon.''

Simon nodded, but didn't speak. Stuart picked up the B-4 bag from the porch. Simon brushed two big tears from his eyes, and took Stuart's elbow gently, ''Come back inside a moment, William.''

Stuart set the bag down, and walked ahead of Simon into the dim parlor. Simon picked up the Bible, and knelt. Until last night, he had never just knelt down with someone and prayed, at least not since he was little. Yet it felt very natural.

Simon placed the book between them. ''This is my good-bye for you, William. We won't need to read the words, just join in.''

Stuart bowed his head and nodded. Quietly they prayed together.

The Lord is my shepherd, I shall not want

He maketh me to lie down in green pastures, he leadeth me beside still waters.

He restoreth my soul: he leadeth me in the paths of righteousness for his name's sake.

Yea, though I walk through the valley of the shadow of death, I will fear no evil, for thou art with me; thy rod and thy staff they comfort me.

Thou preparest a table before me in the presence of mine enemies: thou anointest my head with oil; my cup runneth over.

Surely goodness and mercy shall follow me all the days of my life; and I will dwell in the house of the Lord forever.

25 March 1968   Los Angeles

Stuart turned in his rental car and walked the quarter mile to the TWA terminal. He found the standby desk, and the girl he had spoken to earlier. She smiled, and handed him his standby number. He could see on her list that she had given him a number some twenty-five numbers up from what he was currently holding. She was very pretty. Los Angeles, and California, seemed no longer an unfriendly place. He gave her a smart salute, and felt his juices rising. She giggled, and returned the salute. I'm just beginning to feel good, he thought.

He walked to the gate for the 1030 flight to Washington-Dulles. He gave his pass to the attendant, and found a seat in the lounge for himself, and another for his B-4.

Stuart felt mellow. He sat, and faded inside. Inside his head, images began to rise.

People wish to speak to me, he thought, dozing in the uncomfortable seat. People caught in the past seeking me in the present, in the World. Fair enough, he thought, as Bobby Coles emerged in his brain, lips moving, no sound. Yes, Bobby, I hear. The commitment, the need, the need to manage the fear. Rest, Bobby.

* * *

"Lieutenant."

Stuart opened his eyes. "Yessir?"

Before him stood a TWA captain. Stuart felt groggy, and strangely detached. He wondered how long he had been in whatever dream it was.

"You're riding with us today, to Washington?"

Stuart smiled, "Yes, sir. If you have a seat."

"I'm sure we have. And may I say you're welcome aboard. I'm Captain Kennet." The captain extended his hand, and Stuart shook it. "You must let TWA make you comfortable."

"Thanks, ah, thank you, Captain." Stuart liked the man's craggy face. It fitted with his manner.

"See you on board." The pilot saluted smartly. Stuart felt a bit stupid; his cap was on his lap, and he couldn't return the salute with it off. He did anyway. The captain walked down the jetway and disappeared.

Stuart returned to his reverie. He found himself on the floor of the Elephant Valley, watching Blackjack getting his eye bandaged. They touched, and talked, and the battle was distant. Blackjack's unbandaged eye was bright above his smile.

Billy Hunter rose in his mind, demanding attention. He stretched his hand through the flames, and Stuart grasped it. Billy smiled, and said thank you, with his lips, making no sound. He let go of Stuart's hand, and disappeared, still smiling. Stuart turned, and found the reassuring face of Moser, who nodded, and mouthed one word, which looked like yes.

Stuart stirred in the hard chair. He knew he was dreaming, or hallucinating, but he wanted to go on, to see where it would lead. He knew the spell could break, but he willed himself under. He wanted to know more.

Blackjack and Simon appeared together, speaking silently. Behind Blackjack were the flames of the Elephant Valley, and Stuart felt his numbing fear as he watched the stopwatch tick down. Behind Simon a photo of Bobby and Becky, which dissolved into a picture of a prison yard, and then into a picture of three solemn-faced black boys, and behind them, fire. Simon smiled, and waved a big-knuckled hand. He grasped Blackjack's hand, and they grinned together. Go on, they said, don't grieve.

A band of shouting demonstrators charged through the foreground of his thoughts, led by Professor Frank Bruce, armed with his slick grin. Stuart stood, in his mind, undecided. The men flowed past him, around him. Bobby and Simon, Blackjack and Billy, Moser with his big gun pointed at the ground, and finally, an image of himself. Stuart felt himself soaring above, watching Bruce and his chanting followers throw pail after pail of blood, as the thin line of men stood, stern, but beyond malice, beyond the need of reply. The demonstrators twisted like burning leaves, and crumbled, and faded away, leaving only Bruce's sardonic grin, which Stuart sensed would remain for a time.

"Lieutenant Stuart, you may board now." The ticket agent touched him gently.

Stuart got up and picked up the B-4. "Thanks, ma'am." The boarding pass said 21e. A seat is a seat, he thought.

The lounge was nearly deserted. Stuart hurried to board the aircraft. He handed his ticket to a tiny stewardess, no more than five feet tall, who favored him with a glorious smile, accented by a slight gap between her front teeth. Stuart smiled; she was cute, and sexy. She dialed up her smile, and handed him onward. He hung up his B-4, and walked through first class, looking at the passengers without interest. He found 21, waited while the elderly nun in the aisle seat got up to let him pass, then sat in the middle seat. He thanked the sister, who smiled at him thinly, and resumed her silent rosary. At the window was a real Hollywood type, with long, greasy hair, a black silk shirt, and heavy gold neck chains, who smelled strongly of some Asian-scented oil. He affected an air of amusement as Stuart folded his uniform jacket, stood in the cramped space, and placed it in the overhead shelf.

"Flyboy, huh?" The Chains spoke.

"Sailor," said Stuart, and settled himself into the tight seat. He felt his hostility rushing back, pushing the mellow out of his head. I can't deal with this for five hours, he thought.

"You do it in Vietnam?"

"Yes." Stuart closed his eyes, and pretended sleep.

"Bet you feel like a sucker, now you're back."

Stuart's brain raged. Blackjack looked at him, and smiled sadly. Those who degrade our soldiers do great wrong. He felt the choking sensation return.

"Lieutenant Stuart?"

William looked up into the eyes of the pretty stewardess. "Yes?" The rage receded.

The stewardess tried a salute, then giggled, and read from a piece of paper in her left hand. "Captain Kennet presents his compliments, and asks if Lieutenant Stuart would join him in first class." She giggled again, and reached out and took Stuart by his left hand. Stuart stood, whispered an excuse to the still-praying nun, and retrieved his uniform jacket.

"Hey, why him? I fly this airline all the time," said the Chains, with a sullen frown.

"Veteran," said the grinning stewardess.

She squeezed Stuart's arm as she led him through the curtain into first class. She seemed tinier yet, beside him. The plane had started to taxi, and Stuart sat where he was told. Next to him was a pretty, beautifully dressed black woman, Stuart guessed her age about thirty. Stuart looked at her, and saw fear in her eyes. Jesus, he thought, she's afraid of me, or this uniform. "Ma'am" he said softly, "if my sitting here disturbs you, I'll change seats as soon as the seat-belt sign goes off."

Her expression softened, and she smiled a weak smile. "I am sorry, soldier. It's just that you look so *angry*!"

Stuart put a hand to his face. It felt stiff. He realized he was still showing the scowl from his reaction to the greasy-looking passenger back in coach. "Gee, ma'am, I'm sorry. I guess I was thinking of something else; I certainly didn't mean to frighten you." He grinned gently and settled back as the plane accelerated and took off. She is really pretty, he thought, watching her profile as she looked at a magazine in her lap.

She is more than pretty, man, said Bobby inside his head. You don't know how to look at a black woman. She is a world-class *fox*! Stuart smiled more broadly at the thought. The woman looked up as the aircraft climbed, smiled at Stuart, then returned to her magazine. Stuart settled back, and began to relax.

Once the aircraft reached cruising altitude, the stewardess asked for drink orders. Stuart was ready to ask for a Bloody Mary, but when the lady beside him asked for champagne, he decided that sounded right. She put aside her magazine. He raised his glass to her, and she looked at him quizzically. "To a pretty lady," he said.

"Thank you, soldier," she said, and really smiled, and the smile made her truly beautiful. Bobby was sure right.

"I'm not a soldier, ma'am, I'm a naval officer."

"What do I call you, then, naval officer?"

"William Stuart. William, ma'am."

"All right, William, but don't call me ma'am! I know it's polite, but I don't feel old enough to be a ma'am to a handsome young officer. My name is Anne."

William blushed and felt foolish, but he also felt good. He and Anne talked through drinks and then lunch. She was a buyer for a department store, going to Washington for a meeting. She had once been a fashion model. The tiny stewardess cleared away the trays, and smiled at Stuart, who grinned in return. She then filled both their glasses with champagne, over a brief protest from Anne, and left a half-full bottle on the armrest between them.

Anne and Stuart talked about everything and nothing, and

Stuart noticed that Anne seemed to become more thoughtful as the time passed, as though searching his face for an answer to a question she didn't want to ask.

"Anne, something's on your mind," he said, dividing the last of the champagne.

She twisted toward him in her seat, and leaned close to him, and he could smell delicate perfume. She looked agitated. "I do want to ask you something, William, but I don't want to pry into your life."

"That's all right, Anne, go ahead."

"Well, it's just that we've been sitting here talking for a couple of hours, and you've told me about your new job in Washington, but not a word about what you've been doing. I used to date an army officer, and I recognize at least some of your ribbons. You've been in Vietnam, and in combat."

Stuart felt his stomach tense, and his good mood shatter. Please don't ask me how many I killed, he thought. "Yes."

"Since you haven't spoken about it, I assume you don't want to."

"Ah, that's right, Anne. It's a little too immediate, if you know what I mean."

"I understand, but William, you're a nice person, and I'm very concerned, so I'm going to ask you one question. If you can't answer, just tell me to shut up, OK?"

"Sure, Anne, go ahead." Stuart twisted his empty glass in his hand, and wished for a little more champagne.

"Thank you, William. I have a kid brother, just a baby, who's in the Army. He's a second lieutenant; he just finished parachute training at Fort Benning in Georgia."

Poor bastard, thought Stuart. "Has he been assigned to an outfit yet?"

Anne picked up her purse, and took out a letter. Stuart could see army jump wings embossed on the stationery. "He's going to join the One-hundred-first Airmobile Division, in a place called—I'm not sure how to pronounce this." She held out the letter to Stuart.

"Long Binh," he said, without looking at the letter. The name seemed to ring with sadness.

"I guess so. Anyway, Gary's letters are full of pride and enthusiasm, and he says he's dying to get into the fight." Anne's face twisted with anguish, and she smoothed the letter on her thighs with nervous fingers. Dying to get into the fight, thought William, the phrase bouncing around inside his brain, causing restless movements. Let me talk to him, said Blackjack. "But I know my baby brother, William. He's scared. He's heard things about the war over there. He doesn't know what he'll find, in-in—''

''Long Binh.''

''Yes.''

The stewardess came down the aisle with coffee, and William and Anne each accepted a cup. Stuart was glad for the interruption. How can I possibly help this nice woman, or her brave, scared brother? He looked at Anne, and saw she was looking out the window at the clouds far below. His mind reached back to the first time he had seen Vietnam, riding in a helicopter on a boondoggle with Hooper, their only mission a good lunch and a few bottles of wine. He remembered vividly the monk in the square, silently burning. He saw Moser firing single rounds into the riverbank while he cringed behind the pilot house of the landing craft. He remembered the sick fear in his gut when he had to carry the smoke flare away from the downed helicopter. He saw all the fires of Nam in his mind. He felt the itch in his wounded thigh muscles, and remembered the paralyzing pain of the bullet. His genitals shriveled and his mouth dried from the upwelling within him of accumulated fear. Imagine what it would be like to have orders in hand to Long Binh.

''William?''

Anne had turned back from the window. Her eyes were shiny with tears. William fought a tightness in his throat but didn't trust it. Let her speak, he thought.

''William, if you can, please tell me something positive about this war in Vietnam. Some good thought I can preserve while I worry about my baby brother.''

A line second lieutenant in the one-oh-first probably has a life expectancy of less than ninety days, thought Stuart, bleakly. What can I possibly say that can change that?

''Please, William. I don't know anyone else to ask.''

''Anne, I like you very much, this little time we've had to talk.''

''Don't say it's too difficult, William. I have to have something to cling to.''

It's as though she already knows, he thought. ''And I'm sure I would like your brother. But there is no use in me lying to you. Nam is no fun, for anyone. A soldier is most often wet, and either too hot or too cold. In the field, there are bugs, and snakes, and leeches, and all manner of diseases, from malaria and dengue to skin and foot fungus to big sores that just won't heal. Even in the rear, the camps are muddy mires from the near-constant rain; yet when the sun finally comes out, the ground dries within an hour or so, and then the dust is up, and into every corner of a man's body, and gritty in his nose and under his tongue." Anne reached her hand across the armrest and William took it. "And all that is before you even get to the enemy. The enemy hates with all his being the people he considers invaders and defilers of his homeland. He attacks you in the field, and in your own camps. Every child in a tri-shaw may have a grenade, every tiny prostitute a knife or a piece of sharpened bamboo. A soldier buys himself a little release to put into his veins to stop his horrible fears, and it turns out to be battery acid. The soldier dies, or loses an arm, and the enemy saves himself a bullet." Anne was breathing in short gasps, almost sobbing, but she didn't cry. William squeezed her hand, gently. "And lastly, but maybe the worst, is the way people here in the World—in the USA—will treat your brother. I never had any idea what that could be like, until I got back, but he already knows." Anne bowed her head, and her shoulders began to shake. She hugged herself, and swayed in the seat. William turned to her and put his arm across her shoulders. She pushed the armrest up and out of the way and moved across the seat, and clung to him, her face buried in his chest. He could feel her warm tears soaking through his shirt. "So what is *positive* in all of this? I guess I would have to say it is the sharing, the enduring of hardship together, which is a soldier's lot. Your brother will make many fine friends, he will feel his greatness, and theirs, he will feel himself larger than life, yet humbled in the shadow of the honor and sacrifice of his fellow soldiers. He'll know fear, and despair, and pain, but he will also know honor, and devotion, and comradeship, and courage."

"William—"

"A little more, Anne, only a little. When I was in Nam, I served under a general, a very great man. He could say these things, and they didn't sound trite, or empty. He could rally men, and stir their courage, and bring them close together, and gather their fighting spirit in his hands and mold it into an implacable force through his own love—" Stuart's voice broke, and he brushed away a tear. Blackjack's face rose in his mind, and he looked sad. "He would tell your brother, tell you, what was positive."

Anne sat up, and looked at William. The aircraft seemed deserted around them, dim, and intimate. "Do you remember any words this general said, William?"

"Oh, yes, Anne! Lots, maybe every one! He spoke one day to his entire command, after a major battle, and he spoke about the antiwar sentiment, which was then a new thing, and he called on each man to reaffirm his soldier's commitment, because there had been an incident, somewhere else in Nam, where soldiers had refused to fight on moral grounds. Blackjack—the general—played on the words 'moral grounds.' He told his troops that 'our moral ground is the battlefield secure and under our boots at day's end,' and—''

William could see Blackjack, standing on the reviewing stand before the brigade, proud, and eloquent, and alive. Stuart could feel the cheers of the fighting men rock the ground, crying Blackjack's name. He sat back and tightened his jaw against the pain, feeling his eyes brimming.

''What else did he say, William,'' Anne whispered, touching his eyes and brushing away the hot tears. ''Please, I wouldn't have caused you such pain if I didn't have to know. Please.''

''He said—'' William turned to look at Anne. I think she understands. I hope she does.

''Tell me, William.''

''He said our reward would be glory.''

About the Author

Franklin Allen Leib, a Navy lieutenant during the Vietnam War, served as a gunnery officer, boat officer, and navigator in support of Marine and Army operations. Subsequently, he served as a counter-intelligence officer assigned to the Naval Intelligence Command in Washington. Now an international banker, Mr. Leib has an AB from Stanford and an MBA from Columbia. He lives in Westport, Connecticut. His first book, *Fire Arrow*, is a high-tech military thriller set in today's North Africa.

**Read more
about
VIETNAM**

**from
Ballantine
and
Ivy
Books**

THE BALLANTINE/IVY LIBRARY OF THE VIETNAM WAR

To this day, the Vietnam War represents an era of change in America, but whether that change was for the better or for the worse has yet to be decided.

Many interpretations of Vietnam have been published, both fiction and nonfiction. From an outsider's viewpoint, these books might all seem alike. But the Vietnam books published by Ballantine and Ivy represent a variety of perspectives: oral histories from soldiers, novels by veterans, dispatches from journalists, diaries of officers. Many of these books won literary awards, critical acclaim, and the hearts of Americans who grieved for the soldiers who fought over there.

These Vietnam titles can be better perceived as a group if observed within a historical time line. The war, like any period in world history, went through various stages: the early days before the United States became involved; the onslaught of American soldiers and fierce battles; the drawn-out ending as the United States withdrew in the early seventies; the siege of Saigon in 1975 as the last American was lifted by helicopter off the roof of the embassy; the aftermath at home.

Each stage of the Vietnam War is represented by a book. Whether you enjoy reading these books to educate yourself, to be absorbed in a life-and-death drama, or to find out how your tax dollars are spent, the best place to begin is with an overview.

To clarify the sequences of events, Ballantine publishes two books that serve as an overview of Vietnam, each with a unique perspective. To understand the war's position in world history, it is best to begin with these two books.

THE BIG PICTURE

BACKFIRE: A History of How American Culture Led Us into Vietnam and Made Us Fight the Way We Did by Loren Baritz

An urgent and eloquent expose of how the worst political and military defeat in our history had its roots deep in American culture, how it destroyed the traditional code of honor of many senior military officers, how it bred cynicism and distrust of government at home, and what Vietnam means for America's future.

"Baritz documents in chilling detail how the American military since World War II hardened into a classic bureaucracy that aims towards the mindless preservation of its own interests."   **—The Miami Herald**

SUMMONS OF THE TRUMPET: A History of the Vietnam War from a Military Man's Viewpoint by David Richard Palmer

The story of America's involvement—why we entered, what we did, and how we left. This is a clear and forceful military history that describes significant battles, typifying each stage of America's role, from 1954 until our departure.

"The best military history of the Vietnam War so far."
            —The History Book Club

From here, the best way to understand the perspectives of our Vietnam literature is to look at its setting, which can determine what the reigning interests of our country were at particular stages throughout the war.

1954–65
GATHERING CLOUDS

After the defeat of France by the Vietnamese at Dien Bien Phu in 1954, the Geneva accord divided Vietnam in half at the 17th parallel, giving Ho Chi Minh communist control of the north, and the south to elected President Diem.

U.S. President Eisenhower had not signed the accord because of its concession to the communist Ho, and began sending financial aid to South Vietnam, as well as a group of 700 military "advisors." In 1962, John F. Kennedy would increase the number of advisors to 15,000.

As the North Vietnamese were cutting a 15-mile-wide swath through Cambodia and Laos along the South Vietnamese border, which would come to be known as the "Ho Chi Minh Trail," the guerilla tactics of the Viet Cong in their native land confounded the American military planners.

Buddhist protests of the Catholic President Diem eventually caused his downfall and assassination, not three weeks before Kennedy himself would be killed.

Massive confusion in South Vietnam after these assassinations greeted General William Westmoreland when he arrived in January, 1964. Meanwhile, the unified soldiers under Ho Chi Minh and his heroic general, Giap, were building strength in the North Vietnamese Army and the Viet Cong forces.

While sending more and more troops to Saigon, President Johnson ran for re-election in 1964 declaring: "I would not commit American boys to fighting a war that I think ought to be fought by the boys of Asia to help protect their own land." By 1965, the number of troops in Vietnam would reach 100,000.

After it appeared that North Vietnam had attempted to torpedo a couple of American destroyers, the U.S. Senate passed the Gulf of Tonkin Resolution, which permitted the president to take any and all offensive action in South Vietnam, but was not an actual declaration of war.

In February, 1965, the U.S. began the "Rolling Thunder" sustained bombing campaign of North Vietnam, which would continue for almost four years. The Battle of Ia Drang created a hero of the victor, Westmoreland, who would be elected *Time* magazine's Man of the Year for 1965.

At home, everyone had fallen in love with the Beatles, and it was time to rock and roll.

Nonfiction

FIVE YEARS TO FREEDOM by James N. Rowe
The true story of a Green Beret's five years in a Vietcong prison camp, from 1963 to 1968. A POW very early in the Vietnam War era, Rowe endured grueling psychological

and physical torment, loneliness, and the grief of watching his friends die, while trying to maintain his faith as a soldier for the country that appeared to have turned against him. Rowe returned to the service as a full colonel, commanding ground troops in the Philippines and was assassinated there in 1989.

"If you can read this story and not weep, you are inhuman."
—The Cincinnati Post

THE MAKING OF A QUAGMIRE by David Halberstam
A young journalist's observations from 1962-63 about the dramatic atmosphere and the colorful personalities who played major roles in the Vietnam War. Halberstam's reports from South Vietnam would eventually be awarded a Pulitzer Prize.

A RUMOR OF WAR by Philip Caputo
Pulitzer Prize–winner Caputo landed in Danang in March 1965 as a young infantry officer in the 9th Marine Expeditionary Brigade, the first U.S. combat unit sent to Indochina.

"The troubled conscience of America speaking passionately, truthfully, finally."
—The New York Times Book Review

Fiction

THE GREEN BERETS by Robin Moore
Set in 1963 when the first American soldiers went to Vietnam, the novel is based on the author's participation in the training and secret missions of the U.S. Special Forces team who came to be known as the Green Berets.

"Stirred a fuss in Washington. The official objection to the book apparently is that it is too close to fact."
—The New York Times

PARTHIAN SHOT by Loyd Little
Winner of the 1975 PEN Hemingway Award, this is the witty tale of a group of Green Berets sticking it out in a small Mekong village in 1964.

"Finely balanced satire ... A comic apocalypse."
—The New York Times Book Review
"May be the Vietnam War's CATCH-22."
—Chicago Sun-Times

1965—68
DISTANT THUNDER

The number of U.S. troops in South Vietnam rose to 400,000 in 1966, and would reach a peak of 530,000 the following year. Westmoreland's infamous "War of Attrition" began, the body-count method of determining victories in the battlefield.

New York Times reporter Harrison Salisbury became the first to file anti-war dispatches from Hanoi.

As the public began to question Westmoreland's tactics, the general asked President Johnson for 200,000 additional troops, insisting the "result attained would be a function of the resources committed." The enemy was estimated to be 270,000; although in later years there was some controversy over this figure, which some believed to be far too modest.

President Johnson contended with war protests that began to crop up around the country, as well as the Six-Day Arab/Israeli War in 1967.

Meanwhile, Ho Chi Minh and General Giap began to plan an all-out offensive against South Vietnam. In 1968, this began with the Battle at Khe Sanh, where the North Vietnamese Army surrounded a station of 6,000 Marines. They held fast through a multitude of air strikes by the United States but they never launched an attack and eventually retreated.

At the same time, in cities and villages throughout South Vietnam, the Vietcong filtered in by tens and hundreds amidst the travelers preparing for the Tet holiday. During the traditional cease-fire of this period celebrating the New Year, the Vietcong started a deadly rampage across the country. Their poor synchronization enabled the U.S. and South Vietnamese troops to recover, and to ultimately wipe out this massive offensive from the North.

Even as Westmoreland began further requests for 200,000 more troops, some people were questioning the war's program.

Peace candidate Eugene McCarthy beat LBJ in the New Hampshire primary, and Robert F. Kennedy announced he too would seek the 1968 Democratic nomination for president. President Johnson stepped out of the race.

In 1968, Richard M. Nixon was elected to the White House.

Nonfiction

CHARLIE COMPANY: What Vietnam Did to Us by Peter Goldman & Tony Fuller

A candid look by two *Newsweek* reporters of sixty-five Charlie Company soldiers who toured Vietnam in 1968 and 1969.

> *"The many narratives are graphic and often touching....
> They tend to offset the Hollywood and television view of
> each Vietnam veteran as a walking timebomb, and of the
> war as an olive-drab acid trip. The reader is more in-
> clined to sob over the many quiet tragedies that dogged
> Charlie Company throughout the war and back home."*
> —**Newsday**

THE END OF THE LINE: The Siege of Khe Sanh by Robert Pisor

The riveting, definitive history of the battle where 6,000 Marines held their position for seventy-seven days while completely surrounded and outnumbered by the north Vietnamese Army.

> *"Excellent... A convincing explanation of why the siege
> of Khe Sanh and the Tet Offensive marked America's
> strategic defeat in Vietnam...A good place to start a reex-
> amination of what caused our failures."*
> —**The New Republic**

GUNS UP! by Johnnie M. Clark

The true story of a soldier who arrives in Vietnam with the 5th Marine Regiment during the height of the Tet Offensive in 1968, to serve as a machine gunner along-side Chan, his Chinese-American compatriot, who survived months of active warfare together.

INSIDE FORCE RECON: Recon Marines in Vietnam by Michael Lee Lanning & Ray William Stubbe

The compelling evolution of Marine Reconnaissance and pathfinder units into Force Recon companies that were the eyes and ears of Marine combat units in Vietnam.

INSIDE THE LRRPS: Rangers in Vietnam by Michael Lee Lanning

The original Rangers roamed America during the seventeenth century, when they scouted Indians for European colonists and played major roles in the Revolutionary and Civil Wars. During World War II and the Korean War, the Rangers reappeared, but not until Vietnam did Rangers become six-man teams that fought a guerrilla war as LRRPs, the Army's 75th Infantry, penetrating deep into enemy territory in the war's most dangerous missions. This is the compelling history, and the only reference book of its kind.

THE PASSING OF THE NIGHT: My Seven Years as a Prisoner of the North Vietnamese by General Robinson Risner

In 1965, Lt. Col. Robinson Risner was shot down on a bombing mission over North Vietnam. During his seven years in Hoa Lo Prison, the "Hanoi Hilton," he was subjected to brutal tortures and deprivation. Risner poignantly recounts how he came to terms with himself, refused to be broken, though he was devastated and demoralized.

"Powerful...The total effect is gripping."

—**Publishers Weekly**

Fiction

CRAZYHEAD by John Klawitter

At twenty-one, Dennis Haller has already spent four years in Vietnam, the only member of the four-man "Dimbo Patrol" still in-country, now working for the 33rd Radio Research Unit, which specializes in communications intelligence.

F.N.G. by Donald Bodey

Gabriel Saures is newly arrived in Vietnam, a Fuckin' New Guy who will lose his rawness fast, almost as fast as he can lose his life.

"Raw, profane...A candidly moving portayal of the average American soldier in Vietnam, who often found courage when he did not seek it—but little of anything else."

—**Chicago Sun-Times**

THE HILL by Leonard B. Scott
Ty and Jason, Oklahoma brothers so different in character yet so close in soul reunite in the Battle of Dak To and in the harrowing battle for Hill 875—an insignificant piece of ground that will set stranger to kill stranger for no reason at all, and brother to save brother for the one reason that matters. From the bestselling author of CHARLIE MIKE and THE LAST RUN, a career Army officer who served with the 173rd Airborne and 75th Rangers.

A RECKONING FOR KINGS by Chris Bunch & Allan Cole
An authentic, tightly written novel about the Tet Offensive, from two veterans who were there, from both an American and a North Vietnamese viewpoint."
"A classic war novel."   —San Francisco Chronicle

SEMPER FIDELIS by Johnnie Clark
It was 1968 and Shawn McClellan was part of a fierce but small platoon of U.S. Marines. Fighting anonymous battles deep in the Vietnam bush and also back home, where right and wrong were determined by what was easiest, Shawn seeks refuge in the hardest place of all.

THE SOLDIER'S PRIZE by Dan Cragg
The novel set around the Tet Offensive, an experience of war at its most bloody and its most inspiring. A nightmarish battle of the streets that will test men to their limits, and make lifers into soldiers. By an author who spent five years as an Army NCO in Vietnam.

A STATION IN THE DELTA by John Cassidy
CIA field officer Toby Busch is determined to forget his haunted past, falls in love with a beautiful war widow from Hanoi, and learns about the incredible Vietcong offensive planned for Tet.
"A good companion piece to Graham Greene's masterful THE QUIET AMERICAN ...A readable, intelligent novel."
—The Washington Post

THERE I WAS: *The War of Corporal Henry J. Morris, USMC* by David Sherman

Henry Morris sits down his eighteen-year-old son for a cold beer and a long talk about the war fought in a tiny country that not so long ago no one had ever heard of—and now no one can ever forget. For the grunts in 'Nam, their lives were tales of sweat and sacrifice, moments of swift savagery in searing combat. In the hot jungle hell, if at first you didn't succeed, you died. The author was a Marine corporal who received five citations for his service in Vietnam.

VIETNAM SPOOK SHOW by Wayne Care

Craig Nostrum is in Navy intelligence, tracking enemy fighters, warning U.S. aircraft of imminent MiG attacks, and alerting search and rescue aircraft. Nostrum battles the enemy, but also an infuriating bureaucracy in his own outfit, antiquated equipment and unqualified personnel. His personal war with his commander and his attempts to reconcile his job with his love for Vietnam and its people compose a deft novel of war.

1969—75
THE STORM

In January 1969, Richard Nixon was sworn in as President. While 300 U.S. soldiers died each week in Vietnam, Nixon called for negotiation instead of confrontation, and he called on Henry Kissinger to initiate peace talks in Paris. Kissinger declared that North Vietnam could never be beaten in battle, but Nixon said that to abandon South Vietnam at that point would be to "risk a massacre."

Nixon put into action his "Vietnamization" plan, to strengthen the South Vietnamese Army and its government so they could defend themselves. The number of U.S. troops dwindled to 475,000.

Recovering from the high cost of the Tet Offensive, the NVA made no offensives during 1969. Ho Chi Minh, the great Northern leader, died in September. Nixon invaded Cambodia, until then off-limits to U.S. troops. Cambodians burned down the North Vietnam embassy in Phnom Pehn and ejected the NVA soldiers who, for years, had been a regular presence on the Ho Chi Minh Trail.

In 1971, the South Vietnamese began their own offensives without U.S. troops, who had evacuated completely from Khe Sanh and numbered only 157,000.

In 1972, with only 49,000 American soldiers in Vietnam, the real test of Nixon's "Vietnamization" began when the NVA invaded the South over the 17th parallel. The Southern forces passed the test, with no U.S. assistance on the ground, although the Americans continued to bomb North Vietnam and to mine her harbors.

The United States bombed Hanoi to bring NVA negotiators back to the Paris peace talks.

Actress Jane Fonda met with North Vietnamese soldiers in Hanoi as a protest of the war.

1973 brought a cease-fire throughout Vietnam. The U.S. military presence faded away. Kissinger and his North Vietnamese counterpart, Le Duc Tho, were awarded the Nobel Peace Prize.

In 1975, after defending themselves for two years, the South Vietnamese Army was finally defeated in Saigon, which was renamed Ho Chi Minh City. The remaining U.S. advisers and certain South Vietnamese personnel were airlifted from the capitol. Two Marines shot and killed at the U.S. Embassy were the last two American casualties in Vietnam. The war's total reached 58,000 American dead. The Vietnamese loss was many times greater.

Nonfiction

CHARLIE RANGERS by Don Ericson & John L. Rotundo
Charlie Company, 75th Infantry, provided the six-man teams that specialized in ambushing the enemy, outfighting jungle guerrillas using their own tactics. For eighteen months, the authors braved the test of war at its most bloody.

THE ELEMENT OF SURPRISE: *Navy SEALs in Vietnam*
by Darryl Young
The first nonfiction book to accurately describe the activities of any SEAL unit. The Juliett Platoon, SEAL Team

One, along the Bassac River and on Dung Island in 1970. Underwater demolitions, scuba, parachuting, commando techniques, escape and evasion, patrolling enemy territory, rescuing prisoners of war, and exfiltration by boat under fire. The true stories of fourteen men who conducted over one hundred missions without one SEAL fatality.

LINEBACKER: The Untold Story of the Air Raids over North Vietnam by Karl J. Eschmann
In late '72, President Nixon began bombing Hanoi, to compel the North Vietnamese back to negotiations. Over a twelve-day period, 206 B-52 bombers, 48 F-IIIs, and over 500 other aircraft bombarded the North. This is the first book to examine these missions, allowing nonspecialists to understand modern air warfare. Includes interviews with pilots and with "Hanoi Hilton" prisoners who witnessed the incredible attack.

ONCE A WARRIOR KING: Memories of an Officer in Vietnam by David Donovan
In the spring of 1969, Donovan arrived in the Mekong Delta to work as a military adviser with village chiefs and local militia.
> "Valuable documentation on a relatively obscure part of the American military effort ... how the war really worked on the front line of 'Vietnamization,' the training of local militia. His reflections on his own use of power raise serious and important questions about the American experience in Vietnam." —**The New York Times Book Review**

THE ONLY WAR WE HAD: A Platoon Leader's Journal of Vietnam by Michael Lee Lanning
The author's day-by-day journal of his first six months as a platoon leader with poignant recollections of his experiences.

VIETNAM 1969–1970: A Company Commander's Journal by Michael Lee Lanning
The continuation of twenty-three-year-old Lanning's observations as one of the youngest company commanders in Vietnam.
> "...one of the most honest and horrifying accounts of a combat soldier's life to come out of the Vietnam War."
> —**The New York Times Book Review**

BLOOD ON THE LOTUS by Lawrence C. Vetter, Jr.
Michael Collins is on his second tour; Kim Son is a
woman who has risen to officer rank in the Vietcong.
Michael and Kim Son met one another during Michael's
first tour—and their repeated encounters bring each of
them a very different understanding of the enemy. The
first novel of a former Marine captain who served in the
Third Force Recon Battalion.

Fiction

CHARLIE MIKE by Leonard B. Scott
If war may be said to bring out the worst in govern-
ments, it frequently brings out the best in people. This
is the story about some of the very best. Some led.
Some followed. Some died. Written by a career Army
officer whose combat decorations include the Silver
Star and the Purple Heart.
> *"One of the finest novels yet written about the war in
> Vietnam."* —**The Washington Post**
> *"A hymn on the theme of valor—that of the American
> soldier and that of the North Vietnamese enemy as well."*
> —**The New York Times Magazine**

CHINA WIND by Dan Guenther
From a platoon leader in an amphibious tractor company to a counterintelligence officer, Lt. Sam Gatlin's
career in the Marines is a hell-raising adventure, to say
the least. The author was a Marine Corps captain who
served in Vietnam from 1968 to 1970.

HUEY by Jay and David Groen
A novel by two brothers who are veterans, based on
David's experiences as "The Flying Dutchman," pilot of
one of the U.S. Army's UH-1H "Huey" Iroquois helicopters. Screaming descents into hot landing zones, seven
days of horror in a jungle swamp, battling the brass
when a botched operation spells disaster for the men
under him, in 1970 Vietnam.

THE LAST RUN: The Mission Continues by Leonard Scott

An action-packed story about loyalty in war—and of the unseen wounds our veterans brought home, by the author of CHARLIE MIKE.

"Scott tells the story in plain, readable English but with an ironic humor often heard in a career soldier's language. It is the kind of book that leaves you wanting more when you get to the final page."

—Atlanta Journal Constitution

MEKONG! by James R. Reeves

A novel based on the true experiences of a Vietnam Naval Special Forces SEAL, whose mission was to search and destroy on land and underwater.

COVERT ACTIONS by James R. Reeves & James C. Taylor

The sequel to MEKONG!, coauthored by the former SEAL who inspired the story, this is the SEAL's second mission—a kidnapping, straight out of the stronghold of the enemy.

THE ALLEYS OF EDEN by Robert Olen Butler

An American deserter leaves Saigon during the 1975 evacuation and takes the Vietnamese woman with whom he's been living for five years. Once together in the American Midwest, their differences begin to make themselves apparent and they begin to grow apart, though in Saigon they would have thought this impossible.

"A unique, haunting story that ultimately serves as a metaphor for the pain and suffering caused by this country's participation in the Vietnam War."

—The Washington Post Book World

1963 – 75
A COLLECTION OF VOICES

One of the better ways to understand Vietnam and its effects on the different walks of life, people thrown together in an unpopular war, is through the oral histories, collections of personal accounts that build a greater picture of the human side of the war.

BLOODS: An Oral History of the Vietnam War by Black Veterans by Wallace Terry
Cited by *The New York Times* as one of the Notable Books of 1984, this is the compilation of twenty eloquent voices speaking about the war.

"The story of how members of a race that had been wronged historically were sent off in disproportionately large numbers to kill a colored enemy, protecting a system that had never protected them to any comparable degree...An engrossing, heartbreaking record, full of the drama of real tragedy." —Los Angeles Herald Examiner

EVERYTHING WE HAD: An Oral History of the Vietnam War by Thirty-three American Soldiers Who Fought It by Al Santoli
Nominated for the American Book Award in 1983, this *New York Times* bestseller tells the moving and candid stories of those who were there.

"It is personal, it is authentic, it has great dignity, and it will last...Simply a magnificent achievement."
—The Washington Post Book World

THE EYEWITNESS HISTORY OF THE VIETNAM WAR 1961 – 75 by George Esper and the Associated Press
Not a collection of voices, but a collection of visions from fourteen years of war, accompanied by a chronological narrative from an AP reporter. From the first combat death to the fall of Saigon, words and pictures tell the story. The hundreds of photos include many Pulitzer winners and several photos that were never published before.

A PIECE OF MY HEART: The Stories of Twenty-six Women Who Served in Vietnam by Keith Walker

Selected accounts from the 15,000 women who served as Red Cross workers, WACs, Army nurses, OSU entertainers, etc.

> "U.S. women were active participants in the war although they did not bear arms, they served under horrendous conditions with bravery...The women share stories filled with terror and pathos, and some of their remembrances, especially those from the nurses, are hard to take."
> **—Los Angeles Herald Examiner**

TO BEAR ANY BURDEN: The Vietnam War and Its Aftermath in the Words of Americans and Southeast Asians by Al Santoli

Powerful and moving accounts from 48 different people.

> "Their confused, painful stories point towards a truth more frightening than any of the theories presented so far about America's first 'rock 'n' roll' war."
> **—The Cleveland Plain Dealer**

VIETNAM MEDAL OF HONOR HEROES by Edward F. Murphy

Over one-hundred compelling stories of personal heroism and valor—true stories of action and courage in the face of war. "Many men went to Vietnam with the hope of fulfilling the promise they made to defend their country. The adversities and discouragement awaiting them there made it difficult to keep that promise. Staying true to their commitment made them all heroes. A handful of warriors went far above and beyond that commitment....These gallant men must never be forgotten. For to forget them would mean their sacrifices were in vain." **—the Author**

VIETNAM: The Other Side of Glory by William R. Kimball

Fourteen true stories of rage, violence, and redemption from officers, grunts, medics, chaplains, gunners, and flyers. Their tours of duty and their readjustments to home brought them through alcohol, drugs, and finally to a powerful spirit that helped them help themselves.

1975—90
THE WELCOME HOME

Years after they returned from Vietnam, veterans would recall how difficult it has been to readjust to life at home, with friends and family who, like themselves, still didn't understand what had happened over there. Many would watch the heroes' parade afforded the hostages freed from Iran in 1981 and wonder why their own welcome home had been so shameful.

Nonfiction

OUT OF THE NIGHT: *The Spiritual Journey of Vietnam Vets* by William P. Mahedy
The men who served in Vietnam are consumed by memories of the bloody carnage, the atrocities, the guilt about an unpopular war. They also suffer from a feeling of betrayal by God—He left them in the jungles of Southeast Asia to die. An Army chaplain and counselor in Vietnam recounts veterans' spiritual journey out of the darkness and back into the light of their faith, in a rare look into the spiritual side of the war.
"Disturbing to read but important to us all."
—**San Diego magazine**

PAYBACK: Five Marines and Vietnam by Joe Klein
The post-war experiences of five soldiers who served together in Charlie Company, 1st Battalion, 3rd Marine Regiment, in 1967.
"The most eloquent work of nonfiction to emerge from Vietnam since Michael Herr's Dispatches...We come to know the five Marines as intimately as characters in a novel....Indeed, PAYBACK has that rare quality in a book—the visceral feel of real life, pinned down and clarified through words." —**THE NEW YORK TIMES**

Fiction

AMERICAN BLOOD by John Nichols

Meet Vietnam vet Michael P. Smith, seventeen hours out of Hell and stepping off the Freedom Bird into a shiny, well-fed, antiseptic America. He's as lethal as Typhoid Mary, but it's not his body that's sick. He's got guns, his car, and the open road, and a violent heritage 300 years long.

"The film Platoon *is like* Babes in Toyland *after the almost unspeakable horrors that fill the war days of Michael P. Smith....Nichols' prose is brilliant, captivating."*

—**Pittsburgh Post Gazette**

BUFFALO AFTERNOON by Susan Fromberg Schaeffer

An epic novel from an extraordinary novelist, about Pete Bravado from working-class Brooklyn, who joins the army to get away from home. Pete's numbing experience in Vietnam and miserable return home from the war lead to a breakdown and recovery that will transcend his loss of innocence.

"Remarkable...The entire Vietnam experience (in) one epic narrative. Susan Fromberg Schaeffer's prose is evocative, often haunting. But it's the details that ultimately convince. All the Vietnam material is authentic: the weapons, the jargon, the leeches, the mud....The war almost explodes off the page."

—**The New York Times Book Review**

Look for all of these Ballantine and Ivy books
in your local bookstore.